Ghost Tree

Barbara Erskine is the *Sunday Times* bestselling author of over a dozen novels. Her first book, *Lady of Hay*, has sold more than three million copies worldwide and has never been out of print since it was first published thirty years ago. Her books have been translated into over twenty-five languages and are international bestsellers. Barbara lives near Hay-on-Wye in the Welsh borders.

To find out more about Barbara and her books visit her website, find her on Facebook or follow her on Twitter.

www.barbara-erskine.co.uk
Facebook.com/barbaraerskineofficial
@Barbaraerskine

Also by Barbara Erskine

BARBARA
ERSKINE

The
Ghost
Tree

HarperCollinsPublishers

HarperCollins*Publishers* Ltd.
The News Building
1 London Bridge Street
London SE1 9GF

www.harpercollins.co.uk

This paperback edition 2019
2

First published in Great Britain by
HarperCollins*Publishers* 2018

A catalogue record for this book
is available from the British Library

ISBN: 978-0-00-819584-7

Set in Meridien LT Std by Palimpsest Book Production Limited,
Falkirk, Stirlingshire

Printed and bound in Great Britain by
Printed and bound by CPI Group (UK) Ltd, Croydon CR0 4YY

MIX
Paper from
responsible sources
FSC
www.fsc.org
FSC™ C007454

for
Thomas Owen, Alexander James Erskine
and
Imogen Frances
the new generation

Henry David, 10th Ea...
1710 - 1767

Anne	Isabella	David
1739 - 1804	1741 - 1824	1741 - 1747
unmarried	= (1) William	died as
	(2) John	a child
	no children	

Frances	Margaret	Elizabeth	David Mnt
1771 - 1859	c. 1772/3 - 1857	1774 - 1800	(Davy)
= Samuel		= David	1776 - 18...
(Sam)			= Franc...
			Cadwall...
			(Cadd...
6 children	(unmarried)	no children	5 child...

Mary Ann Catherine
↓ 4 generations
Ruth + her author

TREE

Buchan = Agnes Stenart
d. 1778

...) Stenart	Henry (Harry)	Thomas (Tom)
...-1829 (Earl) ...garet ...gitimate ...ren	1746 - 1817	1750 - 1823

Henry:
= (1) Christian
(2) Erskine (Kate)
4 children

Thomas:
= (1) Frances (Fanny)
(2) Sarah

Erskine
Agnes
Hampden
Alfred ?

Mary	Henry David	Thomas	Esmé
c. 1784 - 1864	1786 - 1859	1788 - 1817	1789 - 1817
= Edward	= Harriet	= Henrietta	= Eliza
no children	8 children	4 children	3 children

N.B. Where source materials have occasionaly been inconsistent, I've had to guess at some details. B€

Prologue

Thomas

'It is ordained that when we die and travel forward on our journey, we forget our previous lives. But sometimes they linger at the fringe of consciousness and sometimes we are forced to remember by the curiosity of others. No man is an island, the poet said, and it is axiomatic that what some prefer to keep hidden, others wish to expose.

'And so one life in particular I recall now, a life like all lives filled with joy and sadness in equal measure, a life of ambition and fame but also of concern and care for the rights and miseries of my fellow men and women, and a life blighted in part by my own foolishness, a life whose danger I bequeathed unknowing to those who came after me.

'We were a large family and an affectionate one, a family imbued with the Christian principles of generations, but there is still much to explore for the diligent burrower after secrets and there is danger there, not of my making, but instilled by the intentions of others for good – also for evil.

'My forefathers came to me with warnings; I heard them but I did not always heed. I now realise how great must have been their anguish as they battered upon my consciousness and I raced on without pausing to listen. I learned but it was hard and it was dangerous.

'It is not within my power to do more than warn those who meddle with what is past; I can only speak to those who listen.

'I am watching over you, child of my children, but if you fail to hear my warnings, or choose not to heed them, I can do nothing to save you . . . '

1

1760

Scampering down the steep, echoing spiral stair, the small boy dragged open the heavy door and peered out into the close. In his family's airy flat on the top floor of the tenement it was still daylight, the south-facing windows lit by the last rays of the setting sun. Down here, where the tall grey buildings closed in to shut out the light, it was almost dark. He closed the door behind him, careful to lower the latch silently so the clunk of metal on metal did not echo up the stone stairway, then he skipped across the yard to the archway that led out into the High Street.

He knew he was forbidden to come out by himself. He knew the crowded streets were full of potential danger for a ten-year-old boy on his own. He didn't care. He was bored. His mother thought he was studying his books, his father was closeted in his study and his brothers and sisters, all older by far than himself, were busy about their own business. Out here on the streets of Edinburgh it was noisy, busy and exciting. He looked this way and that, hesitating for only a moment, then he ran out into the crowds where the din was overwhelming. Music spilled out from a tavern nearby; people were shouting, the sound of hooves echoed back and forth from the walls as did the rattle of wheels on the rough cobbles that paved the narrow street.

He headed up the hill towards St Giles' kirk and the tempting range of shops and booths nestling against its northern walls, and was gazing longingly into the bowed window of a pie shop when a fight broke out only feet from him, the two men shouting at each other quickly surrounded by crowds, yelling at them, cheering them on. The quarrel grew more heated, blows were exchanged, then one of the men drew a dirk. Thomas barely saw what happened next but he heard the gasp of the crowd as the blade found its mark, saw both men hesitate, seemingly equally appalled, as the ribald comments from the onlookers died away and fell silent and the shorter of the men slumped slowly to his knees and then forward onto his face. Thomas saw the scarlet stain spreading down the man's jacket and onto the cobbles as he fell, his face contorted with pain as he gave a final spasm and then lay still.

The crowd scattered, leaving Thomas staring at the slumped figure. Seeing the little boy standing there alone, a woman turned and grabbed his arm, dragging him away. After a moment's hesitation he followed her, too shocked to protest, turning to look over his shoulder at the body lying motionless on the ground as the rain began to fall. Someone had summoned the Town Guard. He heard a whistle and angry shouts. It was too late. The killer had vanished into the network of alleyways beyond the kirk.

As he watched, the boy saw the shadow of the dead man rise up and stand looking down at his own body. He held out his hands in a pathetic, futile gesture of protest, then he looked up. Thomas thought he saw the man's eyes seeking his own, pleading, before he faded slowly away.

He stood watching for one horrified second, then he turned and ran, ducking out of reach of the woman's motherly grasp, dodging through the crowds back down the street towards the safety of Gray's Close. He reached the familiar shadows of the entry, hurtling in, away from the horrors of the scene behind him, crossing the rain-slippery cobbles, desperate to get home. Fumbling with the latch he pushed the heavy door open, pausing in the impenetrable darkness at the foot of the stairwell, trying to get his breath, tears pouring down his face, before heading up the long steep spiral stairs. On, he went, his small feet pounding up the worn stone steps, on and on, up and up . . .

Ruth Dunbar woke with a start, staring into the blackness of the bedroom in her father's Edinburgh house, grasping for the dream, still feeling the little boy's terror as he ran, still seeing the drama unfold, raising her eyes in her dream from the body lying in the dark street to the shadowed grey walls, the crowds, illuminated so dramatically by the flaming torch held in the raised hand of a bystander, her gaze travelling on up to the great crown steeple of St Giles', starkly unmistakable halfway down Edinburgh's spine, silhouetted against the last crimson streaks of the stormy sunset.

She hugged her pillow to her, her breath steadying slowly as her eyes closed again.

In the morning she would remember nothing of the dream. Only much later would it surface to haunt her.

2

The Present Day

'Presumably you're going to sell the house?' Harriet Jervase sat back on the sofa and studied her friend Ruth's face.

There was an almost tangible silence in the room and then, clearly audible, footsteps moving softly through the hallway outside and up the stairs.

Ruth put her finger to her lips and stood up. Tiptoeing to the door, she pulled it open. The hall was empty, crepuscular beneath the high ceiling of the staircase well. She reached for the light switch. The austere hanging lamp with its faded shade threw an awkward cold light which left shadows over the turns in the staircase. Upstairs she heard the sound of a door closing.

She went back into the living room. 'That man gives me the creeps,' she said, throwing herself down in her chair again. 'He was listening at the door, I'm sure he was.'

'Why don't you tell him to go?' Harriet was Ruth's oldest friend. The two women had been at school together and had remained in touch over the years since. To Ruth, the only child of comparatively elderly parents, Harriet had been the nearest thing to a sibling. It was a given that she would have come up to Edinburgh for Ruth's father's funeral.

'I can't just throw him out. He was so kind to Dad.'

6

The presence of Timothy Bradford in the house had been an unwelcome surprise when she arrived. He appeared to have been staying there for some time, very much at home.

'Have you asked him what his plans are?'

Ruth shook her head. 'It's too soon.'

'No, it's not.' Harriet's voice was crisp. 'He's obviously not going to go until you say something.' She gave Ruth a quizzical glance. 'I know you feel you should have come up here sooner when your dad fell ill, but be honest, Ruth, he didn't tell you there was a problem; you came as soon as you knew. And if Timothy was comfortable looking after him, that was his choice. On his own admission, your dad has given him free bed and board in Edinburgh for months, but it's over now. Whatever you decide to do with the house, he has to go.'

'You're right,' Ruth agreed gloomily.

'Do you want me to tell him?'

'No!' Ruth was shocked. 'No, of course not.' She took a deep breath. 'I'll do it tomorrow after you've gone.' She frequently found herself resenting Harriet's calm assumption that she was the more efficient of the two of them, but it wasn't as if they saw each other often enough these days to make an issue of something so trivial.

'So, what will you do after you've got rid of him?' For all their closeness there had been long gaps when they hadn't seen each other, especially since Harriet had moved away from London and down to the West Country. She surveyed her friend fondly. Ruth had large grey eyes, her most striking feature; as a child they had always been the first thing people mentioned about her. Her hair on the other hand was a light golden brown, something she had never bothered about and which had become streaked with silver at the temples at a remarkably early age. It had suited her then and suited her now. Harriet had always felt strangely protective of Ruth. She was one of those people who seemed too vulnerable to exist in the normal world; which was rubbish. At some level Ruth was tough as old boots.

'I haven't any plans yet. I'm not sorry I gave up teaching; I'd been there too long and I was growing stale. I was just learning to appreciate my freedom as mistress of my own destiny when I found out Dad was so ill and I thought I'd have to move up here permanently to look after him.' Ruth sighed sadly. 'No more freedom after all. That was why I rented out my London flat. I didn't realise how short a time he had left.'

'And what of the husband?' Harriet never stooped to giving Richard his name.

Ruth laughed quietly. 'The ex-husband is fine. You saw him at the funeral. We agreed to go our own ways. We still talk occasionally. We're friends.'

There was a painful pause, a silence that covered so much that had happened: her longing for a child and the bleak discovery that Rick was unlikely ever to father a baby, the failed IVF, the decision to give up trying, the sense of empty pointlessness that followed.

Harriet cleared her throat uncomfortably. 'So, you really are fancy-free?'

'I suppose so.'

'With no London flat, at least for now, but instead an Edinburgh house.'

'Yup.'

'Any gorgeous men on the horizon?'

'No.'

'Not Timothy?'

'Definitely not Timothy.'

'So, what did you do with yourself those last few months before you came up here? If you weren't working, you must have been doing something.'

'Living off my share of the sale of Rick's and my house. I bought the flat with my half and that left me some change to give me the chance to stop and think about what I really want to do with the rest of my life. Meanwhile, I was free to read the books I want to read instead of set texts; explore the world, relax; take up hobbies for the first time since I grew up!'

'Stamp collecting?' Harriet's voice was dry, though there was a twinkle in her eye.

Ruth laughed. 'If you must know, I've started researching my family tree. My mother's family tree, to be exact.'

'Bloody hell, Ruth! I thought your father's attitude to your ancestors would have put you off that for life.'

Ruth grimaced. 'On the contrary. I always planned to do it one day, if only to show him I didn't care how much he hated them. Besides, I want to find a family, any family. Dad was my last living relative.' There was a long pause. 'So,' she changed the subject abruptly, 'enough of that. Let's talk about you. You haven't told me what you've been up to.'

'I'm still writing.' Harriet leaned forward, as always intense, her short red hair framing a face focused with sudden excitement. She hesitated momentarily then went on. 'I'm just starting a book about the vital role of women in the Second World War. Code-breakers, SOE – the specially-trained people who went overseas as spies and saboteurs – pilots, that sort of thing, telling the story of one particular woman from each category. I've arranged to go and stay with some friends in North Berwick while I'm up here. Liz and Pete Fleming. Liz discovered that her grandmother worked for SOE. She was dropped behind enemy lines and worked undercover near Paris. Can you imagine how brave you had to be to do that? So I'm writing a chapter about her.' Her eyes were sparkling. 'Another of my subjects is a woman called Dion Fortune who lived in Glastonbury.' Harriet lived in a cottage in the famously eccentric Somerset town. It was there she had already written several well-received popular biographies. 'Dion was a famous occultist. She lived at the foot of the Tor and conducted séances and meditations there. During the war, and this is the fascinating bit, she organised her followers to fight Hitler with magical energies and imagined armies of Arthurian knights with swords. You did know Hitler was into the occult?'

'I think I'd heard, yes.' Ruth was looking bemused.

'Comparatively few people have heard of Dion these days, but that's the point. These are unsung heroines and she's probably the oddest of them all.'

'Magic was my mother's thing,' Ruth put in wistfully. 'She'd have loved Glastonbury. She used to go to crystal shops and buy incense and pretty stones. She kept them in a bag to calm her nerves; she used to meditate. Dad hated her interest in all that stuff. I can still remember the row they had when he caught her looking at them. She tried to stand up for herself, but he sulked like a spoilt child if she tried to defy him and as far as I know she gave it all up.' Her face clouded as she remembered. 'To him, meditation and prayer were pointless at best and childish superstition at worst.'

Intellectually she understood why her father had hated religion, or, his second relentless dislike, anything or anyone whom he regarded as posh, but what she had never been able to forgive was the way he had taken his resentments on both counts out on his own wife.

Presumably it was an instinctive sense of self-defence as she was growing up that preserved Ruth from any interest in history or religion; she left home as soon as she finished school, first to study English literature at Cambridge University, then to learn to teach, then to take up a series of posts teaching English. She had even married an English teacher.

She and Rick supported each other through the heartbreaks and trials that beset the marriage, but something in their relationship died with their hopes of a family. They began to drift apart and it was just after their tenth wedding anniversary that Ruth had rebelled and ended both marriage and career.

'There was a lot about your mother that your dad didn't like, wasn't there,' Harriet said cautiously. 'Even when we were at school. I remember you telling me about her aristocratic ancestors.'

'And those he hated above all. Poor Mummy. I'm not sure why he ever married her, but they were happy as long as she toed the official line.' Ruth paused. 'I suspect he didn't realise when he first met her how well connected the family was, but as soon as he did all his left-wing prejudices kicked in with a vengeance. He found her stories intensely embarrassing. It would have destroyed his street cred if his Marxist pals had found out.'

Harriet smiled. 'But she didn't have a title or anything?'

'Good lord, no. We're talking generations back; hundreds of years even. The blue blood had worn extremely thin by the time it reached Mummy and, in me, well, it's virtually non-existent! No more than the occasional effete gene.' Ruth laughed. 'But back in the eighteenth century one of my great-great-great-great-great-grandfathers,' she was counting on her fingers, 'a chap called

10

Thomas Erskine, was Lord Chancellor of England. It sounded incredibly grand and impressive and sort of out of a fairy tale – what?'

Harriet had let out a strangled squeak. 'Lord Erskine was one of Dion's spirit guides!'

'I beg your pardon?'

'You wouldn't credit it, would you! What a coincidence!' Harriet gave a gurgle of delight. 'I knew I'd come across the name somewhere, but I'd forgotten it was you who had told me about him. A neighbour of mine lent me a book about Dion to read on the train and start filling in some background for my next chapter, and it mentions him! Those séances I told you about? Various exotic people like Confucius came to instruct her in the esoteric arts when she was at the start of her career as an occultist, and Lord E, as she called him, was one of them!'

Ruth gazed at her, bemused. 'Why? How?'

'I've no idea. In fact, you can tell me when you've done your family research! I'll leave the book with you when I go and you can read it yourself. It's a bit intense, to be honest, downright incomprehensible at times, but I love all this mystical stuff! I suppose I couldn't live in Glasto and not know a bit about it. I've friends who are deeply involved in it all. Did your mother ever mention that he had a spooky side?'

'No.' Ruth was still staring at her in disbelief. 'When I was old enough to learn what discretion was and realised what a difficult man my father could be and that I could be trusted to keep quiet, Mummy did tell me stories about them all and I loved listening to them. They were everything our lives at home weren't. Romantic and exotic and part of history, but not spooky, no. Far from it.' She gave Harriet a tolerant smile. 'What I liked was that they all had huge families and, unlike Dad, seem to have been so proud of where they came from. Hence my new hobby. I want to find out about them. And being in Edinburgh is perfect because that was where the story started.'

'And you're not afraid your father's ghost will haunt you if you do this?' Harriet looked at her quizzically.

'If he does,' Ruth retorted firmly, 'I shall have a stern word! I'm doing this for Mummy as much as me. She would have loved it.'

3

Sitting opposite Timothy Bradford at the kitchen table, Ruth found herself studying his face for the first time. He had pale pimply skin and mouse-coloured hair. When standing up he was the same height as she was but he had slumped into the chair and was leaning back, looking up at her, his expression guarded. He obviously resented her knock on his bedroom door and the invitation down to the kitchen.

She had seen Harriet off on the train at Waverley a couple of hours before and walked slowly back towards her father's house in quiet, refined Morningside, in the south-west of the city. A lively autumn wind had risen and caught her hair as she crossed the Meadows, the area of parkland lying between the city and her destination, the leaves flying in clouds from the trees. As she neared Number 26 her pace had slowed. She was not anxious to see Timothy again but, if he was at home, this was the time to face him.

'I wanted to thank you for looking after my dad,' she began. 'It was really good of you. I'm sorry it took me so long to find out he was ill.' She paused, hoping he would acknowledge the fact that he could have made the effort to contact her, but he ignored the remark. He was watching her through narrowed eyes.

'So, when are you going back to London?'

His question threw her completely. This was her line.

'I'm staying here,' she replied after the smallest of hesitations. 'There's a lot to sort out. So, I was going to ask you if you could let me know when you're planning on leaving.'

She saw a flash of something in his eyes. Anger? Shock? Indignation? She wasn't sure what it was, but it was immediately hidden, to be replaced by his previous bland stare. 'I hadn't planned on leaving, Ruth. Your father made it clear that this was my home as long as I wanted to stay here. He told me I was the son he had always wanted.'

In the end, with very bad grace, he agreed to move by the Thursday. The implication in his grudging acceptance of her request after she had threatened to go to her father's solicitor, was that it would only be a matter of time before he returned.

As a house guest, he was for those last few days exemplary. He was neat, tidy and quiet. She barely saw him. She never met him in the kitchen or on the stairs. She wouldn't have known he was still there at all had he not from time to time played his radio very softly in the evenings upstairs. Her father had given him the use of the two small rooms on the top floor and the guest bathroom which sat below it on the half landing. Once or twice she had tiptoed up when she knew he was out and tried the doors. Both were locked.

On the day stipulated in her ultimatum he moved out. She had been to the shops. Pushing open the front door she stopped in the hall. The house felt different; empty. She knew at once he had gone. Dropping her bag on the floor she stood at the bottom of the stairs looking up, then she caught sight of an envelope on the hall stand. It contained a postcard – a picture of the Scott Monument in the rain – and a set of keys.

> Thank you for your brief hospitality. I am sorry I outstayed my welcome. I will return when you have gone back to London, Tim

That was all. No forwarding address, nothing.

'I don't think so!' She found she had spoken the words out loud.

13

She ran upstairs two at a time. Both doors on the top floor stood open. She hesitated in the doorway of the first and looked round. He had left the window open and the room was cold, immaculately tidy, the bed stripped, the furniture neatly ordered. The wardrobe doors were slightly open. She peered in to find a mixed collection of empty coat hangers, nothing else. The second room, which overlooked the narrow parallel gardens at the rear of the long terraced street, was of identical size and layout except that the bed had been pushed against the wall to serve as a sofa. On the table there was a tray with neatly washed cups and saucers, an electric kettle, a couple of plates and an assortment of knives and forks and spoons.

In this room there was a range of fitted cupboards across the full width of one wall. Their doors were closed but she could see from where she stood that at some point they had been forced open; the wood was freshly chipped and splintered around the keyholes. Her heart sank. Pulling open the first door she saw the cupboard was full of boxes and suitcases, hat boxes and cardboard files, carelessly stacked on top of each other. With a sense of rising despair she opened the next door. That too was stuffed with boxes and papers. Only one cupboard appeared to have been left untouched. It contained a hanging rail and on it there were some half dozen of her mother's dresses, some of the tailored trousers she had loved and a slightly moth-eaten fur coat.

It was the first time Ruth had cried since her father died.

She found herself sitting on the makeshift sofa sobbing uncontrollably. These were all her mother's things. She recognised them; she could see letters and papers scrawled with her mother's large cursive handwriting; she remembered the old handbag that lay on top of one of the boxes, the little make-up case, her hair brushes, her faded silk bathrobe, scarves, hats.

Had her father pushed them all in so carelessly, or had someone else forced open the cupboards and ransacked them? It had to be Timothy who had so terribly violated her mother's privacy. Who else would have done it? Her father was a meticulous man. If he had kept her mother's things, he would have kept them neatly. Standing up, Ruth fingered them miserably.

14

Now, when it was too late to talk to him about it, was this a sign of her father's love and his loss when her mother died? He had bullied his wife, and harangued her, questioned everything that made her who she was and made her life unbearably unhappy, and yet he had kept all these memories of her. It doubled the insult that Timothy had gone through the cupboards and then shoved the contents back out of sight, not even bothering to hide his depredations.

Why hadn't she come up to Scotland sooner? Unable to reconcile herself to her father's treatment of her mother, she had never visited him again after her mother died, not until these last weeks, when he was too ill to speak to her. It had been his next-door neighbour, Sally Laidlaw, who had found her phone number and called her. Timothy had done nothing to contact her and seemed to have been surprised that she existed at all. He had been living in this house for several months and her father had not mentioned to him even once, or so Timothy claimed, that he had a daughter living in London.

Suddenly she couldn't bear to stay there a moment longer. Running downstairs, her cheeks wet with tears, she went into the front room. She didn't turn on the light. She just sat there as the colour faded from the sky outside while indoors, behind the heavy net curtains, everything grew dark.

It was only as she was falling asleep that night that it occurred to her to wonder if Timothy had stolen anything.

She had made the room next to her father's into her base when she had moved into the house; the small box room next to it had been occupied by Harriet for the few days she had stayed. A carer had slept there during her father's last weeks, but Harriet's vivacious personality still filled the room now, as did the scent of her various lotions and creams. 'Glasto's best,' she had joked as she was packing to leave. 'All herbal; all guaranteed to give me a luscious skin or spiritual insight or both. Here, have them.' She had pushed several bottles into Ruth's hands. 'Your need is greater than mine. They will soothe your aura. I can always get more. And here's the book I told you about. I've marked the first place Lord E is mentioned, though he seems to have guided her through her whole life.' She clasped her fingers round Ruth's wrists. 'Remember, for a couple of weeks or so I won't be too far away. Call me, any time, if it all gets too lonely.'

It was a complete surprise when next morning Ruth received an email from her father's solicitor inviting her to the office to discuss an 'unexpected problem'.

James Reid had been a friend of her father's for many years. The tall, grey-haired man who rose to greet her with great courtesy, pulled out a chair for her then returned to his own side of the desk and produced a folder which he aligned on his blotter without opening it. This was an office, she noticed, where all signs of modernity – computer, scanner, printer – had been relegated to a shelf along the back wall beneath a solid phalanx of old law books. It was somehow comforting.

'I'm sorry to ask you to come in so soon after our telephone conversation,' he said once she was settled, 'but there is something that needs to be addressed as a matter of urgency.' They had spoken briefly on the phone after her father's death, and again at the funeral. Her father's affairs, he had assured her then, were relatively straightforward. Donald Dunbar had left her, his only child, everything, the house and all his money of which there was quite a substantial sum. Now James Reid glanced up at her with what appeared to be some anxiety. He was a handsome man, perhaps in his mid-sixties, she guessed, and was blessed by a natural expression of wise benevolence. She felt her stomach tighten with anxiety.

'A possibly contentious issue has arisen.' He paused.

Ruth felt her mouth go dry. 'What's happened?' It came out as a whisper.

'Do you know a Timothy Bradford?'

Her heart sank. 'Yes. He was staying with my father in the last months of his illness.'

'In what capacity?'

'Capacity?' She echoed the word helplessly. 'What do you mean?'

'Was he there as a friend? A guest? A carer?'

'A bit of each, I suppose. I don't really know.'

16

'Not a relative?'

'No. Absolutely not.'

'And you hadn't met him before?'

'No. I had no idea he was even there until I came to Edinburgh. I assumed he was some kind of lodger. He claims Dad never mentioned me. It was a neighbour who got in touch to tell me about his illness.'

'So your father didn't tell him he had a daughter?'

'He said not.'

'I see.' He sighed. 'Mr Bradford has written to us informing us that he has a copy of your father's will. A far more recent will than the one which I have, leaving everything to you, which was originally written fifteen years ago.' He paused for a moment. 'The new will leaves the house and all your father's possessions to Mr Bradford.' Before Ruth had a chance to interrupt he went on, 'He further claims that he is your father's son by a liaison formed in the late 1970s before your father and mother were married. I am sorry. This must be an awful shock to you.'

Ruth sat speechless for several seconds. 'I can't believe it. Daddy would never have done such a thing.' She looked across at him helplessly. It wasn't clear whether she was thinking about her father's affair or the fact that he had changed his will.

'I find it incomprehensible,' James Reid said gently. 'I have known your father for over forty years and I remember no mention of such a circumstance, but we are forced to take this claim seriously. The will is, as far as we can see, properly drawn up and signed and witnessed by someone from a reputable firm. I am so sorry.'

'Who was his mother?' At last Ruth managed to speak.

'He doesn't give her name.' He opened the folder on his desk. It contained a single sheet of paper. 'He gives no details of how long he has actually known your father, or of how he came to be living in Number 26.' He looked up at her. 'As soon as the will is processed, he wants vacant possession of the property. In other words, he wants you to leave.'

4

Ruth took a cab back from the lawyers, terrified that she would come home to find Timothy had returned. Her hands were shaking as she inserted the key in the lock, but to her relief the front door opened normally. She closed it behind her and drew the bolt across, then she paused to listen. The house was silent.

Tiptoeing into the sitting room she sat down on the edge of the sofa just as she had the night before. Velvet-covered, under a tartan rug, it was placed in the window so the light fell over her shoulder. She remembered from her childhood how it had been a favourite place for her mother to sit and read. Now it was dusty and faded; the room smelt stale and cold and unloved. The whole house felt abandoned and empty. Even the ticking of the clock had stopped. She had hated that clock as a child. It had underlined the echoing quiet of the place, the passing of time, her loneliness as the only child of two older parents, and she had felt it was mocking her with every jerky movement of its hands.

James Reid had assured her that nothing would happen while he appealed on her behalf against the new will. The absolute worst that could happen was that, if it was proved genuine, she would have to share the inheritance. As her father's undisputed daughter, she was entitled to at least half of everything. He also told her that she was quite justified, at least for now, in changing the locks if she was nervous; after all, whether or not Timothy was related to her, he was still a stranger.

Her phone made her jump. It was Harriet. 'How are things going? I'm loving it here in North Berwick. Liz and Pete are being so kind. I can stay as long as I like, so I'll be here for a while, working on my book.'

The sound of her voice broke the spell. Ruth stood up and, walking round the sofa, drew back the curtains that had blocked half the light from the room. She stood staring out as she relayed the morning's events.

'Shit!' Harriet summed up in one word.

'I'd never given the inheritance a thought; of course I hadn't. I'd spoken to James on the phone after Daddy died; he had told me that my father's will, which he made after Mummy died, left everything to me.'

Harriet snorted. 'I told you Timothy gave me the creeps. What a bastard! So, what happens next?'

'I wait to hear from James. He is formally going to contest the will. Apparently, if Timothy is genuinely Daddy's son, he can claim half the inheritance, whatever the will says, but then so can I.'

'Ouch. I'm sure he'll sort it out. Keep calm, Ruthie. It'll be OK. There's no way that vile toad could be a relation of yours.'

Switching off her phone, Ruth sat for a moment, staring into space.

The house and all your father's possessions, his money . . .

'Don't panic,' James had said as he shook hands with her at his office door. 'Your father's bank accounts are frozen and nothing will happen for a while. These things take time.'

And, she reminded herself, he had told her she was entitled to change the locks.

The locksmith said he could make her his last call that evening. Pulling the curtains across once more after a quick look out into the street, she checked the bolt on the front

19

door and then headed back upstairs to the cupboards on the top floor.

Looking at the rail of dresses and coats she was pretty certain they hadn't been touched; presumably Timothy wasn't interested in clothes. But what about the other stuff, the boxes and cartons? Now she was looking more carefully she could see paler patches in the dust. Parcel tape had been pulled off and not replaced, latches on old suitcases were standing open when she knew her father, even in the act of banishment, would have made sure they were all neatly closed. He had been too ill to have made it up to the top floor for a long time, never mind stir up the contents of the cupboards like this. This had to have been Timothy. He had rifled through all her mother's precious possessions, the things she had treasured and loved, her books, papers, jewellery, pictures. Even the little writing box with its inlaid brass initials that Ruth remembered from her childhood was there, lying crookedly on top of another box in the corner.

Methodically she began to take items one by one out of the cupboards and line them neatly on the floor. Tossed in a corner of one of the cupboards was a teddy bear. He had been hers, her beloved Pooh. She picked him up and held him close, burying her face in his threadbare fur. He had lost the warm comforting scent she remembered and smelt of sawdust. She had loved him above all her other toys and, knowing this, her mother had kept him for her; so too, she realised with a sob, had her father.

The locksmith did not miss the fact that her hands were shaking as she fetched him a cup of tea while he attended to the front door. 'Were you burgled, hen?' he asked sympathetically as he wielded his screwdriver.

'No. Expecting to be.'

'That's tough. On your own here, are you?' He was thorough and efficient, testing the new lock, handing her the keys, doing the same in the kitchen where the back door led out into the narrow garden. 'I'm glad to see you have bolts here. Don't forget to use them. Maybe get an alarm fitted in the house. Motion sensors. If you're scared of being attacked, you can think about a link to the police; or at least a rape alarm.'

It hadn't occurred to her that Timothy might attack her. It was the house and its contents he wanted; her mother's treasures. Surely she ought to hide them somewhere they couldn't be found.

Was there no one in Edinburgh she could go to for help? It was then her thoughts turned to Finlay Macdermott. He had been at school with her ex, and one of their greatest friends. It was worth a try.

'So, what you're saying is, you need to hide stolen goods, eh!' The familiar voice rang out of the phone after she called him and explained the situation. To her relief he had sounded pleased to hear from her.

'Not stolen!' she protested. 'They're mine. Legally. The solicitor said my mother's things would almost certainly be deemed to be mine as my father disowned them and locked them away. The law would presume he was planning to pass them on to me.' She wasn't sure if that bit was true. 'They're probably not worth much either, so I am not cheating the government of tax.'

'Blow the government!'

She realised suddenly how much she had missed Finlay's irreverent humour, which used to echo so often down the line from Scotland and around their living room in London.

'I will be over to see you tomorrow, sweetheart. First thing.'

She smiled as he ended the call.

Whatever had precipitated that final quarrel between her parents had echoed in her head forever afterwards. She must have been very young but her mother's angry denials and pleas and eventual capitulation had haunted her. It was then that her mother's precious things had first disappeared. Ruth looked round, trying to remember what Lucy had brought to her husband's Scottish home from her parents' house in Sussex. One or two of the more robust items were still there, downstairs, the others, the delicate chairs that Ruth as a small child had loved so much, the spindly-legged tables, had vanished overnight. Where were they? There had been portraits of ladies in exotic clothes and bewigged gentlemen and landscapes and drawings and paintings of houses and castles, horses and dogs. Where were those?

There were two boxes of books still in the cupboard, at the very back; presumably Timothy had felt they were valueless. She hauled them out to join the rest of the items on the floor and began to look through them. These were stories of ancient Scotland, the poetry, the works of Sir Walter Scott, a tattered volume entitled *The Lives of the Lord Chancellors* which had, she assumed, included her mother's great-great-great-great-grand-father, the same Lord Erskine who had precipitated her father's rage. She picked them out, handling them with something like reverence. *The Lives of the Lord Chancellors* was signed by the author, John, Lord Campbell. She stared at the title page in awe. It was a first edition, published in 1847. She flipped open a shabby leather-bound volume of Sir Walter Scott's *Quentin Durward*. Another first edition, signed by the author in 1823, and another signed 'Byron'. She sat back and took a deep breath. Her ancestors had known these people.

When, all those weeks ago in London, she had started the research it had been relatively easy. All she did was call up Lord Erskine on her laptop, after she had threaded her way through all the different men of that name until she had found the one she wanted.

She had clicked on the entry, feeling almost guilty looking him up, but thinking of him as a historical reality helped start to dispel the lingering miasma of superstitious dislike her father had created around his name. This man was someone her mother had been inordinately proud of.

Thomas Erskine, 1st Baron Erskine KT PC KC (10 January 1750–17 November 1823) was a British lawyer and poli-tician. He served as Lord Chancellor of the United Kingdom between 1806 and 1807 in the Ministry of all the Talents . . .

He was, it appeared, the son of an earl. That was what her father would have hated most. He would not have resented the fact that the man was a brilliant lawyer, surely, or the fact that to all intents and purposes he was a self-made man. It was the fact that he was the son of the 10th Earl of Buchan, a Scottish aristocrat of ancient lineage, that had got up her father's nose.

She smiled sadly. Over the last weeks of her father's life she had put her lurking interest in genealogy to the back of her mind, but suddenly here, tucked into an untidy heap in a long forgotten cupboard box, was all that remained of her mother's background. She sat cradling Lord Campbell's book on her knee for several minutes, fighting back her tears, before gently putting it down on the carpet beside her and scrambling to her feet to reach for the writing box.

It was about fifty centimetres long and made of some dark wood, perhaps rosewood or mahogany, inlaid with brass decorations and entwined initials and would when unlocked open to make a writing slope. She lifted it onto the divan. The box was broken. There was a deep splintered gouge around the lock and the delicate mechanism itself had been levered out completely; she found it lying on the floor of the cupboard. The body of the box under the leather and gilt writing surface was empty, as were the surrounding small compartments and drawers. Was it her father who had done this all those years ago, or Timothy on his quiet nights upstairs alone after his host had gone to sleep? Whoever it was had used considerable force to lever it open.

She sat back wondering what, if anything, had been hidden there. There had been a secret drawer in it somewhere. She remembered her mother showing her and chuckling at the little girl's wonder as it slid out of the side of the box. Picking it up, Ruth shook it experimentally. If there was something inside it would surely rattle. There was no sound. She put it down again and studied it carefully. Where had the secret drawer been? She ran her fingers over every surface. There were no grooves or ridges that she could discern, save for the vicious damage inflicted by chisel or screwdriver; nothing that betrayed any hidden compartment.

Her mother had pressed something. As she cudgelled her memory, an image of the slim questing fingers with their narrow

23

gold wedding ring the only decoration, popped into Ruth's head. There had been some sort of button inside one of the compartments. There had been a silver-filigree-topped inkbottle there and her mother had lifted it out before pressing the secret place. The inkpot had gone, its former position clearly marked by the faded black stains on the wood. With a sudden surge of hope, Ruth felt the side of the compartment. There was indeed an almost undetectable bump beneath the thin veneer. She pressed it firmly. There was a click but nothing happened.

She pressed again, harder this time. There was no sound. The mechanism, such as it was, had shifted but she couldn't see any sign of a response. Once more she ran her fingers over the outside of the box and then she felt it: a faint ridge at the bottom of the back panel that hadn't been there before. She bent closer and tried to insert her fingernail. Slowly and reluctantly a small drawer began to emerge with her coaxing from the body of the box. It was stuffed with some sort of soft material. Intrigued and excited, Ruth unwrapped the delicate silk handkerchief to expose a portrait miniature. She sat staring at the tiny painting in the palm of her hand. It was of a young man; he wore a short white wig, a pale blue coat and a lace ruffle at his throat. She turned it over to see if there was anything written on the back. There wasn't.

She stared at it for a long time. Whoever had forced open the writing box had missed the secret drawer. She ran her fingers around the back of the drawer once more. It was no more than an inch deep and the handkerchief had stuffed it very tightly, but there was something else wedged in the corner. She pulled out a leather ring box. Inside was a gold signet ring with a blue stone, engraved with some kind of insignia. She slid it onto her forefinger where it hung loosely. The crest, if that was what it was, was difficult to decipher. She would need a better light than this to see clearly what it represented. The last thing in the drawer, also wrapped in a scrap of silk, was a small gold locket on a narrow piece of black ribbon. In it there was a lock of hair.

She felt safest in the kitchen at the back of the house. Pulling down the blind, she put her finds on the kitchen table where the strip-light threw no shadows. Her laptop was already there with the briefcase into which she had thrown all her papers when she had set off north to her father's bedside. Since then she had been back to London only once, leaving her father in Timothy's care, more fool her, to arrange the letting of her flat and to collect everything she would need for what she had expected might be a protracted stay in the north. Struggling onto the train with the two large suitcases and her heavy shoulder bag she had wondered if she was mad to bring so much; now she was glad she had.

She set the writing box down on the far side of the table, together with her much-loved teddy bear, and realised that suddenly another emotion was vying with her sadness as she looked from the box to the portrait miniature to the ring. It was excitement. These must have belonged to her ancestors. Her family. The people she wanted to summon from the past to help assuage her loneliness. They were direct links with the story she was now more determined than ever to uncover. Clues. She pulled her laptop forward. Lord Erskine was the most contentious and famous person in the family who she had heard of and she had begun her research into him back in London. Now it was time to reveal the next chapter in his life. She opened her notebook at a new page and reached for her pen.

Thomas

My career has been followed closely by those who study the history of the legal profession and I am flattered by their attention to detail; my own family over generations have made me something of a hero too, to be enshrined in legend and anecdote. Much, I am glad to say, has been forgotten and much buried, but now I sense the moment has come that I had been dreading. Someone is about to uncover the past in more detail than I care to own and it is this great-great-great-great-great-granddaughter of mine. I find myself being drawn ever more closely towards her; she has inherited more of me than I would have thought possible. She is someone who loves to read and search for detail and she has now at her fingertips, if she chooses to read it, a family archive that will reveal everything I had thought forgotten. Now as I watch her pore over the smallest detail of my youth I smile, yes, sometimes I smile, I wince, I begin to recall it all and I recoil as she draws near to events I had thought buried in perpetuity. Is it thus with us all? I think it is. Though perhaps I had more to bury than most and I sense she is not going to be deflected from her quest. But will her determination to uncover my story awaken more memories than my own? There is one particular ghost in my past I would not want roused under any circumstances, ever.

5

1760

'Mama has said we can go to Cardross!' David Erskine strode into the room, his hair awry. At seventeen he was the eldest son in the family. His brother Harry was thirteen and Tom was ten. 'She said it would be wonderful to have us out from under her feet for a few weeks.'

His two brothers glanced at each other, unable to believe their luck. 'No sisters?' Harry said cautiously.

David smiled triumphantly. 'No sisters!' Their elder sister Anne was twenty-one; Isabella was twenty. 'They will stay with Mama. She can spend the summer finding husbands for them.' All three boys sniggered. They knew their sisters' lack of prospects worried their parents. Anne particularly was studious and religious and she, like them all, had no fortune. Poor Anne was doomed to spinsterhood, but her mother had not given up yet.

David had been working on their plan to escape the confines of the top-floor tenement flat in Gray's Close for a couple of weeks now, since Tom's escapade in the High Street. His little brother irritated him enormously, but at base he was only small and his terror at his experience had moved even David. The boy had come home, white with shock and crying, shakily confessing to their parents where he had been and what he had seen.

Satisfied that his son wasn't able to identify the culprit, and needn't be called as a witness, his father had on this occasion contented himself with a strong reprimand, hastily brushing aside Tom's stammered description of the man's ghostly apparition and wearily agreeing with his eldest son that it would benefit Tom as much if not more than all of them to be free of the claustrophobic confines of the flat for a while. Some good fresh air was what the boy needed to rid him of his dangerously active imagination.

The family castle at Cardross had been sold fifteen years before by their father, and only his elder children, David, Anne and Isabella, could remember it. In David's case, barely. Neither Henry (Harry to the family), nor Tom, the youngest, had been born. David could still picture the ruinous tower, crumbling walls, miles of wonderful countryside, forest, moorland, wild desolate bog, boating on the loch, freedom. Life in Edinburgh was one long round of constraint for all of them. Their father was charming and vague and kind to his children, preoccupied with his own interests. It was their mother who was strict. It was she who taught them all to read, progressing to Latin and then to her great passion, mathematics. It was she who held the purse strings, she who carefully and methodically eked out their meagre finances, she who, though she knew he would deny it, had persuaded her husband to sell the Cardross estates to his cousin John of Carnock, who, as a popular and brilliant professor of law at the university, earned a large enough salary to run the place. John Carnock, amongst his many other duties, quietly kept a fatherly eye on David, who was one of his students, and on the rest of the Buchan brood. His own children were grown and he pitied his cousin's young family, cooped up in the rambling flat on the crowded spine of Edinburgh's heart. He was only too happy to agree to David's plea and allow the children to escape to their ancestral home for the summer.

The Earl and Countess of Buchan still had some of their estates, the Linlithgowshire acres and Kirkhill House at Broxburn, thirteen miles from Edinburgh, but that too was ruinous and leaked, just as Cardross had done. Agnes, the children's mother, had hated living in these ancient castles. She loved the sophisticated delights of Edinburgh's intellectual life, with writers, lawyers, politicians, ministers of the kirk always there, taking tea, dining, discussing excitedly the matters of the moment, the concerts and the theatre. It was a huge relief to her when all that was left of Cardross to the Buchan family was the title. David, as the eldest son, was Lord Cardross; his sisters were Ladies; Harry and Thomas, much to their glee, were styled 'honourable'.

John Carnock sent the trio off in his coach. He knew Agnes, Presbyterian to the roots of her hair, would not have approved such luxury but he persuaded her that as he was sending a load of books and furniture to Cardross anyway it would be a favour to have David there to see them safely in place and to keep an eye on things. He was refurbishing the castle, he explained to her, and there was no one there from the family to oversee matters as he was spending the summer in town working on his latest book. David, it was made clear, would be expected to watch the builders and report back.

No one, least of all Agnes, expected anything of the sort to happen. The moment the boys set foot outside the coach they were off into the park, laughing and shouting, David, far from keeping an eye on his brothers, a child again in his head, leading the way.

Their first big excursion had to be to his favourite place, the loch and the island on it where Mary Queen of Scots had spent some of her childhood holidays.

The two bigger boys rowed; Tom sat in the bow staring round him in awe. The Loch of Menteith, two miles from Cardross House, was peaceful, surrounded by low hills but with the great peak of Ben Lomond off to the west. There was a gentle breeze wafting the sweet smell of grass and heather towards them across the water as they neared the island of Inchmahome.

From the boat they could just see the grey ruins of the ancient priory through the trees, the clouds dappling shadows over the soaring sunlit arches and broken pillars. In the distance they could see someone from the village fishing from the stern of his boat, but he was far away and paid no attention to the boys. As they drew nearer an osprey plunged into the loch alongside the boat and dragged a fish out of the water, flying away towards the west. The island itself was deserted.

Running the boat ashore, the two elder boys scrambled out eagerly. Cousin John's housekeeper had placed some bottles of ale into the boat for them, and pausing only to put them into the water at the edge of the loch to keep cool, the two elder boys raced ahead. David turned. 'Come on, Tom!' he cried impatiently. Tom was still staring through his little telescope, back the way they had come. He stowed it in his bag and climbed out onto the grassy bank. His brothers didn't wait for him; they were used to him dawdling behind, his attention taken by every new bird and plant and dragonfly. He had a small notebook which went everywhere with him; in it he would make laborious drawings and sketches of everything he saw, drawings which even David had to admit were not bad.

Slinging his bag over his shoulder, he made his way after David and Harry along the track towards the ruins of the old priory. The stone arches stood out above the trees, beckoning him on as he followed sturdily in his bothers' wake, pausing to watch the red squirrels chattering angrily in the sweet chestnut trees and a heron standing motionless near the water's edge. He dropped further and further behind the others as they raced ahead to explore the ruins, climbing over fallen trees, watching the dragon-flies that hovered over the crystal-clear water of the loch.

He was slowly catching up with them at last when he realised they were not alone. A man in a long black woollen robe was walking under the arch where the west door of the great church had been. Tom stopped, half shy, half scared. They had every right to be there, he knew that, but there was something about the man and his intense self-absorption which excluded the outer world absolutely. He was praying, Tom realised, and completely unaware of their presence.

He watched as the figure walked slowly away from them into the shadows and disappeared. Only when he could no longer see him did he call quietly, 'Was that a monk?'

David had scrambled up onto the wall of the ancient building, sitting in a window embrasure, his back against the warm stone, his eyes closed against the sunlight. It was Harry who stopped in his tracks. 'Where?' He swung round.

'There. He walked up that way.' Tom was suddenly flustered. 'We shouldn't go after him. I think he was praying.'

David sat up and stared round. 'Where? I can't see anyone.'

'Are you sure you saw someone, Tom?' Harry studied his little brother's face. All three boys had caught the sun as they rowed across the loch, their hair tousled in the wind, and Harry's eyes were bright with laughter. 'It wasn't one of your ghosts, was it?' he probed gently.

Tom flushed a deep red. 'No. He was there.' He dropped his bag on the ground and ran to the arch where he had seen the man walking away from them along the nave that was no longer there. The place was deserted; long grasses grew amongst the stones. A bird flew up as he approached, calling in alarm.

'Oh, Tom, for goodness' sake!' David, ever scornful, allowed a cruel edge into his voice. 'You and your ghosts! They're all in your head, you know. You'll be sent to an asylum if you go on like this.' Nevertheless, he looked round with a shiver and it wasn't very long before he suggested they go and find their food. As he and Harry made their way back towards the beach where they had left the boat, Tom hesitated, hanging behind, and as his brothers' voices grew fainter, he realised he could hear the monks chanting, the sound rising and falling in the distance above the rustle of the trees and the lapping of the water on the shore. He felt the hair standing up on the nape of his neck and, terrified, he turned and ran after them.

They retrieved the bags of bread and ham and cheese and pulled the bottles of ale out of the water. Tom, still chastened and embarrassed by David's scorn and unsettled by what he had heard, sat a little apart. He was determined not to cry. He knew his elder brother could be nasty; it was Harry who was kind and patted him almost paternally on the shoulder as he came over and, cutting off a chunk of cheese with his dirk, gave it to him with an apple.

Tom took a deep breath. 'Why did Papa sell Cardross?' he asked Harry. He had found himself a nook in the stones of an

31

old wall from where he could watch the jackdaws squabbling on top of the broken arches behind them.

'He needed the money.' Harry had already started to share out the rest of the food.

'Mama is always talking about money,' Tom followed his train of thought doggedly. 'Are we very poor?'

'Have you only just noticed?' David snapped.

'Why?'

Harry took pity on his small brother. 'The earls of Buchan were rich and powerful once, long ago. But they kept making mistakes. They chose the wrong side in politics.'

'Politics?' Tom was screwing up his eyes against the sun. He had spotted the osprey again, flying low over the water.

'Like Uncle James, Mama's brother. He fought for Prince Charlie. That's why he has to live abroad. All his estates were confiscated.'

'He doesn't know what confiscated means!' David's voice was muffled by the hunk of bread he was chewing as he lay back on the grass.

'I do!' Tom retorted. 'It means taken away by the government.'

'Well, then. You know why we're poor. They gave some of the land back, but Papa has to live off a measly allowance from trustees who have no idea how an earl should live. That's why we have to live in a flat in Edinburgh instead of a castle.'

'Papa and Mama still like Prince Charlie?' Tom framed it as a question.

'Yes, but you must never, ever, say so. King George is our king now. Remember that.' David sat up. 'If you forget every word I've ever said to you, Tom, remember that one. King George is our king and we are loyal to him. Whatever we may think in private, we keep it private. Understand?'

Tom nodded. He was already watching another bird, but somewhere deep inside his head he tucked his brother's advice away. He would remember it all his life.

It was the most wonderful holiday. They visited the loch and its islands again and again. Tom learnt to row; Harry taught him to swim. They went fishing. David took them outside at night and they lay on their backs in the long grass, staring up at the sky while he told them the names of the stars. They explored the castle and its policies; they made friends with the builders who were constructing a new extension to the castle and with the men working to drain areas of the great moss behind the castle so that it could be turned into rich farmland. Many of the labourers were Highlanders, dispossessed after the Jacobite rebellion fifteen years before; they were full of stories of battles and of grief, legends of ghosts and fairies, and Tom in particular listened wide-eyed to every tale, spending hours sitting listening as they wielded their long-handled spades or sat around their campfires at night. The moss fascinated him. In daylight the colours made him itch to reach for his pens and brushes, trying to capture the emerald of the moss itself, the russets and yellows and the glories of the purple heather. On hot days they saw adders and lizards basking and they heard the calls of distant snipe and the chink of stonechats and the yelp of buzzards. But at night it was lonely and eerie, swathed in mist and moon-shot shadows and the only sound was the haunting call of an owl.

All three boys were devastated when David received a letter from their mother informing them that the time had come for them to return home and that their cousin of Carnock would be sending his coach at the end of the week. The days were not as warm now as when they had first arrived; mist hung in the trees in the mornings and there was a scent of autumn in the air, but even so, they could have stayed there for ever.

Tom wrote everything down in his notebook, careful with the details, including sketches and even little tinted paintings. One of his mother's friends had shown the boy how to use a brush to shade his inks and to grind up pigments to make the watercolour washes that would make his sketches realistic and he practised in the evenings by the light of a lamp as his brothers read or left him alone to walk through the moonlight to take a dram with their neighbours. He didn't realise he was keeping a diary, but the keeping of meticulous records was another skill he would practise all his life.

6

Finlay greeted Ruth with a crushing bear hug when he arrived next morning just after nine. He brought croissants and coffee in a Thermos. 'I wasn't sure whether your father would have proper coffee-making equipment,' he said as he sat down at the kitchen table, the paper bags in front of him. He was a huge man, a larger-than-life character in every way, the same age as Rick, but as they had often joked, he appeared older and was far more worldly wise.

He surveyed her sternly. 'My God, you look knackered, sweetheart.'

She reached in the cupboard for cups and plates. 'I was up late doing family research. It's a good distraction from what's been going on here.'

He studied her for a moment. 'I was so sorry to hear about your father. What a bum summer you've had. And now this ne'er-do-well turns up!' He began to unpack their breakfast. 'It broke my heart when I heard you and Rick had split up.'

When he finally allowed her to speak she told him the whole story as he sat devouring his croissant, his eyes fixed unwaveringly on her face.

'Forgive me asking, but why did your mother stay with your father?' he asked when she finished her story.

Ruth smiled sadly. 'I keep asking myself that. I used to come up to Edinburgh and meet her sometimes secretly; he never knew. After she died I had no contact. He never tried to persuade me to come home.'

'Till he needed you.'

'Even then, it wasn't him who called, it was Sally, next door. To be honest, he barely recognised me.'

They sat in silence for a few moments, then he leaned forward, seemingly re-energised. 'Right, so, you want me to store some of your precious family stuff for you.'

She nodded slowly. 'I don't think it's all that valuable in money terms; I suspect Timothy has already been through it and if there was anything worth having he's probably taken it, but I feel a bit threatened, as if he would take things out of spite if he thought I valued them.'

He leaned forward, elbow on the table, chin in hand, and studied her again with disconcerting concentration. 'I can take as much as you like. You have me to take care of you now.' He grinned boyishly. 'The problem will be to make sure he isn't spying on you. If he thinks you are moving anything out, he might go to the courts. I don't know the law on this. We should check with your Mr Reid. Is there any large furniture you want removed?'

'No, most of the stuff I want to keep is really small. This writing box is the largest.' It was lying on the kitchen table. 'The rest is in suitcases and boxes. I'm still looking for the family portraits. I don't know if they even exist still. Dad really hated them. Mum only brought them here because there was no one else for my grandparents to leave them to. I don't care about the rest of the furniture, to be honest.'

'Right.' He stood up. 'Why don't we go out to my place now with a load. That writing box for a start. I could mend that for you. My car is just up the road. We'll check he isn't lurking. What sort of car does he have?'

'I don't know. I don't even know if he has one.'

Finlay was back at once. 'He's parked right outside, or someone is, watching this house. Take a shifty out of the front window.'

It was Timothy. Cautiously she peered from behind the heavy

curtain. He had made no attempt at being subtle; his hands were clamped on the steering wheel with every appearance of impatience. From time to time he glanced at his watch. 'He looks as though he's waiting for someone. No, he's getting out of the car.' She stepped back from the window. 'He's coming in.'

They heard the sound of a key in the lock. Timothy wrestled with it for a moment, before uttering an exclamation of impatience. Ruth opened her mouth to protest, but Finlay put his finger to his lips and gestured to her to remain out of sight.

He crept towards the door surprisingly quietly for such a large man and opened it. Timothy was standing there, a key in his hand. 'Can I help you?' Finlay stood four-square in the doorway.

'She's changed the lock!' Timothy's anger was barely contained. He didn't ask who Finlay was and Finlay didn't volunteer the information.

'If by "she" you mean Ruth, you're right. She has. On the advice of her solicitor. She suspected, rightly, obviously, that you had kept a key to her house when she asked you to leave.'

'My house.' Timothy was tight-lipped.

'I doubt if any court in the land would substantiate that claim.' Finlay folded his arms. 'I understand you've removed articles belonging to Ruth's mother which are her property and no part of her father's inheritance; that is theft.'

Timothy stared at him, seemingly inarticulate with fury, then he turned and walked back to the car. Finlay closed the door. He put his hand in his pocket and brought out his phone. 'Let me make a note of the licence number for future reference.'

Ruth was seething with anger. 'The nasty sneaky man! What was he planning to do when he got in?'

'I should have asked him.' Finlay slipped his phone back into his pocket. 'I think you should ring your Mr Reid. Tell him what happened. We have to keep the law tight on your side and at the same time warn him that your so-called brother is not playing cricket.'

Ruth stared at him, her mouth open. 'My brother!' she echoed in horror. 'No!'

'Well, half-brother. And almost certainly, no. He will have to take a DNA test to prove it.'

'Of course.' She frowned. 'I hadn't thought of that. That will prove he isn't Dad's son.'

There was a moment's silence. 'Or that he is.'

'Right.' Finlay glanced towards the window. 'Let's see if he's gone. If he has, I'll load up my car with anything you want to save right now before he has a chance to come back. You should also tell Reid that he went through your mother's belongings, and damaged them, and you suspect he may have taken valuables away. For instance,' he paused thoughtfully, 'what about jewellery? Or family silver? Those pictures you mentioned. You showed me the ring and the little miniature, but what else did she have?'

'There was a jewellery box. I can't really remember what was in it, but it lived on her dressing table. I don't think Dad made her lock that away, but she never wore anything out of it as far as I remember. That's not up there.' She gave a miserable little wail. 'Oh, Finlay! If he has taken anything I'll never know.'

'We'll sort it, Ruthie, don't you fret.'

They packed up all the most sentimentally precious things and locked them in the boot of his car, then he helped her search her father's desk for his chequebook and bank cards, things that it had not even occurred to her to look for, and which were conspicuous by their absence. He stood by while she rang the bank and reported their theft, then he took her out to lunch.

When he finally drove away that evening he tried to persuade her to go with him, but she refused.

He didn't argue. 'OK. Good for you. Stick to your guns and stay safe and call me at any time of day or night if you need me.'

She watched him drive away then closed the door and bolted it before wandering back towards the kitchen.

The house was dark and very quiet now that he had gone. As she reached for the light switches by the kitchen door she stopped suddenly in her tracks. She had heard a noise from the kitchen, she was sure of it. She held her breath, listening. Had Timothy managed to find a way in round the back? The silence stretched out and then she heard it again. It was another second before she realised with a flood of relief that it was the sound of the tap dripping slowly into the sink. She took a deep breath and brought her hand down heavily on the switches, lighting every corner of the kitchen. There was no one there.

Of course there was no one there.

For several seconds she stood still as slowly her heartbeat returned to normal then she walked over to the back door and checked the locks. No one could have come in that way. Picking up her laptop, she tucked it under her arm. The wave of loneliness and despair that swept over her was overwhelming.

In the end she turned off the lights and climbed wearily to her bedroom, wishing she had taken up Fin's invitation and gone home with him. Below, in the darkness, the house was very empty. Clutching her teddy bear in her arms she climbed into bed and lay there in the dark, staring up at the ceiling.

7

Timothy's sister, April, was waiting for him in the White Hart, a glass of shandy before her on the table, a bottle of lager for him. She looked up as he walked in. 'Did you get in?'

'Nope! She's changed the locks.'

'I told you she would. You should have taken everything while you had the chance.'

He sat down opposite her and reached for the bottle, twisting off the cap. Taking a large gulp, he wiped the foam from his lip with his sleeve. 'We've got most of the valuable stuff anyway. Do you want to get me another one?'

'Not particularly.' She was very like him to look at; the same skin, the same colour of hair, but while his eyes were brown hers were hazel. She studied his face closely. 'You look rattled.'

'There was someone else there. A big bloke. Some kind of minder.'

She scowled. 'Never mind. You don't need to go there again. We got what we came for: the old man's cash, jewellery, silver. Now you can sit back and wait for the house to fall into your lap.' She took a sip from her glass.

He noticed the packet of crisps at her elbow and reached across for it. 'But she's obviously gone to the solicitor.'

'Of course she has. He will have contacted her the moment he received the new will.'

'Doesn't it worry you?'

'No. It's your word against hers. She hasn't seen her father for years.'

'What about the DNA?'

She gave a grim smile. 'You got it, didn't you? The swab from the old man's mouth.'

Timothy grimaced. 'Disgusting.'

'Proof!' She smiled at him. 'Just don't lose it.'

She reached into her pocket. 'I've been going through some of the stuff you brought back.' She brought out a small cotton bag and tipped half a dozen rings into the palm of her hand.

'Don't!' Timothy let out a cry of alarm. 'For God's sake, April. Someone will see.'

'Shut up, you numpty. You're just drawing attention to us.' She rattled her two hands together then opened them with a smile of triumph as if she had produced the rings out of thin air. 'These are nice. Gold, rubies, diamonds. Victorian, I should say. Not worth a lot these days, but better than a slap in the face. Eighteen carat. They'll melt down well if nothing else.'

They both looked down at her hands. She reached for one of the rings and slid it onto her little finger. It wouldn't go over her knuckle. 'They must have had tiny hands in those days,' she said critically. She shivered suddenly and plucked the ring off. 'It doesn't feel right. Been on a dead person, I reckon. That's why I hate second-hand stuff.' She tipped the rings back in the bag and pulled the cord round its neck to tighten it. 'Best move these on as soon as.'

Timothy frowned. 'We can't risk it. Not yet. Ruth might be able to identify it. Just sit on it for a bit. All of it.' He helped himself to a handful of crisps. 'What is it? What's wrong?' She was staring down at her hand, lying on the bag.

She shuddered visibly. 'I told you. Someone walked on my grave.'

He laughed. 'Stupid mare. I tell you, if you want something spooky, it's that house. It gave me the creeps, there on my own with that old boy. He talked to people I couldn't see. He thought his wife was there with him. He told me she didn't like me. He told me to go away. Then he thought there was someone else there. Her grandfather or someone. He was scared of him. Terrified. He kept saying he was sorry. What?' He realised April was staring at him, her eyes wide with horror.

'I'm not handling these.' She pushed the bag of rings away from her. 'There's something bad going on with these. I reckon we should bail. Go somewhere else. I do not want to be landed with a haunted house.'

'Stupid!' Timothy glared at her witheringly. 'Not after all the trouble I've been to. We've done the hard bit now. As you say, we've just got to wait.' He reached out for the bag and stuffed it into his pocket. 'I need a proper drink.' He climbed to his feet and went over to the bar. 'Two large gins,' he said to the girl behind the till, 'and two hot pies when you're ready.'

Ruth stood looking up at the great crown steeple of St Giles' cathedral. It had been so vivid in her dream, the silhouette against the stormy evening sky, the small boy alone in the crowded street. She shivered. It had been uncannily real.

Number 26 was claustrophobic now, and lonely without her father there. Or Fin or Hattie. She hadn't been able to stand it this morning when she woke. A walk had seemed a good idea, especially now the locks had been changed and she wasn't afraid Timothy would sneak in behind her. She hadn't planned to come here to the Royal Mile, but that was where she ended up, standing staring at the place where Thomas had seen a murder. And a ghost. And it was her Thomas, her five-times great-grandfather, she was sure of that now. The names fitted, the names she had heard shouted out in her other dream, the dream of three excited, happy boys on holiday.

She looked round. This iconic street, stretching along Edinburgh's spine, from the castle to Holyrood Palace, was similar to her fleeting memory, but the booths had gone now of course; the images in her dream were like old photographic negatives, the buildings taller, more crowded, the people wearing darker clothes, the women in long skirts and shawls, carts, horses. The parliament building, and the Old Tolbooth near it, shadowy backdrops to the drama in the street.

Slowly she walked on. Thomas had lived at the top of a lofty tenement in somewhere called South Gray's Close. She glanced at the address on the piece of paper in her hand. She had looked it up on the Internet that morning. It was next to the Museum of Childhood. The actual building in which he had lived had long ago disappeared, it seemed, but there had been a plaque there once, marking the place where Tom and his brother Henry had been born. She came to a halt outside the entrance to the close. There was the rounded archway. Did she remember that from her dream? She thought so, but more than that, she wasn't sure. Everything had been dark then, save for the warm rooms briefly lit by the setting sun before the black rain clouds had swept in. There was graffiti now where, presumably, the plaque had once been. The memory of Thomas and his family in Gray's Close had vanished with her dream.

On her return to Number 26 Ruth went back to her slim file of notes and the Internet. She moved the cursor across to the portrait of Thomas and studied it carefully. He had short wavy dark hair and deep-set piercing eyes. The reproduction was poor; it was dark and hard to make out the detail. She clicked on it. The picture had been painted by Thomas Lawrence in 1802, when Thomas was fifty-two years old.

Sitting back in her chair she thought for a moment, then she rummaged in the zipped pocket of her bag for the portrait miniature. Was it him? The face staring out at her was very different to the arrogant, powerful, quite modern face on the screen. For a start the man in the miniature was wearing an old-fashioned white powdered wig; he was half smiling and he appeared to be very young. She narrowed her eyes, holding it under the light. The glass reflected badly and the picture was, she realised now, very crude in its execution. She dipped back into her bag to bring out the locket. The lock of hair could have belonged to anyone. A woman? Someone from another family altogether? She ran her finger across the glass. She badly wanted to touch the hair. The small oval of glass which held it in place felt loose. She squinted at it, angling it this way and that under the light. Could she prise it off? And if she did, would the hair reveal in some mysterious way the identity of its owner?

She picked up the miniature again, wondering why she assumed everything she had found was to do with that one man, as if he was the only ancestor her mother had. But that was her father's fault, she realised. He was the one with the obsession. It was as if the name, the title, had got under his skin as a personal insult.

Whoever the lock of hair and the miniature had belonged to they had been very precious. With a shiver she dropped them on the table. The thought that the touch of that hair might directly link her to the person from whose head it had been taken felt suddenly like witchcraft.

Thomas

It was the sennachie who first told me I was special. He had come to teach my eldest brother, David. The sennachie is the holder of the family story, the keeper of the genealogy, the remembrancer of all that makes a clan or a family great. We, the Erskines, he said, are both a Highland family and a Lowland clan. That is strange and special and he told us that our name comes from the skein, the little knife that appears on the family crest.

I was there, listening, only about five years old at the time, as the old man talked to my brother of traditions and legends of the earls of Buchan and of their forefathers the earls of Mar, going back to time before time.

There was another boy watching and listening there with us. Not Harry; he had gone out with Mama, and I asked the boy who he was. He said his name was David and he was my brother, the eldest, and he was six.

The sennachie frowned when I mentioned the boy and my big brother told me to be quiet as he could see no one there. The old man reprimanded him and said this other boy, who had joined us so silently and so suddenly, was the eldest brother to both of us, another David, who had died as a wee boy of six and who had come to hear the story of his ancestors.

The sennachie said I had the gift of second sight.

Later Mama told me we had indeed had a brother who had died; as the oldest son he had been named for Papa, but after he had died Papa had given David, our David, who had been their second son, his name and his title as the eldest son of Lord Cardross; before that David had been called Steuart after Mama's family. I was confused. I didn't understand any of this and my brothers were angry with me. They had both known the first David when they were all little together and missed him after he died and David was cross because he felt his name was not his own.

Mama said I must not tell anyone that I could talk to those who had died.

8

James Reid showed Ruth into his office and pulled out the chair
for her. 'I have news for you,' he said as he sat down opposite
her. 'I am pretty sure your Mr Bradford is a fake.' He smiled
triumphantly. 'I called the firm who appeared to have drawn
up your father's new will. Cautiously, you understand. There's
a certain procedure to be followed here. The name at the bottom
of the will is that of a genuine solicitor and I asked to speak to
her. It turns out she's away on maternity leave. She wasn't
working when the will was drawn up and when contacted she
had never heard of Timothy Bradford or your father, and neither,
incidentally, had the young man who is filling in for her.'

'Oh, thank goodness!' Ruth couldn't hold back her exclamation of relief. James Reid's phone call that morning had filled
her with foreboding.

He took off his spectacles and rubbed them thoughtfully with
a handkerchief. 'That would seem to be the end of your problem,
but it leaves one or two unanswered questions. Firstly, is it
possible that Bradford actually is your father's son? And
secondly, whether he is or not, if he has stolen property from
your father's house you would want it back.' He put his glasses
back on. 'In the case of the first problem, you would probably
be quite happy if he disappeared and was never seen again,
thereby proving he is a liar. In the second, I'm sure you would

prefer to retrieve your mother's possessions if it's at all possible before he disappears forever. Either way, he is almost certainly a thief and you are entitled to call in the police.'

Ruth slumped back in her chair. 'How would we find him?'

'There's an address on the will. I doubt if it's real, but it must provide some way of contacting him about his supposed inheritance.' He looked down at the papers in front of him. 'It's my belief that we're dealing here with a man of fairly limited intelligence. He must have realised that we would find out the will was a fake almost at once.'

'But he didn't know there was anyone to query it,' Ruth pointed out.

'That's true,' James said slowly. 'So, what would you like me to do?'

'How long have we got before he gets suspicious?' Ruth leaned forward, her brow furrowed. 'I want him to go away; I want him to leave me alone; but I don't want to spook him into destroying anything he might have taken. To be honest, I really don't know if he's taken anything at all; that's the problem. I remember my mother mentioning pictures and portraits and silver, and there's nothing like that in the house. But it could have been my father who got rid of them.' She looked at him helplessly.

'But from what you told me, you suspect your father didn't get rid of anything.' His voice was gentle; thoughtful. 'Not permanently. He merely locked it all away.'

She bit her lip sadly. 'Mummy had a jewel box she kept on her dressing table. She never wore anything out of it, or opened it at all, as far as I know, except when I was very little. When Daddy was out, she sometimes let me try on her rings and bangles. There's no sign of the box in the house.'

He made a note.

'Where is it he says he lives? He did mention once that he had a sister. It could be her house.'

'If I tell you, you won't go there, will you? I don't want you getting hurt.' James reached for the file.

She smiled. 'No, I won't go there. I don't want to spook him, as I said.'

He studied the letter in front of him. 'He gives a mobile telephone number as his contact and an address in Muirhouse.'

'Where's that?'

'North Edinburgh. Parts of it are pretty rough.'

'As I said, I don't plan on going there. So, what do I do now?'

'That's up to you. If our suspicions are correct, he's committed – at the very least – fraud, forgery and theft. I think we should inform the police as soon as possible. They can then search his house.'

'Can I think about it?'

He nodded. 'Don't take too long.'

The sound of the doorbell pealing through the empty house nearly gave Ruth heart failure. Sally Laidlaw was standing on the step, an umbrella open above her head. Rain was bouncing off it and splashing down onto the doorstep. 'I wondered if you would like to come over and have a cup of tea. This house must be sorely cold and drear.' Sally hesitated. 'It's warmer next door, and I've been baking.' She peered past Ruth. 'Has Timothy gone?'

The difference in the two houses was unimaginable. Sally's was bright and warm and full of colour and in the background Ruth could hear a radio playing. Shedding her raincoat in the hall, she followed her hostess into the kitchen. It had the same high ceiling as Number 26, the same windows looking out onto a narrow garden, but there the similarity ended. The room was lined with pale blue fitments with granite tops; it was immaculate, the small central table adorned with an oilcloth covered with cornflowers and in the middle a jug full of Michaelmas daisies. 'Sit you down.' Sally indicated one of the two chairs by the table. She turned off the radio and switched on the kettle. 'You'll have a piece?' She produced a sticky gingerbread loaf with a pat of butter, closely followed by a pot of tea. 'I'm thinking your house must be very sad,' she said at last as she sat down opposite Ruth. She glanced up. 'Were you planning to keep it when the will is sorted?'

'I don't think so. You're right: it is too sad. It needs someone new to do it up and bring some happiness back there,' Ruth sighed.

'Is Timothy coming back?'

'I hope not.' Ruth gave a tentative smile.

'I didn't take to him,' Sally said succinctly.

'No, neither did I. Can I ask you,' Ruth leaned forward anxiously, 'how long was he here, do you remember?'

'Ages. He visited your father regularly, once a week or so to start with, then twice, then one day he moved in. I asked your father if he was happy with the arrangement and he said yes.' She tightened her lips in obvious disapproval. 'I don't know if you remember, but I was good friends with your darling mother. I had no truck with the way your father treated her, I don't mind telling you, but after she died I kept an eye on him, you know? For her sake.'

Ruth took a deep breath. 'He barely recognised me when I arrived.' She gave a sad little smile. 'I don't know if he told you anything about Timothy,' she went on, 'but a will has turned up claiming my father left him the house and everything in it.' She scanned the other woman's face, waiting for a reaction, and was reassured to see first disbelief then anger there.

'He would have wanted no such thing.' Sally scowled. 'If he signed that will, he didn't know what he was doing. It is my opinion the man forged his signature. He had enough time to practise!'

'My solicitor thinks it's a forgery, but of course he has to take it seriously until we can prove otherwise. Timothy is claiming,' Ruth rushed on, 'to be my father's son.'

Sally stared at her in blank astonishment. 'No.' She repeated firmly, 'No, absolutely not.'

'Dad never mentioned that he had a by-blow somewhere?'

'No. Your father worshipped your mother in his own way, Ruth. She was his first and only love. He was a bully and controlling and even cruel without realising it himself, but he would never have had another woman. If he had, he would have confessed to your mother on his knees and she would have told me, I am certain of it.' She paused for several seconds, as if questioning her own statement. 'Yes, she would. She talked to me often, Ruth. She had no one else to confide in.' She leaned forward anxiously. 'I'm not criticising you, dear, by saying that. I understand perfectly why you didn't want to come here.'

Ruth said nothing.

'Your mother and I were quite close,' Sally went on at last. 'I used to tell her to leave him but of course she wouldn't. She loved him.'

'You knew about his problems with her family background?' Ruth said cautiously.

'Oh yes.' Sally laughed. 'Most people are afraid of reds under the bed; in your father's case it was the lords he found in her pedigree. It was ludicrous! They were so far back, she told me, and I met her parents, your grandparents, and they were lovely, I don't have to tell you that. They were simple, kind folk. I liked them so much when they came to see Lucy. Anyone more unassuming you couldn't find. But then he didn't like their faith either; he had no time for God and your grandfather being a vicar and English was too much for him.' She laughed. 'It was all so illogical. The Erskines are a Scots family, obviously, but here was his wife, sounding as English as they come, from down south. But she was descended from this man who was Lord Chancellor. He pictured the man in the great wig, draped in golden robes, and he had him down in his head as a rampant Tory, though Lucy told me he was a Whig.' She looked worried suddenly. 'She had the second sight. You knew that about your mother, didn't you?'

Ruth looked doubtful. 'I knew she liked crystals and things. We didn't talk about it much. Childish and naive and self-deluding were the words Daddy used when I was a child.'

'He was afraid.' Sally clamped her lips shut and there was a moment's silence.

'Do you believe in it all?' Ruth asked cautiously.

'I have never seen anything myself, but I believe she did. And his being scornful of her did nothing to stop it happening to her. She told me she used to summon the spirits when she was a child; she used to encourage all the things that happened to her. Then when she met your father she realised it wasn't normal and she became terribly upset. She was torn in two.'

Ruth glanced across at her miserably. 'I didn't help. I didn't understand what was happening, then when I was older I just began to hate him because he made her life a misery. I left home as soon as I could.'

'Don't feel guilty. It was a complex relationship. As a child, you couldn't have hoped to understand what was happening.'

'Can I ask you something?' Ruth found she liked this woman and she trusted her. 'In spite of all his threats, Daddy kept all my mother's things. He locked them upstairs in the spare room cupboards. Her clothes and family items, which I thought he'd made her get rid of. I thought he'd burnt them all. That's what he told me, but he hadn't.' She hesitated. 'Timothy appears to have gone through it all pretty thoroughly. I think he has taken some of it away.'

'Oh no!'

'The family pictures are missing and the silver. I remember Mummy showing me spoons and forks, wrapped in soft black cloths; they had what I now realise were family crests on them. There were candlesticks. And there was her jewellery. I know the only thing Daddy ever gave her was her wedding ring, but she had pretty jewellery which she used to let me try on when I was a little girl. As far as I remember she never wore any of it, but it was still there when I left home.'

'And now it's gone?'

'Yes.'

'You should tell the police.'

'I would, but I have no way of proving it was still there. I don't suppose you saw it?'

Sally shook her head. 'I never went upstairs. I very seldom went in at all, to be honest. She came here. I did drop in to see your father every now and then after she died, but we always went into the kitchen. He would give me a cup of Nescafé and we would chat for a wee bit and that was it. He was a very lonely man after she went. I'm not surprised to hear he kept her stuff, the old hypocrite.' There was another pause. 'She gave me some of her books to take care of, Ruth, and I have them still. She was afraid he would burn them after one particular quarrel they had, and I said she could put them in my spare room. She came round sometimes to read them. I kept them after she died. I wasn't sure what to do with them, to be honest. They're yours now. Books about the family and books about all sorts of New Age stuff.'

Ruth felt a surge of excitement. 'I'd love to have them. Thank you.'

There was a pause.

'Your father talked to her, you know. After she died. I heard him once or twice when I came over. I could hear his voice when I was going to ring the doorbell. I confess I listened at the letter box. He was talking, arguing, crying.' For a moment Ruth thought Sally was going to cry herself. 'And he didn't just talk to Lucy.'

Ruth froze.

Sally wasn't looking at her. She was studying her hands in her lap. 'It seemed that he was talking to Lord Erskine. Lucy told me that he would sometimes appear to her. He was kind and understanding and gave her the courage to stay with Donald. Naturally,' she looked up at last with a wan smile, 'I assumed she was going off her head.'

'You're saying his ghost appeared to her?' Ruth found her mouth had gone dry.

'I'm not sure that he was what you or I would call a ghost. After all, why would he haunt a terraced house in Morningside? No. Lucy used to call him up, summon him, in some way; like summoning the spirits of the dead. You know?'

'And you are telling me Daddy called him too?' Ruth felt her whole body stiffen with disbelief. 'That's just not possible. He wouldn't.'

'No, I don't suppose he did.' Sally's shoulders slumped. 'Perhaps he did it without meaning to. Perhaps he called out to him in his anger or anguish or whatever at losing Lucy and never expected, or even imagined for a second, that the man would respond.'

Ruth smiled grimly. 'That must have given him a shock.'

'Your father never stopped loving your mother, my dear.' Sally glanced at her, uncomfortable with the sudden show of emotion. 'He was the kind of man who finds it difficult to express himself. He came from a generation and a background which was . . . ' she hesitated, 'very buttoned up.' She smiled.

'I know he was cruel to your mother, and I know when he hated something he found it easier to say so than when he loved something. But he did love her.'

Later Ruth relayed the conversation to Harriet on the phone.

'Your father talked to him!' Harriet was incredulous. 'Dear God! You have to try to speak to him yourself!' Her excitement was instant and infectious. 'You absolutely have to. What are you waiting for?'

'That's all very well for you to say!' Ruth was once more seated at the kitchen table at Number 26. 'The idea appals me. Oh no, Harriet. I don't believe a word of it. Absolutely not.'

'But we know he was a spirit guide! He knows how to talk to people. Have you read that book yet?'

'No, I haven't. And I don't believe all this stuff. You know I don't!'

'Why not? He's not going to hurt you, is he. You are his however-many-greats-granddaughter for goodness' sake! Did that woman, your neighbour, actually hear his voice through the door?'

'Yes. No.' Ruth was becoming flustered. 'Of course she didn't! She heard Daddy talking to himself.'

'Go on. Try. You have to.'

'No!'

'I dare you.'

'What, and discuss philosophy? Politics?'

'No. Or at least not straight away. Ask him if he minds talking to you. Tell him you're interested in him. Do it now. Then call me back.'

The phone went dead.

Thomas

I knew Ruth wanted to speak with me; but I also knew she was terrified that it might happen. She was a brave woman, and in that she was Lucy's daughter, but she was also her father's child and alone in a dark and gloomy house. My own father had tried to distract me from the consequences of the gift of second sight, and from my precocious insistence that I knew best; if this young woman had the same tendencies, I knew she would have to be brought to the realisation gently and somehow taught, as I was taught, to handle it with care. For the time being, I contented myself with thinking back to my childhood and wondering how she would confront the truths of my life if she persisted in following the paths of her research, and, on this occasion, I left her to her thoughts and dreams rather than give in to the temptation to appear.

9

Lord Buchan studied his youngest son carefully. Tom was twelve now, clever, cheeky and precocious. He was standing in front of his father looking at this moment extremely sheepish. 'Well, boy, did you do it?' the earl sighed. They had been here before. With his eldest brother now in the army and Harry at university, Tom had been left at home with his sisters to be tutored by their mother. Agnes was a brilliant woman and she had taught all her children in turn, imbuing in them her own passion for learning as well as her strict religious views, and yet here was Tom, still running wild in the streets, this time caught stealing from a stall in the Grassmarket below the great castle walls. His excuse, given with passionate indignation, was not a denial but an explanation that there could be no crime for he had stolen from a rich man, who could well afford the loss, to give to a poor one. Lord Buchan sighed. The boy had no idea that, had he been a poor man himself, he would have faced the direst penalties for what he had done. Only a substantial bribe had bought off the indignant stallholder, a bribe they could not afford. Poverty, though, was relative. His paltry two hundred pounds a year would be an undreamed of fortune to the would-be recipient of his son's intended largess.

'I am sending you away, Tom. Mr Buchanan shall be your tutor and you will go to Kirkhill to learn discipline and study until you are ready to go to the High School.' He did not add that they could not afford to send him to the school, otherwise he would have been there already. David and Harry were the lucky ones. Money had been scraped together for their education and now for David's commission in the army, and enough for Harry to study law, but for this third son, probably the brightest of them all, there was little left in the coffers.

Tom looked down at his feet. He managed to master his conflicting emotions; relief that he was not to be beaten; horror at the thought of a tutor of his own and delight that he would once more be in the country. He loved the old tower house of Kirkhill, with the Brox Burn, the broad wild valley of Strathbrock and its distant views of the Pentland Hills, the River Almond less than an hour's walk away. There he would be able to study all the things which fascinated him most, botany and birds and animals, and when the rain streamed down the windows he could read his way through the mildewed books which remained abandoned in the library.

The summer went much as Tom had planned. He enjoyed enormously his lessons in the improvised schoolroom above the stables. Mr Buchanan, though strict, was a brilliant teacher; he was inclined to allow the boy his head between lessons, identifying, as Tom's father had done, a streak of brilliance there that he believed would be best channelled by allowing the boy free rein as far as possible.

When the end of Tom's exile came it was unexpected and deliriously exciting. His brother Harry rode out from Edinburgh with the news.

'We are giving up the flat in Edinburgh. It's too expensive,' Harry said candidly as he sat with Tom over a plate of scones, spread with butter from the mains. He had brought a letter for Mr Buchanan, who sat near them reading it, his expression thoughtful. 'Papa has taken a house in St Andrews and you are to attend the high school there. Mama is pleased with the development,' he hesitated for only a fraction of a second, a hesitation into which Tom read a multiplicity of meanings, 'and we are to go at once.' On the far side of the table Mr Buchanan looked from one boy to the other with quiet satisfaction. Neither noticed. 'Anne is not coming with us,' Harry added wistfully.

Tom looked up. He had stuffed another scone into his mouth and was chewing with much enjoyment. 'What is she going to do? Has Mama found her a husband?' he asked when at last he could speak.

'She's going to Bath.'

'Bath?' Tom stared at his brother in astonishment. 'In England?'

'She has been writing to Lady Huntingdon about the church and God and stuff, and she is going to go and help with all that.' Harry waved his hand in the air expansively. 'Mama thinks she will be happier there. I heard her tell Papa that Anne is not made to marry.' He frowned, catching sight of Mr Buchanan's expression as he glanced up from his letter. 'We'll see her often,' he hurried on. 'Papa says perhaps we'll go and visit her.' Both boys were fond of their eldest sister. She was kind and amusing and had mothered them in ways for which their real mother had little inclination.

Once the plan was voiced it all happened very quickly. Mr Buchanan left for a position at Glasgow University. Friends and servants were left behind with fond farewells and promises of an eventual return. The family's furniture and clothes and belongings were loaded onto a ship at Leith and sent off to Fife ahead of them, and before the autumn gales had set in they were ensconced in their new home.

Tom was delighted that at last he would be going to school, little realising that one of the reasons for his parents' move from Edinburgh was, at the strong recommendation of his tutor, to save enough money to pay his fees. He enjoyed St Andrews. He began to study at the university, taking classes in mathematics and natural philosophy and attending Richard Dick's school of Latin with Harry. He learned to dance, he watched the soldiers on parade and the ships in the harbour, and he explored the countryside and the coastline at every opportunity, striding out with his thumb stick and a bag of food over his shoulder in all weathers. He loved the sea; the waves crashing onto the rocky shore throwing spume high into the air, the roar of the water echoing in the ruins of the castle and the gaunt skeleton of the ancient cathedral that rose so starkly above the cliffs. He shivered as he stood looking out across incalculable distances, setting his shoulders against the long-dead voices that called out from the ancient stones around him.

In the cliff below the spot where he was standing his mother had laid claim to the cave where, so the story went, St Rule had landed on the shores of the ancient kingdom of Fife, bringing with him the precious relics of St Andrew, relics long ago lost to the furies of John Knox and his reformers. The cave was a dark, mysterious place but his mother had had it transformed with seashells, and chairs and tables, and, after she had had steps cut into the cliff to make it easier to reach, she held tea parties there. He disapproved. In some secret place within his soul he thought of the cave as sacred, and besides he knew the locals thought his mother mad. Not that she worried about such things; she had no time for St Andrew, nor for the opinion of her neighbours.

It was here he met the boy. Sheltering in the cave when his mother was busy elsewhere and the icy winds had driven everyone off the streets, Tom caught sight of a lad about his own age, standing by the entrance, looking out to sea. 'Hey!' Tom called. He ran to catch him up, but the boy was ahead of him, jumping down the cliff path towards the rocks below the castle. The boy stopped as he reached the sand, glancing back over his shoulder, waiting for Tom, then he ran on, his hair wet with the rain, his jacket flying open in the wind.

He never found out the boy's name but they played together often, exploring the ruins of the castle and the cathedral, the boy leading him down hidden steps to the sea gate, running along the great curtain wall, balancing high above the sea, climbing off the stones and leaping down the stairs by the postern gate. They spent hours together scrambling on the ruins, on the cliffs, chasing along the sands at low tide, until the reluctant scholar was recalled to his books by his tutors.

It was the day that Harry came to find him and bring him home that he last saw his friend.

'Mama has sent me to fetch you,' Harry called. 'We have visitors from the south with messages from Anne.'

Tom had been throwing stones into the sea, laughing, competing with the other boy as to who could throw them furthest, skimming them above waves that for once were calm.

'I'll have to go!' he called, turning.

The boy had gone. He left no footprints in the sand.

'Who were you talking to?' Harry enquired as they jogged down South Street towards their house.

'No one.' Tom managed to look nonchalant as he stopped to empty some stones from his shoe. 'I was shouting at the gulls.'

He knew Harry didn't believe him, but he didn't care.

He was happy and excited; not for one moment did he realise that he was about to be given the first great shock and disappointment of his young life.

'I can no longer afford your fees!' Lord Buchan was striding up and down the room, his daughter's letter in his hand. Tom was standing before him white-faced. 'I am sorry, Tom. If there was another way I would take it, I promise you.'

'But the university! You promised! I am already going to lectures—'

'No. It's not possible and we can't stay here after all. I am sorry. The fees for your brothers have taken every penny we have.' The earl's face was grey with worry and fatigue. 'You must understand, Tom, that as the youngest your needs have to come last. David will inherit the title when my time comes; and Harry will go into the law. We have to find another way forward for you, and Anne has suggested we join her in Bath. She has a house there, thanks to her friend Lady Huntingdon, and she feels your mother and I could be of use to her in spreading the message about Methodism.' He glanced at his son's face; the devastation he saw there was a physical blow. 'I am sorry, Tom. I know how much store you set by continuing your studies and going on to a profession.'

'And Harry?' Tom asked. 'Is he to go to Bath too?'

'No.' His father shook his head. 'He will visit us, when he can, but he will remain here at St Andrews. I have managed to find him somewhere to lodge.'

'So, what will become of me?' Tom managed to keep his

voice steady. He took a deep breath. 'I suppose it will be the army, like David?' Could he imagine himself as a soldier? The idea had never crossed his mind, but that was the traditional destiny of a younger son.

His father gave him a look of deep compassion. 'Commissions in the army cost money, Tom. But we will face that decision when we must. Anne has many friends and contacts in Bath. I am sure something will turn up. I am praying every day that God will provide for you.' He smiled at the boy, well aware that Tom was fighting back tears. His heart ached for his precocious youngest son.

On his last day in St Andrews, Tom went back to the castle to look for his friend. A fierce wind had arisen, tearing at his jacket, threatening to push him off the cliffs, screaming through the ruins, streaking the sky with rain. Huge waves rolled in over the rocks, smashing themselves against the foot of the cliffs, hurling spray high into the sky. Tom looked round helplessly. Where was he? Somehow he had thought the boy would be here, but there was no sign of him in the remains of the courtyard or beneath the tower or in the shelter of the remaining walls.

His shoulders slumped with disappointment as he stood looking out at the wild sea, its distances shrouded with bellying cloud. His friend was one of the dead. He had always known that, always recognised that the boy must have drowned in the sea and that his longing for companionship and the life he had so cruelly lost so young had brought him back to the shore. 'May God bless you,' he whispered. 'I shall miss you.'

10

'No, of course I didn't try it.' When Harriet rang Ruth the next morning, she laughed. 'This is me you're talking to, Hattie. I do not, never would, try to summon ghosts.'

She looked round the room with a shiver. Even in the mornings the kitchen was such a gloomy place with its high ceilings and shadowed corners, and she was beginning to hate it.

There was a moment of silence as Harriet considered what to do next. Giving up was obviously not an option. 'Pity, but don't worry. I looked up some stuff about Dion and how she contacted ghosts last night. As far as I can gather, she and her companions meditated.'

'I'm not the right person to try this,' Ruth said firmly.

'Yes, you are. You're perfect. You're a relation of his. You must have some sort of link. Besides, your father could do it and he didn't believe in it either and he loathed the man.' Harriet was not going to be thwarted that easily. 'Let me read it up some more then I'll call you back, OK?'

Ruth spent the morning tidying up, going through the drawers in the dining room and the sitting room. Then later she went upstairs. On the first landing she stopped and listened. It was very cold up there and strangely still. It was as though there was a tangible presence in the silence of the house. 'Timothy? Is that you?' She knew it couldn't be, but it felt as though there was someone there listening to the silence with her. She could feel the heavy sadness, the pall of loneliness. 'Daddy?' she whispered at last. One by one she went into the rooms, looked round, then moved on. In her father's room she paused a little longer, her eyes drawn to his empty bed. It was stripped now, but, unable to bear the sight of it with her father gone, she had thrown a tartan rug over it. It did nothing to dispel the emptiness of the room. 'Daddy?' she whispered again.

There was no reply.

The top landing was dully lit from the skylight. She could hear the rattle of rain on the glass above her head. Almost reluctantly she went into the back room and pulled open the cupboard doors. There was nothing left in there now except for some old newspapers on the top shelf. She reached up to them, and then, feeling something more substantial underneath them, stood on tiptoe to drag everything down off the shelf.

There were three large brown envelopes beneath the papers, tied together with thin pieces of ribbon. She carried them over to the divan, surprised at how heavy they were and, sliding off the ribbon, teased one open. On the envelope was one word: COPIES. It contained a substantial collection of letters, all in the same handwriting, which was faded, old fashioned, with a marked slope to the right. She felt a leap of excitement. The letters appeared to have been copied from originals addressed to various people over quite a long period. The top one was headed Walcot. She slid the letters carefully back into the envelope and, gathering them all up, turned back towards the stairs.

The radio and some strenuous house cleaning did nothing to dispel the lonely gloom of the house. Even the letters failed to tempt her and at last she reached for her phone.

Finlay was at home. 'I'll come and fetch you about five,' he said at once. 'Come for supper and stay the night.'

'I've already looked,' Finlay said, as he pulled away from the kerb. He had noticed the nervous way she glanced over her shoulder. 'I can't see him.'

She gave a grim smile. 'He's not going to give up that easily, though, is he.'

'Probably not, but we're a match for him.' Finlay turned into the traffic on Morningside Road. 'I gather he doesn't know yet that we're on to him over the forgery?'

'I don't think so. James Reid is waiting for my go-ahead.'

'So, why are you waiting?'

'I'm afraid he will destroy the things he stole.' She glanced across at him helplessly. 'And I can't prove what, if anything, he's taken. Catch twenty-two.'

Finlay checked the mirror and signalled left as they headed for the centre of town. He grimaced. 'I can see that's a problem.' He drew up behind another queue of cars. 'But I would be inclined to act sooner rather than later. He must realise you're on to him. Why otherwise would you have changed the locks? So,' he went on, 'tell me about the conversation your neighbour overheard between your father and Lord Erskine.'

'There is nothing to tell. Poor Daddy must have been hearing things. That house is so lonely and quiet it would drive anyone round the bend after a bit.' She shuddered.

'And you weren't the littlest bit tempted to try and summon Lord E?' She had told him about Harriet's input. He turned to look at her as they waited at the lights.

She laughed. 'Certainly not. To that extent, I'm my father's daughter. But . . . ' her voice faded. 'But,' she repeated, more strongly, 'Daddy wasn't the sort of man to talk to himself.'

Finlay thought for a minute. 'My house is haunted.' He lived in an old mill near the village of Cramond, about five miles along the coast from the centre of Edinburgh. 'I've seen her several times. A lovely wee girl. She plays in the garden and sometimes round the old stable block at the back. Several other people have seen her too.'

'Ah.'

'That sounds sceptical? Defensive? Disappointed? You wanted me to be an ally.'

'No. I wanted the hear the cold light of reason. I expected the cold light of reason.'

'Sorry. Do you want me to take you back to your father's?'

She laughed. 'No way. You promised me supper.'

'Indeed I have. A soupçon I've taken from the freezer, but I'm sure it will please.' Finlay's cooking was famous. It was also probably responsible for his somewhat large girth. He was a cookery writer and in a small way a TV celebrity.

Glancing in the driving mirror again he indicated right and changed lanes, then he slowed to turn off the main road. Ruth leaned back in her seat, her eyes closed, relaxing for the first time in days. Seconds later she was shocked into wakefulness as Finlay swung the car left and then right again into a quiet housing estate where he pulled in sharply in front of a parked furniture van.

'Finlay! What's happening? What are you doing?'

'Hush! Duck right down.' Finlay was studying the wing mirror. 'I was wrong; he was following us. It's OK, I think I've lost him, but he'll turn round when he realises. I recognised the car. He moved up closer in the heavier traffic just now so I was able to check the number. He must have been waiting round the corner as we left. That's the problem with having a red car; it's easy to spot.' Finlay drove an old maroon Daimler.

They sat in silence for several minutes then Finlay pushed open the door. 'You stay here. Lock yourself in. I'll go up to the corner and peer round. See if he's cruising up and down the road.'

'I'm not staying here on my own!' Ruth reached for the door handle.

'He'll recognise you if he's there.'

'You think he won't recognise you?' She stared at him incredulously. 'You spoke to him on the doorstep. And he's not going to forget what you look like, Finlay Macdermott!'

'Touché! Come on then.' He reached out for her hand.

They looked round cautiously. There was no sign of Timothy's car.

'Do you think it's safe?' Ruth breathed.

'Probably. I won't drive straight home, just in case.'

They drove around for twenty minutes before deciding it was safe to head for Cramond. As they drew to a halt outside the mellow stone-built old house with its long driveway and broad gravelled parking area, it was already growing dark. Ruth followed him through the front door and into his kitchen. 'Ssh!' Finlay put his fingers to his lips. Tiptoeing across the floor, he pulled the curtains and only then did he turn on the lights.

Ruth looked round. The room was warm and full of the succulent fragrance of cooking herbs. It was years since she had been here. Then it had been with Rick and they had had the most wonderful few days in Fin's company. The kitchen was exactly as she remembered it, with a huge oak dresser and refectory table, a bookcase stuffed with cookery books and several framed French posters on the stone walls. The only nod to modernity was a circular ceiling rack laden with shiny saucepans and utensils, and an elegant kitchen island with an attendant cluster of high stools.

'It is lovely to be here again, Fin.' She climbed onto a stool and accepted a glass of chilled Pinot Grigio. 'We had such a lovely time when I came with Rick.' She watched as he slid a dish out of the oven and checked it. Satisfied, he pushed it back, threw down the oven gloves, adjusted the heat slightly then he turned to her. 'I've got something to show you. Wait there.'

The something was the writing slope. He had mended the lock and somehow removed the deep scratches from the wood. Ruth exclaimed with delight. 'You're so clever. You would never know it had been damaged!'

'I enjoy doing things like that. A bit of a hobby. Open it.'

She did so. Inside was an envelope. She picked it up. 'What's this?'

'Something I found when I was mending it. The blotter is made to lift up to form yet another secret cavity.'

She peered into the envelope and extricated a small folded piece of paper. 'It's a letter!'

'A very old one.'

She unfolded it carefully and laid it on the table. The handwriting was small, closely crammed on the page, the ink faded to sepia. Screwing up her eyes, she could just make out the last line of the address at the top. 'It's Sussex. Where my grandparents lived.'

it was signed

Your loving mother, xxx

With a grunt Finlay climbed off his stool to fetch a magnifying glass from the dresser. 'I needed this to read it. Very charming. I've no idea who these people are, but it seems affectionate. Try this.' He pushed the glass over towards her.

Ruth studied the letter. 'I've no idea who they are either.'

'Ancestors of yours?'

'I don't know. I suppose they must be.' She looked up. 'I'm going to try to construct a full family tree. But I'm not sure how to begin.'

'You start at the bottom with you. Then go up to your mum and dad. Then up to your grandparents – on both sides if you can, to keep it fair. You can get that far, presumably?' He grinned. 'Then if there's no one you can ask – cousins? Uncles and aunts? – and no birth certificates and things like that to look up, there's always the Internet these days. And, in your case, you can start the other end, with your Lord High Chancellor himself. His wife, his children and grandchildren are bound to be easy to find as he was famous, and then you can go down from there towards you until you meet in the middle, or backwards to find out his ancestors and on up a tree full of ghosts into this glorious aris-tocratic jungle your father hated so much.' He looked at her mischievously. 'What fun. Count me in for help if I can do anything. This research of yours is a perfect way of taking your mind off the horrors of the low life that is Timothy Bradford.'

Ruth looked up at him fondly. 'I don't know what I'd do without you.'

'You'd manage.' He reached for the bottle to top up her glass. 'Come on. Let's eat.'

Timothy had pulled up at last at South Queensferry near the towering girders of the Forth Railway Bridge. He climbed out of the car and went to stand by the parapet, overlooking the Firth, his hands in his pockets. He shivered as the wind found its way down the neck of his jacket. He had been looking forward to telling April that he had found out where Ruth's minder had taken her and now he had lost the trail. But there was always tomorrow. He would go and stake out Number 26 again and this time he would make sure he followed Ruth everywhere she went.

His mind went back to April. It was odd how she had gone all superstitious on him, shuddering when she tried on those rings, or whenever he mentioned the loot, anxious to be rid of it all. Thank goodness he had the sense to see that as long as they held onto it there was no possibility of anyone spotting it. It would be a shame to chuck it away. His eyes strayed out over the cold grey water. The tide was running fast and there were white-topped waves crashing onto the shingle below the wall.

He turned away and headed back across the road towards the Hawes Inn. The bright lights reflecting out over the wet road were comforting and there was just time for a pint before they closed. Inside there was warmth and food and companionship and escape from the sound of the crashing waves. He saw the door open and then close behind a man and a woman. They hesitated for a moment before the onslaught of the weather, put up their umbrellas and began to battle into the wind. It was only then he realised it was raining.

Thomas

We had always been a God-fearing family. Serious and thoughtful supporters of the Reformation, as the sennachie told us boys, and before that true followers of the old church. Back into the mists of time, as he would say, using his favourite phrase for when his memories no longer served him, although he did mention the Picts and before them the North Britons as others who had been equally devoted to their gods. We were descended from kings, he told us, and when the line of descent strayed away from the throne we supported and served our monarchs with loyalty, if not always skill.

Probity and prayer drove my forefathers into the Presbyterian camp during the Civil Wars of the seventeenth century and through that loyalty they lost their lands and went into exile, first in Holland and then over the sea to the Americas. When they returned to Scotland and the restored Stuart line was replaced, their opinions were split; my mother's brother and my father's cousin fought for Prince Charlie and the lands were forfeit again. My other uncle and my cousin fought against the man they called the Pretender. Although all was now officially forgiven and the various branches of the family, through fines and oaths of allegiance, were once more in favour, in their hearts I suspect more families than ours retained their loyalty to the Stuart cause.

My father was a freemason; indeed, had been grandmaster of the lodge before I was born, and my parents were devout followers of the Calvinist faith; my brothers and I were brought up to go to the kirk with scrubbed necks and hands, our well-thumbed Bibles in our hands. My sisters were even more intense in their devotion.

And me? Did I believe? Oh yes, I believed but I am not sure it was in the same things as my family. I paid careful attention to what was required, but there was a whole universe beyond the strictures of the prayer book which I could see and sense with my own faculties. The sennachie knew; my brothers knew and teased me for it. Anne and Isabella were shocked and horrified. I did not learn in time to keep quiet about what to me was obvious. I was to regret that later in my life, but I never regretted the gift of second sight that I had been given. Ever.

11

Ruth looked with delight round the cosy bedroom. Its stone walls were hung with paintings and there were heavy tapestry curtains at the window. The bedside light threw a warm glow round the room. She went to the window and drew back the curtains, opening the window and leaning out into the clear darkness. The sound of the River Almond far below, splashing over the rocky falls, filled the room. Even over the sound of the water she could hear the hooting of an owl.

Pulling her laptop from her bag she opened it.

There was an email from Harriet:

I've been trying to reach you on the phone. Why don't you pick up, you infuriating woman!! I want to know what's happening.

That was the second vivid dream Ruth had had in the last two days. She woke suddenly, disorientated, staring at the unfamiliar ceiling, trying to grasp at the memory, aware of the boy's shock and misery, his sense of powerlessness, his disbelief that he could be so arbitrarily sent away. She closed her eyes again. Thomas was telling her his life story. In the distance she could hear the sound of the sea, the waves, the rattle of rigging, the tapping of ropes against a mast, the whistle of the wind. In seconds she had drifted back to sleep.

Tom did not like Bath. It was crowded and noisy. He had been used to the press of people living in Edinburgh's old town, but it was more claustrophobic here, prone to fog in the enclosing basin of hills. That it was fashionable, the home of all that was so desirable for the beau monde, escaped him completely.

His sister Anne had found them all lodgings together in a new house in the Walcot area and they settled in swiftly, just the five of them, the earl and countess and Anne herself, Isabella, Tom and their small household of servants.

A short time before, David had resigned his commission and returned to Scotland and, to Tom's intense jealousy, he found that his eldest brother was to return to his education with Harry in Scotland. They would come south to rejoin their family for Christmas.

His parents felt instantly at home in Bath. They attended church and religious meetings and took part in long intense discussions with many of the great and the good who had come together in Bath over the summer, but Tom was lonely and confused. His pleas to continue his education so that he could practise a profession when he grew up fell on deaf ears. 'I told you I could no longer afford your fees. Besides, it is time to earn your living now, Tom,' his father said sternly when at last Tom plucked up courage to speak to him. 'I have been making enquiries and discussing your future with, among others, our good friend, Lord Mansfield.' There was a pause; Lord Mansfield, a fellow Scots aristocrat, had risen to dizzy heights in the English bar and was Lord Chief Justice. The two men were firm friends and Lord Buchan frequently turned to the older man for advice with his wayward brood of children. 'We feel— I feel,' he amended hastily, 'that the Royal Navy would be a good career for you, and it has been arranged for you to sail with his nephew, Sir John Lindsay, as a midshipman.'

'No!' Tom felt the colour drain from his face. 'No, Papa. Please. I hate the sea!'

'You know nothing about the sea,' his father retorted. 'And

you were happy enough to go aboard the ships in St Andrews harbour. You and Harry enjoyed the food they gave you, as I recall!'

'But it was at anchor, Papa,' Tom said miserably. 'I would not like to go to the proper sea. Not at all.'

'And what do you know of the proper sea, Tom?' His father was exasperated.

'I know it can kill you, Papa,' the boy replied softly. 'I watched it from the castle walls at St Andrews. A friend of mine was drowned!' His words died away. His father knew nothing of the ghost boy with whom Tom had explored the ruins.

'I could be a soldier!' Tom said suddenly, brightening at the thought. 'Now David has resigned his commission, I could have it instead.' Anything was better than the navy and he had been covertly watching the dashing young men in scarlet uniforms escorting ladies to the Assembly Rooms, riding up and down the streets, driving their curricles too fast, laughing and shouting with their friends. The idea of joining them one day was rather appealing.

Lord Buchan turned away from him and sat down abruptly. His face was grey and Tom realised that his father looked ill and tired. 'Please, Papa,' he repeated. 'I think I would like the army.'

'The army costs money too, Tom.' Lord Buchan frowned as he looked at his thirteen-year-old son. David, newly promoted to lieutenant, had thrown his chance away, announcing the life was not for him. 'I am sorry. I can't afford to buy you a commission, not even as an ensign.'

'Anne could help,' Tom pleaded. 'She could ask some of her rich friends.'

'No.'

'We could ask them to pray for the money?' In a household fixated on prayer it was a natural thing to suggest, but to his increasing despair he saw his father's anger beginning to surface.

'God expects us to help ourselves, Tom. You can pray to be a good officer in the navy. You will be paid. I am told the starting wage is one pound ten shillings a month and even as a midshipman you will be entitled to a share of any prize money your ship earns from capturing privateers. After a few years you will be richer by far than your father with the miserable allowance he is granted by his miserly trustees!' He forced himself to smile.

Tom couldn't trust himself to speak. He could feel shameful tears clogging his throat. He swallowed hard. He had seen ships of the navy at anchor off Leith; he had seen them off Bristol, the great sails set, heeling slightly before the wind, when his mama had taken him with her to stay with some of her church friends. He had seen the seamen and the swaggering officers and the huge bundles of supplies being lowered into small boats to row out to the great ships at anchor in the fairway. He did not like the idea at all.

His father sighed. 'Tom, we are no longer at war; please God, there is no danger. And Sir John Lindsay is a well-respected captain. He has agreed to take you aboard and train you as one of his young gentlemen; his ship is a frigate, bound for the Caribbean. Your mother agrees with me in all this. You will experience wonderful things, Tom. It will be an adventure, you'll see.'

There was to be no argument.

12

Finlay's idea of a quick breakfast was formidable. Porridge, scrambled egg with smoked salmon, toast and coffee. As they sat over their final cups of coffee he put forward his proposal: 'I think you should stay here with me. I've been thinking about this. That house of yours – and it is yours, or it will be, have no fear – is a gloomy place, an outrage to good taste, and you don't feel safe there. Am I right?'

Ruth nodded.

'And, I'm here, all alone, in a relatively large house which is beautiful, warm, safe and furnished in impeccable style.' He gave a hollow laugh as the sound of a plane flying low overhead rattled the windows. 'God bless Edinburgh airport for its convenience, but the noise I could do without. Don't worry. The wind will change! Now, we can keep a close eye on your place, and ask your friend next door to do the same in case the fearsome Timothy decides to launch a raid, but my guess is he won't. There's too much at stake for him. If he's playing a much larger game, which he seems to be, he is not going to endanger it for the sake of another look round inside Number 26.' He reached for the coffee pot. 'No strings attached. You would actually be doing me a favour being here. It would be lovely to have your company, naturally, but I go away quite a lot and it would save me finding a house sitter. And perhaps I can help with your family research. I propose that you use the dining room as your base. You can spread out your books and papers on the table there, and you can send me off to raid whatever libraries you need. I belong to them all.'

'Finlay!' Ruth looked at him fondly. 'How can I refuse?'

'OK. Soon as you can, ring your solicitor chappy and tell him where you will be and tell him to do whatever he has to do to set the wheels in motion for nailing Timothy, then we can go back to the house and collect those books you mentioned and anything else you might need.'

'It was that simple,' Ruth said later when she rang Harriet back the following day. 'We collected all my stuff and the rest of the books and all the boxes, turned off the gas and electricity, called on Sally Laidlaw, collected Mummy's books from her, asked her to ring me if she sees Timothy poking around, and that was it.'

'And where is Finlay now?' Harriet asked.

'He's gone into town to see someone about his next project.'

There was a thoughtful pause from Harriet. 'I take it he isn't married? You haven't mentioned anyone else being there?' she said.

Ruth smiled. 'No. No wife; no husband; no partner. Rick and I used to wonder about that. I think we assumed Finlay was gay, but he doesn't seem to need anyone; he's just a lovely cuddly person, complete in himself.' She smiled fondly.

'My goodness, Ruth. You have fallen on your feet!' Ruth could hear the amusement in Harriet's voice. 'The only trouble with this paradisiacal set up is that the ghost you need to interview is back at Number 26.'

Ruth laughed uneasily. 'Forget that! I found some letters in the cupboard which are copies of letters Thomas had sent to his daughter. He seems to be telling her the story of his life. I looked at one or two last night and found myself reading about his first days in the navy. Poor kid, he was only just fourteen when they sent him away.' She had looked up the dates. 'It would have been hard not to resent his two brothers for using up their father's money; they were allowed to go to university, which seems to have been his dream, and he was packed off to God knows where with no prospect of coming back any time soon.' And she had dreamt about it, she remembered with a jolt. She had dreamt about it vividly and in detail.

'Any further mention of his being a spirit guide?' Harriet was not to be diverted.

'No. Nothing.'

After the call was ended, Ruth let herself out into the garden and walked down the lawn. Finlay's house had been one of the several water mills along the River Almond, the same River Almond that Thomas had mentioned in his letter. She had mentioned it to Finlay. Apparently Broxburn was less than twenty minutes' drive away and there, somewhere, was Kirkhill, the house where Thomas had studied before leaving with his family for St Andrews. Then the area had been quiet countryside and rural villages. It was in the nineteenth century that industry had come to Strathbrock in the form of shale and coal mining, and to the River Almond.

There was little left here now of the Almond's nineteenth-century past beyond the stone-built miller's house and some old pilings. The garden was separated from the public footpath along the riverside by iron railings and a steep drop, thick with undergrowth. Fin had created a sort of belvedere there and she stood, looking over the railings towards the water far beneath. Behind her the wind was dancing across the flowerbeds and a shower of autumn leaves scattered round her on the grass. She was thinking again about Tom and the fact that she had dreamed about him in such detail and suddenly she shivered. It was as though he was looking over her shoulder.

Easing himself into his car, Finlay sat for a moment staring ahead through the windscreen, deep in thought. The meeting with his agent had gone well. He was planning a new TV series and full of excited enthusiasm for the project. It meant he would be away filming sooner than he had expected but Ruth did not seem worried about being in the house on her own and having her live there would be a relief. He would help her sort out her problems with this wretched man before he left, and when she had custody of her inheritance. The Old Mill House would give her somewhere as an alternative base while she decided what to do with it.

He reached into his pocket for a piece of paper he had put there as he left the house. It was Timothy's address. He had noticed it as she laid out her papers on the table the night before. She had put the file of solicitors' letters to one side and James Reid's note had slipped out. Finlay glanced at it as she reached forward to push it back out of sight and remembered it long enough to make a note of it later. He sat looking down at it, then leaned forward and tapped the postcode into his satnav. It wouldn't take long to drive there and there was no harm in sussing out the enemy's lair. Pulling away from the parking meter he turned on some music. Dvořák seemed like a good accompaniment to a hunting expedition.

As it turned out Timothy Bradford lived on the edge of a run-down housing estate in the shadow of a high-rise block barely ten minutes' drive from Cramond. Finlay slowed the car to walking pace, scanning the house fronts. The one he was looking for turned out to be the right-hand half of a stuccoed semi. The small front garden had been turned, by the destruction of the low front wall, into a parking space adorned by a selection of bins. Finlay recognised the car that was drawn up there, its nose almost pressed against the front wall of the house beneath what was, judging by the array of downpipes on the wall, almost certainly the kitchen window. He grabbed in his glove box for his dark glasses and slid them over his nose as he drove past.

'April!' Timothy was standing at the sink, filling the kettle. 'Look at that! That fat bastard minder of Ruth Dunbar's has just driven by.'

'What?' April had been standing at the cooker. She turned and elbowed her brother out of the way, staring out. 'Where?'

'There. He's stopped to have a good look.' Timothy drew back slightly.

April stared through the blind as the car came to a halt, the engine running. 'I've seen that guy before,' she said after a fraction of a second. 'He looks like someone on the telly. That Scots cook, the one who tells people how to make scones!'

Brother and sister stood side by side, watching. 'It is,' she said. 'It's Finlay Macdermott.'

'Don't be daft, woman. How can you tell from so far away? Besides, what would he be doing here?' Timothy had never watched Finlay's programme. 'He's gone now.'

'Get after him!' April gave Timothy a shove. 'Quickly! Now! Go after him. Whoever he is, find out where he lives!'

'But supposing he's not going home?' Timothy hadn't told her of his previous attempt to follow the man.

'Then stay with him until he does.'

This was one of the few times he was pleased they had an ordinary old vehicle, unlike the one he was following which in daylight stood out a mile. His was dirty, mud-splashed with its number plate barely visible under the layers of crud. Finlay Macdermott. He murmured the name to himself resentfully. A TV chef! April was probably right. He had always been impressed by the way she recognised faces off the telly and she was never wrong. She would dig him in the ribs with her elbow as they walked down the streets and hiss a name at him and point, and he would stare, embarrassed. Luckily she didn't go and ask people for autographs or selfies, but pointing was almost as bad.

Ahead of him, Finlay was signalling a left turn. The traffic was lighter here and it was growing dark. Timothy let himself drop back slightly and settled down to drive with exaggerated care.

Only five minutes later he was following Finlay down the road past Lauriston Castle, towards Cramond. He was much more cautious now. There was hardly any traffic here. He crawled up to the turning into a leafy lane and followed it slowly down towards the river. No cars here. The houses were tucked in amongst the trees with plenty of space to park. They had high walls and fences. There were several turnings and he approached each one slowly, until he arrived at the end. Ahead was a no-through-road sign.

And then he saw his quarry. Through the trees he caught glimpses of a stone house with a gravelled turning area in front of it and there was Finlay, climbing out of his car. Timothy watched intently for a couple of seconds as the man stooped to retrieve a bag of some sort and then locked the door. With a quiet exclamation of triumph he reversed away from the turning, swung backwards onto the muddy verge, then drove towards the main road. He was looking for somewhere unobtrusive to park.

Finlay had never once looked back.

13

'I had a fruitful meeting this afternoon.' Finlay was still thinking about the plans for the next series. 'It calls for a bottle of bubbly, methinks!'

He found his ice bucket in a cupboard, brought a bag of ice cubes out of his freezer and emptied it into the container.

'That sounds wonderful.' Ruth smiled as she watched. 'This is so refined! Rick and I didn't own an ice bucket. If we needed champagne – or to be honest, more likely Prosecco – we stuck the bottle in the freezer for the shortest time possible!'

'Vandals!' Finlay placed the bucket on the table. 'Well, you should be pleased I have standards. I have an image to protect, don't forget.' He glanced at her. 'Which leads me to my news and a favour I need to ask.'

Ruth pulled up one of the high stools at the kitchen island and hauled herself onto it.

'Name it.'

'If all goes to plan, I'm going to have to be away for a time, filming in the Hebrides, far sooner than I expected. Would you be willing to stay here to keep an eye on the house? I know you said you would, but I genuinely envisaged being here to protect you from Timothy for a while at least. I quite fancied myself as Sir Lancelot. To leave you alone now seems churlish.'

'Of course I'd be willing.' Ruth was surprised at the sense of loss which swept over her at the thought of being without Fin, but she hoped it didn't show. 'When are you leaving?'

'Not sure yet. We agreed a format this afternoon, one which I think will suit the producer, and the money men. Then the hard work will start.' He gave her an impish grin, full of almost childlike excitement. 'I've been working on this idea for ages. It is going to be such fun! And I want you to have fun too, Ruthie, so while you're here, especially if you're in charge, you must have a car to drive and as it happens I have a spare.' Before he left the kitchen he reached up to the hooks by the door and she found herself holding the keys to the old MX5 he kept tucked away in his garage.

Champagne flutes in hand, they wandered through the dusk and stood on the belvedere, looking down towards the water, listening to the cheerful babble of the weir in the distance.

'I thought we'd be filming here, in my own kitchen, but the powers that be like the idea of setting it in the Highlands and Islands, perhaps using the kitchens of people who still cook the traditional foods. Old black iron stoves, that sort of thing.'

'Are there still such people?' Ruth asked. She was watching reflected lights dancing on the ripples. Somewhere behind them an owl hooted and they both looked round.

Finlay laughed. 'That's what my editor said. And the answer is, there are a few, though not for much longer, I fear. TV, the Internet, modern technology, they are all conspiring to wipe out the past. People's grannies are no longer wearing long black skirts and checked shawls and aprons,' he sighed theatrically, 'as they are in my imagination; they have supermarket deliveries or fly to the mainland and go shopping in Inverness or Edinburgh or Paris! But, and this is the important part, the recipes do survive, and my show will do its bit to preserve and disseminate them.' He shivered. 'Come away in, it's cold out here. Let's eat.'

Having parked his car, Timothy had crept silently along the side of the house. It was almost dark now and he could see lights on at the far end of the building. The sound of the wind in the trees masked any noise he made as he sidled closer, keeping his back to the wall. There were creepers of some kind there; they provided cover as he reached the lit window and peered in. He could see into the kitchen. It was large and expensive-looking and Finlay was standing by the table talking to Ruth. He saw the champagne bottle and narrowed his eyes resentfully, wishing he dared press his ear against the window. He couldn't hear what they were saying.

When they had moved into the next-door room and opened the French doors he froze, his back pressed into the trellis. If they looked to the side they would see him, but the sudden darkness after the bright light must have blinded them. They stepped outside, laughing, and walked down the grass away from the house without seeing him, leaving the doors open behind them. He hesitated. What was to stop him walking in?

The sound of the owl so close beside him freaked him out. It was eerie, like a horror movie. They heard it too. He saw them both turn. He held his breath. They seemed to be looking straight at him but in the dark they didn't see him and after a moment they went back to their conversation, talking together softly and laughing as they stared out towards the river. His nerve had gone. He took his chance, sliding back round the corner of the house and out of sight. He knew where they were. He knew that, at least for now the house – his house – in Morningside, was empty.

HMS *Tartar* was a 28-gun sixth-rate frigate with a complement of two hundred men and officers. She sailed from Spithead on 28 March 1764. Tom had watched a burly sailor stow his sea chest in the cockpit down on the orlop deck with increasing despair. His new uniform of blue jacket and white breeches sat uneasily on his small frame and his buckled shoes hurt. He sat down on the chest, staring round in the gloom, his cocked hat clutched defensively on his knees. They were below the waterline here and the air was fetid and damp. He looked up at his new friend Jamie and bit his lip fiercely. He would not let himself cry.

'You'll get used to it,' Jamie said wisely. 'We all do.' He spoke from several months' experience as a midshipman. 'We are lucky; we have a good captain and Lieutenant Murray is popular with the men.'

Tom wiped his nose on his sleeve and took a deep breath. 'It didn't sound like it, not from the way that sailor was swearing.'

Jamie laughed. 'That was O'Brian. He is a bit of a troublemaker, but a good sort at heart. Here' – he dived into the shadows and produced a canvas bundle – 'this is your hammock. Let me show you how you hang it. Did you bring a pillow?' As he moved around, the shadows cast by their only light, a candle stub stuck to an oyster shell balanced on the narrow table, leapt and flickered against the wooden walls of the compartment which served as cabin for the midshipmen, separating them from the rest of the crew. They staggered slightly as the ship moved restlessly beneath them and Jamie laughed as Tom threw out an arm to steady himself. 'You will need to find your sea legs quickly, my friend. We're still at anchor here!' he crowed. He was right. As they headed out into the ocean swell, Tom began to feel sick. The feeling grew worse and worse until he thought he might die. Then one morning as he climbed, half asleep, out of his hammock at the beginning of his watch he found the feeling had gone. It never returned.

It must have been climbing trees on the edge of the River Almond and the Brox Burn at Kirkhill that had given Tom a head for heights, that and scrambling round the ruins at St Andrews, or hauling himself up into the ancient chestnuts and oaks and onto the crumbling walls of the priory on Inchmahome Island. Always, when he could, he had climbed.

As he looked up at the towering masts of the ship, the network of ropes, the huge billowing sails and realised that he was expected to climb up there, now, he felt a sudden surge of excitement. 'Can you do it, boy?' Lieutenant Murray looked down at him. There was a certain sympathy in the man's eyes. He had seen too many boys quail and shudder and cling in terror to the lowest rigging.

'I can do it, sir.' Murray saw the glee there and recognised it as genuine. For once there was no bravado. 'Up you go then. To the cross trees and wait there for further orders.'

'Aye-aye, sir!' Tom resisted the urge to spit on his palms as he had seen the sailors do. He must remember he was one of the young gentlemen and expected to behave with a certain decorum.

George Murray watched, shading his eyes against the sun, then he turned to Jamie who was standing beside him. 'Better go with him. Keep an eye on him.'

Jamie saluted gravely. 'Looks as though he was born to it, sir. I expect he could teach me a thing or two.'

The ship heeled slightly in the swell of the sea, heading south. On the quarterdeck the captain paused in his slow patrol. Hands behind his back and seemingly relaxed, he was watching the ship. Early days yet, but it was coming together well. His attention was caught by the movement at the foot of the main mast and he watched the two figures as they swarmed up the ratlines. He gave a barely perceptible nod. Young Erskine would make a sailor yet; and by the time he returned to England he would be a man.

'It's amazing.' Tom was talking to Jamie at the end of their watch. 'You can see the whole world from up there.'

Jamie scowled. 'The whole sea, more like.' He was not going to admit to Tom that he was still unhappy going aloft, clinging to the handholds, his whole body iced with fear.

'It's like being a bird, soaring high over the waves,' Tom went on, oblivious. 'The sound of the wind in the sails and the whistling of the rigging is like music. Doesn't it excite you?'

'No.' Jamie sat on his sea chest and pulled off his shoes. His feet were covered in blisters. 'These are too tight. I will have to see if I can swap them. The purser gets angry if we grow too fast! If I'm lucky, one of the lieutenants might have an old pair he doesn't want any more.' He groaned with relief as he stretched out his toes.

Down below the cockpit was full of the sounds of the ship, the creaking and easing of her joints, the slap of a rope against the masts, the surge of water beneath them in the bilges. Below deck they could smell the stink of it. From beyond the thin partition between them and the seamen's quarters they could hear the low voices of men talking, the occasional burst of laughter, a shout of anger.

Tom was growing used to the routine on board; their lives were ordained by the sound of the bell every half an hour, by the division of their day into four-hour watches, by the longing for mealtimes and for sleep. At first he had thought he would never fall asleep in his hammock, but sheer exhaustion soon won and he was unconscious as soon as his head touched the rough brown canvas. Nearby one of the smaller middies was crying quietly, trying to muffle the sound in his arms as he clenched his eyelids against an intolerable world and Tom found himself aching with sympathy and at the same time relief that he himself felt, if not at home, then at least able to bear it.

As a young gentleman, Tom's main duties were as one of the captain's servants, the young men training to be officers; when called to perform these duties he must brush his own blue coat and make sure his hair was tidily tied back beneath his cocked hat and report to the captain, be it in his cabin or on the quarterdeck. As with everything else, he watched and learned and sometimes, with Jamie at his side, he got into mischief. Once or twice he was invited to the captain's table not as a servant but as a guest, sitting amongst the other officers, permitted with a certain good-humoured tolerance to give his views on subjects of the moment.

Almost as soon as they had set sail, Thomas and the other young gentlemen had been summoned to the quarterdeck to begin their lessons in navigation and it was then Tom discovered that this was to be no ordinary voyage. Not that he had any idea what an ordinary voyage entailed, but he could sense that this was special. The captain himself was there and with him their two civilian passengers, William Harrison and Thomas Wyatt. Sir John was, he explained to the boys, to oversee the sea trial of a special timepiece which would help navigators work out the position of the ship through an accurate knowledge of longitude. A prize was to be awarded to the first person to invent a chronometer that was sufficiently accurate and much was at stake.

With the aid of his calculations Mr Harrison predicted that

the ship would arrive in Madeira on 19 April and the exact distance the ship would have sailed.

Tom stared at the watch. It was beautiful. He had only a vague idea of what the men were talking about but one thing swiftly rose uppermost in his mind. How envious his brother David, with his fascination for the stars, would be of this chance to see these trials. He would write to him and tell him all about it, make his brother envious. He was gleeful at the thought, unaware that at that moment the captain happened to glance his way and caught sight of the fierce excitement on the young midshipman's face. His uncle had told him to keep a special eye on young Tom Erskine and suddenly he understood why. It was more than a benevolent family interest; there was a good brain there and a spark that could be cultivated.

At dinner that night, with Tom amongst the invited guests and, for once without Jamie, who was rapidly becoming his faithful sidekick, Sir John encouraged the boy to listen and to talk with his two distinguished guests. He was impressed that Tom appeared to know so much about the movement of the stars and had so swiftly grasped the basics of navigation. He did not know that the slowly growing pile of letters addressed to Lord Cardross in the bottom of Tom's sea chest were the way Tom was assuaging his homesickness and at the same time proving to his eldest brother, secure in his academic haven in Scotland, that life at sea was something to be envied.

Thomas

Cross though I was with my parents and my brothers, blaming them for my being press-ganged, as I considered it, into the navy, I wrote to them all. To my father I sent a short, polite note, informing him that I was still alive and moderately well. To my mother I wrote in warmer terms, withholding any news which I believed would be upsetting, though my mother was to my mind far better able to bear bad news than Papa. To David I was formal; I would never let him think I had been upset by my sudden relocation into the middle of the ocean. Only to Harry did I unburden myself at length, describing the worst parts of the experience, maybe, in spite of myself, allowing hints of my fear and homesickness, a sorrow compounded by the fact that I no longer knew where my home was. Certainly not Bath. I had been there but a few months. The house of my parents in Walcot was, I suppose, the nearest thing to home that I had known, but in my own mind I considered that they had cast me out. My brothers still lived and studied in Scotland, and Scotland was the land of my birth. It was there that I had grown up; it was there that I had explored a world of confusing contrasts. I was of noble birth, but poor. I was loved, at least by Mama, but I was also their youngest and least important child. I was in my heart a country boy but lived in a city. I had been privy to the conversations of the greatest minds of the enlightened age, encouraged to listen and watch and study, to express, albeit only occasionally, my own small opinions as I grew. I was allowed to make books my friends and to write and have dreams of academe, then told that all of my expectations and certainties were no more than that: dreams.

The place I now found myself was, I supposed, at present my home, the only certainty I knew upon the great wastes of the sea, and I put that at the head of my letters as my current address: HMS Tartar.

I sealed my letters and stowed them away at the bottom of my sea chest. I did not know if they would ever reach their destination. Perhaps it would be better if they did not.

14

April looked at her watch. There was no sign of Timothy and it had long ago grown dark. Presumably he had followed the Daimler for miles, then in his usual clueless way he had got himself lost. She felt a disproportionate wave of hatred for Finlay sweep over her. Everything about him, his complacency, his posh car, his celebrity status – which obviously brought money as well as fame – added to her fury at his decision to get involved and try to thwart her plans.

Sitters they had called themselves. The name had pleased them hugely. Squat. Infiltrate. Take. Hence the acronym. They would look for an empty house to use as a base – surprisingly easy even in this day and age. Then they'd move in, their story of distant relatives ready should anyone ask who they were, and begin to leaflet the area. They offered cleaning services, odd jobs, help with shopping, 'no job too small' and targeted elderly people who seemed to be living on their own. They then befriended them. Hence the sitting; not babysitting, but sitting with the elderly. Timothy at least had convinced himself they were doing the old folk a favour. They were lonely, abandoned by the world. It pleased them to have a friend. They entrusted their money, their credit cards, their PIN numbers, in order to get the shopping done, and she and Timothy had done that shopping, keeping meticulous records in case anyone ever asked. Until the money ran out. Which it inevitably did. That was the point. Sometimes they found the pension was enough to make it worthwhile sticking around, but not usually. Someone might notice. Time to move on. This was business. Their last target had been in Leeds. Before that in Birmingham.

The squats had varied. Some were in empty houses and they had made do with basic second-hand tat to furnish them. Some were already furnished, as this one had been. They knew who had lived here from sorting through the post that still cascaded through the door. Where the old woman had gone they did not know, but she had had good taste. April liked this house. She would be sad when it was time to go. Edinburgh had been trickier than anywhere else had been so far. She had found it harder to make contacts, to know where to go. But this new enterprise was the best so far; a potential gold mine.

They had tried the inheritance scam once before, in Exeter; it had worked like a dream. No one had questioned them, no one had cared. Her only sorrow had been that they hadn't chosen a more ambitious target. 'Start small,' Timothy had said, and she had listened. But now at last they were about to hit the big time. She had looked up the house prices around Number 26 and they were astronomic. Once they had pocketed the deeds to that place and sold it on, she had calculated they wouldn't have to work again. And now it was all being threatened by this bloody greedy daughter who had never cared for the old boy anyway and by Finlay Macdermott, of all people. She could hardly contain her rage.

With a sigh she turned out the lights in the kitchen and stamped up the stairs to the small back bedroom. Drawing the curtains before reaching for the light switch, she hauled a heavy suitcase out from under the bed.

Opening the lid of the case she looked down at the newspaper-wrapped contents. There were candlesticks, spoons and forks, small dishes. She pulled out a large square parcel and unwrapped it. She knew what this was. She had seen it on an antiques programme on the telly. A standish. A sort of pen and ink holder. The glass bottles for the ink had hall-marked silver lids.

90

There weren't any pens with it any more. She ran her finger over the intricate designs carved onto it. Victorian, she supposed. It was sad that it would have to be melted down; the swirls and curls on the silver appealed to her. The other stuff was more austere. Georgian probably. She had made good use of her study of daytime TV. The value of silver had dropped, but it was still all worth a lot of money by their standards.

She couldn't see how Tim's claim to that old boy's inheritance could fail. She had thought of everything, even the DNA. It had been a shock when they discovered he had a daughter, but that almost certainly didn't matter. Donald Dunbar hadn't mentioned her to Timothy in all those months; it would be clear to the solicitor that he had intended to disinherit her. She shivered. It had only been chance that Timothy had spotted the letter on the mat from the solicitors to Ruth that day; otherwise they wouldn't have known what was going on.

She replaced the standish in the suitcase and shoved the case back under the bed. Standing up, she turned away and caught sight of the pictures with their gilded frames stacked behind the door. She wasn't sure he should have bothered to remove them; they would have come anyway with the whole inheritance. But if anyone asked, he could always say it was to keep them safe in case the house was burgled. She gave a wintry smile. Shuddering, she studied the picture facing her. Ghastly woman in a lace-trimmed bonnet. Hideous face! But an oil painting nevertheless and who knows, it might be by someone famous. Or of someone famous. The jewellery she had locked in a drawer, all except the small bag of rings that Timothy had pocketed and she had demanded back as soon as they got home. There was other stuff too, which Timothy had removed little by little over the last few months. He was fairly certain he had taken everything of value. Poor old Donald had been oblivious, pathetically grateful for the attention that had been given him, clinging to her hand when she had gone to visit. She did not allow herself to remember the time when, with tears in his eyes, he had called her Ruth.

She moved over to the table by the door. There was a cardboard box she hadn't even bothered to unpack; odds and ends Timothy had taken from the cupboards upstairs in Donald Dunbar's house. Reaching in, she pulled out a small painted wooden box. She shook it experimentally then wrenched off the lid. There was a bundle of old sticks and rags inside. She stared down at it, puzzled, not making any sense of what she saw. Was it some kind of a primitive doll? Whatever it was, it was a dusty mess which smelled revolting and gave off an icy breath as though it was alive. She slammed the lid back on and rammed the box into the cardboard container. Why in God's name had the idiot brought that here? She shuddered and reached towards the box with the intention of taking the object, whatever it was, downstairs and binning it, but she couldn't bring herself to put her hand anywhere near it again. It emanated evil. She backed away from the table, aware that her whole body was trembling. Reaching the door, she groped for the handle, not taking her eyes off the box, dragged the door open and dived through it before slamming it shut behind her.

Standing on the landing she could feel her heart thumping in her chest. She grasped the newel post and hung on desperately, afraid she was going to pass out; her mouth flooded with bitter saliva and she realised suddenly she was going to vomit. She just made it to the bathroom, throwing herself down in front of the toilet, drenched with sweat as she retched again and again.

It was a long time before she managed to drag herself downstairs to the kitchen. She put the kettle on with shaking hands. It must have been the takeaway she and Timothy had had the night before, she decided vaguely. Prawn curry. Always a mistake. Perhaps that was why Timothy hadn't come home. He had been smitten too. She glanced at the clock on the wall above the bread bin.

Carrying her mug of tea, she went through into the lounge, turned on the light, sat down at the table and reached for her mobile. 'Tim? Where the hell are you?' It was a moment before she realised it had gone to voicemail. The bozo had turned it off. She slammed it down on the table and swore again under her breath.

Upstairs, in the back bedroom, a frosty rime was slowly spreading across the floor.

'If I'd known helping you with research was going to be as much fun as this, I would have cleared my schedule the moment I met you!'

It was a sunny morning and Finlay had volunteered to drive Ruth over the Queensferry Bridge across the Forth and on to St Andrews to have lunch, naturally, and to look for Lady Buchan's Cave.

They were standing at the top of the cliff, looking down at the rocks below, between the cathedral and the castle, the stark stone of the ruins warmed by a sun already low in the west. This was a dramatic coastline, scarred by history and the unrelenting onslaught of the sea, the rocky ribs and sandy coves washed constantly by the force of the waves. They had toured the cathedral and castle and been met with puzzled shakes of the head when they asked about the cave. No one had heard of it. Then at last they had been directed to a local historian. 'I'm afraid the sea took it,' he said mournfully. No one had ever asked him this question before, he said, and he obviously felt he had failed them by having to tell them it had gone. The cave had succumbed to the constant erosion of the cliffs sometime in the nineteenth century.

'But it must have been down there somewhere,' Ruth said sadly, 'and on those beaches below it, Thomas played with the drowned boy.'

Finlay shuddered. 'I'm not sure I'm so keen on that idea. Or chasing up your ghost monks at Inchmahome. Can we leave those as read? What about a quick trip to the Caribbean instead?' and his booming laugh echoed off the walls of the castle tower.

15

By the time the *Tartar* sighted Barbados on 13 May, Tom had settled into the routine of shipboard life as if he had been aboard one of His Majesty's ships for years. He was a good pupil and full of energy. He learned fast and made friends easily amongst the men and the officers; the gunner's wife who was charged with overseeing the welfare of the boys on the ship kept a quiet eye on him, as always trying to avoid favourites and knowing that any signs of preference for one boy over another would lead to jealousies and petty cruelties out of sight down on the orlop deck. One boy had already been badly hurt when the fixings of his hammock had been loosened and he had fallen awkwardly onto the boards beneath.

Jamie and Tom had whispered together that night; they knew who had done it and why. At eight years old, Robbie was the youngest and smallest boy aboard the ship. He still cried at the end of his watches, thinking his tears were inaudible, and when the gunner's wife went to comfort him he clung to her and begged to get off the ship, seemingly unable to comprehend that they were at sea, far from any port. She did her best to reassure him whilst drying his tears and robustly trying to instil what she called backbone. It was of little help. The boy was fading before their eyes, his misery compounded by the vicious bullying of the lad who hung his hammock beside him.

'No, Tom, don't get involved!' Jamie caught his arm and pulled him away as Tom clenched his fists that evening, watching as the little boy's mess tin was grabbed and ostentatiously emptied onto his neighbour's already over-full portion.

'Finished so soon, youngster?' the cocky voice crowed as Robbie stared down, bewildered, into his empty bowl.

'Give it back!' Tom shouted across the table. He was unaware of the sudden authority in his voice. Jamie cowed back out of sight beside him. 'You great bully! What has this poor lad ever done to you?'

'He annoys me, that's what!' Andrew Farquhar stood up, ducking his head away from the lantern swinging from the low beam above their heads. 'With his snivelling and his whining. So?' The face, now turned in Tom's direction, was set with dislike. 'What are you going to do about it?'

Tom flinched back, but he forced himself to stand up. He was a good head shorter than his opponent. 'I'm not going to do anything. You are going to give him back his food,' he said as firmly as he could. He narrowed his eyes as he saw Andrew grab his tin and, anticipating the next move, shouted, 'And you are not going to throw it on the floor. You are going to put it back on his plate.'

'Oh, his plate!' Farquhar's voice had risen into a singsong mockery of Tom's Scots accent. 'We ordinary folk, we eat out of tins. But your lordship has a plate. Where is it then? In your box, is it? All painted with gold and silver, is it?' He launched a kick at Tom's sea chest. Jamie had been sitting on it beside Tom and as he ducked sideways to avoid the vicious attack he slipped awkwardly to the floor.

'I am not a lord,' Tom said through gritted teeth. In spite of his blind fury he was surprised to feel himself becoming calmer as his opponent blustered more and more loudly. 'I am a fair man who hates to see a great blooter like you bully someone small and helpless, and I'm sure our friends feel the same.' He did not dare look at the others round the crowded mess table. The silence after the chatter and laughter was intense.

'I'm sure they do not,' Andrew said, so softly his voice was all but inaudible above the creak of the timbers round them.

Tom became aware that Jamie was scrambling to his feet beside him. He reached over for Jamie's shoulder and pushed him, trying to stop him standing up, but Jamie shrugged him off. 'They do,' he announced staunchly.

One or two of the others nodded, the others remained stock-still, their eyes moving shiftily between Tom and his protagonist.

Andrew dropped the tin on the trestle, splashing the gravy over the scrubbed wood. 'Take it then, if you are so hungry. Eat mine as well. Why don't you.' He turned and pushed his way out of the entrance into the cockpit beyond. They heard his feet on the ladder, and it was only then that Tom became aware of the greater silence from the seamen who had moments before been shouting and laughing beyond the wooden partition which separated the midshipmen from the rest. With a sinking heart, he realised the altercation had been clearly audible to the whole watch below.

Mastering his trepidation, he gave Robbie a smile as he pushed the mess tin towards him. 'Go on, Rob. Take your chance. Eat up.'

The boy seized his spoon and stuck it into the mess of stew but after two mouthfuls he dropped the spoon and stood up, ducking away from the table. Only seconds later they heard him retching into a bucket.

One by one their companions resumed their meal. No one spoke. Tom glanced at Jamie, who grimaced and put his finger to his lips. Robbie huddled against the ship's side in the shadows. He said nothing either.

It was later, as the watch slept, that Tom woke suddenly and saw, in the last flickering light of the candle stub, a figure standing over Robbie's hammock, fiddling with its fixings. 'Hey!' he called, but it was too late. As the burly shadow melted back into the darkness Robbie let out a scream and there was a crash, followed by two great throaty sobs, then silence. Somewhere someone grabbed a flint and lit the lantern. The boy's body was lying awkwardly across the corner of his sea chest and he seemed to be unconscious. The loosened end of the hammock was trapped beneath his body.

A burly sailor carried Robbie up to the sickbay and the acting surgeon and the gunner's wife gave him as much help as they could, waving sal volatile under his nose and burning feathers, straightening his bent limbs, setting a splint on his leg. As dawn rose he opened his eyes but he recognised no one. Tom was called when word below deck identified him as Robbie's friend and only an hour later, with Tom holding his hand, the little boy died. The shadow that left him had no more substance than a wisp of smoke.

Tom was sent for by the captain. Lieutenant Murray was standing beside him as Tom went into the day cabin. Beyond the great stern windows he could see the roll of the waves, a cloud of gulls swooping and diving into the ship's wake.

'I want you to tell me exactly what happened last night.' Sir John had a notebook open before him on his desk and a pen in his hand. Tom looked anxiously at the blank page as the captain fixed him with a firm stare, 'Every detail, if you please.'

Tom told him. At some level he was aware that the code of loyalty amongst his fellow midshipmen would demand silence, but he had been brought up to tell the truth. Besides, he was burning with anger and shock. The sight of the little boy, lying on the bunk before him, the feel of the small hand, so trusting and warm, which had for a moment squeezed his own before falling limp and then oh so quickly grown cold, had moved him beyond measure.

'And did anyone else see Midshipman Farquhar loosen the hammock?' Sir John said, his eyes narrowing.

'No, sir. They were all asleep.'

'How can you be absolutely certain it was him if it was dark?' George Murray asked.

'There was a candle stub still burning, sir. Just enough light to see by.'

'And you are prepared to swear to this on oath?'

'Yes, sir.'

'It has been known for hammock fastenings to be loosened as a joke,' George Murray put in.

'Yes, sir.'

'As it was when I was a middy,' the captain put in, 'and no doubt when you were too, George.'

97

'Indeed, sir,' the lieutenant said slowly. He scowled. 'So this could have been a practical joke that went wrong.'

'Midshipman Farquhar is a bully, sir. He hated Robbie,' Tom put in. 'He had done it before and he must have known the boy would be badly hurt.'

'So you are saying he deliberately set out to hurt him?'

'Yes, sir.'

'But not to kill him?'

Tom hesitated. 'I don't know, sir.'

The captain and the lieutenant exchanged glances. 'Very well. Have Midshipman Farquhar taken up and put in irons, Mr Murray,' the captain said wearily. 'We will have a full investigation and then I will hear the case. Only if a court of officers finds him guilty of murder will we proceed to a court martial when we reach port. Otherwise the matter will be dealt with on the ship.'

'Very good, sir.' The lieutenant sighed. 'We will have to inform Robbie's mother that her son is dead and the navy will have to pay the woman compensation.' He glanced at the captain. 'Shall I draw up the letter, sir?'

'Indeed. Perhaps you can use Tom as your amanuensis so he can see what has to be done. It is all part of his training. And Thomas,' Sir John's tone was stern again, 'I would advise you to watch your step below decks. I would guess you will have made an enemy or two by pointing the finger at Farquhar.'

'Yes, sir. Thank you, sir.' Tom saluted.

'And, George,' the captain added, his voice very weary, 'prepare the ship for a burial at sea.'

'You know I said I was going to go and film in the Hebrides for my TV show?' Finlay said as he walked into the dining room on Sunday evening. 'I'm afraid I am going to have to love you and leave you far more quickly even than I expected.' The table had all but disappeared under an array of papers and notes and Ruth was busy with her laptop. She looked up for a moment, her expression vacant. She had been reading an account of burial at sea in the eighteenth-century Royal Navy.

Finlay peered over her shoulder. 'This looks more like the background to a novel than family research to me.'

Ruth pushed back her chair. 'Harriet has lent me a book which actually mentions Thomas, but it's heavy and weird. Very esoteric. I don't think I'm quite ready for that yet. This is far more exciting. Thomas was only just fourteen when he went into the navy. How shocking is that?'

'It must have been a hellishly hard life.' Finlay grimaced. 'Right, well, I shall have to postpone our trip to Barbados. If you're happy to go on working here and house-sit for me, I'm off to the Isle of Skye instead. I've been doing some phoning around and one of the people I want to interview up there is going away for a few weeks imminently so I have to catch her now if I want her in my programme. It's a bit premature as I haven't signed a contract yet, but I am going to hook up with someone there who will film me with her.' His eyes were sparkling. 'I might stay and do a bit more while I'm there, it all depends. Can I leave you here? I'm so sorry, in your hour of need.'

Ruth smiled. His anxious eager expression reminded her of a puppy that isn't sure whether or not it's going to get a promised reward. 'I've told you I don't mind, Fin.' She meant it. 'I'm just so grateful to have this place to escape to. And I now have a project on top of sorting out Number 26.'

She was, she realised, going to feel utterly lost without his noisy, enthusiastic presence. She took a deep breath. It was ridiculous to be relying on him already. His absence would give her a chance to collect herself, chivvy up the solicitors and start making plans. Stand on her own two feet. And she had her new hobby, not stamp collecting, her mouth twitched with amusement at the thought, but history, and already she had sent off for a couple more books to fill in some of the background to Thomas's life.

When Fin said at once he meant it; he was going the next morning, flying to Inverness. As he assembled his case, his laptop and his overcoat in the hallway, he stopped and dramatically slapped his forehead with the palm of his hand. 'There is so much I have forgotten to tell you! But we will be in touch every day by phone or email or whatever, I promise. Right. I have a cleaning lady, who comes every Thursday, and there is Lachy who comes in to mow the lawns and do the heavy work. He's not regular. It depends on the weather and how busy he is.' He walked back towards the kitchen and the corkboard on the wall near the door. 'Here's his name and phone number, so ring him if you need anything doing. Inside or out. And all the other people you might need are here – gas, electric, doctor, all that sort of thing. They are all brilliant.' He beamed at her. 'And they will all send me bills or wait till I see them, so don't worry about paying anyone.'

Behind him the doorbell rang. 'There, that's the taxi. Goodbye, sweetheart!' He gave her a smacking kiss on the forehead. 'See you soon.'

'But, Finlay—'

She was too late. He had gone, banging the front door behind him.

16

In the end, after driving away from Cramond, Timothy had found his way to the Hawes Inn at South Queensferry, had drunk too much and booked himself in for the night. He expected April to be angry when he returned home next morning; in the event, angry didn't even begin to cover the mixture of rage and fear and indignation she hurled at him. She appeared to have been waiting in the hall for, as he put his key in the lock, the door was wrenched out of his hand and pulled open. He stared at her. She was deathly pale with huge circles under her eyes, her hair unkempt and there was a cigarette in her hand. He stared at it, uncomprehending. Since she had given up smoking two years before, she had been evangelical about not smoking in the house. Not that he ever did smoke. Much.

'What is it? What's wrong?' It was obviously more than his absence overnight that had upset her.

'Where the hell have you been?' She caught his arm and dragged him inside.

'I followed the Macdermott guy, as you told me to.' He wanted to make that point clear. 'I couldn't come back earlier. It was all too interesting. Ruth was out there with him. I think they're an item.'

'So why didn't you ring me?'

'My battery was flat.' That may not have been true last night but it was now. 'What is it, April? What's happened?'

She was still clinging to his arm. 'Come and see.'

She almost dragged him upstairs to the door of the second bedroom; the room he thought of as his own. Abruptly she released him and gave him a push. 'Go in. Go in and see for yourself.' Turning, she ran down the stairs and into the kitchen where she slammed the door.

Timothy hesitated then put his hand on the door handle. Nothing frightened his sister ever.

Slowly he pressed down the handle. There was a squeak in the spring and he stopped, holding his breath, then he nudged the door open. The room looked as it normally did, sparsely furnished with the extra boxes and suitcase and the pictures where he had left them. There was an open box on the bedside table which he didn't remember; apart from that, he could see nothing unusual.

April was sitting at the kitchen table, another cigarette in her hand. He stared at the smoke as it wreathed its way up and around the strip-light, and gave a small smile. Her weakness, her desperate breaking of her own rules gave him a huge advantage.

'What was I supposed to be looking at?' he said, his voice heavy with patience. 'I can't see anything wrong up there.'

She looked up at him and he saw the emotions cross her face one by one. Shock, surprise, disbelief and then, yes, there it was, scorn at his obvious failure. She stood up, pushing back the chair and went to the door. 'You can't have missed it! The cold. The ice! The sense of evil!' She went to the bottom of the stairs and looked up. From where she was standing she could just see the landing. 'You left the door open!' she whispered.

'Why not? What is supposed to have happened?' He looked at her hard, worried now. 'Has the heating broken? The radiator leaked? Tell me what I'm supposed to be looking at.' He pushed past her and took the stairs two at a time.

After a moment she followed him up and peered into the room over his shoulder. 'It's gone,' she said, her voice suddenly flat. 'It's all gone!'

He turned to confront her. 'What's gone?'

She was still staring round the room. 'I couldn't sleep because you weren't here.' At last came the flash of anger. 'I didn't know where you were. I didn't know what had happened to you. I was looking at some boxes of stuff earlier, things you'd brought from Number 26. Silver and pictures and boxes of this and that, and in one of them' – she gave an ostentatious shudder – 'there was something evil.'

'What?' Timothy had turned away from her to survey the room again. He took a step inside.

'No! Don't go in!' she cried.

'What was it, April?' He was scared now. 'What was it you saw?'

'I was on the landing and it felt cold in here.' April shuddered. 'I wondered if the window had blown open, so I came in—' She bit her lip hard. 'The room was full of ice.' She whispered the words so softly he could barely hear them.

'And was the window open?' His own voice, normal, strong, sounded indecently loud.

'No. It was cold as death. It smelt of the sea.'

'Dear God, woman! Have you gone insane?' In spite of himself, Timothy was rattled. He stepped backwards out of the room and pulled the door closed behind him, giving it a little push to make sure it had latched properly. 'Well, whatever it was, it's gone now.'

She followed him back into the kitchen and for the first time seemed to notice the smoke hanging there under the light. Her cigarette had burned to ash in the saucer on the table. 'So,' she said over her shoulder. Her voice was normal again. 'What was so exciting that you couldn't come home? Where does our celebrity chef live?'

He told her everything. Except about his night in the Hawes Inn.

She reached up to the top of a cupboard and produced a half-full pack of cigarettes which she proceeded to crunch in her fist and then throw into the flip-top bin. Timothy wisely decided not to say anything.

'Do you know what it was that you were looking at last night, that made you feel so cold?' he ventured cautiously.

'You had put a box on the side table,' she replied. 'Cardboard. There were various things inside it including a carved wood box. Small. Exotic-looking. I opened it.' She stopped as she sensed the nausea returning. She swallowed hard. 'Inside it was some kind of stinking old doll.' She took a deep breath. 'The evil was in there. I was going to throw it out, but once I took the lid off I couldn't breathe. I couldn't see straight.' She took another deep breath.

'Do you want me to throw it out for you?' Timothy was all big brother now. To his alarm, he found the sight of April in such a state completely overwhelming. She was the eldest, she was the one always in charge. He wasn't sure if he was frightened or if he was pleased to see her weak and indecisive.

Her reaction to his question was far from indecisive though. 'Yes, get rid of it. But don't for fuck's sake open the thing again. Burn it. Or bury it in the dumpster in the next road. Let the council deal with it. Don't try and be clever and take it anywhere in your car.'

He felt his face colour. That was exactly what he had thought of doing. He wasn't sure where he wanted to take it, but of one thing he was certain; he had no intention of getting rid of it, not until he had had a chance to work out what it was.

Luckily, April didn't notice. 'Do it now,' she said. 'This minute. I'll wait in here.'

'OK.' He turned towards the door. 'And I might be a while. I have to do one or two things while I'm out.' He didn't wait to hear if she protested. He was already halfway up the stairs, his car keys in his hand.

It was late afternoon when Ruth went into the dining room and looked at the table with her piles of books, the notebook, the pens aligned neatly beside it, and the brown envelopes full of letters and she felt again that frisson of excitement at the thought of what was in there. Finlay's abrupt departure had distracted her, but now she had time to start again on her reading and, she realised, she was actually pleased to be alone again. This was the freedom she had craved.

First she unpacked Sally's books. Ruth pulled the box open

and stacked the books on the table with the others. There were volumes on meditation and crystals, on past lives and ghost hunting and, she suddenly noticed, a slim volume, half-hidden between two others. *Psychic Self-Defence* by Dion Fortune. 'Oh my God!' she whispered. She picked it up and stared at it. So her mother had heard of Harriet's strange magician. Perhaps she had known, too, about Lord Erskine's alternative career as a spirit guide. She put the book on top of the pile. These books brought her closer in some ways to her mother than anything else she had found. These had been Lucy's special treasures.

She glanced at the bulging brown envelopes. Letters were special. They were so personal, so immediate. She had already looked at a couple of them, documenting Thomas's first months in the navy, and now she reached for one of the unopened packets. This wasn't letters. There were several pieces of paper inside and some small cardboard-covered notebooks. She tipped everything onto the table and shook the envelope to make sure it was empty before picking up one of the notebooks and opening it at the first page.

There was a name scrawled across the top. Catherine Anne. Ruth frowned. The name was familiar. Then she remembered. Wasn't that the name of her mother's grandmother? She turned over the first leaf of the small book and found she was staring at a young girl's diary. A teenager perhaps? The year was 1905. The beautiful, careful writing began neatly and the entries were much like any new diary, detailing a walk through the January woods, a trip to town to buy new boots, a friend's birthday party. Ruth turned the pages slowly. The entries became more sporadic and less neat. Then came one that caught her eye. It had been scrawled with such force that the pen had blotted and the writing had been underlined so heavily that the paper was torn.

> *I had the dream again last night. Or what Papa calls the dream. But it isn't. I know it isn't. He's real!!!*

Ruth read the words several times then turned the page. The next entry was five days later.

I spoke to Dunc last night and he has seen him too. He said not to tell Papa. As a vicar, he isn't allowed to believe in ghosts, but Mama sees them too, Dunc is sure of it. And so did Grandmama.

Dunc was her mother's great uncle, Duncan, killed on the Somme in 1916. She knew that much. The only relation her father had approved of. So, Catherine Anne was his sister. Ruth found herself biting her lip.

There was a gap of several weeks before the next entry.

He came to me again. I don't know what he is trying to tell me or who he is. I don't know what to do. D is still away at school and I have no one to tell. I tried to ask Mama, but she pretended not to understand. She looked horrified when I told her and then Papa came in with his Bible under his arm and Mama went to talk to Cook. Papa looked very stern and made me put my hand on the Bible as if it would protect me. He asked me if I was still having bad dreams and I said yes and he patted my shoulder and said we should pray together.

Ruth could feel small shivers of horror and excitement prickling up and down her spine. She looked up at the window; it was very dark outside. She hadn't realised how late it was getting. Standing up, she went over and pulled the curtains across. Behind her the diary lay in a pool of lamplight on the table.

He still comes to speak to me though I long since stopped trying to tell anyone. He is kind. He knows the future. He tells me that I will marry a handsome man and he smiled as if he knew such things were of importance to young girls. He tells me to listen to my father, that he is a good man and wise and that he only wants the best for me.

Ruth turned the page.

10 December 1912. My 19th birthday. As soon as he heard that he was to receive a living at last, Joseph asked Papa for my hand

106

and Papa agreed. I'm the happiest person in the world. On our
return from honeymoon he will be installed in his new church.

There were only two more entries. The first, dated December, 1913.

How strange it is to read this diary now. The day before my
marriage and once again I saw my ghostly visitor. He gave me
his blessing and told me I would be happy with Joseph. He told
me that we would have four children and said I should give them
all his name. I pointed out that he had never told me his name.
He said he was Thomas Erskine. I told him that I already bore
his name, given to me at my baptism, and he smiled and told me
that he knew it! I have a little girl of my own now, and to her I
have given the family name of Erskine.

Ruth felt she had stopped breathing. Thomas. Her Thomas. But then she had guessed it might be him. The last entry was written after two blank pages and was dated 1916:

Thomas came to me last night. He was gentle and kind and told
me Dunc was dead in France. He told me to prepare my parents
for the coming news as they would find it hard to bear. How
can I prepare them? He told me my children would thrive and
live long lives to comfort me and that my parents would find
joy in my children. I am broken-hearted. I believe him though
even now Mama has written to say she has received a letter from
Dunc, dated some weeks ago. He says he is not allowed to say
where he is but that he is well. Yet I know it isn't true . . .

The remainder of the notebook was empty.

Ruth sat for a long time staring into space then at last she reached for the rest of the papers that had fallen from the envelope. There was the letter sent by Duncan's commanding officer to his parents, saying he had been fatally wounded after showing exceptional bravery leading his men; there was another giving the date of his death.

There was a copy of her mother's family tree. She realised there were tears running down her cheeks as she studied the letters and then the notes her mother had drawn up. Ruth ran her finger from the bottom to the top of the page, pausing when she came to her great-grandmother Catherine Anne, the author of the diary, who was born in 1893. Thomas, Catherine's great-great-grandfather, who had died in 1823, was there, and there above him were lines and lines of names. Her mother had traced her own line of descent from Thomas down through the daughters of the family, every one, save Lucy, married, she noticed, to a man of the cloth. There were other lines of descent, of course there were, the male lines, the direct lines, but this one was hers and Lucy had added Ruth's name at the bottom of the page. Ruth stared at it incredulously. She was there, but this was a version of herself she had never seen before. Ruth Catherine Erskine Dunbar.

Her mother had given her his name. Her father couldn't have known. He would never have countenanced such a thing. It wasn't on her birth certificate. Or her passport. So, it was her mother's secret name for her, the name she had wanted her to carry.

She sat back for a moment, overwhelmed. Then it occurred to her that she didn't need to make a family tree; her mother had done it all for her, but that made her want to know their stories even more. This was her family, the family she had craved since she was a little girl.

She reached for the next envelope. It contained a neat bundle of letters with remnants of broken seals, tied together with ribbon. Had her mother read all these? If she had, it must have been in secret, and when her father locked all Lucy's treasures away he couldn't have realised what they were or surely he would have burned them. Perhaps they had never been read again since they were first opened.

She carefully unfolded the first. This was from Thomas himself, addressed to his daughter, Frances; these had been arranged in order of date of writing, beginning in 1821 – addressed from somewhere called Buchan Hill. Her heart hammering with excitement, she glanced through them, aware that she had something inestimably valuable in her hands, something of national importance and, to her, fantastic interest. She picked out one and looked at it closely. The handwriting was firm and there was a small sketch at the end. Ruth screwed up her eyes, trying to see what it was. A cartoon character of some kind. An old man, with glasses and wild hair, a letter in his hand, at his heels a small attentive dog. It was a tiny, mocking, self-portrait. She put down the letter and stared at the wall for several moments, trying to calm herself, her instinct to ring Harriet and tell her what she had found. She resisted the urge. For now, this was her secret. It was too important, too exciting to be hijacked by Hattie.

This was her route into her family and the first thing she must do, she realised, was to sort everything into chronological order, starting with the first letter from the copies, which were Thomas's letters to various members of his family that had been collected together. Thomas's own writing was condensed and hard to read and she carried it over to the lamp on the side table. It was like finding a route into his head. His style was direct, if wordy, but that was a character of the age in which he wrote, detailed, seemingly with total recall and with a delightfully dry sense of humour.

Pushing the letters aside two hours later, she realised her head was aching and her eyes sore; she felt extraordinarily tired. Going over to the French doors, she pulled back the curtains and looked out into the dark. It had started to rain. The garden was wet and windy, the trees thrashing noisily as she stepped out onto the terrace and felt the rain on her face. The wind tore at her hair and she took a deep breath, smelling the salt in the wind off the churning Forth and the sweeter scent of mountain grass from the far-off Highlands.

It had always been a source of great pride to her Sussex-born mother that her ancestors came from Scotland, that wild, untamed place of history and myth and legend, a place that had pulled at the heartstrings of generation after generation of her family. And now that she was reading about it through the eyes of her Scottish ancestor, Ruth was beginning to understand. How strange that the wiles of Fate should have snatched him away from Scotland so young, first to Bath and then to the heat and sun of the Caribbean. Perhaps it was from these letters, written from so far away, that they had inherited their sense of nostalgia.

Ruth hugged herself with glee. She was at the beginning of the most glorious adventure. This was the world she had seen in her dreams. She was hooked.

17

The entire crew, officers and men, had been assembled on deck to witness Farquhar's punishment. The charge was insubordination and persistent recklessness in such a way as to cause the death of another crew member. They had given him the benefit of the doubt, and decided he had not intended murder. The sentence was to be flogged publicly at the gratings, followed by de-rating, which meant he was to be turned forward as an ordinary seaman with loss of status, pay and patronage.

Tom watched, his mouth dry, as Andrew was brought up from below deck. His face as he came past the line of officers was set, with just the smallest glimmer of defiance in his eyes. His gaze lingered for a second as he passed Tom, who felt a sudden shiver of fear. Andrew was unpopular on the ship, but there were many among the junior officers and seamen who would perhaps have preferred to deal with this matter amongst themselves. Here even Mr Harrison and Mr Wyatt were required to be present. The ship must be shown to be united on the side of discipline. Andrew's irons were removed, he was stripped naked to the waist and secured to the grating that had been lashed to the lee rigging.

As the sound of the cat whistling through the air cut through the hiss of the waves and the thrum of the wind in the rigging, Tom closed his eyes. Farquhar's back was systematically laid open with the full force of the lashes and his blood began to run down on the deck. Later the duty watch would scrub all signs of it away after he had been sluiced with ice-cold sea water and carried below.

Life resumed much as usual after the flogging, but without Farquhar's malign presence amongst the midshipmen. Tom saw him only from a distance, though he was aware of his eyes following him and of the strength of Farquhar's hatred. He tried not to care. He had done the right thing, he was sure of it. He still couldn't get the picture of Robbie's face out of his head, the touch of the small boy's hand, already calloused from his shipboard duties, and the feel of it slowly losing its heat as the chill of death took him away. An innocent, happy child had lost his life after weeks of utter misery and homesickness. That he himself was only a few years older did not occur to him. He was nearly a man compared to Robbie and he felt intensely both his responsibilities and his failure to save the boy's life.

The Island of Barbados was first sighted on 13 May. Tom felt a jolt of excitement as the lookout made the call and the ship's company ran to the rail and saw for themselves the shadow on the western horizon and watched as it grew more and more solid in the haze. As the ship anchored, the whole crew were looking longingly towards the shore. The air was heavy with the scent of trees and flowers and earth, carried on the warm wind with the call of the gulls.

To his joy, Tom found the captain had selected him as one of the shore party escorting Mr Harrison and Mr Wyatt to the observatory with their precious timepiece.

It was strange to be on shore again. The beaten track from the port up the hill to the observatory seemed to rock and undulate under his feet and the scents of the island were overpowering after the clean salt and wind on the sea and the stink of the ship. Tom took in every detail. The boy chosen to come as the captain's other servant was Jamie, and amongst the men rowing the party ashore was, to Tom's disgust, Andrew Farquhar.

By now they all knew the story of Mr Harrison's father, John, and his quest to find a clock accurate enough to maintain perfect time at sea. Tom had listened to the conversation of the two men and the officers at the captain's table and he knew all about John Harrison's race against his rival for the enormous prize offered for a timepiece that could be used to work out a ship's exact position by using longitude as well as latitude.

At the observatory, a clergyman named Reverend Maskelyne was waiting for them. Tom didn't understand the shock and anger with which their passengers greeted the man as he removed his hat in a sweeping bow, but Maskelyne's smug smile alerted them all to the fact that there was something very wrong. It was only later that Tom heard that Mr Maskelyne too was engaged in the quest for an accurate timepiece and that he, who was to be the judge of Mr Harrison's instrument, had recently completed the ocean voyage himself and had already claimed the prize. He dithered as he made the observations of the sun and claimed he could not see it for cloud. It was Captain Lindsay who pointed out that there wasn't a cloud in the sky and insisted the observations be done again and later noted in the ship's log that the watch had worked to perfection, losing only a few seconds on the month's voyage from Madeira.

As Tom looked on, his eyes glued to the proceedings, he became aware of someone standing close at his elbow. He glanced up to find Andrew staring at him, a strange expression on his face. Tom moved away slightly and returned to studying the men making their careful notes. Andrew moved with him. 'That's right, pretty boy. Make sure you don't miss anything.' The whisper in his ear was so quiet it was lost in the sound of the rustling palms and the cry of the birds. 'Are you planning to add Astronomer Royal to your list of titles?'

Tom did not reply. He was busy memorising everything going on between the astronomers, planning already the letter he was going to write to David.

The ship proceeded to cruise between the Windward Islands and up as far as the coast of Florida where they would anchor off Pensacola. As before, the men maintained the ship, scrubbed the decks, watched for distant sails and the midshipmen went about their duties, interspersed with lessons in seamanship and navigation. Once or twice an American privateer was spotted and they gave chase, but to their intense disappointment the ships were too far away to catch and slipped out of sight beyond the horizon.

There was plenty of time for Tom to write his letters and his own diary and to practise drawing, and now there were more frequent opportunities to put the letters in the mailbag to be taken aboard an eastbound ship or a mail packet, and to collect plants on their trips ashore. He discovered too that the ship's officers were invited to the great plantation houses for dinners or sometimes for parties. It was on one of those trips, accompanying Sir John as his personal servant, that, having been sternly reminded of the need for discretion as part of the duties of an officer and a gentleman, he met the captain's woman.

The party was to spend several nights ashore as guests of the plantation owner and Tom gazed as usual in awe at the splendours of yet another great house. He was given a small room adjoining the captain's and it was before the dinner on the first night when there was a knock at the door. Automatically he went to answer it and stopped abruptly at a sharp command from Sir John. 'Leave it! You may go, Tom. You may take the rest of the evening off. I shall not need you again tonight.'

He gestured towards the door which led to the adjoining dressing room. As Tom went obediently towards it Sir John himself went to answer the knock. Tom glanced back and was astonished to see one of the slave women at the door and even more astonished to see his captain seize the woman in his arms, swing her off her feet and kiss her. He caught sight of Tom standing open-mouthed, his hand on the doorknob. 'I said, you can go!' he shouted.

'Yes, sir, sorry, sir.' Tom hastened out of the room.

He sat down on the bed wondering what to do next. He knew some of the officers availed themselves of the services of the women ashore; white women and slaves both seemed equally willing and indeed eager to seek the company of the men from every ship that dropped anchor as they sailed from island to island. That the captain should do the same was not surprising in itself, but the strength of feeling between the two in that short glimpse had been undeniable. The woman was beautiful, he had seen enough of her to notice that, and they obviously knew each other well. With a sigh he levered himself off the low divan and let himself out into the corridor. Suddenly he had hours of free time to himself and he wasn't sure where to start.

Thomas

Black faces I had seen aplenty when I was back in Scotland and in England. Most, though not all, appeared to be servants. I don't think I considered the matter of slavery then. I heard my parents talk about it, and my sisters, but not in any way that engaged me, with my own boyish interests paramount. When I reached the Caribbean I was all at once in a world of men and women and children who had been brought there on the slave ships from Africa. The ships themselves were notorious – some lay at anchor in Bridgetown Bay when we first arrived, redolent of the horrors that went on below decks – but on the plantations we visited, in the houses of the owners and administrators who were our hosts, the slaves seemed content with their lot. I did not then understand the concept of freedom or self-determination. Had my lot been any worse than theirs, conscripted as I was, in my own eyes anyway, into the navy and taken away across the ocean against my will? Their quarters were pleasant, their food better by far than any they could have been used to in their native land, or so I supposed, and better than that on many a ship of His Majesty's navy, their clothing neat and clean. I saw them dancing and I heard them sing. My captain loved one of them, and as I discovered later had a child with her whom he adored. He saw nothing wrong with their situation, so nor did I, then.

And one of them saved my life.

18

Tom could not believe he had been so careless. His sea chest was unlocked, the lid open when he came down off his watch and went automatically to collect his sketchbook. He scanned his belongings. Had anything been stolen? He did not believe it of his shipmates, but occasionally things went missing from someone's gear, probably lost, or put down in the darkness of the gunroom and kicked by mistake into a corner, but there was always the possibility that one of the seamen could have slipped into the midshipmen's mess on the rare occasion when there was no one there.

He knelt before the chest. His writing case was there, the box that contained his pens and inks, his clothes, his precious ring-dial, all his carefully packed and sorted belongings. He wrinkled his nose. An unusually foul smell rose from his body linen as he fumbled beneath it for the packet of letters he had received from home, carried on a sloop from Portsmouth. He recoiled then he reached for the glim, the small candle on the mess table, and held it down over the sea chest to see more closely. A bundle of filthy rags had been tucked in amongst his clothes. In the flickering light of the flame he could see the moist stinking brown stains and was in no doubt what this was. He grabbed the corner of the bundle and ran with it up the companionway to the deck where he threw the offending rags over the side. He saw the querying look on the faces of the men on watch up there but none that he could see looked especially concerned or interested. It didn't matter. He could guess who had done it. He did not immediately guess how truly malicious the act had been.

He found the first sores on his body three weeks later. They looked like raspberries as they swelled and crusted over. Frantic scrubbing did not remove them and at last he confided in Jamie. His friend stared at him, his eyes wide. 'Tom! How could you be so stupid? Who was it? One of the slaves?'

Tom felt himself blush to his ears. 'No! No, I haven't!' he blustered. 'I haven't ever!' He knew where he had got the infection but he could see his friend did not believe him.

He hid the lesions as best he could. He could go to the gunner's wife but he was too ashamed, or he could go to the purser who was acting surgeon in the absence of anyone more qualified and was in charge of the medicine chest with its phials of mercury ointment. He knew that if Jamie didn't believe how he had got the disease then no one else would. Mortified, he scrubbed his body raw with sea water.

It was Andrew who, as Tom walked past, crowingly asked him why he was so obsessed with cleanliness and what he was hiding, and it was Andrew who spread the word that young Tom Erskine had contracted the great pox by sleeping with a slave on a trip ashore. It wasn't long before he found himself being given an evil-smelling ointment by the gunner's wife; he was accused of lewd behaviour and informed a fine would be taken from his pay and then he was summoned by Lieutenant Murray.

To his surprise, however, the officer appeared to believe the story poured out by the humiliated and frightened boy and at once guessed the source of Tom's misery. 'Seaman Farquhar, I suppose,' he said heavily. 'I've seen him watching you; he's had it in for you ever since that affair with the hammock.'

That affair with the hammock! Tom bit his tongue. Did the lieutenant not even remember Robbie's name?

'Yes, sir,' he acquiesced miserably.

Murray arranged for him to go with the next shore party and to Tom's astonishment escorted him personally to the slave quarters behind the governor's house. 'Don't look so worried,

Tom,' he said. 'All is not lost. I am taking you to see the best doctor in the Islands.' He removed his hat as they ducked into one of the small houses behind the governor's mansion and Tom followed suit.

The huge black woman who greeted them smiled at Tom as the lieutenant explained the circumstances. 'So, boy, let me see what's wrong with you,' she said, her voice soft and lilting as she held out her hand. 'You go wait outside,' she added to the lieutenant. 'This thing is bad enough for the child without having an officer leering down his trousers.'

Tom was almost in tears as he undressed, reluctantly removing his shirt and then his breeches, thankful for the dim light of the small house with its palm-leaf roof. He could hear the wind rustling the leaves as the woman pulled him closer to the daylight in the doorway, holding him in front of her with two firm hands.

She gave a crow of laughter. 'You've got the yaya disease, boy. You don't have to panic now I seen you. You not got the great pox. I can fix this, no problem.' She leaned closer, inspecting his wounds. 'You been scrubbing these sores?'

Tom nodded miserably.

'That's good.' She let him go and studied his face. 'Back where I come from, that is how we cure this disease. We scratch our children's skin and rub in the illness, then they get it, but not very badly, and they never get it again. But older people, who haven't had that chance, we scrub the berries!' she chuckled. 'Just like you did. All the dirt and the disease comes away and your own good blood washes it out of you. I will give you medicine and I will give you ointment – I make it myself from herbs and from ground seashells – and you will be as good as new, boy. And you won't get it again. You're a strong child, yes?' She had a wonderful warm smile, he realised, her heavy black face lit with kindness.

'Thank you, ma'am.'

But her face had sharpened. Once again she drew him into the thin ray of sunshine that was finding its way through the doorway so that it shone on his face. 'You one of us, boy?'

He hesitated, confused. 'I don't understand.'

'Yes, you one of us,' she murmured, half to herself. 'You see

118

the dead folk; you feel their loneliness and their pain. That's a hard path for you. I not surprised you go make enemies; people sense you a bit special.' Her mouth widened into a broad smile. 'You can help people – I don't think you go be a doctor like me, but you not made for your king's navy. Why you want to be an officer?'

Tom glanced out of the doorway towards the figure of George Murray, who was leaning against a palm tree, smoking his pipe, seemingly lost in thought. 'My father arranged it,' he replied reluctantly. 'I didn't want to be in the navy, but I quite like it now?' He looked at her anxiously, his answer framed as a question as if he did not know if he was speaking the truth. It seemed important that this woman understood.

She smiled at him. 'It will do for now. When you grow into a man you make decisions for yourself. Now you too open, too much trusting. You must learn to be safe from people, people who are alive and people who no longer here.' She dropped his hand and moved back into the shadows of her house. 'Go tuck your shirt in, boy, make yourself respectable for your officer. I'll give you medicine to make you better and I'm going to give you something special that will protect you from evil which works in shadows. You know prayers, boy? You good Christian?'

'Yes,' he whispered.

'Then I put Christian God and Blessed Virgin in my magic with my own special gods from my homeland who protect me and mine. That'll give you much good and safety.' She smiled again as she fumbled with the baskets on the shelf above her table. 'What I give you, you put in the bottom of your belongings and you keep it safe and you leave it there with you all of your life, and then you give it to your children. You understand me, boy?'

As Tom trotted back to the harbour at George Murray's side he was clutching a bag which contained a bottle of black, strong-smelling tincture, a pot of brown ointment and a carefully wrapped bundle. He had seen Lieutenant Murray dig into his own pocket for some coins with which he had paid the woman, who had swiftly squirrelled them away into the folds of her skirts before turning back to Tom and reaching out to make the sign of the cross on his forehead with her thumb. He had forced himself not to flinch away from her as he made his stammered thanks. He could feel some kind of strange power coming from her which left him scared and awed and, he knew it already, strengthened.

'Thank you for bringing me here, sir,' he ventured shyly.

'I've done it before,' Murray replied easily. 'You've been lucky. It could have been the great pox, which can never be cured.' He stopped suddenly. 'Are we sure it was Farquhar who put the infected rags into your sea chest?'

Tom looked down at the dusty track and shuffled his feet. 'I can't be sure, sir. But he was the one who drew attention to it, who seemed to know about it, who hates me enough to do something like this.' His voice faded.

'We cannot punish him for something that is a mere suspicion, Tom.'

'I know, sir.'

'So, what do you suggest we do?'

'Nothing, sir. It's up to me to be more careful.'

'We can move him to another watch.'

'No, sir.' Tom took a deep breath. 'No, thank you, sir. It's for me to learn to be careful and to learn to make a friend of him, if I can.' He knew he sounded doubtful and he tried to straighten his back and firm his shoulders as he had seen the officers do.

Murray hid a smile. 'We sail to Jamaica soon, Tom. I understand from the captain that you are due some shore leave when we arrive, to visit some of your father's relatives, is that right?'

Tom bit his lip. 'Does the captain know about me being ill, sir?' he asked.

The lieutenant sighed. 'He knows about everything that goes on on his ship.'

'Yes, sir. I see, sir.' Tom glanced at him. 'Will he tell my father, sir?'

'I very much doubt it. Why should he? You're already on the road to recovery. You've been lucky, Tom. You've seen the best healer in these islands and, besides, what happened was not your fault.' He hesitated. 'Just watch yourself. Farquhar has a malicious streak. I'm keeping an eye on him, but I cannot be there every moment of the day. You need to be on your guard and you need to be able to deal with this situation.' He looked down at the boy trotting beside him. 'Be strong, Tom. You have it in you. Don't be afraid to stand up to him.'

James Reid emailed Ruth a copy of the letter he proposed sending to Timothy. 'It has come to our attention that the will forwarded to me purporting to come from your solicitor does not carry an authentic signature, neither has it been possible to contact the witnesses. It is a criminal offence to falsify . . . ' She glanced through the rest of it briefly. James demanded the return of any property Timothy had removed from Number 26 without delay, and threatened to send a copy of the letter to the police if that was not done.

She sat back, staring at her laptop. Perhaps they should send a holding letter first? Give Timothy a little time to return anything he had taken.

'Ruth?' It was Harriet on the phone. 'How are you?'

'I'm good.' Ruth smiled. It was good to hear Hattie's cheery voice. 'I'm discovering lots of stuff about Thomas.'

'Any mention of spirit guides?'

'No, but he does seem to be showing signs of having appeared as a ghost a few times.'

'Now, that is interesting.' Harriet's voice rose with excitement.

'And one other thing you'll be interested to hear: I've found a copy of Dion Fortune's book *Psychic Self-Defence* amongst my mother's books.'

'Have you indeed. Listen, Ruthie. I was ringing because I've had an idea. I've got to come to Edinburgh to interview someone about SOE and check a few things in the library. Liz is lending me her car. I wondered if I could come on to see you the day before and perhaps have supper? Possibly stay the night? Would your friend Fin mind? We can catch up on everything then.'

It seemed like a plan.

19

Andrew Farquhar had hated Thomas from the first moment he had set eyes on him in that little rat hole of a gunroom on the ship. The boy seemed to have the knack of making friends, of being popular. Young as he was, he addressed the lieutenant and even the captain as an equal. Clearly there must be family connections of some sort. It gave Andrew enormous pleasure to set about planning all the petty revenges that would make Thomas miserable. He hadn't intended to kill Robbie. That had been unfortunate, a prank aimed at upsetting the sanctimonious Thomas who had befriended the kid. That prank had gone sadly wrong, and thanks to Thomas he was caught and punished and humiliated.

It had been a petty triumph when he had the idea of stealing the infected rags from the squalor of the seamen's quarters where he now found himself and stashing them in Thomas's sea chest. He had found it unlocked once or twice over the months and spent time searching it, looking at the neat notebooks and pen boxes and brushes and combs, the pile of letters tied with ribbon that had come from his family, the presents his sisters had sent him via a merchant ship from London. Andrew hadn't kept the items he filched, that would have been too easy. One pen, engraved with Thomas's name that he knew had been a gift from his mother, he threw over the side in the dark of the night; the small penknife, a gift from Thomas's father, he kept for two days then slid through a gap in the boards and heard with great satisfaction the small splash as it fell into the noxious bilge water in the hold.

The plan to infect him had worked, but instead of the death-sentence pox Andrew had hoped for, he had caught some disease which turned out to be curable, and even that small misery had misfired when Thomas had gone ashore and come back with bottles of medicine and a jar of ointment. When Andrew had next found the gunroom empty and crept over to look at Thomas's sea chest, he had felt the cold waft of evil coming off it before he even touched it and he fled back to his own quarters. He had never gone near it again, but his hatred had grown, if anything, more entrenched.

Timothy threw the letter down on the table and looked up at his sister. For once he did not protest at the fact that she had opened something addressed to him. 'So that's it, then. We've been found out.'

'No. He only says there's a delay. Even if they suspect something, they can't prove it.' April glanced at him. 'And we still have our trump card: the DNA. We can prove you're the old man's son.'

'You really believe that will work?'

'It will work,' she said emphatically. 'And that would at least give us half the house and half the stuff.'

'Us? It will give me half the house,' he said mildly. He gave a grim smile. 'After all, it will prove you are not my sister.'

He looked away when he saw the ice-cold fury in her eyes. 'Don't even think you're going to cut me out of my share,' she said quietly. 'It was all my idea and my planning. You haven't the brains to tie your own shoelaces!' The scorn in her voice was cutting.

He gave a small shrug of his shoulders. 'It was me that sat with that old man for months.'

'And why not? It's not as if you had any other job.' She stood up. 'Now, what do we do with the silver and stuff?'

'We're going to deny having it, right?'

'Of course.' The tone was withering again. 'They can prove

123

nothing if they can't find it.' She put her hands on the table in front of him and leaned forward, right in his face. 'What did you do with that box of muck?'

It was the first time she had asked. 'I put it in the rubbish skip down the road, like you said.' He didn't meet her eye.

'Good. Right. Now, we have to get everything out of here. We can smash up the pictures and burn them; they aren't worth anything. The rest is easier to stash.'

'I know where we can hide the stuff.' His voice was quietly triumphant. 'Somewhere they will never even think to look.' Her casual dismissal of the pictures hurt. They were old and so probably valuable.

'Where?'

'Macdermott's place in Cramond.' He grinned.

She opened her mouth to protest, then sat down opposite him and stared at him hard. 'Go on.'

'When I was poking about there in the garden I came across an old shed behind the outbuildings. Looks as though no one has been in there for years. It's full of spiderwebs and dead leaves. I can put it there.'

She thought for a moment. 'It could work.'

'Can you think of anywhere better? Short of chucking it in the Forth?' His courage was coming back. 'And you can't exactly have a bonfire here, can you! Mr Nosy next door would want to know what you were doing and there would be forensic evidence, even if it was ashes.'

'No, you're right.' She made up her mind. 'Let's load the car.'

'I can't do it in daylight.'

She hesitated. 'We've got to risk it; we can't risk keeping the stuff here in case the police come. We were stupid to use this address on the will, but we had to give them somewhere to contact us.' She scowled. 'Load the car then park it somewhere until it's dark.'

Once her mind was made up, they were a team again.

The family visit had not gone as well as Tom had envisaged. The *Tartar*, having cruised north to Pensacola, turned to patrol southwards again and finally arrived in Jamaica, anchoring off Kingston. Leaving the ship, his chest carried ashore by one of the sailors and passed on to one of his cousin's slaves, it was with some relief that he turned his back on the sea for a while.

If he had expected a hero's welcome from his father's cousin, he was sadly disappointed. She turned out to be an elderly lady, comfortable in her own world, with little interest in a fourteen-year-old boy. It was a huge relief to both of them when she announced that they were expecting a visitor. 'Dr Butt,' she told him. 'I think he will be better suited to entertaining you, Thomas. I fear I have no conversation for a boy your age.' She smiled that cold austere smile that he had so quickly grown to dislike. He had hoped to find the warmth and welcome here that the word family conjured in his mind. Her next sentence was like a slap in the face. 'He can fill in the time by teaching you till you go back to your ship.'

Dr Butt, however, turned out to be an agreeable and affable man, recently appointed to the position of physician general to the island militia, who swept the lonely boy under his wing and took him back to his own house where Tom spent a most enjoyable time, studying, drawing, exploring the island and flirting with Dr Butt's daughters, who helped him choose a tortoise to ship home as a gift for his mama in Bath.

It was to Dr Butt that he finally confided the story of his illness. The doctor examined the medicine the slave woman had given him and he nodded, sniffing the mixture and examining the faint scars left on Tom's body. 'Yaws,' he said. 'Horrible, but not fatal. It is incredible how clever some of these African women are. Obeah women, they call themselves. They practise the magic of their own religion. Some are genuine healers with far more knowledge than many of us so-called educated doctors.' He smiled. 'We could learn so much from them if we only let ourselves listen.'

Tom did not mention the strange doll the woman had given him, sensing the doctor would not be so approving of that. It was tucked in the bottom of his trunk, wrapped in a necker-chief. He could feel its power, but it didn't frighten him; on the contrary, he knew it would somehow keep his belongings safer than any padlock.

It was with genuine regret that he prepared for his recall to the ship. Having packed his trunk and dispatched his last batch of letters home, he headed back to the harbour, hoping against hope that he would not find Andrew Farquhar waiting for him.

20

Timothy pulled the car under the trees where he had parked before, reached over to the passenger seat for his backpack and the large torch he had bought that afternoon, and let himself out into the cold night.

The air was heavy with moisture, a damp mist hanging low over the garden as he tiptoed across the grass at the side of the driveway. There were no cars parked outside the house and there was no sign of life. Perhaps there was no one at home.

On the face of it, this was a brilliant plan and he had sold it to April easily, but there were one or two snags he hadn't mentioned, the first and most obvious being that he had not actually looked inside the shed. He didn't know what sort of condition it was in and he had to find a way of freeing the door from its curtain of ivy and bindweed in such a way that there would be no trace of him afterwards. In his sack there were kitchen scissors and a large knife and some secateurs. He was pretty sure he could hack his way into the shed with those, but what to do to put it all back and restore it to its desolate appearance of never having been touched in fifty years was a problem he would have to solve when he got to it.

As his eyes grew used to the misty darkness he could see thin lines of light around the curtains drawn across the French doors at the back of the house out of which Ruth and Macdermott

127

had appeared last time he had been here. He had no way of knowing Ruth was even still there, but it was she he pictured in the house. He waited for several seconds. The darkness made him feel safe. Even if she opened the doors and came out onto the lawn, she would not see him. He backed away. She wouldn't be able to see the outbuildings from there anyway, screened as they were by a line of trees and shrubs. She could walk all the way down to the river, as she had done that evening with Macdermott, and she still wouldn't see him.

The jungle area behind the garage looked even more wild and impenetrable in the cold beam of the torch. He surveyed it carefully. In daylight he had been able to see the shadow of the door behind the ivy. Now it was all black moving shapes and crawling stems. There was a sudden disturbance among the leaves and a blackbird shot out of its roost with a deafening shriek of alarm. He jumped back, his heart thudding with fright. Turning off the torch he waited, expecting to see lights coming from the direction of the house, expecting shouts and police sirens. There was nothing. The darkness fell back into silence.

It was a couple of minutes before he dared turn on the torch again.

The biggest mistake he had made, he realised very quickly, was not to bring gloves. He gave a grim smile. Obviously he wasn't a seasoned crook or hiding his fingerprints would have been the first thing he thought of. And since he wasn't a seasoned gardener either, it hadn't occurred to him that nature would fight back, that the undergrowth would tear at his skin and be full of thorns.

He managed it in the end, freeing the door of everything but cobwebs, the rusty latch hanging off, the padlock that had once secured it dangling uselessly from its hasp. He gritted his teeth and pulled. The door didn't move. He pulled again, careless of the blood dripping from his fingers and from the deep scratch across the back of his hand. He was sweating from his exertions, the cold seeping into his body now he had stopped, and he was exhausted. When the door resisted, he wanted to sit down and cry. He gripped the edge of the rotten boards once again dragging at it with the last of his strength and reluctantly it began to move. He pulled one more time and with a deafening squeak and groan of rusty hinges it opened. He was past caring if anyone had heard as at last he shone his torch inside.

The shed was a lean-to, mostly empty. In the far corner was an ancient mower, draped in rotting tarpaulin; there were broken rakes and spades leaning against the wall and a pile of ancient flower pots. The ground was beaten earth. He shone the torch upwards and saw the underside of the roof, some of it tiles, some rusty metal, all precariously balanced on split and sagging beams. It looked as if the slightest breath of wind would bring it down.

He bit his lip. It would do as a temporary hiding place but not for long. It was not secure and it was far from weatherproof. If the paintings were left in here for more than a few days they would be destroyed. He cursed again. He should have thought of bringing something waterproof to drape over everything. He shivered. He could not change his mind now. There was no plan B. His only option was to cart the stuff from the car, stack it in here, behind the mower, refasten the door and drape the ivy back into place as best he could. Once he was safely home in the warm and dry he could try and think of somewhere better to hide the stuff. He glanced towards the house. It was all in darkness. They must have gone to bed. He was amazed at the shot of jealousy and disgust that knifed through him at the thought of Ruth and that fat slob together.

Ruth was eating a bowl of breakfast muesli the following morning when there was a knock at the kitchen door. She froze, her spoon halfway to her mouth.

Slipping off the stool, she opened the door to a tall, lanky man with fiery red hair and bright blue eyes. 'I'm Lachy.' He held out his hand.

'Lachy?' She shook it, bewildered.

'Did Finlay not mention I'd be coming to tidy the garden?'

He accepted a cup of coffee, and stood leaning on the sink as he sipped from it. 'Have you heard from Finlay?'

'No. I was going to text him to see if he had arrived safely.'

129

'He's not very good at keeping in touch when he's on one of his research trips.'

She laughed. 'You obviously know him very well.'

'We go back a long way. I come in from time to time to keep an eye on things here. If I didn't, Finlay would be lost in the jungle by now. The man doesn't understand that things grow and when you cut them down they grow again.' He laughed.

'Isn't that odd. You would think as a cook he would have a fantastic kitchen garden. There's plenty of room here.'

He blew the steam off his coffee and took a sip. 'Gardening needs to be a passion to keep on top of something like that. He hasn't the time. And he knows someone who grows wonderful organic veggies for him.'

'You?'

'Me.' He laughed again.

'And is that your main job?'

'No, I design software. That's why I have to get out in the air sometimes. I have my allotment and I have this place to indulge my need of sun and wind and rain. Sun today, so I thought I'd rake up some of the leaves.'

'And he pays you for all this?' It was none of her business, but she was intrigued.

'No. He offered, but I told him he couldn't afford me! We keep it informal. My wage is the joy of being here. Besides, I like Fin. I bring my kids sometimes to play; they adore him.'

That was a side of Finlay she had never suspected.

Lachlan drained his cup and put it in the sink. 'I will be on my way out then. If there's anything you need, give me a shout or call me. Fin's got my number on his corkboard over there. I'm very happy to come over. And don't be afraid to explore the garden. It needs to be loved.'

She sat for a long time after he had let himself out. It was strangely reassuring to know there was someone there for her.

She had started building a timeline of Thomas's life. The night before she had read a copy of the letter he had sent to his brother about his stay in Jamaica and how he had sent a tortoise to his mother. She wondered idly if the creature ever reached

England safely and what Lady Buchan had thought about the strange animal destined to wander in her garden.

She picked up her pen. It was a year later. HMS *Tartar* was sailing north towards Florida on her regular patrol up and down the western seas. The sea was blue, a pod of dolphins leaping and diving under the bow of the ship, the wind steady from the north-west. She had discovered there were actual log books from the ship still in existence and online. The lieutenant had spotted the tell-tale signs of a storm on the horizon. She wondered at what point he would have made sure the captain knew. Was that when they would take in sail and batten down the hatches?

In the garden, Lachlan went on raking the leaves into piles ready to put them on the bonfire. Methodically he worked his way across the lawn, as usual lost in thought. It was a while before he noticed the trail of footprints in the long wet grass. They led from the front drive round the back of the garage and into the undergrowth behind the fir trees. Puzzled, he stared at them for several seconds, then he decided to follow them to see where they went. Leaning his rake against a tree, he ducked into the cold wet shadows.

21

The sea was unnaturally calm. The dolphins that had been escorting them for some time, first on the starboard bow, then to larboard, had disappeared. The sky was growing increasingly black and threatening and what wind there had been had dropped away to nothing. In the distance they could hear the grumble of thunder. The men were uneasy, glancing up at the sky as they worked, taking in the last of the sails. There was no need to urge them to hurry. They all knew what these sudden storms were like. They could see the lightning now, flickering on the horizon, and again the growl of the thunder becoming more distinct. The storm was coming ever closer. A slash of lightning sizzled out of the sky and hit the sea nearby, followed by a much louder crack of thunder. 'Order your watch below, if you please, Mr Erskine.' The captain was watching the storm, a frown deepening on his face.

'Sir.'

Tom had become used to commanding the men now. Much younger than many of them, it was part of his training and when Lieutenant Murray had been promoted to command the sloop HMS *Ferret*, Thomas had assumed some of his duties. He had stepped forward, ready to give the signal, when a second lightning bolt knifed out of the sky and hit the mizzen mast immediately beside him.

He dropped like a stone.

He wasn't sure how long he had been unconscious. He came round feeling as though his arm was on fire. As his eyes were flickering open, two men seized him and carried him down from the quarterdeck towards the companionway. 'Take the injured below.' The captain's voice was harsh. 'Call the purser and the gunner's wife to attend to them.'

Tom cried out with pain as he was half carried half pushed down into one of the officers' cabins and dropped unceremoniously on the bunk.

'My God, sir!' the seaman who tried to straighten him said in shock. 'You look like you've been hit by a cannonball.'

'What was it? What happened?' Tom was delirious with pain.

'Lightning, sir. It hit you full on.' The man gently pulled the scorched shreds of Tom's sleeve away. 'You're badly burned, sir.'

'But I didn't hear it. I didn't see it,' he protested.

'Well, everyone else did, sir.' The man stood back as the gunner's wife bustled in. She had her box of medicines with her. 'Go and help bring the others down,' she ordered the seaman. 'There are at least four more injured. Take them to the sickbay.'

She bent over Tom and examined his arm, noticing the tell-tale flowery pattern of marks and the burns under the skin. 'This is going to hurt, young sir, but I know you will be brave. I have to rub in spirits to prevent gangrene. After that it is up to God how scarred you are. You have been spared by a miracle.'

Miracle or not, Tom found it hard not to scream as she poured on the spirit from her small blue bottle and dabbed it over the burn. She was putting the stopper back in the bottle when there was an enormous explosion. The whole ship trembled and shook and was enveloped in noise and smoke.

Tom shot up on the bed as the gunner's wife ran to the door. 'Sweet Jesus, we've been hit again! We're going to sink!' she screamed. They could hear the crashes and splintering of wood above deck and smell burning. Forgetting his injuries, Tom followed her up the companionway and stared round at the scene of destruction in horror.

'The main mast has gone, and the main top and the top-gallant!' a voice called out of the smoke. There is fire below, sir.'

The deck was covered in splintered wood and shredded canvas from the sails. Another flash of lightning hissed down into the sea near them, followed by a deafening crack of thunder. The sea was churning now as though eager to swallow the injured vessel.

The men were pouring up on deck and already the well-practised fire drill was in operation, with men passing buckets of water hand to hand. The captain saw Tom standing, watching. The boy's face was white, streaked with sweat and soot, his arm hanging useless at his side. 'Get below, Tom. You can do nothing to help. The ship is safe.'

Safe? How could it be safe? Someone had said they were sinking. Tom gulped as he looked at the devastation around him then he obeyed. He managed to scramble back down the ladder, one-handed, and staggered back to the cabin where he fell on the bed in a fog of delirious pain. In seconds he had lost consciousness again.

At first the sound of knocking was a part of the noises in the cabin, the creaking of damaged wood, the slap of ropes, the shouts of men, the furious crash of the stormy sea. Ruth had been so engrossed she had been aware of nothing beyond Tom's account of the storm. She looked up at last and saw the figure outside the windows. Seeing he had her attention, Lachy knocked again.

'Sorry, I was miles away.' For once that cliché was no more than the truth.

'I didn't want to disturb you.' He stayed outside on the terrace, with a gesture at his wet boots. 'I just wanted to check, did you put some stuff in the shed behind the outbuildings, or is that Finlay's?'

'I'm not sure I knew there was a shed. It certainly wasn't me.'

'It must be Finlay then.' He looked around doubtfully. 'I'm

not certain what to do. It will be spoiled if it's left there. Perhaps he didn't realise the roof has gone. He's covered it up a bit, but that's not going to keep it dry. What should I do, do you think?'

'What kind of stuff is it?'

'Boxes and suitcases. Maybe he planned to take it to a charity shop. I could move it all into the garage. It would stay dry in there.'

'That sounds like a good idea. Would you mind? I'll mention it when he gets in touch.' Automatically she reached for the phone and glanced at its screen. Nothing. 'He's still not answering my calls and his voicemail isn't switched on.'

'Probably forgotten we exist.' Lachy didn't look the least put out by the thought. 'He's lost in his world at the moment. Good luck to him.'

Thomas

I recovered from the lightning strike and wrote home to my brother David as soon as I was able, describing the events of that fateful day, making light of my injuries as I knew he would pass on the information to Mama and Papa. Unbeknown to me, David had my letter published in St James's Chronicle. *If they paid him for it, he never passed the money on to me.*

Of one strange occurrence I told no one then or since.

I remembered nothing of the strike itself; I neither saw nor felt the flash, though now I think I smelt a strangeness in the air moments before it happened. I did not hear the crack of doom as the thunder clapped, but I presume it was much as the second strike that took out the main mast, the sound so loud and awful and the shudder so great it was as if every cannon on the ship had been fired at once.

As I lay on the first lieutenant's bunk I was at first aware of nothing but the pain in my arm. People came and went; the gunner's wife brought a cold towel to press on my forehead and redressed my arm. All was a blur, my eyes unfocused and my head blind with pain. Then Jamie, ever the cheerful soul, looked in to see if I was alive and I opened my eyes and saw for the first time. It was as though some connection had been made in the depths of my brain. Everything around me was bright and fluid with swirling lights and Jamie, above all, was surrounded with a halo of reds and greens and yellow colours. As he talked and laughed, a wild shaky laugh, I saw the lights around his head and shoulders reflect his true feelings, I saw his fear for me, his shock at what had happened to the ship which was the centre of our world, saw he was not telling me everything. I saw that men had been killed or injured far worse than me by the lightning blast and by the flying splinters as the mast disintegrated and by the fire that followed, and I realised I was reading his thoughts. He did not stay long. The whole crew had been mustered on deck to help the poor Tartar *limp into Pensacola Bay under a jury rig, and there repairs were made. I was left alone to thank God for my life and to puzzle the strange gift of deep sight that had been opened to me. I wished the sennachie was there to explain to me what had happened to me and failing his presence I wondered when and if we would ever return to Barbados so that I could visit the slave woman who was so brilliant a doctor and who had read the secrets of my soul and could, if I had the chance to ask, no doubt do so again.*

22

'Are you sure you covered your tracks?' April had subsided onto the nearest chair. She opened and closed her hands on the table and Tim smiled maliciously, guessing how desperately she wanted a cigarette.

'Of course. Is everything tidy here?'

She glared at him. 'I've even run the vacuum round the room. There's no trace of anything from Number 26.'

'So we're cushty?' He grinned.

'Unless the police come about the will.'

She hadn't spotted the utterly brilliant part of his plan. If ever the shit hit the fan he had only to say that he had rescued the valuables to keep them safe for Ruth. Why else would he have taken them to the place where she was staying? It was April who had forged the other signatures on the will after he had guided Donald's hand to sign it, April who had found the old will forms in the first place. He had been an innocent bystander who had genuinely liked the old boy and had looked after him. He had had no idea Dunbar had any family; he had thought he was doing him a favour.

'The police won't come,' he said confidently.

'You don't know that.' She gave up the struggle, climbed to her feet, went to the drawer under the draining board and extricated a battered packet of cigarettes. She shook it experimentally, found three inside and ignoring his raised eyebrow turned on a gas burner and bent to light one. She inhaled deeply. 'I will be sad to move on from here. I like this house.'

He gave a grim smile. 'Better than Number 26?'

'Don't kid yourself we'll ever live there. If we inherit it, we'll sell it. Do you know how much houses in that part of town are worth?'

'Of course I do. You think I didn't check?' He waved away her smoke with a look of distaste. 'Have you thought about where we'll go next?' It was a grudging admission that she was the one who made the decisions. He went to the window and pushed it open. A thread of fresh air entered the room, mingled with the waft of the bins outside; anything was better than the smell of her smoke.

'Maybe London this time.'

'Won't we have enough money to retire?'

She pulled a face. 'Not unless you plan to go to work.'

'I was working, April,' he retorted mildly. 'I worked damn hard.'

She acknowledged the fact with a dubious inclination of the head. 'I'll give it some thought.'

He gave up on the fresh air and pulled the window shut. 'I might go out for a bit.' He wasn't good at waiting and that was all there was to do now.

'Please yourself.' She was looking forward to her next programme on the telly. If he was out of the house she could enjoy it more, maybe even have another cigarette.

Harriet arrived just before six, and Ruth showed her round the house. 'Isn't it lovely? I haven't actually asked Fin if you can stay – I can't get hold of him – but I'm sure he wouldn't mind. Sit down there and I'll make us a G & T.'

Searching through Finlay's drinks cupboard she found some gin. She studied her companion for a moment as Harriet hitched herself onto a stool. 'So, your book is going well so far?'

Harriet nodded. 'Liz's grandmother was the most amazing woman. Awesome! I wish I'd met her.'

Ruth poured a hefty slug of gin into each glass. 'So, how long will you be staying up north?'

'I should think another couple of weeks.' Harriet reached for one of the glasses and took a sip of neat gin. 'You were telling me on the phone that Thomas saw ghosts? Yuk!' she pushed the glass aside. 'Haven't you got any tonic? This is far too strong.'

Ruth gave up on the search for tonic. 'Let me make us a Negroni. Finlay has all the ingredients.'

She stood stock-still, thinking, as she reached for the bottle of Campari.

'Ruth? What is it?'

'I was trying to remember where Thomas mentions ghosts.'

'You haven't tried to summon him yet?'

'No way.'

'I think you should. In fact,' Harriet looked up, her whole face suddenly animated, 'why don't we both give it a try tonight, while I'm here?' She took the bottle out of Ruth's hand and screwed the top back on. 'That's it. We'll hold a séance – a proper séance this time – and get him to come and talk to you.' She shoved the bottle towards Ruth. 'Come on. If you're going to make this concoction, get on with it. After supper we are going to repair to a candlelit room and we are going to ask Lord Erskine to appear and tell us the truth behind all this.'

The captain's woman had died in childbirth. The whole ship knew and the mood was sombre. Thomas and Jamie had accompanied him ashore when he was summoned by a slave from the estate. The two boys waited nearby as he went into the house to see her. They had been too late.

When Sir John came out hours later he had his little daughter with him. His face was ravaged with grief. 'I am staying ashore for a while,' he told them. He handed a letter to Thomas as the little girl clung to the skirts of his coat. 'Return to the ship, Mr Erskine,' he said formally, 'and give this to Mr Barton. He will assume command until I return.' He stooped and picked up the child. 'I have to see to my little one.'

They stared after him as he went back into the house. 'He

must have really loved her,' Jamie said wonderingly. 'Even though she was a slave.'

Tom nodded doubtfully. Something about Jamie's words did not seem right to him. Just because a woman was a slave, why should that make a difference to how a man felt about her? He had seen the strange mixture of emotions swirling in the air around the captain's head and shoulders. Above all there was anger, there was grief, there was love, love for the woman who had gone and love for the little girl with her dark skin and her huge uncomprehending eyes, and there was guilt that he had caused the death of the beautiful woman who had loved and trusted him so unreservedly.

They were so preoccupied they did not at first see the black woman who walked heavily out of the house and down the steps towards them, the burden of her own grief all too evident. As she came closer Tom recognised her. He gave Jamie a push. 'Go on. I will catch you up. I need to speak to this lady. She is like a doctor on the estate.'

As he approached, she looked up and saw him. 'So, it is the young man with the yaya. You are better?' Her face was streaked with tears and she looked exhausted.

'Thank you, yes. You were trying to save the captain's lady?' Tom hesitated. The sight of Sir John completely unmanned by his loss had moved him greatly.

'The captain's woman,' the old woman corrected him. Seeing her for the first time in daylight, he registered that she was old, her face lined, her hair threaded with grey, her hands knotted and rough. 'It was her time. She was too frail to birth that child.' She led him over to the shade of some palm trees and looked at him closely. 'So, you know your destiny now, boy.'

'My destiny?'

'That's right.'

'I know I can see things now. I was struck by lightning.' He held out his arm and pulled up his shirt sleeve to show her the burn. She barely glanced at it. 'I wanted to come and see you. I needed to know what happened to me.'

'You have special powers, boy, I told you that before and now you know it. You're greater than your brothers.'

He stared at her. The wizened face was wise with years, the eyes bright and all-seeing. 'How did you know I had brothers?' he stammered.

'I see everything.' Suddenly her gaze became intense. 'As you do, now, boy. You can see as well as me now. The great god in the sky, he turned you on with that lightning bolt!' She gave a weary giggle. 'Use those powers well, boy. Use them for good. Learn to control them. You must be able to call them to you, and send them away again when you don't need them. You will be a great man.' She reached up and pulled him round so he faced the intense afternoon sunlight and she studied his face for several seconds. 'I see so much in you. I wish you well, boy. Now, you go back to your ship. Your captain won't come back. You can see that, can't you.'

He stared at her and he realised it was true. He had seen it in Sir John's face. It was as if something had been extinguished in the man's soul. 'How is it possible to love someone so much?' he stammered.

She giggled again. 'One day you'll find out. You will love someone as much as he did. Now, go, boy. I'm so tired and I want to pray for that girl's soul and for that of her baby. Your gods and my gods, they are all the same. They got compassion for the innocent ones. In all the misery and the pain, they are there. Don't you forget that, boy, you with your godly sisters!'

With a last exhausted peal of laughter she gave him a little push and walked away, the slap of her bare feet on the path throwing up dust as she went.

'What was all that about?' Jamie had been waiting for him, watching.

'She's the woman who cured me when I was ill. She's some sort of doctor.'

'A witch doctor?' Jamie's eyes rounded.

'No! Yes!' Tom screwed up his eyes in the sun. 'She's a wise woman. We have those in Scotland. She can see the future.'

She had known he had brothers, and she had known about his sisters. And, he glanced down at the sealed letter in his hand, she knew the captain would not return to the *Tartar*.

Thomas

A spey-wife we in Scotland would have called that woman. She was right. Sir John Lindsay did not return to his command. He took leave of absence and booked passage home, taking his little daughter Dido Belle with him. I did not know it then but he gave her to his mentor and mine, his uncle, Lord Mansfield, to raise as a lady in London with Lord M's orphaned niece, Elizabeth, who was already in his care. And in the meantime I went back to my duties as a midshipman under our new commander, George Johnson. He was a tough man; not likeable but fair and in due time I was made acting lieutenant.

And the halo of lights? In the busyness of my life they went away. Just sometimes as I looked at someone I saw them again and slowly I learned that, as the old woman had told me, I could command the lights, but it took practice and I was young and the mental effort required was mostly more than I could summon.

It was in the final months of 1767 that I received a letter from my brother warning me that our father's illness was likely to be fatal. Papa had never been strong, but the shock of those words as I read them, penned so many weeks before the letter was in my hands, was overwhelming. I took myself to the bulwarks and stared out to sea as the sun set into the purple haze and in my mind's eye I was there in Walcot at my mother's side in Buchan House, as Anne's residence was now called, as Papa breathed his last on the first day of December, and I was there with her and my brothers as they and so many others, strangers to me, sang a hymn and prayed as his coffin was taken to Lady Huntingdon's chapel. His funeral was the focus of so much attention in Bath that David, now the new Lord Buchan, the 11th earl, no less, issued tickets to attend.

It was strange that later people reported I was there, at the funeral, when in reality I was thousands of miles away in the Caribbean Sea. Perhaps there were people there who could see as I saw, but I know not who they were. Certainly not my brothers.

My father's coffin was taken to Bristol from where he was transported by sea to Edinburgh and there interred with all due ceremony in Holyrood Abbey, and I watched it all through my strange far-seeing gaze.

Sometimes I smiled through my sadness to think how grand David would now be. Though I was wrong about that, at least at first, for he seemed to have become the most devout and religious of men and followed his new mentors to London. He was mocked by society for his religiosity but to do him credit he ignored the gossips and for a while he continued to pray.

In time both my brothers returned to their previous lives, and our mother left Bath and went home to Edinburgh, perhaps to be nearer to my father. My sister Anne resumed her duties at Lady Huntingdon's side and it was through their zealous offices that my brother David now had the services of no less than three chaplains! I wondered if they shared his love of the stars.

23

'We shouldn't have drunk so much!' Harriet was quite giggly. 'But I want to get on with this. I've been to séances before in Glastonbury and it was amazing!' She was not to be dissuaded and eventually Ruth stopped trying to think of excuses not to go ahead. She did not, after all, expect anything to happen.

They carried their glasses through to the sitting room after supper and Ruth lit the wood burner. She threw herself down on the sofa and closed her eyes with a sigh of contentment. 'We are in no fit state to do this.'

'Rubbish. Alcohol loosens the inhibitions and if we have one fault, you and I, it is that we are far too inhibited.' Harriet sat down opposite her. She took another sip from her glass.

'So,' Ruth said, 'we're going to sit here with a tumbler and lots of bits of paper with the alphabet written on and ask, "Is there anybody there?" like a couple of drunken students?'

'We are a couple of drunken researchers, though, aren't we?' Harriet giggled. 'It's probably not that much different. So, you have done this before?'

'Of course I've done it before. As a student. It was the most cumbersome, idiotic pastime. If dead people wanted to talk to us, they would talk, not force us to spend hours with a glass – not an empty one, anyway – racing backwards and forwards across the table while we try to make out what it's trying to say.'

'What happened when you were a student. Did it work?'

'We scared ourselves silly, if I remember, and in the end the glass flew across the table and smashed against the wall.'

'So it did work.'

'Doesn't it always? Because someone always cheats. Oh, come on, Hattie! Grow up; you didn't think it was real?'

'I've never done it.' Harriet took another sip.

'What a sheltered life you've led!' Ruth looked at her in mock despair. 'You're not really qualified to write this book of yours, are you.'

'Isn't that the whole point?' Harriet climbed to her feet and went to stand in front of the wood burner, which was beginning to throw out some real heat. 'Anyway, tonight I was planning to do something different. A proper séance.'

'And how does one do that?'

'One has to go into a trance.'

'And you really think it will work?' Ruth tried to keep the mockery out of her voice. 'No, don't answer that. You go ahead. I'll watch.'

'Aren't you going to do it with me? I thought we were going to contact His Lordship.'

Ruth gave a derisive snort. 'I don't believe in this, Hattie. Remember? And I don't think it's supposed to be a communal activity!' she added severely. 'Come and sit down again. Finlay has a candle there on the side. That's perfect. I'll turn down the lighting and you can relax and ask him to come and talk to us and I'll watch.' She took a sip from her glass then went to turn out the lights, leaving one small table lamp in the corner of the room. She carried the squat red candle to the coffee table and lit it, then she sat down on the sofa and gestured at Harriet to begin. For a long time neither woman said anything. The only sound was the crackling of logs in the wood burner. The flames behind the glass filled the room with a dull glow that threw faint shadows on the walls. At last Harriet spoke. 'Is there anybody there?'

Ruth subsided into giggles. 'Oh, come on. That's such a cliché!'

'Shut up!' Harriet glared at her. Sitting back against the cushions in her chair she closed her eyes again. The silence lengthened and deepened. Ruth took another sip from her glass, then closed her eyes as the berry scent of the candle began to permeate the room.

Harriet still hadn't spoken out loud when Ruth became aware of a sense that they were not alone. She sat absolutely still, not daring to open her eyes. The feeling grew stronger.

'Who's there?' Harriet must have felt it too. 'Can I ask you a question?' Her voice was soft, barely audible.

For a long minute nothing happened, then there was a loud, deep, very male chuckle. 'Thank you, ladies, for your invitation!' The voice was husky, with a slight West Country burr.

'Oh my God!' Ruth's eyes flew open. 'Hattie, was that you?'

Another chuckle, so quiet it was almost inaudible. 'My name's not Hattie.'

'Harriet!' Ruth whispered urgently. 'Hattie! Wake up.'

Her friend was sitting exactly as she had been before, her eyes closed, a half smile on her face.

'Hattie!' Ruth called again. She was terrified.

'Two beautiful women! How lovely,' the voice whispered. 'Let me come closer.'

Appalled, Ruth felt the cushion move on the sofa next to her as if someone had sat down, though she could see no one. She cowered from the unseen presence. 'Who are you?'

'A passing friend, at your service, ma'am.' She could feel hot breath on her cheek and then, to her horror she felt a hand on her breast. She leapt to her feet with a scream.

Harriet opened her eyes. 'What? What is it?'

'Dear God!' Ruth was already at the door groping for the light switches.

In the sudden brightness they both blinked. Ruth stared round wildly. 'Someone touched me!'

Harriet scrambled awkwardly to her feet. She still seemed dazed.

'It was horrible! He groped my breast. He was sitting beside me on the sofa. I could smell his breath!' Ruth put her hand over her mouth. 'I still can.' The sweet smell of the scented candle had been replaced in the room by a pervasive stink of stale sweat. The candle, they both realised at the same moment,

147

had gone out. A trail of smoke curled up from the wick towards the beams, gathering under the low ceiling.

Harriet wrinkled her nose. 'Oh God, I can smell it too. Oh, how vile. I don't understand.' Her eyes were darting round the room. 'There must have been someone in here. Someone real.' She broke off, looking at the floor-length curtains over the windows.

Ruth followed Harriet's gaze in increasing horror, watching as she tiptoed across to the chimney, picked up the poker that was lying in front of the wood burner and turned towards the windows, flinging back the curtains on their heavy wooden rings. There was no one there.

Harriet turned to survey the empty room.

'I'm not making it up.' Ruth was defensive.

'So the séance worked,' Harriet whispered. They stared at each other in dawning horror. 'Could it have been Thomas?'

'No!' Ruth was vehement.

'And it definitely wasn't your imagination?'

'No.'

'Perhaps it was a real person and he was out of the room before we turned the lights on.' The suggestion sounded almost like a plea.

There was only one way to find out.

They searched the house, keeping close together. They found nothing.

They did not return to the sitting room, going instead into the kitchen. Ruth had changed her sweater, throwing it into the washing machine, unable to bear the thought of wearing something that the invisible hand had touched. She switched on the kettle and reached for the coffee pot. 'I can't believe it happened. I just can't. I must have imagined it. We were obviously more drunk than we thought.'

Harriet shook her head. 'You weren't drunk, Ruthie. Merry perhaps, but not drunk.' She sat quietly, lost in thought. 'I've been trying to remember stuff I've heard about séances.'

'I thought you'd been to some.'

'I have, but as an observer. To be honest, nothing much happened, but I remember the person conducting one of them was very insistent that everyone followed the rules and I've realised that we broke one of the very basic things you're supposed to do.'

'What?' Ruth spooned some coffee into the cafetière and poured on the hot water.

'I said, "Is there anybody there?", didn't I.'

Ruth felt her mouth twitch into a smile. She nodded.

'And I opened a door to anyone who wanted to come through it. I wasn't specific who I wanted to talk to. I think, inadvertently, we let in a passing rogue spirit.'

'You. You let him in,' Ruth pointed out.

'Yes, me, it's my fault. A little learning is a dangerous thing and all that. It's one of the reasons people say séances are so dangerous.' Harriet made a valiant attempt at laughter.

Ruth shuddered. 'Every rational bone in my body says it isn't true. It can't be true. But I didn't imagine him, Hattie. I truly didn't.'

Harriet reached for the pot and filled two mugs. She slid off the stool and went to the fridge to retrieve the milk. 'If he was a spirit, do you think he's gone?' she said as she came back. 'Really gone?'

'I don't know.'

'At dawn, doesn't he have to go back to his grave?'

'I think that's vampires.'

In the long silence that followed they heard the old clock in the hall chime. It was midnight.

'We have to go back in there, don't we,' Harriet said eventually. 'This is a lovely house. We can't allow ourselves to be spooked by some passing evil spirit. We have to make sure he's gone and say some prayers to seal whatever channel it is I've opened up.' She slapped her forehead suddenly. 'The book. You've got the book. *Psychic Self-Defence*. What does it say to do?'

'I've never even looked at it.' Ruth stood up. In the doorway she hesitated, looking at the closed door to the sitting room, then she turned along the hall and went to the dining room. Grabbing the book from the table, she hurried back to the kitchen, closing the door firmly behind her.

'Nothing is going to work if I don't take this seriously,' she said as she hauled herself up onto her stool. 'My grandfather, Mummy's father, who was a vicar, would have prayed. I remember how fervently he believed in prayer. Once he told me when I was little that I could wrap it round myself like a warm blanket. We were staying with them at the vicarage and I had a nightmare. Next morning, I told Mummy what he'd said but my father was in the room. I was too young to have understood the need for discretion, and Daddy laughed. It was such a cruel, dismissive sound and I was made to feel as if I was the stupidest child in the world. He made it quite clear such a thing could never work, and that Grandpa was a gullible fool who shouldn't be trusted to talk to me.'

'Oh, Ruthie. What a beast your father was.' Harriet reached over and touched Ruth's hand. 'What did your mother say?'

'I can't remember. I pretty much blotted the whole thing out. That was probably the last time we went to stay with my grandparents.' She sighed. 'So, I have a mountain to climb in the faith department.' She handed Harriet the book. 'Do you realise that we seem to be absolutely cold sober?' Ruth reached for her coffee. 'Nothing like being groped by a ghost to instil instant sobriety.'

Harriet gave a shudder. She was still looking very white. 'She has chapters on what to do.' She turned towards the end of the book. 'My neighbour lent me her copy when she knew I was going to write about Dion. Let me see if I can find the place. The one thing I remember reading which really struck me as being right in so many contexts, was . . . here we are: "What the imagination has made, the imagination can unmake." As well as a psychic, Dion was a trained psychologist and counsellor. So, on every level she knew what she was talking about. But if you think what happened was your imagination, we know it wasn't. No one could imagine that stink and I smelt it too!'

There was a long silence as she read, skipped a few pages and read again. Ruth sipped her coffee and poured herself some more. In the hall the clock chimed the half hour, then one.

'OK,' Harriet looked up. 'There is so much technical stuff

here which we couldn't possibly do, but the absolute simplest seems to be garlic.'

'But that's vampires too, isn't it?'

'Garlic and onions absorb noxious energies, physical and psychic, if I'm reading this aright. We could use holy water – and she gives instructions on how to make it – but I don't think either of us is qualified to bless it with sufficient conviction.'

Ruth let out a snort. 'If only we'd known. You could have brought crystals from Glasto!'

'OK. We don't have any crystals and we can't pray or don't want to, so why don't we put some garlic and onions in the room overnight. I need to sleep! If I don't go to bed soon I will collapse. Then in the morning, in the blessed daylight, we can decide what to do.'

Ruth slid off her stool. 'Blessed daylight!' she remarked. 'I assume you don't see the irony of that comment. So, garlic it is. That sounds good. It sounds earthy and physical and rational, and as we are in the kitchen of a celebrity chef there are more onions and cloves of garlic here than probably anywhere else on the planet! And I will bet money they are all organic.'

There were baskets of both in the pantry.

'How much do we need?' Ruth asked.

'She doesn't say. Enough to place round the room. What about half a dozen of each?'

It was Harriet who pushed open the door and peered in. They had left the lights on and the wood burner was still glowing but the room felt cold. They crept in cautiously. 'Put them all round the room,' Harriet whispered. 'Evenly spaced, I should think. Like Christmas decorations. Do you think we should say something? "Begone, foul fiend!" or the Lord's Prayer or somesuch?'

'We ruled out prayer, remember? It would be pure hypocrisy, at least on my part. Can you feel anything?' Ruth was standing near the sofa, a bulb of garlic in her hand.

Harriet was silent for a moment. 'No.'

'Nor me. He's gone. I think he went as soon as I turned the lights on.' She laid the garlic bulb down on the coffee table. 'This will soak up anything that is left, then in the morning presumably we dispose of it all. I can't believe I'm saying this! It occurs to me that what we have here was mass hysteria.'

'Mass?' Hattie looked quizzical.

'I'm sure if they're drunk enough, two is sufficient,' Ruth said firmly. 'Now, to bed before we both collapse.'

She spent a long time in the shower, scrubbing every inch of her body, washing her hair, trying again and again to rinse away the memory of rough, insolent hands on her breast. When at last she dried herself and pulled on her pyjamas, she could still feel him.

This couldn't be happening. She didn't believe in it. She took Dion's book to bed with her and left all the lights on, but it was a long time before she fell asleep.

Thomas

In the year 1768 Tartar *was directed back to England, her mission over. At Portsmouth, the crew was paid off, and I became aware that there would be no new berth for me as a full lieutenant; the navy had sufficient. I had enjoyed my time in the Caribbean Sea and learnt much but I had no wish to go back to being a middy, so with my wages in my pocket I took the stage to London to seek my fortune elsewhere, my time in the Royal Navy done.*

Imagine my chagrin when, as I climbed aboard the coach, I saw the face of my nemesis, Andrew Farquhar, in the crowds and watched him settle in one of the roof seats near me. He was still wearing his sailor's canvas slops, a much-patched linen shirt and short jacket. Even to avoid him I was not prepared to pay the extra to be inside the doubtful comforts of the stage. Instead I pulled my hat down over my eyes and pretended to sleep.

The weather was cold and wet and there was no inclination or possibility for talk amongst the passengers as we made the dismal journey to the capital huddled in our greatcoats. At the staging posts I avoided Farquhar, contenting myself with the warmth of mulled ale and a pie by the fire as they changed horses, wondering why I had not stayed in Barbados! From Portsmouth to London is some seventy miles and I was near dead with cold when we arrived but finally we were there and I found my lodgings with my sister, Anne, in the house of Lady Huntingdon, where they had made their base after moving from Bath. I had neither acknowledged nor bid farewell to Andrew. I trusted earnestly to God that we would not meet again. Unfortunately, God did not keep his side of the bargain.

24

April had taken the car. When Timothy asked if he could go with her or at least get a lift into town she rudely refused. 'You've had the damn car for days!' And with that he had to be content. She had not said where she was going or when she would be back.

Without her there the house was depressing. When April was there it was her personality that filled it, her noise, her scorn, her presence. This one was nicer than anywhere else they had stayed. It was decently furnished with a settee and a couple of easy chairs, even a telly that worked. Someone must have paid the electricity bill before they left. They had in the past camped in houses that were cold and dark and even smelly – though April did not tolerate that for long. She was right. If you knew where to look and how to find them, there were always places to stay. She relied on him to get them in. He had taught himself the gentle art of burglary. He could pick locks, bypass meters, hot-wire cars. She thought she was the brains department, he was the muscle, but he knew better. He had brains; he just preferred to keep them hidden.

By midday he was going stir crazy. He couldn't stay on his own another minute. He walked up to the bus stop and caught the westbound bus to Cramond with only minutes to spare.

There were no cars outside. The place felt empty. In a way he had wanted Ruth to be there. He liked the feeling that she thought she had escaped him, but she hadn't. She had dared to order him out of his house, the house her father had meant him to have, and she wasn't even staying there, she was camped out in this beautiful place with a rich famous man. It wasn't fair.

He studied the house for a while, then withdrew into the bushes and crept around the back. While he was here he would go and make sure his stash was safe and all traces of his passing were hidden. It had been hard to be sure in the dark.

He paused, hidden by a tree trunk, and studied the back of the house. At the far end there was the kitchen, then came the dining room with the French doors, then a long low room which he supposed was the lounge. He tiptoed sideways behind the hedge to get a better view. He knew he was going to have to go closer, to peer into the windows. He would not be able to resist.

Sprinting across the lawn, he flattened himself against the wall and waited, his heart banging with excitement. There was no sound, no shout of indignation. He tiptoed to the corner and looked round. There were some big black birds pecking at the lawn. They saw him and flew off squawking. He held his breath.

There were no lights on in the kitchen and the room was shadowy but he could see in perfectly well and he took the time to study every detail. Slowly he scanned the dresser, the cupboards, the work areas, the hanging pans and kitchen utensils, aware of how much April would love to see this. There was a bowl of fruit on the worktop, a huge electric range cooker, lines of jars on shelves, their labels handwritten though from the window he couldn't read them.

It was a long time before, with a quick glance over his shoulder, he moved on to the dining room windows. The long table was still strewn with books and papers. Her laptop was lying half buried beneath a notepad and there was a discarded coffee cup amongst the debris. He studied the rest of the room. There were some nice-looking pictures on the wall and a long low sideboard; his gaze focused on one or two pieces of silver, then it moved on.

The last set of windows belonged as he had suspected to the lounge. The room was more shadowy than the previous two; he could feel the cold emanating from the window panes. Raising his hand to shade his eyes and block the reflection of his own face he noticed that there was an onion on the window-sill. He stared at it, puzzled, then he adjusted his gaze to look further into the room. He could make out a long low couch, a couple of large easy chairs, a coffee table. He moved closer, trying to see more clearly. There appeared to be an onion lying on the coffee table, and a scatter of garlic cloves. There were several large lamps on side tables and there too he could see onions. He stared round in amused bewilderment. Was it some kind of culinary game? His gaze moved on and there, standing in front of the fireplace, he could see the shadowy figure of a man staring back at him. He was hunched, deformed, ugly. For a full second Timothy felt his heart stop then with a small cry of fright he turned and fled.

'I've found us a possible new house,' April greeted Timothy as soon as he appeared through the door. 'It's the other side of town. Down Craigmillar way. A bit rough, but somewhere to go if we need to. We can go on using this if we're careful, but we don't want to be here if the police start nosing.'

'When are we going to sell the stuff?' Timothy had completely forgotten to check it was safely hidden in his panic at seeing the man through the window.

'Soon. There's always a market for silver as bullion if you know where to go.' April bent to the oven and removed a carton which had been keeping warm. 'I bought chicken and chips.' The kitchen filled with the aroma of vinegar on the chips as she put it on the table and Timothy felt his mouth water. They didn't use plates, helping themselves from the trays. He didn't mention where he had been that day and she didn't ask.

Thomas now had his own room, new clothes provided by his sister and a valet. The young man, Stephen, had unpacked his trunk for him, removing his books and writing materials from the bottom. He then produced a small bundle and held it up with an expression of disgust.

'Shall I dispose of this, sir?'

Thomas looked up. It was the obeah woman's doll. He hesitated; for a moment he wavered then he shook his head. 'Keep it. Leave it in the chest.'

He was a little abashed by the atmosphere of his sister's dining room at breakfast. Prayers; excited talk, yes, but of churches and meetings and Bible classes for the poor. As he helped himself to kedgeree at the sideboard, he frowned. This was at odds with his dreams of London life.

Excusing himself from accompanying Anne on her morning visits, he set out to explore on his own as soon as he could decently escape, running down the steps of the house and into the noisy crowded streets. It was exhilarating and it was dizzying. The smell was atrocious, and yet as the sun fought free of the clouds and the streets were aglitter with reflected sunlight it was the most exciting place he had ever been. Anne and Selina Huntingdon listened patiently to his account of his day as, bathed and changed, he joined them to sip wine by the fire in the withdrawing room before dinner that evening.

'It must all seem strange indeed after so long at sea,' Anne put in at last. It had been hard to get a word in. She regarded her brother fondly. He had grown so tall since she had last seen him in Bath, taller than either of his brothers, and he sported a weathered complexion that suited him. She sensed a new strength there which was to be expected after his experiences in the navy. She found herself hoping he would not find a new ship too quickly. It would be fun launching her baby brother into society.

The young lieutenant became something of a trophy guest. His good looks and his quick wit were appreciated particularly by hostesses with daughters who could do worse than a brother of the Earl of Buchan. The lack of fortune was the problem. Four years' worth of earnings seemed riches to Thomas, but he soon found the money would not go as far as he had hoped and, at the same time, his dream of a new ship was quickly dashed. The only berths available were for midshipmen – Jamie signed on again at once – but having returned to England as an acting lieutenant Tom could not bring himself to take a demotion. He dared to dream for a while of going back to university but that would only be possible if David would subsidise him and his letters from his eldest brother following a cautious enquiry were succinct on that point. The new young earl was not going to squander any of his precious but slender patrimony on a brother who had proved himself quite capable of earning his own living, although he did grudgingly pass on the small bequest left to Tom by his father.

Tom spent his days exploring bookshops, where he browsed to his heart's content. It was Anne who suggested that he visit his parents' former advisor, Lord Mansfield, His advice was simple and so obvious Tom wondered why he had not thought of it himself. He might not be able to afford his idea of an academic career, but he could fulfil his previous dream of joining the army, sporting at last the coveted red coat which had so attracted him as a boy. Strings were pulled, introductions made and Tom found himself laying out his inheritance and most of his precious savings on a commission under the Duke of Argyll in the second battalion of the Royal Scots, the 1st Royal Regiment of Foot. His first posting would be Berwick-upon-Tweed.

The day before the regiment left he went for a last walk alone. He had only gone a few hundred yards when he stopped. It was there again, that feeling that he was being followed. Several times in the last few days he had glanced over his shoulder at the crowds surging to and fro behind him, the sea of faces, anonymous beneath tricorn hats and hoods and caps, hunched beneath the cold rain. No one seemed to be watching him but he had been warned of cutpurses and thieves, of which there were plenty in the teeming alleys and roadways. He turned sharply across the street, dodging between a heavy coach and a laden waggon, and retraced his steps to stand in a shop doorway, scanning the crowds. Rain teemed off the roof and the galleried upper storeys into a puddle at his feet and he stepped back, glancing at the distorted image of himself in the bulbous panes of the window next to him. There was someone standing close beside him, a face, leering into the shadow of the doorway. He turned swiftly back towards the street, but there was no one there.

He could see no one suspicious but the feeling remained, a slight shiver down the spine, an awareness of eyes following him. With an involuntary shudder he walked on, uncomfortable until he was safely in the warmth of the coffee house, where to his gratification he was greeted at once by a shout of welcome and was within minutes seated at a table with two gentlemen he had met some days before. By the time he returned home the incident was forgotten.

25

Ruth lay staring up at the ceiling. Harriet had left early in the morning, as originally planned, with some reluctance at leaving her alone, but Ruth had insisted. The house felt cleansed, if slightly garlicky, and she had gone back to her research without any qualms at being alone. It was late when she finally went to bed and she had fallen asleep at once but something had woken her. Groping for her phone, she stared at it, trying to focus on the bright screen. She had only been asleep for an hour. Slamming it back down on the bedside table she looked towards the window. She had left the curtains undrawn and the window was open a crack so she could hear the distant burbling of the river and, above it, the hoot of the owl. That must have been what had woken her. The sky had cleared and she could see the moon, low above the black outline of the trees. Pulling the covers over her head she tried to go back to sleep.

She must have dozed when she was awoken by a sound in the room near the bed. She lay still, rigid with fear, listening. There it was again. A sigh. And then she felt it, something pulling at the duvet. Someone was climbing into bed beside her, a hand was reaching out to her, touching her, and she smelt his breath as he leaned across her and tried to kiss her, to force his tongue into her mouth. She couldn't move. She was paralysed. She couldn't scream.

And then as suddenly as he had come, he had gone.

She leapt out of bed and turned on the lights. The room was empty.

It had been a dream.

She didn't sleep again that night and it was still dark when she made her way down to the kitchen.

She was sitting at the kitchen table nibbling at a piece of toast an hour later when she saw a movement outside the window. A shot of adrenaline stabbed through her and for a moment she thought she was going to be sick, then she realised it was Lachlan. She didn't wait for him to knock.

'Come in. I've made coffee.'

She saw him raise an eyebrow but he kicked off his boots and walked in, pulling off his muddy gloves. 'I thought I would catch up on some more tidying early,' he said as he took the proffered chair. 'The forecast is for storms next week and I might not get up here for a few days.'

'Is this house haunted, Lachy?' Ruth blurted out the question as she put the coffee pot down on the table.

He looked astonished. 'Not as far as I know. Why?' He surveyed her face curiously. 'Have you seen a ghost?'

She forced herself to smile. 'It was probably a nightmare.'

'I don't believe in ghosts myself.' Lachlan grinned at her. 'But they make good stories. I think Fin claims to have seen something. A little girl I think it is. Not very frightening.'

'No. Fin mentioned her to me. But he said she was in the garden. No this wasn't a little girl. It was a man. In my bedroom.'

'And it's rattled you.' He stood up and went to the dresser to find the sugar bowl. Subconsciously Ruth noted that he seemed to know his way round. 'And I'm not surprised. But, I'm sure you're right. It was a dream.'

She nodded. 'I couldn't get back to sleep.'

'I can see that would be frightening.'

'You haven't heard from Finlay, have you?' She didn't want to sound so desperate.

''Fraid not.' He took a sip of coffee then she saw him frown. 'You're not thinking of going?'

'No, I promised him I'd stay. It's just . . . ' she flailed about for the right words. 'It's a big house.'

'Not really.' He grinned again. 'Do you want me to make sure there isn't anyone lurking?'

She nodded, afraid that if she spoke she would start to cry.

'Wait here.' He pushed the chair back and stood up.

She did as she was told, listening as his footsteps faded into the distance. She could hear him opening doors, the rattle of curtain rings, then the pad of his socked feet as he ran up to the first floor. Five minutes later he reappeared. 'All clear. There's no one here, living or dead. I even looked in the attic.'

'Thank you.' She was embarrassed. 'I feel such a fool.'

'I don't see why. Nightmares can be very scary. I tell my kids they have to shut the door in their imagination after a bad dream and then push the bolts across. One two three.' He laughed. 'Luckily I don't have nightmares any more. I reckon one usually grows out of them.'

'I thought I had. Worrying dreams, exam dreams, yes. But not men who try and attack you.'

He gave a small whistle. 'That does sound bad.'

She looked down at the table. 'Maybe,' she said. 'I'll remember your advice if it happens again. Bolts sound reassuring.'

He paused as though waiting to see if she was going to say anything else then he stood up. 'I ought to get on.'

She smiled up at him. 'Thanks, Lachy.'

He pulled on his boots, then paused on the doorstep. 'Do you know Mollie Fisher, next door?'

'No.'

'Nice lady. I reckon if you were worried about anything you could pop round to hers and you can always ring me, don't forget. I'll come over with the kids. That would scare any ghost, believe me.' He laughed and was gone.

She walked slowly out into the hall and looked round. He had left all the inner doors open, the curtains in the rooms drawn back and the downstairs was flooded with watery sunshine. The sitting room was its old self, neat, attractive, benign; the dining room, as before, littered with her books and papers. Finlay's study was tidy with its usual slight spicy aroma of aftershave combined with the musty smell of old books. Upstairs Finlay's bedroom was tidy, again that faint smell of vetiver and cedar. It was a lovely room, unexpectedly masculine compared to the rest of the house, with dark blue curtains and a wall of books which made it look more like another study than a bedroom. There was a second guest room, where Harriet had stayed, also lined with bookshelves. Her own was a mess, the bedclothes trailing across the floor, the light still on in the bathroom, an uncapped tube of toothpaste lying in the basin, her dressing gown dropped in a heap on the floor. She felt a wave of embarrassment at the thought of Lachlan surveying her clothes and the rumpled bed. She walked over to the window and pushed it open. The morning was cold and blustery and she could see him raking the leaves in the distance. The sight of him was reassuring. She turned back to the room and set about tidying it. The house felt empty and clean. Whoever – whatever – had been there, had gone.

Thomas

We were stationed for several months in the large barracks, designed some years previously by the architect Nicholas Hawksmoor, in the town of Berwick-upon-Tweed. It did not escape me that this garrison, on the Scottish border, was created as a defence against my own countrymen, but then we were a Scots regiment and in the complicated politics of our time there were many, now good subjects of King George, who had in the years immediately before my birth wholeheartedly supported the Jacobite cause and perhaps still in their secret hearts yearned after their royal line. Even my mentor Lord Mansfield was accused of being of Jacobite sympathies. It had not done his career any harm.

I enjoyed my training as an ensign on this bleak, exposed corner of the east coast and even more my free time and my leave. I was able to visit Mama in Edinburgh whence she had returned with my sister Isabella soon after my father's death. She took me to see his grave in Holyrood Abbey, which had escaped the roof fall in a terrible storm earlier in the year. And I met up with Harry, now well embarked upon his legal career, and we shared a few drams together.

I rode out whenever I could to explore the countryside around Berwick and on one of my visits I had an experience which drove me back to Edinburgh to seek out from my mother the whereabouts of the senna-chie, the recorder of our family history. I had seen a ghost.

26

The wind was whistling round the ruins of Berwick Castle as Thomas rode up towards the collapsing stone walls and tethered his horse in a sheltered corner. He nearly always explored alone, preferring his own company to the gossip and ribald laughter of a group of young men, though he missed Jamie who was now back in the Caribbean and who had written to him but once, care of his sister in London.

Tearing up some handfuls of rich grass for his horse to eat he turned towards the castle, clinging to its perch high above the River Tweed near the old stone bridge. He felt it as soon as he drew near: misery, defiance, longing. One person's call from the distant past. He paused, looking round, aware that it was a woman's voice reaching out to him, then shook his head to free himself of the echo and stumbled on towards some steps which led down towards the great wall.

An old man was dozing in the shelter of the wall, huddled in an ancient greatcoat. He scrambled to his feet as Thomas approached.

Thomas sighed. He felt in his pocket for a coin. No doubt the man would demand to be paid whether or not he was allowed to act as guide.

'You can hear her then?' The man waved Thomas's hand away.

'Who was she?' The clouds were rolling in from the sea and the sunlight had been extinguished as though it were no more than a blown candle flame. Thomas shivered.

'The Countess of Buchan.'

Thomas stared at him, startled. His skin, he realised, was suddenly crawling with fear. 'Buchan, you said?' he spoke more sharply than he had intended and he saw the man's eyes narrow.

'Aye, Buchan.'

'My brother is the Earl of Buchan.' It came out as a whisper.

The man eyed him curiously. 'Then she would have been a kinswoman. Poor lady, hung there on the ramparts in a cage, the price to pay for crowning a king of Scotland and displeasing a king of England.'

Thomas stared round as the sky grew darker. 'When was this?'

'Hundreds of years ago.' The man stood staring out across the river. He didn't seem inclined to say anything else.

'Did she,' Thomas cleared his throat, 'did she die here?'

'No,' the old man muttered almost reluctantly, as if it spoiled his story. 'She was released in the end, but no one knows what became of her.' He paused. 'Perhaps the cage sent her mad, perhaps her soul could never escape.' His voice took on the singsong tone of a story often told. 'She haunts these ruins and her voice can be heard wailing in the wind.' He glanced back at the young soldier curiously. 'Very few people hear her though,' he added censoriously.

'Show me. Show me where the cage hung,' Thomas said sharply.

The old man hesitated, visibly trying to decide whether or not to relay the answer he usually gave to that question. Visitors expected to be taken to a specific spot. They wanted to imagine the poor woman's sorrow and pain and they needed a particular stone upon which to focus their delighted horror. He obviously decided that it was not worth the risk of lying to a kinsman of the lady in question. 'No one knows,' he replied mournfully.

'But she is seen?'

The man glanced up again, noting the stern face of the young man. 'Not by me, sir.' It was apparent that it hurt him to say it.

'But by others?'

'So I'm told.' He hesitated, then, deciding he could contribute no more to the discussion, he touched his forelock. 'I'm away to my lodgings, sir. I will leave you to your thoughts.'

As the old man scuttled away Thomas scrambled up towards a better viewpoint and stood staring round. He could feel her so closely now, her defiance towards her captors, her fear of the future, her hopeless resignation as time passed and she was forced to realise that rescue was not coming and she must accept her fate. He could feel the cold in her bones, hear the scream of the wind around the ramparts.

The old man had been right. He felt the need to touch the stones that had imprisoned her, to try to send her healing and comfort across the centuries, to reassure her spirit and let it understand that it had the freedom to soar away from this godforsaken place towards the sky.

A spatter of raindrops blew across the walls and he heard a rumble of thunder in the south. 'Rest in peace, sweet lady,' he whispered. 'Your bravery will not be forgotten.'

As he turned away from the river he thought he saw her, standing on the rampart wall against the flicker of lightning, a defiant, slim figure, wrapped in a dark cloak, her hair torn from its hood by the wind, then she was gone.

Lachlan left at tea time. He knocked on the kitchen door to say goodbye. 'Remember, you can ring me any time if you're worried.' And he handed her a piece of paper with his mobile number on, even though he knew it was on the wall there in the kitchen. She watched him climb into his car from the window then she turned back to the dining room.

With the lights on and an electric fire to boost the warmth of the radiator, the room felt safe and friendly. She had closed the door on the sitting room and refused to let herself think about what had happened there. It was growing dark and she was missing Harriet's extrovert presence. She reached for her phone and dialled her number. The phone was switched off; she tried Finlay again, not even expecting it to ring. No answer there either.

The cheerful little screen on her laptop seemed almost friendly as she switched it on and stared at the last notes she had made in her timeline. *TE stationed at Berwick on T. Visited the castle. Saw ghost.* She was puzzled. She looked at the scattering of books on the table. She knew her notes mentioned the start of his career in the army. He seemed to have enjoyed his time in the Royal Scots and his first posting had indeed been to Berwick, but seeing a ghost? Her gaze shifted to the letters. One of them must have mentioned it.

She pushed the laptop away and sat, deep in thought. The Countess of Buchan in a cage? Was that true? If only she could ask Thomas. If only she still had her mother's treasured portraits of him, it would perhaps be easier to conjure him up. Not through a séance, never again would anyone try that in her presence, but surely it must be possible to imagine him. She glanced sideways along the length of the dining table, trying to picture him sitting there on the far side, benign, perhaps smoking a long-stemmed pipe, a true grandfather figure, telling her more of his story. Would what he told her be true? Of course not, but it might be interesting.

Duncan Erskine, who had been his father's kinsman and senna-chie, had taken up permanent residence at Kirkhill House at the invitation of the young new earl. Thomas had vivid memories of studying here as a boy, in the gloomy room above the stables which their father had designated as a schoolroom but now he found the old man ensconced in the library, as quick-witted as ever, and Thomas saw his face light up with interest when he mentioned his visit to the ruined castle of Berwick. Duncan sat back slowly in his chair, pulling a plaid around his shoulders. Behind them a fire roared in the hearth; there were mugs of mulled ale on the table as the wind whistled and moaned in the crumbling tower.

'Isobel of Buchan was a courageous woman, a daughter of the house of Macduff, and it was in that respect that she took upon herself the hereditary duty to place the crown upon the head of Robert the Bruce,' he said. 'But she was of no kin to our house, my boy; she died without children and the Comyn earldom fell into abeyance. The earldom of Buchan has been a

169

great and ancient force in the land, always in the gift of the kings of Scotland and given as a prize to their descendants; that is how our family came to inherit it.'

'Papa told me we were descendants of kings,' Thomas said thoughtfully.

The old man smiled. He reached for the enormous ledger which was lying on the far side of the table and then drew towards him a pile of ancient scrolls. 'See here. I have your ancestry drawn up. Your brother, the earl, asked me the same question, though he does not have the gift of sight.' He opened the book. 'Your line comes through the lords of Cardross and from the earls of Mar. You have ancestors who died at Flodden Field, men who were always close beside the king and to Mary Queen of Scots, and you, my boy, are descended, not from Isobel Macduff, but from King Robert the Bruce himself, not once but twice over, and before him from the blessed St Margaret.' He sat back and reached for his tankard of ale. He studied Thomas's face as the young man turned the pages of the ledger digesting the information, and he nodded with satisfaction. 'You will do your family credit, and you have inherited from somewhere amongst these men and women of old the ability to see true, to see beyond the immediate. That is how you came to see that poor lady.'

'Can you see my future?' Thomas looked up again.

The sennachie shook his head. 'Your brother is heir to the titles and the lands, such as they are,' he looked round at the cavernous room thoughtfully, 'and your brother Harry stands as his heir until the earl should have sons of his own. To my mind, this leaves you to carve your own destiny with no weight of expectation. You are free to fulfil your dreams.'

'When I was in the West Indies I met an obeah woman amongst the slaves there,' Thomas confided. 'She said much the same. She was very wise, with the knowledge of her ancestors from Africa.'

'She was indeed wise, then,' the old man agreed. 'But you must learn to control your gifts, Thomas. And you must learn to hide them, too. This is an age when such things are questioned and mocked and held to be the domain of silly women. You must use them for good. I sense, and it is no more than a sensing, that you are destined to walk with kings as your ancestors did, but I sense too that you already have enemies.'

Thomas stared at him, shocked. 'Enemies?'

The old man took a gulp from his tankard. 'I fear there will always be those who let jealousy and anger and bitterness sway their emotions,' he said sadly.

'But who? I have no enemies!' Thomas was indignant.

'I'm afraid you do, my boy.' There was a long silence as he stared into his tankard as though seeking further inspiration in the depths of the thick brown ale.

Thomas stood up and walked across to the fire, holding out his hands to the flames. The only enemy that he could think of had been Andrew Farquhar, who was, as far as he knew, long gone from his life. 'I've been naive. All my life I thought people liked me,' he said sadly.

'And by and large, I'm sure they do. You're lucky to have a supportive family and powerful friends and you are blessed with charm and talent.' The old man chuckled. 'But those very things can incite others who are less lucky to look on you with resentment.' He pushed back his chair and stood up, groping for his walking stick. 'It's time for you to go. Think on what I've told you and come and see me again when you're next in Scotland.'

Thomas turned his back on the fire. 'Do you know where I'm to be posted next?'

'Across water,' there was another small chuckle. 'Where I fear you may discover that you've lost your sea legs.' The old man gathered an armful of scrolls from the table and carried them across to the shelves on the far side of the room. 'What skills for reading the future I have, I learned from my predecessor in this role, young Thomas, but I see darkly and without inspiration.'

'Do you see the lights around people?' Thomas blurted out suddenly. 'After I was struck by lightning I found I could see moving lights, colours, almost like music, as people thought and laughed and shouted.'

'And can you see them now?'

Thomas sighed. 'Only sometimes.'

'That is one of the gifts God has given you, Thomas. As I've told you, your talent is altogether more natural and more fiery and more frightening and more powerful than mine. Learn its control well. Learn to read those lights.'

'But who from? Can't you teach me?'

'That is not in my remit, I fear.' The old man's eyes were full of regret. 'No doubt the teacher will come in good time. Read. Read the books by those who have trodden this path before you. Some write with wisdom, some with foolishness, but you will find, there, kindred spirits and feel less alone. And in the meantime, beware.'

Ruth rubbed her eyes. Had she dozed off? Outside it was dark and she could hear the wind in the chimney. It had grown more wild, like the wind at Kirkhill. There was no fire in the fireplace now, no dark chamber lit by candles smelling of tallow and beeswax with an undertone in the air of old parchment and books and hot ale.

She had imagined that Thomas had been talking to her, sitting at the far end of the dining room table, one leg swinging as he balanced on its corner, looking into the past. He was relaxed, smiling at first, then his face had clouded as he described the warnings of the sennachie.

'I rode back to the barracks, deep in thought, to discover that the regiment was indeed to be posted south and over the water, as the sennachie had predicted, to the island of Jersey where we were to form part of the garrison on constant watch against any possible depredations by the French.'

It was as though he had been talking to her, telling his story, as if he were in the room with her. She surveyed the table. She remembered now; she had quite deliberately pictured him sitting there. He had been extraordinarily real. She had found herself listening, seeing through his eyes, not from information she'd read or looked up on the net, but detail she could not possibly have known.

She stared down at her notebook, open on the dining table. There was nothing there that had not been there yesterday. She looked her laptop. It showed the desktop screen. She clicked back to her browsing history. Nothing since yesterday.

So write it down. The words echoed in her brain. *Now, before you forget the details. Don't question it. Don't try and rationalise it. Don't even believe it, just write it down.*

With a sigh Ruth closed down her laptop and pushed back her chair. Going over to the window she drew back the curtain to stare out into the garden. There were no stars; bitter cold struck off the glass which was spattered with raindrops. She could hear the roar of the wind in the fir trees. Lachy had been right about the weather. It had turned into a stormy night. She left the light on in the hall, pausing to stare at the old clock as the hands slowly ticked round towards midnight and with an exhausted sigh she turned towards the stairs.

She paused on the landing and listened. The house was very quiet. Then, from somewhere downstairs, she thought she heard a door close. She stood still, frozen with terror for a fraction of a second before diving into her own bedroom, slamming the door and turning the key. The room looked serene, peaceful in the light of the bedside lamp. The only sound came from the radiator as it ticked gently under the window.

She slid under her duvet fully clothed and it was then that the daughter of her atheist father, who had long ago scornfully discarded the Lord's Prayer and everything to do with her grandfather's church, found herself murmuring a child's rhyme she summoned from some deep well of memory. She must have been taught it by her mother or her grandmother when she was very, very small. It had comforted her then in the terror-filled dark, and it comforted her now.

> *'Matthew Mark Luke and John*
> *Bless the bed that I lie on.*
> *Four corners to my bed,*
> *Four angels round my head,*
> *One to watch and one to pray,*
> *And two to bear my soul away . . . '*

She couldn't remember any more.

27

Cautiously Timothy made his way down the side of the Old Mill House, keeping his head bent against the wind. There was a small Mazda sports car outside. Was that Ruth's? As far as he knew, she didn't have a car, but if she was living here now perhaps she had bought one. There was no sign of the Daimler. He felt a small shiver of excitement at the thought of Ruth close by. April had suggested he needed to collect some of the silver to give them some more cash. He hadn't needed telling twice.

The grass was wet, soaking his trousers as he pushed through it towards the shed. He had brought a screwdriver with him in case the warped door had swollen even more after all the rain and under his arm he carried a couple of large canvas bags to put the stuff in.

Even from several feet away he could see that something had changed. The door had been pushed flush with the lintel and the hasp wedged with a thick piece of twig. He didn't remember doing that. He felt a prickle of suspicion as he glanced round to make sure he wasn't watched then drew closer, running his hand over the hasp. It had been wedged tight. 'Shit!' Someone had been here. He could see it now. The grass had been trampled and the brambles cut away to make it easier to open the door. He had been careful to pull them across when he left.

He twisted the twig free and inserted his screwdriver to force the hasp, dragged the door open and, fumbling for his torch, he shone it into the shed. The stuff had gone. All of it. The pieces of old carpet and tarpaulin he had covered it with had been pulled away and folded against the wall and he could still see the imprint of the heaviest suitcase in the earth floor.

'No! No, no!' He flung his torch down on the ground and stamped his foot furiously. Someone had found it. Ruth! Bitch! Why would anyone want to go poking around in a falling-down lean-to at the arse end of a garden in the middle of nowhere? He had been so sure it was the perfect place. He'd told April it was the perfect place. He froze. April was going to be beyond furious. She would kill him. This was their insurance, their income for months to come. He turned slowly round as though by looking again he could conjure up the boxes. He had to get them back.

Slowly his brain began to work again. Surely, whoever had found the stuff would have taken it into the house. All he had to do was wait until the place was empty and break in. He needn't tell April the things had been discovered. He would tell her he hadn't been able to bring anything away as there were people around. That would be explanation enough.

He carefully wedged the door shut behind him, even looking on the ground for the twig he had thrown away to hold the hasp shut, then he tiptoed back to the edge of the lawn and studied the back of the house. It must be possible to get in. He ran across the short distance of mown grass and, edging towards the corner of the building, peered round and began to creep towards the dining room windows.

Ruth was sitting at the table, tapping into her laptop, her back to the window. There were books all over the table and as he watched she sat back in her chair and he caught his breath in terror as he realised there was also a man in there. He was sitting on the edge of the table, his arms folded, and as Timothy saw him he looked up and for a fraction of a second he seemed to hold Timothy's gaze.

*   *   *

175

April was waiting for him on the corner of the street. As he drew up she pulled open the car door and climbed in. He noticed her casting an eye over the back seat and he got in first. 'Too many people around to risk trying to move it. I'll go back another time.' He pulled out into the main road. 'So, did you get anything for supper?'

Thomas

I was quite the man about town on leave before the next posting and Anne and Lady Huntingdon were kind and generous in their further attempts to integrate me into London society. I met the great and the good and the fashionable and enjoyed myself enormously. I neglected my studies, but then what were they for, but my own interest? When I repacked my boxes for our posting to Jersey I would include my books and sketching implements. Time enough then to catch up with my learning. And the obeah woman's fetish? I still had it, tucked away in my belongings. My talk with the sennachie had reminded me of its power to repel those who might be my enemies and, just in case, I put it in an empty tobacco pouch and kept it with my pens.

It was walking down the street one day that I once again experienced that strange feeling that I was being watched. London was hot and unpleasant. Soon people would be leaving town for the summer pleasures of Brighton and Bath but in the meantime the streets were crowded with acquaintances and I tipped my hat to several ladies as I walked towards the park. It was a prickling at the back of my neck, much as I imagined a rabbit would feel as the fox crept closer. I stopped and turned round swiftly, almost bumping into two men who were walking close behind me. I apologised and stepped round them to stare into the crowd but there was no sign of anyone who appeared to pay me more attention than usual.

177

The next day it happened again and this time it was outside Lady Huntingdon's house, almost as soon as I had descended the front steps. I was certain someone was following me.

I returned to the house, informing the footman when he opened the door for me that I had forgotten something. Then I left again, to the intense surprise of the servants, by the back door. I went on my way without any further worry, but again the words of the sennachie came back to me. I had enemies.

28

Andrew hadn't intended following Thomas to London. Paid off like everyone else when the *Tartar* docked, with a pocket full of cash he had wandered along the quay wondering what to do. He had opened his letter when it found him on the ship back in the Islands much as the other men did, excited to have news from home. It was from the local rector, in England, informing him that his father had died. He had sat, stunned, reading and rereading the cramped words on the page. Andrew and his father had never been close. He had no mother, no siblings or indeed any relatives that he knew of, and the rector made it clear, with careful tact, that there was no money left after the expenses of burial. Andrew knew why. His father, gentleman though he might have been once, had drunk away his patrimony and what he hadn't been able to drink he had gambled in the gaming houses of his hometown of Gloucester.

Andrew kept the news to himself. He had made few friends on the *Tartar* but life on the ship was all he had known for the last six years. Now as he was paid off with the others it dawned on him that he had no home, no relations, nowhere to go and no prospects until he signed on again.

The nearest tavern beckoned but then he had seen Thomas heading for the London stage; Thomas, who was responsible for destroying his career; Thomas who had watched as he was flogged and humiliated, Thomas who dined at the captain's table and exchanged letters with an adoring family, Thomas with whom he had vowed to get even. Eyes narrowed with resentment and hatred, he joined the queue and bought himself a ticket on the same coach and as the final boxes and bags were thrown into the luggage net he climbed onto the roof and settled into the last seat. Thomas had pulled up the collar of his greatcoat and, with his hat down over his eyes, already appeared to be asleep. One by one the passengers dragged the waterproof covers over their knees and settled down for the first stage of the cold and uncomfortable journey. At no point did Thomas appear to see him and at the staging posts amongst the crowds and noise and the shouts of the ostlers changing horses they did not exchange so much as a glance of recognition. Andrew saw Thomas buy himself mulled ale and a pasty and go to stand by the fire in inn after inn as they made their painfully slow way towards London. Perhaps if he had offered to buy him a drink, to share a pie, things would have been different, but Thomas preferred to cut him dead.

When they arrived at last, Thomas hailed a hansom cab to take him and his luggage who knew where. Andrew watched him leave, feeling a strange sense of abandonment, then as the horse pulled out into the solid mass of churning wheels and shouting drivers he realised he could walk as fast as the cab could travel and he set off in pursuit, his sea chest on his shoulder. They did not go far. He paused, sheltered in a doorway to watch the young lieutenant climb down, pay the man and heave his belongings up the steps of an elegant townhouse where the door was opened by a footman in livery who stooped to lift his luggage inside before shutting the door, leaving Andrew outside in the cold. For a fraction of a second Thomas had paused on the doorstep and looked round.

Andrew found passable cheap lodgings in St Giles and for several days he did what every sailor does when newly ashore. He ate and drank and whored and slept, trying to get used to the strange hours of the landlubber when his whole body was used to a timetable of watches. His plan to re-enlist evaporated, and then he had his first bit of luck. As he walked down the street he happened to glance down and there in the mud of the gutter he saw what looked uncommonly like a purse. Within seconds he had stopped and picked it up, whisking it away into an inner pocket. He glanced round. No one had noticed. He slid towards the church and in the shadow of the wall he pulled out the purse and cut the thong that tied it shut. It contained four gold guineas, a few coppers and a small silver ring. He couldn't believe his eyes.

The next day he strolled again past the house where Thomas was staying. It was something he found himself doing every day, rubbing salt into the wound of his bitter loneliness in this heaving lonely city. Enquiries of a loitering passer-by he had met on that first day revealed that the house belonged to a countess, no less. Who else. He spat on the ground as he walked away.

The door opened and Andrew saw Thomas in smart new clothes and shiny buckled shoes running down the front steps. He set off at a swift pace, threading his way through the busy streets, and Andrew fell in behind him, dodging through the crowds, keeping him in sight, falling back only when he saw him turning into a coffee house. It was when he saw Thomas hesitate in the doorway and glance behind him that he realised his quarry knew he was being followed.

He laughed out loud. The young man had looked worried. A cloud of uncertainty had crossed the sun of Thomas's happiness. Andrew leaned against the wall and folded his arms. He would wait for him. He had no reason to go anywhere and the thought of causing even the smallest uncertainty in that young man's world gave him intense pleasure.

Carefully he planned a secret war of attrition. It was imperative Thomas never saw him closely enough to identify him, that would spoil the fun. All he had to do was follow, with here a glimpse and there a trailing shadow as a linkboy guided him home from an evening engagement. Andrew's only disguise was a selection of hats, tricorn, brown felt, old top hat, cap. People never seemed to look at the face beyond it.

Thomas was a skinflint, that was for sure, walking everywhere, never once wasting money on a hansom after that first day. It never occurred to Andrew that Thomas was, at least for the time being, probably poorer than he was. He himself was relatively rich. After his first find of treasure in the gutter he had kept his eyes open and several times had found coins of various denominations lying in the mud. You had to be quick to find them; there were boys out there who made a career of retrieving such things and they carried knives. He watched and learned. Within weeks he had taught himself to pick pockets, to lift purses from the reticules of ladies shopping in the arcades, to tip his hat to someone and offer to carry their bags, his thoughtful good manners blinding them to the thought that he might duck down a dark alley with their belongings and disappear before the hue and cry was raised.

His torment of Thomas had ended when Thomas appeared in the regimentals of the Royal Scots one day and Andrew's perusal of the *Gazette* told him the regiment was to be posted north to Berwick. He knew Thomas's next posting almost before Thomas did himself. Never mind. He could bide his time. He wasn't going to give up on Thomas Erskine. Every man needed a hobby. If and when Thomas returned to London, he would be waiting.

In the meantime he had found an exciting and lucrative career of his own. He had discovered that he enjoyed the heady rush of excitement as he planned and executed each new theft; it was almost as gratifying as the counting of the money and treasures he took home to his lodgings. He was good at this. What he would eventually do to Thomas he wasn't sure yet, except that it would be very satisfying to bring him to ruin. Or worse. It was only occasionally in the dead of night that he thought of his former home life, of his sweet gentle mother who died when he was a boy, and the kind old rector. Both would have been horrified if they could see him now. His father wouldn't have cared; he would just have asked if he could have some cash to tide him over, then sent his son away.

29

'How are you, sweetheart?' It was Finlay. 'Sorry I haven't been in touch. I've been staying with this gorgeous woman who lives in a deep deep glen in the Cuillins with absolutely no Internet or phone coverage. I'm hoping to be back tomorrow or the next day, not sure yet, but we've done masses of filming. It has been fabulous. See you soon – all right, I'm coming!' That last obviously addressed to someone else, then a click and silence.

'Finlay?' Ruth looked hopelessly at the phone in her hand and then pressed it back against her ear. 'Finlay?' But he had gone.

She wasn't sure that she had said a single word to him, but it didn't matter. He was coming home.

She had caught something of his energy. Her night had been restless and, if she were honest with herself, nervous. Each time she closed her eyes she would open them, and stare round the room in the semi-darkness thrown by the small lamp on the chest. She had fallen asleep at last, but then woken at first light.

Slipping her phone in her pocket she went through into the dining room, pulled back the curtains and opened the French doors. It was a clear sunny morning; the rain and cloud of the day before had gone and been replaced by a brisk skittish wind that was busy whirling Lachy's neat piles of leaves across the lawn. As she turned to go inside, her phone rang.

It was Harriet. 'How are things? I feel so guilty leaving you there on your own after what happened.'

'I'm fine. I had a nightmare and it scared me a bit. Lachy came and searched the house for me to make sure there was no one hiding anywhere; he's such a nice man.' Ruth headed into the kitchen. 'He gave me the name of the next-door neighbour in case I want backup and he said I could ring him any time, and Fin is coming back, so I'm OK, I promise.'

'Thank goodness. Talking of neighbours,' Harriett sounded animated as she changed the subject. 'I rang my neighbour in Glasto to ask her advice about séances.' Ruth heard the chink of a spoon on china and realised Harriet was taking a coffee break. 'She said don't do it – I know, too late – and she also said the best thing we could do was to read Dion's book from cover to cover, so I've ordered one for myself, and you'd better start reading yours now. And,' she took a deep breath, 'she knew a lot about Dion's stuff. Not the war, but what she got up to in Glasto. According to her, it was all very genuine and powerful. I mentioned spirit guides and she said they were referred to as "ascended masters". I said that you were interested in Lord E as he was your ancestor and she said it sounded as though you should consider him as your guide. You would have a different relationship to him from the one that Dion had. For her he was a spiritual force. He was a voice in her head, a teacher. For you it's different. To you he is coming closer and in a form designed not to frighten you.'

Ruth reached into the cupboard for a mug. 'Frighten me!' she echoed. 'So, you're saying that when I imagine I see him, I'm seeing my spirit guide trying not to frighten me!'

'So, you are imagining you see him?' Harriet kept her voice carefully neutral.

'Well, I've certainly dreamt about him.' Ruth thought for a moment. 'And deliberately imagined him. And he did seem quite real, I must admit. He sat on the edge of the table and chatted about his life. Friendly. Nice-looking. Not particularly old.'

There was a short silence. Harriet exhaled loudly. 'You are keeping a careful note of everything he says, aren't you.'

'I am, as it happens. But it can't count as real, can it? It's fiction. Or fantasy. My fantasy.'

'You know, Ruthie, this is incredibly exciting.' Harriet sounded almost wistful. 'Isn't it an irony? It's you who has the psychic ability. I want to believe in it passionately, but can't do it. You don't believe it, whatever happens, but you seem to be able to summon him with ease.'

Ruth shivered. 'No. I just have a really good imagination.'

Hattie laughed. 'If you say so.'

'And,' Ruth added, 'the story is incredibly compelling.'

'We move today! Now.' April's face was strained and anxious.

'Why?' Timothy was eating handfuls of Rice Krispies straight from the packet. He crushed the inner waxed envelope, hurled it towards the bin and dusted his hands together. 'I thought we agreed we'd wait.'

'We can't wait. There are police out there.' She had been standing at the window. 'They've been past twice this morning. Are you packed?'

'No.' He was indignant. 'I didn't think there was any hurry. You haven't even told me where we're going.'

'I have. Craigmillar.'

She gave him five minutes while she stuffed her own belongings into the car boot. She didn't care who saw them.

They managed to take everything they needed and she agreed that Timothy could come back if it seemed safe to collect a second load, but for now it was time to go.

Timothy hated the house on sight. He couldn't believe April had chosen it. It was a ruinous bungalow, run-down, dirty, isolated, the kitchen window broken, and there were obviously mice; probably rats. There was a weed-grown concrete driveway down the side where they could pull the car out of sight of the road. Beyond it was a plot of derelict land full of nettles and brambles, almost beneath the legs of a huge pylon. At least there were no neighbours.

April surveyed her new domain with some satisfaction. 'I admit it's a bit more run-down than I thought, but no one will ever know we're here.'

Timothy was aghast. 'I hope you don't expect me to be able

to connect the electricity; no way I'm going to try plugging into that thing.' He pointed at the pylon with a sarcastic laugh. 'And the toilet hasn't been flushed in years.'

'It'll be fine when you fix it.' April seemed oblivious to the problems. 'Make a shopping list. There are fireplaces. All you will need to do is clear the chimneys of birds' nests; the roof looks fairly sound. The water's off, and when we turn it on we might find a few burst pipes but you can sort that. We'll get sleeping bags and camp beds. There is a trading estate up the road where we can find everything we need and there's an old solid-fuel Rayburn in the kitchen. That'll still work; they go on forever. We can use it for cooking and hot water and keeping us warm.'

Timothy shuddered. 'Are you out of your mind? I'm not going to live here!'

'Well, I am. I suppose you think it's too far from Cramond!' She gave him a malicious glance. It was about as far as one could get from Cramond without leaving the city confines. 'Go if you want to. Find somewhere nearer Ruth.'

He ignored the remark.

'Oh, and we'll need a saw,' she went on. 'There are enough trees and things out there to keep us in logs for months. This'll do nicely.' She was using her patronising smug tone. It infuriated him. Who was going to do all this sawing and chimney clearing and plumbing and roofing? He was. And what for? A few weeks in this foul dump before they had to move on again.

He walked outside into the blustery wind to start unloading the car. How could this happen? He all but owned a lovely house in the city. He had been bequeathed it legitimately by that old man. Maybe the will wasn't proved, but it still might be. They had never been caught yet. They had stayed under the radar all their lives. Until now. But the time had come; they needed to stop running. He was not going to live in some ruin on a dump under an electricity pylon. He wanted that house, Number 26. Only Ruth was standing in his way.

'Timothy!' April was impatient. 'Come on. I'm cold. Let's put on the kettle.'

Kettle. What kettle? Theirs was electric.

He unpacked the car and then they found the trading estate and stocked up on necessities. She didn't want to bother with the camping stove, but he pointed out the Rayburn had a huge hole in the back. It was never going to work. The tap reluctantly spewed rusty water and he was sent out again as it grew dark to buy a six-pack of mineral water and two portions of fish and chips.

As they wriggled into their sleeping bags side by side on the floor and piled the duvets on top of themselves, April reached over to turn out the lantern. For the first time in ages, she felt safe.

Thomas

I ignored my instinct that trouble was stalking me in London. I was on leave with money in my pocket, or at least enough to make me feel a king of the world. I had a smart uniform and I was preoccupied with having fun. I was nineteen and in love. Or, at least, in love with the idea of love. I had discovered the joy of having girls hang on my arm, of having them gaze up into my eyes and listen to every word I uttered. I had also discovered that I might be the son of an earl but I was only the third son with no fortune, and the eagle-eyed mamas of these pretty girls had an extraordinary way of knowing one's prospects to the last farthing and, while they might permit their daughters to flirt harmlessly on the arm of a handsome and gallant beau, they were in no way going to allow any relationship to develop.

Our leave over, the regiment was sent to St Helier on the island of Jersey some dozen miles from the coast of France. My duties were not onerous and I filled my time as was my habit with exploring the beauties of the island and, mindful of my lessons with Dr Butt, with drawing and painting its botanical specimens. I read extensively; following the sennachie's advice, my choice of reading matter was expanded to include the works of Newton and Swedenborg and similar authors. I wrote, too. I continued to send letters to my brothers, David still based in London and much involved with Anne and her church activities, and to Mama and Harry in Edinburgh. By writing I was, I suppose, teaching myself the way of words. I wrote sermons and I wrote essays and short treatises on subjects that interested me. I was, I suspect, always more of an academic than a natural soldier, though I enjoyed the martial life. We were not at war, our postings were purely protective, showing the flag to anyone who might at the time have contemplated invasion. It was an ideal life.

The subject of one of my essays was Sir Thomas More. I had brought his book Utopia with me and I was fascinated by his career, his rise and his fall from favour, his horrific death after so faithfully serving his monarch. The other subject of my literary efforts was ladies. I liked them. Greatly. I set out to list the properties of the ideal wife. I wanted her to be fair, yet modest; I wanted her 'to delight rather than dazzle, shine like the mild beams of the morning rather than the blaze of the noon and I wanted winning female softness both in person and in mind'. I was a bit of a prig.

The one thing I had not realised was that one of their number might make me fall hopelessly in love, at which point I would have no further say in my destiny.

30

James Reid leaned back in his chair and studied his hands, steepled before him on the desk. 'My informants tell me that the Bradfords have left their former address, a place it turns out where they had been squatting. They had no legal right to be there. They have, if nothing else, an enormous amount of chutzpah, those two.' He gave a wintry smile. 'I am only sorry that all this nonsense is delaying the processing of your father's will. I suspect you would like to be able to dispose of the property as soon as possible.'

Ruth nodded. 'That house has a great many unhappy memories.'

'Nevertheless, your father has left it to you, and we can be certain it was to you that he meant his bequests to go, a very nice inheritance. We have the valuation of the house now.' He opened the leather folder on his desk, withdrew a piece of paper and pushed it towards her. 'Obviously there will be tax to pay on that sum when the house is sold, but it will still leave you with a decent amount, and I think we can be certain that you will not be sharing it with Mr Bradford. He would find it very hard to prove a relationship with your father. He claims to have a DNA sample but he seems to be unaware of the fact that we would require the sample from him to be taken by our agent in front of witnesses. We have proved from handwriting experts and from the solicitor whose signature he forged that his copy of the will is not genuine. I think that you can be confident the inheritance is yours alone.' He shut the folder again and smiled up at her.

'And the things he stole?'

He shook his head regretfully. 'There we are less hopeful. Unless you can give me details of what has been taken, there isn't much we can do.'

Ruth had felt safe in that old-fashioned office, reassured by the calm friendly manner of the man sitting opposite her, but as soon as she was back outside in the street, surrounded by bustling pedestrians and traffic, it was a different matter. She had one more visit to make before going back to the Old Mill House. She needed to go to Number 26 to check everything there was as it should be. Even the thought of going there seemed to conjure up the malign presence of Timothy following her wherever she went. She glanced over her shoulder, but if there was anyone there she would find it impossible to spot them.

Thomas's posting to Jersey was over, and once again Anne arranged for her brother to spend his leave with her and Lady Huntingdon. He was allotted the same bedroom and looked around it with some pleasure as the footman deposited his luggage near the foot of the bed.

And so it proceeded. Each day was full of delight and adventure. He put his notebooks away, stacked his pencils and sketchbooks on the table in the corner and did not look at them again. Instead he went to the coffee houses and met with men who remembered him from his previous visits and were now becoming friends. The conversation excited him; they would sit for hours discussing the latest politics and scandals. Then Thomas would make his way back to change for a dinner or a ball and the heady delight of flirting with the clusters of pretty young ladies who surrounded him as he arrived at the latest party.

It was late in the evening and he was standing by the table in a side room at yet another ball, sipping a glass of wine, when he saw her standing nearby. She had been led to the table by a tall, well-dressed young man. He gave her a glass of sherbet, bowed

191

and then left her there alone. He saw her glance round, as though desperately searching for a familiar face amongst the crowd. In the ballroom the orchestra was striking up a minuet and men were bowing before the partners of their choice; ladies were fluttering their eyelashes as they scanned the room from behind their fans for the men who had booked their dances, but this girl turned away shyly and sipping from her glass began to edge towards the door. As she did so the glass slipped from her gloved hand and fell to the floor. She stared down at the spilled drink, appalled.

Thomas was at her side in an instant. 'Excuse me. Can I be of assistance?' he bowed.

She looked at him, startled, and he found himself confronted by a large pair of dark eyes and a face which combined extraordinary attractiveness with a quirky inquisitive charm. He could see her embarrassment and then her shy admiration as she noted his good looks and his dress uniform. He hastily retrieved the glass, thankfully unbroken, and found her another which he filled from the punch bowl. 'I'm sorry, ma'am. We have not been formally introduced, but perhaps on this occasion we may assume the introductions have been made by our hostess in inviting us both to the ball.'

She seemed struck dumb by his shocking suggestion but then he saw the spark of mischief light in her eyes. 'Indeed, I believe they have, both by our hostess and my aunt, who brought me.'

'And were she here with us, would she tell me your name?' This was highly improper but he couldn't bring himself to bow and walk away.

'It is Frances, sir. Frances Moore.'

Behind them the minuet finished and after a pause they heard the orchestra striking up once more. He laughed in delight. 'A Scotch reel, I think, Miss Moore. Would you do me the honour of dancing it with me?'

She hesitated for only a second. 'I suppose as we have now been introduced there would be no harm.' She set down her glass with a determination which he found extremely attractive. He held out his hand and with just the slightest of hesitations she rested her gloved fingertips on his and allowed him to lead her back into the ballroom.

192

31

The loud banging downstairs was followed by a furious ringing on the doorbell. Ruth sat up in bed, her heart thudding with fear, then she reached for her bathrobe. Her glance at the little clock beside her bed told her it was just after 6 a.m.

'You bolted the door!' Finlay had paid off the taxi by the time she had the door open.

'Oh, Fin, I am so pleased to see you!' She flung herself into his arms. 'Why didn't you tell me you were coming back today?'

'I thought I did.' He sounded plaintive. He dragged his suitcase inside, left it in the middle of the hall floor and headed for the kitchen. 'So, what's been happening?'

'You wouldn't believe. So much!' She clambered onto the stool, watching as he reached for the kettle. 'You first. Tell me about Skye.'

'Skye was magical as always, Elspeth is a darling and I am in love, her food was to die for and she will be the absolute star of my show.' He poured his coffee, sipped it as it was, black, then pushed the cafetière towards her. 'You look washed out, sweetheart. Tell Uncle Finlay all about it. How are things with the horrible Timothy?'

Once she had started she couldn't stop. She told him everything: Harriet, the séance, the ghost, Lachlan, Thomas and his story, seemingly dictated by her imaginary co-author. By the time she had finished, Finlay had drunk two mugs of coffee, prowled round the kitchen and put everything back the way he liked it, dived into the freezer for bread, made toast and scrambled eggs for them both with smoked salmon from Skye which he produced from the cool bag he had left in the hall by his case.

'So, basically I leave you in charge of my house for a few days and you are engulfed in mayhem and black magic.' He had insisted that they adjourn to the sitting room, light the wood burner and continue their coffee drinking in there in comfort. He noticed the smell of onions at once and roared with laughter at her explanation. 'Dear God! Ruth! What are you like! I can't turn my back for one minute.' He pulled up a chair and put his feet up on the coffee table. 'So, has our evil spirit returned?'

'No.'

'Good. We don't want to waste good vegetables one minute more than we have to.' He closed his eyes for a minute and she realised suddenly how tired he must be. It turned out he had been given a lift back from Skye as far as Perth and from there he had found a taxi to bring him home.

'I'm sorry, Fin. I have exhausted you with my whingeing. Now you are home, everything will be all right.'

He gave a guffaw of laughter. 'Thanks for the vote of confidence. But at least you won't be on your own now. I can't imagine how scary it must have been after Harriet left. That was a bit unfair of her, wasn't it? To leave you by yourself like that.'

'She had meetings to go to.'

'Really?' The word was loaded with disbelief.

'Yes, really. I'm tough, Fin. I can take most things, though I must confess I wasn't happy here on my own after the séance. I don't believe in ghosts, but . . .' her voice faded.

'What we need is an expert on such matters.' He drained his last cup of coffee and stood up. 'My dear, I am going to have to get my head down for a few hours. Can I leave you to your own devices until lunchtime? And while I shower and dream of Hebridean delicacies I will see if I can think of someone who can advise us on what to do should the nasty spooky man return.'

It had been Frances who had let slip that her parents planned to take her with them to Ranelagh the following night. She and Thomas had danced together three times at the ball and it was when they withdrew to a quiet corner behind a huge flower arrangement so that they could at last talk that Frances's chaperone finally caught up with them and whisked her away. Thomas had stood watching her go with the strangest feeling of loneliness. His head was full of the memory of those merry eyes, her quiet laugh, the touch of her gloved hand on his, her gentle but acerbic remarks. He had watched her go, seen her glance back over her shoulder and the quick regretful wave of her hand, and then she had moved out of sight. He began to follow but the woman with her had taken her arm and ushered her into a group of older people and they had all headed towards the doors.

He didn't sleep that night and by morning he was plotting a way to see her again. He would go to Ranelagh. It had seemed like fate that he had spotted her with her parents strolling up the main avenue of the pleasure gardens almost as soon as he arrived. He saw her father frown as he approached and realised too late that he should have engineered this meeting better. He should have had someone with him to make the introductions. As it was, it was Frances who spoke first.

'Papa, Mama, this is Tom Erskine. We were introduced last night at the ball. Tom, my parents, Mr and Mrs Daniel Moore.'

Tom bowed over her mother's hand. Her daughter resembled her in stature and the colour of her hair, but the eyes were different. They were blue and a little calculating, he thought, as she looked him up and down. He shook hands with Frances's father. 'Sir, it is a pleasure to meet you both.' As they walked on together as a group with Mrs Moore talking abstractedly about the lights and the music, the two young people exchanged glances. Frances was, if anything, more beautiful than he remembered. Tom manoeuvred himself to walk next to her but her father had already turned to him again. He stopped and gave a slight bow. 'I am afraid we are joining friends, Mr Erskine, so we must say farewell at this point.'

Tom was left staring after them, chastened. The introductions had not been made well. He cursed himself for not thinking the situation through. Of course her father would be suspicious of him. The woman the night before would probably have told her parents that he had danced with their daughter three times, an unforgivable breach of etiquette. He and Frances had not been properly introduced. Worse, he had stammered like a shy boy when he spoke to them. He did not even know where they lived.

Andrew Farquhar was finding life surprisingly enjoyable in London. He had found more comfortable quarters now and was building for himself a successful double life. At night when the crowds were leaving the theatres and chop houses and taverns, when Oxford Street or Drury Lane were teeming with people, or in the dark alleys full of drunken revellers, he had proved himself an adept thief. It had been laughably easy to wrest a purse here, a pocketful of change there from the rich and incapable, to pull a ring off the finger of an all but insensible playgoer, to brush against a pretty lady, accidentally touch a breast here, a buttock there, right her with a gallant apology and leave her flustered and indignant and without her reticule or bangle. In the daytime he donned a sensible coat and hat and made his way between the coffee houses, reading the newssheets, listening to discussions, joining in here and there as his views became more informed and confident.

He had all but forgotten Thomas Erskine, languishing still as far as he knew in Jersey, out of sight out of mind, until one day he saw a soldier in the regimentals of the Royals and learned that they were on leave before their next posting. He found his way, almost unaware of what he did or that he was driven by a sudden lurch of hatred which surprised even himself, to the London house of the Countess of Huntingdon and looked up at the darkened windows.

A farthing here, a penny there and, disguised as a passing tradesman of tinware from the East Indies, he had found his way into the servants' hall, suitably humble, afraid to speak out of turn, sold Lady Huntingdon's usually astute butler some lacquered trays and discovered that while Her Ladyship and Lady Anne Erskine were at present in Tunbridge Wells, Lady Anne's brother was staying in the house until his regiment was posted overseas. And he heard the footman chuckle with a housemaid about the gay young dog and his social life and his popularity, and the fact that he had been to yet another ball last night, and today planned to join a party of friends at Ranelagh Gardens to hear a concert in the Rotunda.

Andrew walked down the street and out of sight, pushing his bag of wares into the hands of an astonished beggar. Thinking about the opulent house he had just left, the pleasant well-fed staff, the affectionate banter about Tom and his social life, his visceral hatred of Thomas Erskine deepened.

Joining the queues at the gates of the pleasure gardens, he paid his two shillings and sixpence to join the huge crowds wandering around in the lantern-lit darkness and headed slowly towards the Rotunda where the music had already started. It was a busy evening; the crowds were everywhere, and Andrew smiled grimly. He could make himself a rich man ten times over at his chosen trade here, but tonight he was a respectable man. As he had approached via the King's New Road, watching the coaches and carriages backed up for a mile along the road, he had wondered how anyone ever managed to meet up with their friends amongst such a throng, but despite the crowds, he had no trouble spotting Thomas, staring out across the lake towards the prettily illuminated bridge. He was with a group of fellow junior officers; they were laughing and talking and flirting with the passing girls, and then as he watched Thomas drew suddenly away the others. He had seen someone he knew. Making his way closer, confident no one would see him in the throng, Andrew saw him bow to a middle-aged couple; he then turned to the girl with them and kissed her hand. He saw the girl introducing them and watched the expression on the faces of the two older people, obviously her parents, the father politely friendly, the mother suspicious. Andrew felt a prickle of interest. This was more than a casual, accidental meeting and he found himself wondering if it had been pre-arranged. He was only a few yards away now and he could see the girl clearly. She was tall for a woman, swathed against the cold wind off the river in a fur-trimmed wrap. Her hair was simply dressed beneath her hood and looped around an oval face with large dark eyes, and he saw the expression with which she was regarding Thomas, a combination of conspiratorial amusement, adoration and demure reserve which made even him want to laugh. Within seconds he had formed a quiet resolution. One way or another he would have that young woman for himself, and if he broke Tom Erskine's heart, so much the better.

By the next morning Thomas had a plan in place. By lunchtime he had presented himself at the house of their hostess at the ball where he had met Frances. He pressed his note of thanks for her hospitality into her hand, accepted a dish of coffee and confided his problem to her with so much candour she was enchanted. When he left the house he had learned that Daniel Moore was one of the two MPs for the constituency of Great Marlow, that he leased a house in Charles Street, that Frances was his favourite and youngest daughter, twenty years old, like Thomas himself, and that his hostess would without more ado arrange a formal introduction. 'Fanny's mother is the most tremendous snob, dear Tom,' her ladyship announced. 'When I tell her that you are the brother of the Earl of Buchan and reside with your sister at Lady Huntingdon's, she will welcome you with open arms.'

There was no sign of Frances when Tom was shown into Mrs Moore's drawing room. It appeared that she had gone out with her sisters to see the Shakespeare Gallery in Pall Mall and knew nothing of his visit. Mr Moore was not there either. Tom took the proffered chair, accepted a dish of tea and prepared to charm Mrs Moore as he had never charmed anyone before.

She was not to be charmed.

'I assume that you are interested in my daughter, Mr Erskine,' she said. 'I should tell you that you that my husband and I consider you both far too young to contemplate any kind of a close friendship. We leave London for Marlow when the House rises and will be away for the summer. You may visit us in Marlow.' She paused for a few seconds, as if with the intention of testing his resolve to the utmost. 'I have read your glowing testimonial' – she brandished the letter he had presented as though it were a suspect forgery – 'and I will look into your circumstances, but I have to say Frances has many admirers; we look for a man of fortune for her. I understand that you are the younger brother of Lord Buchan.' She did not seem as impressed as he had hoped. 'From your accent, I assume that to be a Scotch peerage.' She paused just long enough for her scornful views of the unacceptable nature of David's rank and nationality to be made clear. 'My husband will make enquiries as to your brother's position and circumstances.'

Tom went cold. 'I am only asking if I may be permitted to call upon her, ma'am,' he said, crestfallen. This was the first time he had had a close encounter with the forensic eye of the mother of an unmarried daughter. He had heard his friends joke about such dragons, but he had not given a thought to what one of these ferocious animals would make of his prospects, his brother, or his accent. He was a lowly subaltern, true, but in a good regiment and with excellent prospects of promotion, but beyond that even he could see he was not a good bet. He looked up and met her eye in an agony of disappointment. 'I shall make a point of calling upon you all in Marlow, ma'am,' he said with his bravest smile.

As he ran down the front steps of the house into the street he heard a low whistle from the basement area behind the railings. He paused and turned and there was Frances, lying in wait. He stared down at her, appalled more by the whistle than the fact that she had evaded her companions in order to meet him. She was alone and swathed in a cloak, the hood pulled up well over her face. She giggled when she saw his expression and ran up the steps towards him, reaching out for his hand. 'This way, quickly. I have only a few minutes. My sister wanted to meet a friend of her own so I told her I would come home ahead of her.' She dragged him towards the corner of the street and into a quiet garden square where they found a shadowy bench beneath a tree. 'So, how did it go?' Her face was alight with eagerness.

'Your mother was not impressed with me.' He gazed at her, almost speechless with surprise and delight. 'She didn't like anything about me: my future prospects, my brother, my accent. I fear she has great plans for you, Frances.' For all his candid words, the overwhelming depression that had enveloped him as he left Mrs Moore's drawing room had vanished.

Frances gave a gurgle of laughter. 'Some hope! I have no fortune either. We are two poor church mice, Tom. Besides, I have no intention of marrying for a long while yet. That does not mean we can't be friends, though, does it?' She was still holding his hand, and he looked down at her slim white fingers. She had a tiny pearl ring on the little finger of her right hand and he ran his thumb over it gently, amazed at the bolt of excitement that went through his body at the touch of her skin. 'We shouldn't be here,' he stammered. 'It is most improper for us to be alone.'

She bit her lip, and lowered her eyes chastely. 'Oh dear. I am so sorry. I had not had you marked down as a man to give up so easily.'

He was devastated. 'But I haven't. I'm not. I was thinking of your good name.'

She gripped his hand more tightly. 'Leave me to look after my good name, Mr Erskine,' she said coyly. 'No one saw us come in here. My sister Cassandra and I, we look after each other. If I ask her to give me an alibi she will, as I will give her the same, should she ask for it.'

Tom looked up at her in amazement. His sisters were both much older than him, both sober and serious without a flirtatious bone in their bodies. This sparkling, laughing girl with her warmth and daring dismissal of the social norms was something so new and exciting he couldn't believe his good fortune. He was struck dumb. She took the opportunity to lean forward and give him a quick peck on his cheek. She pulled back before he could react. 'I've never kissed a man before,' she said, still half joking, half abashed at her own daring. 'No,' she pushed him away as he leaned towards her. 'No, I shouldn't have done that.' She was all demure damsel again now.

His head was in a whirl, his whole body aflame with excitement and longing. 'Fanny, my love,' he stammered. 'I must see you again.'

'And you shall, I promise.' She looked him up and down critically. 'I like you too, Tom. We can meet here. It's a safe place. Very private. And we can walk in the park too. I am sure there are shady little avenues there amongst the trees and shrubs.'

'But you're going back to Marlow.'

'Not right away,' she said indignantly. 'Papa has to go back to his constituency, I suppose, but surely not yet.'

'Your mother said you would be going as soon as the House rose for the summer recess.'

'And when is that?'

He shook his head in mock despair. 'Very soon.'

She frowned. 'Mama promised that we would go to Bath this summer so my sisters could meet suitable husbands. I expect she meant that for me too.' She was suddenly thoughtful. 'Papa said he couldn't afford such expense, so I suspect you're right, we'll go to Marlow. We always do. He will claim work calls him there, and Mama will be furious and disappointed. But Marlow isn't far away. You could come there, Tom, and you haven't really met Papa yet. He's a nice man. Kind. He loves me.' Her face warmed at the thought. 'It's Mama who deals with the business of his daughters. She knows he can refuse us nothing if we wheedle him.'

Tom laughed. 'I can imagine no one at all could resist you if you wheedle.'

'Not even you?' She had a way of putting her head to one side that enchanted him.

'Especially not me.'

'Good.' She jumped to her feet. 'But for now, that must be all, Tom. I must go home or Cassandra and Jane will arrive before me and then Mama would discover our subterfuge. Go and see Papa. Make him like you.' Again that head on one side. 'That shouldn't be hard.' She stood on tiptoe and pecked his cheek again, then she caught his hand and ran with him towards the gates. Only when they had rounded the corner and were in sight of the house did she release him, blow him a kiss and run towards the front door. She didn't look back.

He stood where he was, watching until the front door was opened and she disappeared inside. He had caught a glimpse of the maid who answered her knock, the quick exchange between them, Frances running in past her, the girl glancing surreptitiously out into the street before she gently closed the door and he could imagine that the servants in the house were as much in thrall as he was. Her mother would never know where she had been.

Slowly he turned away and almost without thinking where he was going he retraced his steps along the street to the square and to the bench where they had been sitting. His heart was aflutter and his brain whirling with conflicting emotions. If he hadn't realised what had happened before, he knew it for certain now. He was in love.

32

It was the perfect place to meet. Frances and her maid Abigail would leave the house to walk in the sunshine or to buy ribbons or embroidery silks and as they passed Berkeley Square Frances would slip through the gate in the iron railings into the garden, with its gravel paths and central lawns, neat concealing shrubs and shady plane trees, leaving Abi to go on alone. It had been Frances's idea and Thomas had seized on it with alacrity. It was she who sent him the note, she who dictated the best time for her to be able to leave the house without her mother's close scrutiny and Abi was a willing double agent, carrying letters back and forth, choosing the prettiest silks for her mistress to carry back in triumph to the house and keeping absolute silence on the subject so that the servants in the Moore kitchen had no idea at all that anything was afoot.

Thomas was in thrall. She gave him a tiny portrait miniature of herself and demanded one from him in return – something that cost him far more than he could afford. When the kissing stopped, sometimes they would talk, sitting side by side on a bench under a mulberry tree. He knew everything there was to know about her now, the books she liked to read – novels – the fact that she liked animals as much as he did, the fact that the injustices of the world could fan her into a fury of impotent rage, and indignation that her father could so order her life that he decided whom she could see and entertain and eventually marry. 'He owns me, Tom!' she cried in wild indignation. 'That's the law!'

'But he doesn't oversee your every excursion,' Tom soothed. His hands moved gently down her arms as he drew her closer for another kiss. 'You wouldn't be here if he did.'

'No, I could be open and honest and tell them how much I love you!'

Tom froze. 'You love me?' He had never dared hope, never thought beyond these moments in the shadows.

She grinned impishly, not realising how much the frank declaration had affected him. 'We are going to a masquerade ball next week. Can you be there? Then we can be together openly. Mama cannot object to my dancing with you once or twice if you come and bow and be charming to her. She admits you're a good-looking young man.' She smiled up at him archly.

He pulled her close again. 'I shall do my best, my darling.'

'And it appears you are well connected,' she added. She knew her mother had been asking about him amongst her friends.

'To my brother, the earl, perhaps.' Mrs Moore hadn't appeared to think much of his connections when he had spoken to her.

'Especially to your brother, the earl.' She snuggled into his embrace. 'She was impressed. He is of ancient lineage, I gather. Me, I don't care if your brother is a pedlar. I would still love you as much.'

He pulled her close. 'It's nearly time for Abi to come back.' He glanced over her head towards the gates. There was someone there, a silhouette against the sunshine. A tall figure who stood for some seconds looking in their direction, then stepped back out of sight.

She felt him tense and pulled away. 'What is it?'

'There was someone there. I thought he was watching us.'

'No! Who?'

'I don't know. No one I recognised.'

'Has Papa sent someone to spy on us, do you think?' She jumped to her feet, thoroughly frightened.

'But he doesn't know. Abi would never betray you.' He stood

up too and caught her hand again. 'Don't worry, sweetheart. I'm sure it was a stranger.'

But that was the trouble, he wasn't sure at all. Just for a moment the figure had seemed familiar and the man's presence, in a landscape of moving shadows and crowded pavements, had made him uneasy.

'Let's abandon our meeting tomorrow, my darling. We shall see each other in any case at the ball,' he said. 'Perhaps we have been too regular in coming here and someone has become curious. Best to be safe. I don't want your papa to be suspicious. We must do everything by the book.'

'Everything?' She looked up at him, startled, her eyes wide with anxiety.

'When I ask him for your hand.'

'Oh, Tom.' She flung her arms round his neck. 'When?'

He laughed. 'Perhaps after the ball. We must see whether or not your parents are pleased to see me there.' He stepped back from her, her hands still warm in his own. 'And besides, I have to find out whether you would agree to the match first. I don't believe I've asked you yet. If I did, do you think you would say yes?'

'Mistress Frances?' They hadn't even noticed Abi's arrival. 'We should go. It's getting late.' She was looking anxiously over her shoulder.

Frances blew him a kiss and she was gone. She never answered his question.

33

'It all depends how we go about finding a ghost expert.' Finlay had brought back a selection of cold cuts, the components of a salad and a bottle of his favourite white wine for lunch from a short meeting with his agent. 'Max was a mine of information on the subject when I asked him. Starting at the top: there is a ghostly department at the university. Did you know that? The Koestler Parapsychology Unit. Serious scientific stuff. He knows someone there who you could talk to. If you don't want to take the academic route, there are the churches, most of which have blokes for dealing with this sort of thing and will exorcise and bless your house, or you, if you're lucky.' He glanced at her face. 'Perhaps not the church! Then there are the private operators. Ladies who tiptoe out of shady streets and appear swathed in shawls at psychic fairs.' He chuckled, passing her a glass of wine. 'According to Max, some of them actually know their stuff.'

Ruth clinked glasses with him. 'How on earth does he know all this? I thought agents were down-to-earth businessmen who brook no nonsense.'

'They are.' He gave a wicked chuckle. 'That's why useless wimps like me need them. But he gathers a lot of usually useless information along the way and occasionally it comes in handy.'

Ruth climbed onto a stool and leaned her elbows on the island amongst his waxed paper packets of cheese and prosciutto, sipping from her glass. 'None of that quite helps me though. I don't want a scientific bucket of cold water, which is what the university probably administers; I don't want a dotty old lady. And you're right about my view of churches. But I want to believe in Thomas.' It came out as a wail. 'And I don't want that awful other . . . ' she hesitated, unable to bring herself to even describe him, 'that being from the lower circles of hell.'

Finlay smiled. 'How lovely to have a literate guest who can ascribe a ghost to the correct department in Dante's inferno. But, sweetheart, you addressed the problem with garlic and onions. That surely is advice from the shady ladies' department.'

'I don't think Dion Fortune was quite a shady lady. But as far as I know, she wasn't university either.' Ruth sighed as he leaned forward and topped up her glass. 'I gather she was Christian if a bit unorthodox, and into some very complicated ancient magical studies,' she went on thoughtfully. 'Come on, Fin. We need another category. An expert who believes it all and knows how to handle it. I don't want validation, I want discrimination and then maybe explanation. I want Thomas encouraged and I want the other bloke banished forever.'

'I'm not sure who else to ask.'

'I thought all Scots were psychic.'

Finlay put his head on one side. 'I think that's an over-generalisation,' he said gently.

'But you said you had seen a ghost here.'

'That's the kind of ghost who wafts around charmingly in the distance from time to time.' He began to lay out the food on a wooden platter. 'I don't think I could cope with any other kind. Leave it with me. We'll find someone, I promise.'

'I'm coming with you. I want to see inside his house.'

Timothy stared at April in horror. This was the last thing he wanted. The Old Mill House was his private place.

'I've seen his kitchen on the telly,' she went on dreamily, 'with pots of herbs and lovely pans and things.'

They were sitting over a fish-and-chip takeaway by an oil stove. Timothy had been over to Muirhouse again that afternoon to see if there was any post. There wasn't and he had a strange feeling someone had been in there. 'They make the programme in a studio,' he said, deliberately pouring cold water on her idea. 'It would just spoil it if you saw his real kitchen. It is very ordinary. I've seen it through the window.'

She stared at him and for a moment he saw something like devastation in her eyes. He really had destroyed it for her. He glanced down at the table. They were eating off newspaper in a condemned house with almost nothing to call their own except their dreams and he had knocked hers on the head. But then it was her fault they were living the way they did. He had always followed her lead. Ten years older than him, it had been April who had brought him up. He didn't even remember their parents. Even when he was a little boy she had been pursuing some agenda he had never quite fathomed, as though she were trying to pay life back. He sighed. He wasn't going to take her to the Old Mill House. If he went, and he knew he would, it would be alone, with a torch, wearing gloves. One way or another he intended to make damn sure they would have enough money after his visit to see them through the winter.

It was time to move on again. Find another crib. Andrew lay on his bed, his hands behind his head, staring round the room critically. Unlike his previous berth this place was shabby and dirty and dark. He could afford something much better and he was beginning to dislike the way the landlord looked at him so calculatingly when he came to collect the rent. On the plus side these knots of narrow noisy streets in the Rookeries, with their filth and their bawds and the perpetual dusk of the tall buildings reaching across towards one another beneath strings of washing, were the perfect hideout. Even if anyone had spotted him when he was out and about on his own particular business, they wouldn't dare follow him back here. He frowned. Somewhere down in the street a child was screaming.

There were shouts and he heard the wail of a woman. No doubt some dirty brat had got under the wheels of a cart.

He stretched and reached for the bottle by his bed. Perhaps a short doze then he would get dressed up and go out, wander the smart areas around the park and pick some more pockets or collect some more coins from the gutters. Whoever had said that London's streets were paved with gold had been right. It was astonishing how often the gentry, drunk or just careless, dropped their money without realising it or without wanting to scrabble in the muck to pick them up.

He smiled lazily to himself, wondering how Thomas was doing. He was still on leave, in London, living like a prince in the house of that weird countess. No doubt he was still following that dark-eyed doxy around, all doe-eyed and lustful. When Andrew had seen them kissing under a tree it had been all he could do not to puke!

He settled back more comfortably on the pillow and went back to one of his favourite daydreams: getting even. Perhaps it was time to make an advance on Miss Moore himself. Oh yes, he had made it his business to find out her name and exactly what number Charles Street her father lived at. An MP, no less. Andrew had spent a great deal of time thinking up the perfect trick to play on the lovers. The ever-so-proper MP and his wife wouldn't be pleased to know that their daughter was hanging out in secret with a sailor boy who had picked up the pox in the West Indies, indeed they wouldn't. Then when Miss Moore was at her most devastated he would move in to comfort her. She was clearly not averse to secret rendezvous. Once he had her alone in an avenue between the trees without her maid he would find out just what it was that attracted Tom to her so much. He licked his lips. She would be ruined, of course. But that was the whole point.

When he went out an hour later he had in his pocket a neatly folded and sealed letter addressed to Mr Daniel Moore, MP. He was particularly pleased with the seal he had bought at a printer's and stationer's shop in Little Britain. It depicted Hermes the messenger of the gods.

* * *

Their leave was nearly over. Thomas stared at his fellow ensign, shocked. He had lost track of time over the past few weeks and been so distracted by the delightful dalliance with Fanny that everything else had gone out of his head.

'We are posted to Minorca, my friend. The most boring of the overseas postings, I hear!' Alex was sitting on the far side of the table in the Cheshire Cheese. 'How could you not have seen the notices?'

Tom was dismayed. 'I can't go.'

'You have to, old boy. Unless you can buy yourself out. Don't be stupid. Why would you not want to go? You'd enjoy it with your endless sketchbooks! And at least we're not bound for the West Indies!'

Tom could only think of one recourse. He hadn't seen much of his brother David over the last few months. The Earl of Buchan was lodging in London, not far from his sisters, but Tom had little time for the religious fervour his eldest brother had displayed since his father's death; he had enough of that at the breakfast table in Lady Huntingdon's house now she was back in residence. Today, however, he made a point of catching David before he was out of the house in the morning.

'I have to buy myself out of the army.' Tom made no bones about why he had come. 'There must be some more money due to me from Papa's estate.'

'What on earth makes you think that?' They were in the morning room and David wandered over to the sideboard to pour himself some coffee. He had sent the servants away after one look at the agitated expression on his youngest brother's face. 'You and Harry seem to think I have become the family's bank.'

That gave Tom pause for thought. Harry was in Edinburgh, working as a lawyer, and a very successful one, by all accounts. Why had he been soliciting money from his brother?

'What does he need it for?' As soon as the distracting thought had occurred to Tom the words were out there, hanging in the silence.

David raised an eyebrow. 'I don't think that need concern you. But, for that matter, what do you need it for so urgently? You have a commission—'

'Which I paid for myself with every penny of my savings from four years' sweat in the navy!'

'That was well done and a good investment. You are showing signs of acumen, Tom, but I don't want to destroy that by handing you money on a plate. As I told Harry, far better you work for your money and then you will appreciate it the more.' David carried his coffee over to the table and sat down in the ornate chair at its head. Briefly Tom wondered whose house this was. Some rich Methodist friend, no doubt. David could never afford the rent even if he could have brought himself to part with the money. He scowled and turned away to pour himself some coffee before sitting down at the far end of the table from his brother. 'There is a reason I need to buy myself out,' he said. 'I want to get married and we are being posted overseas. I could not bear to be parted from her for even a moment, never mind for months.'

If he hoped such an appeal would soften David's heart he was disappointed. His brother sat up and studied his face. 'Who is this lucky lady?' He barely kept his sarcasm out of his voice.

'Her name is Frances Moore. She is the daughter of the Member of Parliament for Great Marlow.'

'And her father approves of the match?'

Tom looked down at his hands, clasped on the table. 'I haven't asked him yet.'

'I see. And this young lady is the possessor of a considerable fortune I take it?'

Tom looked startled. He remembered now the remarks Mrs Moore had made to him. It had not occurred to him that his brother would be as interested in the couple's potential income as her mother was. The matter of money was, it appeared, a matter of great importance when marriage was being discussed. 'I've no idea.'

'Then I suggest you make it your business to find out. If she's an heiress, you needn't worry.'

David made it clear the topic was closed, but as his brother stood up and bade him farewell, he put down his coffee cup and added: 'One thing, Tom. Don't forget that you're not yet twenty-one. As a minor, you cannot get married without my permission as head of the family.'

Tom stopped in his tracks. 'But you would give it if Frances turned out to be an heiress?'

David folded his arms as he considered the matter, his head on one side. 'That would depend. If she were that much of an heiress I might decide to marry her myself.'

His brother's laughter followed him down the front steps and along the street.

Thomas

My senses were overwhelmed by that, my first experience of love, and perhaps also by the noise and lights and crowds of London. I enjoyed walking the smart streets, looking in the shops and dreaming of the gifts I would buy for Fanny when I had the money – jewellery and silks and pretty ornaments – and for myself I enjoyed trawling the shops of Little Britain, that area between Smithfield and Aldersgate, where the booksellers and stationers and printers abounded, and of course I enjoyed the coffee houses where I found friends and gossip and talk of politics and of war. The latter interested me particularly, given that I was in the army and I didn't fancy getting killed – though, like most young men my age, it didn't occur to me that this was a real possibility.

It was an exciting time but, even though overwhelmed with thoughts of love, I was finally realising that all was not well with my planned courtship. David's reaction had stunned me. He had refused me any kind of financial help and that last quip had shot home with unpleasant accuracy. I had always admired my eldest brother, but also been nervous of him. He was eight years my senior and had treated me with alternate absent-minded fondness as though I were some small pet animal, and with contempt. And yet I fawned on him, I wrote him endless letters, I craved his approval. And I was, I now realised, since the death of our father, totally in his power. Until I came of age I was his to command.

Luckily a healthy sense of rebellion began to rise in me within seconds of walking out of his door and I upbraided myself for not demanding whatever payment had been made to him by the St James's Chronicle *in which he had, without my permission, published my letter describing the lightning strike four years before. The very memory of it made my arm burn and I found myself rubbing the scar as I made my way down the street. I had known nothing of the article until Anne had shown it to me. She had clipped it from the paper and proudly stored it in her desk. My next thought, thoroughly rebellious in perfect harmony with the age, was that I was not prepared to wait on his pleasure for permission to marry. Somehow I would sidestep that technicality. The permission of Frances's father was a far more pressing problem. Her parents had shown no inclination whatsoever to accept my tentative approaches. I was a man without fortune. Compared to that, my aristocratic blood was of no importance; my lack of money was enough reason to slam the door in my face.*

By the time I reached the far corner of the street I had begun to work out a shocking and daring plan which filled me with excitement. The question was, would Frances agree to it.

34

Finlay's agent Max had given them the address. 'I couldn't tell you without asking him first,' he told Finlay, 'but he's happy to see you.'

Leaving the Old Mill House to the tender care of Fin's cleaning lady for the morning, they left early for the hour's drive south into the lowland hills. Making their way up a long winding drive, they parked and they sat staring at the building in front of them. 'It's a bloody castle!' Finlay said. They looked at each other and smiled.

'Come on.' Ruth climbed out first. The garden appeared to be no more than an area of roughly mown grass holding back the surrounding woods and the only car in sight was an ancient mud-splashed four-by-four. The house was turreted, yes, and tall; it seemed to have about five storeys but it was comparatively small. A flight of steps led up to the front door which opened as they headed towards it. A man appeared to greet them. He was dressed in shabby jeans with a checked shirt beneath a lovat green sweater and two springer spaniels raced past him to meet them. He appeared at first glance to be between forty and fifty years old, of wiry build and looked anything but the stereotype of a mystic.

'No shawls,' Finlay whispered out of the corner of his mouth. Ruth frowned at him but she knew what he meant. The man looked more like a TV gardening expert than a psychic. She went up the steps first and held out her hand. 'Mr Douglas?'

'Mal, please.' He was of middle height with springy grey hair and hazel eyes. Shaking hands with them both he led the way inside. A small vestibule, littered with boots and walking sticks, led to a spiral stone staircase up which they followed him, the dogs scampering ahead.

'What a wonderful building!' Ruth exclaimed as they arrived in the first-floor sitting room. The windows were narrow but they looked out on all four sides of a room that was lined with books. A fire burned in the huge fireplace and the whole place smelled of apple smoke.

'Please, make yourselves at home.' Malcolm Douglas took the low chair by the fire for himself and the two dogs immediately lay down at his feet. 'This is what they call a tower house. Fifteenth century. It belonged to my late mother's family. Now,' he leaned forward, 'I gather from Max that you have need of spiritual disinfection.'

For a moment neither Ruth nor Finlay spoke.

Malcolm laughed. 'Sorry! Too abrupt. It's one of my faults. Shall I start by telling you a bit about myself?' He looked from one to the other and took their continued silence as acquiescence. 'I was for years pretty much self-taught at this stuff. From my childhood I had a certain facility which had always fascinated me and I read up on it. It became a hobby and then an obsession. Then I decided I wanted to meet other people who could talk about the same things and I began to go on courses. All helpful and interesting, but I was put off by the money side of things. If people need to earn a living that's fair enough, but it's very easy to start to improvise, and then the temptation is to form groups which have a tendency to become cultish. I didn't like that side of it so I moved on, kept quiet and only confided in the occasional friend. Max is one of those. He has been my agent for quite a few years now – in my other life, as he probably told you, I'm an author. As for my interest in spiritual matters, he thinks I'm completely dotty, but he keeps me in mind if ever he hears of people who have a house that needs a bit of attention. I don't charge. I don't give guarantees. I come over, I look round, do a bit of feely stuff and perhaps chat to the intruder. That generally does the trick. Oh, and I ask people to keep my involvement confidential.' He felt in his pocket, extricated a biscuit, broke it in half and gave a piece to each of the dogs. 'Questions?'

'What are the dogs' names?' Ruth knew that wasn't what he meant.

'Castor and Pollux. The heavenly twins. Cas and Pol to their friends. But, I really meant questions about the way I go about things. Supposing you tell me the nature of the problem.' Malcolm sat back and crossed his legs comfortably. He was younger than she had first thought. Early forties, perhaps, rather than fifties. A log shifted in the fireplace sending up a shower of sparks.

Ruth glanced at Finlay. 'It's a long story,' she said. 'But if you don't mind, I'll start right at the beginning.'

Malcolm leaned forward, his elbows on his knees, concentrating on Ruth as she told her tale, moving only once to throw another log onto the embers as the fire burned low. When at last she fell silent he thought for a few moments longer then he looked up. 'Fascinating,' he said.

Both dogs sat up and looked at him expectantly. He raised his hand and they lay down again, resigned. 'I have heard of your friend Harriet. She is a competent biographer. Her involvement adds a certain piquancy to this whole scenario.' He looked gleefully boyish. 'But for now we'll concentrate on you. If I have understood you correctly, there are many layers to this problem as well as many generations. You want to know if your Thomas Erskine is "real".' He emphasised the last word. 'And, you want to be rid of this lustful uninvited drop-in. At the same time, you want to assure me that you don't believe in any of it.'

Ruth looked down, abashed. 'That's about it.'

He smiled again. 'An interesting conundrum. Do you think they might be connected in some way, Thomas and the drop-in?'

She hesitated long enough for him to nod. 'I sense you do. Fascinating. Getting rid of a random passer-by should be relatively easy, but if he's involved with the story of your ancestors he may be harder to dislodge.'

Ruth grimaced. 'And I gather garlic was never going to work?' Her tone was self-mocking.

'On the contrary, it's a lot better than nothing. Fortune's book is a good primer for this sort of enterprise.' Malcolm was thoughtful. 'I'm fascinated by the way this all fits together. What an extraordinary tale.'

'So, will you come to the Old Mill House?' It was the first time Finlay had spoken.

'Try and stop me!' Malcolm said gravely. 'I sense – and yes, I do mean that as a technical term – that there are huge complications in this story. When can I come?'

'Now? This afternoon? Tomorrow?' Ruth glanced at Finlay.

'Why not tomorrow?' Finlay put in. 'I am out all day and that will give you plenty of time on your own. I take it you don't need me there?' He gave Malcolm a self-deprecating smile, his head on one side.

Malcolm narrowed his eyes, catlike. 'No, Mr Macdermott, I don't need you. Your aura is as clean as a whistle, and your thoughts are pure as the driven snow.'

Finlay let out a guffaw of laughter. 'I'll take that as a compliment.'

'I'll arrive about ten tomorrow morning.' Malcolm turned back to Ruth. 'Don't worry about it. Don't expect claps of thunder and flashes of lightning. In fact, don't expect too much. We may achieve nothing at first. This will be an exploratory visit, nothing more. The only thing I can promise you is that you have found someone to confide in.'

'I'm sorry, Mr Erskine, she's not coming.' It was Abi, at last. He had been waiting for hours, or so it seemed. He felt his spirits plummet. 'Why?'

Abi looked away uncomfortably as though seeking inspiration from the trees. 'She gave me a note, sir.' She held it out to him. 'Mrs Moore is going down to Marlow today, and she is taking the girls with her, sir. I'm sorry.'

And she was gone, running away from him towards the gates of the square.

I'm so sorry, Tom. Mama won't tell me what is wrong but she has received a letter about you. Whoever wrote it seems to have known we've been meeting. Besides that, it told her something about your time in the West Indies which made her very angry. I have been forbidden to see you ever again, my dearest. F

It had been scribbled in haste and badly folded. He could almost feel her despair and anger coming off the paper. He ran a few steps after Abi but she was long gone. David? Would David do anything so unkind as to write to her parents? Surely not.

It was then he saw him, standing watching in full view some fifty yards away. It was Andrew Farquhar. Smartly dressed, his hands resting lightly on his cane, his hair combed and tied into a neat queue under his hat, he was smiling, not the smile of a friend, but a smile of utter triumph. He wanted to be recognised. When he saw Thomas had seen him he gave a small malicious bow and turned away.

Thomas stood utterly still. Why hadn't he guessed? His suspicions that someone had been watching him had been correct. How could he have been so careless and so stupid as not to pay attention to his instincts? He could guess what Andrew had done. He had followed Frances home. He had found out who she was and he had written to her parents.

So, what had he told the Moores?

Too dejected to think clearly he walked around the streets for hours, nursing his hurt and disappointment, wearing her miniature on a ribbon next to his heart. Then at last he began to formulate a plan. He had to speak to Frances. He had to know what the letter said. Whatever it was it could not be that bad. She already knew he had no money. She had said she didn't care. She had implied that she would be happy to be a soldier's wife. They must have forced her to write that note; they would have had to drag her away to the country. But he would follow. It would be easy to find Mr Moore's house in Marlow then somehow he would find a way to speak to her.

One of Lady Huntingdon's grooms procured a horse for him and he was on his way the next morning. It was good to be in the saddle again and out of the fug of the London streets. There was no hurry, he kept reminding himself. When he arrived he would have to make contact with Abi and arrange a safe meeting place. He doubted if Andrew would be following him but, even so, from time to time he found himself turning to survey the road behind him.

It was a strong horse, a rangy roan cob, and they made good time towards Marlow through the beauties of the Thames Valley. He put himself and the horse up in the Bell, a coaching inn in a village only a couple of miles or so from Marlow, and the first person he asked knew exactly where their MP lived.

The Moores' house was well cared for and there was smoke coming from the chimneys. Servants appeared from time to time but there was no sign of Abi or any of the ladies. Worried, he waylaid the boy he had seen several times coming and going on errands to the town and was pleased to find him quite prepared to deliver a covert letter to Abi for sixpence.

Excited at the thought of a secret assignation, she was quite willing to continue her role as go-between. 'Miss Frances has been beside herself,' she informed him. 'She was so angry and upset when her mother told her we were coming back early, we all thought she would work herself into the megrims. Mrs Moore threatened to lock her in her room.'

'But she hasn't?' Thomas was horrified.

'No, of course not.' Abi seemed shocked. 'She threatens her with what will happen when Mr Moore joins them. He's remaining in London until the House rises.'

'Will you tell Frances I'm here. See if she can find a way to meet me. Please.' Thomas caught her hand. 'I'm lost without her.'

Abi was enchanted by the whole situation. 'I'll see she meets you. Leave it with me.'

It took two days. Thomas walked up and down the towpath

endlessly, wishing he had his paints with him, watching the birds and the river barges, relieved that he had the money from his army pay to put himself up in comfort at the inn until finally the message came.

He watched as Frances approached, his heart thudding frantically. She was dressed in a pale-blue day dress with a matching bonnet and holding a parasol to shield her face. Abi was walking a few demure steps behind her, carrying a basket, the perfect lady's maid.

'Abi must stay,' were her first words. She glanced over her shoulder anxiously. 'Mama has forbidden me to go out alone.'

'Of course Abi must stay.' He caught her hand. 'My darling, I know your parents received a letter about me. But what did it say?'

'Papa received the letter.' She looked down suddenly, embarrassed. 'He wouldn't tell me what was in it, but Mama did.' She took a deep breath and drew him a few yards along the path out of Abi's hearing. 'It told him you had a' – she glanced round unhappily – 'a disease.'

Thomas stared at her incredulously. This was beyond anything of which he could have imagined Andrew capable.

'No. That's a lie!' He tried to calm himself. 'Listen, my darling, I know who sent that letter. I saw him loitering near Charles Street. He was with me on the *Tartar*. He was my enemy then and seems to be my enemy still. I bore witness at a hearing on the ship, as a result of which he was flogged and demoted. Clearly, he hasn't forgiven me. He means to have his revenge by spoiling our happiness.'

'So you're not ill?'

'No, my darling, I'm not ill. I was, briefly, when we were based in Barbados. My lieutenant and I suspected someone had put some infected rags in my sea chest deliberately. We both guessed it was him but there was no proof. Lieutenant Murray took me ashore to see a doctor and I was completely cured. I swear, I would never put you in danger. That's an outrageous slur.'

To his horror, she shuddered. 'I don't know, Tom. Mama said it meant you would go mad and die.'

He stared at her, speechless with horror. 'No, no, no. No, my darling, darling Fanny. I am not mad or dying! I am fit as a flea and I love you. I want you to be my wife.'

'But you have no money.'

'Does that matter? Really matter? I have my army pay. You yourself said that you would like to be married to a soldier.'

She gave a coy smile. 'I did, didn't I.'

'And you must believe me. I am well and strong.' He drew her to him.

She threw herself into his arms. 'Yes, I believe you. You know I believe you.'

Their kiss was long and deep. A few yards away Abi, who had been studying a pair of ducks paddling up and down the river bank, turned and watched them with equal interest. They didn't notice.

When finally they drew apart he held her two hands and studied her face. 'Listen, my darling. I've had time to think what we should do. Everyone is trying to prevent us from marrying. My brother, the earl, has forbidden it, and as the head of the family I need his permission as long as I'm underage. You need your father's permission. We are completely hamstrung. Either we wait until I'm twenty-one, or . . . ' he hesitated. He had dreamed of this so long he was afraid to say the words out loud. 'We go to Gretna Green.'

She stared up at him, her eyes bright with excitement. 'We run away together?'

He nodded.

'And then we can be married in Scotland? Oh, Tom. Yes, please.' She sobered. 'But how will we manage it?'

'We'll need Abi's help. She must somehow contrive to get you out of the house at night so we'll have several hours' start. Your mother might guess where we're going, and she would have us pursued.'

'She would.' Frances was crestfallen. 'And she would send for Papa at once and he would call the Watch. She would not forgive this. We would only have the one chance.' She looked up at him very seriously. 'To my mother, Jane and Cassandra and I are investments. She told me so. I don't think my happiness is of any interest to her.'

'I'm sure that's not true.' He looked troubled.

'Oh, believe me it is.' She set her mouth in a straight line. 'Will you get into terrible trouble with your brother?'

'He obviously would prefer it if I married a lady of means, but I will be twenty-one soon; then he will have no say over my life. I believe I will be in more trouble marrying without my commanding officer's permission, but I will cross that bridge when we reach it. Once you are my wife they're not going to undo our marriage.'

'And the marriage will be a proper one?' Judging by the sparkle in her eye, it did not bother her much.

'It will be a proper marriage. Legal. Though not in church.' He frowned. That thought troubled him. But surely with all Anne's contacts they could find someone to bless their union.

His prospective bride seemed to have no such qualms. 'When shall we go? Today?'

'Tonight.'

To his relief, Abi was keen to help. 'But what will happen to me?' she asked at the last moment. 'Mrs Moore is bound to suspect me. I'll be sacked.'

'You will come to London, to my sister's house. Fanny will need a lady's maid. As soon as we are back from Scotland we will meet you there. I will give you a letter for Anne and another for Mr Phillips, Lady Huntingdon's butler, to give you lodgings until we return.'

His plan seemed simple. He would leave the inn, covering his trail, then double back and wait with the horse until Fanny arrived with Abi, and he would take his beloved up behind him. Casual enquiries in the taproom of the inn had given him easy instructions to follow as to the route. In High Wycombe he would hire a fast chaise to take them on the first stage of the journey towards Stokenchurch and on towards Oxford. Speed would be everything.

The question eating away at the back of his mind was, when it came to it, would Fanny have the courage to go with him?

35

Ruth had replayed her conversation with Malcolm Douglas in her head a dozen times and the more she thought about him, the angrier she became. 'He was so patronising!' she burst out when Finlay asked her what she thought of him. 'Did you hear what he said about Harriet? "Competent!" And "adds a certain piquancy". How dare he!'

'It was an odd thing to say, I agree. Did you get the impression he knows her?' Before she could answer, Finlay went on, 'I have looked him up on Google. I'd understood from Max he was some sort of low-key psychic, but when he said he was an author as well I thought it would be worth finding out if he was there.'

'And?'

'And he's a historian. He's written four hefty tomes on the Georgian period. Bestsellers. He's a serious player.'

'No wonder he's keen to downplay his psychic powers,' she retorted tartly. 'Oh God! The Georgian period, you said? Thomas's period? Why didn't he say? The name must have meant something to him.'

'He did look quite keen, Ruthie.'

'I thought that was because of the ghostly conundrum, not because he wanted to sign up Thomas for an interview.' She was pacing the floor. 'Shall we put him off? I don't think I can cope with him, and I doubt very much that he'll be any help.'

Half an hour later she was on the phone to Harriet.

'So, you have heard of him?'

'I've just told you. Naturally I've heard of him. He's a brilliant biographer.'

'Implying that you aren't?' Ruth was feeling defensive.

'I'm not in his league, no,' Harriet confirmed coldly. 'Why do you want to know about him?'

'Fin and I met him this morning.' Ruth wondered if it had been a good idea to mention him but it was too late. 'Do you know him?'

'We've met.'

'And?'

'And nothing. How did you hear about him?'

'We were given his name by Fin's agent. He's an expert on psychic phenomena.'

Silence.

Ruth waited, then she heard the snort of laughter. 'You're joking!'

'No. It's an interest of his.'

'Then it isn't the same man.'

'I think it is. Fin looked him up on Google and there's a picture of him.'

The low whistle down the phone made her smile. 'My God! He must keep very quiet about that particular interest. People would think he was bonkers. In fact, it would blow his street cred clean out of the window if that was generally known.'

'So please keep it to yourself!'

'I shall have to see about that.' Harriet was crowing. 'So, how did he handle himself as a psychic?'

'Cautiously. He wants to come and see the house. I was scared by what's been happening, Hattie, you know I was. I've got to talk to someone about it.'

'What was he like?'

'Nice enough.'

'*Nice*?' Harriet echoed derisively.

'Yes.'

When she finished the call, Ruth realised she would have to go through with the meeting if only to satisfy Harriet's curiosity.

When Malcolm arrived the next morning, Ruth gave him a tour of the house, visiting every room in turn. He had driven up in the old Defender, minus the dogs. 'They get too excited, ghost hunting,' he said with a smile in response to Ruth's enquiry. 'Don't worry, they stay quite happily with my neighbour if I'm out for any length of time.'

'It's not the actual house that's the problem, is it?' Ruth felt tense and uncomfortable as they finished the tour in the sitting room.

'I would say not, no.' Malcolm went to stand in front of the wood burner. Ruth had lit the fire as an afterthought before he arrived, and it had not yet warmed up. The flames seemed unusually yellow and unreal.

She had finally looked Malcolm up herself, the night before, and found he was indeed a respected academic. Looking at the list of titles credited to his authorship, all given five-star ratings by reviewers, she felt embarrassed at not having recognised his name. There was no mention anywhere of his interest in the supernatural.

Malcolm headed towards the door. 'Let's go to the kitchen. Perhaps now is the time for that coffee you offered me when I arrived.'

As they sat opposite one another at the kitchen table the sun appeared briefly and shone across the floor, showing up the irregularities in the flagstones. The room was bright and warm. 'Our walk round the house was revealing.' Malcolm sipped his coffee. 'It's very clean. In my sense of the word. Strangely so, for an old building. I suspect it has something to do with being so near the river; there may be underground springs beneath the building which would keep it fresh, and it may have been spring-cleaned – again, in my sense of the word – by someone in the past. You say there is a little girl ghost here, but I have no sense of her.'

'I think Finlay said she was in the garden.'

'We'll go out there later and see. Right now, I'm more

interested in you.' He was holding his mug in both hands, staring down into it. 'I'm so sorry, Ruth, I can see you're nervous. I can feel you warding me off and I don't blame you. First let me put your mind at rest. I am not going to go all bell, book and candle on you. If you want that, you need a priest. And I am not going to produce crystals and smudge sticks and bells. But we do have one prop to discuss, so let's talk about the garlic. I had a quick glance through Dion Fortune's book again last night. It's a long time since I read it.' Having spotted it lying on the worktop, he went to bring it over to the table. 'Did you notice the subtitle? *A Study in Occult Pathology and Criminality*? It gives one a strong clue as to how seriously she took this stuff. You could do a lot worse than study this book. She suggests garlic and onions because of their ability to absorb what she calls noxious emanations. People also use them, you know, when someone has a bad cold. They work with physical as well as psychic gunk. But in the same section of the book she says something very telling. I can quote it verbatim. I have used it over the years and I had forgotten where I got the phrase from. "What the imagination has made, the imagination can unmake." She applies that to thought forms, things and beings that we or others have imagined so strongly that they have taken on an actual reality, however tenuous.'

'How odd. Hattie remembered that quote too.' Ruth gave a tentative smile. 'So you think Thomas is a thought form?'

'Dion certainly didn't if she called him an ascended master. I will have to look all that up. For her he was a different league of being, but for you . . . ' He left the words hanging and took another sip from his mug, giving Ruth a moment to absorb the suggestion.

'I don't think I invented him, if that's what you mean.' Somewhat to her own surprise, her words came out as thoughtful rather than indignant. 'And others have seen him. My father seems to have talked to him. His neighbour in Morningside heard them chatting to each other.'

'His thought form, fuelled by guilt?'

Ruth scowled. 'I suppose it's possible. I admit I imagined Thomas quite deliberately, sitting on the edge of the table through

227

there, talking to me,' she glanced towards the dining room. 'At least, I think I did. I must have imagined him,' she repeated desperately. 'I'd been reading so much about him and there was so much I wanted to ask him.' She looked up at Malcolm. 'I don't suppose you ever do that when you are writing?'

'We are not talking about me,' he replied firmly. 'So, how did he seem, your thought form? Friendly? Helpful? Resentful, trying to keep secrets back?'

'Friendly. Reassuring. Slightly rueful about his past exploits.'

'And did he refer to your unpleasant ghostly visitor?'

'No.'

'I sense there is a connection.'

Ruth frowned. 'I didn't pick up on it if there is. I assumed that it, he, the nasty ghost, was something in the house.' She reached for her mug and then put it down again untouched. 'So, my version of Thomas is not real. You're saying I invented him so it's up to me to disinvent him.' She was astonished how disappointed she felt.

Malcolm smiled. He wondered if Ruth knew how transparent her face was. It can't have been a help in her job as a teacher. 'I'm saying nothing. I'm making suggestions at this stage and explaining some of the possible phenomena that might be at work here. It may be that Thomas is as real as you and I.'

'Really real?'

'It's possible. To digress for a moment and fill in some background information: you told me your father had no faith and instilled that lack of belief in you. So, you would describe yourself as an atheist?'

'I suppose I would, yes.'

'As in, you don't believe in God, but you can accept the other stuff? Spirits and angels and, yes, ghosts?'

'Not angels!'

'OK, so angels belong in the God department. But the rest?'

'I don't know. That's the problem. If I did, perhaps I wouldn't need you. Perhaps I should more honestly say I'm an agnostic, but that would really be a cop out, wouldn't it.' She tried to soften the words with an apologetic smile.

Malcolm laughed. 'Fair enough. The situation means, though,

that you've been left without a basic set of tools to work with. It's not that you don't know the stuff – prayers, blessings, charms, signs against the evil eye – it's that you cannot bring yourself to use them. And you have nothing to replace them with. I suspect even the act of strewing garlic round the house embarrassed the rational, intelligent, educated, liberal, twenty-first-century woman that you are. You could not under any circumstances admit the possible efficacy of their use. Nature spirits, how do you rate them?'

She felt her resentment flare again at his assessment of her, accurate though it was. 'Fairy tales,' she snapped.

'But as a student of English literature you have an interest in the origin of fairy tales?'

'Of course.' She was impatient now. 'They contain legend, history, myth and morality lessons, we all know that, but they're not real. The ogre in the castle is metaphor; whatever is lurking under the bridge is human threat, not a dryad or a troll; paedophiles not wicked gnomes.'

'Do you cross your fingers when you tell a lie?' Malcolm sprung the question on her.

Ruth looked shocked, then in spite of herself she smiled. 'Not any more.'

'Do you know the words of the Lord's Prayer?'

'I'm old enough to have been taught that at school. Besides, my grandfather was a vicar. Daddy might have dissed everything his father-in-law believed in, but he couldn't quite wipe my memory banks. Why are you asking me all this?'

'I am trying to get an idea of what we're working with. You are, in my opinion, a very conflicted woman.' He raised his hands in defence as Ruth opened her mouth to object. 'You don't need me to address your worries and hauntings and fears, you are completely capable of doing it yourself, but you have closed down deliberately and slammed the door on everything that you consider – what word would your father have used? – nonsense? Twaddle? Tosh? I'm sorry to say this, but you are intelligent and educated. That much you will concede?' He did not wait for Ruth to acknowledge the words, rightly sensing her rising fury and indignation. He leaned forward and shook his finger in her face.

'There is no point in resenting everything I say. If you want my help, you'll have to put up with my vocabulary. We don't have time to be subtle here. I'm not trying to sneak superstitious garbage past you. Your knowledge of the world is very specific, self-censored and academically based, so you have a deep-seated resistance to much that's around you. When it comes to intuition, observation, instinct, you've switched off, or been switched off. You tell me you escaped from home, but you took all your father's angst with you. I am not interested in where he got it from, probably his own father before him, but *you* have to wake up and acknowledge that there is more in heaven and earth than are dreamt of in your narrow philosophy.'

Ruth stared at him, stunned at his sudden passion. 'You've been talking to Finlay,' she said at last.

'I'd never met Finlay before yesterday.'

'You have no right to say all this about me.' She felt confused and angry.

'OK. I'm sorry. May I remind you, you came to me for my help.' Malcolm was trying to suppress his frustration. He stood up. 'I can't help you at the moment because there's nothing here. Your unpleasant visitor seems to have left no traces in the house that I can pick up on. It's you and your friend Harriet he attacked and for the time being he's gone. I will go too now and give you time to think. If you want to contact me again, you know where I am.'

'But aren't you going to do anything?' She wanted to kick herself for sounding so pathetic.

'Not without your cooperation. Consider what I've said carefully, Ruth, please. You are a woman of great power. Potentially, that is. I felt it yesterday and I feel it today, but it's all banked up like a reservoir behind a dam. I know you resent me. For that I'm sorry. I have obviously antagonised you and that is my fault. But talk to your father. He is hanging around. He will tell you he was wrong. He knows it now. Just be careful. There is so much energy swirling round you. I think you need me and I will be there if you call, but it must be your unqualified decision. And you can safely call on your however-many greats grandfather. He's there for you too. Listen to him.'

Thomas

I had tried to reach Ruth and I thought I had succeeded but she did not truly believe in my existence. To her I was some fictional figure, drawn from the past. She did not feel the beat of our blood, the kinship that linked us. She is interested only in my story, so it is with my story that I must try and reach her.

Frances and Abi were late arriving at our rendezvous and I had died a thousand deaths, imagining that they would not come. But there they were, two small shadowy figures in the darkness, nervously creeping up the lane towards me. We fixed Frances's small bag to my saddle and she came up behind me on the roan. There was no time for speech. We were all frightened and excited. She bade farewell to Abi and I, in my gratitude, did the same. I don't think either of us looked back.

It took us several days to cover the three hundred or so miles to Gretna in post-chaise, curricle and even, once or twice, the common stage, always looking behind, always afraid. It was there that we were married over the anvil. Under the laws of Scotland we were man and wife.

We spent our wedding night in a roadside inn and then headed up the post roads towards Edinburgh, where I presented my new wife to Mama, who, pragmatic and intelligent as ever, welcomed her with open arms. We stayed with Harry, who was also welcoming, slapping me on

231

the back and rumpling my hair as though I were still a boy of ten. My cheery, boyish brother had gained a certain gravitas; he been made a member of the Faculty of Advocates two years before, and his house in Shoemakers Close on the Canongate, though a bachelor abode, was nevertheless warm and welcoming and it was full of interesting conversation in which my Fanny took a spirited part. I was beginning to find that my beguiling and attractive wife had a brain as good as my mother's, and though she had not had the benefit of a deep education she was well read and intelligent and held her own in any conversation.

It was with great reluctance that we headed back to London. We took our time, happy and in love. It was only as we drew nearer that another emotion began to intrude: trepidation at the nest of wasps we knew we would encounter when we arrived.

My sister Anne had returned home from her busy tour of rural parishes in order to confront us and Fanny was overjoyed to find Abi there waiting for her as well. Within hours we knew that Mr Moore had indeed sent the Watch after us when he realised his daughter had flown, but hours too late to catch us. Beyond that he had made no efforts to follow us. He had summoned poor Abi and dragged the truth out of her, informing her that it was her fault he no longer recognised his youngest daughter before sending her off without references. Fanny's mother had been distraught and angrier than her father, if Abi's opinion was to be believed. My darling proved to be made of strong stuff. She sighed resignedly as she heard the story, but she did not cry.

From my commanding officer I faced a stern dressing down but was granted extended leave; we weathered Anne's stern reprimands, and laughed off the fact that some of the cheaper gossip sheets had obtained the story of our elopement, naming me only as the Earl of Buchan's brother, my identity subsumed in his. The Earl of Buchan himself did not deign to see me, only sending a message that I need never ask for help from him again. As he had not helped me in the first place that did not weigh for much with us. Far more alarming was the sight of Andrew Farquhar, lounging in the street outside the house, a supercilious smile on his face as I caught sight of him from our bedroom window. By the time I had the front door opened and hurtled down the steps, footman in tow, to confront him, he had gone.

The sight of him rattled me. I checked my writing case and made sure the obeah woman's fetish was still there, though I did not show it to Fanny. I confided my fears about Farquhar to Anne. It appeared that she had anyway been thinking hard of where Fanny and I should go. A publicly acknowledged reprobate like me could not be allowed to remain under Lady Huntingdon's roof. I was informed that the perfect solution had been found. We would for the time being go to our sister, Isabella, who three months before had married a successful barrister by the name of William Hamilton. She had, it appeared, generously offered us a home for as long as we needed it. And so we decamped to their house in Tunbridge Wells.

Our destination was kept secret from Lady Huntingdon's household, lest Farquhar find out where we had gone. The man worried me. How had he the time to spend stalking us through the streets of London? It was as if we had become an obsession, and I feared for Frances's safety, especially as by now she was expecting our first baby.

Little Frances was born in Tunbridge Wells early in 1771 and baptised later in the church of St Mary in Marylebone. Isabella, who I had always found a little distant as I grew up, being like Anne so much older than me, now proved a warm and generous friend. She had no children of her own yet and adored little Frances, to whom she stood godmother.

Fanny and I were establishing a firm and fond friendship with her and William, and felt safe at last with them in Kent when Farquhar reappeared on the scene and this time his threats were far more real and more sinister; this time he was on our doorstep and he was ready to strike.

36

To Timothy's joy and relief, April had announced this morning that she would be busy all day. It meant he could go back to Cramond with no fear of her demanding to go with him.

Cautiously he looked left and right and pulled the French window open a crack. He couldn't believe his luck. Ruth hadn't locked it before she went out. He had watched from the bushes as she drove away from the house, half disappointed to see her go, half excited that it meant he could explore without the fear of being seen. There were no other cars there. The place was empty.

Slipping into the dining room out of the rain and kicking off his wet shoes by the door, he went over to the table. It was still strewn with books but the laptop had gone. He reached down to flip open a notebook. It was full of Ruth's untidy writing, clusters of words, scribbled numbers, looping lines joining paragraph to paragraph across pages. He didn't try to read it but he was tempted for a moment to take it away – it looked as if a lot of hard work had gone into it and it was amusing to think of her anger and frustration when she found it was missing. But he didn't want her to know he had been here. Not yet. He looked up with a shiver. The room was ice cold. His rain-soaked jacket was, he realised, dripping all over the carpet.

He tiptoed to the door and opened it. The house was shadowy. It spooked him slightly, as did the solemn ticking of the clock in the hall. If they had brought the silver and stuff into the house, where would they have put it? Somewhere out of the way probably. A spare room maybe?

He climbed the stairs on tiptoe, holding his breath in case they creaked, but there was no sound. On the landing there were four doors, all of them open. He crept towards the first. It was obviously Finlay's bedroom. He looked round, automatically noting the little silver dishes and the ornaments on the chest of drawers, the nice pictures, but touching nothing. There were bookshelves and matching curtains and bedcover. Posh. And there was a private bathroom which smelt of expensive soap. The next room was clearly where Ruth was sleeping. So, they weren't an item, then. He stood in the doorway, taking it all in. It was a pretty room, with flowery curtains, and a cream bedspread. He walked over to the bed and pulled the covers back. He could smell the scent she always wore; it had a musky edge, flowery and something else, something deeper that made him want to sniff and sniff again. He leaned forward and smelt the pillow, then pulling back the duvet lowered his face to the sheet where she must lie, night after night, warm and safe, thinking she had got rid of him for good. He could smell her there. It turned him on.

It was several minutes before he pulled away and carefully remade the bed. He went over to the dressing table and pulled out a drawer. There were some T-shirts in there and a couple of bras and some pants. He pulled them out. Pretty, lacy underwear. Not particularly sexy, but just handling them made him feel powerful. He shoved a pair of her knickers into his pocket and carefully replaced the rest. She too had a small bathroom off the bedroom. He looked at her toothbrush and cosmetics without interest and turned away. The next room was another spare room, then there was a large bathroom and another flight of stairs. Up in the attics were three more bedrooms, all furnished simply, all attractive but cold. The cupboards up there were empty. There was no sign of what he was looking for anywhere. Turning, he ran back down to the ground floor.

He walked across the landing and looked into the living room.

The wood burner was out, a slight smell of wood smoke in the air and that room too was very cold. He turned away with a shiver and made his way towards the kitchen.

Silently pushing open the door he found that Ruth had left a light on. This room was cheerful and bright. April would like it. He had never seen Finlay's TV show and he didn't know where it was set, but this place would be perfect. It smelt faintly of cooking, garlic and something he couldn't quite identify. It was tidy, but not too tidy, full of shiny gadgets and wooden bowls, and yes, on the windowsill there were some terracotta-potted plants. He didn't know if they were herbs. April would have known. He paused, wondering if he would bring her here. She would adore it. He could picture her wandering round the kitchen and for a moment he visualised the wistful longing in his sister's eyes. It made him uncomfortable even thinking about it.

He turned sharply out of the room. There was one more door off the hall and he headed for it and pushed it open. Finlay was sitting at the desk, the telephone to his ear. For one brief second neither man moved as they stared at each other in mutual astonishment.

Finlay reacted first. 'Oi!' he shouted. 'What the hell are you doing here!'

But already Timothy had fled, back along the hall and through the dining room, grabbing his shoes, out of the French window and into the rain in his socks. By the time Finlay had got to the open door and peered out after him, he had disappeared.

Timothy's heart was still palpitating under his ribs, and he was feeling sick as he let himself back indoors. Thank God April wasn't there! He had been stupid. Careless. Why hadn't he realised that Finlay would be there? Why hadn't the Daimler been outside the house? He sat down shivering, still in his wet jacket, his hands shoved deep into his pockets. Finlay had recognised him. And he had called the police straight away. The patrol car had passed Timothy, light flashing, as he headed along Whitehouse Road. Most people would have had to wait hours but Finlay was a rich celebrity so they had shifted their fat arses and moved. He never doubted that police car was for him. Shit! Shit! Shit! April would kill him. If she knew.

But she needn't know. If he didn't tell her, how would she find out? Slowly his breathing returned to normal. One thing was certain. He could never risk going there again.

'I thought we had done with him!' Finlay was still pacing up and down furiously when Ruth returned from the shops. 'I cannot believe it! The man was brazenly wandering round the house.'

'Which means he knows where I am. Surely the police can arrest him now?' When she heard what had happened, Ruth had run upstairs to her bedroom, terrified he might have been in there, taken something. There was no sign of him that she could see and her laptop was lying untouched where she had left it, but even so his escapade made her feel uncomfortable and, somehow, soiled. And she was the one who had left the French window unlocked.

'It's only a matter of time before he's picked up.' Fin led the way into the kitchen. 'Don't worry, Ruthie. It's all going to be OK. So, tell me. Have you spoken to Malcolm again?'

'Sorry. My nerve failed.'

He swung round and stared at her. 'Do I gather you have given up on him?' He plonked a crystal glass in front of her and poured a hefty dose of whisky into it.

She acknowledged his question with a weary smile. 'I'm a wimp, I know. I thought about it after he had gone and all last night. And I do need the conversation to continue. But he made me feel like an ignorant fifth former.'

'And as a teacher you know all about ignorant fifth formers.'

'Indeed I do.' She sipped from the glass, recoiled and went over to the sink to add some water from the tap. Finlay looked at her aghast but said nothing.

'I have to find a way to lever open my closed mind, I realise that. Oh, Fin, I don't know what's wrong with me. I love poetry, I love art. I believe in the beauty and magic I see depicted there but for me it isn't real. It isn't something I can touch. It is a delightful but foolish construct.' She paused then went on. 'I want to talk about it with Thomas, but if I invented him it wouldn't be a valid conversation.'

'Excuse me, love. Is that what Malcolm actually said?' Finlay heaved himself up onto the stool opposite her and leaned forward, his glass balanced between his fingertips. 'If he did, he's no use to us at all.' He thought for a moment. 'But even if you had invented Thomas, then it would be like talking to your subconscious, wouldn't it? Which is probably a hell of a lot wiser than your conscious right now!'

He let the remark sink in as she sipped her whisky. 'Do you think Timothy will come back?' she said suddenly.

'God knows! Wretched man. Not if the police catch up with him. But for goodness' sake keep the dining room doors locked in future.'

'He scares me and he shouldn't. He is a weedy, nasty, small-time crook, but there's something about his persistence I don't like. What does he gain by poking around here?'

'I told the police he'd been stalking you.' Finlay began to unpack the shopping bags and laid out their lunch. Bread, cheese, salad.

Ruth shuddered. 'You don't think he's plotting some awful revenge?'

'You mean plotting to burn the house down after being thwarted in his scummy little plans? I doubt it, but I think he might have a bit of an obsession with you!'

'After lunch I'm going to move all my writing stuff upstairs to my bedroom. You don't mind, do you? I've had the feeling that someone has been looking through the window at me more than once, and I don't think I'd feel safe working in there any more.'

They carried a table into the bedroom, large enough for her laptop and notebook, and they stacked her books on the floor. Ruth looked round in despair. 'Supposing Thomas doesn't come to me up here?'

'Because it's your bedroom?' Finlay put a small vase of flowers on the dressing table as a finishing gesture.

'Silly, isn't it.'

'But if he's a construct of your mind, why would it make any difference?'

'It wouldn't, unless it's my own inhibitions.'

'You can always move down again. We can have blinds put up.'

He left her with a cup of Earl Grey tea and a dark chocolate ginger biscuit.

She stood looking round the room for several moments. There was no sign that Timothy had been in here, or anywhere upstairs for that matter, but even so, the thought made her skin crawl. She had to try and forget him. Think about Thomas instead. She went over to the velvet-covered Victorian nursing chair in the corner and pulled it up near the desk. 'There. That's for you. If you could sit there when we talk. Please.' She was addressing the construct.

She laughed to herself, hoping Finlay hadn't heard.

'Where's Fanny?' Thomas had just come in. He had shrugged off his greatcoat and made his way to the drawing room where little Frances was lying kicking in her cradle while Isabella crooned over her.

'She and Abi went to buy some dress material.' Isabella looked up. 'This child is adorable, Tom. Look how she smiles at you.'

Thomas reached down to give his daughter his finger. She grabbed it with a small gurgle of delight. 'It's getting dark. Surely they should be back by now.'

Isabella glanced towards the windows. 'I was so preoccupied with my goddaughter I hadn't noticed.' She went over to the table and rang the bell. 'Susan, has Mrs Erskine arrived back yet, d'you know?'

'No, ma'am. They've been a long time.' The maid went over to the windows and began to draw the curtains. 'Shall I bring tea, ma'am?'

'Yes, please, Susan. And put another log on the fire, there's a dear.' Isabella glanced at her brother. 'They weren't going far. I don't understand what could have delayed them.'

Thomas stood back from the crib. 'I'll go and meet them. I'm sure there must be a good reason. Perhaps they met someone they knew in the Pantiles?' He couldn't hide his anxiety.

Snatching up his coat, he ran down the steps and out along the street, straining his eyes through the dusk in an effort to spot the two figures on the road ahead of him. There were still a lot of people about but no sign of Fanny. He could feel panic rising as he reached the corner. They hadn't planned to go far. Why would they delay?

And then there was Abi, running towards him. She caught at his sleeve and pulled him after her. 'Here. Round the corner. We were hiding!' There were tears running down her cheeks.

Behind her, Fanny emerged from the shadows and threw herself into his arms. 'Tom, thank God you came! I didn't know what to do. Has he gone?'

'Has who gone?' Thomas guessed the answer. 'Not Farquhar?'

'I didn't know who it was. He came up to us in the haberdashery. I didn't recognise him. I'd never really seen Farquhar before. He was very civil and he offered us a lift in his carriage. It was starting to rain and there seemed no harm. He introduced himself as James Hardy and told us he was a friend of Isabella's. He seemed to know the house, and he said he was a colleague of William's.' Her voice was unsteady and she still clung to him. 'If Abi hadn't remembered where she had seen him before, we would have got into the carriage. He had opened the door and was ushering me in. He had his hand on me, round my waist. I thought it overfamiliar, but it was raining hard and he was trying to help me into the dry, then Abi screamed at me and pulled me away and he turned round and' – she let out a sob – 'he punched her in the face!'

Still holding her close, Tom looked over her head towards Abi. She had pulled the hood of her cloak around her, but now he could see the bruising and the trickle of blood near her eye. 'We ran and there was a lot of shouting,' Fanny went on. 'Someone had seen what happened, but we didn't wait to find out. Abi dragged me away and we ran down an alleyway.' Her voice broke into a sob. He could feel her shaking in his arms.

'Where did he go? Did they catch him?'

It was Abi who'd seen what happened. 'He leapt onto the box and whipped up the horses, straight at the crowd. There was a terrible to-do and a lot of shouting, but when I looked back he'd gone.' She was still crying. 'I heard people calling after us to come out, it was safe now, but we didn't dare.'

Somehow he got them home. Isabella's housekeeper ushered Abi away to the kitchen and tended her with hot sweet tea and a warm vinegar sponge for her bruises, while Isabella and Thomas sat Fanny down by the fire in the parlour.

Thomas looked at his sister in despair. 'If he knows where we're living, we're no longer safe here.'

'The man is deranged!' Isabella said stoutly. 'We'll talk about it with William when he returns home. He'll know what to do.'

William instigated enquiries the next morning. There were many witnesses to what had happened and they all agreed it was an attempted kidnapping. It turned out the carriage had been stolen only minutes before. Farquhar must have followed Frances and Abi as they were strolling round the shops and decided it was the perfect opportunity to pounce. What he intended to do with them once he had them in his power, they could only guess.

Thomas and William sat up late into the night discussing the situation. When Thomas was a single man he had been able to take care of himself, but now he had family responsibilities. They had no way of tracking down Farquhar, so the only solution, as far as they could see, was for Thomas and Frances to disappear. It was a hard decision.

The army had anyway recalled him from leave. He would abandon all thoughts of buying himself out and make himself available once again for duty. So it was that Thomas, accompanied by Fanny, found himself bound for the island of Minorca in the Mediterranean Sea.

No amount of argument and pleading from Fanny had changed Thomas's mind about going. Abi and little Frances were left to the care of Isabella and Tom's mother, who made the long journey from Edinburgh to be with her daughter and her little granddaughter.

'I know it's hard, my darling,' Thomas whispered as they set sail, 'but I have to earn my living and Frances will be safer without us. Mama and Isabella will take care of her, I promise.' He couldn't bear Fanny's agonised sobs at being parted from her baby. He folded her in his arms. 'By the time we go back to England that bastard Farquhar will have forgotten we exist.' And in case he hadn't, Thomas had left the fetish in Abi's care with strict instructions to make sure it never left little Frances's nursery.

37

Finlay was working in his study. The house was very quiet as Ruth opened her laptop and began to try to make sense of her notes. There was so much information, and so many family threads to tie in besides the details of Thomas's life. She had copied out the family tree as far as it affected him, his parents, his grandparents, his brothers and sisters and his own children. They were such a widespread family, and because they seemed close they were all relevant. All there in his story; her story; ghosts from her past.

She sighed. As the only child of two only children she could only imagine what it was to be brought up in the rough and tumble of a family nursery. As a teacher she had known many big families, but big by modern standards was three or four children on the whole with perhaps extended families as well, but Thomas was one of six, only one of whom had died young. The others had all flourished.

She glanced up, and there he was, sitting on the velvet chair. He had short dark curly hair, only slightly grey at the temples, and a high complexion. He was handsome, slim, with dark alert eyes. He winked at her.

She took a deep breath, trying to focus, but he had gone.

She looked back at the laptop, but her concentration was all over the place. He had looked so real, so solid and, yes, so humorous. 'Well, talk to me then!' she burst out. 'Please. Don't tease me like this!'

Outside she could hear the wind in the trees. A stem of the wisteria was tapping against her window. She looked towards it, suddenly frightened. Could Timothy climb up to her that way? She leapt to her feet and went over, lifting the corner of the curtain and peering out. There was a moon high above the streaming clouds and for a moment it illuminated the lawn, but there was no one out there.

Letting the curtain fall, she threw herself down on the bed with a sigh. She awoke two hours later and realised that it was midnight and that she had fallen asleep fully dressed. The wind seemed to have grown stronger; she could hear the splatter of raindrops against the window. Wearily she climbed to her feet and began to take off her clothes. Still half asleep she pulled on her nightdress, brushed her teeth, reached across to turn off the light and fell back into bed.

The hand on her shoulder was part of her dream. It was caressing, gentle, awakening longings she hadn't felt for a long time. She felt herself turn to meet it, relaxing, and she knew she was smiling. The touch grew stronger, massaging her breasts and moving down over her stomach; she felt the weight of a knee on the edge of the bed and then hands were holding her down, pushing her back into the pillow, tearing at her nightdress, forcing her legs apart. As she tried to fight back she felt the weight of a hand across her face as he slapped her down.

'No!' She was awake now and struggling. 'No, leave me alone! Help!'

'Let her go you bastard!' Another voice. Help had arrived, flickering candlelight appeared in the room, a figure bent over the bed, dragging him off her. She heard the smack of a blow land, a groan as the man fell backward and scrambled away.

And then Finlay's voice, outside on the landing. 'Ruth? Ruth, are you all right?'

The door opened and light flooded the room as he reached for the switch. Finlay was wearing a thick woollen dressing gown, his hair standing on end. 'I heard you calling!'

Ruth had shot out of bed and was standing with her back to

the wall, her pillow clutched in her arms. She was shaking all over. 'He tried to rape me!'

'It's all right Ruth,' Finlay said gently. 'It was a bad dream. There's no one here. Look.'

She was looking, scanning the room. 'Was it Timothy?' she gasped.

'There's no one here,' he repeated. He went to pull back the curtains. Rain was streaming down the panes and the creeper outside was thrashing against the glass. 'See. The window's locked.'

'You came in. You pulled him off me.' She was too confused and frightened to think straight.

Finlay grimaced. 'No, darling, I didn't. There was no one here. Honest.'

'Look in the bathroom.' The door in the corner of the room was half open, behind it, darkness.

Finlay obliged, turning on the light, pushing the door wide. 'Nothing.' He turned the light off again. 'Let me go and find you a cup of tea.'

'No. Don't go!' It was a reflex action to reach out to him but he had already turned away. 'Thank you, I'd love some,' she whispered faintly at his retreating back. She hadn't moved. She could still feel the man's hands on her; feel his foul breath in her face, hot and moist as he sought her mouth. She gave a little moan of disgust at the memory. Slowly she moved away from the wall. Dropping the pillow on her bed to reach for her bathrobe she realised that her nightdress was torn open from neck to hem.

When Finlay returned she was perched on the edge of the bed, her bathrobe knotted tightly round her. 'You hit him in the face, Fin,' she said wearily. 'Thank you.' Her hands were shaking as she reached out for the mug of tea. She sipped it and scowled. 'You put sugar in,' she added reproachfully.

'That's what they tell you to do for shock,' he said. He sat down on the velvet chair. 'I didn't hit anyone, Ruthie. I'm sure I would have if I'd been here, and if he'd been here, but it was a dream.'

'He tore my nightdress.'

It was lying on the floor at the foot of the bed where she had let it fall. They both looked at it for several seconds then at each other. 'I suppose you are going to tell me I did that myself,' she whispered.

Malcolm arrived at half past eight. He left Finlay and Ruth downstairs and climbed up to the bedroom alone. He didn't need to wait to tune in. The place was electric with lust and anger and an extraordinary vicious hatred. This man had not been imagined by anyone.

He glanced across at the table, at the piled books, the closed laptop, then he made his way across the room and pushed the window open. The storm had blown itself out in the night. The garden was full of sunlight but in here – he turned round slowly and surveyed the room – it was putrid.

He sat down on the bed and waited. He was utterly calm, safe in his own protected space.

'Let's walk down to the river,' he said to Ruth and Finlay an hour later.

They followed him across the wet grass, out of the back gate down the steep flight of steps to the riverside and stood together on the bank, all three mesmerised for a while by the glittering, racing water. 'I want you to move all your books back downstairs to the dining room,' Malcolm said eventually, addressing Ruth. She was shocked at how exhausted he looked in the unforgiving sunlight. 'Your concentration on the past is leaving you open. I spoke to Thomas,' he went on after another thoughtful pause. 'It was he who hit your assailant and drove him away. He's full of remorse that his troubles have followed him to your door.' He pushed his hands deep into his pockets. 'I wasn't strong enough, Ruth, to hold the link and find out more about what's going on. I'm sorry.'

Ruth and Finlay were staring at him. 'Has he gone, this vile pervert?' Finlay asked. 'I can see you're serious about this, but how could the man be a ghost? He tore the nightdress off her, for God's sake! He tried to rape her!' He was finding it hard to contain his anger.

Malcolm folded his arms. 'He is a strong presence.'

'Will he come back?' Ruth's whisper was all but inaudible against the roar of the river.

'In my experience, entities such as this one make use of what energy is there,' Malcolm replied cautiously. 'You were tired and unprotected, focused on his story, and he would have gained strength from the storm. But you can fight him off. I'll show you what to do.'

'Do we need a minister? Prayers?' Finlay glared at Ruth. 'It's my house! You may not want the kirk involved, but I sure as hell do!'

Malcolm smiled. 'That's for Ruth to say. Thomas would like you to use prayers, Ruth. To give yourself strength. You are all over the place because you don't have a strong perimeter, but it's for you to decide. Prayers, if they're an empty gesture, would be no use at all. When you rang me this morning you were looking for my help. You should have been looking inside yourself. You have an amazing ally in your ancestor Thomas; you have taught yourself to contact him, you're almost there.'

Ruth looked at him miserably. 'I can't believe any of this.'

'You do believe it.' Malcolm sounded as though he was about to lose patience. 'You are just too stubborn to admit it. Your father has a lot to answer for!' He sighed in exasperation. 'Think of this as like jumping off a diving board. Allow yourself the courage to do it. You will find everything suddenly makes sense and you will then be able to use the tools you need to deal with the situation. If you don't, you will remain open to attack.' He stepped forward and took Ruth's hands in his own. 'I'll help you all I can, I promise, but as I said to you before, you already have the inner knowledge to do all this yourself. This man must be persuaded to go and seek rest and peace and you are the only one able now to give it to him.'

Ruth gazed at him in something like panic. 'Do you pray?' She was still holding Malcolm's hands. They were warm around her own cold fists.

'Yes, I do. I'm not strong enough to do this job alone. I pray to angels and spirits and ancestors and I pray to God.'

'So, you go to church?'

Malcolm smiled. 'Not often. You don't have to go to church, though I would always recommend a bit of meditation in an ancient kirk in the country. They have a serenity that would do you good.' He let go of Ruth's hands abruptly. 'The house is safe and calm for now. Do you want me to help you clear your books out of that room?'

38

Timothy was tight-lipped and seething with anger. April wanted to go to see the Old Mill House. She'd been itching with curiosity and wouldn't let it go. He hadn't told her he had been there alone, almost been caught, and that he had vowed never to go there again.

'Get a move on, Timothy!' She was bad-tempered, even when he gave up arguing and agreed to do what she wanted. She had got dressed up, put lipstick on, for heaven's sake! Silly cow.

He drove the car jerkily, every gear change reflecting his mood, but she took no notice, blithely looking out of the window as if they were on some fun outing, which, she was. She didn't know that there was probably a police guard there, that maybe Finlay had installed security cameras. Well, she would soon find out.

He parked further away than usual and insisted they keep to the grass verge so her shoes were soaked from last night's rain. To his fury, she seemed to enjoy the subterfuge and hardly noticed that her shoes were ruined, though no doubt he would hear all about that later. Like him she harboured grudges.

Ruth's car was outside the house, along with another, an old four-by-four of some kind.

April was close on his heels as he stopped to think and she blundered into him. 'Watch where you're going!' he snapped. 'There are people there. We should leave.'

'His Daimler's not there. They could be out in that,' she retorted.

'It'll be in the garage.' Timothy dived into the shrubbery and down the side of the house. Both garage doors were closed as they always were. He sprinted across the driveway and went to the first door. He opened it a crack and peered in. There was the car.

Behind him, April pulled at his coat. 'Is it there?'

He smiled. Closing the door with infinite care he confronted her. 'He's home. Let's go.'

'We can't go! Not when we've just arrived.' She looked as disappointed as a child told it can't go to a party. 'There must be something we can see. If we're careful we can look through the windows.'

She didn't wait for his approval. She was off, running clumsily on her toes as if that made her less conspicuous, heading towards the trees. With an exclamation of fury and frustration he followed her and caught her up as she paused to peer across the grass. Her eyes were shining with excitement. 'Supposing we go round the front. There are lots of bushes and things there. We can try the other side of the house. Are there any windows that side?'

He opened his mouth to reply and realised he didn't know. He was about to lie when he saw her looking at him. 'You've never checked, have you.' That edge to her voice was there. It implied that he was an incompetent idiot. She didn't wait for his reply.

There were windows on the far side of the house but they were in deep shadow and there were no lights showing. They crept closer and cautiously peered in. 'This is some kind of cloakroom.' Her voice was heavy with disappointment. She moved on to the next, more cautiously now. They could both see there was a light on. The window looked into the kitchen and she caught her breath with excitement. She could see the whole room, the worktops, the table, the hanging pans, the larger window opposite with the row of terracotta pots and the herbs she had so admired. It was the kitchen she had seen on TV. This was where he cooked.

'OK. You've seen it. Now let's go!' Timothy pulled at her arm. He kept glancing behind them.

'No! Not yet.' She was glued to the window, taking in every detail. There was a book lying face down on the worktop only feet from where she was peering in. She could see a photo of the author, Malcolm Douglas, on the back.

'April!' He was getting desperate. 'We have to go. We'll get caught.'

'One more minute.' She hadn't taken her eyes off the scene in front of her when she froze. The door in the far corner had opened and Ruth walked in, followed by a man. It was the man on the back of the book. She held her breath with excitement, watching avidly. Ruth was laughing. 'I would have expected ghostbusters to drink something more esoteric than coffee,' she said. 'But you're welcome to some more before you go.' April held her breath. She could hear every word. He declined the invitation but she could see he would have liked to say yes, to stay a bit longer. She smirked. 'I've bought one of your books,' Ruth was saying to him now. She seemed embarrassed. She had picked up their empty mugs and she walked across to the sink and put them down on the draining board then she turned and saw April. Their eyes locked for a moment, then April ducked back.

'She's seen me! Quick!' She was already running, back through the bushes towards the gate. Timothy plunged after her, almost sick with terror as they ran up the lane.

There was no sound of pursuit as they found their car. April threw herself in and suddenly she was laughing. 'That was exciting!' She looked across at Timothy as he followed her, slammed the driver's door and reached for his seat belt. 'What a buzz!'

'Are you insane?' He was still fumbling with the car key, trying to insert it with a shaking hand. 'We could have been caught. We could still be caught. They know what sort of car I drive.'

She lay back against the seat, trying to get her breath back. 'But it was worth it! It was glorious.'

He wasn't sure if she meant the kitchen or the adrenaline rush or the whole experience.

He kept to the back roads, trying to lose any possible pursuer. When he finally drew in and round the back of the Dump, as he had officially christened their latest house, he glanced across at her. To his astonishment, she seemed to be asleep. He studied her face, looking at the slack jaw, the untidy pepper-and-salt hair, the ugly cheap jumper which he could see under her jacket and he felt an unexpected wave of affection. Poor April. What she would give for a kitchen like Finlay's. For a moment he had a glimmer of understanding at the way she felt. She had never had a kitchen of her own; never had the chance to collect shiny pans and pots of herbs. Once she had brought home a plastic pot of parsley from the supermarket and watered it carefully, but the plants grew long and floppy and in the end they became mouldy and died. He couldn't see why she had bought them in the first place. He'd refused to let her cook with the stuff. He wasn't even sure she knew how.

'There was someone outside the window!'

Finlay followed Ruth and Malcolm into the kitchen and saw her peering out. 'Timothy?'

'I'm not sure. It might have been a woman. I only caught a glimpse.'

'I'll tell the police.' Finlay groped in his pocket for his phone. 'Bloody man! He's obsessed.'

'Do you want me to go after him?' Malcolm had followed Ruth to the window.

'No! No, I don't think there's any point. He – she – will be long gone.' She sighed. 'He'll get bored with spying on us in the end? Don't bother the police again, Fin. As long as we keep the doors locked what can he do? He's cross because he was caught out as a crook.' She was trying to convince herself to stay calm.

'He's a stalker, Ruth.'

She shivered. 'I know. But I suppose I'm a bit sorry for him.'

'Why? Because he failed to trick you out of your inheritance?' Fin was fuming. 'Get real! I'm not asking the police to rush out here. But I am going to log the fact that he was here again and

I'm having security cameras installed. And in future we must remember to always set the alarm. These things can escalate, Ruthie. You must not underestimate him.'

Ruth saw Malcolm studying her face and gave a sheepish grimace. 'You must wonder what kind of people we are!' she murmured.

'You are people having to cope with a huge amount of stress,' he replied gently. 'I can't deal with your physical stalker, but at least I can be of some use with the other one. And please don't buy any more of my books,' he added with a grin. 'If they will help with your research I will gladly give you copies.'

Thomas

The man, Malcolm Douglas, is a strong and calming force. If anyone can persuade this stubborn young woman to see the light, it is he. Ruth, if you won't listen to me, why won't you listen to him?

My own story from this point is well documented. Little Frances thrived under the adoring care of Mama and Isabella, who wrote often. In turn I wrote long letters from Minorca to Mama and to Harry; I stopped writing to David, under the impression that he was no longer my friend, and so it was Harry who told me that our brother had married our cousin Margaret Fraser, returned to Scotland and installed himself at Kirkhill with the intention of supervising its restoration! I sent him a wedding gift from Minorca. I'm not sure it ever arrived.

Harry himself married a lady called Christian Fullerton and they were living, he told me, in Shoemakers Close while he furthered his career in the law. I confess I felt a pang of jealousy that my brothers were doing so well, but I enjoyed my life as a soldier and no one could deny that I, though the youngest, had the prettiest wife – though in retrospect I realise I had no idea what my new sisters-in-law looked like!

The garrison at St Philip's Castle in Port Mahon was there to make sure it was held securely for the British. As neither the Spanish nor the French were at that time focused on war in the Mediterranean, we were not in a state of alert and I installed Fanny in a pretty house in the town and for the first time we found ourselves with a home of our own. My career progressed with promotion to senior ensign; I resumed my studies, reading widely, and was called upon to preach twice to the men in the absence of the chaplain who had returned home on leave. I found I enjoyed preaching, though perhaps it was the sound of my own voice I was beginning to enjoy! I also began to write in a more serious vein and study the reports of politics back in England.

Fanny and I were ecstatically happy together. I realise now how extraordinarily lucky I was to have found her. We married too young, of course we did, carried away on the tide of first love and rebellion and adventure, but to our delight and perhaps to our amazement our love grew ever stronger. My darling was the perfect match for me, reining in my over-enthusiasms, my tendency to pomposity (which I had not recognised, but she assured me might have been a problem without her gentle teasing) and sharing my love of books and plants, planning, even then, the garden we might one day create together when we returned to England.

If it hadn't been for Fanny missing our little girl so much, I could have stayed happily in Port Mahon forever, but an opportunity for a further six months' leave came up and it coincided with the discovery that she was expecting our second child so we embarked once more for London. As we stood at the ship's rail looking out across the azure sea and as the beauties of the Minorcan landscape faded into the sea mist, my thoughts returned as they so often did to Andrew Farquhar. Had we been away long enough for him to have forgotten us? I could only live in hope but my instincts told me he was waiting and my instincts were always right.

39

Andrew Farquhar put his hand in his pocket and brought out a farthing. He passed it to the urchin who had brought him the news and smiled, well satisfied. So, Tom Erskine was back in town.

The coffee house was crowded, noisy and full of pipe smoke. He called for another cup of chocolate and reached for a news-paper. He kept an eye on the *Gazette* and he knew Tom's regiment was still in Minorca, so what was he doing back here? The papers kept him informed of most things but his network of boy runners was more efficient. There wasn't much he missed in this seething, festering city and anything he had missed he would soon discover.

It was still extraordinarily easy to obtain money, he found, when he put his mind to it. Keeping it was harder, but all he had to do was lay off the gin and porter and keep away from women.

He moved lodgings once and then again, each time to somewhere more salubrious, he bought new clothes – still inconspicuous – the kind of garments a lawyer's clerk might wear, and he learned to walk with an unthreatening gait. Occa-sionally he carried a bag of books or papers to add to the image, but they tended to impede his nimble fingers. Constables, members of the Watch, Bow Street Runners, he could spot them at a hundred paces and melt into the crowd long before they came near him. If there was a patrol in the street he moved on; there were, after all, plenty of places where there was no one on the lookout. He was aware now that he was gaining something of a reputation. They called him the Invisible Man. He liked that.

The moment April and Timothy had left the car behind the Dump she reached for her phone. She hadn't been able to use her laptop since they had moved here and there wasn't much charge left in the phone. She would have to go back to the corner shop where Mr Singh let her plug into his boss's electric every now and then and gave her a mug of coffee in exchange for a chat. Malcolm Douglas. She typed his name into the search engine. He was a writer. A good one. Real history books. It didn't mention being a ghostbuster. As the battery died she filed away his name in her head for future reference.

Fanny was ill again. Abi knocked on the door and peered in. 'Mr Erskine, she's ever so sick. I think we should call a doctor.' Thomas was sitting by the fire with William and Isabella. They had all moved back to London from Tunbridge Wells at the end of the season in time for the Michaelmas law term.

Isabella stood up. 'I will go and see her. You stay there, Tom. Abi, I think I heard Frances crying.'

With no children of her own, Isabella was enchanted with her year-old niece, and endlessly hospitable to her brother and his wife. She dropped a kiss on her husband's head. 'We'll dine soon, William. I'll tell the servants,' and she was gone, bustling towards the stairs.

The doctor's diagnosis was an imbalance of humours.

'Rubbish!' Abi retorted under her breath when she heard. She didn't think much of doctors. She had a solution of her own. The Hamiltons' cook had a niece who was young and clean and willing to learn and loved children, being the eldest of seven herself. She could look after Frances, freeing Abi to take more care of her mistress. The arrangement worked well;

the young woman, whose name was Martha, was an able, intelligent girl who learned quickly and within weeks was indispensable to the household. Little Frances adored her and Martha endeared herself to Fanny by making decoctions of dried chamomile flowers to dilute with warm water.

The great John Wesley had in the 1740s written a book for the general manner of people who could not afford doctors. The book was called *Primitive Physick*, and all his followers owned copies. Isabella and Anne were both sworn devotees and Fanny, having studied it closely, decided it was infinitely preferable to the advice of the pompous doctor. For whatever reason, the remedies prepared by Martha worked. Fanny stopped vomiting and began to bloom.

It was a blustery October evening when Martha cornered Thomas in the hallway as he came in. She was clearly agitated.

'What is it, Martha? Is something wrong with little Frances?' He adored his pretty flirtatious little daughter and was constantly worrying about her though she seemed a remarkably healthy child.

'Something happened this afternoon, sir.' Martha twisted her hands together in her apron. 'I was out walking with Mrs Fanny and little Frances and Abi and I lagged behind them only a few yards, sir.' She looked scared.

'What happened, tell me?' Thomas felt his anxiety soar at the expression on her face.

'A man came up to me. He was a well-dressed gentleman, sir, and he had a nice smile. He asked me if that was the Honourable Mrs Erskine, sir, and I said yes. I didn't think, sir.'

Thomas froze. 'And what happened next?' He kept his voice level with difficulty.

'He said I was to give her a letter, sir.' Martha felt in her apron pocket. 'There was something about him that frightened me. His eyes were,' she stopped, visibly searching for the right word, 'hungry, sir.'

'And then what did he do?'

'Abi turned round to look for me and he disappeared, sir. He was there one minute and then the next he was gone. I think he must have slipped up an alley. I didn't know what to do so I thought I'd better tell you.'

'You did right, Martha. Thank you.' He put out his hand for the letter. 'I don't want my wife upset in her present condition. Go back to the nursery now and tell little Frances her papa will be up to say goodnight soon.'

The letter felt cold in his hand. He could feel the evil emanating from it even before he opened it.

Carefully written in a literate hand it contained a string of obscene threats and promises of what he would do to Fanny and to little Frances when he had them in his power. Thomas only glanced at the sheet of paper once then he dropped it in the fireplace. He reached for a spill from the jar on the mantelpiece, lit it from the candelabra and, putting a flame to the sheet of paper, he watched it burn, feeling very sick. It had been unsigned but he was in no doubt as to who it had come from. Andrew Farquhar knew that they had returned to London.

Thomas

Within a week we had moved back in with Anne and Selina Huntingdon. We felt safer in the larger household and if Fanny or the children went out it was with a footman in attendance.

Fanny, preoccupied with the coming birth, did not begrudge me my London friendships. I was a published writer now, having produced a much-acclaimed book on the shortcomings of the army, something which strangely did not seem to alienate my superior officers who promoted me to lieutenant. The book was published anonymously but it was widely known who had written it. I was making contacts I hoped would see me succeed in London society and, to Fanny's joy, I appeared to have gained sufficiently in gravitas and respectability for my parents-in-law, who were pleased with their gorgeous grandchild, and the prospect of another on the way, to make the decision to forget the unseemly haste of our marriage. After what they presumably considered a timely exile to forget our escapade, and with me in the uniform of the Royal Scots, I found myself a guest in their house at last.

I met the great and the good of the literary world; at a dinner with Sir Alexander Macdonald I met and impressed Dr Johnson, no less, and, thanks in part to my brother-in-law William and to my former mentor and hero, Lord Mansfield, I began to move in legal circles. It was while I was visiting Lord Mansfield at his magnificent seat in

Kenwood that I saw again Sir John Lindsay's daughter Dido Belle. Mansfield had adopted her to be a companion to his niece and the children ran rioting round the great rooms and corridors of the house while we talked of politics and law, particularly the matter of slavery, which he made one of his especial interests; in a memorable case he had established that such a state had no basis in common law in England and as such came it to be recognised as the end of legal slavery in this country.

On one occasion I went to a trial presided over by Lord Mansfield to listen to the proceedings and he summoned me forward to sit on the bench beside him while he heard the rest of the case and it was at that moment that I acknowledged that since I was a boy all I had ever really wanted was to study law myself.

40

Ruth watched Finlay head off down the drive in his car. He had mentioned the boxes stacked in the garage. 'They're not mine!' he had said as he climbed into the Daimler. 'We'll get Lachy to clear them out next time he comes. It's difficult to fit the car in with them at the back there.'

Was it a suspicion? An instinct perhaps, inspired by the way Timothy was hanging round? She pulled open the doors, letting the sunlight in. Beyond the patch of oil on the floor where the car normally stood she could see cardboard boxes, two old suitcases, a couple of cheap plastic storage containers. She felt a leap of hope. She pulled the smallest towards her and levered off the lid, peering in to see a sheet of newspaper. Under it there were a dozen or so packages. She picked one up and unrolled the paper to reveal a bundle of silver forks. She stood staring down into the box, her heart hammering with excitement as she saw the family crests on the handles.

A sound behind her made her swing round, the forks still in her hand. Timothy was standing there, staring at them. 'Those are mine!' he burst out.

'I don't think so.' The wave of fury that swept over her took even her by surprise.

'Your father gave them to me!'

'He did no such thing! You stole them.' She dropped the

bundle back into the box and groped in her pocket for her phone. 'I'm calling the police! I've had enough of your trickery and forgery and your spying and following me around!' Her voice rose, she was angrier than she had ever been. 'You have made my life a misery, and it's going to stop!'

She hadn't expected him to leap at her. His face white with anger, he threw himself towards her, knocking the phone out of her hand. 'Those are my things!' he shouted. 'Mine! You're not going to call the police! You're not going to get in my way again!' As he lifted his hand to hit her, he lost his balance, staggering backwards with a cry of fright. Ruth was aware of a figure there beside her as Timothy half fell, recovered himself and lunged forward again. She managed to sidestep, looking round desperately for her phone but Timothy had recoiled violently and dodged away from her. With a scream of terror he began to run.

The police arrived shortly after Finlay. There was nothing they could do. Timothy was long gone, they already had his car number, they could only repeat their warnings to keep the doors locked and as a final gesture help Ruth and Finlay move the boxes into the main house.

'Thomas was here. I saw him!' Ruth waited for the police car to disappear down the drive before she told Finlay what had happened. 'Timothy was about to hit me; he completely lost it! I know I told the police he changed his mind and ran away, but he changed his mind because there was this figure beside me. It was Thomas, I know it was. I don't know if he was solid, but Timothy saw him and he turned and ran. He was terrified!' She stared at him wide-eyed. 'He was real, Fin.'

'I believe you,' Finlay said slowly. 'Hopefully, that will scare Timothy too much to ever come back here.' He led the way into the sitting room and threw himself down in a chair. 'The policeman said it would only be a matter of time before they picked him up. They will give it a higher priority now he's threatened violence.'

Ruth shivered. 'I should go, shouldn't I. I'm making your life difficult and if I'm not here any more he'll leave you alone.'

'You will stay here as long as you want,' Finlay replied firmly.

'I'm not allowing that low life to chase any guest of mine out of this house.' He paused. 'As long as we can keep you safe.' He smiled. 'Forget him for now. Let's have a look at the treasure.'

There were forks and spoons, pretty silver filigree dishes, a set of glasses, some of which were broken. Finlay held one up. 'Oh, this is a complete tragedy. Look at these. They're eighteenth century. See, the lovely spiral twists in the stems? And this.' He held another up to the light. 'This is an Amen glass. I've only ever seen them in the museum. The faithful used to drink the toast to the Jacobite Pretender and then smash their glasses, which is why they're so rare. See, James Stuart's face in the glass?' He stood up and carefully set it on the mantelpiece.

There were several paintings, three of which were small portraits; several sketchbooks; scrapbooks full of pressed flowers and ferns; and in one of the cardboard boxes Ruth found her mother's jewel box. She put it on the coffee table and opened it gingerly. It was half empty. She stared at it in dismay. 'Her rings have gone. And there was a locket, I remember, and a charm bracelet.'

Finlay leaned forward and gently took the box out of her hands. 'Don't think about it now. If they're sold, then there's little chance of finding them. But you've recovered so much. Be positive.' He put the box down on the coffee table. 'Why on earth did he hide all this here?'

She gave a grim smile. 'It seems like a good place to me. Where better? After all, we didn't find it, did we? If Lachy hadn't gone into the shed and moved it to the garage you might never have spotted it. And it meant Tim could keep an eye on me and the stuff at the same time. No wonder he kept coming back.' She shivered.

Finlay was dipping into the cardboard box again. 'Good God, look at this!' He had pulled out a tea towel and unrolled it. Lying on the faded cotton picture of the Forth Rail Bridge was a small doll made of straw and stones and beads strung together on red thread with feathers and plaited hair. They both stared at it in silence. 'It looks like some kind of voodoo fetish,' Finlay said. He rerolled the tea towel round it with a distasteful shudder and stowed it back in the cardboard box.

Ruth reached out as he put it away then withdrew her hand. 'That's exactly what it is. I read about it in his letters,' she whispered. 'When he was in the West Indies, Thomas was ill. He went to an obeah woman, a doctor, and she gave him something to keep him safe. He kept it in his sea chest and he was sure it warned off whoever had been messing with his stuff.'

Finlay glanced at her with a look of scepticism. 'It doesn't still work then, does it. So you're telling me that lump of stuff is over two hundred years old?'

She smiled wanly. 'So are most of the things in here.'

'True.' He stood up. 'Well, let's find somewhere to store it all. Shall we lock it in the landing cupboard for now and decide what to do about it later?' He closed the flaps of the box over the contents with a look of extreme distaste. 'You might want to run that thing past Malcolm next time he comes. It would be interesting to see if he gets any vibes off it.'

It was to Lord Mansfield that Thomas at last confided his worries about Andrew Farquhar. There had been no further word from the blackguard and no sign that he had followed them back to Huntingdon House but he could not rest safely in the knowledge the man was free on the streets of London.

Mansfield listened to the story and sighed wearily. 'A man can hide himself in the underworld forever, my boy. A change of name, a change of lodgings and he's gone back into the cesspit of back streets. You could have a word with the Bow Street Runners but the trouble is you have no way of knowing how this man lives, how he earns his living. You say your wife's maid said he was smartly dressed. For all you know, he's a gentleman, albeit with a lewd and vicious tongue. I'll have a word with John Lindsay and see if he remembers him from the *Tartar* days. He may still be in touch with some of the officers from the ship; perhaps one of them will recall something of his background. In the meantime, my boy, have you given any more thought to leaving the army and taking up the law?' He smiled fondly. He knew Tom had thought of nothing else.

As he mounted the roan cob to ride back to London, Thomas was still thinking about the enormous step of giving up his army career, something he enjoyed and at which he was reasonably successful, to go back to his studies and once more face the idea of extreme poverty until he had qualified as a lawyer. It would be a huge decision.

It was a glorious evening, and, dazzled by the setting sun, he did not notice the man loitering outside the gates of Kenwood House. He was just another beggar, dressed in a rough jacket and filthy breeches. He did not even toss the man a coin. Had he looked at him more closely as he kicked his horse into a canter, he might have recognised the ice-cold stare.

'That's it!' Timothy was beyond caring what April would say. 'We have to get rid of the car and we have to leave town now. I've had it with this place! I was attacked! This man was there with Ruth, and he hit me!' He was genuinely aggrieved. 'She found our silver. She called the police! It's all gone to shit!' He was shaking visibly.

She had been snoozing in the folding chair by the oil stove when he got back and now, slowly and stiffly, she stood up. 'You went back without me?' She stared at him in disbelief. Then his words sank in. 'The silver's gone? You stupid, stupid man!'

He had grabbed one of the bags from behind the door and was already stuffing things into it at random. He groaned. 'It's not my fault. It's her. She won't leave me alone,' he whined.

'Stop it, Timothy!' April shrieked.

He froze.

'I saw this coming. I knew you were losing it.' Her voice was full of venom. 'And I take it you drove straight back here and left the car outside the house?' Registering the guilt on his face, she yelled, 'I thought so. Dear God!' She looked up at the ceiling for a moment. 'OK. As long as they didn't follow you?' She looked at him, waiting for an answer and saw the look of blank terror. 'You didn't even look in the mirror, did you! Give me the car keys and wait here. Can you manage to do that without getting it wrong?'

Fumbling in his pocket, he gave them to her and stared after her as she went out, banging the door behind her. Already she was talking to someone on her phone. He could not have moved if he wanted to. He was still paralysed with fear.

It was dark when she finally came back. 'I've had the number plates changed. I'd already ordered them, so I collected them, then got a guy I know in Muirhouse to meet me at our old place and put them on for me. That'll buy us a bit of time.'

'Time?' He looked up at her blankly.

'Yes, time. To see what we can retrieve from this farce. All our planning wasted! We could have made a killing from this and you've blown it, you cretin!'

He barely heard her insult. 'So, what do we do now?' he asked dully.

'We wait and we lie low,' she replied. 'As far as Madam Ruth and the police are concerned, we'll disappear. They'll assume we've run away and their guard will drop. Eventually.' She gave a cold smile. 'Then we'll decide what to do next.' She fixed him with a gimlet stare. 'Have I made myself understood, Timothy? You will leave Ruth alone. For now.'

41

'You didn't bring the fetish with you?' Malcolm guided Ruth into his kitchen. The windows here were small slits in the thickness of the wall. Spotlights shone brightly down onto the scrubbed wood worktops, and there was a jug of autumn flowers on the table.

'No. We locked everything in a cupboard. I didn't really want to touch it.'

'Fair enough, but I'm going to have to see it to form an opinion.' He had made some thick black coffee and almost as an afterthought dug in the fridge for some milk.

'So.' He sat down opposite her at the table. 'From the beginning.'

When she had finished, he looked at her steadily for a full minute. 'I'm getting the impression you are beginning to concede that Thomas is a bit more than an imaginary construct. Am I right?'

'Timothy certainly thought so,' she admitted.

'And we now know that Thomas is able to intervene on your behalf, and he has done it twice, once against Timothy and once against your ghost stalker.'

She smiled. 'I suppose so.'

'However nasty Timothy is, I am, to be honest, more worried about your lascivious ghost.'

She felt a prickle of unease run across her shoulder blades. 'You think he's dangerous? I mean genuinely dangerous?'

268

'Oh yes. I think we have to accept that. It's because of him I wanted you to come to talk here. You and Harriet invited him in, but he must have been hanging around before that. Maybe just waiting for someone to give him some attention.' He sighed as he picked up his mug of coffee. He drank his black.

The door opened behind him and one of his dogs poked its head into the kitchen. It trotted in, followed by the other, and they settled down together on a heap of cushions in the corner, obviously a designated dog bed area.

They watched the dogs in silence. 'It's such a relief to have someone to talk to. I feel so lost.' Ruth hadn't intended her words to sound so bleak.

'In a metaphysical desert.' Malcolm smiled. 'As I've said before, your father has a lot to answer for. He destroyed your spiritual mojo.'

She laughed out loud. 'I suppose he has.'

She liked his face when he smiled. The wrinkles round his eyes, the almost reluctant softening of the line of his mouth. It lit up his expression with genuine warmth. He met her gaze and she looked away hastily. 'So, can I rebuild my mojo?'

'I am glad to hear you ask.' He reached for the coffee pot and topped up his mug. He noticed she had barely touched her own but he said nothing.

'And are you going to tell me how?'

He shook his head slowly. 'I can give you pointers, but this is something you have to find in your own heart and soul. Talk to Thomas about it.'

Her mouth fell open. 'Seriously?'

'Why not? He has been talking to you about everything else, hasn't he? He knows you're there and he's interested in your welfare.'

She hesitated. 'I'm reading so much about him, but when I read my notes I keep thinking they're turning into a novel.' She looked down at her clasped hands on the table. 'I'm a teacher, Mal, I encourage my pupils to write fiction. I can tell the difference between a good story and history. I'm afraid I'm making this up. Then he wouldn't be real.'

'History is a good story, in my humble opinion,' he said at last.

'And at best it's a matter of interpretation of selected facts, which may not even be genuine facts. Few historians have the chance to interview their subjects first-hand. Don't knock it, Ruth. Listen. Write. Work out what it is you've written later.' He took another gulp of coffee. 'In the meantime, what you have to deal with is a leakage through time. You and Harriet opened a crevice, door, portal, however you like to describe it, and for whatever reason this guy has come through it. I've been doing some extra reading around Thomas too.' Malcolm ran his fingers through his hair. 'Would you let me see the letters you have been working from, Ruth? It would help me get things into context. The books I've looked up have been largely concerned with his legal career and to study your notes about how he arrived at that point would help me understand him and his relationship with Farquhar.' He saw the doubt flash across her eyes. 'Doesn't matter if you'd rather not,' he added hurriedly. 'Think about it.'

He stood up. 'What we need is a change of scene. D'you fancy taking the dogs for a walk?'

He reached to unhook her jacket from the back of the door and helped her on with it, then picked up his own. Shrugging it on, he clicked his fingers at the dogs, who were watching the proceedings eagerly.

'I think better out here,' he called over his shoulder as he walked ahead of her across the driveway and into the woods. The dogs had disappeared into the undergrowth. A stiff breeze was blowing, whirling the fallen leaves across the path, tugging at their hair.

'Where are we going?'

'Somewhere very special. It's not far.'

She felt her spirits lifting as the path wound deeper into the woodland. It was far more sheltered here than at the Old Mill House, which was so close to the stormy Forth. Even with a sharp wind in her face she felt at peace here. Eventually they turned a corner in the path and arrived in a clearing in which stood a small stone building. She stopped and gazed at it in delight. 'What a magical place.'

He smiled. 'You have chosen the right word. This is my chapel, if you will. I come here to think and meditate and pray.'

'Your own chapel?' She felt herself grow cold.

'Why not?'

'No reason, I suppose. It's just that I haven't been very complimentary about religious people.'

'You came to me for spiritual help.'

'I came to you for help with a haunting.'

'Same thing, in my book.' He pushed open the door. 'Come in and see.'

She hesitated for a moment then followed him inside. On a small sturdy oak table by the far wall was a candlestick, the candle in it hung with stalactites of wax. Beside it was a beautiful pottery statue of the Virgin and Child, a basket of crystals, and a cut-glass dish containing a box of matches. She glanced round. 'I'm sorry. I don't belong in here.' She backed away towards the door.

'Why not give it a few minutes.' He indicated an easy chair in the corner. 'Just sit and see what happens. Relax. This place belongs to the wood. See, the green man on the wall?' He pointed to a plaque, half shaded by the curtain of leaves hanging outside the window. He reached for the matches and lit the candle. 'I'll wait outside. Don't worry. I'll be there as long as you like. Just give the peace of this place a chance to work. If it does nothing else, it will relax you. You don't have to pretend anything. Don't try and pray. Don't picture anything. Don't think. Just sit and rest and listen to the birds.'

She sat down uneasily. He stepped backwards out of the door. 'Don't shut it!' she called desperately. She heard him chuckle. He left it half open and she heard his footsteps fading away as he walked across the clearing.

She found him half an hour later, sitting on a log, his back against the trunk of a tree. His dogs were lying on the grass in a patch of sunlight near him. He smiled up at her lazily as she appeared in the doorway and made her way across to him. 'OK?'

'I fell asleep.'

'That's good.'

'Is it?'

'It means you could relax in a place that is full of religious symbolism.'

'It's a lovely place.'

'Somewhere you felt safe?'

'I suppose I did. I didn't think about it.'

'It was because you were protected. It's what these days is called a safe space.'

'You mean my would-be rapist couldn't get me there?'

'Exactly.'

'But he can get me at the Old Mill House?'

'Not if you make that a safe space too.'

'And you're going to tell me how.'

'That's what you came to me for.'

She smiled. 'OK, fair enough. What do I need? A picture of the green man?'

'Only if he is deeply meaningful for you. The same goes for the Virgin and Child. If they hold no significance or resonance for you or fill you with superstitious horror, then they will not be comfortable in your space or you in theirs.'

'And crystals? You said you didn't do crystals.'

He grinned amiably. 'OK. I confess. Just a few crystals.'

'But not for me. So what should I put there?'

'Ah, that is for you to discover. Come, we'll walk back to the house while we think about it.' He set off ahead of her towards the path through the trees.

Symbols of nature seemed like a good start. She admitted she collected seashells when she was a child. 'I have a box of them at home in London. They make me feel happy. And pressed leaves from trees. And pictures of the countryside. Are you telling me I have to scatter these things round Finlay's house?'

'Thinking about them makes you smile, right? Their presence brings back happy moments. You keep them near you to make you feel secure.'

'Ah.' She gave him a quick look. 'I am beginning to understand.'

'You build your own safe space inside your head. It's full of the things you love. You do not allow anything in that space which is discordant or scary or a bad dream in any sense. It is somewhere you can retreat to at any moment.'

'No sign of the cross? No holy water?'

'Nothing that makes you uncomfortable.'

'Just raindrops on roses and whiskers on kittens,' she laughed. 'Oh please! It can't be that easy.' Her scepticism had returned. 'So, I make a safe space. But this guy is waiting outside it. What do I do then?'

'Ah, that's the next lesson. That's harder.' They had reached the Tower House now. They paused beside her car. 'Feeling stronger?'

She pulled a face. 'I'm not sure.'

'Practise. And before you sleep, ask for help. If not angels, then your teddy. As long as someone is looking after you.'

'Teddy indeed!'

He laughed out loud. 'I saw it. On your bed.'

She felt herself blush scarlet. 'It's only there because I found it in my father's house. He'd kept it.'

He stepped forward and raised a finger as if sealing her lips but not quite touching. 'I'm not mocking. It was a wonderful sign of hope as far as your spiritual welfare is concerned. Now, go home; I have to see a man about an eighteenth-century archive. I'm sorry to hurry you away, but we'll talk about this again, and in the meantime if you're worried or bothered or truly frightened, put my number on speed-dial and I will come, I promise.'

Thomas

I attended several trials presided over by Lord Mansfield after that first time and it took very little persuasion on his part to confirm to me that my true calling was to the law. I would, if my earnest calculations were correct, have enough money, by selling my commission, to put myself through law school. I consulted Harry, who had qualified as a lawyer the year I returned from sea, and through him Mama, whose views I always valued, and only then at her insistence, with David. They were all gracious enough to encourage me, though none could offer pecuniary help with my studies should I embark upon them.

Strangely, it was through my re-established contact with David and his fascination with the stars that I heard the outcome of the sea trials of the chronometer that had been tested on that first outward voyage on the Tartar. *He told me how badly the Board of Longitude had treated poor John Harrison, refusing to pay his reward, and how the old man, our William Harrison's father, had had to appeal to the king. In the end, parliament had awarded him nearly £9,000.*

It was only after my discussions with the family and much further thought that I broached the idea of resigning my commission with Fanny and my darling love proved ecstatic at the idea. She no longer enjoyed the idea of having a soldier for a husband, especially with riots in London and the threat of revolution in America. My duties took me often away from her, and although I had been granted long leaves of absence, we missed one another sorely when I was gone. Our time in Minorca had been a blissful interlude, but now with the world growing uneasy again, and hungry little mouths to feed, I was feeling the financial strain intensely.

Fanny was the mother now of three little girls, the apples of my eye, but we were presuming too much upon my relatives' hospitality. I had to find somewhere to lodge us all together in safety.

And so I embarked upon my new venture, one which I hoped desperately would prove more lucrative than the life of a lowly lieutenant with little prospect of further promotion. Besides, I knew I would be good at it. I was not slow in putting myself forward in print or at dinner parties. I was good at voicing my views and my views were sound and passionately Whig and, after realising that my Scots accent was a drawback and even a source of mockery in some circles, I worked at lessening the effect of my rolling r's and my Edinburgh lilt. All well and good. In the meantime, Fanny and I had to eat and clothe ourselves and it was all going to prove hard to afford.

I had seen nothing more of my bête noir. Andrew Farquhar had disappeared into the miasma of London low life and I fervently hoped he had lost interest in us. As far as I could tell, he had ceased to follow Fanny; that was all that mattered.

275

42

Andrew lay back on the bed with a sigh. The room smelt of soiled linen and spent lust. He reached out for the tankard of porter on the chest beside the bed and found to his surprise and disappointment that it was empty but for some grounds in the bottom which he spat on the floor in disgust. He already knew his stash of coins would be gone. He had slept too deeply, too long and too carelessly and the doxy who had shared his bed had no doubt crawled back to her pimp in triumph, the money hidden in her grubby cleavage, leaving no trace but the smell of stale cheap perfume on his pillow. He lay back with a groan, his arm across his eyes.

When he next awoke it was in time to hear a distant church clock chime in a rare gap in the sound of passing traffic outside the window. It was midday and he was hungry.

Stripped to the waist he stood at the pump in the freezing yard behind his lodgings, holding his head beneath the feeble stream of water until his brain began to clear. Dressed, his hair combed and knotted into a neat queue, he padded down the stairs, managed to pass his landlady's door without being importuned for the rent and let himself out into the street, heading for the West End. Within an hour he had stolen enough money to buy himself a hot pie from a street seller and a mug of hot chocolate at the local coffee house. Retreating to the far end of the long table with his drink he helped himself to a copy of the *Gazette* from the rack and began to study the front page. Ten minutes later he was still sitting staring at the same paragraph. The Honourable Thomas Erskine had sold his commission in the army and had moved his family back to London. Mr Erskine intended to study law.

Law!

Andrew threw back his head and laughed out loud. He returned the paper to its rack and pushed his way out of the crowded coffee house and into the street. He needed to make some serious money in the next couple of hours and he had no need to study to achieve it. He was the best. Turning abruptly to cross the road he bumped into an elderly gentleman who was hesitating before trying to fight his way between carts and carriages to reach the other side. Escorting him across, his hand beneath the man's arm, Andrew was at his most helpful and charming. He listened attentively to the old man's effusive thanks, allowed him to shake his hand and watched him walk away, leaning heavily on his silver-topped cane. When he ducked away down an alleyway two minutes later he had relieved the man of his purse, a fine pocket watch and a silk handkerchief. He was back on form.

'It is going to be hard, my love.' Thomas looked round the main room of the small house they had rented in Kentish Town. 'But it will be worth it!'

Abi would sleep with the children in the larger of the two bedrooms, he and Fanny would have the second bedroom – so small it was scarcely more than a shoebox, and there was a closet barely large enough to hang their clothes. The main living room was where they would all live and would be where he would study.

He saw Fanny glance round at the shabby furniture, the scratched wooden table, the boxes which contained their worldly goods, still strapped and labelled from the last move, and his heart ached for her. She had thrown in her lot with him with so much excitement, so much unqualified love, and this was all he could give her. The door opened and little Frances crept in. She looked from one parent to the other and ran to her father, scrambling up onto his knee. She was a pretty child with long ringlets and large dark eyes that seemed wise beyond her years. He gave her a hug and gently pushed her back onto the ground. 'Go and help Abi with the little ones, sweetheart,' he said softly. Abi was with them still, loyal, unquestioning, frequently unpaid. To Fanny's immense regret they had had to let Martha go. He sighed. He had to keep focused on the future.

The money from the sale of his commission would not last forever, but if he budgeted carefully he thought he could make it last the five years it would take to qualify as a barrister. These lodgings in the hamlet of Kentish Town, just north of London, were the cheapest he had been able to find. The terraced house was small, two-storeyed, built of the local grey brick and the area was pleasant enough, with fresh air for the children. Fanny would be safe here, and happy. He tried not to see the exhaustion and despair in her face as she glanced round the room. He would help her all he could, but the important thing was to qualify as soon as possible. With another sigh he bent to his book box and began to unstrap it.

Later he went out alone to walk along the bank of the River Fleet and clear his head. The air was fresh out here and away from the noise of the children it helped him to think. He had enrolled as a student at Lincoln's Inn. To do so had cost him the sum of three pounds, three shillings and four pence. He was on his way. He could walk there from Kentish Town in less than an hour to attend lectures and already he had discovered a way to reduce the length of time it would take to qualify. If he obtained a university degree it would cut two years of study time. Having settled Fanny here and promised her a home of her own at last he wasn't sure how he would break the news about Cambridge, but it had to be done and it had to be done at once.

As they sat together in the twilight the house was unusually quiet. Abi had cooked their supper and put the children to bed, falling asleep herself in her truckle bed in the corner of their room.

Fanny looked at Thomas fondly as he poured them both a mug of ale. 'I thought we would settle and be happy here,' she said with a gentle smile. 'But you are restless as a cat about to give birth. Is it another idea?' She waited, her eyes on his face. By this time she knew her husband only too well. It was like living with a grass fire, every moment threatening to spark and flare in another direction. 'Go on, tell me what is eating you up, my darling.' She reached across the table and took his hand.

She was silent for several seconds when he told her, then she made herself smile reassuringly. 'Then that's what you must do. It will reduce our penury by two years.' She tried to make a joke of it, already hearing her father's harsh voice in her ear: 'You made your bed with this penniless good-for-nothing, so on it you must lie.' Her father, less enchanted than his wife by the children, had refused to lend Thomas money, but her mother quietly passed her a few guineas each time they met. Fanny didn't know where the money came from, probably her father, did he but know it, but she blessed Mama for it. She was no longer too proud to take it.

She had dreamed of attending dinner parties and soirees and balls with her dashing young husband, of joining the company of intelligent women, but her children had put a stop to that. Thomas could not afford to buy her gowns and wigs and jewellery. All the money they could spare from food and rent must go on Abi and the children. Already Thomas was beginning to look like a beggar, seemingly unaware of the shabbiness of his clothes. She had pleaded with him to see to his wardrobe but he was too immersed in his books and his writing to notice and his friends, enchanted by his wit and his ideas, seemed to forgive him sartorial blunders they would never tolerate in other men. She glanced across the room at their only table, the table where she and the children and Abi would eat in an ordinary world. Already it was strewn with books and papers and inkpots; she must warn her husband about leaving the ink within reach of small hands; little Frances had shown an extraordinary keenness for drawing. Thomas would make it all come right in the end, she reminded herself sternly. She had absolute faith in him.

43

'Bradford and his sister are no longer living in their old squat.' The young woman police constable perched on the edge of the sofa in the living room at the Old Mill House. 'But they are still going back there from time to time. It was a tip-off following another investigation: a back-street business manufacturing false number plates we'd been watching. A woman turned up on foot and then left with a parcel under her arm. Our DC followed her to Muirhouse, where the plates were swapped onto the car she was driving.' She looked slightly embarrassed as she added, 'Unfortunately, it was a couple of days before they realised that this was the car connected with your case.'

'Timothy Bradford's car?' Ruth was biting her tongue, trying not to interrupt the young woman's monologue.

'When they checked the original number to see if it was a stolen vehicle and saw it flagged they sent a couple of my colleagues round, but she was long gone.' The policewoman glanced down at her hands. 'Too slow, I'm afraid.' She raised her head again and flashed Ruth a helpless smile.

'How could they be so stupid?' Ruth wailed at Fin later. 'They could have had them! And they let them get away.'

Finlay shook his head in despair. 'I should put them out of your mind. Timothy must guess there's a warrant out for his arrest after he attacked you, and he's lost the stuff he stole from you, so there's nothing to hang around for. Let's hope he's cut his losses and gone off to try and fleece some other poor sod.'

Ruth sighed. Common sense told her that what Finlay said was true. 'You don't think he'd try and get into Number 26 again, do you?'

He scowled. 'You've checked it, haven't you? And the woman next door is keeping an eye on it.'

They went again, just to be sure.

'So, hopefully we can have some peace now,' Ruth said to Thomas later. Finlay had gone out for the evening and she was once more ensconced in the dining room with some new cardboard files they had bought when they were out. She looked around half hopefully but there was no sign of anyone there.

Her thoughts returned to Malcolm as, she had to admit, they did quite often. He intrigued her. He was an enigma, no doubt about that. A serious academic, a knowledgeable man and no fool, that was certain, and yet he genuinely believed in all this stuff which most – no, all – intelligent people dismissed as total garbage. She sat back in the chair and folded her arms. She liked enigmas.

It was a guilty pleasure walking through the countryside into London each morning. As Thomas kissed Fanny and the children goodbye and closed the door with relief on all the noise he knew only too well how much his wife had invested in his dreams and he was determined that, not matter how hard he had to work, he would make them come true.

The last person he expected to see on his walk was old Duncan Erskine, his father's sennachie; his brother's now, he reminded himself, as his brain tried to compute the strangeness of running into the man here of all places.

He held out his hand, but Duncan ignored it. 'Were you coming to find me, old friend?' he asked. 'This is astonishing luck. Two minutes either way and you would have missed me. How are you?'

'I came to say goodbye.' Duncan bowed slightly. His face was grey and drawn and he looked immeasurably tired.

'Goodbye?' Thomas stepped back as a chaise rattled down the road past them, raising the dust. 'But why? Have you left Kirkhill? Are you no longer in my brother's service?'

'Alas, no, but before I leave, I have warnings for you, my boy.' The shadow of a smile illuminated the old man's face. 'You will do well now you have found your calling and one day you will have riches beyond everything you can imagine. Don't let it go to your head. Remember your friends and beware your enemies.'

'Enemies?' Thomas repeated the word with a frown. He had not seen or heard of Andrew Farquhar since they had moved. As for riches, that was nothing more than a dream. To be able to put food on his children's table and buy them new clothes would be enough reward.

Duncan did not reply. The morning stage from Highgate was approaching. The thunder of the four sets of hooves, the rattle of wheels, the blast from the coach horn were deafening. Clouds of dust from the hooves and the wheels swirled in the air. When it had passed, Thomas looked for the old man again. He had disappeared.

'Duncan?' he called. He turned full circle on the roadside, staring round. There were no turnings off the road here as far as the eye could see. He was alone.

44

Harriet had been plucking up courage for days. Ruth had made the biggest mistake of her life in trusting Malcolm Douglas. The more she thought about it, the angrier she became and with Liz and Peter out for the afternoon this was her chance.

It took just over an hour to drive across country from the coast at North Berwick into the border hills where the Tower House nestled in its beautiful valley. When she drew up beside the shabby four-by-four, she still wasn't certain what she was going to say.

The barking dogs had alerted him to her arrival as, before she climbed out of the car, the front door had opened. She recognised Malcolm immediately.

She held out her hand with a frosty smile. 'Mr Douglas? I am sorry to intrude on your privacy. As I believe she told you, I'm a friend of Ruth Dunbar. You may remember me? Harriet Jervase.'

'Indeed.' He took her hand and shook it firmly. 'How could I forget you. Ruth did mention you, but not that you were coming to see me.'

'She doesn't know. We need to talk.'

He led her up the long spiral stairs to the second floor and into his study. A wood burner was throwing out heat and the two dogs lay down at once in front of it. He gestured her towards the only spare chair in the room and resumed his own in front of his desk, swivelling slightly so he was half facing her. The computer was switched on, the desk full of open books, a tall lamp throwing a pool of light onto the area around the keyboard. 'So, how can I help you?'

'I gather you claim to be some kind of psychic.' Harriet sat down, still wearing her coat. The room was very warm and she was already feeling uncomfortable.

He leaned forward, resting his hands on the desk, his fingers loosely interlinked in front of him. 'You sound cynical, if I may say so. Strangely so for someone who, I understand, is writing about Dion Fortune.' His voice was low with the faintest trace of a Scots accent.

'Ruth is very vulnerable,' she replied, her tone repressive. 'I don't want to see her made a fool of.'

'There is no possibility of that, I assure you.'

'Do you have qualifications for what you do?' Even as she voiced the question, Harriet knew how stupid it sounded.

His face remained serious. 'I take it you are referring to my psychic activities, as you call them? No, I have no qualifications. I'm not sure what they would be? Perhaps you would enlighten me.'

'Reputation. Experience.'

'I have both.'

'I saw no mention of them in any of the articles about you online.'

'My activities in this area are my business. I don't choose to broadcast them. And I ask my clients to keep them confidential, something that Ruth has presumably failed to do.' He looked like a stern Victorian schoolmaster, she realised. 'That's sad,' he went on, 'if it means I can no longer go on working with her. Mutual trust is extraordinarily important in any area of this nature.' He stood up. 'I don't think we have anything to discuss. I'll show you out, Miss Jervase, if you don't mind. I am, as you can see, working and I don't normally see people without appointment. As a writer yourself I am sure you can understand.'

The two dogs had leapt to their feet and were standing by

the door, panting with excitement. He went to open it and they ran ahead down the stairs as he waited for her to precede him.

She didn't move. 'I'm sorry; I didn't mean to offend you.'

He inclined his head slightly. 'I think you probably did, but I'm not offended. I just see no purpose in continuing this conversation. Ruth spoke very highly of your friendship and clearly trusts you. That's fine. I hope you can give her the support I'm afraid I can no longer provide.'

'Are you that touchy?'

He smiled. 'No, Miss Jervase, I'm not touchy, I merely treasure my privacy. I make that clear to anyone who comes to me for help. I assume Ruth felt she could trust you, but sadly, that doesn't seem to have been the case. I'll leave you to explain to her what's happened. I'm truly sorry as I thought I could help her. Now, please leave my house.'

She stood up, aware that she was dripping with perspiration inside her coat. The heat of the fire and the agony of embarrassment had combined to make her face scarlet. She walked past him without looking at him, on down the stairs, then out to the car. She climbed in and started the engine without a backward glance.

The narrow drive widened at its junction with the road; she pulled up onto the grass, killed the engine and sat with her face in her hands. Dear God, what had she done? What had possessed her? It was a full ten minutes before she groped in her pocket for her mobile and called Ruth. There was no reply. She didn't leave a message. What was the point? The damage was done.

A packet of letters was waiting for Thomas when he returned to the house in the last week of the month. There was one from each of his brothers. He opened the one from Harry first. It was full of gossip. He and Christian had moved from Shoemakers Close and were now living in a lofty tenement in Halkerston's Wynd which afforded them more space for Christian's tea parties which, he said, were the toast of Edinburgh society and a way of keeping up with family and friends. Thomas paused wistfully in his reading to glance round the room in which he sat, imagining the scene. Here in Kentish Town they knew few people and had time and money for nothing save the basic necessities of life. As if reading his thoughts, Fanny put down her sewing and came to stand beside him. She put her hand on his shoulder. 'It will be worth it,' she whispered.

He looked up at her and smiled. 'How did you know what I was thinking?'

'I always know.'

'I miss my family. It has been so long since I saw them.'

'I know.' She stroked his face. 'But we've done something neither of your brothers have achieved.'

'We have?'

'We have given your mama three lovely grandchildren, Tom.'

'I wish she could see them now.'

'She will. When you have your first position at the bar we shall have the money to go to Edinburgh. Is the other letter from David?' Her sharp eyes had missed nothing.

He picked it up, slid his finger under the seal and unfolded the sheet of paper. It was sent from Kirkhill. 'I am sorry to have to tell you that our old sennachie, Duncan, died this last week. He had been ailing for some months and kept to his chamber. He was very insistent that I tell you and that you be reminded of his final instructions to you. It must be a long time since you saw him, Tom, but he always had your well-being particularly at heart.'

Thomas looked up. His eyes were full of tears.

'What is it? What does he say?'

'Duncan, our sennachie, is dead.'

'But you saw him only a few days ago. You told me.' She put her hand to her mouth. 'Oh, Tom. Was he a ghost?'

He nodded slowly. 'I should have realised. I should have listened.'

She stepped away from him, studying his face. 'Tom, I know you have this ability to see things beyond this world but it always scares me.'

He reached out to her, winding his arms around her waist, clinging to her, burying his face in her skirt. 'It scares me too.' He glanced up at her through his tears. 'It's a gift, Fanny, something I've been chosen for, to use for the good the knowledge brings, but sometimes I don't understand the messages I'm being given. Duncan could have, would have, taught me more if I'd listened to him, but I was always too far away, always in too much of a rush to learn from him.'

She hugged him more tightly. 'That is all part of your talent, my darling.' She put her hands on his shoulders and pushed him away so she could study his face. 'It would be easier with your family around you, I know that. Your mother is such an inspiration to us all, but especially to you. We could move to Edinburgh, Tom. To be near them all.'

'No need. I have Anne and Isabella to hold me steady here.' He gave her an impish look. 'I mean to rise in the law, Fanny. I love my brothers dearly but in Scotland I would be eclipsed by them as I always have been. The earl, who will always be the earl, and the lawyer so many years ahead of me and already a rising star of the Edinburgh bar. No,' his grin widened into a smile. 'We will leave Scots law to Harry. I am going to make English law my future. There are enough Erskines in Scotland already. London is where this one is going to make his mark.'

45

'You still haven't told me why you're here.' Ruth greeted Harriet at the door in astonishment, glancing beyond her to the borrowed car and then standing back as Harriet pushed in past her.

'Is Finlay here?' Harriet headed for the kitchen.

'No, he's gone into town.'

'Good, because we need to talk.' Harriet stopped in the middle of the room, her back to Ruth. Her fists were clenched as she turned to face her. 'I've done something terrible.'

'Go on.' Ruth eyed Harriet's face with a sinking heart.

'I went to see Malcolm Douglas. I'm sorry. I was angry. I wasn't thinking straight.'

She waited for Ruth to say something. The silence stretched out between them as Ruth closed her eyes and sighed. 'Go on,' she repeated. 'You'd better tell me what happened.'

'I wanted to protect you.'

'From what?'

'I don't know. I just felt he was bad news.'

She stepped back as Ruth walked past her and went to sit at the worktop. 'I think you needed a far better reason than that to go and see him.'

'I know.' It was a whisper.

'So, what was it?'

'It just didn't sound right, OK?' Harriet was almost shouting. 'So much secrecy, so much pseudo modesty. Not charging. Keep it quiet and don't tell anyone. Having secret sessions with you all alone in the woods. It sounded dangerous. Creepy. And I'll bet he's spying on your work as well. You know he's writing about William Pitt?'

'Yes, he told me.'

'I saw some stuff on his desk. You know Erskine and Pitt hated each other. They were on opposite sides politically. Has he asked to read any of your notes?'

Ruth didn't reply.

'He has, hasn't he.'

There was another silence, then, 'I thought I could trust you, Hattie.'

'You can.'

'So, what happened?'

'This was our thing and he's taking over. He's deliberately sidelining me.'

'Why on earth should you feel that?' Ruth rubbed her forehead. 'You know as well as I do that we couldn't cope.'

'No. We needed an expert on psychic stuff, not a bestselling historian.' The words were so loaded with venom they sounded like an insult.

'I'm not writing a history book. Even if he does write about Thomas, it wouldn't matter.' Ruth slid off her stool. 'Hattie, you're sounding unhinged.'

'D'you fancy him?' Harriet hadn't moved. 'You do, don't you.'

'No! For God's sake, Hattie!'

'He's a good-looking man. I wouldn't blame you. Is he married?'

'I have no idea if he's married. It never occurred to me to ask. I do not fancy him, as you put it.' Ruth was furious. 'I never had you down as having a jealous streak.'

'And I'm not. Usually.' Harriet took a deep breath. 'I haven't told you the worst yet.'

Harriet saw Ruth's shoulders tense as though warding off a blow. 'Tell me.'

'He said he can't trust you any more because you spoke to me. He doesn't want you to contact him again.'

'Ruth?' Fin had returned at lunchtime. He walked into the kitchen and threw his keys down on the worktop. Reaching into the cupboard he produced two tumblers and set them down next to the keys then he called again. 'Ruthie! Where are you? I have good news.'

When she eventually came downstairs he could see she had been crying. Without a word he poured her a whisky and put it into her hands, folding her fingers round the glass. 'Take a slug of that then tell me.'

When she had finished he gave a small sigh. 'What is it with women?' he said. 'This always happens. They tell each other everything, then they wish they hadn't. It invariably ends badly.'

She gave a watery smile. 'So speaks the expert on female psychology.'

'Why d'you think I never married?' He put his hand over his mouth. In mock remorse. 'Don't answer that. So, what do we do? Have you rung Malcolm?'

She shook her head.

'Maybe a dignified silence is best for now.' He sipped his drink thoughtfully.

'You haven't told me your good news,' she said at last.

'Max has got me a wonderful tie-in. A book to go with the TV series.' He kissed his fingertips. 'Fantastic deal.'

'That's great.'

'It is. Let's drink to it.' He raised his glass. 'Where has Harriet gone?' he asked after a moment.

'I've no idea.'

'Would it help if I had a word with Max? He can always explain to Malcolm—'

'No!'

'OK.' He glanced at her under his eyebrows. 'Lunch? Food always helps in a crisis, in my opinion.'

'Which explains your less than sylphlike figure.'

'Ouch. There's no need to be nasty just because Harriet has dissed you.'

'Sorry.' She took a gulp from her glass and spluttered. 'This is strong!'

'That's for the best.' He headed for the pantry. 'Now, let's see what food we can rustle up to cheer madam out of the vapours.' He glanced towards the window. 'You haven't seen any more of Timothy and his sister, I take it?'

'No.'

'Then let's be thankful for small mercies.'

She watched listlessly, every now and then glancing at her phone, which stayed resolutely silent, as he busied himself at the counter, collecting a chopping board, some mushrooms from a pottery bowl on the windowsill, a bottle of olive oil and a jar of Arborio rice, slicing onions with small assured strokes of his knife, sweeping them into his pan on the stove, filling the kitchen with luscious smells.

'I am so lucky. There must be a million of your adoring fans who would give their right arm to eat the food you prepare,' she said.

'Indeed, you are lucky. So you're going to eat it.' He opened the fridge and brought out several packages. 'I fear it's Max's proximity to wonderful shops that dooms my potential for being a sylph,' he muttered, almost to himself.

She smiled. 'What happened to self-control?'

'Not in my job description.'

'What am I going to do, Fin?' She held her hand over her glass as he picked up the bottle for a refill.

'I suggest you do nothing. You have plenty to occupy you. You're researching the life of Thomas Erskine, for your own interest, and it's no one else's business but your own. Whether you see Harriet again is up to you.' He collected a bottle of wine from the counter with two glasses. 'Don't look at me like that. You have had only the smallest dram and now a wee glass of wine will do you no harm at all. I know Harriet's your oldest friend and all that, but friends, real friends, don't act like this. What was she thinking of?'

'She thought she was saving me. Apparently.'

'From what?'

'She said Mal was a charlatan. And that he was out to spy on my work.'

'That makes no sense. We went to him; he didn't know what we wanted; he certainly didn't know what your interest was.'

'He did ask to read Thomas's letters last time I saw him.'

'To help find out who the ghoul is?'

'I suppose so.'

'There you are then.'

'But supposing Harriet's right? Supposing there's historical stuff here that Mal doesn't know about. He would be interested, wouldn't he?'

'Of course.' He poured the wine and sat down again. 'Forget them both for now. One or other of them will come back to you eventually and then you will have to respond. My guess is that that response will be instinctive. You'll say what you really feel. Until that happens, don't give it a thought.' He edged a glass over towards her and reached for his own. 'So, who was the Whig and who was the Tory?'

She smiled. 'Thomas was a Whig.'

'Ah, pity. I always had rather a soft spot for eighteenth-century Tories. They supported Bonnie Prince Charlie. Much more romantic.'

'Thomas's family seem to have had Jacobite leanings. But like so many Scots families, they were pragmatic. They kept their views to themselves.'

'So they didn't spoil their job opportunities.'

She gave a wry smile. 'Cynical but sensible.'

'My history is a bit shaky. Was Pitt a Tory then?'

'I think so. But not a Jacobite.' She sat staring into space for a while as he stirred the pan, then almost visibly shook herself out of her reverie. 'So, what are you, Fin? Twenty-first-century Tory or are you a Whig as well?'

'I'm not sure there is such a thing as a Whig these days. But it's immaterial. I don't do nowadays politics. Far too fraught.'

'That's what I think too.' She picked up the wine glass and took a sip.

'It won't be Mal,' she said after a long pause.

Fin frowned. 'What won't?'

'Who comes back to me. I made a promise and I broke it. He only made one stipulation about helping me. Just one. And I blew it.'

Fin spooned steaming risotto onto her plate. 'Didn't you tell me that he has already taught you what to do if the bad guy comes back?'

'He told me what to do, but not how to do it. I need to strengthen my spiritual core.'

'Like Pilates?'

She smiled again. 'Something like that.'

'So, perhaps you don't need him any more anyway.'

'Perhaps not,' she sighed.

Thomas

In January 1776 I became what was known as a Fellow Commoner of Trinity College, Cambridge. As, at the same time, I was studying at Lincoln's Inn and was a pupil successively of two top counsel, I exercised my right, as the son of an earl, not to attend lectures or take an examination to obtain my degree. But I had to pay for everything, even the bedmaker who looked after my rooms, and those rooms were a haven of peace after the chaos of my home life, so when I could I took time to travel to Cambridge and go to a few lectures, where I studied English composition, and I am sorry to say I felt not a moment's guilt in leaving Fanny and Abi to take care of my family while I enjoyed those short interludes of the kind of academic rigour I could only dream of when I was a boy.

I was leading an exhausting double life. I found it hard to study at home, reading late into the night and growing ever more cross and irritated with the children and their noise. Abi would take them out all day, attempting to tire them out, but at night when I was sitting with my candle and a tankard of porter, trying to read, one or other of them would begin to cry. Though I would clamp my hands over my ears to block out the sound, I could hear Fanny's urgent whispers as she endeavoured to soothe them, and the patter of Abi's feet as she ran up and down the stairs on her pittance of a wage, which sometimes was nothing at all. Even though my door remained closed I lost the thread of my reading and would have to go back to the beginning of the page yet again as the ink scattered droplets across the page or dried on the nib of my pen.

One day when I came home with my usual package of cheap meats for our supper, the house was empty and I found a note from Fanny on the table. 'I have found the perfect solution. The children and I are staying with my cousins near the Fleet Ditch. We are welcome there and we will return home when you go up to Trinity again. Call in on your way to Lincoln's Inn and we will kiss you good morning. Enjoy the peace, my darling.'

I smiled with relief and fervently kissed the note. My perfect wife who understood all and everything about me had solved our problems at one brave stroke. Her cousins, the Moores, lived in a chaotic crowded house at the foot of Ludgate Hill. They were successful jewellers and the most charming and kindly people who used to refer to me as 'our Tommy'. I had no idea how they would accommodate Fanny and Abi and the children, but I tried not to think about it beyond giving thanks to the Almighty and blessing them all as I spread out my books and in a fit of extravagance lit a second candle as I ate her and Abi's portion of cold cow's heel and tripe with my own.

I would not have been so joyful had I realised that Fanny was again with child and that living where she now did she was going to be walking daily into the stamping grounds of Andrew Farquhar. And neither of us remembered the fetish, tucked in a drawer in Kentish Town, where it could protect neither my family nor me.

46

Malcolm was lying staring up at the ceiling. When he was a child he had chosen a fourth-floor room in the tower as his bedroom and he used it still, in spite of its vaulted stones and narrow staircase. It had a larger window than the bedrooms on the floor below, inserted by a previous Douglas before some petty bureaucrat had invented the concept of grading buildings, forbidding alterations to one's own house, and it gave a view across the treed valley with its broad river and up to the wild hills beyond. The version of the window story he preferred was that an ancient enemy had created the casement by lobbing a cannonball through the wall. Job done. Building alteration. Perfect. He levered himself out of bed and went to look out, pushing the casement open and leaning with his elbows on the broad sill. One of the great things about living in a castle: thick walls meant wonderful windowsills.

The night was still and cold. Somewhere in the distance an owl hooted as it hunted along the river. He was thinking about Ruth. The overriding thought in his head when he had awoken so suddenly was that she was in danger and that he hadn't helped her. He had spent his time telling her what was wrong with her, poor woman, but he hadn't given her the tools to deal with her problem and he hadn't concentrated on the scariest part of her predicament, the lascivious ghost.

Harriet would have gone straight over to see her and told her what a narrow escape she had had and he had been unfair, he knew that. He shouldn't have expected or even asked Ruth to keep the fact of his involvement secret. He sighed. He had remembered Harriet, of course he did. He gave a wry smile. The woman sold a hell of a lot more books than he did, and they were popular. Readable, if her reviews had been anything to go by.

The owl hooted again, closer this time.

The dogs were waiting as, having pulled on sweater and jacket, he let them out into the icy dawn and headed for the woods.

Lighting the small wood burner in the chapel, he sat down and waited for his thoughts to settle as the first light began to creep in through the small windows.

It was mid morning when he reached the Old Mill House. He rang the doorbell and waited, wondering if he should have phoned. Finlay opened the door.

'I need to see Ruth.'

'Does she need to see you?' Fin folded his arms.

'Yes, she does. Urgently.'

Fin stood back. 'You'd better come in then. She's in the dining room.' He gestured behind him.

Malcolm went in without knocking. 'I'm sorry I was hasty. Harriet made me very angry.'

Ruth had been sitting staring at the screen of her laptop. She looked up at him, her eyes blank, as though for a moment she didn't recognise him, then her face cleared and she smiled. 'I thought I'd never see you again.'

'I didn't intend that you should. But you need me.'

He pulled a chair out from the end of the dining table and sat down, leaning towards her. 'Have you had any more trouble?'

'I watched Thomas dream. It was so odd. I suppose I was dreaming myself.' She looked at him steadily. 'I was devastated when Harriet said you'd washed your hands of me.'

'Is she staying here?'

'No. She has friends in North Berwick. She came to tell me what she'd done and I told her to get lost. I was very angry. I apologise, for her and for me. I didn't keep my word. I shouldn't

297

have told her about you. I thought as she was part of it I could trust her.' She hesitated. 'I need you, Mal.'

'I think you do.' He held her gaze. Neither of them spoke. In the silence the door opened and Finlay walked in.

'Sorry, am I interrupting? Does anyone want strong black coffee? If you do, come out to the kitchen.'

As he retreated, Mal stood up. 'Coffee's good.'

When they walked in Finlay turned and surveyed them both. 'Have you forgiven Ruthie? If I lay my hands on Miss Jervase I'll give her a piece of my mind, I can tell you. We have enough problems going on without her sticking her oar in.'

'It's sorted.' Mal pulled himself onto a stool.

'I gather she thought you wanted to plagiarise Ruth's story of her ancestor.' The kitchen was full of the rich scent of the coffee.

'Fin!' Ruth objected.

'No. She was right to be worried,' Malcolm put in. 'Harriet and I belong in our own ways to a cut-throat business. There's a lot of competition between historians. Colleagues can be deadly rivals. We guard any exciting new facts we dig out carefully. We frequently accuse each other of trying to upstage our new theories. It's one of the few ways we create enough excitement to engage the interest of the press. And I confess, I am fascinated by Ruth's ancestor, but alas, in the form in which he talks to Ruth, I can never quote him. I can quote his papers, and his letters and contemporary newspapers and Hansard, but I cannot cite the conversations of a ghost, however well meaning.'

'And anyway,' Ruth put in. 'I'm not writing a book. Please, Fin, that coffee must have sat for long enough.'

Fin obliged and pushed the milk towards her. 'Are we allowed to know what your quarrel is with Harriet?' he asked.

'We were on stage together at a book festival with a chairperson who took great delight in setting Harriet and me quite deliberately at each other's throats. Unfortunately, she has rather a short fuse, and perhaps didn't realise that we were being manipulated. It was implied that she wrote for a popular market to make pots of money and therefore wasn't as intelligent a historian as me, with my more academic approach. She took it

298

as an insult and stormed off the stage. Headlines in the press next day, which pleased both of our publishers immensely and did wonders for our sales, but she was obviously deeply hurt. I did write to her to try to smooth things over but she never replied. We hadn't seen each other since.'

'You probably need to speak to Harriet again, Ruthie, before she goes to the press with this,' Fin said.

Ruth looked at him, horrified. 'She wouldn't.'

'I'd guess she might if she's still angry. One of your charms, and your failings, is that you are a bit naive.' Fin glanced at Malcolm. 'I suspect you would agree with me.'

'Indeed.' Malcolm winked at her.

Ruth blushed. 'OK. We've established I'm an idiot. I'll do it now.' She fished in her pocket for her mobile. 'It's switched off.' She threw the phone down on the table and reached for her coffee. 'Oh God! What if it's too late? Oh, Mal, she could tell everyone about you. I'm so sorry.'

He smiled. 'Not the end of the world. In fact, an interesting footnote to my career. Don't worry about it.'

'I do worry. Your street cred would be in tatters.'

He laughed out loud. 'And my career as a psychic advisor to the stars would be launched.' He leant forward and put his hand over hers. 'Please, don't give it another thought,' he repeated.

His hand was warm and firm and reassuring. She noticed Fin looking at their two hands on the table. Malcolm saw the direction of his gaze and gently removed his. 'I must go. I have a chapter to write while I still have a publisher. In the meantime, I want to remind you that you can call me any time if you need me. I'll be there for you.' He drained his cup and stood up. 'And I would be grateful if you can find a way to defuse Miss Jervase. She's probably learnt enough by now from studying Dion Fortune to be capable of sending some psychic bullets my way if she saw fit, never mind the columns that might appear in the *Daily Mail*.'

'Column inches in the *Daily Mail* are things we lesser mortals dream of,' Fin put in. 'Don't knock the idea. It would do wonders for your sales figures, my friend.'

47

Ruth had wanted to slap Fin. He had asked Malcolm as he left if he had a wife at home waiting for him, then glanced at her with a huge wink. She sat back in her chair staring at the screen. Was she giving off some kind of signal that she was unaware of herself? Did she fancy Mal? Hattie had seemed to think so.

He was a good-looking man, obviously. Attractive. And she liked him, maybe even fancied him a little, but she didn't want to get involved. She and Rick had parted amicably; there had been nothing there to put her off men; she liked men; she had several men friends, like Fin. It was more that she had revelled in her new-found freedom and had no wish to give it up. Perhaps that mojo had been switched off as well as her spiritual one. She smiled wistfully.

Outside the window something moved over towards the shrubbery. She stood up and went to look out, her heart thudding. Not Timothy, surely. Not in broad daylight. The rain had blown away and the sky was blue this morning. The garden sparkled with hanging raindrops. The birds pecking at the lawn didn't appear to have been spooked by anyone. There was no one there. She glanced at her watch. Half an hour to read some more. It was as if Thomas was calling to her, urging his story onward. Fin was cooking and she knew better than to offer to help; they were expecting Max for supper. She turned back to her laptop and within seconds she was once again engrossed.

Winning the English Declamation prize at Trinity was the high point of Thomas's career to date. Having celebrated long and late with his friends and walked back with them along the bank of the Cam, he fell into bed as dawn was breaking.

He dreamt about Fanny. She had kissed the children goodbye, four of them now, his three adored little girls, Frances, Margaret, and Elizabeth, and his son, two-year-old Davy. She waved a hand to Mrs Moore, and then to Abi, and let herself out of the front door onto Ludgate Hill. She had a shawl about her shoulders and her reticule was hung from her wrist by a cord and he could see the happy smile on her face. She was still beautiful, his wife, and strong and happy in spite of their impecuniousness. In his dream he was gazing at the ceiling of his room, planning to tell her about his prize, how he had stood up in the chapel with its painted ceiling and looked down on the sea of faces listening to his every word, captivated by the power of his oratory.

Fanny paused at the corner of the road, looking for a gap between the carriages so she could cross to the other side and walk down Fleet Street. Why was she alone? His brain was befuddled and he couldn't understand. 'Fanny!' he called out to her sharply. 'Wait for Abi. Don't go out by yourself.'

A horse trotted by, pulling a chaise, and she couldn't hear him for the sound of wheels on the cobbles. She stepped out onto the road and he heard the whinny of another horse behind her, the shout of a postilion, the scream of a woman on the pavement. 'Dear God! Fanny!' Thomas heard himself shout her name but there was someone there to pull her to safety, grabbing her elbow, swinging her out of the road and into his arms as he half lifted, half dragged her out of harm's way. Thomas saw her face, the frightened 'o' of her opened mouth as she turned and screamed his name, 'Thomas!', the relief with which she clung to the man who had saved her and then as passers-by gathered round them, a glimpse of the face of the man who was holding his wife in his arms. It was Andrew Farquhar.

301

'Come on now, Mr Erskine, sir. This won't do.' Light flooded into his bedroom as the curtains were drawn back and his bedder was standing looking down at him. 'Been celebrating, have we, sir?' The old man stooped and began to pick Thomas's scattered clothes off the floor. 'Shouting fit to wake the whole stair you were, sir.' He hung Thomas's hat and his neckcloth on the bedpost and began to shake his jacket free of its creases. 'Shall I fetch you some coffee, sir? That will clear your head.'

'Dear Lord, Fanny!' Thomas was tangled in his sheets, struggling to get out of bed. 'The bastard has her! I have to save her!'

'I think you'll find you were dreaming, sir. Coffee will rectify the situation.' The servant was already halfway out of the door.

Thomas lay back on the pillows. His head was thumping and he tried to comfort himself. It was a nightmare. Fanny was at home, safe. She would never go out alone; the streets of London were too dangerous. Mrs Moore would go with her, or Abi.

But his dreams were often too accurate for comfort. She had called for help and he had to go to her. He dragged himself out of bed and ran to the door shouting for his bedder to come back.

An hour later he was galloping along the road towards London on a borrowed horse. Please God he would be in time to save her.

They all slept late after the supper party. Max had spent the night in the end and it was ten next morning before Fin began to concoct breakfast for the three of them.

'So, has Mal been able to help you with your ghost problem?' Max asked as Fin busied himself at the cooker.

Ruth nodded. 'Thank you for the introduction.'

'Mal's a nice man. A bit reclusive. I had no idea for years that he had a spooky side.'

'He seems very gifted.'

'He certainly is as a writer.'

'He's writing about Pitt, I gather?' Ruth put the question casually.

'Indeed. Almost finished.'

She liked Max. He had a kind, lived-in face with a small beard and wire-framed glasses that made him look, she thought, a little like Einstein. 'I like his house,' she said.

'Isn't it wonderful. It's been in his family for centuries.'

'He seemed very pleasant when I met him.' Fin had produced a pan of scrambled eggs and a huge pot of coffee. 'Does he live in that great house all alone?'

'As far as I know. He's an intensely private person, as I expect you found out. We've never discussed his family. I've only ever met his dogs. What?' He had noticed as Ruth reached to give Fin a playful slap across the table.

'Private joke, old boy,' Fin replied.

It was getting on for midday before Fin and Max left for the city; Ruth went into the dining room and switched on her laptop. There on the screen was her calculation of how long it would have taken a frantically worried Thomas to reach London from Cambridge on horseback.

She had been trying to remember her own journeys up and down the A10 to Cambridge with Rick before they were married, and she had reckoned on at least fifty miles. Obviously she had consulted the Internet.

Distance to London 54 miles; eighteen hours on foot.

By stagecoach, in 1750, two days.

A fit horse could do it in one day as long as well rested afterwards. Fastest way to travel, probably post horses?

Prince Regent rode London to Brighton (similar distance?) in four and a half hours and back the same day!

Poor Thomas, he had been out of his mind with worry. But he had reached London and all had been well.

She then reached for her copy of Lord Campbell's book. It mentioned Thomas's studies at Lincoln's Inn and his time at Cambridge. His prize oration had been on the subject of the Glorious Revolution of 1688. She looked back at the screen and began to scroll up to the top of her notes. She appeared to have written several pages, describing his life as a Cambridge under-graduate, the celebration after his dissertation in the Chapel of Trinity College, drinking with his friends, staggering happily along the Backs in the early hours, tiptoeing past the porter's lodge, his finger to his lips, avoiding the wrath of the porter for his late return when he saw the man slumped across his desk, his head in his arms, snoring. And then it was Thomas who was snoring in his bed in his set of rooms on the narrow staircase.

Ruth read her own description of Fanny as she slipped out of the house onto the busy street. She didn't remember writing any of this. Fanny was wearing a green riding habit, slightly faded and worn, and a neat feathered hat beneath which her hair had escaped into a tangle of ringlets. The street was busy, and the pavements were crowded. She was trying to cross the road and she stepped out behind a loaded handcart almost under the hooves of a trotting horse. The man who caught her arm had been immediately behind her, his hand outstretched; it was almost as if he had pushed her. Then all hell had broken loose. The scream, not from Fanny, but from a bystander who had seen what had happened, the whinny of the horse as it reared up in the shafts and the rattle of wheels, the shouts, and there before Thomas's eyes and so before her own, the man who had pulled Fanny back had turned for a moment to leer directly up, almost as if he sensed the two people watching him, Thomas and Ruth, some two hundred and thirty years apart and she had seen him clearly. His was the face of the man who had come to her bedroom; the ghostly figure who had tried to ravish her in her bed was Andrew Farquhar.

Thomas's story stopped on her screen as he threw himself into the saddle and galloped along the turnpike, away from Cambridge. No telephones, no emails, no one to contact for help; no way of knowing if Fanny was safe.

Farquhar! Ruth tried to steady her breathing. She had seen him. He had touched her! Out for some kind of perverted revenge then, was he still out for revenge now? Still, over two hundred years later, obsessed, able to leap off the page, leap out of the past? She shuddered, hugging her arms around herself. Logic told her none of this was real, it couldn't be, but logic no longer had any part in this.

She reached for her mobile.

'Mal. The ghost is Farquhar! I recognised him.'

'Is he there now?'

'No.' She took a deep breath. 'Sorry. I shouldn't have rung you. It's just – I was dreaming. At least, I suppose I was—'

'Do you want me to come back?'

'No.' The sound of his voice reassured her and she pulled herself together with an effort. 'I'll be OK. You didn't sound surprised. You knew it was him?'

'I had a suspicion. Remember, keep yourself strong. Don't let him intimidate you. If he appears, tell him to F off!'

She gave a shaky laugh. 'I love your esoteric language.'

'It will work. And surround yourself with light.'

Putting down the phone, Ruth turned back to the screen. She had to know what happened next. With the benefit of hindsight, she knew Fanny had lived to tell the tale, but she didn't know what had happened in those moments after Farquhar had caught her arm. Had she recognised him? Had she pulled away and run back towards the house? Or had she gone with him, grateful for his help?

There was nothing about this in Thomas's letters to his daughter, written some forty years after the event. She needed to talk to him directly. This was no time for scepticism. She looked across at the empty chair. 'So, tell me what happened next,' she whispered.

'I knew you'd seen it happen.' Fanny nestled into Thomas's arms as they sat together on the settee by the fire in the Moores' front parlour. 'I tried to tell you I was all right. Oh, my darling, I'm so sorry. You galloped all that way to save me.'

'What happened to him?' Thomas was holding her so tightly she could barely breathe.

'I told you. He disappeared almost as soon as I recognised him. So many people crowded round us and there was such a to-do about the horse, which had gone down in the shafts, and I was being jostled on every side and when I looked round he had gone. And then a lady only a few feet from me started shrieking that someone had stolen her purse and people's attention went to her and then I saw old Abraham who works for

305

my cousins had come out of the house and seen me and he offered to take me back indoors. There was no harm done, my darling.'

'But Farquhar was waiting for you. It can't have been chance that he was there in the crowd.'

'No,' she sighed.

'So, what were you doing out on your own? Could you find no one to go with you?' He knew he sounded more stern than he intended.

'I didn't think there was any harm. I wanted ribbons for the girls' hair. They have so few pretty things.' She caught her breath. 'Oh, Tom, I'm sorry. That sounded petty and cross. We'll have all we need as soon as you're qualified.' She reached up to kiss his cheek. 'I hadn't given Mr Farquhar a thought in a long time. I assumed he'd gone. But he didn't hurt me. Tom,' she hesitated. 'I did wonder . . . ' she paused again. 'I wondered if he had pushed me in front of the horse.' She looked up at him anxiously. 'But he couldn't have. Could he?'

'Someone would have spoken up if they'd seen him do it. Was the horse injured?'

She smiled. 'As always you think of the animal rather than your poor wife.' She punched him affectionately on the arm. 'No, it was only frightened. And the driver didn't beat it. He soothed it just as you would have done. And talking of horses, what happened to the animal you rode here on, all lathered and sweaty and exhausted as it was?'

Thomas hugged her. 'The horse is fine. Abraham sent it round to Lady Huntingdon's stables for me and it's being cossetted and spoiled and the groom will see it is returned to its owner.'

'Then no harm is done and my clever husband is come back to me with his prize and his honours and his new degree. I'm so proud of you and the children will be so pleased to see their papa.' She turned to him and pulled at the collar of his jacket. 'Muddy and dusty though he is. When you're called to the bar, my darling, you will have to smarten yourself up. You dress like a travelling tinker. Mrs Moore told me she felt you should be admitted by the back door in case her neighbours saw you. She said it as a joke, but I think there was a friendly admonishment there.'

He hugged her even closer. 'You will be saying I smell of horse next.'

'You do, Tom. And worse.'

'Then I must go home to Kentish Town. It isn't fair to inflict myself on your fastidious relatives a moment longer.' He sat up straight. 'Come home with me, Fanny. We can all have some time together before I need to study again. I've missed you so much.'

She looked up at him longingly. 'I should like that. But are you sure? You work so hard, Tom. I don't want you to be cross with the children for getting under your feet. Here they have a whole floor to themselves in this rambling house. We're so lucky to be here.'

'Abi will hold them at bay.'

She smiled. 'You know she can't always control them. They're a wild bunch, your daughters, and now little Davy is doing his best to outshout them all.'

'They take after their mama!' He pulled her towards him again. 'And I wouldn't have it any other way.'

48

Andrew Farquhar had rented a room in a dark courtyard off Whitefriars. He had acquired the services of a boy, Dickon, to act as a servant and a runner and a spy, and the person on whom he spied was Frances Erskine. She appeared to have acquired another child in the last two years, which made the total four. For some reason she had moved out of the rented house in Kentish Town and was living with the family of a jeweller on Ludgate Hill. Perhaps the marriage was unhappy. He hoped so.

The boy found it easy to break into the Kentish Town house. It was small, terraced, poorly furnished and full, so he told Andrew later, of books and papers and pens and ink. The inventory with which he carefully regaled his master was so boring that he screwed up his grubby little freckled face in disgust as he relayed the list.

Andrew smiled. 'And he will not know that anyone was in there?'

Dickon shook his head emphatically. 'Anyway, it was such a mess, how would he know?'

'Oh, he would know.' When he wanted Tom Erskine to know he had been in his house it would be on his own terms and it would be with such drama and frenzy that there would be no doubt at all as to what his visitor had done. Andrew briefly pictured the scene; Frances spread out across her husband's work table, ravished, her pretty clothes torn and ruined, and he smiled. He thought of the brief touch of her skin, the scent of rose water when he had caught her arm and pulled her away from the rearing horse. Yes, he had pushed her towards it, an instinctive move, but the second he had done it he regretted it and pulled her back. What fun would there be in her finishing up in a coffin as the result of a street accident? He gave a shudder of something like ecstasy and quickly pulled himself together as he saw the boy's eyes thoughtfully studying his face. 'Get out. Go and buy me some gin, you impudent urchin.' He felt in his pocket for some coins and tossed them onto the table. 'The Erskines are not worth bothering with at present. No money, nothing worth stealing.' He could not quite keep the smile off his face. 'We're going to bide our time.'

'Why?' The boy looked at him with his head on one side. 'What did they do to you?'

Andrew narrowed his eyes. 'That's personal and my business.' His voice hardened. 'Remember that if you value your filthy rotten skin!'

The sound behind her made Ruth whirl round. A pencil on the table was rolling towards the edge. As she watched it fell to the ground and lay still under her chair. She must have dislodged it when she stood up. She went over and picked it up, putting it back on the table. The screen of her laptop had gone blank, and she realised the room had grown very cold.

'No!' Suddenly she was furious. 'Go away, do you hear me!' *Visualise a ring of light. Don't let him see you're afraid.* She wasn't afraid. She was angry. *Strengthen your core, strengthen your protection*, as Mal had reminded her. She took a deep breath as she turned and scanned the room. It was empty. No figures, no wispy presences. He had gone. If he was ever there.

Thomas

My studies were over. I had my Master's Degree and on 3 July 1778 I was called to the bar of Lincoln's Inn. I was a barrister at last and optimistic that clients would flock to my door.

Which did not happen. Until, one day, I fell over into the mud.

I was planning to spend the evening with yet another relative of Fanny's, heading towards the lady's house with her son Charles when, cramped and bored after another abortive day at my desk, I attempted to leap a ditch as we crossed Spa Fields. I slipped and fell and sprained my ankle and had to be helped home. This was fortunate because when I arrived there I found an invitation to a dinner that, if I am honest, promised to be far more genial than an evening with old Mrs Moore.

I made an instantaneous miraculous recovery and went to the party. During the course of an animated tirade on my part I was unaware that a guest, seated further down the table, was listening to my every word. We did not meet then, but the next day there was a knock at my door and I was handed a retainer to appear at the King's Bench Court on the gentleman's behalf and with the note came my first fee, one golden guinea.

49

As he walked into their bedroom in Kentish Town, Thomas was pulling off his neckcloth. The room was dark and the candle in his hand threw wildly leaping shadows up the walls. He hadn't called for Abi to take away his clothes to brush them ready for the next day. She had enough to do now they were all back home together, and he could perfectly well do that himself. He set the candlestick down on the nightstand and threw the cloth on the bed. It was only then he noticed the figure standing in the corner of the room. 'Mama?' He stared into the shadows, screwing up his eyes. He was exhausted and his head ached. He was seeing things. He took a step forward. 'Mama, is that you?' he repeated softly.

She turned towards him and she held out her hand. *Tom.* He heard her voice clearly against the whisper of sleet against the window panes. *Always know I'm so proud of you, Tom.* He stepped forward but she had gone. There was nothing there but a crooked wall joist at the corner of the room.

'Thomas!' Fanny found him standing in the semi-darkness. He was staring at the pile of little presents for the children that she and Abi had been secreting in the chest at the foot of their bed. 'I wish I could afford more for them,' he said wearily. Christmas would be upon them in only three weeks.

Fanny looked at him, seeing at once the tears on his face in the flickering light. 'Tom. What is it?'

'Mama. She's dead.'

'When did you hear? Was there a letter?' She sat down on the bed, reaching out for his hand and pulling him down beside her. Of course there was no letter. He would have told her at once if there was.

She squeezed his hand gently. These moments of his still unnerved her, but she had learned to live with his gift of the sight. Letters would follow in due time for Anne and Isabella, and for Tom. Agnes would be buried with her beloved husband in the Abbey of Holyrood; David and Harry would be there with her. They would follow the coffin and grieve at the graveside and mourn in their own way, but in the meantime Tom had already said goodbye to his mama, alone.

'I wanted to say sorry again. I'm truly sorry I interfered.' It was Harriet.

Ruth stared out of the window as she took the call. It was almost dark.

'Have you managed to speak to Malcolm?'

Ruth hesitated. 'Yes.'

'And he's agreed to go on helping you?'

'Yes.'

'That horrible man hasn't come back, has he?'

'Yes. He has.'

'But Malcolm can get rid of him, surely?'

'I hope so.'

'And you believe in it all now? That's a far cry from the cynical lady who didn't believe in anything,' Harriet said.

Ruth laughed. 'I don't believe in quite everything,' she said drily, 'but I'm getting there.'

'So, do we assume he was someone Thomas knew?'

'Yes.' Ruth didn't elaborate.

'Oh God!' There was another pause. 'Thomas must have come across some low-life people in his career as a barrister,' Harriet went on cautiously. 'Apparently when some of Dion's followers queried who Lord E was, they said it couldn't be our Thomas as his life wasn't exemplary enough for him to be an ascended master.'

'You didn't tell me that!' Ruth was indignant.

'I only just read it.'

'Well, I've read that he achieved his greatest fame as a champion of civil liberties. That must count in his favour,' Ruth retorted.

'You'd think so,' Harriet sighed. 'Call me on my mobile if you need me, Ruthie, and apologise again to Malcolm for me. Please.'

As she switched off her phone, Ruth thought she heard footsteps outside the door. She went out into the hall and looked round.

'Fin?'

There was no one there.

The house was in uproar. Little Frances was screaming, then Lizzie and Margaret joined in. Shadows raced across the walls as Abi managed to light a lamp and ran into the girls' room from the tiny closet, emptied now of clothes, she shared with toddler Davy.

Thomas threw open their bedroom door. 'What is it? What's happened?' Fanny followed and scooped her daughters into her arms.

'A man,' Frances sobbed. 'He put his hand over my mouth, he had a knife—'

Thomas turned and pelted down the stairs. The front door onto the narrow dark, deserted street was hanging open. He did not try to follow. There was no point. Slamming the door shut he bolted it and taking the stairs two at a time went back into the bedroom. The flickering light showed blood on the child's sheets; her nightgown was torn.

'Was it Farquhar?' Fanny was cradling Frances in her arms as Abi comforted the other girls. In the next room, little Davy slept on next to Abi's truckle bed.

'I didn't see him.' Thomas was tight-lipped. 'Is she all right?'

'It's only a scratch,' Fanny pointed at the knife on the nightstand. 'It could have been so much worse.'

They looked at each other, their eyes full of unspoken horrors.

Thomas

I bought a pistol, and we moved into accommodation closer to town. There was no further sign of Farquhar but I had no doubt it had been him. Perhaps he couldn't find us. Perhaps he was content with having scared us. Perhaps he was just biding his time.

Time passed quickly. It was a matter of serendipity that I had won that first case. The substance of it appalled me, involving as it did my two passionate hates, corruption and injustice. I stood before the court and gave what might have been the best and most impassioned speech of my life. It certainly was, up to that point, as it was my first! I can still see the expression on the face of the presiding judge, my mentor, Mansfield, as he listened to my eloquence.

From that moment retainers poured in.

My handling of another case, that of Admiral Keppel, resulted not only in my fee but a personal gift of a thousand pounds from the admiral himself; I had after all saved him from the gallows. I paid off my debts. I bought Fanny dresses and shawls and fans, and toys and ribbons for the children. Later I bought a country house in Hampstead, so popular with the haut ton with its new assembly room and attractive houses. Mine was across the lane from Lord Mansfield's estate at Kenwood. I bought elegant furniture in the latest style. And best of all, I bought myself a Newfoundland dog. I called him Toss. He was a wise dog, with huge sympathetic eyes, and I trained him to sit in my chair in my chambers, spectacles on his nose and a wig upon his head. The expression on the face of clients who came in to be so greeted was wonderful to behold. My clerk was shocked but I thought it hilarious and I took Toss with me when I joined the Home Circuit of the Bar, travelling around the southern counties.

It was then, when riding between Lewes and Guildford with my friend William Adam and Toss at our heels, I had the strangest episode. Poor William thought I had gone insane. He tells me I dismounted from my horse as we walked them loose-reined over the heathland and I stood staring before me in a trance and started to talk as though thunderstruck. I proclaimed that one day I would be Lord Chancellor and carry on my chest the diamond star of the Thistle. The poor man didn't know what to do with me, so, sensibly, he stooped to a puddle and doused me with cold water. I remembered nothing of it afterwards and swore him to keep silence. What embarrassment, even for me! Dear Toss was afraid of me for several minutes after, as was my poor horse.

William was as good as his word and made no more mention of the occurrence.

And Farquhar? My little Frances did not seem disturbed by her ordeal. A few times she had nightmares, but on waking had forgotten their substance and now I could afford servants, all of whom were warned to keep their eyes open and tell me if they saw anything suspicious. I hid the fetish in the girls' bedroom, but I had lost faith in it. It had not kept the man at bay. I lulled myself into a false sense of security. I had forgotten the danger of the streets.

50

Andrew dodged into a doorway, watching Thomas walk down the street. It had been a slow morning. He had found only one or two coins in the mud. He had walked towards Lincoln's Inn out of boredom more than anything else, but then coincidentally had spotted Thomas emerging from the gatehouse, turning away from him up Chancery Lane.

An old man drove past him in a cart pulled by an emaciated pony. Andrew grinned to himself. In two steps he was alongside the cart, dragging the man off his perch on the front and leaping up in his place. He grabbed the whip and laid about the pony, forcing it into a canter, driving it straight at Thomas. The frightened animal veered across the road, tripped, staggered and almost fell as Andrew aimed another vicious swipe at its head. Already a crowd was forming. Thomas turned and found the vehicle almost on him. Still flailing blindly, Farquhar hit the pony again and the panicked creature let out a scream of terror. It tried to escape, the wheel of the cart caught a costermonger's barrow and cart and barrow overturned.

Oblivious to his own danger, Thomas dropped his blue bag and lunged furiously with his walking cane at the man he saw driving the cart. He grabbed the man's wrist, trying to wrest the whip out of his hand and managed to hit him over the head. 'You will not beat that horse!' he shouted, to the cheers of the watching crowd. He was beside himself with rage, so angry he still had not recognised the man with whom he was fighting.

'I'll do what I like!' Farquhar managed to shout through gritted teeth. 'It's my horse!'

'And this is my stick!' Thomas hit him again. Suddenly he had recognised him and his fury doubled. He was far stronger than Andrew had expected. He tried to dodge the blows, scrambled to his feet and ducked away, pushing through into the crowd.

Thomas didn't try to follow; his first and only thought was for the pony. Panting, he went back to the animal and began to soothe it as it stood, trembling, by the wreckage of the cart, stroking gentle hands over its skinny frame, horrified when they came away streaked with blood.

'That's my horse!' The original driver finally fought his way through the onlookers to reclaim his property.

'Then you should be ashamed of yourself. It's starving.' Thomas did not bother to argue. He threw a handful of coins from his pocket at the old man, ten times what the horse was worth, and, grabbing his bag, led the limping animal away.

Somehow he managed to coax it back to the stables at Lady Huntingdon's. Her groom thought he was mad. 'Not even the knacker would pay for that,' he commented, staring in disgust at the poor animal, but Thomas wouldn't listen. 'His name is Invincible,' he said. 'And we are going to feed him and tend his bruises and cuts and groom him until he shines like new.'

Not until the horse was bedded down in a safe, warm stable did he have time to wonder if Andrew Farquhar had seriously intended to kill him and if so, why?

Half an hour after she had spoken to Harriet, Ruth's mobile rang again. It was Fin. 'Max is jumping on the train to London this evening to meet up with a colleague of his and he has suggested I go with him. I would only be a couple of days,' he said. 'I'll buy a toothbrush down there. Would you be OK on your own, Ruth? I don't like leaving you again.'

Her heart sank. 'I'll be fine,' she said automatically.

The house was silent, save for the sound of the grandfather

clock ticking in the hall. She stood up, and held her breath. She had been so completely engrossed in her reading, she hadn't consciously acknowledged that at some level she had been listening. The place seemed full of strange noises tonight. Then she heard it again. Someone was looking for something, opening a drawer, pushing papers about on the hall table. 'Fin?' she called. 'Did you come back after all?'

She opened the door and looked out. 'Fin?' She heard her voice waver as she reached for the light switch. There was no one there. The front door was still closed.

She knew it wasn't Fin. He was on his way to London.

She stood for a moment looking down at the hall table. Nothing had been touched as far as she could see. There was the glass bowl, in which Fin kept the keys to the clock, the usual jumbled pile of junk mail and bills, the small japanned dish, empty now, where Fin tossed his car keys when he came in. The kitchen was in darkness too. Turning on the lights she closed the blinds and reached for Fin's little radio, sitting on the worktop. The room filled with the sound of a piano and she stood listening. It sounded like a Chopin prelude.

She wanted badly to go on with the story. It was forming in her head, weaving round her scribbled notes. Thomas's cases were all high profile and he obviously relished the challenge of the public defence against what he saw as the deep injustice and corruption of the times.

She pictured Thomas sitting elegantly on the far side of the dining room, his legs crossed, his arms folded as he sat at an angle to the table, his eyes sometimes focused on her face, sometimes staring into the far distance where his memories lay buried. It was as if she was acting as his amanuensis, putting down the facts – and surely they were facts, as he remembered them – telling the story the political biographers only skimmed over.

And if he was there with her, surely, she was safe.

So, do you intend to tell the truth about what happened to me?

The voice hissing in her ear was laden with sarcasm.

The voice wasn't Thomas's. She clenched her fists. 'What happened to you?' She spoke out loud.

There was no reply.

'Go away!' She couldn't, wouldn't, let this vile incubus frighten her. He wasn't real.

But nor was Thomas.

She wanted to ring Mal again. She needed to hear his voice. She wanted to run out of the house, slamming the door behind her, and drive back to his magical tower. She did neither. She took a deep breath, visualised a clear bubble of light around herself, held it there for a couple of minutes and then she went back into the dining room. Thomas was real. The other was not. She had to hold onto those two thoughts.

But if they were both real?

She took a deep breath. Farquhar was already in her story. After all, every tale needed a villain.

The sound of Chopin followed her down the hall.

51

Andrew Farquhar stretched out in bed with a groan and opened his eyes. Beside him, the woman was still asleep. She was snoring, her mouth slightly open. Was it Moll or was it Georgie? He screwed up his eyes and peered over the pillow towards her, his head spinning. It was neither. This one had straggling fair hair. She was pretty. Younger than Moll. Much younger. He debated whether it was worth waking her for some more of the same, then lay back with a sigh. His limbs ached and his head was throbbing from the beating Thomas had given him. He scowled. His mouth was dry and tasted like an open drain. He remembered now. His glorious attempt at running over Thomas had failed dismally and he had staggered back to his crib, bleeding. He hadn't intended to kill him; what would have been the fun in that? Just hurt him, annoy him, frighten him and throw him into the mud.

There was nothing left in any of the bottles they had drunk the night before; no food either. His pockets were empty. No doubt had they had anything of worth in them they would by now have been ransacked by the girl and she would have disappeared into the night. He gave a cynical smile. Easy come, easy go. He would have to get up; he needed a piss. He rolled out of the bed and groped for the chamber pot under the bed. It was almost full already and stank. He groaned again. This time the noise woke her and she sat up. He was right. She was young, no more than a child, and she was, she announced, hungry. He eyed her distastefully. She was scraggy, with almost no breasts. He liked his women buxom, with a bit of experience. What had possessed him to choose this one? He bent and picked her dress up off the floor. It was muslin and had been pretty once. His face softened for a moment. Had it been hers in her earlier life, bought for her by a loving mother perhaps, or had she stolen it from a washing line hung across some dark alley? He laid it on the bed. Pulling on his trousers he buttoned them wearily. He would have to go out and find something for breakfast, he owed her that much. He had no money to pay her, that was for sure. She was clutching at her dress, holding it up to hide herself, and he saw her eyes widen in a panic as he made for the door. 'Don't worry. I'll be back with something to eat,' he reassured her. He meant it.

The air was cold and comparatively fresh as he walked along the alley and out into the street. It had rained and the sun had come up; he paused and looked round. The world was beautiful this morning. He seldom noticed these days; his was a world of shadowy streets and the people around him, any one of them, a potential victim. He sniffed distastefully. He had no desire to go back to that room ever again. The girl had been verminous. He shuddered. Perhaps he wouldn't bother to go back to her. There was nothing worth stealing in the room, nothing of any value at all. He couldn't remember the last time he had had enough money to rent a decent crib. Better to cut his losses. When she was hungry enough she'd leave and find herself some other mug to infect.

There were more people around now. Ahead of him he saw an elderly man emerge from a doorway, descend the steps and turn away from him, leaning heavily on a cane. His eyes narrowed. He saw the old man grope in his pocket for a handkerchief and bring it out, wiping his nose vigorously. In three steps he was alongside him, cannoning into him, knocking him off balance. The watch was his, the silver snuffbox, the guineas in the breast pocket. With a final vicious push he left the old man lying in the gutter, sobbing, and ran straight into the arms of two Bow Street Runners.

He struggled frantically, but they had him fast. Two other men joined in. 'I saw him, the bastard! He robbed that old gent!' A costermonger had dropped his crate and joined in with alacrity. Andrew threw himself from side to side like a madman. One of the men lost his grip for a moment and he was almost free, but then another market trader joined in the affray and another. He felt rope slide round his wrists, his arms were wrenched behind him and he was lost. He was dimly aware of two women bending over the old man. He was sorry for hurting him but sorrier for himself as he felt the rope tighten as they dragged him away along the middle of the road. He was shouting and cursing, kicking out with his legs and it took four of them to hold him, lifting him clean off his feet. Someone must have hit him for he could feel his jaw aching; he barely noticed. He only stopped struggling when he was thrown into a cell and left in the darkness, his arms still bound behind him, lying on the floor as they slammed the door on him and he heard the lock grate shut.

It was several hours before two jailors appeared. They searched him roughly, removing his spoils, then untied the ropes that bound him and pulled his arms forward to fix manacles round his wrists. In the light that filtered through the open door he saw he was in a small cell without windows. 'Wait!' he called.

But they had already gone, dragging the door shut behind them. No word had been spoken. He swore viciously as the darkness descended again.

The magistrate was a tall thin man who wore wire-rimmed spectacles. There were a dozen or more witnesses there, including the old man whom he had robbed and the two women who had helped him and, to his extreme puzzlement, the girl who he had left lying in his bed and who it seemed had not trusted him to come back and had followed him. It appeared they knew who he was. He was confused. He was the Man from the Shadows; the Invisible Man. No one knew his name, but here they were claiming he was a well-known thief. They thought he was in disguise, that he had a rich house somewhere, that he had a fortune hidden away. That might have been true once, but no longer, not for a long time. He wanted to laugh but his cry of derision turned into a moan of self-pity. He had been rich, he had had everything they claimed and he had drunk and gambled it all away. He drew himself up in the dock and faced the magistrate. He could at least pretend to be an officer and a gentleman even if he stank like a street beggar. 'If I am to face a court, sir,' he said clearly, 'I need to send a message. I want my man Dickon to be fetched and a letter delivered by him on my behalf. I wish to be represented by a top barrister. I wish to be represented by Thomas Erskine of Lincoln's Inn.'

Malcolm stood looking out of his living room window towards the woods. The sun had set in a stormy blaze and it would soon be pitch-dark. Since Ruth's revelation that she had recognised Farquhar he had been growing increasingly uneasy. He had had his suspicions, but somehow the fact that she knew made her more vulnerable and this evening his anxiety quotient had been ratcheting up tenfold. His planned meeting had been postponed. That had left him time to think.

He felt one of the dogs lick his hand and he smiled. 'There's something wrong, isn't there, boy.' He felt in his pocket for his phone and scanned the screen. Nothing. It wasn't Pitt's American policies that were worrying him, he knew that. It was Ruth. He scrolled down to find her number.

'Ruth? Are you OK?'

'Hi, Mal. I think so.' She sounded distracted.

'Is there anything wrong?'

'Fin's gone down to London.'

'Do you want me to come over?'

'No.' And suddenly she was speaking in a rush. 'I was thinking, can I come to you? I don't want to be here alone. I'm sorry, tell me if it's inconvenient—'

'Come now.'

'Are you sure?'

'I'm sure. Now, Ruth.'

'OK. I'll be there as soon as I can.'

'Don't worry about collecting anything, just get in your car,' he shouted. He looked down at the phone in his hand. Call ended. He wasn't sure she had heard him.

Thomas read the note again, then he stood up. 'Is there a reply, Mr Erskine?' Charles Bevan, his clerk, was watching him anxiously, not quite sure what to make of his master's reaction. Thomas usually greeted potential retainers brought to him in chambers with interest, enthusiasm, anger on behalf of the wronged person anxious for his aid, or an instant gracious refusal, pleading overwork and lack of time if the brief failed to attract him, but this letter had been read with a mixture of emotion which puzzled him. Anger, pity, frozen indifference, each succeeded the other on Erskine's face. He threw the letter down on the desk and went over to the window, standing, his hands clasped behind his back, staring out without a word.

At last Bevan cleared his throat, reminding him that he was not alone. Thomas turned. 'Have you read it?' he asked, his voice husky.

'Yes, sir. I opened it, as I always do unless marked confidential.'

'What do you make of it?'

'It is not your usual kind of retainer, sir. It was brought by a rough-looking boy who is still outside awaiting your answer. Normally I would have thrown it on the fire, but the . . . ' there was the slightest hesitation, 'the gentleman who penned it claims to be an acquaintance of yours.'

'He claims to be my friend,' Thomas corrected sharply. 'Which he is not. We were midshipmen together in the navy many years ago.' He went back to the desk and sat down, picking up the letter again. It was a sheet torn from a notebook, crumpled and written in pencil. 'Since those days he has proved to be a charlatan and a blackguard. He has threatened the safety of my wife and my children.'

Bevan frowned, his heavy jowls making him look more like a bloodhound than ever, something which usually endeared him to his employer. 'Then there can be no possibility of your helping him, surely. Particularly as it appears that there is a string of accusations against him, and as he freely admits, the stolen goods were found on his person after his crime was witnessed by some dozen people. He claims he was framed, but I find myself wondering as to the nature of his veracity.' Bevan pursed his lips primly.

Thomas was silent. He rolled the paper into a tube and tapped the leather-topped desk in front of him. 'You are right, it is not my usual kind of case,' he said after a few moments, speaking more to himself than to his companion. 'But,' he favoured his clerk with his most charming smile, 'it would be a triumph to save the man from the gallows, for that is where he will surely end if I don't take on his case.'

'It sounds as if he is a man who deserves to swing if anyone does,' Bevan retorted briskly.

Thomas raised an eyebrow. 'Not a charitable response.'

'He does not appear to be a charitable person. If the letter is to be believed, he is accused of robbing a man of eighty who is yet likely to die of the shock. In which case he will be arraigned for murder.'

'Since the days of the Greek lawgiver, Draco, there has been a clear difference between intended and unintended homicide,' Thomas corrected him absentmindedly. 'In this case, it was clearly unintended.'

'Unless he's done it before, armed,' Bevan stated flatly. 'When has a cutpurse ever gone out without a knife about his person?'

'Was he armed this time?' Thomas responded thoughtfully. 'We would have to ascertain from the arresting officers.'

'You are not going to take the case?' Bevan was incredulous.

'I will think about it, and perhaps interview the prisoner.' Thomas sat back in his chair and laced his fingers together on the desk in front of him.

'I can enquire for you,' Bevan reminded him tentatively. 'See what word is on the street about him. Try to find character witnesses.' He cast a doubtful glance towards the letter.

Thomas looked up. 'Do that. Let us see what we are dealing with.'

That evening he told Fanny what had happened. 'You are not going to defend him?' She was horrified. 'He threatened my life, and your children! He cut little Frances with a knife! And he tried to crush you with that horse and cart. No, Thomas, you can't even think it!'

He went to stand in front of the fire. They were living now in a smart rented house; Abi had been promoted to housekeeper, though she was still more of a friend than a servant and somehow she had tracked down Martha, who was now the children's nanny. He looked forward to this part of the evening. His growing family were upstairs in their own quarters. Fanny was able to buy rich gowns; she had a personal maid and Abi had enlisted nursemaids, house servants and a wonderful cook, besides a valet and a butler. Thomas was smartly dressed though he still showed no interest in his clothes and if Fanny let him he would have gone to work in a dressing gown and slippers, distracted by a head full of his latest case.

She went to him now and put her arms around his neck, snuggling against him. 'My darling, you cannot do it. I know you. You will see this as a challenge. You against the world. But supposing you get him a discharge. Would you be proud of yourself? Would you be happy knowing he was free to prowl the streets of London again, robbing old men and women, for all we know, cutting people's throats! You and I know what kind of a man he is. We know he's guilty.' She gazed up into his eyes. 'We *know* it, Thomas,' she repeated firmly.

He nodded slowly.

'And you owe him nothing.'

He smiled at her. 'You would make a good advocate, Fanny. I've always said so.'

'Yes. I would.' She was always so certain about things. And she was usually right. 'He is not going to disturb your dreams, Thomas. Give him not another thought. The man turned to a life of crime and violence and disgusting debauchery. Abi has told me some of the things written about him in the newspapers. If he is truly the Man from the Shadows he doesn't deserve to live. Leave him to God's judgement!'

'But . . . ' he said thoughtfully.

326

'No! There are no buts! You are not God, Thomas Erskine.' Her stern face softened into a smile. 'Even though you sometimes think you are.'

'But,' he went on firmly, 'are we sure that he is the Man from the Shadows? What does he say the papers call him, the Invisible Man, a title he seems proud of. Do we allow the gutter press to make the identification, to scream of his guilt? Yes, he's a thief, we know that, and he made threats, but he never actually hurt you, Fanny. You told me he saved your life when he pulled you away from in front of the horse in the street.'

'No! You saw what happened, Tom.' She stood back from him and grabbed his arms in her small hands, tightening her grip until he winced as she held him in front of her, forcing him to look into her eyes. 'You saw it! You told me how it was. You saw, when you were still in Cambridge. You saw as if you were there. He pushed me. Yes, he rescued me, but he pushed me in front of that horse. Maybe he changed his mind about seeing me dead, but he pushed me. He tried to kill me! And he took a knife to your daughter's throat, Thomas. How can you even consider this?'

Thomas gave an agonised moan.

She released his arms and walked away with a rustle of silk skirts to stand in front of the window, staring across the street. 'So, that's settled, you will not defend him. In any case, you told me you have no time to take on new cases.'

'As always you are right, my darling.'

'So you will tell Bevan to send back the request.'

He knew everything she said was correct but he was still uneasy.

'Thomas!' His attention had wandered. His determined wife was in front of him again. 'Did you hear what I said?'

He smiled at her. 'Remind, me, my darling.' He caught her in his arms.

'I said we are going up to Hampstead tomorrow to stay in the new house. You promised. The children are looking forward to it.'

His smile broadened. He was drawing up plans with the architect to alter their new home to suit his ever-growing family.

He was full of plans for it; already there was one extra incumbent of the stable. The pony, Invincible, had responded to his new regime and become a firm favourite with everyone. He was now a family pet and would follow them round the garden like one of the dogs. The gardens, already being replanted with a huge array of flowers and trees and shrubs under the care of a wonderful Scots gardener, would be full of beauty and peace and children and animals – if the two concepts could ever be made compatible! As if on cue, the door opened and one of the dogs pushed its way in, coming to him at once and thrusting its nose into his hand. Frances shook her head good-humouredly. She was used to sharing his affection with his pets. 'I have ordered the carriage and the phaeton. Enough room for children plus servants. If the dogs are coming you can ride and they can follow with you. There will be no room for us all in the carriages!'

It would be a pleasant day. But first he had to pen the instruction to Bevan. Best do it quickly and acknowledge that he had no choice. This was one case he could not, would not take on.

52

'Why don't we go to the Old Mill House tomorrow?' Timothy had spent four days working on the Dump, trying to make it more habitable. They had bought a second oil stove and another gas camping cooker, and one room was now more or less free of draughts.

'Why?' April was sitting wrapped in a rug, listening to their portable radio. 'I told you we were going to lie low.'

'We have. We've been bloody stuck here. And we'd get the place nicer quicker if you would help.' He glared at her.

'You're supposed to be the handyman.' Her voice was laden with sarcasm.

'Don't you want to know what's happening over there? We could go and see if we can find the silver. It's there somewhere. It must be. We could burgle the place.'

'And look what happened last time you tried that.'

'So, what are we going to do?'

There was a long silence. He glared at her, waiting.

'I haven't decided yet.'

'Well, I'm going out,' he said at last, defiantly. 'I might go and have a look at Number 26. I reckon I could get in there easily enough. There's a garden at the back; no one would hear if I broke in.'

'And supposing Ruth is there?'

He grinned. 'I might take the chance to remind her how much she misses me.'

April finally looked at him. 'Are you out of your mind?'

'Only joking.'

'I wish I thought you were. You're obsessed with that woman. You stay here. Forget Ruth. Forget Number 26. We'll pay the Old Mill House a visit when I say so, and not before, do you understand?'

'So we are going back there?'

She thought again. 'Yes, we're going back there. Once they're off their guard.'

Dickon had brought Andrew the news. Thomas Erskine could not or would not defend him. He did however recommend another barrister to take on the defence and offered to defray the expenses of the case, 'for the sake of our former acquaintance on HMS *Tartar*, and ignoring your subsequent unwelcome attentions to my family'. So, Andrew found he was to be lodged in a private cell at Newgate Prison until his trial, bed and candles were to be provided and Dickon would be given the money to bring in food. 'To assuage his conscience,' Andrew sneered as he looked round his new abode. Dickon wisely held his tongue.

The barrister, though eloquent, did not succeed and Andrew Farquhar was found guilty of a whole raft of crimes, from petty theft to murder.

Word was brought to Thomas as he sat at the breakfast table with Fanny. He was tempted not to tell her after he had read the letter, but, seeing her watchful eyes upon him, changed his mind. 'They found Farquhar guilty last night.'

She closed her eyes and took a deep breath. 'Will he hang?'

'Yes.'

'God rest his soul.'

'Indeed.'

They sat in silence for several minutes then Thomas rose to his feet. 'I must go to my chambers.' He walked over and kissed the top of her head. 'It's no more than he deserves.'

'No.' She reached up and clasped his hand. 'I will tell Abi.'

'Of course. It will in any case be in all the newspapers. They love a good hanging.' His voice was grim.

'Will you visit him in prison?'

'No.'

He kept his word, but on the morning of the hanging he found himself in the crowds making their way to Tyburn in the company of his friend, James Boswell. 'I went to a hanging once before,' Boswell had confided. 'As you know, I went with a kinsman of yours. I did not intend to go again.' But he had reluctantly agreed to Thomas's persuasions. Thomas had to go. He felt he owed it to the man, he wasn't sure why.

The night before, he had a dream. If it was a dream. Voices were calling to him, voices he somehow knew were from the past.

Don't go.

Who were these people, gathering round him, wise men, and women too, ancients, his ancestors, why did they bother themselves with his affairs?

Don't go.

How could he not? It was his duty. If he had chosen to represent Farquhar, could he have saved him? He doubted it. For all his confidence in his own capabilities, he could not in all conscience try to save the neck of a man whom he knew in his soul to be guilty, to be evil through and through.

So he ignored the voices in his dream.

He and Boswell had tickets for the stands erected to give those prepared to pay for a better view of the proceedings over the heads of the milling crowds. Thomas stared round. Hanging days were one of the popular sights of London. The air was full of the smell of food from the stalls set up along Oxford Street; pedlars circulated with printed texts of the full confessions of the men about to die. There were no women today, which would disappoint some. His eyes kept going back to the stark silhouette of the gallows, empty for now, and he realised he felt sick.

They could hear the carts coming from a long way away by the roar of the crowds that accompanied them. He could feel the palms of his hands sweating. Farquhar was, it appeared, the star of the show today. The Invisible Man, the gentleman thief whose knife had a silver blade, murderer, blackmailer and all-round low-life crook.

He was dressed for the occasion in smart new clothes, his hair tied back jauntily, smiling, acknowledging the swelling roar of the crowd. The cart in which he stood pulled round in front of the stand and Thomas felt the man's gaze. The two men looked at one another for a full minute as the horse was brought to a halt by the press of people and Thomas felt the full force of the man's stare as the mocking insouciance adopted to please the crowd fell away for a moment to show the icy hatred beneath. 'My God!' James Boswell whispered. 'He doesn't care for you, my friend.'

'No.' Thomas's voice was husky. 'If I were a papist I would be tempted to cross myself.'

Boswell chuckled. 'Papist or not, I would do it.'

'Hanging should not be made a public spectacle,' Thomas muttered. 'This reduces people who watch to the lowest of the low.'

'And that includes us?'

'No.' The retort was brisk. 'We are not here for fun.'

Each man was allowed his time to address the crowd. Farquhar was the last to speak. As he stood up, ignoring the clergyman who stood beside him, Bible in hand, he looked down at the crowd, bowed and smiled and gave them a few words of wit and wisdom that had his audience howling with approval. It was as the hangman stepped forward to pull the cap over his eyes that they heard him utter the one word, 'No.' The man shrugged and stood back to adjust the noose, leaving Andrew's face uncovered as he turned towards the stands. His eyes once more sought out Thomas. He gave a small bow. 'We will meet again,' he called, his voice carrying over the howls of the crowds around him. 'Don't think you'll escape me.'

The gleeful yell of the crowd as the rope pulled taut was deafening. Farquhar kicked desperately for a long time before the movements grew feeble and at last he was still, his neck bent at a grotesque angle, the only one to have elected to leave his face bare.

Thomas sat still, mesmerised by the bloated, terrifying rictus of the mouth, the staring eyes. He had seen the thing he dreaded most, the shadow lifting from the body, drifting towards him and hovering at the end of the row of seats, and he saw the shadow's lips move, the repeated words drifting like smoke.

Don't think you've escaped me.

Boswell sat beside Thomas for several seconds, then put his hand on his friend's shoulder. 'It's over. Let's find a drink.' His voice was hoarse. Around them people were already moving, the entertainment over, vacating the benches, setting off back into town, still in festive mood.

Thomas climbed to his feet and followed his friend down the rickety steps. He gave one last glance over his shoulder towards the scaffold. Around it the ground was rapidly emptying, the grim structure under guard, the bodies left to hang until they were taken away on the carts. There was nothing now but wind-blown rubbish left to show for the vast numbers of people who had been there.

The two men followed the crowd for a while then turned off Oxford Street and ducked into the first tavern they found. Boswell pushed his friend into an empty booth and went to order two double brandies. He put a glass into Thomas's hand. 'Let's drink to the man's soul, may it rest in peace.'

Thomas shivered. 'That man's soul will never rest in peace.'

'Aye. I got that message loud and clear. I'd not want to be haunted by the likes of him.' Boswell tipped his drink down his throat. 'But a God-fearing man like yourself has nothing to worry about, surely.'

'Nothing at all.' Thomas threw back his own drink and felt in his pocket for some change. 'Let's have another of those. When I get home I want to be too drunk to remember anything at all about today.'

53

Ruth had been about to gather her books and papers into her bag. She glanced at the story she had been reading, the scribbled, breathless account in Thomas's journal of the hanging of Andrew Farquhar and in spite of herself she read on, seeing the scaffold in her head. The carts, the horses, the crowd. The condemned men, their elbows strapped to their sides, leaving their hands free to pray, the thick ropes around their necks, their nightcaps ready to pull down over their faces. It was horrific.

She couldn't stop reading. Only when James Boswell stood up and prepared to help his friend home from the tavern did she close the notebook and shakily stand up. She wished she hadn't read it. She felt sick.

The Chopin recital had long ago finished and now there was something orchestral on the radio. She listened for a moment without recognising it. Closing her laptop, she slid it into its bag. Notebooks, files of letters, the little journals she was only now beginning to explore, and textbooks joined it and she was ready to go upstairs to grab some overnight things.

The light on the landing was on and as she looked up she thought she saw a shadow move. She hesitated then forced herself to climb the stairs. All she needed was a toothbrush, a change of clothes.

The light was flooding out of her bedroom door. She must have left it on. She took a deep breath. Surround herself with the bubble of protection then go in, collect her stuff and leave. It would take two minutes. Somehow she made herself approach the door.

The room appeared normal. There was no one there. The curtains were stirring gently as the night wind blew outside the window. She walked over to it, made sure it was closed and locked, then she turned towards the bathroom. Brush and comb, washing things, a few cosmetics, tossed with her clothes into her holdall. She grabbed it and turned towards the door then she paused. Her mother's jewel box was sitting on the dressing table. In the bottom was a fine gold chain and, strung on it she had noticed, there was a gold cross that the Bradfords seemed to have overlooked. Her mouth dry, she fastened it round her neck. She paused and looked round. If she had forgotten anything that was tough. This time she remembered to turn off the light.

Before she left the house she carefully set the alarm, then ran the few steps to her car, throwing her bags into the boot, almost crippled with sudden panic. Her heart rate had tripled by the time she had climbed in and slammed the door and she sat, her forehead resting on the steering wheel before she leaned forward and with shaking hands inserted the key. Only when the engine began to purr quietly and solidly and she felt the little car respond to the accelerator did she begin to calm down.

Behind her, in the house, the radio played on in the kitchen. This time it was the sound of a Beethoven piano sonata that filled the silence.

Thomas found Fanny waiting for him in her small parlour. It was almost dark in there, lit by a single candle. He gave her a look of helpless misery. 'I'm sorry. James and I got drunk.'

She had risen to her feet; she went to put her arms around him. 'Was it awful? You mustn't blame yourself. Even you could not have saved him. He deserved everything he got.' Her determined tone made him realise she had been rehearsing the words, probably for hours, waiting for him to come home.

Thomas flung himself down on a chair. 'He saw I was there.'

'Here.' She poured him a brandy from the decanter on the sideboard and handed him the glass.

'Sweetheart, I'm already drunk.'

'So, another won't hurt. Then we can call Benjamin to help you to bed.'

'He bowed to me and he shouted something,' Thomas mumbled. 'James thought he cursed me, but the man in front of me said it sounded more like a promise.' He took a gulp from the glass. 'A promise to meet again.'

Fanny paled a little as she went back to the sideboard. 'Here. Take some more. Put him out of your head.'

'He swung there and he kicked so desperately and he didn't die. Not for ages. It is a barbaric death, Fanny, with the crowd baying like hounds. It is despicable. If it must be done, it should be done decently behind walls.' His hands around the glass were shaking.

She sighed. 'He threatened me and your children, Tom. He attacked our daughter; he tried to push me under a chaise.'

'I know.' He straightened, sitting back in the chair and reaching for her hand. 'You are right, my darling. He deserved all he got. And he did not repent nor make his peace with God. I pray for him that his soul at least will rest quiet now.'

'And at last we are safe, Tom.' She dropped a kiss on the top of his head. 'What will happen to his body?' She moved away from him and stood facing the mirror over the sideboard. 'Will they bury him in a pauper's grave?'

He shook his head slowly. 'They'll take the body for anatomical research. Under the Murder Act it must be either hung in chains on public display or publicly dissected, so "that some further terror and peculiar mark of infamy be added to the punishment".' She could hear the quotation of the law in the tone of his voice. '"*Pour encourager les autres*," as Voltaire said.'

'Oh, Tom.' She shuddered. 'Then he will never rest in peace!'

'No.' Tom took another swig from the glass. 'I fear not.'

'He will not haunt you, Thomas!' She knelt in front of him and reached up to hold his arms, her fingers white with the strength of her grip, her face anxious and determined. 'I will not let him. I will protect you, with my own dying breath if need be.'

'Sweetheart!' he leaned forward. 'My brave wonderful darling. I fear no one can stand in his way if he has made it his last wish.' He leaned back with a deep sigh.

'They can. I can. And you have your lucky talisman.'

His eyes flew open. 'The charm from the obeah woman? It was always directed against him.'

'You still have it safe?' she whispered.

He nodded. 'I have it safe.'

'And you have prayed, Tom?' She sounded stern.

He smiled. 'I have prayed, my darling.'

'Then he can't harm you. All his curses will be useless.' She scrambled to her feet, smoothing her skirts as she stood up. 'Now, go to bed. You need to sleep. Today is best forgotten.'

She went to the sideboard and reached for the little bell. Benjamin, Thomas's valet, must have been waiting outside the door. He gave his master his arm and steadied him as he stood up, guiding him towards the door. Fanny waited until they had disappeared then she sat down in her turn in his chair. She had left her Bible on the little side table, the page marked with a silk ribbon. In St Matthew's Gospel Jesus had rebuked a devil and cast it out and told his disciples if they had faith the size of a grain of mustard seed then they would be able to move mountains. She closed her eyes. 'Please, Lord,' she whispered. 'I have more faith than a mustard seed. Give me the strength to keep Tom safe.'

Ruth swung the car out of the lane and drove down into Cramond village, turning into the car park. Her panic had returned and was growing stronger. She couldn't get rid of the feeling that someone or something was with her inside the car, clinging to her jacket, tangled in her hair.

Flinging open the door she scrambled out and ran through the hedge and down towards the beach to stand staring out across the stormy Forth. The wind had risen. It tore at her hair and her jacket, thrashing the water into waves that crashed onto the shore and over the causeway that led to Cramond Island. She was tempted to try to walk across to the island before it was completely covered. Surely Farquhar, if it was Farquhar, couldn't follow her there? The force of the sea would purify her, purge him out of her system. This was Thomas's battle, not hers. She groped at her throat for the little cross and held onto it tightly, part of her even now unable to believe she was doing such a thing.

The gold was warm and reassuring in her cold fingers.

In her pocket her phone rang. She fumbled for it. 'Mal?'

'Where are you? Are you all right? What's that noise?'

'It's the wind and the sea. I was afraid I'd brought him with me and I thought I could blow him away.'

'Good idea. Are you OK?'

'I think so. I'm on my way now.'

She climbed back into the car and reached for the ignition key. It had worked. For the time being, Andrew Farquhar had gone.

Thomas

I tried to put all thought of Farquhar away. I would not let his memory haunt me. And for a while my resolution held.

The sadness engendered by the death of my sister Isabella's kind husband, William, did much to distract Fanny and me from thoughts about the wretched man, as did my involvement with the defence of Lord George Gordon, one of the cases that was to establish me as England's most successful barrister.

The following year England's most successful barrister allowed himself to be involved in the idiocy of fighting a duel. In Lewes, of all places. My opponent was an apothecary, but as conscious of his honour as I was. Luckily neither of us was hurt (I had taken the precaution of writing a will) and the matter was dropped before we were discovered. I decided to forget the incident. Just as well. It was soon after that Lord Mansfield suggested I take silk.

I was a rich man now and my own family, my darling wife and children were happy. We called our house in Hampstead, Evergreen Hill. The air was good and there was land, the gardens we had dreamt of so longingly when we were first married with our own Scots pines, obtained from Kew at the behest of my garden designer, Humphry Repton, to join those already there. There were views across the heath-land towards Windsor Castle in the far distance to the west and London to the south, space for the children and the animals, farmland behind us. It was heaven on earth.

As my workload increased I needed a base closer to Lincoln's Inn so I bought a house there as well, at Number 36. It was the perfect balance. I did not forget to write to my brothers, informing them of my new addresses.

Modesty must prevail. I did not win every case in which I was involved but my speeches continued to be admired; I entered politics and became Member of Parliament for Portsmouth. I cared neither for Portsmouth nor politics. And I did not care at all for Prime Minister William Pitt, nor he for me; my loyalty was as ever with his rival, Charles James Fox. Speeches before parliament did not set me (or I regret to say my audiences) on fire! When I lost my seat after the fall of the government it was with relief that I returned to the practice of the law, and found all my enthusiasm and my natural wit and brilliance returned. Do I boast? I was often accused of it, especially by Fanny. People did not always appreciate my sense of humour. It didn't worry me. I was passionately enjoying my life and, I confess, hoping that, from faraway Scotland, my brothers were watching my success as I travelled round the country, on one occasion as far as St Asaph's in North Wales.

And then as a great meteor soared across the skies of London to the terror of the general populace, my nightmares began again.

54

'It was a pencil. Just a pencil, rolling across my desk.' Ruth was still mystified by her own reaction. 'It scared me more than any of the vile things he has said and done.'

Malcolm sighed. 'I think I can understand that.'

They were sitting by the fire in his living room, listening to the rain and wind battering against the tower.

'And then Fin rang and said he wasn't coming home. I thought I could stay there by myself, I thought I was strong enough, but I kept hearing noises . . . ' Her words died away. 'I was reading about the hanging. It was awful. I couldn't stay. I was terrified. I climbed into the car and I thought I was safe, then I sensed he had come with me after all and all I could think of was to get to the sea. It was wild. Primeval. Cleansing. I somehow knew he wouldn't like it; he wouldn't stay with me, if he was there at all.' She sat back in her chair, staring into the flames.

'You are one brave lady,' Mal said softly.

She sighed. 'Mad, more like. I can't seem to stop reading the story even now it scares me so much.'

'Because you want, even need, to know what happened. I know how that feels better than anyone. But, Ruth, you must accept that, if you go on reading, you will go on seeing things that frighten you. If you want all this to stop, stop reading.'

'I can't. It's my history, My family. I want to know about

341

them so badly. I suspect my mother never read this stuff, Mal. Maybe that's why Farquhar left her alone.'

'If he did.'

'He must have. Otherwise she would have been in an asylum.' She was silent for a while. 'Where do they go between times, Mal? Is there a waiting room somewhere where restless spirits queue up ready to launch themselves into the world they used to live in? Harriet said I was muddling ghosts up with vampires, but I would like to think that Farquhar crawls back into his coffin at dawn.'

'He wouldn't have had a coffin.'

'No. Dissected.' She shuddered. 'In public.'

'A grim end.'

'Do you believe having the vicar at your hanging laid your soul to rest? He was there, but Farquhar wouldn't pray with him.'

'I suspect it depended on whether you were repentant.' Mal stood up to select another log for the fire. 'I don't subscribe to the authorised view of hell as depicted by Dante or Bosch, but I do believe people make their own heaven or hell, both before they die and maybe after. If Farquhar had a conscience about what he did in his lifetime, he would have repented. But he clearly didn't. He is angry and full of resentment.'

He threw the log onto the fire. They watched the sparks fly up the chimney. An extra strong gust of wind blew back and stirred the ashes, whisking smoke into the room. Watching it she tensed, then relaxed again.

'It may be that reading the letters has reactivated him in some way,' Mal said after a long pause. 'Perhaps you are, in his eyes, fair game as Thomas's descendant.'

'I tried to do what you told me. I pretended to surround myself with light.'

He schooled his face not to show the despair he felt as he looked at her. 'Well done.' He kept his voice neutral.

She was not fooled. 'I did a crap job, didn't I? Obviously it didn't work. I expect you can see the holes in my aura.' She was either mocking herself or him. Or both.

He inclined his head. 'For the word to even cross your lips is a step in the right direction.'

She smiled sadly, holding out her hands to the fire. 'How do we get rid of him, Mal? Do you think he will have gone back to the Old Mill House?'

'I don't think it works like that. I think he drifts in and out of existence. He draws on the energy of the environment, or of particular people, and recreates himself. Then he clings to whatever – or whoever – he has fixed on. His grasp is not very secure, I'm pleased to say, but he is persistent and, don't forget, originally, he came by invitation.'

'We were so stupid.'

'You did nothing thousands of other enthusiastic seekers after ghosts haven't done before. The worst that usually happens is that people scare themselves witless.'

'We were trying to be mediums. "Is there someone in the audience wearing a blue dress. John says to take care of your-self",' Ruth mimicked.

Malcolm gave a tolerant smile. 'I have met genuine mediums. They are formidable in their knowledge. Just as I have met people who can read one's aura and tell one everything that has ever happened in every lifetime and often everything that is going to happen as well.'

Ruth folded her arms on her knees. Near her feet, Pol stretched out his legs with a sigh. His brother had retreated behind Mal's chair, too hot near the fire.

'You are a sensitive, Ruth. You could do it.'

She shook her head.

'Well, shall we say you are potentially sensitive, but were indoctrinated from birth.' He grinned. 'You're work in progress.'

'I told you that I pretended to surround myself with light.'

'Pretended.'

'You said pretending was better than doing nothing,' she defended herself. 'And it worked. Or at least I thought it did.'

Mal glanced up, looking round. 'Cas?' he called sharply. His voice was full of anxiety. The spaniel had shot to its feet and was standing huddled against the door, trembling. He walked over to let it out. It fled down the stairs and was immediately followed by Pol.

'Was it something I said?' Ruth enquired shakily.

Malcolm had turned back into the room, his hand still on

the door handle, and was studying her with a strange expression on his face.

'What?' She stood up, frightened. 'What's wrong?'

'We have a visitor.'

Outside on the stone staircase a light bulb was flickering. And then she felt it, a cold touch on the back of her neck. She could smell him now too.

'Stand still, Ruth!' Malcolm stopped her in her tracks as she whirled round in a panic.

'I command you to leave this place. Now!' He had raised his hand and was making the sign of the cross as the room filled with the sound of insane male laughter. Ruth let out a scream as someone or something pushed her aside. She cannoned into the table, sobbing.

Malcolm ran to the window and pushed it open. 'Out!' he shouted. 'Out. Now! You are not going to have her. Do you hear me? This is a place of light!'

Silence.

Then his phone started ringing.

The sound rang out round the kitchen for several seconds, then it stopped. Their visitor had gone.

55

The old stone church was deserted. It smelt of damp and candlewax and ancient rotting hassocks. Thomas had looped his horse's rein over a gravestone in the churchyard before removing his hat, reaching for the iron ring on the door and lifting the latch.

It had been a surprise to find out from his brother Harry that he had once wanted to be a vicar in the English church, that law had been very much a second choice. At the time it had infuriated him. Harry had walked into the career he hadn't even wanted while he, Thomas, had had to struggle and fight to study something he had dreamed of since he was a boy. The curse of the third son. He walked slowly up the narrow aisle and stood staring at the altar. It was covered in a dark blue velvet cloth with a small brass cross and candlesticks. To his amusement, he saw one of the sticks was dented, immediately unable to resist visualising the vicar losing patience with a recalcitrant churchwarden and hitting him over the head with it.

Like Harry he found himself drawn towards the Church of England. It was in any case a prerequisite of his present position to attend. Methodism, which so attracted David and his sister Anne, was not for him. Nor was any religion, if he were honest. But this was where he felt at home, in the dark, spidery shadows

345

of a country church where the only liturgy was a dim echo of the past and the prayers were whispered pleas from long-dead parishioners.

And that, he realised, was why he was here. He had ignored the voices in his head for too long. The rumbustious world of politics and the intensity of the study of law had left no time for silence. Fanny found peace in the gardens at Evergreen and he was there with her when he could, but already he had had to resign his sketches and plans for the garden to Repton. A man of his standing had no time to dig his own flowerbeds.

Or to pray.

Opening the door to the front pew, the one that no doubt belonged to the local squire and his wife, he sat down and looked up at the cross on the altar. Someone was there at the back of his head anxious and determined to make themselves heard. All he could do was wait. He glanced round. There, lying on the narrow seat beside him, was the squire's lady's prayer book, and her Bible, and a slim pamphlet hidden beneath them. He pulled it out, curious to see what it was, opening it at the page marked by a length of silk ribbon and found to his delight it was a privately printed copy of 'The Diverting History of John Gilpin'. He laughed out loud. The poem had been written by his late lamented friend William Cowper. He closed the book and carefully replaced it under the Bible where the lady's husband would not see it. He would have loved to send William a note telling him what he had found. He would have been cheered and utterly charmed to be so subversive an influence during the no doubt boring lengths of a country sermon.

When he looked up he wasn't surprised to see the figure standing on the chancel steps. 'Duncan, my good friend. I'm sorry, I have been ignoring your attempts to speak to me. The duties of a lawyer seem to preclude the good manners needed to listen to my first and best advisor.'

The old man was fading, reaching out a hand towards him, almost clawing at the cold air between them. Thomas leapt to his feet. 'Duncan!'

But it was no use. In seconds he had gone. Thomas stood still, staring at the space where his old friend had been, bereft.

Duncan had been trying to warn him of something, but what? He was still too unfocused to be able to hear him.

He heard his horse whinny and he turned abruptly and strode down the nave to the door. He had been in the church longer than he thought. It was growing dark. The shadows of the great yews cast black bars across the pathway. He closed the door behind him and walked over to the horse, pulling the rein off the gravestone and leading it away from the porch. 'Sorry, Ebony.' He rubbed its ears. 'Did you get bored waiting?' He led the animal out through the lychgate and halted it beside the mounting block. As he gathered the reins the horse sidestepped, and laid its ears back as he swung into the saddle. It was staring round nervously. High hedges blocked the last of the light from the lane as he turned it back towards Hampstead. There was something or someone out there, he could feel it as easily as could the horse. Cursing the fact that he had no pistol or sword with him, he urged the animal into a canter. Whatever it was would be easily outstripped on the heath. Ebony had raced at Newmarket in his day; there wasn't a horse in London could outrun him.

But no horse could outrun his nightmares. There in the background, never far from his waking thoughts, was the hate-filled, dying face of Andrew Farquhar. Was that what Duncan had been trying to warn him about? He shuddered at the thought.

Fanny was waiting for him in the schoolroom with the children. They ran to him as he appeared. 'Papa!' Frances was now thirteen and a real young lady, her sister Margaret twelve, Elizabeth eleven and Davy ten.

'They all have work to show you, Tom.' Fanny smiled wearily. After years of blessed respite from pregnancy she was with child again and her body was heavy beneath her exhausted thin face.

'And so they shall.' Thomas sat down at the table with them. 'My darling, you should go and rest. Leave the children to me. I shall expect them to line up neatly, youngest first, and present their best efforts of the day.'

'Oh, Papa! That means I'm last!' Frances stamped her foot.

She was turning into a beauty, his eldest child. He eyed her fondly. 'So, you have most to learn, sweetheart.' He reached out and drew her to him, kissing the top of her head. 'And, you must wait. Davy will be going to school soon. He must show me his efforts as he might have the most to correct.' He looked severely at his only son, who instantly reacted by going red in the face, and opening his mouth to protest. Thomas patted Frances on the behind and pushed her to the back of the queue. He adored his children.

He helped Fanny to her feet and escorted her to the door. 'Rest,' he said sternly. He pulled her to him and kissed her gently on the lips. 'Later, when the brood have gone to bed, I shall need your advice.' She was the only person now who knew about his tussles with the visions in his head. Only Duncan knew besides her, and he had failed Duncan today.

Later when the children were dispatched to their bedrooms he let himself out into the gardens, followed by Toss. This was a magical place, surrounded by trees. He went over to the stables first to check that Ebony had been bedded down. He heard the horse give a throaty whicker of welcome while he was still outside the stable yard. He opened the door and went into the loosebox, putting his arms round the animal's neck and kissing its nose. There was no one there to see; Jake the groom had gone in for his food. 'You could tell me who it was out there on the road, old fella, couldn't you,' Tom whispered in the horse's ear. The ear flicked knowingly, but the horse said nothing. He toured the stable, speaking to each horse in turn, the coach horses and Fanny's mare and the children's ponies and, last of all, little Invincible.

He told Fanny later about the old church and its visitor. 'It worries you,' she said softly. 'But there is no danger, surely. Unless it's your own foolishness in riding round the country-side alone. Supposing there was a footpad lurking, or a highwayman.'

He laughed. 'I don't think I was in danger there, my darling. Your husband was a soldier, don't forget. I just need to get away sometimes. I am so busy. I travel with my clerk and my driver in a grand coach; I work on my briefs as I travel, I read till the early hours and my eyes close of their own volition when all I want to do is take my darling wife in my arms and make love to her.'

She giggled. 'You have found plenty of time to do that, husband mine! With all these children of ours to prove it.'

He sat with his arms round her in silence for a while. The logs on the fire were turning to ash and the candles in the candelabra were burning down, leaving trails of wax. 'I couldn't bear it if anything happened to you,' he whispered.

'And nothing will. You know I drop children with the ease of one of your bitches whelping.' She laughed. He reached over and patted her stomach gently. 'Will this be another boy?'

She shook her head. 'Abi says it's a girl.'

'What?' He pretended to be shocked. 'Am I to be drowned in women?'

'Serves you right for being such a doting father. You spoil them too much.' She sighed. 'Do we have to send Davy away to school?'

'Of course we do. This female household will be the ruin of him. All those big sisters to spoil him and now a baby as well. Winchester will knock some sense into him.'

They both fell silent at the sound of the owl somewhere close outside the window. He heard Fanny take a sharp intake of breath. She clutched his hand. 'Do you ever think about Farquhar?' she whispered.

He felt himself grow tense. 'No!' he lied. 'Why do you mention him now?'

'I saw some of Mr Hogarth's prints today when I went to take coffee with Lady Mansfield. One of them showed the body of a highwayman being,' she paused, unwilling to frame the word, 'dissected, by a surgeon. In front of an audience. It made me think what an awful fate it was.' She took a deep breath. 'How could any man's soul rest in peace, Tom, after such a thing? Supposing he still walks the earth, looking for some kind of restitution?'

'You must not think such things, my darling.' He put his arms round her. 'You are bound to be fanciful, in your condition. What was Elizabeth Mansfield thinking of, showing you such things? He has gone, his soul fragmented and scattered as his ashes must have been at the end of the experiments.'

'Is that what they do? Do they burn the . . . ' she shuddered, 'the remains?'

'I have no idea.' He sounded cross. He should know, he realised. If such a fate was the result of a case in which he had been involved, it was his duty to know such things. As to Farquhar, he had tried to forget him. But it hadn't worked. He was always there, at the periphery of his consciousness.

Gently he released her and stood up, walking over to the window. It was dark outside. He could hear the trees stirring in the wind. The owl had gone, winging its way no doubt over the lane and out across the neighbouring grounds of Kenwood towards the heath and a night's hunting. In Scotland the owl was a messenger of death, carrying the souls of the departed to the underworld.

56

April appeared to be asleep when Timothy let himself out of the house into the cold wet dawn. He had spent yet another sleepless night sitting by the defunct Rayburn and only crawled out of his sleeping bag in the early hours when he was too stiff and uncomfortable to stay there a moment longer. He tiptoed towards her and stood looking down at her. She let out a sharp snort but lay still. Cautiously he reached for her purse. There was a twenty-pound note inside and some pound coins. Silently he extricated the money and replaced the purse, then he crept towards the door. Ignoring the car, still drawn up behind the ruined building they called home, he walked slowly and pain-fully away from the Dump. On autopilot he found his way towards the main road and the all-night burger bar and ordered himself a bacon butty and coffee before retreating to a seat in the corner as far away from the counter as possible. The place was empty, but it was warm, condensation running down the windows. The guy behind the counter retreated behind his newspaper. Timothy reached for the brown sauce with a heavy sigh.

Somehow he would have to persuade April to do something soon. He wanted to go to the Old Mill House. He couldn't get Ruth out of his head. Either they could go to break in, in one last attempt to recoup their losses, or leave town and write off the whole stupid episode as a complete failure. Then they could start a new life in a new place. Yet again. Anything but go on staying where they were, with him working pointlessly day after day at holding back the tide of rot, while April sat there and watched. He sat staring down at his plate, fighting back tears of frustration and disappointment. April. Always April holding him back, getting in his way.

The door opened and two men came in. The place filled with cheery conversation. A huge lorry drew into the car park outside, turned off its lights and subsided with a hiss of brakes. Moments later the driver joined the others at the counter. There was more easy banter, laughter, the smell of coffee and frying and toast filled the air. With a wail of misery, Timothy pushed away his plate and stood up, staggering away from his table, unaware of the silence behind him as he pushed open the door and made his way out into the rain.

He hitched a lift from a lorry at the service station on the main road. He rubbed his face as he sat back in the high seat and breathed a sigh of relief. He was on his way. He need never see April again.

'Where're you going, mate?' he asked as the driver leaned forward and fired up the engine.

'Leeds do you?' the man replied.

'Sounds just about perfect,' Timothy said. In minutes he was asleep.

When the fire had burned down and Ruth could no longer stay awake, she admitted her exhaustion at last. In the silence that followed the disappearance of their unwelcome visitor Mal had put his arms around her until she stopped trembling. The dogs had come back. Everything was normal again. Now he showed her upstairs to a guest room somewhere in the lofty heights of the tower. It was a small room, comfortably furnished. The windows were set deep in the thick walls and had shutters to close off the night. 'You will be safe here,' he said. 'Call if you need anything. I'm just downstairs.'

When she made her way down the steep spiral staircase to

the kitchen the next morning it was almost nine. The lights were on and the room smelt of coffee but there was no sign of Mal or the dogs. The table was laid and the coffee pot on the side of the stove was hot. She poured herself a mug and went to stand by the window. The rain in the night had blown away and the sunlit views were stunning. She was still lost in thought when Malcolm returned with the dogs.

'How did you sleep?'

'Surprisingly well.' She watched as he sliced a loaf of bread for toast. He put butter and honey on the table. 'Why can't Thomas save me, Mal, if he's an ascended master?'

'We don't know that he can't save you. And we don't know that he's an ascended master. Or perhaps he is, but it's part of his remit that he cannot interfere with the world he left behind.' Mal refilled her mug.

'You mean there are rules?'

'Of course.'

'Set by whom?'

He laughed. 'God? I'm not sure of the hierarchy, but there is one. For millennia the teachings of adepts in every corner of the world have told us of the structures and progressions of spiritual beings.'

'Like cherubim and seraphim?'

'Exactly.'

She sat down. 'And you believe all this is real.'

'I'd like to think so, but I know no more than the next man. Or woman,' he added hastily.

She acknowledged the amendment with a movement of her eyebrow. 'You're supposed to be the expert.' She helped herself to a slice of toast.

'But I'm not an expert, that's the trouble. Not at this.'

'As far as Farquhar's concerned, obviously the garlic didn't work.'

'It worked temporarily, but long term it apparently did no more than get up his nose,' Malcolm's mouth twitched. 'Sorry, bad joke.' He sat down on the chair opposite her. 'We need to find out what we're dealing with. I think we can assume he's not one of the world's brightest. Powerful, yes, but he appears to be motivated by the basest of emotions and instincts.'

'So you, we, should be able to outwit him.'

'In theory, yes; but he's working to a different set of laws and in a different space and time to us.'

Ruth sighed. 'How do we find out what we need to do?'

'You know the answer to that as well as I do.'

'Ask Thomas?'

He nodded.

'I have,' she hesitated before going on, 'I have tried to speak to him, and he has sort of spoken to me, as he seems to have spoken to my father and to some of my ancestors, but I don't think we were having a conversation. I think it's like a crossed line on an old-fashioned telephone. I felt as if I was dropping in on a dialogue that happened a dozen lifetimes ago.'

'An echo through time.' He was thoughtful.

'It was relevant to what's happening, but we were out of sync.'

'That sounds like a good description. So, when you talk to him, or listen to him talking, how do you do it?'

'I just sit at my desk.'

He waited. 'And?'

'And that's it. Sometimes nothing happens. Sometimes, after I've been reading some of his letters and journals, he seems to go on with the story in my head.' Her voice tailed away.

His face had lit with interest. 'His journals? You have some of his journals?' he said eagerly.

'One or two,' she said cautiously.

Some of them had been written by Fanny. She had only realised when suddenly the writing had changed. Fanny's were delightful, humorous, honest. Riveting. Ruth had sorted the letters, the little journals, the larger notebooks, all from those cupboards at Number 26, chronologically, so that she could follow the story day by day, month by month, sometimes year by year. There were letters from other lives, other dates, but for now she had put them aside, saving them for later. After all, it was Thomas's story she was following.

Mal was watching her intently. 'Will you show me? Please.'

She hesitated.

'Oh, come on, Ruth!' he said. 'Don't believe what Harriet's

told you.' He had picked up on her thought immediately. 'I'm not going to poach your information. But I do want to know. I want to see. Do you realise what a priceless resource you have? And not just for their history, but because touching these things, holding them, puts you in touch with the people who wrote them. First-hand. Literally. You are touching what they touched, feeling what they felt, being a part of their lives.'

Ruth looked away uncomfortably. 'I see that, yes.'

'I hope they are somewhere safe. Timothy couldn't have found them?'

'Timothy wouldn't have been looking for them,' Ruth said slowly. 'He was looking for valuables. But no, he wouldn't have found them.'

Malcolm nodded.

'Why don't we go back to your chapel?' she said after a moment. 'Assuming Thomas is all in my imagination,' – she glared at him, daring him to contradict her – 'perhaps he could be persuaded to appear for real there. You must have created some kind of channel into the next world with all those crystals and statues and candles.'

He gave her a quizzical glance. 'There are only a couple of crystals,' he said, his tone reproachful. 'But it would be worth a try.' He drained his mug and stood up. 'Now?'

'Now,' she said. She wanted to get outside, away from his intense scrutiny, away from her sudden need to confide in him, to believe in all this.

The dogs went with them, racing through the trees, barking with excitement. The sun was shining and the wind had dropped a little, making it seem warmer, but the chapel itself was shadowy; the light was green and flickering, full of shapes and silhouettes cast by the ivy over the windows. He reached into his pocket for some matches and lit the candle. 'This is just to create a relaxed, welcoming atmosphere. So, what do you say when you want to talk to him?'

Yes, what do you say when you want to talk to him?

The voice was in her head, amused, rough, sarcastic.

Ruth looked round in fright. 'Did you hear that?'

'Hear what?'

'The voice, asking me . . . Oh God! It's him. It's Andrew Farquhar. He's in here with us.' She clutched at Malcolm's arm. 'I've brought him to your chapel.'

He wasn't coming back. April waited all day for her brother, huddled in her coat as the rain poured down the windows and through the leaks in the roof. She hadn't given it a thought when she found the sleeping place next to her empty and his sleeping bag discarded. Neither of them slept well here, but she had drifted off in the end, overwhelmed with sheer exhaustion in the early hours. When she opened her eyes it was after nine. She assumed he had gone to fetch them both some breakfast and lay huddled under the covers, shivering, waiting for him, looking forward to coffee and perhaps a bacon sandwich. An hour passed and she climbed out of the improvised bed, needing to have a pee. The car was parked outside, which meant he was on foot.

He should have been back by now. She was beginning to have a bad feeling about him. She went over to the chair in the corner where she had left her shoulder bag and groped for the purse which should have had about twenty quid in it. It was empty. 'Bastard!' she swore. He must have gone through her things while she was asleep. She turned and went over to her shake-down bed. There was a loose board under it, one of many in the house, and she had stashed the rest of her cash in there. He wouldn't have been able to get to it while she was asleep on top of it, even if he knew about it. Sure enough, the envelopes were still there. She smiled grimly. If he thought he could get the better of her he could think again.

It didn't take her long to go through their meagre belongings. The car keys were still in her pocket. His rucksack with some clothes in it was leaning against the wall. So, he hadn't planned to leave, else he would have taken that at least. She stood for a while, jingling the keys in her hand, thinking. The car was a liability. The police knew the new number by now and it would be picked up by the first APNR she drove past. Better to leave it. She began to pack her stuff carefully into Tim's rucksack.

There wasn't much she wanted to keep. There was more than enough cash to see her through for a while and she would find a way of getting more. She always did. Strangely the thought of being on her own filled her with exhilaration. Tim dragged her down. She had been looking after him since they were children. Now he had made a choice and she was free of him.

The last thing to go into the rucksack was the small bag of trinkets from Ruth's jewellery box. She had flogged a couple of the rings, both set with diamonds in heavy Victorian 24 carat gold, which had brought her several hundred quid Tim didn't know about. She smiled. The rest, the smaller rings, the locket, the brooch set with pearls and plaited hair, she would keep until someone made her an offer. They were in her shoulder bag, securely held against her body by a strap. Pulling on her coat, she looked round the room without regret. The one thing he had been right about: the place was a dump.

The last thing she did before she left was to pull out a box of matches and set fire to some rubbish in the Rayburn. The cracked stove would spew the flame onto a pile of old newspapers and it would spread fast around the room to wipe out all traces of them, and by the time anyone bothered to come and look she would be well on her way up the road to the petrol station where, unbeknown to her, Tim had thumbed a lift twelve hours before.

Thomas

Our lives in Hampstead progressed with much happiness. My darling Fanny, as confidently predicted by the stalwart Abi, produced another gorgeous daughter, whom we christened Mary, and two years later a second son, who we named for my brothers and my father, Henry David. I had builders provide more room for my growing family and in addition had them design and enlarge a top-floor entertaining room which my friends teased me by calling the banqueting hall. It was in the latest style with elegant square windows, giving views across the heath. In the garden I procured more trees from Kew and grew vegetables and flowers and, finding the gardens too small for my ambitions, negotiated with Lord Mansfield to buy a further area of land from his estate across the lane from my house. We had them dig a tunnel under the road, from behind my wall to behind his to create an easy and private access to our extended estate which was safe for the children and gave them – and, I own, me as well – a place to play endless games of secret pirates and hide and seek. The games were greatly enhanced by a gorgeous macaw that we taught to talk.

We entertained often and in style, Fanny sometimes content to sit quietly at the end of the table listening to the conversation of her guests, sometimes contributing witty and amusing asides, absorbing their opinions and anecdotes and later writing them in her journals. When she showed me an extract we would laugh and enjoy the evening anew. I saw mention of my own practical jokes: I brought to the table one evening the jar in which lived the leeches with which I had been bled after a short illness. I told the assembled company they were as much my pets as the dogs. One of the ladies swooned. It was very diverting, as was the effect produced by our wicked macaw. Unknown to me, Davy had added to its vocabulary. Fanny and the ladies were not amused and the bird was banned from parties thereafter.

Those parties were always a great success. I invited literary ladies like Hester Thrale and Fanny Burney, political friends, Fox, Burke, Sheridan. Lord and Lady Mansfield came and my friend James Boswell with many other writers over the years and painters like Sir Joshua and Lady Reynolds. I was pleased to call the Prince of Wales a friend, and hoped he might one day come to join us. He didn't, but his brother, Prince William, did. More than once, now that I moved in such circles, I was to remember my brother David's insistence we forget any romantic attachment to the Stuart line and cleave to the House of Hanover. However unpopular, even despised, they were in many quarters, theirs was a patronage one needed and I was prepared to court it. Within reason.

Another trial of conscience was to come, however, and this one brought me almost to disaster. The shade of Andrew Farquhar reared its ugly head once more in our household and brought me and my beloved Fanny near to breaking asunder. It was in the year 1786.

57

Thomas was working in his chambers in Lincoln's Inn when his clerk brought in a letter; the seal was broken. 'I believe we should turn down this brief, sir,' he said. 'This is not a case for you.'

Normally he would look up from his reading and wave away anything Bevan advised against. The old man was a sure barometer and they had so many requests it wasn't possible for him to read through them all. On this occasion, however, he held out his hand. 'I'll take a look, Charles, while I wait for my coffee. The office boy has sent out for it to help me wake up after last night's late hour.'

The old man smiled tolerantly. 'It was a roisterous time, sir?' he asked.

Thomas laughed. 'Interesting. Political discussions of the liveliest kind at Carlton House.' He unfolded the piece of paper Bevan handed him and began to read. Bevan bowed and withdrew, leaving Thomas in the silence of the room.

Bevan was right. This was not the kind of case with which he would normally become involved. It was a squalid and unfortunate tale of assault and rape in a Sussex town. He began to read, sitting comfortably at ease in his chair, looking up only when the boy brought in the jug of coffee. He set it down on the side table, poured a cup and put it at Thomas's elbow then hesitated as though awaiting further instruction. Thomas waved him away. He had not lifted his eyes from the paper.

The complainant was an army officer, on behalf of his daughter, a young lady of sixteen. She had gone with a friend to her first ball. They had returned together in the friend's carriage and the young lady had been dropped off at her father's front door when she returned at ten o'clock that night. It appeared that the defendant, lurking nearby, had grabbed her before she could reach the door and dragged her to the local churchyard where he had raped her. There appeared to be no doubt about his guilt. The man had a bad reputation, and was, besides, deformed and ugly and highly unpopular locally.

So, it's not a matter of sedition! Not a matter of the freedom of the press! It will bring no great praise, nor piles of golden guineas. It is merely the prosecution of a poor man who will swing from the gallows if convicted. You didn't save me. Why would you save him?

Thomas dropped the page on his desk. His pulse was racing uncomfortably as he stared round the room. 'Go away!' he shouted. It was Farquhar's voice.

The door opened and Bevan looked into the room. 'Did you call, sir?'

'No. No, I'm sorry. I burned my mouth.' Thomas indicated the cup on his desk.

Bevan withdrew, closing the door softly behind him.

Thomas looked up. 'Are you there? Why should I have tried to save you when you threatened me and mine and made our lives a misery?'

There was no reply.

He took a deep breath. 'Besides, I'm being asked to appear for the prosecution.' If the case was won, as was inevitable given the man's obvious guilt, Farquhar was right, the man would die.

Suddenly Thomas's hands were shaking. He was sitting again beside James Boswell, watching as the rope tightened round Andrew's neck, seeing his eyes widen with terror and then slowly begin to bulge and glaze over as the breath was choked out of him and he saw again that final look of agony and hatred as he swung towards them and fixed in his dying moment his stony gaze on Thomas's face.

'Sir?' Charles Bevan had reappeared, a bundle of papers under his arm. He looked at Thomas's desk in horror and rushed to mop it with a cloth. Thomas hadn't realised he had knocked over his cup and soaked the letter which was lying in front of him in a pool of coffee. 'I will take this and reply for you.'

'No!' Thomas grabbed it. 'No, Charles, I shall take this one.'

'Sir? You can't!' His clerk looked scandalised.

'Book it in. I shall take this case. This girl was scarcely more than a child. The same age as my daughter.'

But the nightmares that followed his decision were unceasing. In his dream, he could feel the rope around his own neck, he could feel his feet desperately trying to maintain contact with the cart, kicking reaching, stretching, even as the rope tightened.

'Thomas!' Fanny was standing by his bed in the dressing room, a candle in her hand. 'My darling, you were shouting. You'll wake the children.' She sat down beside him and put her hand on his forehead. 'Calm yourself. Don't think about it.' She had guessed the source of his agony and why he had insisted on taking on the case. A young girl, scarcely older than Frances, had been cruelly deprived of her maidenhood and her honour. Of course he wanted to take it.

'I am to confirm this man's guilt. I am to see him swing for what he has done. But you do see,' Thomas repeated to Fanny as they sat near the fire in the library the next evening, 'the trial must be fair. The evidence must be gone through. Even if he is ugly and she is pretty and young the presumption must not be that she is therefore telling the truth, until the evidence has been heard.'

While Thomas sipped his glass of brandy, Fanny went over the case again in her head. It seemed to her that there was no question as to his guilt. 'My darling, you mustn't be too zealous,' she said cautiously. She looked up from her embroidery. 'This child's reputation is at stake. The least she can expect is some kind of retribution.'

'But if the trial goes against him, he will die,' he insisted. 'We have to be sure. The locals are prejudiced against him.' He looked at her, his face shadowed by the flickering firelight. 'No one gave Farquhar that benefit of the doubt.'

'No, because all knew him guilty.' Fanny frowned. All at once she understood. He still felt he should have tried to defend Farquhar. 'There were so many witnesses then, Tom, and one of them, though I was not called, would have been me!'

He was chewing his lip. 'I have to see this man gets a fair trial.'

'But you are to speak for the Crown.' She put down her embroidery frame and sat forward in her chair. She was beginning to get angry. 'If you can't be committed to your side of the argument, you shouldn't take this case. It may be a small village affair, but there will be so many eyes watching because it's you. Your celebrity will have preceded you. You have to be clear about whose side you are on.'

He had grinned, the boyish grin she loved so much. 'But supposing I manage to win for the defendant, though I seek to prosecute him. How cunning would that be?'

She stared at him, appalled. 'You can't, Tom. You absolutely mustn't! This poor girl will be vilified forever if the jury find for him and say that she has lied.'

'You are right. I mustn't do it.' He looked quite forlorn for a moment then he climbed to his feet. 'I must go to my study and read through my speech once more. There are alterations I must make.'

She did not try to dissuade him. What was the point? Once he had made a decision he would stand by it.

He called for candles and a fire to be lit in his study, then as the door closed and he was alone, he went over to the window and stared out across the garden. The owl was there again. He saw the dark shape take off from the tall pine beside the gate, glide across the high wall in the moonlight and swoop down into the moonlit gardens of Kenwood.

So, you think that getting this man off will prove how clever you are and make up for your betrayal of a fellow shipmate.

The voice was quiet, in his ear, almost at his shoulder. Insidious. Persistent.

You're doing this to assuage your conscience. About me. Do you really think you can do it? I'll bet you can't. Would you like a wager? Can you wager with a ghost?

* * *

'I've changed my mind.' Timothy was sitting opposite the driver of the lorry at a truck stop somewhere between Scotch Corner and Darlington. He was hanging onto the last of his change, just in case, so he could only afford coffee. The other man had not offered to sub him – and why should he? – so he'd had to sit for the last twenty minutes, watching the guy stuffing bacon and eggs, sausages, black pudding and baked beans into his mouth, drenching his plate with sauce and wiping it clean with one of the extra slabs of toast he had ordered on the side.

'Changed your mind?' The guy looked up briefly then turned back to his plate.

'Yup. I'm going back north.' Tim stood up. 'Thanks for the lift, mate. Appreciated. It's given me the chance to think.'

It took him an hour to find a lift back up north and it was nearly dark when he found himself standing in the rain staring at the burned-out shell of the house they had so briefly tried to make into a home. What was left of the car was still there, the paintwork blistered, the seats destroyed, the windscreen and windows shattered. The pylon above it seemed to have escaped the fire unscathed. The place was deserted.

What had happened? Where was April? He bit back the lump in his throat.

A forlorn length of blue-and-white police tape fluttered along the road's edge, knotted to the telegraph pole one end and to the broken gatepost the other. Someone had designated it a crime scene. Did that mean she was dead?

He stood there, unable to move, overwhelmed by utter misery. There was no one to ask, nowhere to go, no one to talk to unless he went to the police and that wasn't going to happen. A car drove up the road behind him, its wheels swishing on the wet road. It threw up a curtain of spray as it swept round the corner and out of sight, leaving him wetter than before. The sudden cold of the water finally galvanised him into movement. He turned away from the ruin and began to walk slowly up the long road towards town, groping in his pocket to see how much money he had. He had his phone but the battery was flat, he had the clothes he stood up in, now soaked, and he was alone, genuinely, absolutely alone.

58

Fanny was waiting for him in Hampstead when he returned from the Sussex Assizes and seeing her standing there by the fireplace in the drawing room, her face alight with pleasure at the sight of him, Thomas quailed.

'So, what happened?' She ran to plant a kiss on his lips.

'The prisoner was acquitted,' he said.

She pulled away and looked up into his face. 'Tom?'

He shrugged his shoulders and turned away. 'I cannot win every case, my darling.'

She ran after him and caught his hand, forcing him to turn and face her. 'But this case, you should have won. You told me that the man was guilty!'

'The jury did not find him so.'

'And the girl? The girl who was attacked?'

'The feeling was that she was mistaken in what happened. Her virtue was preserved, I made sure they understood that.' He looked downright shifty. 'Her story was not sufficiently convincing for them to find the man guilty. She was young and inexperienced and perhaps a little foolish. A girl with much imagination, who had no knowledge of the world of men. Her reputation was intact, as was she, as far as we know.' His voice tailed away.

'Thomas Erskine, you are being disingenuous!' Fanny cried. 'How could you?' She stamped her foot.

He looked down at her sheepishly. 'The judge did not question my address, my darling. He found it proper.'

'And did her father find it proper, as you call it?' Her eyes were blazing.

Thomas looked uncomfortable. 'The case was dismissed, Fanny. I did not see her father afterwards. My carriage was at the door of the court and I came straight home.'

'Did you realise you were holding your cross?' Mal and Ruth were walking back from the chapel.

'It's not my cross.' She was embarrassed. 'I found it in Mummy's jewel box.' He was right, though. Instinctively her hand had flown to her throat when she heard Farquhar's voice. And in that moment of terror, she had hung onto it as though her life depended on it.

He grinned. 'Whoever it belonged to, it worked.' The voice had not returned.

'The cross is only because I can't carry my teddy bear everywhere,' she said, half laughing.

He nodded. 'Fair point.'

'I think I might keep wearing it.'

'I sense a touch of defiance there.' He smiled at her. 'That can only be good.'

Later, Ruth went back to her bedroom. Somewhere there, in all those letters and journals, must lie the answer to how to deal with the problem that was Farquhar. She picked up the letter she had been reading. She would continue from where she left off. She didn't want to miss anything.

Half an hour later, she laid the letter down again and sat staring into space. Why had Thomas told his daughter, even many years later, this complicated story about the Sussex rape? It obviously made him uncomfortable to remember it. It was a misjudgement, in his own mind a terrible miscarriage of justice, so why had he done it? Had it been a challenge just to prove how clever he was? The guilty man had got off scot-free and the young woman had been left with doubt hanging over her. What had happened to her after the case? The poor girl had presumably gone home with her parents, mortified, accused of being a fantasist, her reputation gone, her father left without recompense, perhaps never able to hold up his head in public again, perhaps never able now to find the husband he had dreamed of for his daughter.

'But, as you had won the point, did Farquhar pay you the wager?' Ruth wasn't aware that she had spoken out loud, that she was addressing the figure standing looking out of the window of her tower bedroom, leaning on his elbow on the sill.

'Of course not. He was a ghost!' The response was sharp.

She was tempted to strike her forehead with her fist. 'Duh!'

He turned towards her with a smile. 'I am not proud of that day's work.'

'And am I supposed to write that down in my notes?'

'It's the truth,' he sighed.

Behind her the door opened a crack and one of the dogs nosed his way in. When Ruth glanced back at the window the figure had gone. She bent to fondle the dog's ears. 'Are you Pol?' she said quietly. 'I still can't tell the difference between you. Did you see him, Pol? He was my imagination, wasn't he?'

The dog sat down, panting, then turned and ran back to the door. He had obviously come to fetch her.

Malcolm was in the sitting room, lighting the fire. 'Are you OK working up there?' he asked as she appeared. 'Do you have everything you need?'

'It's perfect.'

'I've been thinking,' Malcolm went on, scrabbling in his pocket for his matches. 'We have to resolve this situation.'

'I'm sorry. I know it's inconvenient having me here. Fin will be back—'

'No! That's not what I meant.' He lit the kindling, paused to make sure the flame was steady and turned to face her. 'I'm very happy for you to stay as long as you like. And I hope you will. It's nice having some company.' He smiled a little wistfully. 'No, I was referring to your foul-mouthed ghost and also to the evil Bradfords. It's a nonsense that they're all stalking you like this. The whole thing has to be sorted.'

'At least Timothy doesn't know where I am now.'

'True.'

'As far as he's concerned, I'm a bit like Rapunzel at the top of her tower. Unreachable.'

'Unless you let down your hair.'

'Oh, I won't be letting my hair down, I assure you.' She shook her head.

He laughed out loud. 'Pity. I was quite hoping you would at some stage.' He saw her sudden embarrassment as she realised what she had said and shook his head ruefully. 'Quick change of subject.' He reached for a log and placed it in the hearth. 'We need a plan. We have to assume that the police are still trying to find the Bradfords and that you're safe from them for now. Unfortunately, the police can't help us with the other matter.'

'Will Fin be safe when he gets back?' Ruth put in. 'The Bradfords don't know I've left the Mill House.'

'Fin has burglar alarms and bolts.'

'And he's put in a couple of cameras. But it's such an isolated place.'

'You mean compared to here.'

It was her turn to laugh. 'No, not compared to here.'

'I think you have to let Fin manage his own security, Ruth. Let's worry about you. Let's work out a way of getting rid of Andrew Farquhar for good. I think I might have thought of something.'

She sat down.

'The facts seem to be that he's working out a long-term grudge against Thomas. So, we have a vicious, vengeful, unshriven soul—'

'All this depends on what one believes happens after death,' Ruth interrupted. 'If one believes anything happens at all.'

'You still have doubts?' He looked at her, askance. 'After everything you've been through?'

She hesitated. 'I suppose I'm prepared to believe that some do not rest in peace,' she conceded.

He acknowledged the remark with a quizzical nod. 'That's a start.'

'I'm sorry to be so perverse.' She was cross with herself. 'I

368

can see something is going on; my surroundings seem to be crawling with ghosts at the moment so how could I deny it? And yet there's still a part of me that says, no, this is not logical, and I am denying the evidence of my own eyes because I can't get past that stupid rational glitch.'

Malcolm chuckled. 'It is fascinating, isn't it. Your father must have been some powerful personality! Someone should write a thesis on your dilemma. OK, we'll just have to go back to the pretending bit, pretend you believe, pretend you can accept the evidence of your own eyes, pretend this is all quite normal and pretend, above all, that this peculiar man you are staying with can fix it.'

'OK.' She grinned at him, surprised at the warmth that engulfed her. 'So how is he going to do it?'

'Consult Dion Fortune.'

She frowned. 'In a séance, you mean? That was how we allowed Farquhar in in the first place!'

'No, not a séance. In the first instance, we read her book. Both of us. Carefully.'

'We are talking about *Psychic Self-Defence*?'

'Indeed, and perhaps some of her others. Don't forget, we're going to assume that Thomas was one of her teachers. He must have believed in her skill, knowledge, powers, whatever you like to call it. Now, what is Farquhar trying to do? For now, he seems to be concentrating all his energies, in so far as they exist, on a single-minded pursuit of physical gratification and intimidation.'

'Of me and Harriet?'

'It's a possibility.'

'So a pair of middle-aged women, dotting about the house and playing at spooks, were fair game?'

He looked up, appalled. 'Is that how you see Harriet and yourself?'

'It might be how he sees me.'

'OK, let's drop the middle-aged bit and you could be right.'

She laughed. 'Thank you, kind sir.'

'And now, a middle-aged man and a beautiful woman are going to play spooks again but this time with a lot more knowledge and hopefully a few carefully aimed weapons.'

She looked away, afraid she was blushing. 'Not so much of the beautiful.'

'Sorry.'

She glanced up at him. 'You aren't sorry at all. You're laughing at me.'

'No, I'm not. Truly. This is not actually a funny situation, but maybe keeping it in perspective will help us to fight this bastard. And I'm not sure Harriet is part of this. It might be that he wants to humiliate and threaten you specifically as Thomas's descendant and representative. Whichever it is,' he looked at her solemnly, 'we have to deal with it. You haven't asked me what the weapons are.'

'Prayers?'

'Not for you, no.'

'Sonic screwdrivers?'

'Be serious.'

'Sorry. So, tell me what my weapon of choice will be.'

'Courage. The ability to hold your own when he tries to scare you. Refusal to be spooked. Both of which you've demonstrated. Think about it, Ruth. We're not talking about a physical body here. He's nothing but energy. His psychic presence is strong, we have established that, but in some ways he is nothing but air, hot air, if you like. He's the uncomfortable feeling you're left with when you walk into a room after two people have had a quarrel. Bombast. Emotion. That's what spooking is about. Fear. He loves the energy of your fear. It feeds his lust. So, instead of running away and fending him off, you go for confrontation. You've proved it works. I very much doubt if he can cope with a strong woman.'

Ruth exhaled loudly. 'My goodness. You make it sound so easy.'

'It is. And I'll be with you.'

'Supposing he doesn't fancy that sort of confrontation? As far as we know, he's gone two hundred years or so without feeling the need to assuage his lust.'

'As far as we know.'

She made a face. 'So, how are we going to arrange this battle of wills?'

'I haven't worked that out yet.' He sighed. 'I'm not too keen on inviting him here; certainly not into the chapel.'

'The Old Mill House then? That makes sense. Though I'm not sure Fin would be too pleased. We are talking about a séance, aren't we?'

'Not as such. No. We could do it while Fin's away. With his permission. And promise to clean up after ourselves.'

'When you say clean up, you are not talking blood and spattered brains; you mean no garlic residues?'

'Exactly.'

She stood up. Walking towards the window, she gazed down at the treetops for a while, deep in thought, then she turned to face him. 'All we need to do is to imbue me with enough courage. Simple.'

59

Fin and Max were already on their way home when Ruth finally managed to get through to Fin on his phone. It turned out he was planning to be out the next day anyway; he and Max were going to sort out the final contracts for his show then take themselves out to a slap-up lunch to celebrate. He sounded dubious about their plan but was only too willing to promise he wouldn't return before 6 p.m.

He left food in the fridge in case they got hungry, threw his papers into his briefcase, grabbed his tablet and put it in as well, with his favourite signing pen, grabbed his car keys and was giving a final glance round his study when the doorbell rang. He looked at his wristwatch. They were early.

'Darlings!' He pulled open the front door and his greeting died on his lips. Timothy Bradford was standing there. He had a large knife in his hand. He stepped in, pushing Fin back as he did so, and slammed the door behind him.

Fin was too stunned to react. He dropped his keys and the briefcase with a small cry of fright and backed against the wall, his hands in the air. 'What do you want? Ruth isn't here. The police will come. They'll know it's you. There's a camera!'

Timothy was scruffy and wet through, his shoes soaked and covered in mud and he looked exhausted. He stood, the knife

372

pointing at Fin's stomach, glancing around him. 'Keep still,' he hissed. 'Let me think.'

Fin swallowed hard. His mobile was in his pocket, his hands up, level with his ears.

'April is dead,' Timothy said.

Fin felt himself go even colder. 'Did you kill her?'

'No. There was a fire.' Timothy was shaking. Fin could see the point of the knife making tiny jerky movements only inches from his body. 'She's gone. She's left me alone.'

'I'm sorry.' Fin knew he couldn't keep his hands in the air much longer. His arms were aching already and he felt dizzy. 'Look, why don't we go in the kitchen and make a cup of tea.' He managed to keep his voice steady. 'You look done in.'

Briefly, he thought Timothy was going to agree, but he shook his head. 'I've got to lock you up. I've got to stay here. I've nowhere else to go.'

'You don't have to lock me up, old chap. It's better to talk. And have a hot drink. It will make you feel better. Then you can think what to do.' Fin lowered his arms a fraction.

Timothy tensed. His fingers tightened round the knife handle. 'I told you not to move.'

'I can't help it. I can't stand like this.' Fin lowered his arms and closed his eyes as he felt himself sliding to the floor. Any second he would feel the knife blade between his ribs. His last thought was that it was a cruel irony for the best chef in Scotland to end up filleted.

Harriet was sitting on her bed, her legs stretched out in front of her, a cup of tea on the bedside table. This, she thought, was the ideal way to be entertained; her hosts had gone out for the afternoon, leaving her to write. Outside, the sky was rapidly blackening as another autumnal storm drove in from the east and even through the window, one street back from the beach, she could hear the waves crashing on the shore. She laid her book down on her lap and stared towards the window. What were Malcolm and Ruth doing, she wondered. She screwed up her face. What did it matter? It was nothing to do with her any more.

With a weary sigh she reached for her teacup. Firmly she pushed the thought of Ruth and Malcolm out of her head and turned her attention back to the history of the Second World War.

Malcolm pulled up outside the Old Mill House and peered through the windscreen. 'It looks as though Fin's car is still here. I hope we're not too early.'

'Just don't get here till I've gone,' had been Fin's last words on the phone the night before.

Ruth looked at her watch. 'Maybe Max came and collected him. They were going out somewhere nice for lunch, so he might have done.' She felt in her pocket for her key. They climbed out and stood looking up at the house. There was a small camera above the door now, linked to Fin's phone. Ruth glanced at Malcolm, wondering if he felt as nervous as she did. He gave her a reassuring smile. 'It'll be OK.'

He followed her up the steps as she put the key in the lock. 'He's forgotten to set the alarm,' she said as she pushed the door open.

The house was silent. 'Fin?' she called. There was no reply.

'His briefcase is still here, by the door.' Malcolm was staring round, frowning. The house felt unsettled, the atmosphere uncomfortable, jagged.

'I don't suppose he needed it. He could put his lucky pen in his pocket.' She walked towards the sitting room. 'In here?'

Malcolm had stopped in the hall. Something had happened here. He could feel it so clearly, something that did not involve Farquhar.

He followed Ruth into the sitting room, unsettled. His concentration was in pieces.

'I can feel him already,' Ruth murmured. 'A kind of presence, as though someone is waiting for us.'

She was right. Mal took a deep breath. He could not afford to be distracted.

'Shall I put the lights on?' Ruth's mouth had gone dry. The room was shadowy. The sky outside was black and, almost on cue, an ominous rumble of thunder echoed from the distant hills.

'No, I think we'll keep it like this.' Malcolm produced a box of matches and a candle from the game bag he carried over his shoulder. He was focused now. 'Our man was from the shadows. He likes it that way.' He glanced at her with a reassuring smile. 'Ready?'

She licked her lips nervously. 'Ready.'

'This might get a bit melodramatic. B movie stuff, I'm afraid, but then, that's how it's done.' He pointed to the sofa and she sat down nervously on the edge of it, clutching her coat round herself tightly.

'Right, Mr Farquhar,' Malcolm said clearly. 'It is time for you to show yourself. We need to ask you some questions.'

Ruth held her breath.

The candle flame flickered. 'Oh come, Andrew.' Malcolm's voice was firm. 'Don't be bashful. Ruth is here, ready to talk to you. Let's see you. Isn't this what you want? Come and show Ruth what a fine figure of a man you were. You fancy her, don't you. You like her, she's everything you miss about having a woman in your arms. A real live woman.'

Ruth gave a small strangled gasp.

Malcolm glanced towards her, then he went on. 'Come on. This might be your last chance. Her attention will make you strong; virile again. Isn't that everything you dream of?'

Ruth clenched her fists. She was waiting to feel his hands on her, smell him, but there was nothing there. Outside, it was beginning to rain.

'Come on, Farquhar! Show yourself.' Malcolm's voice was more powerful now.

Ruth cowered back against the cushions and it was then she felt someone near her. She gave a whimper. 'He's coming.' She was trying to resist feeling for her cross.

'That's it. But we want to see you.' Malcolm was standing with his back to the fireplace. 'Let's see you. Now!'

60

Thomas had ridden hard and fast, trying to reach home before the storm. Ebony was sweating, his coat steaming beneath the rain. To the east, a flash of lightning sliced down through the cloud, lighting up the heath like day. It had been foolish not to wait until the storm was over, but he had to get back to Fanny. The baby was due and he had promised. He had won his latest case, as he had known he would, and he was exhilarated, sending his clerk and the papers home in the carriage. He hoped they were back by now and that Fanny wasn't worried. The builders had finished their work and the family had moved back to Hampstead from Lincoln's Inn so she could be comfortable for her lying in.

Ebony skidded to a halt as another flash lit the sky. Thomas slid from the saddle and soothed the horse. 'Come on, you've seen storms before. I'll lead you and we'll head down there and find shelter.' But even as he spoke another lightning bolt came down, close to where they were standing. Ebony reared with a scream of terror, tore the wet reins out of his hand and galloped off into the dark. Thomas dragged the collar of his greatcoat round his head and began to run, but it was too late. All he heard was a loud crash and then nothing.

When he woke, he was lying in his own bed. He tried to move

and heard himself groan. Fanny was there at once, bending over him, her hand on his forehead. 'Tom? Oh thank God, are you all right? One of the grooms has gone for the doctor. The dogs found you when the horse came home without you. Oh, my darling, you're so badly burned.'

Abi was there now, and there were more candles round his bed. She was dabbing at his shoulder with a cold wet compress that smelt of vinegar.

'What happened?'

'You were struck by lightning. Or the tree beside you was. It went up like a Roman candle. Oh, Tom.' Fanny was crying.

'And Ebony. Is he hurt?'

'No, he isn't hurt. Just very frightened. What possessed you to ride through the storm?'

He could hear the dogs whimpering as they cowered by his bed. There was a strong smell of singed cloth from his greatcoat which was lying on the floor where someone had thrown it after they had torn it off him. His shirt was in shreds and he could feel the agony of the burns now as the shock began to wear off. The children were there too, he realised now, in a huddle by the door. Little Mary was crying quietly and Frances had her arm round her sisters, trying to soothe them. 'Come here, my darlings,' he called. He was trying to stop himself groaning; the pain was agonising. 'Don't be afraid. Just learn from your papa's stupidity. I should never never have tried to ride home. I put my most favourite horse at risk and probably my own stupid life as well, just for the sake of an evening ride.' He lay back on the pillows and blew them all a kiss. 'Go now, leave your papa to rest,' he said. It was all he could do to keep his voice steady. 'I can hear the doctor coming.' The commotion below announced the arrival, the removal of the doctor's soaking coat, and the sound of firm steps on the stairs. The children vanished as a footman appeared carrying more candles and showed the doctor into the room.

Thomas woke much later, fighting his way up through a fog of laudanum to hear the birds singing in the trees outside the window. The rain had stopped and a faint light came through a crack in the curtains. 'Fanny?' Thomas's mouth was dry and his voice no more than a whisper. He heard the scurry of feet and a small face appeared. It was Frances. 'Are you all right, Papa?'

He tried to nod.

'Would you like some water?' She brought him a glass and held it to his lips. The pain of moving was excruciating, but he managed to swallow some before falling back on his pillow.

'What are you doing here, darling? You should be in bed. Where is your mama? Is she getting some sleep?' He managed to smile at her.

Frances shook her head. 'I said I would stay and look after you when the doctor had to go. Mama is having the baby.'

'What? Now?' Thomas half sat up, then lay back with a groan.

His daughter adjusted his covers anxiously. 'Abi and Martha and the midwife are with her. She is being very brave. He will be here soon.'

'He?' Thomas felt sweat running down his face. 'Is it a boy, then?'

'Abi says so.' His daughter gave a knowing smile. 'Don't worry, Papa. Everything is under control. Would you like some more drops? The doctor showed me how.'

He watched her pour the dose from the little blue bottle, her face grave as she counted the drops into the glass of water. She helped him sip it. In minutes he had drifted away into sleep.

'So, Andrew, did you know that Thomas was struck by lightning again?'

It had been in the last letter from Thomas to his daughter that Ruth had read the night before, reminding Frances of the drama of that evening so long ago. Ruth was sitting on Fin's sofa, clutching a cushion to her chest. Malcolm had told her to talk to the shadowy figure hovering in the corner of the room. 'He was exhilarated by the storm; he couldn't resist riding through it. He loved the feel of the rain on his face, the energy of the wind as he galloped over the heath. He said later the horse saved him. It reared up and threw him. Seconds later and he would have been killed. The lightning struck an ancient oak tree only feet from him.'

Her voice was stronger now as she gained confidence. The phantasm that was Andrew Farquhar was still there.

There was a new tenseness now about the shadow, as though his attention had been caught, a flinching from the quiet words that circled the room like predatory birds. 'You can't forgive Thomas for what happened on the ship, can you. Though you know it was your fault, all of it. Did you think he betrayed you? Or were you so ashamed of what you did to that boy you couldn't bear to think of everyone knowing about it.' Another long silence. 'Even there, on the ship, Tom was among friends, wasn't he. His family knew the captain. You were a bully and a cheat and a cruel vicious boy and then you were a bully and a cheat as a man. I've read all about it in his letters.'

For a long time there was silence, then they heard it.

The apparition laughed.

Appearances are everything. April had been shopping. New top and skirt, pants and two bras, tights, shoes, an upmarket jacket, as good as new from a charity shop for £5. She bought a tote there too, in which she could carry her worldly belongings, and a document case to tuck under her arm. Her laptop just fitted it. She changed in the ladies in a department store, stuffed her old clothes in the much re-used plastic bag from the charity shop and, wandering down a quiet street, found a wheelie bin to dump it into. The only thing she needed now was an umbrella – she glanced up at the swiftly approaching black clouds – then she would have to find somewhere to think about what to do next. If she thought about Timothy at all it was as a huge weight lifted from her shoulders. He was no longer her responsibility. He had taken his life into his own hands. She didn't care where he had gone, so long as she never saw him again.

The last thing that needed fixing was her hair. She was too embarrassed to go into a hairdresser, but there the storm saved her. She stood in the street allowing the rain to pour down on her head and by the time she went into the shop, laughing and gesturing at her head, there was no need to explain the dirt and the grease because her hair, wet and straightened, had been washed clean and was ready for a change of style and colour. The April that emerged from the hairdresser later was a different woman.

Her ambitions were simple. She didn't see any reason to move on from Edinburgh. She liked it and she had got to know the place. She wanted comfort and security, a risk-free existence and space to dream. There was no limit to dreams, after all, but she didn't yearn to make them come true any more. It was enough that she didn't have to look after Timothy. She didn't intend or expect to see him again. Ever.

She had not lost her skill as a shoplifter. The rest of the day was spent happily wandering round the antique markets collecting what she thought of as stock. Small things, that fitted easily into her bag. Next morning she visited one of her trusted colleagues and cashed in her booty, walking away with a tidy sum that covered the cost of her purchases and a night in a cheap hotel. It was heaven. It had a room with a door that locked, hot water and a comfortable warm bed. A cooked breakfast was included. The only item she had forgotten amongst her purchases was a nightdress. She would get that tomorrow. And she still had her store of trinkets from Ruth's mother's jewel box in the little bag, now safely tucked into the zip pocket of her tote.

Thinking of Ruth reminded her about the Old Mill House. She had unfinished business there. Smiling to herself, she plugged in her laptop and opened it on the hotel dressing table. Malcolm Douglas, the ghostbuster. Ruth liked him, that much had been obvious, so he had made himself a target. Working her way steadily through the links she found everything she needed to know about him, including an obscure reference in an interview from ten years before for an American small-town paper in which he had confessed to the fact that he was interested in ghosts, had helped exorcise one or two houses 'back home in Scotland', and, pure gold this, had once or twice been tempted to consult the dead to check facts for his biographies. '"I never have," Malcolm joked,' the article quoted. '"And I promised not to tell anyone this, but I can't help wondering . . . "'

April paused thoughtfully at that. Then she smiled. She knew from more recent entries just how serious a writer Malcolm was. As far as she could tell, he had never mentioned his interest in the supernatural in public since. It would be enormous fun to bring it up again and, the perfect touch this, make him think that Ruth had done it. Almost certainly it would seriously piss him off.

By the time she had drunk two coffees and a tea from the box of sachets on the little tray she had found in the drawer with a kettle, she even knew his address. She smiled in triumph. 'Got you, Ruth bloody Dunbar!' she crowed.

It didn't take long to set up new Facebook and Twitter accounts in a name which would mean nothing to anyone but those involved: RuthieD. She smiled as she tapped away in the small silent room. Nothing cruel, nothing libellous, not yet, just hints, seeds sown in the night.

A certain serious historian is said to be obtaining his research through spirit mediums. Whoa! Watch this space to find out who. #Malcolm Douglas

Better check your history books. Ever wondered where biographers get their information? Do they dream it? Or do they interview the dead?

Famous Edinburgh author turns out to be secret psychic. You can get your home exorcised by him for free #Malcolm Douglas

Now she had started to think of suitable tweets she couldn't stop.

She switched off her laptop and sat back with a smile.

Next morning, she switched on her laptop again. It took only seconds to find RuthieD. She stared at the screen, then slowly she began to smile. Perfect. His name was already out there. Not exactly a Twitterstorm, but one or two trolls were starting to sharpen their pens and other people were expressing their shock and disappointment. Give it another few hours and the papers would pick up the story. He had hardly been discreet, even if it was ten years ago. 'Screw you, Mr Douglas,' she muttered. 'And then screw you, Ruth.'

As she made her way later towards Princes Street and the crowds of people looking into the shop windows or standing staring up at the great castle on its rock, she felt one of them at last. She was no longer a woman on the run, she was a person in her own right, and free. And she was on a mission.

61

Timothy couldn't hear anything from where he was hiding in the smallest bedroom on the landing. At the beginning, Ruth and Malcolm's voices had been clear. They were in the hall at the foot of the stairs, then they had walked into the sitting room and closed the door behind them. He heard the murmur of their words every now and again, but then he lost the thread of what they were saying. They were talking to someone else, someone called Andrew. He held his breath. All the more reason to be careful. He didn't want to be confronted by three of them.

He crept out of the room and looked down the stairs at the sitting room door. It was closed. He could faintly smell a scented candle. It was incensey, exotic. He screwed up his face, afraid he was going to sneeze. Pulling off his shoes, he tiptoed down the stairs and over to the door and listened. They were silent, then he heard Ruth's voice quite clearly. He hadn't heard a word from Andrew yet. He turned away. He couldn't risk being caught. He ran in his socks across the hall and back up the stairs, pausing halfway with a catch in his breath as a step creaked under his weight, then on up towards the attic. He would stay up there until they had gone.

He was wishing already he had stopped in the kitchen to grab some food. He was desperately hungry but best be safe. He could eat all he wanted once they had gone.

There were three bedrooms in the attic. He pulled a blanket off one of the beds and wrapped it round his shoulders, then he lay down against the pillows, prepared to wait. In seconds he was asleep.

Fin could hear nothing. When he had woken from his faint he was tied hand and foot, blindfolded, and there was something stuffed into his mouth, almost choking him. He groaned and received a kick in the shin. 'Shut up you fool or I'll kill you.' Timothy grabbed him under the arms and began dragging him backwards across the floor. He felt himself being bumped down a couple of steps and suddenly it was very cold. They were outside. He could feel the rain soaking into his clothes, then they were out of the rain again and Timothy was propping him up against the wall in a sitting position. He knew exactly where they were. In the outhouse, outside the kitchen door. 'Now listen.' Timothy's mouth was close to his ear. 'If I hear a sound from you, I will come in and stick this knife between your ribs, is that clear?'

Fin felt himself nodding vigorously. He heard the door bang and the key turn in the lock outside, then all was silent but for the sound of the rain on the broken slates. He waited several seconds then he began to wriggle. His wrists were agony, lashed behind his back, his shoulders twisted and aching, his feet tied so tightly they were going numb. He couldn't stop himself groaning. He was crying now too, hot tears running down his face from under whatever was tied round his head. The only part of himself he could move was his neck. He rubbed his head against the wall, which was cold stone and rough, and almost at once he felt the bindings round his eyes and mouth loosen. He wriggled to get a better purchase and within a few minutes he had managed to spit out the gag, retching, then the blindfold slipped down off his eyes onto his shoulders. It was his own scarf from the coat hooks in the hall. Encouraged, he began to work on his feet. They were tied with orange string. He could feel it loosening. It hadn't been knotted properly and had somehow caught in the hem of his trousers. Another couple of hefty kicks and his legs were free. He was calming down now, his brain beginning to function rationally.

Timothy had panicked, that much was obvious. He hadn't expected Fin to be there; the man was evidently quite mad. He thought hard. Where were Ruth and Mal? Dear God, had they walked in on Timothy? Were they all right? He began to struggle even more frantically.

Fin was not the most athletic of men and his bulk made it difficult to manoeuvre, but he was determined somehow to get to his feet, albeit with his hands still lashed behind him. He knew the one thing in his favour was that the shed he was locked in was so old and rotten that one good kick would smash the door off its hinges. Once he was outside, he could head for the drive where, if he kept to the bushes, he could escape unseen. He wriggled some more, harder this time, trying to get his feet under him. It was raining harder now. A trickle had found its way through the roof and was running down his neck.

Please God, let him get free before Timothy came back. He tried to move his feet and gasped with pain as one of his legs seized with cramp. He took a deep breath and made another attempt and this time he managed to get his feet under him. On levering himself upright, he found his head wedged under the damp rotten beams. His face was covered in spiders' webs as he took a step forward and threw himself against the door. His prediction had been right. One shove and the doorpost splintered and wrenched free and the whole frame fell out onto the path, followed by him. He sprawled full length in the rain, but he was free. He managed to scramble to his feet and ran, his arms still bound behind him.

It was almost dark. It had been lunchtime when Timothy had attacked him; it must now be late afternoon; the stormy sky made it darker still but a streak of light between the clouds showed him a car outside the front door. It was Malcolm's. So they were here. His overwhelming relief was followed by a stab of panic. Supposing Ruth and Mal had been attacked by Timothy?

Shivering violently, he forced himself deeper into the shrubbery, and tried to work out what to do.

'Andrew?'

They had been here for a long time. First Ruth, then Malcolm had been talking patiently to the hovering shadow, as if to a recalcitrant child, trying to coax him to respond, but to no avail. After his first few responses he had remained silent and now the figure was fading until they couldn't see him any more. The room felt empty.

'He's gone,' Ruth whispered.

Malcolm glanced at his watch. 'We ought to go too. We promised Fin we would be out of here before he came back.' He looked round the room. 'Nothing of him left, as far as I can tell.' He blew out the candle. 'Fin won't know we've been here.'

'I'll ring him later and thank him.' She followed him into the hall. 'Shall I go and check round the house? Make sure everything's all right?'

He shook his head. 'I'm sure it's fine. Farquhar's gone. He's not going to stay when there's no one here.' He reached to turn off the lights behind them.

'Do you think he's gone for good?' she asked.

'Sadly not. I was hoping for more of a confrontation.'

She shuddered. 'That was enough confrontation for me.'

'You faced him off at the beginning. That was the main thing. You didn't let him terrorise you and he didn't or couldn't find enough strength to hang around. It proves to me he feeds off your fear. We're on the right track.'

They were heading for the front door. Ruth set the alarm and they let themselves out into the cold. The rain had finally blown away towards the west. They climbed into the car and it was as Malcolm started the engine and turned on the head-lights that he let out a cry of alarm. There was a figure staggering towards them across the lawn.

'Oh my God! It's Fin! What's wrong with him?' Ruth scrabbled with the door handle.

'Drive! Drive away quickly!' Fin was sobbing so hard he could barely speak. 'Lock the doors. It's Bradford – he has a knife.' He was crying as they pushed him onto the back seat. Malcolm glanced round the wind-swept garden then dived into the car to find the Stanley knife he kept on the shelf under the steering wheel. It took only moments to saw through the twine and cut Fin's hands free. Ruth grabbed one of the dog blankets from the back to tuck round him, before climbing in beside him, gently trying to rub some life back into his arms as Malcolm accelerated out of the drive.

They rang the police from the main road and waited there under a street light until the patrol cars arrived. One drew up immediately behind them, the other swept round the corner down the lane towards the house.

'Your alarm has been activated, so we were already on our way.' One of the policemen climbed into the front passenger seat beside Malcolm. He turned so he could talk to Fin and Ruth in the back.

'I set it just now as we left,' Ruth said.

'He must have still been in there,' Malcolm said, 'and let himself out as soon as we drove away. Oh, Ruth! And you nearly went upstairs alone!'

The house was empty, though the police found at once where Timothy had spent the afternoon. The discarded blanket and the crumpled bed were clear to see.

Fin refused to go to hospital, and was too distressed to be interviewed. It was agreed the police would come to the Tower House next morning to take a full statement and at last they were able to drive away.

'I don't think I will ever feel safe in that house again,' Fin was sobbing. His teeth were chattering.

'Shall I pick up the dogs on the way past?' Malcolm called back over his shoulder as they neared home. 'I can leave them if you like, till tomorrow.'

'No. Fetch them. I think we'd all feel happier and safer with them there,' Ruth replied. She was holding tightly onto Fin's hand. It was warmer now, but it was still trembling.

When Malcolm opened the rear door, the two dogs leapt into the four-by-four with huge enthusiasm, overwhelming them with yaps of joy and the smell of excited dog. Ruth was right. They all felt better for their company.

With Fin warm and bathed, wrapped in a huge woollen dressing gown, courtesy of Mal's late father, and ensconced in front of the fire in the sitting room, a large glass of whisky in his hands, he reached for his phone and found all the missed calls from Max, wondering where he was. Max was there in an hour with a bag of hot food, wine, more whisky and two large dog treats.

It was only much later, as they all sat round the fire again, the horrors of the day behind them, that Max reached for his tablet. 'Sorry, folks. One of the joys of being an agent: always on duty.' He began to scroll down his emails and after a few moments he looked up. His face was white.

62

Timothy had been waiting on the top landing when Mal and Ruth came out of the sitting room. He leaned over the bannister to look down the stairwell and heard Ruth suggest she look round the house. He tensed. He could see her shadow as she moved across the hall. He smiled. If she did, he could creep up behind her, put his hand over her mouth and she would be in his power. It had been so easy to overcome Finlay. The man had collapsed at his feet. He hadn't decided yet what to do with him. Whatever it was, it would be a delicious moment. How April would have loved it. To have her idol at her feet. But then, he reflected, perhaps she wouldn't. It would have spoiled her image of him as a shiny, cheery chap always surrounded by lovely food and pretty pots of herbs when in fact he had shown himself to be a stupid, scared, fat man who had probably wet himself by now. He sneered at the thought. He was almost disappointed when he heard Mal tell Ruth not to bother going upstairs.

He sat down to wait as they put on their coats and opened the front door, then he stood up and ran down the first flight of stairs. He could still smell the candle they had used downstairs.

Unable to resist making a detour into Ruth's bedroom, he opened the door to find all her personal stuff had gone since he had last been there. The bed had been made, the bedspread pulled over it smoothly. On the bedside table was a little old-fashioned travelling clock and an almost empty box of tissues. He was about to move on when he spotted, half-hidden by the box, a set of keys. He stared at them for a second then grabbed them. These had to be the keys to Number 26. In her rush to pack and move out, she had overlooked them. He felt an enormous leap of excitement as he shoved them into his pocket. He was almost home.

Timothy was heading for the door when he heard a voice close behind him.

That's her bed. If you can't have her, don't you want to lie down there; pleasure yourself?

He spun round, shocked. 'Who's that? What do you want?' The room was empty but he could sense the presence of someone near him, feel him, smell him. He felt his skin crawl. His hands grew clammy as he backed towards the door.

You and I could get along.

The presence was nearer now, overpoweringly close, but he couldn't see anyone there. He took another step back. 'Go away!' He put up his hands to ward off the voice.

Alike as two peas in a pod, you and I. I think we'll suit nicely.

There were hands on him now, feeling him, clutching at his biceps and then dropping to grab his crotch.

Timothy let out a howl of rage and fled out onto the landing and down the stairs, taking the last three steps in one leap. He ran for the front door and somehow managed to drag it open. As he flung himself down the steps he heard the alarm go off, wailing deafeningly behind him.

The four-by-four had gone. There was no one there. He ran as fast as his legs could carry him for the drive and then on up the lane, careless of who might see him, stumbling in the dark, splashing through puddles. At the main road he pushed through a gap in a hedge and across someone's garden, into some kind of copse. There, he collapsed, gasping for breath, unable to run another step.

As he huddled onto the ground, his head cradled in his arms, he heard the sound of ugly laughter ringing in his ears. Whoever, whatever, had touched him in the Old Mill House had come with him.

Malcolm was studying Max's tablet. He was silent, intently scrutinising it, then he handed it back without a word.

'What?' Ruth said anxiously. 'What's happened?'

'Show her,' Malcolm said.

Max leaned forward and handed it to her. She looked at the line of tweets and the colour drained from her face. 'Oh, Malcolm! RuthieD. That's not me. You do know, that's not me!'

It was Fin's turn to hold out his hand and she passed it on to him. He glanced at it then he looked at them all in turn. 'Of course it's not you,' he said. 'But it's someone who knows you. It's Harriet.'

Ruth stared at him. 'No. I don't believe it. She wouldn't. Would she?' She put her hands to her face and rubbed her cheeks miserably. 'No, it can't be.'

'If it is her, it's my fault,' Malcolm said. 'I didn't realise how hurt she still was.'

Ruth was chewing her lip miserably and he leaned towards her. 'Don't look so upset. None of this is your doing.'

'Oh but it is!' she flashed back at him. 'Me and my big mouth. If only I hadn't told her. I never dreamed—' She rubbed her face again. 'You told me not to tell anyone.'

'Need this necessarily be bad?' Fin put in. He glanced from Malcolm to Max. 'Isn't all publicity good publicity, if you handle it right?'

Max nodded slowly. 'I think you're right. There is no point in trying to stuff the cat back in the bag. All the history snobs are having far too much fun to let this drop.' It wasn't the original tweets that were so bad, it was the vicious enthusiasm with which other people had piled in with their scornful ridicule. 'I think we should maintain a dignified silence for a while, then Malcolm can put out a suitably amused response.'

'Amused?' Malcolm raised an eyebrow.

Max nodded again. 'The reviews from your esteemed colleagues over the years, Mal, are evidence enough that your work is sound. If those same people jump on the bandwagon to diss you, they are going to be admitting that they have made huge mistakes in judging your books; that they couldn't spot hokum when they saw it. Admit your interest in the paranormal, ask why it should prove so amusing to RuthieD' – he shook his head at the name – 'who obviously doesn't realise it's a serious subject with a chair at the university. Then wish her well.'

Malcolm smiled uneasily. 'So, we leave it for a while and let the hordes claw me to pieces?'

'They are condemning themselves, no one else. Max is right. That's a good call,' Fin said.

'And if RuthieD asks why you kept it so secret?' Ruth whispered.

'It's because it's a private interest that has no relevance to your work,' Max answered. 'How many people know Mary Berry is a twitcher?'

'Is she?' Fin looked astounded.

'Probably not, so don't quote me or she might sue, but you get my point. It's not the end of the world whether she is or she isn't, it's irrelevant to her day job, and the only person who looks an idiot in the end is the person who first spreads the gossip. Especially,' he added, 'if it turns out it's someone who might be thought of as a professional rival.'

'Poor Hattie,' Ruth said sadly. 'Why would she do it?'

'She still hates me, and she's even more cross because she thinks I fancy you,' Malcolm put in softly.

Ruth blushed scarlet. 'She's being very silly. It's not like her at all.'

'She's being protective of you. She sees me as a bounder.' Malcolm grinned broadly. He stood up. 'Now, let's change the subject and leave Ruth alone. Max, are you staying the night? There is a sofa bed in my study if you would like it; we'll need your input in the morning for a council of war. Fin can have the second spare room if he can climb that high and Ruth is where Ruth is, which is as far away as possible from me to keep her safe.'

Tim was hungry. Very hungry. His twenty pounds was long gone. He was too tired and cold to think. He didn't know what to do.

You steal food, you fool.

The voice in his head was still there, mocking, persistent. He ignored it.

What would April do? Shoplift. Sell the stuff for cash and live the life of Riley. Except there weren't any shops here and he would probably get caught. What did the rough sleepers do? He had seen them often enough. They went through bins and they queued for handouts from the do-gooders with their woolly hats and their cheery smiles and their steaming cauldrons of soup. His mouth watered at the thought.

Sheltering from the rain under a tree, he groped in his pockets in the desperate hope that he would find enough cash for a bus. All he found were the keys. He looked at them carefully, jingling them gently in the palm of his hand. The keys to Number 26. They had to be. All he had to do was hitch a lift into the city centre.

Ruth sat on the end of her bed for a long time that night. She had pulled her jacket round her shoulders to ward off the chill of the room, staring into space. So much had happened, her thoughts were a jumble. The exorcism had been a failure as far as it went, although Mal kept reassuring her that they had made good progress, and if they hadn't tried it they wouldn't have gone to the Old Mill House and they wouldn't have rescued Fin. The thought of the loathsome Timothy Bradford threatening to kill him filled her with overwhelming horror. And now Hattie had turned on her. Her thoughts went back to Malcolm. He had more or less admitted in front of them all that he liked her, but she had known that and, she had to admit, she liked him. She smiled wistfully. She wasn't ready for this. Not yet. Perhaps not ever. It would be better if she left. Now Fin was back, they could look after each other in Cramond, or perhaps she should go back to Number 26.

The two police officers, a man and a woman, arrived just after ten the next morning. They seemed to find it amusing that they had all taken refuge in what the senior officer described as a castle. 'Not that it isn't sensible,' Detective Inspector Sue Grant added hastily. 'This man, Bradford, appears to be extremely dangerous.' She glanced from one to the other. No one disagreed with her.

'I think,' Fin reminded her gently, 'that we have been flagging this man up for weeks now as being a stalker and basically off his rocker. He has been following Ruth ever since she evicted him from her late father's house. I just happened to be in the wrong place at the wrong time. My own home, granted, but it's Ruth he's after. The police have not been taking this seriously.'

'I assure you we have, Mr Macdermott,' DI Grant bristled. 'We have been looking for Mr Bradford and his sister for some time now. As a matter of fact we are very concerned about his sister. The house in which they have been squatting has been burned to the ground.'

The group round the table were shocked into silence. 'He told me she was dead. He mentioned the fire,' Fin whispered. 'But I don't think he killed her. He seemed angry that she had left him.'

'We're not assuming anything at this point,' DI Grant said crisply. 'There were no human remains at the scene. Does he know about this place?'

Malcolm shook his head. 'Not as far as we know. But, as long as we keep the front door locked we're safe in here.'

'You should have been safe at the Old Mill House,' she commented reproachfully, 'but on your own admission,' she addressed Fin, 'you let him in, sir.'

Fin bit his lip. 'Touché!'

'I think my colleague was just pointing out that it would be as well to be doubly careful,' the younger police officer, Jack Jordan, put in tactfully. 'I'm glad to see you have dogs here.'

Pol, who had made a huge fuss of the young man, was now leaning against his legs, though both dogs had barked loudly when the police car first drew up outside.

'There's another matter,' he went on, 'which would not normally concern the police – at least not at this stage. I don't know if you are aware, sir,' he turned to Malcolm, 'but you appear to be the victim of some unpleasant trolling on social media and this has only occurred within the last twenty-four hours.'

Malcolm scowled. 'We are aware of it, yes.'

'Is it possible it could have been initiated by Mr Bradford?'

Malcolm stared at him. 'It never occurred to us. We assumed it was started by someone known to us who has a professional grudge against me. I don't honestly think it's a police matter. Anyway, I somehow doubt that Bradford has the knowledge to do something like that.'

'Never underestimate people's computer literacy,' DI Grant put in. 'A two-year-old child can do it these days.'

'Can you think of anywhere he or his sister would hide out now their latest squat has been destroyed?' Jack Jordan put in.

'He is obsessed with the Old Mill House,' Ruth broke her silence. 'He keeps on going back and there are quite a lot of places he could hide there. Sheds and garages and undergrowth.'

'Undergrowth!' Fin protested faintly. 'Carefully curated shrubs and trees, if you please!'

Finally Sue Grant smiled. 'We are watching the Old Mill House,' she said, 'and we'll keep an eye on this place too. As I said, please keep your doors locked and don't open them without checking who it is. Now, it would help obviously if we had photos of them. I have some blurred camera footage here from your doorstep.' She glanced at Fin and then her colleague, who produced some A4 sheets of paper. 'I would be grateful if you could take a look and see if we have the right people.'

Jordan pushed them towards Ruth. She glanced at the top one and sat forward. 'Yes. That's Tim.'

'He was also caught on someone's CCTV near your house in Morningside.' She looked at Ruth. 'You didn't think to mention that you owned a house in the city? Is it possible he might seek refuge there?'

Ruth gave a weary sigh. 'Our problems all go back to that house. He claimed that my father left it to him, but my solicitor has proof the will was a forgery. I suppose it's possible he would go there but I would have thought it would be the first place he would expect us to look and he knows I've changed the locks.'

'Make a note, Jack,' DI Grant turned to her colleague. 'We should step up routine security there. And this woman in the picture with him. Is that his sister?' She pointed to a second printout which showed two people walking side by side down a pavement towards the camera.

'I've only seen her once, and I didn't get a good look,' Ruth said, shaking her head. 'I wouldn't recognise her.'

'No matter. At least we have him.' Sue pushed back her chair and stood up. 'We've put out his description, and we'll add this picture. It's not too bad. Enough to identify him. We'd better not include the woman in case she's an innocent bystander.' She sighed. 'Take care now, all of you.' For the first time she seemed to soften. 'I very much doubt if he would use his knife, but we don't want to take any chances.'

Thomas

As my burns began to heal, it brought back all too vividly the pain and shock of the lightning strike all those years before, on the Tartar. *I had been spared almost certain death then, and I had been spared it now. Both my horse and I recovered, in his case thanks to the care and warm mashes administered by his groom, and in mine, thanks largely to the attention lavished on me by my clever eldest daughter and my darling wife, who, as soon as she was able to leave her bed, brought me our latest child, a lusty boy whom we agreed we would name Thomas after me! 'Just in case we need a replacement,' Fanny quipped with a wicked gleam in her eye, 'if you continue to act like a foolish boy instead of a senior member of the administration of this country.' As soon as possible and with her usual tact and charm, she dispensed with my doctor and replaced his care with her own loving tenderness, augmented by Abi's herbal potions.*

As soon as I was able to walk I went down to the stables to visit the horses, including the faithful Invincible and Ebony, who made it clear he did not blame me for our mishap. Indeed, he had undoubtedly saved my life. As soon as I had the strength, he and I went for gentle hacks across the heath and round the ponds. Before long, apart from the scars upon my arm and shoulder, and apart from the occasional searing headache, I was as good as new.

My recovering strength meant I could resume my duties and I was summoned to Carlton House by HRH the Prince of Wales and informed that he was going to do me the honour of making me his Attorney General. My friend Fox was there to shake my hand and after the formalities had been completed the prince called for his favourite dry champagne to toast my position.

Fanny came from Hampstead to stay at 36 Lincoln's Inn Fields so she could accompany me to the banquet at Carlton House and she made a beautiful and gracious consort, but later she confided she did not enjoy it. 'Please, Tom. Let me stay at home with the children.' I tried to argue. She was a brilliant and lively companion and could hold her own with the brightest minds there, but she was adamant. In future I was to make her excuses, if necessary, on the grounds of health. As if to reinforce her argument, she informed me only a few months later that she was expecting another child. In due course our fourth son and eighth child, Esmé Stuart, was born.

It was then, in the midst of all the excitement and when I was near to overwhelmed with the work of my office, that I saw Andrew Farquhar in the street. I had taken a chair from Lincoln's Inn to Westminster and we were making our way along the Strand when something caused me to pull back the curtain and glance out at the bustling crowds. At that same moment a figure on the pavement stopped and fixed me with a stony gaze. I saw the street empty round him, passers-by gave him a wide berth, a horse shied and another pulling a chaise near overturned it in its panic to avoid him. It seemed to me the street had grown silent, all the usual sounds of wheels and hooves and shouting dying away. I rapped the roof of the chair with my cane and the bearers came to a halt and lowered it to the ground, but I did not try to descend. I had no intention of accosting him. Then I realised the figure had gone, the noise of London slowly came back and the space where he had stood filled and swirled again with the bustle of the street. I commanded the men to carry on and sat back in my seat, the curtains once again closed. My heart was hammering in my chest and I could feel my hands sweating with fright. I did not do myself justice that day, I own. I did not tell Fanny what had happened, although, observant as usual, she asked me what was wrong. I tried to convince myself it was my imagination or a dream, but in my soul I knew it was real. The chill I had felt could not have been caused by even the worst nightmare. Andrew Farquhar still did not rest in peace. As we had feared it would, his shade was drifting unfettered through the streets of London.

63

Ruth found Malcolm in his study. 'Fin and Max have just left.'

Max had taken Fin to stay with him in his flat in Heriot Row in Edinburgh. For the time being there was no question of him returning to Cramond.

'If ever,' he had said shakily after climbing into Max's car.

'Oh, Fin. What have I done?' Ruth was anguished.

'You have done nothing,' Max said firmly. 'And Fin will be fine once this oaf is apprehended. We will have the most wonderful party at the Old Mill House and reclaim it for the side of righteousness.'

Ruth sat down near the fire and began to scratch Cas's ears. 'Have you looked at the tweets this morning?'

'Of course. I've decided there was no point in trying to pretend it hasn't happened. God, it's amazing how vile people can be, even people I thought of as friends!'

'You mean you know some of them?'

'Some. Not many, I'm glad to say.'

'What are you going to do?'

'Take Max's advice and make one single dignified response.' He was staring thoughtfully at his screen. 'You can help me compose it.'

'Mal, I think maybe I should leave. Go back to London.'

'Why?'

'I am nothing but trouble, to you and to Fin. To everyone I talk to.'

'Ruth, I think you would find the police might be worried if you left.'

'Surely I'd be safer down there?' She glanced up and caught his look of disapproval.

'No. I want you where I can keep an eye on you.'

'I beg your pardon!' She was genuinely indignant.

'I mean it, Ruth. I'm not talking about Bradford. I'm talking about Farquhar. We did not dispose of him. He knows we're interested in him and he knows your research is going to expose him, if it hasn't already, as the low-life scum he was.'

Ruth sat back with a sigh. 'The crux of the problem – one the police haven't even guessed at.'

'Though they are sniffing round my reputation as a psychic fraud.' He didn't sound particularly worried.

She smiled. 'Being rational twenty-first-century people, they don't believe in psychics.'

'Any more than you do.'

'Oh, I have come to believe in something,' she said. 'I think my rationality balance is beginning to swing the other way. If not ghosts, who are these people who keep popping into my life? I desperately want to believe in Thomas and I've been forced to believe in Farquhar. So, you can chalk me up as a victory.'

She looked away, suddenly embarrassed that he might misunderstand.

The silence that ensued seemed interminable.

'OK.' Malcolm leaned towards her. 'Shall we address the elephant in the room? To stop all this potential for saying the wrong thing.' He hesitated. 'I do seem to have grown very fond of you, Ruthie, and I'm so sorry if I've made you uncomfortable. As you must have realised by now, I'm not very good at this sort of thing. I shall in future shut up and concentrate on the matter in hand, which is Farquhar. As for anything else, I shall remain on my best behaviour. The last thing I want to do is add to your worries.'

She found her mouth had gone dry.

'And I would like you to stay here, if you want to. But the one is not predicated on the other.'

She gave a snort of laughter. 'Predicated! Oh, Mal. You clearly never had lessons on how to sweet-talk someone!'

He gave her a quizzical smile. 'I think by now you must have realised that I am an inarticulate academic.'

'Rubbish. You are extremely articulate.'

'So, have I made myself understood?'

She hesitated. 'I think so.'

'And to assuage your friends' anxious enquiries, I am not married. I had a partner,' he hesitated, 'a much-loved partner, but she died ten years ago, and since then I have been wedded to my work. Passing girlfriends. Nothing serious. As to the future, I leave that up to the gods.'

She laughed again. 'I think I'm comfortable with that idea. I would like to stay very much, thank you.' She bit her lip. 'And I'd like to keep my room in the top of the tower.' She was trying to work out how to explain. 'I was enjoying my freedom after Rick and I were divorced; I had no plans to get hooked up again at any level. And besides,' she hesitated, 'you and I have barely got to know each other. We might have fallen in love slowly, given the chance, but we have been thrown at each other and people around us keep suggesting things that we're not ready to deal with. At least, I'm not. Not yet.'

'They're suggesting things because to them they're obvious.' He paused. 'Go with your instincts, Ruthie,' he said gently. 'You're analysing everything again. But at least you haven't freaked out and run for the hills. I will respectfully stand back and wait.'

'And say nothing about this conversation to anyone.'

He saluted with crossed fingers. 'Scout's honour.'

April took the bus out to Cramond the next morning. As she got off, she ran her hand self-consciously through her hair. No one would recognise her even if they knew what she looked like.

There were very few people around as she walked down the lane. At the gate to the Old Mill House she hesitated, then she walked on down the drive. She mustn't look suspicious. If anyone asked, she was looking for Mr Macdermott.

The place looked forlorn and deserted. There was one security camera over the front door that she could see. If she gave it a wide berth she could go round the back of the house unobserved. She crept round, past the padlocked garages, moving cautiously until she could see the whole of the back lawn, then tiptoed towards the rear windows of the house, which looked as dark and blank as the ones in the front. The dining room, when she peered in, was neat and tidy and deserted. The kitchen was dark and empty. The herbs on the windowsill were drooping. No one had watered them. There was no one there.

She stood still for several minutes, drained of energy. There had been a small part of her, she realised, that had hoped Tim would be here. She wished fervently she hadn't come.

As she began to trudge back towards the main road she realised she had no idea when the next bus would arrive; she would probably have to wait hours.

Behind her, the driver of the unmarked car parked under the trees nudged his companion. 'Did that woman come out of the Old Mill House drive?'

'I didn't see.' The young police constable had been doing the crossword in yesterday's *Evening News*. He reached for the printout of the picture of Timothy and April that had been circulated round the force. 'Doesn't look like her to me.'

They watched the retreating figure plodding away from them as the rain began to fall. 'We could offer her a lift back to town,' he said with a malicious grin.

The man at the wheel considered the idea. 'I don't think so. We'll give this another half hour then we'll go and get something to eat in the pub.'

In the distance, April disappeared round the corner and headed towards the bus stop oblivious to the fact that she had been observed.

64

Ruth liked her room in the tower. It was quiet and cosy and, since Malcolm had carried an extra gate-legged table upstairs for her to work on, suited her very well. She smiled as she sat before her laptop thinking of the struggle he had had getting it up the spiral staircase on his own. 'Wait till there's someone to help you,' she had begged.

'There isn't anyone else, in case you haven't noticed.'

'What, no varlets?'

'No varlets, sadly. Not since my mother's time. Varlets are out of fashion.'

'Even Fin has a gardener.'

'Fin is a celebrity chef; he's probably a rich man.' He had sat on her bed until he got his breath back, then he left her to work.

There had been no word from the police. Fin had rung that morning to say he would be staying with Max for a few days if they needed him. Harriet's phone was still switched off. The Twitter account of RuthieD had not displayed any new comments for several hours.

When they convened in the kitchen at lunchtime, Malcolm handed her a glass of wine. 'Can you work up there OK?'

'It's perfect. I feel safe there.'

403

'Good.' Neither had mentioned their conversation of the previous day. He studied her face. 'Are you making progress with your research?'

She nodded. 'I would like to think Thomas wants me to set the record straight.'

'You mentioned he was struck by lightning a second time.' Malcolm sat down at the table and took a sip from his glass. 'Where did you hear about that?'

She hesitated. 'He mentions it in one of the letters. And it's a family story. Mummy told me about it when I was very little and I was hugely impressed. He is supposed to have been struck by lightning three times and lived to tell the tale. She used to say he was in the *Guinness Book of Records*.'

'Not the sort of story that even a doting family would make up.'

'No.' She sat down opposite him. 'Do you mind if I don't show you my own notes yet? They are all a bit mad; ad hoc; unintelligible in places; not really suitable for a serious historian.'

'You forget I am no longer a serious historian,' he sighed, somehow not managing the light-hearted tone he was looking for. 'Have you managed to get hold of Harriet?'

She shook her head. 'Her phone is still switched off.'

'I wonder how she's planning to do her research into ascended masters without you. She must realise she will have upset you as well as me.'

Ruth reached for the wine bottle and topped up her glass. Almost as an afterthought she leaned across and poured some for him too. 'We don't know it's her, Mal. I keep thinking about what the policeman said. Supposing it is Tim.'

'Whoever it is, RuthieD will get bored soon.' He was thoughtful for a minute or two. 'You're right. We shouldn't be too hard on Harriet. Not till we're sure it's her.'

'Whoever it is intended to ruin your career, but people can live with the slur of believing in the paranormal,' she added mischievously. 'Thomas for one. He was much mocked for his beliefs.'

'Well, there you are then. If he can, I can.' He pushed away his glass. 'Bread and cheese OK for lunch? I'm afraid I can't compete with your Masterchef.'

Thomas handed his greatcoat and briefcase to a servant. He carried the fetish with him everywhere now, carefully wrapped in a silk neckerchief, hidden amongst his papers, and so far it seemed to have kept Farquhar at bay. He walked into the drawing room surrounded by his dogs to find Frances there alone, practising the harpsichord. 'That sounds lovely, my darling. You have a real talent,' he said. 'Where is Mama?'

'She's lying down. She was tired.' Frances rose from the music stool and came over to her father. She patted the dogs. 'They wait for you to come home all day, you know.'

'Rubbish. They love playing with you all, especially the boys.' He walked over to the fire and sat down in his chair. 'Come and talk to me. There is something I wanted to discuss with your mama but my intelligent daughter will do just as well. It is a problem I have at my office and I need some advice. Have you heard of a man called Thomas Paine?'

Frances sat down on the chair next to him, arranging her skirts with care, glad to have her father to herself.

'Of course.'

'Tell me what you know.'

'He is a revolutionary and a troublemaker and he has just written a book called the *Rights of Man*.' She gave a small smile. 'He supports the American cause.'

'My goodness, I have an informed daughter.'

'He interests me because you yourself told us all those stories about your visit to America when you were in the navy and your stay with our cousins in the Windward Islands, and Mama has told us so much about her grandfather who was Attorney General in Pennsylvania.'

'I know,' he teased, 'and her uncle who was a privateer!'

Frances giggled. 'He was only a privateer briefly, Papa. Mama's heart has always had a soft spot for her American relatives, you must know that.'

'Indeed.' He tried to look stern.

'And it makes us all interested in America. Davy wants to go there when he finishes at university.'

'Does he?' Thomas's children never ceased to surprise him. 'So, please don't tell me you have all studied Thomas Paine's ideas?'

Frances looked at him knowingly. 'Mama has a copy of the *Rights of Man*; she has Mrs Wollstonecraft's *A Vindication of the Rights of Woman* as well.' Her expression had become quite coquettish.

'Oh, does she now.' Thomas laughed. 'So, let's keep to Mr Paine for now. Tell me, how is he regarded in England?'

'As a traitor and a troublemaker for his demands for parliamentary reform.'

'And what if I were to tell you that he is to be indicted for sedition and that I have been asked to defend him.'

She turned so she could look into his face. 'The Prince of Wales would not like that, Papa.'

'No, indeed he wouldn't.' She was very wise, this child of his. 'No more than does the noble Lord Loughborough, who accosted me on the heath this very evening as I was on my way home and begged me not to take the case.'

'But you are going to?' Like her mother, she knew him so well.

'I think I must. Whatever his views, he has the right to express them.'

'And if you take the case, what will happen?'

'His Royal Highness has already told me that he could no longer employ me as his Attorney General. And I would be very unpopular in certain circles.'

Her troubled gaze lasted a few more seconds, then it melted into laughter. 'And as long as you were doing the right thing by your conscience, you wouldn't care at all what people thought, would you.'

'No.'

'You must tell Mama.'

'Of course. She will back me up.'

'She always backs you up, Papa.' Frances reached for his hand. 'She is so proud of you.'

* * *

Ruth's hands paused over her laptop. Was it really like that? An affectionate supportive family, a talented daughter who could giggle with her father? A man sitting by the fire with his dogs sprawled around him, a glass in his hand, his feet stuck out to the warmth of the flames, listening as she gave a very passable rendition of a minuet. Ruth listened, her head on one side. The minuet was finished. Now she was playing a Bach prelude. This was nonsense. Malcolm must be in his study with some suitably themed music playing as a background while he worked. She stood up and walked over to the door, opening it gently to look down the stone steps as they wound away into darkness. She listened. Silence. The music was in her room. In her head. Gently she closed the door and went back to her laptop. She knew what happened next. Almost every breath Thomas took during this period had been documented, pored over, analysed. The quest for parliamentary reform in the face of corruption, the fear of revolution.

She read over the last section of her notes. Frances had kissed him goodnight and left him sitting by the fire. A servant had come in and put on more logs, and Thomas had told him to leave the candles so one by one they had burned down in their sconces and the room had grown dark. It was then the voice of Andrew Farquhar had returned. 'So now you're an advocate for the people.' It was mocking, insidious, hissing in Thomas's ear.

The dogs did not react. They couldn't hear it. 'You, in your fine house with your lovely children, standing up for the poor and disenfranchised.' Farquhar was there, a shadow in the flickering light from the glowing logs, sitting on the chair on the far side of the hearth.

'And you're claiming to be an advocate for the poor and needy?' Thomas looked up. 'You, who raped and murdered and robbed your neighbours. I would ask our parson to pray for you if I thought it would do any good. Leave me to do what I can for the good of mankind and go back to the boiling runnels of hell where you're at home.'

He stood up and went over to the sideboard, reaching for the whisky decanter.

'So, it's for the good of mankind, these high fees you collect. The silver, the servants, the coach and the horses.' The voice was mocking.

'Yes, by God!' Thomas spun round. 'It is.'

'Thomas?' The door opened behind him and Fanny appeared, a chamberstick in her hand. The shadows ran across the wall and over the ceiling. The figure in the chair had gone. 'Who were you talking to, my darling?'

Thomas put down his glass. 'I'm sorry. Did I wake you?'

'No, Frances came up to say goodnight and she told me she was worried. You take on so much work and you give yourself so little time to sleep.' She went over and put her arms round him. 'Was it Farquhar?' she murmured.

He dropped a kiss on the top of her head. 'When I'm tired, I can't get rid of him.' He had realised that he had left his briefcase with its precious hidden talisman in his chambers.

'Ruth!'

The voice, cutting through the quiet of the room, was followed by a loud knock. Frances and Thomas vanished. The elegant, shadowy drawing room in Hampstead disappeared. For a moment Ruth sat still, bereft, then she looked up.

'I've brought you a cup of tea.' Malcolm was standing on the threshold. 'I'm sorry.' He took in her blank look. 'You were working and I've interrupted. I should know better, shouldn't I. I would kill anyone who walked in when I was in full flow.'

She shook her head, trying to dislodge the voices from the past. 'I was lost in the story.'

'Just so long as Farquhar wasn't there.'

'But he was. He's there all the time, in Thomas's head. Mocking. Deriding everything he stood for.'

'Keep your boundaries strong, Ruth.' Malcolm turned away, the cup still in his hand.

'No, don't take it away. I need it.' She reached out. 'Come in. I'm quite glad to stop, actually. I am stiff and cold. I've been reading and typing for hours.'

They both looked at the table with its lamp and the laptop, the books, the notebooks, the pencils. Malcolm smiled. 'A familiar scene. The ingredients we use to bring the past back to life.'

'And music. Do you ever play music to put you in the mood? Bach?'

'Not when I'm working, no.'

'Just now, Thomas's daughter was playing the harpsichord in my head. It was beautiful.'

Mal perched on the edge of the chair by the window. Outside a quarter moon was struggling to emerge from the clouds. 'You really were there.'

'It felt real, yes.' She sipped the tea.

'And Farquhar was there with them?'

'A shadow, by the fire, when Thomas was alone. The moment Fanny walked in, he disappeared.'

Malcolm was looking thoughtful.

'Thomas told Farquhar he would ask the parson to pray for him if he thought it would do any good.'

'Interesting. So was the doubt there because he didn't believe in the power of prayer, or the power of that particular parson?'

'I got the impression it was because he thought Farquhar so imbued in evil he was beyond redemption.'

'Ah. That might explain our problem in the present day.' Malcolm walked over to the window and stood looking out. It was almost dark now, yet if he looked west he could still see the line of pale light on the horizon where the hills fell into a V at the end of the glen. For the first time in his life he sensed something sinister out there and he shivered.

'What is it?' Ruth was watching him.

He stood back and reached up to close the shutters. 'I was wondering where Bradford has got to.'

'You think he's out there?'

'No. But I would feel happier if I knew he was under lock and key.' He turned back into the room. 'Shall I leave you to it? Supper in the kitchen later?'

'Yes, please.'

As soon as he had gone she went over to the window and opened the shutters again. But she could see nothing out there now. The woods had shrugged themselves into the night.

65

Tim hadn't bargained with having to walk the whole five miles or so to Morningside. He had found shelter for a few hours in someone's garden shed, but the cold had woken him up in the early hours and he had set out again in the dark, thankful only that it had stopped raining at last. The sky was full of stars; there was no traffic, no one to thumb a lift from, but as dawn broke his spirits lifted. It turned into a glorious day. He had forgotten how beautiful Edinburgh could be as he trudged towards the West End, passed the huge black bulk of Edinburgh Castle high on its rock above the streets, and more by luck than good judgement arrived in Morningside as Sally Laidlaw was closing her front door and heading up the road. Stupid woman! He had never forgiven her for summoning Ruth. If that hadn't happened the will would have gone unchallenged and he would now be warm and cosy in the house he still thought of as his own. One day he would get even. But not yet. For now he would keep his head down and concentrate on finding food and warmth. He waited for her to walk out of sight round the corner then he groped in his pocket for the keys he had stolen from Ruth's bedside table.

He closed the door behind him and leaned against it, smiling.

She hadn't touched the old man's tins of food. He pulled them out of the cupboards eagerly. Baked beans, tinned pears and, bliss, sausages in tomato sauce. Tuna, potatoes, packets of this and that, some old and distinctly past their sell-by date, but the tins were OK. The gas turned on easily, as did the electrics, though he must remember not to switch on the lights at night if he wanted to keep his presence secret. He made himself a meal at once, and only when he had eaten every last scrap on the plate did he turn his attention to the rest of the house. There was always the faint hope that he would find some cash in the back of a drawer.

The desk in the dining room had been emptied; the chests in the old man's bedroom contained only rubbish, pens that no longer worked, rusty paper clips, a few old pre-decimal coins that were no use to anyone. The cupboards on the top floor containing the rubbish left after he had removed everything he had thought of value had finally been emptied completely. Never mind. His stomach was full, he had a choice of comfortable beds and he had a base from which he could venture forth to try his hand at a bit of petty thieving. It was astonishing how many people still nipped out to the shops leaving their back doors open, or left their cars with the passenger doors unlocked and a glove box full of loose change.

Time you learned to pick pockets, my friend.

He frowned and rubbed his forehead. The voice in his brain was like an interloper, mocking, insidious. 'April?' he responded out loud. 'Is that you?' Of course it wasn't her. The voice belonged to a man, a coarse powerful voice that seemed to whisper but was insistent. As he pulled blankets and sheets from the cupboard on the landing he stopped, suddenly in a complete panic as the realisation hit him again. April had gone.

'Who are you?' Timothy dropped the blankets and turned round slowly, scanning the open doorways. There was no one there. He was hallucinating through lack of sleep. Stooping, he scooped up the bedclothes. He could live without April very well. If he missed her it was only because she always knew what to do, always had a fiver in her pocket. Well, it was time for him to step up on his own. After all, her plans had in the end gone disastrously wrong and now his were back on track.

* * *

April walked on through the crowds looking this way and that, enjoying the buzz. She had more sense than to try to do any business; she was here like everyone else, to enjoy herself. Later she would make her way back to one of the bigger antique markets, but on a Saturday one had to be careful. They often upped the security. She pulled the strap of her bag further up onto her shoulder and pushed on through the crowd. She had enough cash to treat herself to an upmarket coffee and a cake. It was as she was sitting at the table sipping the froth off the top of her cappuccino that the man at the next table opened his newspaper. Timothy was headline news and there was a Photofit picture of him, with a woman at his side.

She sat without moving for several seconds, frozen with terror before it dawned on her that the picture looked nothing like her. It was an invention. The woman staring back off the front page had a wooden, fixed expression, wispy light-coloured hair, weird straight eyebrows. She smiled as she lowered her lips once more into the froth. No one in a million years would identify that desperate-looking loser with the smart, vibrant woman with intensely deep chestnut hair and designer jacket sitting here in a West End coffee shop. Even so, she had to force herself to stay put as she finished her cappuccino, trying to look casual as she pushed the cup away and extricated herself from the table. As she eased past the man with the paper he looked up and seemed to stare at her for fully three seconds. She held his gaze, paralysed with fear, then managed to smile and moved on. He went back to his paper without any sign of recognition.

'I am so sorry to have inflicted all this junk on you.' Ruth was standing in a ground-floor room in the Tower House, with Malcolm at her shoulder. They had made a trip back to the Old Mill House that morning to collect the boxes and cases from Fin's cupboard, unwilling to leave them in the empty house, a house that seemed forlorn and very quiet as the police constable on duty waited on the doorstep for them to lock up and leave.

What Mal referred to as her treasure was now piled on the floor in front of them in a mostly unused sitting room.

'It's dry and safe here, and I never use the room so you can leave it as long as you like,' he reassured her yet again. 'My mother used to entertain unwelcome visitors here, like the poor women from the Mothers' Union and the WI.' He laughed at the memory. 'She was a feisty soul. Unclubbable.'

'She was the laird's wife, presumably, and therefore a great prize.' Ruth was bending over one of the boxes, pulling back the flaps to see what was inside.

'She was the laird.' He smiled affectionately. 'As far as the local ladies were concerned, my poor father was just an add-on. They weren't interested in him, they didn't even notice when he died, poor guy, but I don't think they ever gave up trying with Mum.'

'So, are you the laird now?' She stood up and looked at him quizzically.

'For my sins.'

'What does that mean. Being a laird?'

'It means those same women flutter their eyelashes, but from a safe distance, and send their husbands, who are on the PCC or the committee of the golf club, to see me instead, and I ask them upstairs for a dram.'

'Wow. Overwhelmingly hospitable.'

'I try,' he sighed. 'But I expect word will get round now about the tweets and even the husbands won't dare come any more. I'll be identified with Dracula, or worse.'

'Is there anyone worse than Dracula?'

She held his gaze. Again, that strange feeling of warmth. And longing. They were standing very close to each other in the semi-darkness of the room and she found herself reaching up to put her hand on his chest. 'Mal—'

The kiss was brief and she pulled away almost at once.

'Why, Miss Dunbar, I do believe you are trying to seduce the laird?' His voice was strangely husky.

She laughed awkwardly. 'I don't know what I was thinking of.' She was trembling, she realised. 'Perhaps I should go back to the top of my tower before I get carried away.' She turned hastily back to the box. 'But before I go, I just wondered what this was.' She dived in to cover her embarrassment and came up with a bundle. 'I was going to ask you about it.'

'Let's take it up to the kitchen.' He had turned away a little too quickly.

She took a deep breath and followed him.

Putting the bundle on the kitchen table she began to unwrap it. 'I thought you might know what it is.'

In the bright lights the crudely woven doll with its beads and feathers looked like a moth-eaten scrap of rubbish. Over by the stove the two dogs sat up. Pol growled in his throat. Malcolm glanced at him and back at the doll.

'Can you feel it? This has power,' he said softly. 'What an extraordinary find. This is very special. It was created for the purposes of magical manipulation.' He pushed back his sleeves and reached out tentatively. 'Do you know where it came from?'

'Thomas brought it back from the West Indies.'

He glanced up sharply. 'So this is eighteenth century?'

'It is.'

'Part of the slave culture of the time.'

'Voodoo?' she whispered.

'Possibly. It depends which island it came from. But not all voodoo was bad. I have a feeling this one is protective.'

'He refers to it as a fetish. I know how he got it. He went to a black woman doctor when he was ill. His lieutenant took him and I gather a lot of the men on the navy ships held her in great esteem. I don't know if she was what we would call a witch doctor, but she knew her stuff with herbs and things.'

'Probably a great deal more efficient than a British doctor. At that time in Britain they were peddling lethal stuff and trying to get old women herbalists if not burned as witches, then mocked and derided, to protect their monopoly on new medicines like arsenic and opium!' He gave a resigned sigh. 'Typical men, taking over something that wasn't broken and deciding they could fix it by making new rules.'

She gave a reluctant smile. 'Shouldn't that be my line?'

'Probably.' He was still looking at the doll. 'Can I ask how you know about all this?'

'His letters home.'

'Of course.'

She waited for him to ask again if he could see them, but he didn't. He carried the doll over to the lamp in the corner and examined it more closely. 'This is a fascinating thing. Beautifully made. I've come across such things before but they've always been modern. They tend to give off an unpleasant aura and people are frightened of them.'

'How on earth do people get hold of them?'

'Tourists bring them back from the West Indies or Florida, places like that, as souvenirs from voodoo and Santeria shops, then they don't dare throw them away. But this is an old one, the real thing, and I would definitely say it is protective rather than imbued with hatred. You can see here, the typical mix of traditions: tiny crosses, little carved figures that represent the Virgin Mary and Baby Jesus, then other figures and gods – totems from her African background. My guess is that the old woman who made it for Thomas did so in order to keep him safe. Perhaps she fell for his charms.' He smiled.

'So, what do I do with it?'

'Oh, keep it. You are one of his descendants, one of his children, in a manner of speaking, and I suspect she included you all within its magical remit.'

'So, we are talking black magic here.' She couldn't quite keep the incredulity out of her voice. 'Doesn't it scare you?'

'No, it doesn't. On the contrary. This is a wonderful thing.'

'But the dogs don't like it.' She looked towards them. They had gone back to sleep.

'They can feel its power, but it isn't disturbing them now.' He touched it tentatively again then rested his hand over it, his eyes closed. 'It is amazingly strong, though I sense it has been asleep for a long time. See if you can feel it.' He pushed it towards her.

She pulled a face. 'You know me, I don't feel things!' She touched it with a finger. 'I think Fin could though. He was there when I first found it.'

'Ssh. Stop talking. Stop thinking. Close your eyes,' he remonstrated.

Reluctantly she obeyed his bidding, trying to empty her thoughts. The doll felt icy cold beneath her fingertips then slowly she realised she could feel it growing warmer. She withdrew her hand abruptly, her eyes flying open.

He was watching her. 'You felt it?'

'Only that my hands were warming it up.'

He smiled at her. 'You know, I can't help wondering if this wasn't made to keep our friend Andrew Farquhar at bay.'

Ruth nodded. 'Thomas kept it for that reason. He had great faith in it.'

'Rightly. I'm inclined to think that as long as you have this with you, you might be safe from Farquhar's attentions as well.'

'But if that's true, why didn't it work before? It was there all the time, in my mother's stuff.'

He was thoughtful for a moment. 'Perhaps it needed you to wake it up; to acknowledge its presence in your life. Perhaps it needed to be near you.' He glanced up at her. 'Just think of it as something that brings you luck.'

'But it's—'

She was going to say horrible, but she changed her mind. She was looking at it more closely. It was partly carved wood, partly some kind of fabric, but it had so much else in its makeup: sticks, dried berries, red thread, little bits of black wire, fragments of what looked like leather and, as Mal had seen, tiny crosses and carved beads and what looked like icons.

'Touch it again. Let it know you acknowledge it,' he said quietly, 'then take it upstairs and put it somewhere in your room. Look after it carefully, it's very fragile.'

'And it will keep me safe?'

'There's a good chance it will.'

'Even from marauding lairds?' She smiled.

'Ah, now that depends on whether you welcome their marauding or not.' He gave a cautious grin. 'Now, away you go and put it somewhere safe while I, in the tradition of your English compatriots, hastily put on the kettle.'

She went upstairs, carrying the doll, and tucked it tenderly in the drawer of the little table beside her bed. She preferred to think of it as a doll rather than a fetish. Horrible word. It was rubbish of course to think it had any more power than a mascot of the kind they all used to carry at school when it was time for exams.

Nevertheless, mascots worked. Just carrying them gave one confidence.

As she pushed the drawer closed she smiled to herself. That was not what was happening now. She wasn't stupid. The strange breathless excitement she felt, a tingling all over her body, was less to do with the power of the precious thing she had hidden away in the drawer and more to do with the man downstairs in the kitchen with his teapot and the fact that she was aching to kiss him again.

Thomas

In spite of my passionate defence of Paine's right to freedom of ideas and his right to express them, he was found guilty of sedition by a rigged jury. King and government clung to their right to maintain control on society.

Those were exciting times and I was in the thick of them. The country, with its eye on revolutionary France, was in a ferment of unrest, with terror and anger finely balanced in the streets of London.

At the same time Fanny and I were saddened by the death of my old friend and mentor, Lord Mansfield. The subject of slavery was one which engaged all thoughtful people, and he had raised it again and again in the House. With no children of his own, he left a substantial amount of money to his niece Elizabeth and a further amount to his ward, Sir John Lindsay's daughter, Dido Belle, who had lived at Kenwood as part of the family for nigh on thirty years. Philosophically, the idea of one man owning another was insupportable in an enlightened age. The slaves on the plantations of our relatives had seemed happy. They danced, they sang. I did not, when I had seen them as a boy, understand the loss and yearning in their hearts for a homeland they would never see again. No one is morally justified in removing a man from his own soil, taking him to a faraway country and keeping him there by force. And no man is morally entitled to own another.

But each time I held my talismanic doll in my hand I remembered the old slave woman who had given it to me. If she had not been there I might long ago have fallen victim to the malign curses of Andrew Farquhar.

Oh yes, he still haunted my dreams. Every time I looked into the crowds I was subconsciously searching for that bloated, hate-filled face. Somehow I knew he was there somewhere, waiting his chance. But his chance to do what? And how long could I hold him at bay?

66

For a moment Ruth couldn't think where she was. She stretched out, feeling for her pillow, and her hand touched a shoulder. Her eyes flew open. She was in Malcolm's bedroom.

'Good morning.' He turned to smile at her.

She groaned. 'Please tell me I didn't.'

'You did.' He raised himself on his elbow. 'See what happens when you take a fetish to your bedroom. All your inhibitions fly out of the window. And I'm very glad they did.'

'I came downstairs looking for you?' She was beginning to remember. She pulled the duvet over herself, covering her face. 'What must you think of me?'

'I think it's wonderful.' He sat up, leaned over to give her a lingering kiss before reaching for the dressing gown that was lying on the floor beside the bed. 'And I wish we could start all over again, but I have just realised what the time is and that my esteemed agent will be arriving in about half an hour from now. Too late to put him off alas, so we'll have to take a mutual rain check, and resume our very enjoyable encounter later. Agreed?' He did not wait for an answer. In seconds she heard his bath running.

Slipping out of bed she headed for the door. In her own room she found her bed hadn't been slept in. The light was still on. She gave herself a little hug. She felt extraordinarily happy.

When she was showered and dressed she found Max and

Fin with Malcolm in the kitchen. The room smelt of coffee, there was a plate of croissants on the table, and an armful of Sunday newspapers lay on the chair.

'No further news about the Bradfords,' Fin said as he saw her. 'The police have confirmed that April wasn't in that burned-out house.'

'Thank goodness.' Ruth slipped into the chair at the head of the table.

Malcolm passed her a cup of coffee, his face solemn. 'Did you sleep well?'

'I did, thank you.' She managed to keep her composure.

'It means,' Fin went on, oblivious to the exchange, 'that they are probably together again, working as a team.'

'What is happening at the Old Mill House?' Ruth asked suddenly. 'Are the police keeping an eye on it?'

'There was a guy there yesterday,' Malcolm put in, 'when we went to fetch Ruth's treasures. But then we did tell them we were coming.'

'Well, Lachy's there now. He moved in last night with his family and his very large scary brother, just for the time being.' Fin grinned happily. 'Max has kindly offered me his spare room for as long as I need it and I take it Mal will allow you to stay here for a while.' Fin met Ruth's gaze straight on.

'Of course she can,' Malcolm put in.

'So,' Fin went on, 'all we have to do is keep our heads down till the police catch them.' He sighed. 'I'm not sure whether you want to know what's in the papers. There are several articles about you, Mal, I'm afraid. Not all bad. Not all mocking.'

'Which implies that some of them are?'

'You weren't expecting anything else, were you? We thought it better you know about it.'

'There's nothing there that will do you any damage,' Max put in. 'I think it will all blow over. So, how are things on the Internet? Have you checked this morning?'

'I haven't had time to look,' Malcolm responded cheerfully. 'Better things to do.'

Ruth kept her eyes determinedly on the coffee mug in her hands.

421

'And unless my publisher decides to pull my contract for conduct unbecoming, I shall concentrate on my writing,' Mal went on. 'And I shall continue to do so.'

'There's no way Timothy could find out I'm here, is there?' Ruth asked suddenly.

'I don't see how. Unless . . . ' Max stared at her thoughtfully. 'Harriet wouldn't put it online, would she?'

Someone had.

Supernaturally inspired biographer #Malcolm Douglas has been consulting about haunted houses with celebrity chef's friend, Ruth Dunbar.

'Shit! How could she!' Ruth cried out in despair as they all stared at the screen. 'She must realise how dangerous this is.'

'She's out to hurt us, I'm afraid,' Malcolm said sadly.

'If it is Harriet,' Fin put in.

'Who else could it be?' Ruth looked up at him wildly. 'Who else knows? Look, here's another one.'

I wonder if historian Malcolm Douglas has company in his lonely tower. Eagles and ghosts witness what's going on under his ancestral roof.

'Poetic.' Malcolm's tone was dour. 'What are the chances of Timothy seeing this?'

'It's unlikely he'd follow Twitter, isn't it?'

'If he does, it pinpoints your possible whereabouts. Where I live is not exactly secret,' Malcolm sighed. 'Not that it matters if we keep the door locked. She is one bitter lady, Harriet. My own stupid fault.'

And her phone was still switched off. Ruth left a message. 'I'm not sure what you're playing at, Hattie, but you're putting my life in danger. Is that what you intend?'

The others were listening. 'That's telling her,' Fin commented.

'Sorry. I'm fed up with sitting here and taking whatever she cares to throw at us,' Ruth defended herself. 'I know. I should be dignified and silent.'

'No way. Dignified and silent is for Mal,' Max put in. 'You go for it. If you're sure it's her, keep texting her and remind her how stupid this is. She must know by now what these people are capable of. She needs to think what she's doing. And tell her to switch on her phone and speak to you.'

Thomas

My eldest son, Davy, progressed to Cambridge, and to Lincoln's Inn, and was admitted to the bar; then, as had been his dream since he was a little boy, he went to America to seek his fortune and there he found a wife in his cousin, Frances Cadwallader, Caddy, he called her, there being already too many Franceses in the family.

Our two eldest daughters, Frances and Elizabeth, went up to Scotland and learned there to love the country of my birth and of their heritage. My brother, David, made them welcome at his newly built house beside Dryburgh Abbey and Elizabeth fell in love with David's son. David never had legitimate children, alas, but this young man was as dear to him as an heir would have been. Fanny and I travelled north for the wedding and gave them our blessing, unaware when we returned south with Frances after our joyful visit that we would never see our darling Lizzie again. She had never been strong and became increasingly ill. Her husband and her father-in-law cared for her with every ounce of their love but could not save her; she died in August of the year 1800 and was buried in St Monan's chapel within the walls of the ancient abbey. Fanny and I were devastated but I had too heavy a workload to travel north for her funeral. All we could do was weep and pray that she rest in peace in the country of her ancestors she had come to love so much.

When my darling Fanny became ill, weakened by her grief at Lizzie's death, I sensed Farquhar's glee as I sat with her one night and I grew afraid and scrabbled in the bottom drawer of my desk for the doll. I had ceased to carry it around after one of my clerks had found it amongst my papers, and it looked dull and forlorn. Instinctively I held it against my heart until I could feel its power rekindled, and I hid it in Fanny's room, learning a valuable lesson, the power and protection of love.

We drew comfort in our sadness from an unexpected quarter, our fashionable new young doctor, Samuel Holland. Busy as always, I did not notice that he came more and more often, that Frances was always there to conduct him to her mother's apartment, that the two of them talked earnestly and long, their conversation straying from the medical to philosophy, to music, and on to particulars of religion. My Frances was a devout young woman, inheriting the passions of her grandmother and her aunt, not sharing their love of Methodism but favouring the Church of England. It appeared Dr Holland felt the same.

Frances's sister, Margaret, meanwhile, busied herself overseeing the education of her youngest four siblings. Without Fanny's oversight they might have run wild, but Margaret, knowing how distracted I was, conscientiously stepped into her mother's shoes. Mary, Henry, Thomas and Esmé, aged at the time of their sister's death, sixteen, fourteen, twelve and eleven respectively, lived mostly at my Evergreen haven, surrounded by horses and dogs, the boys going in turn to school and, in Henry and young Thomas's case, to Cambridge, in Esmé's into the army and in Mary's to study with her sisters' governesses.

And I, ambitious, clever (not modest, as was constantly pointed out by astute commentators, both those who called themselves my friends and those who were conspicuously not so), ploughed my furrow deep and earnestly as ever.

67

Thomas had been at a dinner party at Carlton House the night before. It had been noisy, raucous even, Prinny in fine voice, full of jokes and laughter, Fox and his colleagues leaning across the table, thumping their fists down amongst the glasses, gesturing vehemently to emphasise their ideas.

Having promised himself a weekend in Hampstead, Thomas had called for Ebony early, eager to clear his head with a gallop over the heath. Much as he enjoyed the cronyship of the prince and his circle, the world of politics, law, the theatre and the music of London, there were times when he longed to be alone in his garden. He missed Fanny. Her constant tiredness was an excuse not to accompany him to the soirees and parties, the dinners and plays, all things that she no longer enjoyed, but it would all have been so much more fun with her at his side to giggle and whisper late into the night as they had when they were young.

She was sitting in the morning room when he arrived and greeted him with a hug and a kiss. 'My darling you look awful. Is the prince leading you all astray? What time did you get to bed?'

He laughed. 'You are right as always.' He pulled a chair up beside her. 'So, what news from Hampstead? How are the children?'

'They flourish.' She smiled ruefully. 'They drain my every last drop of energy. And I have had a letter from Davy in America. He is so happy with his beautiful wife. They are returning to England soon and at last we will be able to meet her.' She glanced at him. 'And Frances has news which I will leave her to tell you as she has forbidden me to mention it.'

He raised an eyebrow. 'Indeed?'

'Indeed.'

He did not have to wait long. His daughter was loitering in the hallway and all but dragged him out into the garden. 'I have decided to marry Dr Holland, Papa. So, when he comes to you to ask for my hand, you will say yes.'

Thomas was astounded. She was so strong-willed, this his eldest child, he was inclined to agree as meekly as she no doubt expected. He managed to look stern. 'I cannot agree to anything of the sort!' He tried to picture her as an opponent at the bar in Westminster Hall. 'How could you imagine that I would? He's hardly suitable. My daughter cannot marry a doctor!'

'Why?' She pulled at his hand until he was facing her. 'Surely my father is not a snob? Besides, Sam is of ancient lineage, as ancient as ours, no doubt.' She saw his face in time. 'Well, perhaps not quite as ancient as ours, but nevertheless ancient. Not only descended from kings as we are, but from the princes of North Wales, near where you went to stay with the Dean of St Asaph. His father died when he was young, but he was a rector in Essex and' – she had the expression of a conjurer about to produce the rabbit from his hat – 'he is himself a man of the cloth. You didn't know that, did you? Before he decided to become a doctor, he studied for the church. That was his first love.'

'Then why,' he managed to ask, 'did he change his mind?'

'Because like you he's interested in everything. He couldn't imagine having to give up his studies in natural philosophy and his fascination with medicine. And I very much like his sister, Anne,' she went on breathlessly. 'She has become my best friend. And she has confided in me that he worships the ground I walk on and would like to make an offer for me. She has told him I would accept and I have told her to tell him that you would welcome him as a son-in-law.'

'It sounds as though you and your best friend Anne have everything in hand,' Thomas said drily when at last he could get a word in. 'And what does your mother think?'

'Oh, she adores Samuel.' His last line of resistance crumbled at her words. 'After all, he has made her better. He is an amazingly clever doctor. And,' she added almost as an afterthought, 'he's rich.'

She didn't tell him that the proposed marriage was as yet a dream conjured by Anne and herself. She didn't think Samuel had even begun to guess what they planned for him. No matter. It was true that he worshipped her, although so far it had been from afar. Anne would soon fix that. The date of their first encounter alone was already decided upon.

The night before the wedding Thomas called Frances to his study in Lincoln's Inn Fields and gave her his wedding present. It was a heavy gold signet ring. 'It belonged to your grandmama,' he said. 'She looked after you when you were a baby and your mama and I went to Minorca with my regiment. I want you to have something of hers. The stone is said to have belonged to Mary, Queen of Scots.'

It was too large even for her forefinger. 'Did your papa give it to her?' Frances said, holding it in the palm of her hand.

'I think he did.' He gave her a hug. 'And I have something else for you, my darling, something strange and special which I want you to keep forever and then pass on to your eldest daughter in turn.' He reached down beside his chair for a small carved box. 'This was given to me by an old lady in the Windward Islands when I was a midshipman in the navy. She told me it would always keep me and those I love safe.' He was about to add that she shouldn't open it but already the lid was off and she was gazing at the contents of the box. She looked up a little quizzically. 'What is it?' He noticed she didn't touch it.

'A doll.'

'Is this one of your fey Scots charms?'

'If it helps to think so.'

'And something I should not tell my husband about because he would surely disapprove.'

'I would never ask you to lie to your husband, Frances.'

'But better I don't show him?'

'Maybe.'

To his astonishment, she nodded and closed the box. 'I will lock it in my writing desk.' She reached over and kissed him. 'Thank you, Papa, I know how much these things mean to you.'

That night Andrew Farquhar came back in his dreams, laughing. 'As though I would want to harm your strait-laced daughter! Far more fun to torment you and your precious wife now you are no longer guarded by the slave woman's toy.'

Thomas woke, sweating, aware of daylight feeling its way through the curtains. Frances's wedding day. He would not let a phantom from his nightmares spoil it.

Harriet had seen the headlines about Fin. She picked up her phone and switched it on.

She listened to Ruth's last message twice, then deleted it. She could feel her face reddening with indignation and embarrassment as she switched the mobile off again and laid it gently down on her bed. Liz and Pete had gone out for lunch and she had turned down their invitation to go with them. Now she wished she'd gone. At least that would have distracted her from the thoughts whirling round in her head.

How had she put Ruth in danger? She didn't understand. Timothy Bradford was some sort of psychopath, that was obvious. No one was going to deny that. And he had targeted Ruth for coming between him and her father's supposed will. Of course she was in danger, but how was that her fault? She took a deep breath and redialled Ruth's number.

Ruth picked up at once. 'For pity's sake, Hattie, what are you thinking about? Have you any idea how much damage you've done? But of course you have or you wouldn't have done it!'

It was a minute or two before Harriet worked out what Ruth

was talking about. 'Ruth, it wasn't me, I swear it! I'm not even on Twitter. I promise you faithfully I would never have done such a thing. How could you think it?'

There was a moment of silence the other end of the line.

Harriet took a deep breath. 'I rang to tell you I had only just seen the news about Fin. Is he all right? Listen,' she rushed on. 'I've decided it's best if I go home.' That was true and however much they denied it, Liz and Pete would probably be pleased to see the back of her. 'As for putting your life in danger, I think Timothy is responsible for that, not me. Perhaps he's behind these tweets. Or April.'

She ended the call, unable to hold back her tears. It was only seconds before Ruth rang back. 'I'm sorry, Hattie,' she said remorsefully. 'I didn't really believe it was you, but I couldn't think who else. No one else knows about me and Mal. And I knew you hated him—'

'I don't hate him,' Harriet interrupted. 'A bit resentful, perhaps, but whatever they did to me, I would never try and harm someone's reputation, I swear it. Listen, I'm going tomorrow. If you find out anything to help my chapter on Dion, let me know.' She took a deep breath. 'You take care of yourself, Ruthie. And let Malcolm look after you. He's a good man, I'm sure. You have my blessing.' She gave an unhappy laugh. 'Bye, for now.'

She sat on the bed for several minutes after ending the call, tears pouring down her face, then she reached for the phone again. If she booked her seat on the train for next morning she wouldn't be tempted to change her mind.

You should carry a knife.

Timothy shook his head. The persistent voice was beginning to bug him. It was mocking, singsong, like tinnitus, always there, never allowing him any peace.

He had been surveying the kitchen cupboards with some gloom. There was probably enough to keep him going for another couple of days but that was all and already he was fed up with the diet of tinned food. He knew what he had to do and he had already targeted a couple of supermarkets he felt he would be safe places to nick some stuff. He had stood and watched a guy shovelling things into a sports bag in the back of a shop once. He had zipped up the bag, sneered at Timothy and walked out, brazen as you like. It wasn't usually that easy, he knew that, but he had no money. He had no choice.

A diver; that's what we call the best at picking pockets, and that's what you need to be. I made a fortune. Gold, quids, silk wipers—

'Shut up!' Timothy yelled.

He stamped round the kitchen, slapping his ears. 'Leave me alone!'

He went out and bought a paper. While he was choosing it in the corner shop he pocketed two packets of sweets. It was a start.

He had almost reached the house when he saw a policeman walking towards him. He crossed the road as casually as he could and strolled past on the other side. The policeman didn't give him a second look. He was too busy studying Number 26.

When the doorbell rang later he almost died of fright. He crept into the front room and sidled up to the window. The curtains were half drawn and he managed to peer round them in time to see a woman standing on the doorstep. He held his breath as she rang the bell again then she turned towards him and he felt a shock of sudden recognition. Under the dark glasses and weird hair, it was April.

'You stupid idiot!' He dragged her inside and, finger to his lips, pushed the door quietly closed behind her. 'The police are watching the house; and the woman next door is always peering at the windows when she goes past.' He led the way into the kitchen. 'How did you know I would be here?'

'It was a guess.' She sat down at the kitchen table, dived into her bag and pulled out a crumpled newspaper. 'So, what the hell have you been up to? You tied up Finlay Macdermott, threatened him with a knife? You are to be considered armed and dangerous?' Her explosion terrified the daylights out of him.

'I didn't hurt him.' Timothy snatched the paper away from her. 'What a whingeing wimp he was.'

'So, what were you planning to do with him?' Her eyes bored into his head. 'I leave you alone for a few hours and that is what you do!' She took a deep breath. 'So, what did you go there for? Did you nick anything worthwhile?'

'No. Well, the keys to this place. Then someone came.'

'Someone came!' She echoed his voice nastily. 'Ruth and Malcolm Douglas, it said so in the paper. You were disturbed and you ran away!' The sarcasm was biting.

'I didn't know who it was,' he tried to defend himself. 'A car arrived – it might have been the police.' He changed tack abruptly. 'The Dump burned down. I thought you'd died in the fire.' He heard the pathetic wobble in his own voice.

'I torched the place when you didn't come back. Best thing for it. I assumed you had finally grown a pair and gone off on your own.'

His eyes became flinty. 'I did go. I hitched a lift out of here, then I worried about you. I thought you wouldn't manage without me.' He saw her lip curl. 'I see you managed fine. I like the new look.'

'Which is more than I can say about you.'

He scowled. 'I've been living rough. I'll get you to cut my hair now you're here.' He grinned. His relief at seeing her was only just beginning to kick in. To his immense surprise he wanted to give her a hug.

'I've been staying in a hotel,' she said thoughtfully, 'but it uses up cash. I'll get my stuff and move in here. I take it that it's safe if we avoid being seen?'

While she returned to the hotel he went shopping with the cash she gave him. The cupboard was no longer bare.

It was after supper he asked her straight how much cash she had.

'None of your business.' She opened her laptop and went to her Twitter account.

He managed to hide his fury. 'Well, will it buy us train tickets? We can't stay here forever. What about Newcastle? I always fancied Newcastle.' He stood up and stared at the screen over her shoulder. 'It says here that Ruth has moved in with this man, Malcolm Douglas.' He took a deep breath, astonished at the wave of jealous fury that gripped him. 'He lives in a tower house in the Borders,' he went on. 'Ruth is twittering about them.'

He saw April's shoulders tense.

'It's not Ruth, it's you!' He sniggered.

'That's the man we saw her with at the Mill House. Hopefully this is making Ruth squirm.' She laughed.

But Ruth's not going to get away that easily, is she?

That voice again. Now. With April here. Timothy rubbed his face with his fists.

April looked up. 'Did you hear what I said?'

Timothy scowled. 'I did. Yes. So, what do you expect me to do about it?'

'Probably nothing. At least she's not likely to come here if she's cosily tucked up with him. And you're right, we need to get away. You've messed up enough.'

He looked at her with dislike. So, it was back to normal. Her giving him orders, handing out just enough money to keep him in line, her, with her ugly, humourless face, treating him like a child.

Whoa there. Not yet. We'll get even soon enough. First you need to find Ruth.

'You're right,' he told the voice in his head, 'we have to find Ruth first.'

'Why?' April looked at him sharply.

'Because otherwise she will live happily ever after and that would be unfair. Why should she have so much when we have so little?'

He wasn't aware that he was using someone else's words, but he did see the odd expression on his sister's face as she looked at him.

'It seems an unnecessary risk.'

He smiled. So, at last she had listened to something he had said. 'It's no more than you've been doing online. We could at least find out where this place is.'

That night he had the most disturbing dream. He woke sweating and aroused, not quite sure where he was. He had been in a room with several scantily clad young women. They had been touching him, crooning, plying him with drink, laughing as they beckoned him on, then running away, demanding money before they would let him grab them. He was getting more and more desperate, unable to contain himself, intoxicated by the smell of stale perfume. And then he awoke, all alone in the dark silent bedroom.

He sat up, shivering. He had never been all that keen on sex. The few times he had tried it, it had left him and his partner unsatisfied and let down and the last time he had failed entirely. He did not try again, but now he was desperate. He reached down to rub himself miserably.

Well, that's not going to get us very far, is it. We need to go out and find someone.

Almost without realising what he was doing he was reaching for his clothes, opening his door and creeping along the landing. He paused, listening. He could hear April snoring. Quietly he tiptoed downstairs, opened the front door and stepped out into the ice-cold night.

The streets were deserted. He found the young woman, paralytically drunk, weaving about on the pavement three streets away. She didn't fight him as he dragged her up into someone's driveway, tore off her clothes and slammed her against a tree.

Good. That's good. You see, you can do it. The voice was panting exultantly. *Now, don't hurt her. You don't want a murder charge hanging over you. That's what did for me. Give the lady back her clothes.*

Somewhere a clock was chiming as he made his way back to the front door. He let himself in quietly. April was still snoring. Silently he climbed up to his bedroom and dropped on the bed. He slept at once.

In the morning he assumed it had all been a dream.

'You're looking very pleased with yourself.' April was sitting at the kitchen table when he went downstairs. Her laptop was open in front of her. 'Here. Take a look at this.' She pushed it towards him.

He sat down opposite her and tried to focus. He was looking at a small castle. An ancient building, anyway, with several storeys, narrow windows and a moss-covered slate roof with a little turret. It stood against a background of cloud-swept hills. He scrolled down to the caption:

One of the ancient seats of a southern branch of the Douglas family, at present occupied by current laird, biographer and historian, Malcolm Douglas.

Timothy looked up at April triumphantly. 'Bingo!'

'As you say.' She sat back smugly. 'If that is where she is. Trouble is, we don't have a car.'

'That's my department, I think. What would madam like this time? A Bentley? A Roller? A Ferrari perhaps?'

She reached over and punched his shoulder. 'Anything that goes. We aren't going to keep it for more than one journey.'

He did a double take. 'What do you mean?'

'Well, we aren't going to hang around, are we. The police patrol up and down the road every few hours here, I've been watching. Whatever we do, it'll have to be quick, then we're on our way out of here, for good.'

68

Thomas smelt burning as soon as the shouts of the servants woke him. He leapt out of bed grabbing his dressing gown and opened the door. 'The stables,' Roberts shouted as he ran past him. The place was in uproar, all the servants awake now, Fanny and Margaret, wrapped in shawls, hurrying towards the front door, the dogs barking, one of the maids screaming hysterically.

Thomas ran outside and stood still for a moment in horror, seeing the flames licking out of the stable block. 'The horses!' he shouted. As the menservants streamed across the lawns to help he saw one of the grooms leading Ebony away from the building, then another with one of the carriage horses. There was a crash as a roof fell in in a fountain of sparks that seemed to reach the sky, then the sound of a horse screaming. Thomas grabbed a bucket and joined the chain of men pouring water on the flames but there was nothing they could do. It was dawn before the fire was out. Men had come from all over Hampstead and from the Kenwood estate to help. Exhausted, they gathered on the lawn as the morning light allowed them to view the scene. One end of the stables had gone completely. Two carriage horses had died and they had found Invincible on the floor of his loosebox at the end of the building. He was covered in blood. 'His throat was cut, sir.' The head groom had tears in

436

his eyes as he and Thomas stood looking down at the little horse.

It was a moment before Thomas could speak. 'The fire was deliberate then?'

The man nodded. 'I fear so. I don't understand. Who would do such a thing?'

Fanny had come up behind them. 'Oh, Tom!' She began to cry. She was still coughing from the smoke, exhausted, like them all. 'Oh no.' Behind them a crowd had gathered, looking down at the body of the pony.

They could find no clues as to who had done it. Thomas knew though. Somehow Andrew Farquhar was behind this atrocity. No bolts and locks or night watchmen could keep them safe from him. He had given away the obeah woman's doll and the horses had paid the price.

By six o clock that evening Timothy and April were back at Number 26 having left the stolen car almost where Timothy had found it. The nearly full tank of petrol had put him in a good mood that morning; the realisation that the Tower House was an impregnable fortress depressed him totally. No one appeared to be at home. There was a muddy Land Rover parked in front of the house, but it didn't look as if it would go very far and the old outbuildings that might have served as garages were deserted; the woodland was forbidding, as were the surrounding shadowy hills. After a cursory tour of the place from the shelter of the trees, they climbed back in the car, disgruntled. 'If she's there, she's safe, from you at least,' April said dismissively as they set off towards Edinburgh. 'Forget her, Tim. She's not worth it. There will always be others.'

'Others?' He ground the gears and swore. He'd be lucky if the engine lasted till they got back to civilisation.

'Other people to scam. Other houses. Other hoards of jewellery.'

He did not reply. His teeth gritted, he set the reluctant car at another of the interminable lonely hills. What a place to live!

'Other fascinating women,' she added with a snide smile.

He didn't bother to answer.

The voice waited until late that night when April was asleep, before pestering him again.

Don't tell me you didn't enjoy it. A woman in your power. The excitement, the passion, the raw smell of her, the screams. Do it again now. We'll find someone easily.

He sat on the edge of his bed, rocking backwards and forwards, feeling the urge building somewhere deep in the pit of his stomach. He looked at his watch. Eleven. It was too soon. There would be too many people about.

He hadn't given yesterday's young woman much thought at all. At first he had thought it was a dream but then he had begun to wonder. The voice had convinced him. She was probably too drunk to remember what had happened, it said. He hadn't hurt her, or done anything a dozen men hadn't done to her before. And this time he would be better at it, he would prolong the glorious rush of excitement and exultation. The voice in his head, whoever, whatever, it was, was an experienced teacher.

Come on. What are you waiting for?

The voice was getting impatient; desperate.

He found this girl on her own doorstep, fumbling to get her key into the lock. She was trying to juggle her handbag with a tote full of books, a student then, with clean shiny hair and stylish wedged shoes and pretty clothes. He didn't give himself time to think. Creeping up behind her he had his hand over her mouth and dragged her into the bushes in seconds. This girl fought. She fought tooth and nail, but he overpowered her in the end, panting in triumph as he forced himself into her. The exultant cry he let out as he fell away, exhausted, was not his own voice. He dragged himself to his feet and ran for it, leaving her lying on the ground. He didn't wait to see if she was all right. He didn't give her another thought.

* * *

438

SERIAL RAPIST STRIKES AGAIN

It was headline news.

Timothy had slept late; when he went downstairs April had been out to buy food and a newspaper. She pushed it towards him without a word.

DNA testing on the first victim confirms a link to a violent attack on celebrity chef, Finlay Macdermott, in Cramond. Police report that another vicious attack on a student as she returned to her digs in Bruntsfield last night was almost certainly by the same man. The girl, nineteen, is recovering in hospital this morning, being comforted by her parents and her boyfriend. Police warned that this man's violence is escalating. They are telling people to lock their doors and advising women not to walk in the streets alone at night until he is caught.

'Perhaps you would like to explain?' April's ice-cold voice cut through his thoughts as he pushed the paper away.

'What do you mean?' He looked up and held her gaze.

It had all been a dream. When he woke this morning he knew it was a dream.

'What do you think I mean? Where did you get those scratches?' There was one across his face, another on his wrist. He had stared at them in the mirror this morning and wondered how he got them.

'I don't know,' he said. His bewilderment was real.

The voice was silent.

Malcolm had seen the movement in the trees from the window the day before, as he had gone down to the kitchen to make coffee.

'Ruth!' he called up the stairs. 'Come and see this.'

They had watched April and Timothy scouting round the house, saw Timothy run across the open ground to try the front door, and saw him immediately scurry back to where his sister waited in the trees. 'So, we can assume they are tracking us through the bloody social media,' Malcolm said thoughtfully. 'I wonder if there is something we can put out there to throw them off the scent. Fight them in their own swamp.'

Ruth gave a reluctant smile. 'I thought I was safe here.'

'You are safe here.' He put his arms round her. 'Look, they're heading back towards the road. Ring the police. I want to see where they're going.'

Making her lock herself in, he followed them soundlessly back towards their car, saw Timothy hot-wiring the engine, watched April climb in with a final look over her shoulder. He waited till they had driven out of sight before he went back indoors.

The police had not come round until the following morning. Their faces were grave. 'Unfortunately we missed them yesterday. He returned the car to the same car park he stole it from and no one spotted them.' Jack Jordan pursed his lips. 'We didn't join the dots. Vehicle theft is not a priority these days but this man is. His violence is becoming more and more marked. Two rapes in two days, the second far more vicious than the first. We have to catch him.'

'I can't believe Timothy's a rapist,' Ruth shuddered. 'He is a nasty, creepy little man, but it just doesn't sound like him. He's greedy and he's a swindler, but rape?'

'There's no mistake,' Jordan confirmed. 'At least, not in the first case. We don't have results yet from the second, but from the victim's description it's the same man. He wasn't masked. He made no attempt to hide his face.'

When the police had gone, she brought her books downstairs to be near Mal while he chopped onions. They were taking turns at cooking their meals.

'I can't believe Tim has turned into a vicious rapist.'

'I can.' Malcolm pursed his lips. On the stove behind them the onions sweated gently in a heavy pan. 'He's repressed, he's a failure. No woman would ever find him attractive. What has he to lose?'

'I've always wondered if his sister is the brains behind their schemes,' Ruth said thoughtfully. 'And she could be the one behind the tweets.' She paused. 'But this violence just doesn't seem like him. Unless. You don't think . . . ' she hesitated. 'Tim was in the Old Mill House when we summoned Farquhar. Is it possible . . . ?' She paused again.

'That Farquhar possessed him?' Malcolm finished the sentence for her. 'If I'm honest, I've been wondering about that. We summoned Farquhar and we were protected, I made sure of that, but Timothy is without boundaries. He's weak and who knows what suppressed lusts the man has.' He paced slowly across the floor and back. 'Possession is the stuff of horror movies, but it can and does happen. Even if that theory's true, though, there's no way of proving it or doing anything about it until he's caught, and then it would be a matter for police psychiatrists.'

Ruth shuddered. 'You don't think the Bradfords have gone back to the Old Mill House?'

'Not if they know what's good for them. I gather Lachy and his brother are a formidable team. And the policeman said they're making regular patrols past Number 26 in case he goes there.'

'When I think of all the nights I spent under the same roof as him!'

'Don't think about it. They're going to catch him very soon and when they do they'll throw away the key. You'll never have to worry about him again.'

'And meanwhile, what do I do? Stay here?'

'Rapunzel, at the top of her tower.' He came over, drew her to him gently and kissed the top of her head. 'It means you're safe. And perhaps we'll find a Lachy of our own for backup. If it comes to it, it would be interesting to find out how quickly the laird can raise an army to defend his lady.'

'Am I your lady?' She felt a warm glow pushing away her unease.

'Oh yes.'

'An army sounds impressive.'

'Well, we'll have to see about that. It may consist of a team of old codgers from the pub, but they are a loyal bunch round here. They adored my mother and though I'm not so good at baking for the WI I think they would be there for me if I called.'

'And they wouldn't mind your new reputation for being a sorcerer?'

He laughed. 'It was from my mother I inherited the gift.'

'I'm glad you think of it as a gift still, and not a curse.' She put her arms round his neck. 'And, for the record, I feel safer here than I have felt anywhere for a long time.'

Thomas

The sennachie taught me once how to create a secure space. I only half listened at the time but I remembered now, at Evergreen Hill, visualising the ring of light around the garden, the trees, the lawns, the stables where already the builders were at work, the coach house and the house itself. This place would be inviolate.

But I couldn't do it at Lincoln's Inn. Too many strangers came and went in the house there who needed to be made welcome and it was there that I heard the voice again, laughing, always laughing. 'You miss the pony then? Did I make your children cry?' And when, frozen with horror, I looked around, there was nothing to see but shadows, movements at the corner of my eye and that voice in the distance, that mocking laugh.

One place he never came was the country church I had discovered once by accident. I would ride there alone, or with a groom who would wait with the horses outside and I would sit quietly in the front pew. It was there I learned to contact my ancestors and speak in prayer to God. The sennachie had told me my teacher would come and in this dusty little church with its murky stained glass and its shadows and its cobwebs I found the ability to pray. Perhaps that was what he had meant.

Davy and his American wife, Caddy, presented us with our first grandson, named Thomas in my honour, and then, only a few months later, Frances and Samuel produced their first son, another Thomas. It should have been a time of joy but both times Farquhar came to torment me, reminding me that through my fault, or so he claimed, he had no children. It was then he made his most chilling threat of all. That he would pursue my children and my grandchildren, and their descendants, for generations to come.

Then he tried to kill me.

As I walked along Pall Mall towards Carlton House to a meeting with the Prince of Wales, a hand at my back pushed me violently in front of a coach and four as it trotted swiftly down the road. I stumbled and managed to find my feet in time as the driver reined in the horses, swearing. I knew who had done it. No living being had been near me, at least not near enough to push me. I stood there, at the edge of the road, as the crowds parted to walk past me, the incident forgotten immediately by those who had witnessed it. People were being knocked down in the road all the time; some were lucky and lived to tell the tale, others were maimed or killed; they were picked up and taken away and a bucket of sand was thrown down to absorb the blood. I had been lucky. This time.

Only minutes later as the doors to Carlton House opened I was swept into the noisy, jovial presence chamber to greet my friends and tell them about my recent trip to France. I had taken the opportunity while the courts weren't sitting to visit Paris to meet the first consul, Napoleon Bonaparte. I did not trust the man and did not like him. Later I learned that the feeling had been mutual. I told the story as a joke to make Prinny and Charles Fox laugh. It was no longer a joke when my suspicions were proved right and Napoleon declared himself emperor and openly prepared for war.

69

With the threat of invasion by France, regiments of militia were set up all over the country. Two in London were made up of lawyers and Thomas, as a former soldier, found himself colonel of the Temple Corps. When he told the king his troops were all lawyers, the king replied drily that they ought, in that case, be called the Devil's Own. The name stuck.

It was hard to concentrate on his cases when, beside the threat of war, personal news of loss and despair came thick and fast. Letters from Edinburgh told of the death of his brother Harry's wife, then in October their sister Anne died. He was stunned. He had grown used to consulting her on all manner of problems, regarding her advice as a rock upon which he could lean. The eldest of them all, she was so like their mother in many ways he found it hard to grasp the fact that she had gone.

'She will go on watching over you, my darling,' Fanny reassured him. She took his hand and gave it a gentle squeeze. 'You above all people must know that.'

'Unless her faith precludes her from returning.' He pulled off his jacket and threw it down, walking across to the fireplace. 'She quoted the book of Deuteronomy at me once, saying that to talk to spirits was an abomination. She's hardly likely to return to speak to me and risk putting my soul in jeopardy as well as her own.'

'It may be an abomination to talk to them, but that's not to say they don't exist,' Fanny retorted. She gave a wistful smile. 'So, she may not have the choice. Besides, she knew you don't seek to speak to the spirits of the dead. If they return to you it is because you have the God-given gift of hearing them.'

In the silence that followed they were both thinking of the same thing. The ghost of Andrew Farquhar.

'He hasn't returned,' she said. 'Has he?'

'No.' He was not going to tell her that the man haunted his dreams, his office, his library, the corridors in the Lincoln's Inn house, his every waking moment, a shadow at the periphery of his vision, sometimes distant, no more than a hint of trouble on a stormy horizon, but sometimes there beside him in the road, or in the carriage or even standing at the head of his horse. His dogs and horses sensed him too. He would hear a quiet rumble in the throat of one of the dogs, see his hackles rise, or his horse would jib and sidestep and lay back its ears. Only in the silence of his garden in Hampstead, ringed with a safety cordon of magic, was there relief.

In the Lincoln's Inn house, no one was safe. And it was there Farquhar struck again. It was the day after Christmas and Thomas had been out walking in the snow. As he arrived home the door opened. The footman who greeted him was white in the face and so agitated he forgot to bow. 'Mr Erskine, sir, please come quickly. It's Mrs Erskine, she's had a fall.' Thomas dropped his folder of papers and ran after him, his heart in his mouth.

Frances's bedroom was hot, the fire blazing up the chimney and candles everywhere providing enough light for the two doctors who were bending over her as he burst into the room. Margaret and Abi were standing at the foot of the bed.

'What is it? What happened?'

'She fell, sir. Down the stairs.' He did not recognise either doctor. The first straightened, spectacles on the end of his nose. 'It is a concussion. She is already stirring.' He glanced down at his patient, and leaning forward slightly took her wrist to feel her pulse. He looked up again. 'It's stronger. Nothing is broken, sir, I'm pleased to say.'

'Mama has been unconscious a long time, Papa,' Margaret

put in softly. She came round the bed and took his hand. 'I was there. I saw it happen. She must have tripped at the head of the staircase. One second she was talking to me, laughing as we prepared to go downstairs, and the next she gave a little cry of surprise. She seemed to fly out into the air.' She choked on a sob. 'It was awful.'

The second doctor, a younger man, looked up. 'My colleague is correct, sir. There are no broken bones, her neck is undamaged and she is beginning to stir. If it please God, she will recover.'

'Where is Samuel?' Thomas asked suddenly. 'Has someone sent for him?' He had enormous faith in his son-in-law's capabilities.

'Of course we have, Papa. We have sent messengers to find him and Frances. They will be here soon.' Margaret squeezed his hand. 'She'll be all right. She's waking up.' Her voice was tight with fear.

'How did she fall?' He looked at Margaret and saw the bewilderment in her eyes. 'She was pushed.' He answered his own question at last, his voice bleak.

Margaret was distraught. 'How could she have been? I was the only one there. Papa! You don't think it was me?'

'No, I don't think it was you!' he shouted. He knew who it was. Farquhar, who had pushed her once before. Farquhar who had no physical body but who could use the sheer power of his energy to knock people over, drag them from the saddle, push them in front of galloping horses, in front of carriages and now down the stairs.

He sat by her bed all night. At some point Frances and Sam arrived. Sam spent a long time examining her, then shook his head. 'My colleagues were right. I can find no broken bones, no sign of damage to her head or neck. We must wait for God to send her back to us.'

God chose to take her away. She lingered, unconscious, for several days, then one icy dawn she died in Thomas's arms, surrounded by her children.

'Ruth? What is it? What's the matter?'

Malcolm, on getting no reply to his knock, had pushed the

447

door open to find her sitting at the table, her face wet with tears. He knelt at her feet and reached up to stroke her face. 'Ruth?'

She held out the piece of paper to him. It was a letter, folded, a piece of wax still clinging to the outside, addressed to the Rt Honourable, the Earl of Buchan, Dryburgh Abbey, Berwickshire. He glanced at her, then unfolded it carefully.

The letter began formally then turned into a wild outpouring of grief. It was signed 'your unhappiest of brothers, Thomas'.

Malcolm glanced at the table in front of her. There were several similar letters, all in the same slanting hand.

'What happened?' he asked gently.

'Fanny died. She fell down the stairs. He loved her so much.' Ruth rubbed her eyes on her sleeve. Behind them there was a click of claws on the stone stairs and one of the dogs nosed his way into the room. He came to sit beside Ruth, licking her hand.

She patted his head. 'It's silly to be so upset about something that happened over two hundred years ago.'

'How old was she, do you know?'

'In her fifties. Like him. She had survived childbirth eight times and seemed so strong, then this.'

'Was it Farquhar?' Malcolm pulled up the other chair and sat down opposite her.

'He doesn't say so in the letter, but that is what he believed.' She didn't say how she knew.

'He wouldn't tell his brother. I was wondering how he got the letters back.' Mal had noticed the length of ribbon now, lying on the table. It had obviously held the letters together.

'Frances had them. His daughter. Lord Buchan must have sent them back to her. They must have been in her writing box.' And tossed aside by Timothy.

Mal felt a tingle of excitement. This was history, first hand. He wanted to read them so badly it hurt, but carefully he refolded the letter and put it back on the pile. 'So, was Farquhar satisfied with that, I wonder.'

'If he had been satisfied he would have stopped haunting, wouldn't he?' She fished a tissue out of her pocket and scrubbed at her face with it. 'And yet now, two hundred years later, he is still here, still full of anger, haunting me.'

'All went well for Thomas after that, though, didn't it?' Malcolm sat back on the chair, his face thoughtful. 'Only a year after the date on that letter he reached the peak of his career and was given his title.'

Ruth laughed sadly. 'The title my father objected to so strongly, and which the family have always been so proud of. But the irony was it meant far less to Thomas because he couldn't share it with Fanny. She wasn't there at his side as Lady Erskine.'

'She'd have hated all that flummery,' he said wryly.

Ruth stared at him. 'How do you know? You talk as though you knew her!'

He looked surprised. 'I suppose it's because you've told me so much about her. It's true though, isn't it?'

'She seems to have been a very special woman. He was surrounded by strong women. His mother, his sisters, his daughters.'

'Perhaps their ghosts kept Farquhar at bay,' Malcolm said thoughtfully.

'Seriously?' She gave him her quizzical look.

'I'm still interested in why Farquhar has reappeared on the scene now. I know you and Harriet invited him in, but why now? Why like this? You need to find out if there was any further mention of him in Thomas's letters. This is where my knowledge of Thomas's history is sketchy. I haven't followed his career except where he and Pitt came up against one another. Were there any other calamities to show that Farquhar was on the rampage again?'

'Apart from the fall of the government?'

He nodded. 'I don't think we can credit Farquhar with that.'

'Perhaps it was then Thomas began to store up the wisdom that led to him becoming Dion Fortune's super-guide.' Ruth pulled a notebook towards her. 'Apparently, later in his contact with her, he called himself the *Magus Innominatus* – the Master with No Name. But why? Did he feel that to be associated with his worldly life would detract from the important messages he brought through from the other world? Harriet told me he went on being Dion's main contact throughout her life. He was important to her.'

'Curiouser and curiouser.' Malcolm folded his arms. 'The Master with No Name and the Man from the Shadows. There's only one way to find out. Go on with your story.'

Thomas

Grief is a strange thing. It rises and falls like the tide, at times over-whelming and inundating, and at others a distant, gentle murmur lapping on a faraway shore. We buried Fanny in the church at Hampstead, in the village she had loved above all other places in the last years of her life, and there I raised a memorial to her memory.

I was not given the luxury to grieve for long.

After Pitt's death his ministry fell, to be succeeded by that of Lord Grenville, in which my friend Charles James Fox was foreign secretary and to my great honour and delight I was made Lord Chancellor, on 7 February, going to the Queen's Palace to receive the great seal of England from the king. I was elevated to the peerage in my own right as Lord Erskine of Restormel, the title suggested by the Prince of Wales – Restormel being, I was told, a beautiful but ruined castle in his Duchy of Cornwall. I would have liked to choose a title from my homeland of Scotland but my position was an English one; my brother Harry was now Lord Advocate of Scotland!

I was heartbroken that my darling Fanny, who had uncomplainingly shared so much hardship and grief with me in the early days of our marriage, could not share my honours and my title, but my children were ennobled with me. They all took the title of honourable. Davy would succeed to my title after me, and the burden of work did not

451

stop me from giving a hand up to my two sons-in-law as well; Mary's husband, Edward Morris, I made a Master in Chancery. To Frances's husband, Samuel, who, after much heart searching, abandoned his profession of physician in order to enter his first love, the church, I was able to give two parishes in the preferment of the king, and therefore in the gift of the Lord Chancellor, Beaudesert in Warwickshire and Poynings in Sussex. It was to Poynings that they moved from London with their growing family. The parsonage was old and dilapidated, but very beautiful in its way, large enough for my Frances to make her home and for her to have her much-longed-for piano, and Samuel told me at once of his plans to rebuild the house one day in the latest style. But for the time being they were happy in their country retreat and near enough to Brighton, where the prince spent so much of his time, should they wish to join with the finest society.

I missed Frances very much. She reminded me so much of her mother and in my heart, secretly, I dreamed that maybe one day if I ever came to retire, I would move to Sussex to be near them. Not yet, though. The excitement and ambition of my early days were still with me. I was not planning on retiring for a long time yet. I enjoyed sitting on the Woolsack where one of my greatest triumphs was to be able to support the bill for the immediate abolition of the slave trade, ending my speech with the words, 'Let us now set an example of humanity and justice which may be followed by all the nations of the earth.' It fell to me to announce the royal assent to the bill.

70

It was time for RuthieD to make a new appearance. April smiled to herself as she bent over the keyboard.

> So, our sexy historian has given up ghosts for a lady writer. She in turn has abandoned chef Finlay MacD for life in a Border Tower.

> So much gossip and scandal in the wilds of the southern upland glens. Out there, no one can hear you scream.

She liked that one especially. And then,

> Watch out. Your nemesis is on the way. A man with a knife is creeping through the trees even now.

April knew Tim wouldn't be able to keep away. She had caught him looking up bus routes down towards the wild Moorfoot Hills, part of the endless lonely uplands around Malcolm's stronghold and she had scoffed, 'Trying to plan how to break into the castle now?' He had glared at her and no more had been said, but today he had gone out early without a word. The longer he was absent the better. He had changed. His few days without her had made him coarser, more violent, less dependent on her. And if the police were to be believed he was a depraved vicious rapist. She found that hard to believe, even now, but they had the DNA. What an irony that he had been identified the very way they had planned to convince the authorities that he was Dunbar's son.

It was time to go. She wasn't going to hang around to find out what had really happened. She had been stupid to hook up with him again. She went into the sitting room and peered out through the curtains towards the road. Better to leave.

Where would she go? Somewhere with a uni where she could study English Literature. She would love that. Even as she thought about it she could hear Timothy's wild laughter in her head, not his old nervous snigger but the raucous, scornful laugh he had developed lately. The laugh that told her she was rubbish and he would as soon dump her as she him. Well, she would save him the trouble. By the time he returned she would be gone and hopefully her tweets would ensure the police were waiting for him should he make it as far as Malcolm's Tower. The decision made, she was astonished at the sudden feeling of release that overwhelmed her.

There was very little to pack. Her spare clothes and her laptop went into the new tote.

She never had, never would, trust Tim with her money. It was hidden under a loose floorboard she had found under the carpet in her bedroom. Pulling out the envelopes, each one with a thousand pounds in cash, she shoved the board back in place, looked round the room with a satisfied smile, turned off the light and headed for the stairs.

Bag in hand she opened the front door and stepped outside.

'Going somewhere, Sis?' Timothy was standing on the doorstep.

Ruth made the decision to show Mal everything that evening after removing another bundle of letters from a leather folder she had found amongst her mother's books.

She sighed. 'I know so little about this period. Why didn't I pay more attention at school?'

'Can you tell me the problem?' Mal grinned. 'I'm probably the nearest thing you're going to find to a world expert on the Georgian period in this glen.' He had been making some coffee and he wiped his hands and sat down opposite her at the kitchen table.

She smiled. 'Modest with it.'

'This is an underpopulated glen. Can I give you a tip: less is more. Pick out the most salient bits. You can read round any more details you feel you need later. And ask Thomas. I'm sure he would love to discuss his world with you.'

'As would you. I'm sorry. I've been selfish. You must read this stuff.' Impulsively she pushed the folder towards him.

'Are you sure?' He hesitated, then reached out towards it.

With the letters were several more of the small notebooks. They had all been wrapped in a sheet of paper, headed Poynings Rectory. A neatly written inscription read: '*Papa's writings. To be preserved. One day they will be valuable.*'

'I don't think she meant monetary value,' Ruth said.

'No. She seems to have been a rather saintly lady in her old age.' Malcolm had picked out a faded page from a magazine which, tucked in amongst the other papers, had turned out to be a copy of Frances's obituary. He studied it for several minutes before putting it back in place and reached with extreme care for one of the small notebooks. This was clearly another journal. 'I was looking through some of my own sources last night to find references to your Thomas and I found two quotes from Sir Walter Scott.' He fished a piece of paper out of his pocket. 'This will amuse you!' he grinned. 'This one is his comment on the Erskine brothers: "The earl's wit was crack-brained and sometimes caustic, Henry's was of the very kindest, best humoured and gayest sort that ever cheered society; that of Lord Erskine was moody and muddish—"'

'What!' Ruth looked up indignantly. Then she laughed. 'But then, Thomas and Scott didn't get on. There was a row, wasn't there, later, over some play in Edinburgh? The crowd stood up and applauded Thomas when he came in, rather than Scott who was the author of the play. And in one of his letters I saw him quote that Scott had said "Tom Erskine was stark mad"! He seemed quite pleased with the remark.'

'Praise indeed! This one is more complimentary. Lord Byron this time: " . . . anything in Lord Erskine's handwriting will be a treasure gathering compound interest for years".'

'Lord Byron was biased. He was a good friend of his.'

'As was practically everyone of note at the time.' Malcolm glanced at the scattered letters that lay between them. 'What are you going to do with these?'

She shrugged her shoulders. 'They should be preserved, shouldn't they.'

He thought for a minute. 'Use them for family history. That is your right, but after that?'

'Perhaps I should give them to the nation. The British Library or something.'

'That would be very generous. They are probably worth a lot of money. Think about it.'

Those letters are private!

The words tore through her brain, abrasive and angry.

She sat back at the table abruptly.

'What is it? What's wrong?'

They are not to be published!

'I don't know. Perhaps it's a migraine coming.' Ruth glanced up at him, rubbing her forehead distractedly. 'Sorry. They hit sometimes.' She flinched again.

'Farquhar?'

She shook her head. 'Thomas.'

Malcolm glanced round the room. 'Obviously there are things in these papers he would rather you, we, the world, didn't see. But would he have told his daughter such things?'

'We will have to read them to find out.' She gave him a faint smile. 'When I know what's in them, then I will decide.'

Burn them!

Ruth put her hands over her ears. 'Stop it!'

Malcolm reached across and gathered the letters together into a pile. 'Leave her alone,' he said sternly, looking round, unsure where the voice that was addressing her was coming from. 'She has to read them, you must see that. Then she can decide. She is of your blood, Thomas. She will do the right thing.'

Ruth looked up, her hands, palm down on the table in front

of her. She sighed. 'He says I don't understand,' she said helplessly.

'And you never will if he doesn't give you the chance to examine them.' Malcolm put the letters into the box and closed the lid. 'Leave them for now. No one can touch them up here.'

'Couldn't Thomas destroy them with a blast of psychic power?'

Malcolm smiled. 'If he could, he would have done it by now. If Dion Fortune is right and he's an advanced soul, then he knows that the truth is paramount and must prevail. If he made mistakes, it was because he was human. Perhaps his incarnation as Thomas Erskine was one of many and he has gone on to live more perfect lives that have exonerated his mistakes. He lived in turbulent times, at the heart of power amongst men who changed the world. We need to know what happened.'

The room was silent. If Thomas was still there he did not, presumably, disagree with what Malcolm had said.

Thomas

To my enormous sadness, Charles Fox died that same year. I was a pall-bearer at his funeral in Westminster Abbey and found it hard to contain my grief, so much so that later the Duchess of York presented me with a ring containing a lock of the great man's hair. The government could not survive without him; when it fell months later, I fell with it. I was disappointed and sad and angry to have to relinquish the great seal so soon. I had not had the chance fully to exploit my talents in what became known as the Ministry of All the Talents, but in many ways I was pleased to resume my legal career, although this time in the House of Lords.

We entertained as we always had. My daughter Margaret at my side, we welcomed our old friends to dinners and soirees and with them came princes and dukes and earls, and, so important in a household of animal lovers, a new puppy came to live with us. I called him Fox.

I now had time and opportunity to pursue a cause very dear to my heart and introduced in the House of Lords a bill against animal cruelty, something one saw everywhere, every day, in the streets of London. If any piece of law was to be attached to my name, I wanted it to be this one. To my delight it was passed in the House of Lords, but alas, due mainly to the campaign of one man, it was thrown out of the Commons. My speech was published as a pamphlet and I gained much support nationwide and I did not give up. The law was passed the following year.

Life was good, though often I thought of my darling Fanny. She would not have revelled in the company as I did. She would have craved the peace and beauty of the gardens and the joy of watching the children and grandchildren at play, and with her there I would have enjoyed them the more.

In my desire to be near Frances and Samuel and their ever-increasing brood I bought a country estate of several thousand acres near Crawley in the Sussex Weald. I felt I could grow to love Sussex with its forests and Downs and sweet air, but I craved a wilder landscape too; watching my family grow up and away I thought of my own childhood and dreamt of taking them all one day to Scotland.

But they were busy building their own lives and I suppose I was lonely.

For then I met Sarah.

71

Thomas was about to go out when he heard the harpsichord playing in the drawing room. He handed his greatcoat back to the footman and went to the door. Margaret didn't notice him as he stood there silently listening. She was enraptured by the music, rocking back and forward a little as she played, completely transported. She was a far better player than Fanny had ever been, or Frances either, but she steadfastly refused to play in public, shyly shaking her head and withdrawing from the company whenever he tried to persuade her. He didn't move until she finished then quietly he applauded. 'That was lovely, my darling. What was it? I don't believe I have heard you play it before.'

She blushed a little and stood up. 'It is a sonata by Scarlatti. I have been learning it when there was no one listening.' She smiled reproachfully. 'I didn't see you there.'

'You are too modest.' He went over and kissed her cheek. 'I am going to Lincoln's Inn. Would you like to accompany me in the carriage? I can easily wait until you have your maid pack a valise.'

She shook her head, then almost as an afterthought she caught his sleeve. 'Papa, wait. I have an address for you.' She hesitated anxiously. 'I took tea with Caddy yesterday.' They all referred to Davy's beautiful American wife by her nickname. 'She was telling me about a young woman she met. A bonnet-maker, as I understand it.' She paused again and catching sight of her father's raised eyebrow she gave a nervous giggle. 'She is a talented medium. Genuinely gifted. Caddy thought she might interest you.'

Thomas gave no sign of having heard her for several seconds then he sighed. 'These people are often tricksters,' he said gravely.

'But this one is good, so Caddy said. Apparently, the woman said . . . ' Margaret paused and took a deep breath, 'she said she could contact Mama.' She turned away to hide her tears.

Thomas closed his eyes. Of all his children only Margaret, he suspected, understood his deep loneliness, the visceral ache he experienced when he thought of Fanny and how much he missed her.

'Have you seen this woman yourself?' He spoke more sharply than he intended and she flinched.

'I wouldn't dare go. I think Caddy was planning to, but she couldn't go on her own and Davy would laugh her out of it. He has no time for . . . ' again she hesitated, 'for things like that.'

Of course he didn't. Thomas didn't think any of his children had inherited his ability to see beyond the immediate. Once he had guessed that his daughter, Frances, could do it, but she had never told him outright and now she was married to a man of the cloth she would never admit it. He thought fleetingly of the doll he had given her for her wedding day and wondered if she'd kept it.

Margaret had gone over to the escritoire which stood between the windows and she pulled open one of the small drawers. Inside was a piece of paper. She handed it to him. 'If you want to contact her, this is where she lives,' she whispered.

Preoccupied with preparing an important speech, Thomas did not give the piece of paper another thought for several days. It was only when he pulled it out of his pocket when looking for another address that he had stuffed inside his wallet that he stopped in his tracks and looked at it hard. Miss Sarah Buck, bonnet-maker, lived off St Martin's Lane. On a whim, he picked up his hat and cane and set out on foot.

It appeared that the lady in question lived with her brother's family in Stonecutters Court, a narrow shabby court off the main thoroughfare. Mr Buck was a plasterer by trade. One of his assistants directed Thomas to a dark staircase in the corner of the yard with a jerk of his thumb.

Sarah was sitting by the window stitching a frill of lace onto an elegant blue hat when he arrived. She looked up as he pushed open the door. She was a small woman, in her thirties, he guessed, neatly dressed with a thin face, a prominent nose and high cheekbones. She studied him for several seconds as he stood looking across the room at her, then tucked her needle into her work and set it aside on the table. 'Have you come for a reading?'

She did not stand up and he was forced to approach her. 'I have heard that you have a certain talent, madam,' he said cautiously.

'I charge sixpence for half an hour,' she said, indicating the chair opposite her. She watched as he put his hat and cane and gloves down on a side table, her eyes narrowing slightly as she noted the expensive cut of his clothes and the gold signet ring on his finger. 'Lord Erskine, I presume,' she said quietly.

'My face is familiar to you from the newspapers, madam?' he sat down on the edge of the chair.

She ignored the question. 'Normally I would ask for something belonging to your deceased wife to help me focus on her, but she is here, waiting to speak to you,' she said. Glancing up she noted how he clenched his fists on his knees. 'And normally,' she went on, keeping her voice cold and disinterested, 'I would require payment in advance, but I am sure a nobleman such as yourself can be relied upon to pay me fairly for my services.'

He reached into his pocket and brought out a shilling. He put it down on the middle of the table without a word.

She resisted the urge to grab it and put it into her pocket, leaving it lying where it was as she closed her eyes and took several deep breaths. She could feel him watching her closely and forcing herself to ignore him she searched in her mind for something to say. They were sometimes there, the people on the other side, and sometimes they weren't and then she had to improvise. It was important her customers were not

462

disappointed or they would not return. Just enough to keep them satisfied, to make them curious, to comfort them. She read her clients very well, something she had been good at since she was a child. For all his flash clothes and confident manner, this man was lonely and unhappy. She had to be convincing. The silence spun out round her and then she heard a voice out of the darkness. 'Tom? Tom, my darling, I miss you so.'

The voice when she spoke was hers but the intonation, the accent wasn't. She heard her own tongue curl round the unaccustomed speech patterns, the words coming without plan or pretence. 'I am so proud of you and of the children, my darling, and I am so pleased Margaret looks after you. You must make sure she finds a husband, Thomas. I do not want any of my girls to grow up old maids.' And so it went on, the happy rush of words, inconsequential as they so often were when the dead contacted the living, continuing with conversations just as they used to. No revelations of the afterlife, no comments on their surroundings or their new companions. Sarah relaxed and let the words flow until at last Fanny was silent. 'I'm tired, my darling,' were her last words. 'Come and speak to me again, but not too often. Not too soon. Let me rest in peace.'

When Sarah opened her eyes she saw he was crying and she closed them again quickly, giving him time to compose himself.

'Sixpence is enough, my lord,' she said, pushing the coin back towards him. 'I do not require more.'

She heard the muffled, indignant, exclamation on the stone stair outside and knew her brother had followed her client up to listen at the door. She hoped he hadn't heard. If he had, he gave no sign. Lord Erskine stood up and turned away to gather up his things, leaving the coin untouched. 'She said not to come back too soon,' he said. His voice was husky.

She hesitated before she replied, 'And she was right. She must be allowed to continue her journey.' Her conscience would not allow her to lie. 'But,' she went on carefully, 'it may be that she has much to say to you before she can calmly and composedly move on, so . . . ' again the hesitation, 'it may be that she will use me to pass on further messages now that she has found a way. If she should wish to use me in that way, how may I reach you, my lord?'

She lowered her eyes, strangely moved by the look of anguish that crossed his features.

'Send to my chambers,' he replied. 'I will come to you.' He turned away and walked back across the room leaving the coin still lying on the table.

When he opened the door, the stair was empty.

When Ruth awoke the next morning she was alone in bed. Descending the spiral staircase she found Malcolm standing staring out at the hills. The sky was full of racing clouds. His laptop was open on the table behind him. Hearing her come in he gave a deep sigh and turned towards her. 'I've a problem.'

She sat down at the table and waited, reaching down to fondle Pol's ears as the dogs came over to greet her.

'I need to go to London.'

She had not been expecting that. 'Why?'

'I've been trying to find someone else to give a talk I'm scheduled to deliver. I'm so sorry. So far, it's proving impossible to sort this out. Apparently, I signed a contract of some sort. These wretched events are booked so far in advance.'

She swallowed hard. 'You're not my keeper, Mal,' she said gently. 'You can't put your life on hold because of me.'

He pulled out a chair and sat down opposite her. 'I need to be here.'

'No. You don't.'

He looked up to study her face and for several seconds they were both silent. He reached out and took her hands. 'No, you're right,' he said at last. 'I don't need to, do I. You are much stronger now.'

Max, when he heard, suggested she join him and Finlay in Heriot Row but she refused. 'Malcolm will only be away a day or so. I'll be perfectly safe here.'

'Alone?' Finlay's voice boomed at her from her mobile as he grabbed Max's phone. 'I don't think so. If you won't come to us, then we'll come to you.'

'There's no need.'

'There's every need. Let me speak to Malcolm.'

She was being manipulated again, looked after, but suddenly she realised she didn't mind. They cared. They all cared very much and she was so lucky to have them.

April put out her hand, pushing it flat against Timothy's chest, stopping him in his tracks. 'Don't try to intimidate me, Tim. You don't scare me and you never have. If I choose to leave, that is my choice. It seems to me we both did perfectly OK on our own. Maybe it's time we branched out. We can always meet up now and again.'

He smiled. 'What makes you think I would want to meet up with you?'

He raised his hand and fastened it around her wrist, slowly twisting it off his chest and pushing it away.

'Ow! Let go, Tim.'

He went on twisting, a strangely dispassionate smile on his lips. 'Do you know how upset I was when I found the Dump burned down and I thought you were dead.'

'Let go, Tim!'

'I thought I was alone in the whole world.' They were still standing on the doorstep.

'I only left because you never came home that day. I assumed you'd gone for good!' She was determined not to struggle, sensing it would only excite him, and then over his shoulder she glimpsed movement at the end of the street. She relaxed, smiling. 'Our friendly police patrol is approaching. Shall I call him? How long do you suppose it would take him to recognise you?'

'Shit!' He shoved her inside and, stepping in after her, slammed the door behind them with his foot. 'Did he see us?'

At least he had moved his hand. He walked past her into the kitchen.

'I don't think so.' She followed him.

He sat down at the table and put his head in his hands. 'Go, if you want to,' he said, defeated.

'I don't want to. I'm just afraid of what you might do next. Why did you attack that girl?'

'I told you, it wasn't me. It can't have been. I don't remember it.'

'They have your DNA.' She leaned against the cupboard, her arms folded, studying him intently. 'Tim, you're a sick man. We've never done violence. We never hurt anyone.'

He looked at her defensively. 'You think people haven't been hurt by what we do?'

'I'm talking physically, Tim. You raped those girls. You nearly killed Finlay Macdermott. That is not you.'

No, it's not him.

Tim groaned and smacked his forehead. 'Go away!'

April shrank back against the wall. 'Who are you talking to?'

'The voice in my head.' Suddenly he was a little boy again. 'He won't leave me alone. I don't want to play with him, I don't want to do these things, but he won't leave me alone.' Tears were running down his face.

April pulled out the chair opposite him and sat down. She studied him, torn between sympathy and fear. 'How long has this been going on?' she asked. The sight of his intense misery touched her as it always did. She was his big sister. She looked after him.

'Since I was at the Old Mill House. He was there waiting for me. He was there with them. He clawed his way into my head.' He looked up at her pitifully, his face swollen with tears. 'It's not my fault, none of this is. It's him.'

'And who is he?' She managed to keep her voice calm.

Andrew. I'm Andrew. Tell her she's a fat cow and it's none of her business what you and I do. And we can do it again tonight. You'd like that, wouldn't you.

Tim let out a shriek of rage. He was sobbing loudly. 'Go away!'

April stood up and backed away from the table.

'He's called Andrew,' Tim whispered piteously.

'Jesus Christ!' April clutched her coat round her tightly. 'They said in that American article that Malcolm Douglas was an exorcist. That's what he was doing, wasn't he, when you barged into that house. It was haunted and he was going to get rid of it and you've brought the bastard thing home with you. You're

466

weak and stupid and it's clinging to you.' Her voice rose in panic.

Give the lady a prize!

'I'm not weak and stupid!' Tim thumped his fists on the table.

April took a deep breath. She didn't know what to do. Half of her wanted to comfort him, the other half wanted to run. She glanced towards the door, trying to judge whether she could make it before he reached her.

'It's all right.' All at once he relaxed. He smiled miserably. 'He's gone. Go if you want.'

She hesitated. 'You need help, Tim. We have to find someone who will get rid of him.'

'Malcolm bloody Douglas?' He laughed sarcastically.

'If necessary, yes.'

'And you think he's going to say, "Of course, Mr Bradford. Why not, Mr Bradford. Let me help you. No don't worry about the things you've done, Mr Bradford, none of them were your fault."'

April's eyebrow twitched. 'So,' she said quietly. 'What do you think we should do?'

He sighed. 'I've no idea.'

'Why don't you go and find a car,' she said after a few moments' thought. 'Then at least we'll have the option of going to ask for his help.'

He looked up and rubbed his face hard with the palms of his hands. Surely she wasn't serious? 'Could do, I suppose.' He stood up and looked at her bitterly. 'I suppose you'll be gone by the time I come back?'

She met his gaze squarely. 'I haven't decided yet.'

'Let me know when you have.' He headed towards the door.

72

It was less than a week before Thomas found himself once more climbing the stairs in Stonecutters Court. This time there was no sign of anyone in the workshop below Sarah's small sewing room. She was neatly attired in a grey woollen dress with a white lace-trimmed cap and apron. 'Come in, my lord.' Curtsying, she showed him to a chair which had been placed near the window.

Her note had been sent to his chambers, delivered by an urchin who had demanded sixpence from his clerk. He had been sent packing with a halfpenny for his cheek. It was only luck that Thomas had received the note at all. Had he not at that moment walked into the inner office it would have been consigned to the wastepaper bin in the corner. He scrutinised the neatly folded piece of paper, frowning.

My Lord, your wife has asked me to speak to you again.
If you would be so good as to visit at your convenience, I
have messages for you from beyond. Yours respectfully,
Sarah Buck

Thomas sighed. He was no fool. He knew he had laid himself open to this, that she would exploit him and probably make a fool of him and maybe blackmail him into the bargain. But the woman had seemed sincere. She had not snatched at the coin he had left her; she had seemed to know what she was talking about. He would give her one more chance, just one, then he would call a halt.

She sat down opposite him and tucked her skirts neatly around her ankles – shapely ankles, he noted in spite of himself – then she gave him a sad smile. It was somehow complicit, drawing him into her confidence. 'I am sorry to say your lady, Frances, is unhappy. She is concerned about your family, and anxious that I should pass on her worries. You have several grandchildren, I understand, and one of them is ill?'

Thomas frowned. 'Not that I know of.'

She seemed flustered. 'Then perhaps I have misunderstood. Perhaps a child has been exposed to infection. She is very concerned.'

'As she would be,' Thomas returned. 'Children are always being exposed to infections, Miss Buck. This is hardly news.' He was about to stand up when she interrupted. 'Little Frances. She is called for her grandmother.'

Thomas froze in his chair. 'What's wrong with her?'

Sarah was silent, listening, her head to one side. 'It is hard to make out, but she's here now to speak to you. She's trying to tell me. The little girl's father is away from home. No, they are away, staying with an aunt in Ramsgate, so they are not at home?' She looked at him almost fearfully. 'Her papa would know what to do, but he may not be there in time. The child has a quinsy, no, a croup, perhaps,' she hesitated, screwing up her face to hear something that Thomas could not, 'perhaps the chin cough—'

'Enough!' He stood up abruptly. 'If you are right then she is seriously ill and my sister will have sent for a doctor!'

'Wait!' Sarah raised her hand anxiously to catch at his arm. 'Your lady says she had a receipt for a cure. Someone called Abigail always used it on the children. A remedy made from wild thyme on the hills, coltsfoot, honey—'

Thomas paused long enough only to toss a couple of coins onto the table and he was gone. Sarah sat staring at them sadly then she shivered. 'I did my best, my lady,' she said sadly to the empty room. 'He will help if he can.'

He sent messages to Ramsgate and to Poynings by the fastest horses possible. And another to Abi who, nanny-in-chief to the whole family, was with his youngest, Esmé, a man of twenty-one now, and his wife, Eliza, to supervise the first months with their first child, yet another Thomas to add to the clutch. Fanny was right, Abi would know what to do.

It was several days before he heard back from Frances, whose note confirmed that little Frances had indeed contracted the whooping cough. At the first sign of illness they had bundled her into a chaise and taken her back to Poynings, where there was an old lady in the village who had nursed generations of children through the disease, using herbs picked on the Downs. Her recipe had been much like Abi's and the child was on the mend. She gently chided her father for panicking and assuming she would not know what to do. She did not ask how he had heard of the illness.

He sent Sarah a purse containing three shillings, with a brusque note of thanks.

It was only two days later that she sent him another message:

My lord, I fear that too much bothering will make you angry, but my lady, your wife, keeps speaking to me in my head. She wants to tell you about her fall. Sometimes she is so clear, at others she speaks as though through the clouds. Please come when you can so that I may relay her words.

Thomas unfolded the note and, spreading it flat on his desk, sat staring at it, reciting the words to himself in a hoarse whisper. Why would this woman, this uneducated, almost illiterate woman, have been chosen to relay Fanny's words? Why could Fanny not speak to him directly? His gaze fixed on the one sentence 'She wants to tell you about her fall.' How would Sarah know that was how Fanny died? But it was general knowledge surely. Perhaps they had even put it in one of the newspapers. He sighed.

'My lord?' His clerk had been hovering. 'Is this woman pestering you? I could have her taken up—'

'No!' Thomas looked up. 'No, thank you,' he added more gently. 'I need to see her. She has information on a subject that is of some importance to me.'

This time he did not sit down. He stood in the doorway to her work room, still holding his hat and cane and gloves. 'Miss Buck, this cannot go on. You seem to feel that I am free to be summoned at your every whim—'

'Not my whim, my lord,' she interrupted angrily. 'Are you saying that your grandchild was not ill? If so, that is not my fault. Perhaps Lady Erskine was mistaken—'

'My wife was not Lady Erskine!' he burst out. The fact that Fanny had died before he was given the title and had never been able to share the recognition it bestowed was a lasting misery for him. 'You may call her the Honourable Mrs Erskine.'

She looked astonished but made no comment.

'Very well. So, was the child not ill?' she challenged crossly. 'It's not my message. I merely report what your wife tells me! Don't imagine I'm making all this up.' She had not risen from her seat this time, and she had not curtsied.

He found he was looking at her with more respect. 'You were right,' he said quietly. 'The child was ill.'

'And were you able to help it?'

'The child's mother already had everything in hand.'

She looked up at him, her chin set stubbornly. 'I am pleased to hear it.' She paused then gave an ostentatious sigh. 'No, I'm sorry. There is too much negativity in this room. I cannot ask her to speak to me when I'm upset.'

'Then I will leave.' He turned to the door.

'No, wait,' she called. 'I can at least tell you what it's all about.'

He paused without turning round and waited.

'She told me when she bade me call you back to speak to her again. She wants you to know she did not trip. She was pushed.' She stared at his back, her lips pursed, defying him to leave now.

He turned slowly. 'You are saying my wife was pushed down the stairs?'

Sarah hesitated. 'Wait!' She raised her hand. 'Now she's here. She is stamping her foot, insisting you listen. She is cross that you won't believe me. It was,' she hesitated, her head to one side, her eyes half closed. 'It was Andrew,' she finished in a rush. She opened her eyes triumphantly. 'Andrew. And you must be careful because he wants to kill you too. There! Now you know. That's all. She's gone. And you have no need to give me more money. I see you think I am a fraud, but I have done no more than repeat what she told me.'

He was staring at her in silence and she met his gaze steadily. 'Do you know an Andrew?' she asked at last.

'Indeed I do,' he replied.

'He's not one of your sons?'

'No, he most certainly isn't.' He frowned impatiently. 'What made you say that?'

'It sounded as though she knew him well. She was irritated, cross.'

'She had reason to be cross if he killed her.' Thomas put down his hat and cane and came to sit down in the chair opposite her. He leaned forward slightly. 'Did she say anything else?'

'No, she didn't.' She paused for a few seconds. 'Will you have him arrested?'

Thomas shook his head.

'Why not?' She looked up in despair. 'Of course. I'm no use as a witness. Who would believe a stupid woman like me?'

'You are right. No one would believe a clairvoyant as a credible witness in a court of law,' he said sadly, 'but that is not the reason he can't be arrested. The reason is, madam, that he's already dead. He has already paid the ultimate price for his misdemeanours. I watched him hang.'

She stared at him and he saw disbelief, then horror then disgust play across her features. She shuddered. 'So how . . . ?' She swallowed hard. 'You mean he's an evil spirit? A ghost? He pushed her as a ghost?'

Thomas closed his eyes with a heavy sigh. 'You must tell my darling that I have her message, but I do not know what to do.

472

I am the greatest lawyer in the land, and I don't know what to do. I don't know how to bring Andrew Farquhar to justice.'

'Only God can do that, my lord,' she said softly.

He smiled sadly. 'You reproach me for my hubris, and you're right. Only God can deal with this, so why doesn't He?' The last sentence was an anguished cry.

'I don't know what hubris is, my lord, but, I'm sure you will know what to do when the time comes.' She cocked her head slightly at the sound of footsteps on the stairs.

Thomas didn't move. He was lost in thought. Only when the door opened did he turn angrily to face it, to be confronted by a neatly dressed lady's maid in a cloak and bonnet. The woman stared for a moment at the man seated in the chair then addressed Sarah haughtily. 'I have come to collect my lady's hat, if you please.' She glared at Thomas again then glanced swiftly back at Sarah. 'You may come to the house tomorrow to collect your money.'

Sarah stood up and went over to a side table. She picked up a hat box by the cords that fastened it closed and handed it to the woman. 'I will come tomorrow to her ladyship to see that she is happy with my work,' she said meekly.

'Do so.' With one final glance at Thomas the woman turned away and disappeared back down the stairs.

He stood up. 'I must go. My thanks for your help. I doubt if my wife will want to speak to me again, so our business is done.' He reached into his pocket for two shillings and sixpence and dropped the coins gently on the table in front of her then he turned away. It did not occur to him that the maid would have recognised him or that by the time he reached his office a cartoonist was already sketching out a depiction of him consulting a woman with a crystal ball.

The Tower House was very quiet without Malcolm there. Ruth stood in the kitchen, her arms folded tightly across her chest, staring out of the window. The larch trees on the hills were beginning to turn to gold and the sky was a brilliant blue behind them. The dogs had gone too, to the neighbour who always looked after them when Malcolm was away. Max and Fin had again offered to come and stay with her if she didn't want to go to them, but again she had gently rebuffed their offer.

'Are you sure you don't mind being alone?' Mal asked as he left.

'Quite sure. I am perfectly safe here. I don't even need to go out if I don't want to.' He had insisted they stock up the larder and freezer so she need never unlock the front door. 'Max and Fin are only a phone call away if I change my mind, and I won't have time to miss you.'

She did miss him. Within minutes of watching his car disappear down the long drive towards the road, she was feeling desolate. She brought her laptop down to the kitchen and poured herself a glass of wine, then she turned on the radio. It was tuned as always to Malcolm's favourite Radio 3 and she found herself listening to the joyful cadences of a harpsichord. She sat in front of her laptop without opening it, lost in the music, picturing a ball of the kind Thomas would have gone to, the room lit by hundreds of candles in candelabra, crowded with men in elegant evening dress and women in colourful gowns, all of them bewigged and hot, the huge chamber noisy and crowded, smelling of pomanders and flowers and the lavish food laid out in the next room, but above all smelling of sweat.

She shuddered. The smell was rancid in her nose as the music grew louder, filling the kitchen, bouncing off the walls, jangly, threatening, overwhelming.

'No!' She stood up abruptly and slammed both her hands down on the table. 'I am not having this! Go away!'

The sound of the harpsichord stopped dead. The little red light on the radio went off. The room was completely silent. She wasn't frightened, she realised. She was angry.

He had gone.

She ran upstairs to her bedroom, took the fetish doll out of its drawer and brought it back downstairs with her.

When she turned the radio back on there was a discussion programme in progress.

* * *

Timothy was laughing to himself as he climbed the stairs. He had told April to go if she wanted to. See if he cared. The presence in his head had disappeared. It had happened quite suddenly. The banging migraine above his eyes had vanished between one breath and the next and he was left with the most extraordinary feeling of peace. He went into his bedroom and sat down on the edge of the bed. Downstairs he heard the front door open and then close. April had gone out but he wasn't worried. She had said she would go up to the store on the corner and buy some fresh food from the deli counter. Clearly she had money and for some reason she had started being nice to him. He smiled. He would find her stash, but just for now he was content to let everything go. He was himself again. He lay back on the pillow and stared up at the ceiling. The street lights outside threw strange square shapes on the walls of the room and he watched them grow brighter as the darkness outside deepened. Half an hour later he heard her footsteps on the pavement outside, that quick tap of her new shoes. She had found them in a charity shop, she had told him. They had heels and made her look quite different; she walked, she even stood, differently. They seemed to give her confidence. The footsteps paused at the front door and he heard the key in the lock. He had given her the key when she had said she was going out. Why not? He knew she would come back. The front door opened and then closed and he heard the tap of heels in the hall. She turned on the lights in the kitchen and he saw a narrow strip of brightness appear under his door. He wriggled down more comfortably on his bed and smiled to himself. Everything was going to be all right now she was back. He was safe.

The smell of cooking woke him. He identified frying onions and sausages; he could hear her humming to herself. She looked up when he appeared. 'I thought the thought of food would bring you down.'

'It smells good.'

'I haven't cooked for so long.' She picked up a heavy saucepan and carried it, steaming, over to the sink. She drained potatoes and put the pan on the table. 'Mash?'

'Yes please.' He sat down and watched her. 'We could be really happy here.'

'I suppose we could.' She went over to the fridge and as she opened the door he saw there was milk in there now and one or two small packets. He hoped they were cheese. She brought out some butter and cut a slab into the spuds then reached for the masher she had found in a drawer.

It wasn't until they had finished the meal and were sitting over a cup of tea that his headache began to return. She noticed him put his hand to his forehead, frowning slightly. 'What is it?'

'Just a twinge.' He reached for his cup and drained it then he put it down. His hand was shaking.

'Why not have an early night.' She was still happy, thinking about cooking again tomorrow. Secretly she had decided to go up to Princes Street and look for a bookshop and find one of Finlay Macdermott's books. Tim needn't see it. If he did, she would tell him that she had found it in the house.

He stood up and she saw him screw up his face as if he had felt a twinge of pain. Just for a moment he stood looking down at her and she felt a tremor of fear. It was as though someone else was looking out of his eyes, then he was himself again. 'I will go up,' he said. 'Thanks for the meal, Sis, that was really nice.'

She heard his footsteps on the stairs and his bedroom door banged. Minutes later it opened again and she heard him race into the bathroom. The sound of retching went on for ages; she put her hands over her ears, then sadly got up to do the washing up. The clank of pots and dishes drowned out the noise. When she had finished she went to the door and listened. Everything was quiet again.

Are you ready to go out? Let's see what we can find. April will be asleep soon. You don't want to wake her.

Tim sat on the bed shivering, his head in his hands. The bastard voice was back, insisting, pushing, going on and on.

We'll find something a bit juicier this time. A girl with a bit more meat on her. A girl with a bit of fight, shall we? Think how good it will be to lie between her thighs, knowing how much she's enjoying it, however much she squeals.

'No!' Tim cried out loud. He froze, looking at his door, but there was no sound from April who had finished tidying the kitchen and gone to bed. He had heard her door open and shut. He hoped she hadn't heard him being sick. He had enjoyed the meal so much.

'I'm not going out,' he murmured. 'Go away. I don't want to do it again.'

Oh, but you do. Did you wonder where I was? I went to see Ruthie this evening. You want to screw Ruthie, don't you. We could go together. We could knock on her door and persuade her to let us in. She's all alone there, waiting, longing, begging for it—

'Shut up!' Tim banged his ears with his fists.

The sound of mocking laughter filled his head. Soon he would give up trying to fight it, he knew he would. He would go out. To resist was too hard. He wanted to go. He wanted a woman so badly it hurt. He lay back on the bed and pulled the pillow over his face, moaning.

In the room next door April heard him call out and she shivered. Quietly she prayed to a god she didn't believe in, 'Please, don't let him go and do it again,' and she slid out of bed to turn the key in her own door.

Thomas

I saw her again, of course I did. And again and again. Most of the time her messages were authentic, or so they seemed to me. It was Fanny's tone, her wit, her humour and more often than not her concern over the family and for me. I asked and begged she give me details of how she had fallen down the stairs; I had again interrogated Margaret, who was with her when it happened, asking if my darling could have been pushed, but my sweet gentle daughter merely looked at me as if I were mad and said, 'I've told you. There was no one there but me.'

I disliked going to Stonecutters Court and I disliked even more Sarah's brother who lurked there amongst the dust and rubble of his trade as a plasterer. He was a greedy man, with a sharp eye for my fortune and status and I did not trust him.

In the end it was easier to bring her to Hampstead. I gave her a place as under-housekeeper, much to Abi's fury, my butler's indignation and Margaret's disgust. None of them liked or trusted her or believed in her mediumistic gifts. I did not require her to work with the other servants and gave her two small rooms of her own. It made them hate her the more, though she tried to befriend them as best she could. Poor Sarah, neither fish nor fowl, she wandered sadly through the house with no one but me to talk to when I was at home and in those days I was more often at the House of Lords or at Lincoln's Inn. My children

478

were united in disliking the situation. They saw her as an interloper and a fraud and all hated the rumour and mockery in the broadsheets.

It was Margaret who stayed at home, Margaret who for the sake of civility tried to talk to Sarah, and Margaret who came to me one evening when I had returned from dinner with the Prince of Wales, to sit me down in the drawing room at long past midnight and talk to me seriously. 'She must go, Papa. I'm sorry. She means well and I think she may well be honest, but if she is, have you not thought how hard it must be for Mama, to see this woman beginning to play you like a caught fish, to wind you round her fingers, speaking in her name? It must distress her beyond all comprehension and Sarah herself admitted to me that you are keeping Mama earthbound, unable to take her place in heaven.'

I stared at her, appalled. 'Sarah told you that?'

Margaret nodded. She pursed her lips. 'It is not right, Papa, any of it.'

She was correct, of course, and it was not right in more ways than that. I wondered if she knew the truth? Presumably not. Margaret was a well-brought-up lady. She could not have dreamt how far I was about to go in error.

73

Thomas told his butler to send the servants to bed and then to go himself. He would not be needed again that night. It was windy and the great trees outside were particularly noisy, their branches thrashing to and fro. New logs had been stacked on the fire and the candles replenished and he was sitting in his favourite chair poring over a speech he was to deliver the next day, with a glass of port beside him on a side table. Margaret had gone to bed an hour since after playing for a while on the harpsichord for him. When the door quietly opened he looked up startled and for a strange displaced moment thought he saw Fanny there, a chamberstick in her hand. It was the kind of thing she would do, wondering where he was and why he had not come up to bed and still, all this time later, he half expected it to be her, about to chide him for working too hard. The woman in the flickering candlelight was wearing a nightgown, a shawl about her shoulders and her hair was loose down her back. A part of him knew full well it was Sarah, but even so he put down the papers and beckoned her over to the fire. She came at once and without hesitation sat on his knee and put her arms around his neck. 'You miss her, don't you,' she whispered. 'She has told me to come to you, to comfort you, to tell you to close your eyes and imagine I am she.' Her mouth was close to his ear, he could feel her warm breath on his neck, as slowly she felt for his neckcloth and began to unknot it.

He could have pushed her away, he could have dismissed her from the room and from his employ but he did neither. With a small groan he buried his face between her breasts and began to kiss her warm scented flesh.

It was Sarah who slid from his lap and caught his hand. It was she who led him up the stairs to his own bedroom and who then slid under his counterpane and waited with a slow sleepy smile as he tore off his clothes.

When he woke in the morning he was alone. His trousers and shirt had been neatly folded and lay on the chaise longue at the end of his bed. There was no trace of his companion in the room. He rang for his valet and within half an hour was shaved and dressed and had called for his horse. He ordered his carriage to follow him, to bring his books and papers to Lincoln's Inn. What he needed was a gallop on the heath. He did not return to Hampstead for more than a week.

Sarah crept back to her own room at dawn before the servants were awake and slipped into her own bed. When she awoke again it was full daylight and she lay there for a while, feeling warm and sated and triumphant. Later she would go down to the servants' hall and order the housekeeper to appoint her her own maid and tell them that in future she would take her meals alone in the small morning room. It did not bother her that Thomas had already left for London. He would come home soon enough. She knew him too well by now. He would ponder and rationalise and probably feel anguish at what he had done, but now that the longing had been reawakened, he would not be able to stay away. He was a passionate man, older than she might have liked perhaps, but he was rich beyond her wildest dreams and last night had proved that she had him caught fast in her web. He had thought he was making love to his wife. He had called out Fanny's name. He had kissed the face he remembered with so much love and anguish. She, Sarah, had brought the past back to life, that was her gift to him.

481

She saw the shock and dislike in the housekeeper's eyes before the woman hid her feelings and she smiled condescendingly. 'Lord Erskine said I could make these arrangements,' she said smugly. 'If there is a problem I can send to Lincoln's Inn—'

'There will be no need for that,' Mrs Ford said quietly. She glanced at Martha, who was sitting sipping tea at the table in the servants' hall. The two women had been talking quietly when Sarah had walked in. Only Mrs Ford had risen to her feet. 'If Miss Margaret says it's all right, I will see that the morning room is prepared for you.'

'Miss Margaret will be only too pleased, I can assure you. Thank you, Mrs Ford.' Sarah turned on her heel and walked out of the room, feeling their eyes boring into the back of her skull. It didn't matter what they thought. The only person who mattered in this house was Thomas.

Wrapping her shawl around her, she let herself out into the gardens and walked slowly down the path out of sight of any prying eyes that might be watching from the windows. She didn't like the country. The village here was not to her taste at all, but she knew she couldn't expect to live at Lincoln's Inn. The house was too busy, there were visitors constantly coming and going. At least here there was only Margaret and the staff to contend with. She walked on a little way, shivering as the wind caught at her skirts.

So, you have ensnared your prey.

The voice in her head was no more than a whisper.

A triumph, no less. And you will bring him down.

She took a deep breath. Voices were something she was used to, had been used to since she was a child. This was a man, from the West Country by his speech, and instinctively she shrugged him away.

No. Not so easy. I'm not some passing tosspot, I have had dealings with Lord E for many years. Since we were boys. And he is mine.

And suddenly she knew who this was. 'It was you who pushed Thomas's wife to her death,' she said out loud. 'You are Andrew Farquhar.'

There was no reply and she turned slowly round on the wind-swept walk. 'Speak to me!' she commanded.

Again there was no reply.

She smiled. 'So, you wish to play games with me. I don't advise it, Mr Farquhar. You have met your match with me.' She paused, hearing only the rustle of leaves, and the moan of the wind in the Scots pines. 'You thought you had destroyed Thomas when you killed his wife. Think again. I can bring her back to him any time I choose.' She smiled. 'That is power, Mr Farquhar. Something you will never have. Leave your petty grievances in whatever hell you inhabit and stay there with them to rot.' She raised her right hand and snapped her fingers. It was a definitive dismissal.

One of the under gardeners, rake in hand, was watching her curiously from behind a stand of holly. He pushed his hat back and scratched his head thoughtfully. He could see her talking into the wind and that there was no one near her and he could see the look of triumph on her face as the wind caught the rim of her bonnet and blew its ribbons backwards across her shoulders. He shivered. Later, over a tankard of ale in the Spaniards Inn, he relayed what he had seen to Thomas's groom. 'She's mad as a hatter,' he said. 'Whatever His Lordship sees in her I cannot imagine. I hope he ditches her soon. She's no good for him, that's for sure.'

Ruth had laid out the letters on the kitchen table. This new bundle seemed to have been kept less carefully than the previous ones she had been reading. The pages were torn and faded. She unfolded the first and reached for Malcolm's magnifying glass. 'The best friend to researchers after ancient secrets,' he'd said with a smile. 'You'll find it helps enormously, especially when the ink's faded.'

It seemed Thomas's staff weren't the only ones worried by his dalliance. This letter to his sister, Frances, was from Davy, Thomas's eldest son by now returned to England from his post as ambassador to America. He seemed to be living in London with his family and, Ruth seemed to remember from her notes, did not have enough to do – code for he was interfering in his father's private life. And here was proof.

I went to Evergreen Paradise yesterday to take luncheon
with Margaret. THAT WOMAN is still there, playing the
lady, and to my horror I saw that she is enceinte! How
can this be? Please, my darling sister, speak to Papa. He
might listen to you. His career will be ruined. Even if he
cares nothing for his family's reputation, surely he has
some regard to his own. At least persuade him to put her
away and find her a cottage somewhere far away.

Ruth pushed the letter aside and sat back in her chair, wishing
Malcolm was there to share her excitement. This was so
intriguing. Just imagine the scandal!

Sadly, there was no copy of Frances's reply to her brother,
or her subsequent note to her father, if there was one. Ruth
switched on her laptop and called up her own draft notes. There
was her own account of Sarah's seduction of Thomas. The
woman had channelled – wasn't that the word? – Thomas's
beloved wife. Had he really thought he was making love to
Fanny? Surely not. He was an intelligent man. Yes, he believed
in the paranormal but this was something else! Ruth sighed,
wishing, as she did almost daily, that her mother was still alive.
Her mother had known so many stories about Thomas: that he
had been struck by lightning three times; that he was haunted
by a fellow crew member from the *Tartar*, and this one, that
Sarah Buck had been a clairvoyant and thus had somehow
gained a hold over him. And was it her mother who had inherited and somehow inadvertently passed on to her the curse of
Andrew Farquhar?

There, on her screen, she carefully reread her own words.
Andrew Farquhar had tried to climb into Sarah's head and she,
strong and experienced in her art, had snapped her fingers at
him and he had disappeared in a puff of metaphorical smoke.

Pushing back her chair, Ruth stood up and went over to the
kettle: reflex action when trying to think. Sarah had snapped
her fingers at him. Was that all it took? She gave a grim smile
as she reached for the tin of tea bags. In a sense that was exactly
what she had done herself. When he had come sniffing around
earlier she had stood up to him, sent him away and he had

gone. She had reacted without thinking – with anger rather than fear – and it had worked. So where was he now? Where did he go when he was not showing himself to her? Malcolm hadn't been able to answer that question but now she found herself wondering again if it was at all possible that their lascivious, vicious ghost had climbed into Timothy Bradford's head.

Timothy had dozed off, lying on his bed with only the side lamp on, the curtains tightly shut against any possibility of someone seeing the light. He woke suddenly and raised his arm to see his wristwatch. It was midnight.

Perfect timing. Partygoers, staggering home, drunk.

He didn't even bother to try and argue; he didn't want to argue. Climbing to his feet, he reached for his jacket. On the landing he could hear April's steady snoring. He gave a grim smile and proceeded to tiptoe down the stairs. He scanned the parked cars outside carefully. There was no sign of the police. So, Mr Plod didn't bother to patrol at night. It was too cold for him, perhaps.

He set off towards the town. No point in looking round here at this time of night. He needed to go where the nightclubs were emptying and party girls were staggering out into the streets, scantily clad in spite of the cold, falling out of their shoes, dodging the waiting arms of the Street Pastors who were trying to save them and ducking into the alleys and wynds to vomit in the dark.

He found the girl he was looking for so easily. She was standing in a doorway fumbling in her bag for cigarettes. No coat, no sense, only one shoe, almost insensible from the vodka slammers he could smell on her breath. At least she didn't smell of vomit. She struggled frantically, trying vainly to push him away, and as he ripped down her skimpy dress she began to scream. What had she expected, going out dressed like that? Presumably she had wanted to pull, but maybe not the kind of man she was confronted with now, a man from the meanest streets of eighteenth-century London, a man who wanted to hurt her badly.

He left her lying where she fell and faded back into the night, walking and jogging, back towards the quiet streets of Morningside, too excited and energised to want to go home yet. He wished he had something to drink. *Grog*, the voice muttered, *that's what we need.*

As he turned the corner of the road at last, exhausted, heading for bed, he was appalled to see a police car parked up outside Number 26. He shrank back, his heart thudding with fright. The voice in his head had gone; he was alone. Shaking, he turned and walked away. When he returned, much later, the car had gone.

Next morning Ruth was standing in the kitchen surveying the table with its neatly stacked papers and letters. The sun had risen behind the hills and it looked as though it would be a fine morning. Already she knew what she was going to do later. She would walk through the woods to the chapel and sit there for a while, on her own, in quiet mindfulness, just to see what would happen. Timothy was long gone and she would keep her eyes open. There would be no danger in broad daylight.

But first she would eat some scrambled eggs. She was hungry and unaccountably cheerful. The phone rang as she was lifting the heavy iron pan off the stove and she felt a leap of excitement. It would be Malcolm. Today he would be giving his talk; the next day he would be setting off for home.

'Ruth? It's Sally Laidlaw, from Number 24.'

Ruth's heart sank instinctively. Please let it not be any more bad news. She set down the pan. 'Hello, Sally, how are you?'

'I'm fine, dear, thank you. Look, it's not my business but I just wanted to check. Were you over here last night?'

'No.' Ruth felt a tremor of unease. 'Why?'

'I went out late to bring in my washing. I had forgotten about it in the garden. And, well, I could smell cooking. I'm not sure it was coming from your house, but I remembered what you said about keeping an eye on the place.' She hesitated.

'Aren't the police watching the house?' Ruth found her mouth had gone dry.

'Oh yes, they come by all the time. Ever such a nice young man was here last evening. He sat outside for a while in his car so I went out and asked him if he'd like a cup of tea.'

Ruth smiled. 'That's OK, then. Thank you for letting me know. But I will call in, Sally, next time I come by.'

She laid her phone gently on the table and stood staring down at it. Somehow she had gone off the idea of scrambled eggs and her plan for a walk in the lonely woods no longer seemed such a good idea, either.

April went out early, her laptop in her bag, leaving Timothy a note saying she was going into town and would see him later. He was still asleep. She could hear him muttering as he slept. She wasn't worried about getting back into the house; when she had gone shopping the day before she had had a key cut for herself at the corner shop.

She opened the front door cautiously and looked up and down the road before stepping outside but there was no sign of the police car. The sun was shining and she allowed herself a brief moment of glee as she set off up the road in the cold glittering air. She planned to stay out most of the day and she would start with coffee. She found a patisserie in Rose Street, sitting unobtrusively at the back of the shop, in a corner, with her laptop on the table in front of her.

So, Malcolm Douglas was in London. She sipped her coffee thoughtfully. The post came from his publisher and that meant that presumably Ruth was alone in her tower. She wondered if Timothy would go over there today, unable to keep away, and she smiled. She didn't care what he did as long as he didn't bother her. Before she went looking for a bookshop, the fact that Malcolm was away needed to be addressed. She clicked onto his Twitter account. No, he hadn't mentioned it himself.

So, MD is in London today, RuthieD typed industriously. *Have they heard the gossip? Is he going to lecture about using source material from the Beyond!*

Pleased with herself, she ordered a second cup of coffee and a croissant with jam. Then she turned her attention to Ruth.

Nothing there either. Ruth was as always conspicuous by her absence on the Internet. Quickly bored by the search, April began idly to look through some of the day's news and there it was, scrolling across the bottom of the screen.

Breaking news: THIRD EDINBURGH RAPE VICTIM FIGHTING FOR HER LIFE

It was as if the world had disappeared. The gentle hubbub of the coffee shop died away and she was left in a silent bubble of horror as she read:

After a third vicious assault in Edinburgh last night, police are hunting DNA suspect Timothy Bradford, wanted for his attack on TV chef Finlay Macdermott and implicated in two rapes in the city.

It couldn't have been Tim. She would have heard him if he'd gone out last night. She found she was holding her breath.

74

She called the boy Erskine.

Thomas was furious.

Margaret moved out. 'Papa, you cannot expect me to live under the same roof as your mistress,' she said quietly. 'You have refused to set her up somewhere discreetly. No one would have blamed you for that, but to move her into your home, Mama's home, that is an insult to her and to me.'

She went to stay with Davy and Caddy and within two days Davy had come to see his father in the Lincoln's Inn house.

'You realise you are the mockery of the whole town,' his son said, tight-lipped. 'If you have no care to your own reputation at least have some for the rest of your family.'

How could Thomas explain that with Sarah came Fanny, their mother, the woman he still loved to distraction? None of them understood.

The baby boy was an angry, bawling, bundle of fury, his tiny fists clenched as he screamed his outrage at a world that he seemed already to have perceived as unfair and cruel. Thomas looked into the cradle with huge compassion, all too aware of the disservice he had done to the child's mother and to the rest of his children, but he didn't know how to extricate himself from the mess he had made of things.

His son, Esmé, came to see him on the eve of his embarkation to the continent. The war with the French Empire had intensified; Esmé, resplendent in his scarlet regimentals, was now adjutant general to the Duke of Wellington. Thomas was very proud of his youngest son.

'Papa. Sir, I had been going to leave Eliza and my boys to your care while I am at the war, but I feel I can't. I am sure you know why.' Esmé stamped restlessly up and down the room, his spurs rattling. He could barely contain his frustrated anger. 'You have caused so much unhappiness to us all, you must see that. Margaret is distraught. I went to see Davy and Caddy yesterday, to say goodbye, and Margaret was there, in tears.' He waited for a reply and when one was not forthcoming he went on: 'I have asked Davy to take care of my family. As my eldest brother, that seemed my only choice. I'm sorry.'

Thomas was tight-lipped.

Esmé waited for a full minute then he turned to the door. 'I'm sorry to leave you in anger, Papa, but it seems this woman has bewitched you and there is no way of making you see how terrible this is for us all.'

There was no hug, no smile. Esmé gave him a formal salute and turned to the door.

'Wait, my boy.' Thomas's voice was husky. 'I cannot have my family dictating to me the way I run my life. You must see that.'

Esmé grimaced. 'Then we would seem to have reached an impasse, sir.'

He hesitated for one second then he clicked his heels, bowed formally and turned for the door.

Thomas sat down at his desk and closed his eyes, trying desperately to block out the peal of sarcastic laughter in his head, the laughter not of Sarah Buck but of the man he had last seen dangling from the end of a rope at Tyburn.

It was several days before Thomas returned to Evergreen Hill and Sarah was not happy. She greeted him with scowls and a stamp of the foot. 'The nursemaid you sent me is useless. I have spoken to the housekeeper and she says there is nothing she can do as the woman was your choice. So you must choose me another.'

Thomas flung himself down in his favourite chair. The room was cold; no one had been called to light the fire and there was only one branch of candles near burned down on the mantelpiece. When he mentioned it she turned on him. 'How was I supposed to know you would finally be returning home? Call the butler yourself, he pays scant attention to me!'

He noticed she referred to none of the staff by name. Perhaps she had not even taken the trouble to find out who they were. He took a deep breath. 'Sarah, I have decided that it would be more convenient for you to live in your own house.' He saw her face redden with anger and he went on, his voice slightly raised, 'It would be somewhere quite close and I would be able to make sure that you, we, were more comfortable there.'

She subsided, thinking. He could see her calculating, trying to work out if she would be better off in town.

That night she came to his bedroom freshly bathed and wrapped in a lace-trimmed bed gown, her hair loose down her back. She had regained her figure; her breasts were losing their voluptuous curves thanks to the wet nurse her mother had found for her, a neighbour in Stonecutters Court who had lost her own baby only weeks after its birth. She suspected Thomas would be horrified if he knew where the woman had come from but he had seemed uninterested in the technicalities of her life; no one on the staff was prepared to help her so she had been forced to turn to her family who were all too eager to intervene.

'Fanny came to me this afternoon,' she said with a flutter of her eyelashes. 'She thinks it would be fun to be together in a small house.' She had curtly dismissed his valet who after a helpless glance at his master had bowed and left the room. In here there was a warm fire and Thomas had ordered dozens of candles to be lit. Outside, the wind was roaring across the heath and for a moment he wished he was out there, on his horse, galloping into the dark. Did she not realise that the very act of wearing the same perfume as Fanny was an insult? But it wasn't an insult. It wasn't Sarah at all. His beloved wife had slipped effortlessly into the woman's body.

She climbed onto the bed, exposing a length of shapely leg as she did so. 'Tom, my darling Tom.' It was Fanny's voice. Sarah saw him tense, and she gave an inward smile. She had been practising Fanny's mannerisms. She had been the mouthpiece for his wife so often now she could switch on the persona at will. Fanny did not always come to her any more but Thomas did not know that. She could see the longing in his eyes as she slipped her nightgown off her shoulders.

Below stairs Abi and Mrs Ford, Roberts the butler, Thomas's valet, Benjamin, and two or three of the maids gathered round the table in the servants' hall. They too could hear the wind outside. Abi shivered. One of the maids who had been allocated to Miss Buck had been telling them what she had heard in the nursery earlier. The woman had been talking to her baby, not crooning and singing but hectoring, telling it what it had to do, who it would be when it grew up, how it would win its father's heart. 'I saw her face,' the girl said, her eyes growing round as she remembered. A gust of wind blew back down the chimney and a puff of smoke strayed out into the room, making the candles flicker. No one spoke. 'It wasn't her,' she whispered. 'It was a vicious cruel man I saw there. If it wasn't for that innocent little mite in the cradle, I would give my notice now, this minute. I swear it was witchcraft.'

Abi caught Mrs Ford's eye and grimaced. 'What nonsense, girl,' she said sharply. 'You keep such imaginings to yourself. If I hear another word from you I will send you off.'

The girl looked down meekly, but her expression was defiant. 'I did, so there,' she whispered. The words were not quite inaudible and the silence that followed was uneasy. Mrs Ford stood up and bustled over to the stove. 'Hot toddy for everyone,

I think,' she said firmly. 'On a stormy night like this it will help keep out the cold.'

* * *

'Witchcraft!' Ruth shivered. She reread the last paragraph she had copied down and glanced back at the letter from which she was paraphrasing. It had been written by Margaret to her brother Henry's wife, Harriet. As an ordained priest, Thomas's second son was perhaps the most concerned of all about his father's liaison.

He has at last moved her into a small house where he can visit her discreetly, but people talk. The servants talk and again and again they mention this word. Can't Henry have a word with him? Surely as a priest in the Church he can drum some sense into Papa's head. The woman is dangerous. I went to stay with Frances and Samuel in Sussex, and they too are worried sick. Samuel volunteered to speak to Papa but it would come better from Henry.

Ruth smiled. Family gossip. This was what she had so missed in her own life and was, perhaps as much as anything else, why she was so engaged in this story. It was so much more than an enthralling tale, it was her own family and she shared their deep concern for Thomas. Sarah had wormed her way into his affections through her skill at channelling Fanny; whether that was real or pretend she had no way of knowing, but it was obviously compelling. And intriguing. She turned the page in Margaret's letter:

One of her nursery maids was sacked for claiming she saw Sarah's face change into that of a man. A vicious cruel face, she said. Abi told me. Mr Roberts had dismissed the story as women's gossip but then the girl saw it again and she ran screaming out of the nursery and Miss Buck sacked her on the spot. Papa gave the girl some money and a reference, but it didn't stop her telling the whole world what had happened.

A vicious cruel man. Ruth swallowed hard. Farquhar.

Her thoughts were interrupted by the sound of the doorbell echoing up the stairs. She went over to the window looking out towards the front of the house. There was no sign of a car. The doorbell rang again more insistently this time and then she saw him as just for one second he stepped back and looked up. It was Timothy. She froze. He can't get in, she told herself firmly. You know he can't. She turned and grabbed her phone off the table.

'He's here now.' The emergency number she had been given by the police picked up instantly. 'On the doorstep. He rang the bell.'

A local police car was there within fifteen minutes, followed sometime later by a second from Edinburgh. 'I'd rather you didn't stay here alone until we've located him,' Jack Jordan said to Ruth after he had conferred with the local officers. She couldn't wait to go. The shock of seeing Timothy there, on the doorstep, looking up at the windows, perhaps spotting her before she ducked back out of sight, had left her sick with fear. Leaving his backup to search the hillside, Jordan waited for her to pack her bag and grab her laptop and briefcase, then he drove her to Edinburgh.

On the way, she told him about the smell of cooking from Number 26. He grinned. 'Good to know your neighbour is keeping her eyes open. Why don't we go past and check?'

The policeman on duty said no one had been near the house, and Sally, when questioned, was overwhelmed with embarrassment. 'I'm so sorry to have brought you all this way. It turns out it was my neighbours at Number 22. I checked and they said they were having a barbecue.'

They didn't go in.

Jordan dropped Ruth off at Max's flat in Heriot Row, at the heart of Edinburgh's elegant Georgian New Town, and waited until he had opened the door and let her in.

'Why can't they catch him?' She found her hands were shaking as Max handed her a cup of strong black coffee. She was sitting next to Fin on the sofa in the sitting room of Max's beautiful first-floor flat.

'They will.'

'But what about Farquhar? He can walk through walls. I couldn't tell Jack Jordan about him.'

'I think you should,' Fin said. 'He must be used to dealing with people who are, or think they are, possessed.' He paused, aware of the expression on both Ruth's and Max's faces. 'OK.' He raised his hands in mock surrender. 'Perhaps not. So, what do we do?'

As she sat on the edge of the bed in Max's second-best spare room that night she was clutching her folders of papers to her chest as if her life depended on it. Max had smiled at her as he showed her in. 'It's a box room really. I'm sorry it's so small. But there is everything you need and you're next to the bathroom.'

Curling up against the pillows she reached for the latest little volume of Thomas's diary. Beside the bed, sitting next to one another on a small chair, sat her teddy and the voodoo doll.

As Ruth was driven away from the Tower House, Timothy was high on the hillside above them peering down from the woods. He had seen the police cars, gaudy in the sunshine, parked outside the front door, the uniformed figures first on the door-step then separating to circle the building. Well, they wouldn't find him there. He leaned back against the trunk of a larch tree, adjusting his back to the sharp stubs of old branches and he watched, enjoying the show. They reconvened at the front after a while and stood staring round. He saw them look up to scour the hillside and he held his breath, afraid they would spot him, but they couldn't possibly see him from there. He felt a surge of triumph which was dissipated somewhat when he saw Ruth emerge and climb into the back of one of the cars. So, she had been there all along.

He wondered whether they had found his car. This one he had taken from a petrol station forecourt while its idiot owner had gone to pay, leaving the keys in the ignition. He knew the CCTV would have caught him at the pumps. No matter. The keys to the stolen car were in his pocket. Unlike its owner, he had locked it when he left it tucked into the trees further up the brae. He turned and began to lope down the path.

When he had awoken late that morning to find that April had gone out, he was furious; he wanted her to cook him breakfast. However, on second thoughts he could not face her shrewd narrow-eyed gaze and sour ill humour, and he had a bit of money in his pockets; he would go out and have a fry-up somewhere. He went back upstairs to find his jacket and it was while he was searching through the pockets that he found the blood. The jacket was torn, the zip broken and there was blood all over the sleeve. He stood staring at it as his night's activities came back to him in a rush. He remembered the thrill of the busy late-night streets, the lights, the noise, the crowds of young people out enjoying themselves; then the dark alley, the confidence with which he had stalked his prey. The girl had fought. She might have been drunk but she had been strong and furiously angry. He remembered hitting her hard to subdue her. He felt no regret; in fact, he felt nothing at all. It was as if it had happened to someone else. He went on systematically emptying his pockets, carefully collecting every last penny.

Now, as he watched the police below him, he found himself wondering if the girl was badly hurt. If she was, it would be on the news and April would be incandescent with rage. Perhaps he would leave it until later to go back to Edinburgh. Besides, the police might search Number 26. If they did, they would find out that he and April were living there. But why should they search it? They had been patrolling the street and not spotted him. He felt a flash of intense disdain. He was so much cleverer than them; what chance had they of catching him?

The sound of the helicopter in the distance didn't register at first, it was so far away, but it was coming closer. He could see it now as he craned upwards through the branches of the trees, a tiny dot in the sky. It seemed to be making straight for him. He felt a stab of fear as the sound of the rotor grew louder. He watched, holding his breath as it hovered over the conical roof of the turret, then began systematically to sweep in ever-growing circles the surrounding hillside and the woods. Dry-mouthed, he turned off the path and forced himself into the thicker undergrowth where they couldn't see him as the sound of the rotor grew deafeningly loud.

It was only a few yards further on that he spotted the clearing in the trees and saw the small stone building standing in a patch of sunshine.

After dropping Ruth off at Max's flat Jack Jordan had gone back to his headquarters to find DI Grant. 'At least she's safe where she is for now,' he reported. 'That woman must have a death wish; to stay all the way out there alone is insane.'

Sue looked up from her screen and sighed. 'I know how she feels. She doesn't want to be victimised by the creep. You reckon he's still out there?'

Jordan nodded. 'Yup! I could feel the bastard watching me.'

She looked up and he saw the flicker of humour in her eyes. 'Another psychic in our midst?'

He held her gaze. 'Don't knock it. It's called police intuition.'

'Have we left anyone there?'

'A couple of local guys are keeping an eye on the place.'

'Good. I've called for a helicopter search and dogs. This man is dangerous. If his latest victim dies he will be up for murder. When is Malcolm Douglas coming back?' She squinted back at her screen.

'A day or so, I think. That's another thing I don't understand! How could he let her stay there by herself?'

'Maybe he agrees with her. She needs to feel in control of the situation. I can't imagine he could stand up to her if she was really determined.'

Jordan grimaced. 'Heaven save us from powerful women!' He caught her eye. 'Sorry, ma'am. I didn't mean you, naturally.'

She ignored the remark. 'Out,' she said firmly, 'or you'll find yourself back there, patrolling the woods for a month!'

* * *

Pushing open the door, Timothy ducked inside. The helicopter wouldn't be able to see him in here. He closed the door behind him and looked round the shadowy building, expecting to see a derelict ruin. The light seeping in through the small narrow window and the cracks around the door showed him the table, the chair, the crystals, the statue, the candle on the table. It was a little church. His eyes strayed to a small dish, on which lay a box of matches and he tiptoed over to pick them up. Whoever came to this place, and he guessed it was Douglas, obviously cared a lot about it. It took only seconds to break up the chair and pile the remnants in the middle of the floor, then the table, smashing everything on it as he did so. Striking a match, he dropped it onto the pile where it flickered and went out. Scooping up a handful of the dry leaves that had drifted into the corners of the building he tried again and this time the flame caught. He watched it lick over the wooden splinters of the furniture and stood smiling, distracted by the satisfaction of seeing the fire catch hold. It was only the sound of the helicopter in the distance that reminded him it was time to go.

Thomas

Esmé, my youngest and bravest son, was wounded at Waterloo at the side of the Duke of Wellington. When finally he came home he told me he remembered little of what happened. In the midst of the fury and the fire and the crash of artillery and the screams of horses and men he kept as close to the duke as he could, protecting him, sword in hand, trying to keep him in sight, which was difficult as the duke wore, as was his custom, dark clothes so he did not stand out as a target for the enemy. The cannonball that brought Esmé down he remembers only as a crash like the day of doom. His arm was amputated by a field surgeon and for weeks he lay between life and death, but he lived to return to his wife and children and to his father who, stiff upper lip to the fore, patted him on the back and congratulated him on his survival as though he had been at nothing more than a skirmish or an afternoon following hounds. I was proud of myself, but later I confess I wept a tear for my beautiful youngest son.

75

The helicopter hovered somewhere below, sufficiently far away for Timothy to be sure it hadn't spotted him. Something else must have caught the interest of the pilot. It stayed there for ages, just hanging above the woods, and then it rose up in the air and shot off northwards. Slowly the sound of the engine died away. Pressed against the bole of an old dead tree he peered down the hillside. He thought he could hear shouting in the distance. Perhaps they had seen the smoke from the burning chapel, or seen someone in the trees. Backing carefully away into the shelter of the larch forest he made his way cautiously along the shoulder of the hill heading always north. He had long ago given up any thought of going back to his car. It was several hours now since he had rung the bell of the Tower House and the police did not seem to have given up their chase. He was hungry and tired and, as the adrenaline wore off, beginning to feel afraid.

It was as he breasted the brow of the hill that he had his first ray of hope. Far below in the glen, in the angle of a winding burn, lay a farm steading, barns, outbuildings, an old square stone house. In the yard behind the house he could see cows, crowding together around a hayrack, and nearby there were two cars. Old, muddy, but both looking as if they were still capable of going somewhere.

Carefully he began to make his way down the steep slope, sliding between the trees, slipping on loose scree, less worried now about leaving the shelter of the trees as long as the helicopter was grounded.

Keeping his eyes skinned, he edged towards the yard. The gates to the outer yard were open and he could see fresh tracks in the mud. Hopefully the farmer and his family were out. Crouching low, he ran to the first of the cars and grabbed at the door handle. It was locked. Swearing under his breath, he ducked back to the other one and this time the driver's door opened. He only pulled it a few inches then stopped and looked round. A cow in the inner yard had started mooing loudly and he froze, terrified someone would come to see what was going on. Nothing happened. A few hens were pecking round the gate. They ignored him. He moved forward, still bent double so he could see inside. There was no key in the ignition. He swore again. Inch by inch he edged the door open until he was able to feel his way to the wires under the steering wheel, and spark the contact. The engine caught almost immediately with what sounded like a deafening roar. He leapt in, engaged gear, spun the wheel and began to back out of the yard. As far as he could tell, only the hens noticed him leaving.

Thomas was standing by the fire in Sarah's sitting room in her house in Hornsey, warming his hands. He had been to see Esmé and was still distressed. His son had bravely tried to hide his pain as he talked to his father, but he was pale and terribly thin, and kept pushing away the children as they tried to climb onto his lap. His eyes were huge and haunted and his surviving hand was shaking so much he could hardly hold the cup of tea he had been given. Secretly, Thomas felt it would help the boy to talk about his experiences, to get them off his chest, but Eliza, his wife, frowned and whispered that the doctors had told her not to mention anything about the battle, to pretend it had never happened. Eliza had been ill and she was uncomfortable and thoroughly irritated by her father-in-law's visit which meant she had to bring out the best china and make what she saw as polite conversation. The visit had not gone well.

It was a mistake to go straight round to see Sarah.

'I expected a better welcome than this!' Thomas complained as Sarah flounced into the room. She was expecting another child, and the pregnancy was obvious though she had draped a shawl artfully around herself to try to conceal it; Thomas prayed it would be a while yet before his grown-up children realised what was happening.

He threw himself down on the chair nearest the fire. 'Call the maid and get her to put more coals on. I pay your servants enough! They should be here to attend you. And I would like a glass of port.' She couldn't keep her servants, he noticed, and he could see why. She was rude and ungracious to them when he was there. He dreaded to think how unpleasant she would be when he wasn't.

Unerringly she seemed to read his thoughts. When the boy had carried away the empty scuttle to refill it in the yard she stood for a moment looking at the flames, then she turned back to him. 'I'm sorry, my darling.' It was Fanny's voice. 'I'm not well. The baby kicks so.' She sank down on the floor at his feet and rested her head on his knee. 'This waiting is interminable.' He said nothing, his thoughts still with Esmé. His son's three small children had climbed over Thomas like puppies, gladly making do with their grandpapa as they weren't allowed near their father with his empty sleeve pinned across his chest and his spasms of agonising pain.

'Where is Erskine?' He loathed the fact that she had used his name for the child.

She gave a careless shrug. 'I think one of the nursery maids took him out for a walk.'

'At this hour?' His voice was sharp.

She looked up, startled. 'I'd forgotten it was late. Perhaps they're back.'

'Then why is he not here to greet me?' He stood up, pushing her away from him, and walked over to the door. The house-maid came running.

'He's in the kitchen, my lord.' She sketched a curtsy. 'I'm

sorry, I didn't think to bring him in. Mistress Sarah' – was that the slightest of sneers in her tone? – 'doesn't like the child near her.'

'Well, I do,' he snapped. 'Bring him up here at once.'

The little boy was neat and clean, but, as always, he seemed scared when his father beckoned him over and he shrank from his mother's hand. 'So, have you been a good boy?' Thomas felt in his pocket for a sixpence. He wished he could love this child as he loved the rest of his family, but the little face was narrow and pinched and hostile and already the eyes were over-shrewd and he resembled no one save his mother.

Sitting down again, Thomas pulled him onto his knee, aware of Sarah's anxious gaze as she stood close by, ready to snatch the child away if anything went wrong. Erskine sat rigidly upright, perched precariously, careful not to relax against him. As soon as he could, he slid off Thomas's knee and ran to hide behind Sarah's skirts. Thomas saw her give the boy a none too gentle push. 'Go back downstairs,' she whispered. The boy didn't need telling twice.

He sighed and rose to his feet. 'I am glad to see you well, Sarah. Be sure to tell me if you need anything. Are the midwife and wet nurse booked?'

He knew they were. She had asked him for the money weeks ago.

She laid her hand on his arm. 'I need more servants, Tom.' He loathed it when she called him Tom, in Fanny's voice. 'You must see, these children are yours; it is not right that they have to stay in the kitchen with the servants.'

He didn't bother to point out that the second child had not yet been born and that she already had more than enough staff for the small house. It was easier to acquiesce than argue.

'Send your housekeeper with the details when she has found someone suitable,' he said wearily.

His carriage was outside. Leaning back against the opulent leather-covered seats with their cushions, coachman in front, valet and footman on the rear box, he felt a moment of shame. Sarah should be here in the warm with him, but he knew that that would never do.

His new daughter was born the following week. To his enormous distress, Sarah called her Agnes after his mother.

Within two weeks she was visited by the voice of Andrew Farquhar. What he suggested was beyond even her imagining.

Ruth had been poring over the fragmented last pages of the small leather-covered journal for more than an hour and her head ached. Fin had gone to the Old Mill House to see Lachy, promising to return before dark, and Max was lunching with an author.

Feeling safe and peaceful in Max's beautiful flat with its polished floors and its combination of Georgian elegance and modern chic she had brought her laptop and papers into his sitting room to sit by the window, looking down into Queen Street Gardens.

She had read about Esme's part in the Battle of Waterloo. The next passage, as intensely personal and painful as it was, transported her into Sarah Buck's small home; she felt Thomas's pain and his dilemma over these two unwanted children on whom he could never and would never turn his back. Pulling her laptop onto her knees she began to write, putting herself into the picture, painting the scene.

Then the last piece of the jigsaw came unbidden to her screen and what she saw appalled her.

Sarah was dozing on the sofa by the fire in her sitting room. The coals had been banked up and the curtains were half closed; it was stiflingly hot. There was no sign of the baby. Sarah groaned, trying to arrange herself more comfortably on the cushions, and closed her eyes. She could feel someone pushing at her mind, someone who wanted to speak, and she shook her head irritably. She did not welcome intrusions when she was alone. Thomas was her only client now; she didn't dare antagonise him by allowing others to come to the house, but that didn't mean she was not sometimes pestered by spirits who needed to talk. She did not encourage them. She was good at this. A natural, as people said. The only voice she permitted was Frances Erskine and she, to Sarah's intense frustration, came less and less often.

But now this. The man's voice was loud and strong, bullying.

He'll do anything you want. I've been watching. Imagine having one of the most powerful men in the land in your pretty little hand.

His laughter was cruel, mocking.

Where was Fanny? Sarah was afraid. She wasn't sure she was strong enough to shut the voice out any more. She knew he was trying to use her and she was frightened by the growing realisation that she couldn't control him.

You should welcome me, as an old friend of Tom's, he crowed. *But don't tell him I'm here. Let's surprise him.*

Ruth took her hands off the keyboard, afraid to go on. Andrew Farquhar. Was there nowhere he couldn't go? She pushed the laptop away and leaned across to pick up the little diary, leafing through the pages towards the back of the book. The ink was faded, the handwriting sometimes barely legible. There were places where Thomas had squashed in so many words she could imagine him writing at top speed, trying to fit it all in, sometimes writing vertically in the margin as well as across the page. It was Sarah she was looking for. Comments about her and the children, but there was nothing there. Instead he said that he was ill.

'It is an inflammation of the lungs such as you had before.' His son-in-law Samuel had, at his request, come up from Sussex to see him.

'I need your doctoring skills, not your prayers,' Thomas commented hoarsely as Sam approached his bedside. The younger man smiled gravely and pointed to his medical valise. His hand was cool on Thomas's burning forehead. 'I have both here. I will give you some medication, and then some laudanum to help you sleep, then I will pray for you, and I will tell my wife to stay away and leave you in peace until tomorrow.' He smiled gravely. 'She is very angry with you.'

'About Sarah?' Thomas could feel his eyes closing.

There it was. Ruth leaned closer, holding the little book closer to the light.

'Indeed, and we hear now that Miss Buck has not one but two children . . . ' Samuel kept his voice carefully neutral. His words were growing unintelligible, fading. Was that the sea Thomas could hear? It sounded like the waves on the rocks at St Andrews when he was a boy, or was it the tide racing up over the pebbled beach at Brighton? He couldn't breathe and now he was coughing again. Samuel was still talking: ' . . . the sea air at Brighton is most beneficial. You shall come and stay with us when you are well enough to travel and perhaps, when the warmth returns, dip in the sea as Dr Russell prescribes. His therapies are very popular. They are said to be almost miraculous in their efficacy . . . '

When he drifted back to consciousness Samuel's words were still weaving in coloured threads around the room: ' . . . as you know, I plan to rebuild our parsonage. It is too small for us. It may be that Frances and I will have to move house in the interim . . . ' The voice faded again.

When Thomas opened his eyes once more the room was almost dark, a single candle burning on the mantelpiece. He could hear someone talking quietly; no they were praying. Samuel was still there, by the fire, a little prayer book clasped in his hands.

He had dreamed he was Sir Thomas More, another Lord Chancellor. How strange. He had studied the man's life as a student and now he realised he and More were of the same cloth. But that couldn't be. More had died on the scaffold for his Catholic faith, and now, two hundred years later, on his own desk was the draft of a speech he himself was to deliver in parliament on the contentious subject of Catholic emancipation. He groaned. The prayers stopped and Samuel came across to the bed. He felt the cool hand on his brow again. 'You should be a doctor.' His lips were too dry and his throat too sore to speak clearly. He heard his son-in-law chuckle and then felt the cooling drops on his tongue. More laudanum and he was back in the Tower of London, awaiting execution. Then as the door began to open he saw the figure standing there waiting to escort him to the scaffold. It was Andrew Farquhar.

When he woke again it was full daylight and his daughter, Frances, was standing over the bed.

'At last, Papa. We were so worried. Your fever broke last night and you will be better now.'

He reached out and took her hand. Beside her his dogs were crowding round, wanting to jump on the bed. As long as she was there, he knew they wouldn't dare. 'My darling,' he whispered hoarsely. 'It is so good to see you here.' Margaret was there too and Samuel, Bible in one hand, doctor's bag in the other. Thomas lay back on the pillows, exhausted.

With his children around him, surely Farquhar would be unable to reach him.

The police car came into view just as Timothy was unlocking the door of Number 26. He dived in and slammed it behind him. Had they seen him? He leaned against the door, waiting. He heard the car wheels on the road as it drew up outside, then nothing. He waited a full five minutes then he moved away from the door and tiptoed into the front room. He edged towards the window and peered round the curtain. The bastard had parked right outside, staring through the windscreen, then he unclipped his seat belt and pushed open the car door. He climbed out and stood for a moment on the pavement, staring at the house. Timothy held his breath, but as he watched the guy turned abruptly and ducked into the car again, reaching for his radio. Timothy saw him listen and nod briefly. In seconds he had started the engine and raced away from the kerb.

Timothy sagged with relief. It was several minutes before his heart resumed its natural rhythm. Throwing back his head, he began to laugh. The dumb, stupid pig had almost had him! The man was within a few metres of him! The euphoria that flooded through him was overwhelming. Even if he had failed in his main objective, which was to find Ruth, he had enjoyed his day, rounding it off by abandoning the stolen car, engine running, on a double yellow line in the middle of the city and now he was back under his own roof and hungry again.

Ruth's eyes were sore from studying the faded writing and her head was thumping. Abruptly she put the book down on the table by the sofa, desperate for some air. The others wouldn't be back for hours yet. What she needed was a walk.

Slipping the keys to Number 26 into her coat pocket, she let herself out of the house and set off towards Princes Street and the West End, then on up Lothian Road towards Tollcross. She had never given a thought to the spare set of keys she had left behind at the Old Mill House.

Thomas

I remember that fateful year for many other things. His Royal Highness saw fit to fulfil the second part of my own strange prophecy of all those years before and make me a Knight of the Thistle in recognition of my service and my noble Scots blood. The family were pleased but Sarah grew more and more bitter at her exile in her little house where she saw nothing of the great and exotic men and women who were my friends. She did not take well to being discreetly put away as my children had insisted. Not well at all.

That was the year I concluded my novel. I had been writing it for years on and off, dreaming of fame for my literary skills. I was missing life as a barrister far more than I had ever expected; for one brief year as Lord Chancellor I had forfeited my chance of ever again practising at the bar. But then, look what I had in return. Title, wealth, fame, notoriety perhaps, and enormous influence at another bar, the Bar of the House of Lords. I called my book Armata, *and the first edition sold out within weeks, which was gratifying. It went into several more editions before it was forgotten.*

The last of the good things of that year was the appointment of Samuel as Precentor and Prebendary at the great Cathedral of Chichester, in Sussex. He deserved it. He was proving himself yet again an able and talented man. My daughter had made a good choice in her husband.

But then came tragedies. Esmé died, no longer able to withstand the trauma of his wounds, and close on that devastating loss came the news that my brother Harry was no more. He had built himself a beautiful house in the Italianate style, so he had told me, on the banks of the River Almond, on the family land at Almondell, less than two miles from Kirkhill where we had spent so much time as children. Sadly widowed, he had remarried a lady, ironically called Erskine, but whom he called Kate after her mother, whom he loved dearly. He had written poetry on and off all his life, but now the subject was this new house and the tumbling river and the woods and gardens around it and one day I promised myself that I would go there, a promise that was to prove more fateful than ever I dreamed. But now after years of happy retirement, he was gone and with him my dreams of our reunion. My heart ached for him.

I bought another house, this one in Arabella Row. It was a pretty, terraced home near Buckingham House which was still known then as the Queen's Palace, and for a while I thought of moving Sarah from Hornsey and giving it to her, to make her more a part of my life. But swiftly I dismissed the idea. She would never fit in my circle. This, like my estate in Sussex, would be my own retreat. There was a cottage there I was having converted into a house and I had called it Buchan Hill. I loved it there with its forest and woodland and wild heaths. One day soon, I realised I would have to give up our house in Lincoln's Inn. I dined in hall there occasionally, and that pleased me greatly, but it did not warrant keeping a large establishment nearby, not when I could retreat to my Sussex fiefdom. There, Sarah could not find me.

But I could not let her go, not when she spoke to me in the voice of my darling, and begged me to stay.

76

April had gone back to the hotel. Sitting on the bed, biting her nails, she surveyed her document case and tote and handbag gloomily. Every item she possessed in the whole world was there, lined up in front of her on the carpet. On the plus side, she had several thousand quid in cash in one of those bags. She wondered briefly whether Tim had gone back to the house yet. Reaching for her phone she scrutinised the screen. No messages, no texts. Nothing. From anyone. There was no one to call her except Tim. The words echoed bleakly round her head. No one. If she ditched Tim and left Edinburgh she would be totally and completely alone.

Lying back on the bed she felt tears of self-pity leaking down the side of her face and into the bedspread. She should call the police. He had spiralled out of control. She didn't recognise him any more. He had always been weak, easily led, and that had suited her when they were growing up with no parents, or none that cared. She, the elder by a decade, had taken care of him, made sure he went to school, wiped his snotty nose, collected her mother's benefits. It was easy to go on doing that when, one day, her mother went out and never came home. Neither of them wondered much where she had gone. No one questioned anything until one day a nosy neighbour knocked on the door. It was then they packed everything they could carry, Tim had nicked his first car and they had taken off into the night. And done very nicely up to now.

She sat up wearily and reached down to find her laptop. Plugging it in she signed in to the hotel's Wi-Fi. To her relief there were no more screaming headlines. Yet. She sat for a long time, staring at the screen, unable to decide what to do. She knew she ought to shop him. What if he killed someone? She would not be able to live with the knowledge that she could have stopped it. She knew she was not what you would call a moral person, though there had been a teacher at school who had taught them all right from wrong. It was just a sad fact that wrong paid so well. But not this. Not rape and not murder.

To distract herself she clicked on Twitter. She wondered if Malcolm Douglas was still in London and what Ruth was doing without him. Ruth had friends. And family. So, her dad had died, but at least she had had a dad. She and Tim had never known theirs.

A few people were defending Douglas now. Telling her to shut up. As if.

So, did the ghosts follow you to London? Bet that went down a ball!

She pressed tweet and suddenly she felt better. Tim hadn't hurt anyone in daylight. It was as night fell on the city she would have to decide what to do. In the meantime, she would send some more tweets and then take herself out for some food.

Making up history must be fun. Everyone believes someone like you. How does it feel to be able to rearrange the past to suit you?

Back at police HQ Jack Jordan sighed as he read the report that had just come in. Following a sighting by the helicopter a police team with dogs had threaded their way up into the hills behind Douglas's house and tracked down a man who ran away as soon as he saw them. An arrest was made, precious time lost. It was only some poor bloody rambler.

Leaning forward, he clicked on his keyboard and sat staring at the screen. RuthieD had tweeted only twenty seconds ago. Ruth had confirmed it wasn't Harriet Jervase. She still thought it might be April Bradford and in his mind that fitted. Only a guess, perhaps, as he knew so little about the woman, but it felt right. Cop's intuition. The tweets weren't vicious or obscene, just full of innuendo, designed to cause trouble.

As he watched another tweet appeared.

Has it ever worried you that you might be seriously pissing off the dead. I wonder if ghosts can kill.

'I tried to visit you when you were ill.' Sarah was looking thoroughly bad-tempered when Thomas finally confronted her in her sitting room. As always the room was over-hot and this time the two children were there. She insisted that Erskine bow formally and call him my lord. Baby Agnes was red-faced and grizzling in her cradle.

'I was not aware that you called,' he defended himself, sheepishly. He had not given Sarah a thought for several weeks.

'Your housekeeper said you were too ill to see me, and then Margaret appeared and said that I should go away as you might have something catching and I should not risk my children's health. She offered to pay for a chaise to take me back to London, as though I were a common pauper.'

'I'm sure she meant to be kind.' He had brought a box of toy soldiers for Erskine. The boy inspected them, clearly puzzled as to what he was supposed to do with them, then abandoned the box and went to his mother, shyly clinging to her skirts. She pushed him away.

'This isn't good enough, Tom.'

He tensed. She had lapsed into Fanny's voice.

'You have to make an honest woman of her. Do you want her to be insulted and sidelined at every turn forever?'

He stared at her, shocked, trying to read the message in her eyes. Was that really his Fanny, speaking through her from the worlds beyond, or was this woman playing with him? He knew what his sons would say, and Frances and Margaret, but he couldn't be sure. As he studied her face he saw it change infinitesimally. She was Sarah again. 'I will ring for some refreshments,' she announced stiffly, and he guessed she realised she had gone too far.

She rang for the maid and sat rigidly waiting for the tray to be brought, watching as Erskine, his curiosity finally getting the better of him, went back to the box of soldiers and started to arrange them on the table. Thomas ached to put his arm round the little boy, to play with him, but he felt he had to be cautious. Her words had scared him: to make an honest woman of her. To marry her. That was unthinkable.

In the hall later, as her footman helped him on with his greatcoat, he heard a man's voice coming from the sitting room. Frowning, he turned back to the door and walked in. Sarah was standing in front of the fireplace. There was no one else in the room but for the children. 'I heard you call?' he said abruptly. Then he heard it again. Singsong, mocking.

She means to have you. She will make your life a living hell until you do, and I shall show her how. Between us, we will bring you and your spawn down.

Sarah clamped her hands over her mouth, a look of agony on her face. 'That wasn't me!' she gasped.

'I am fully aware who it was,' Thomas retorted. Without another word, he turned and left the room, slamming the door behind him.

He told his coachman to take him back to Hampstead. Leaning against the carriage cushions he closed his eyes with a shudder. He had to find a way to deal with this man. If he were a real, living being he would have no problem, he would have at his fingertips every form of law enforcement agency there was, but this vile incubus was another matter. He had wondered on several occasions whether he should discuss this with Sam, but always he held back. Sam might feel he had to tell Frances, and that could not be supported. What about his sons? There was no question of discussing anything that might reflect back on Sarah with Davy or Thomas. Both men would demand instantly that she be taken up as a fraud. She would find no sympathy with them, or excuse that as their father's mistress she should be given some kind of special consideration. Both men were astute, they had seen through her from the start. What about his second son, Henry? He was an ordained minister of the church but that was his only similarity to Sam, who as a man of the world would confront the problem thoughtfully and perhaps wearing his medical hat. Henry had been married for only two years and Thomas saw him and his new family less often. He could not confide in him. His thoughts travelled on to his friend, William Blake. Many thought the man mad, but he considered him a mystic and a genius and a kindred spirit; he would understand, but could he be counted on to keep his counsel, and if he could, would he know how to remedy the situation? He somehow doubted it.

With a deep sigh he realised for now he had to deal with this matter himself. For the whole family's sake, he had to find a way of neutralising Farquhar, and soon. If this restless and vicious spirit really had found a mouthpiece in Sarah there was no one, absolutely no one, whom he could trust to discuss it with and if he didn't do something, there would be no way of stopping her.

As the horses slowed to climb up towards Hampstead he leaned forward to look out of the window, half expecting to see the spectral figure of Farquhar jogging alongside. It had started to rain and the road was rapidly growing muddier. Behind them he heard the distant sound of a coach horn. The evening stage would soon be wanting to overtake them. 'Pull over,' he called to his coachman. 'I shall walk the rest of the way.'

'Shall I follow you, my lord?' His valet, Benjamin, was reaching for his pistol and already climbing down from the box.

'Please do so.' It would not be worth risking the anger of his family if he came home alone, besides which, it was stupid to risk his life that way. More and more footpads were frequenting the heath. Thomas didn't allow himself to suspect that he was afraid that if he was alone Farquhar might appear. As the evening stagecoach north raced past them up the road at full gallop, accompanied by the thunder of hooves and the sound of the coach horn, he beckoned his young escort after him and turned his face to the rain. In minutes his headache had gone.

In the end he talked to his trees, and as always, the noble pines listened, the wind shushing through their branches. In the sound of the trees he heard the crash of the waves and the moan of the wind on the Scottish moors, and there, through the song of the pine needles came the voice of the sennachie.

I warned you there was danger. You have to strengthen the armour of your soul and spirit. You have to call on the name of Christ. You need to summon the generations of your forefathers and the masters of the ages to stand at your back and you must call upon the generations to come to keep guard with you upon your children.

'How did Farquhar get such power?' Thomas heard himself shouting against the roar of the wind and knew his gardeners had withdrawn out of earshot. They were loyal. They would not gossip in the Spaniards Inn about the madness of their employer in talking to the trees.

You gave it to him as he swung on the gibbet. You acknowledged the evil in his soul and recognised in it the ability to roam your world unfettered and you are the only one who can take that power away.

'How?' The rain was running down his neck, soaking into his coat and his neckcloth. His hat had long ago blown away. 'Please, tell me. You have to help me!'

But there was no answer.

Ruth stopped at the end of the street, staring along it towards Number 26. Her scalp was prickling uncomfortably. The terraces of solid grey stone houses were quiet, the road as usual lined with parked cars. She resumed walking, more slowly now, on the opposite side to Number 26, surveying the house fronts. It hadn't occurred to her that Timothy might be there. There was supposed to be a police presence here, but she couldn't see any police cars and the strange uncomfortable sense of awareness at the back of her neck was growing stronger. She was moving even more slowly now, near enough to scan the house front.

Where were the police? Standing still she took in every detail. Had she left one of the upstairs windows open? Had she, for that matter, left the downstairs curtains closed?

Her gaze shifted next door to Number 24, with its brightly painted front door and the welcoming, uncurtained, downstairs window with its huge display of orchids clearly visible from the street. On impulse she crossed the road and went over to ring Sally's doorbell.

There was no reply.

77

The ghosts had followed Malcolm to London. In his hotel bedroom he was glued to the small leather-bound journal that he hadn't been able to leave behind. Reaching for a tot of whisky from the minibar, he read on.

The man was like some wild animal inside Sarah. She couldn't fight him off. His rage and vicious fury seemed to possess her utterly and all her experience, all her knowledge of the spirit world, stood her in no stead at all. On those days she would lock herself in her bedroom, her hands clenched in the covers of her bed, her teeth gritted and she would beg him to leave her alone but all he did was laugh.

He is putty in your hands, woman. Reel him in! He cannot resist the wiles of his wife. Speak in her voice and he will do everything you say.

Now his voice changed. He was persuasive, kind, whispering.

He loves you; how could he not? Make him promise. Now while he is at his lowest. He is lonely and sad without his beloved wife and his children have gone. And think how angry his family would be if you were to marry him, you, a woman from the gutter.

That made her angry. 'Gutter!' she shouted. 'I am not from the gutter. That is your place, you vile creature!'

'Mama!' She could hear Erskine outside her door, scrabbling

with the handle to get to her. Then the little fists were desperately beating on the door. 'Mama, let me in.'

Could the boy see him, this vile thing that possessed her? He was so like his father, brave, intelligent, even though the rest of the family wouldn't even recognise his existence. 'I'm coming, my darling,' she called.

Make him marry you. For the boy's sake.

'Go away!' she screamed. She stuffed the corner of the bedspread in her mouth to stop herself screaming again.

She climbed wearily from the bed. The terrifying presence had gone as abruptly as he had arrived; she sensed it instantly. Trembling, she scrabbled with the lock and pulled open the door. Erskine ran in and flung himself at her, clinging to her, crying.

She pulled him to her. 'Can you see him, my darling? The bad man who comes to Mama.' She held Erskine in front of her, forcing him to look at her. He struggled to get free.

'Answer me!' she shouted.

The little boy had huge tears running down his face. He peered round the room, still clinging to her. 'He's gone.'

'What does he look like? Tell me!' She caught him by the shoulders and shook him hard.

'Can't you see him, Mama?' He was sobbing so hard he could barely speak. 'His head is all sideways; there's a rope round his neck.'

She pushed him away, horrified. 'Jesus Christ, no!'

Erskine turned and fled out of the room and down the stairs. She could hear the patter of his little feet and he ran down and she knew where he would be going. To the kitchen where Janet, the latest of the nursery maids, would welcome him into her arms before spreading the story down the length of the narrow street.

She turned towards her dressing table and picked up her brush. She should call a maid to help her with her hair, but she didn't. She didn't want to see the look of frightened pity on the woman's face. For a moment she felt herself sinking into utter despair.

Her hair was beautiful; she was proud of it, long and thick as it was, and she knew Thomas liked it. He used to run his fingers through it, feeling the weight of it in his hands. She removed her combs and pins one by one, slowly, and pulled the brush through the heavy locks, her eyes fixed miserably on the mirror.

It was then she finally saw the man who haunted her, standing close to her shoulder, his eyes staring, his tongue protruding, his neck bent at a sharp angle by the hangman's rope that still hung there, tightly knotted around his throat.

Malcolm stopped reading, unable to get past the vivid picture of the man with his distorted neck, fully aware that it was his own mind filling in the gaps in the story; that he was seeing in his head so much more than Thomas had actually written. He felt sick, hypnotised by the immediacy of what he had visualised in that small overheated room in a terrace of newly built Regency cottages in Hornsey with Sarah, feeling her fear and her helplessness as the spirit possessed her.

He wanted to ring Ruth, to tell her what he had seen in Sarah's house, that he understood completely now how she was being swept helplessly into the story. Instead he took another sip from his glass and read on.

'You promised me!' You promised me marriage!' Sarah was clinging to the lapels of Thomas's coat. He was still weak from his illness and he hadn't the strength to pull her hands away. 'You promised to make me and your children honest!' She was crying noisily. 'How could you go back on your word? Ask her, ask your beautiful Fanny. She was here, she's here now, she's always with us, listening to your ramblings and your wrigglings. She heard you promise. She told you to do it!'

Thomas was shaking his head, trying to step back, pushing at her. 'Sarah! Stop it!' His voice at least was still strong. 'When did I promise that? I never did any such thing. You are deluded, woman!'

She stepped away abruptly and stared at him. 'Deluded!' It was a hiss.

'I cannot marry you, Sarah. You must know that. I am taking care of you, and your children—'

'Our children, Thomas! They are yours too. You cannot do this to them!' She was shouting now. She knew the servants, and probably the children too would be listening, hearing every word they yelled at each other as their voices echoed down the steep narrow stairs. 'You are a dishonourable man! Fanny is horrified that you could be so cruel. She is here, in my head,' she slapped her own cheek with the palm of her hand and suddenly her voice changed. Suddenly she was Fanny, in voice and gesture. 'Thomas! Thomas, please, don't do this to the poor woman. Your name will be vilified all over London.'

That was the word that did it. Vilified. Not a word a bonnet-maker from the back streets would use. He stood away from her and she saw the fight leak out of him as his shoulders slumped.

'Fanny!' his voice broke. 'My darling—'

Sarah snarled. 'Oh, she is your darling, but I am nothing but a drab! Not worth your concern. Not worthy of being treated with honour.'

'No, Sarah! My dear! Please, calm yourself. You don't understand. A man of my standing cannot marry just anybody. My children would be appalled. I work for the prince regent. I would have to consult him if I were to remarry. I would have to consult my advisors.'

Anything to get out of this unhappy, haunted house.

He stared round in the silence that followed his plea. He knew Farquhar was there now. He could sense him. The man had a stink about him, a vile rotting stench that clung to his spirit as it would have clung to his body when the final remnants of his dissected corpse had been consigned to the pits of night soil outside the city walls.

He realised that the little boy, his son as much as Davy or Henry were his sons, was peering in at the door, clinging to the handle with small desperate hands, and he took a deep breath. None of this was the child's fault.

Ruth looked round surreptitiously. A couple were walking along the road on the opposite pavement, and another woman with a pram was approaching her a hundred metres or so away. Everything was going on as normal yet she felt exposed, terribly vulnerable. The guys were right. She shouldn't have come out. Turning away without even trying the key in the lock she set off, walking fast, glancing back over her shoulder every few paces, down Bruntsfield Place, Lothian Road, across Princes Street with the castle at her back, and up Charlotte Street at last. Turning into Heriot Row she almost ran the last few yards, scrabbling with the lock on the street door, and hurtled up the stairs.

The men were still out. She stood looking down at the vase of lilies in the middle of Max's elegant dining table as her breath steadied. She was, she realised, near to tears. Miserably she walked back into her bedroom and automatically she reached for her files. They would distract her until Fin and Max came home.

She selected the next group of letters clipped together with a tortoiseshell loop she assumed was a Regency paper clip. They were from Davy to his sister Frances. Always Frances, who had kept everything.

The marriage would have to be secret and it would have to be swift.

Thomas pushed Sarah and her two children into a hired carriage that bore no insignia to make the journey north. There had been no time for banns, no chance of a special licence. There was only one option. Scotland. So, once again, he found himself on the road to Gretna Green.

In the corner of the coach Sarah slumped back against the cushions, her face white with exhaustion. For weeks she had been speaking in the voice of Thomas's first wife, wheedling, begging, praying and now that they were actually on their way, her own voice had deserted her. She was hoarse and exhausted and only too aware of the reluctance of the man who sat next to her as the horses galloped up the great North Road through the October gale. Their two children sat huddled on the seat opposite them, wrapped in rugs, and there were foot warmers between them on the floor, the coals glowing gently through the holes in the containers. Each time they stopped to change horses, Sarah would usher the children into the inns to relieve themselves and to buy pies and drinks; they had brought no maids. It was imperative, Thomas had said, that no word leaked out of their plans and yet Davy had found out. Davy had guessed what his father was planning and there was no doubt he would be following them, perhaps with Henry and Samuel, all insisting Thomas must not do this terrible thing.

Thomas pulled down the window and leaned out, looking behind as though he could see the dust of the following horses.

'Please, close it, Tom dear,' Sarah pleaded. 'It is so cold in here.'

It was growing dark. At the last inn they lit the carriage lamps and the horses were moving slowly now, led by a linkman who knew the road, but still pressing on as fast as was safe.

As he pulled up the window and fastened the strap that held it shut, Sarah reached out for his hand. She smiled though he couldn't see her face in the dark. 'When we're married, will we go on to visit your brother, the earl?' Her voice was husky with exhaustion but he could hear the eagerness there.

Thomas closed his eyes. 'We'll have to see,' he said after a moment. He knew it wouldn't be fair to her to expose her to David's scrutiny at Dryburgh House any more than he would demand that his older children entertain her. He would take her back to Evergreen Hill, and perhaps, though it pained him to think of her there, to his special retreat, in Sussex. She could have the trappings of being a lady and his title, and he would insist that his servants and staff treat her with respect, but he knew he would never present her to the royal family or to his friends and his heart ached for her. This was all his fault and somehow he had to make amends for allowing her to think she would fit into his world.

The coach hit a rut in the road in the dark and veered sharply, throwing them together. He reached out to put his arm around her. There would be no going back from this marriage. He hoped Fanny would realise, wherever she was, that he was doing this for her.

Things grew worse as they drew nearer to Scotland. Sarah was terrified that Davy would catch them and her fear was infectious. 'He's following us, I know it. At every inn we stop at our description will be remembered.' She clung to him, her hands cold, the shrillness of her voice waking the children from their exhausted sleep. In the end he lost patience. 'All right! Have it your way. I shall travel in disguise. Where is your hat box!' He had the coachman lift their boxes off the luggage rack and pulled box after box open there in the muddy road, helping himself at last to one of her bonnets and a heavy silk skirt. He pulled the skirt up over his trousers, and tied the bonnet firmly on his head. 'Will this do? Will this fool them?' He was furiously angry.

'Stop it! Stop being such a fool!' Sarah cried. She pulled at his sleeve.

'Reload the boxes,' Thomas snapped at the coachman and he climbed back inside, still wearing the bonnet. Sarah followed him, weeping tears of anger and embarrassment. As he sat beside her he was aware of the astonished face of his son as he awoke from his cocoon of rugs and sat up, considering his father's new attire. There was a long silence as the driver climbed back on his box and picked up whip and reins and the coach lurched into motion, then the little boy started to giggle. In seconds they were all laughing.

78

'Ruth? Wake up!'

It was Max. He began to take off his overcoat and scarf. 'Any sign of Fin?' he called over his shoulder.

'No. At least . . . ' she hesitated. 'I don't think so. I was reading.'

'So busy reading you didn't hear me shout. You didn't know where you were or who I was.'

'I was very involved in the story,' she said defensively. She avoided his intense scrutiny, looking back at the pile of letters in front of her.

'Ruthie,' Max stretched across the table and put his hand over hers, 'being involved is one thing, being obsessed is another.'

'I'm not obsessed!'

'You weren't here, Ruth. You were so engrossed the house could have burned down round you.'

'Maybe that's the way I read.'

'Then it is a dangerous way to read. I read. I become immersed in stories. Dash it, I'm an agent. Reading is my business, but not like this. You were not in your body, Ruth.'

'Are you saying you couldn't see me?'

'No, I am not saying that. Mal is the same,' Max said softly. 'He becomes wrapped up in the period he is studying to the exclusion of the world around him that it's dangerous, Ruthie.'

'In what way dangerous?'

'In case you get stuck.'

'Stuck?'

'In the past. It's like a drug, that's what he told me. You are there, you are watching it as if it's a film before your eyes. You can see it, perhaps smell it, taste it, but it doesn't touch you. You can never properly be part of it. It doesn't know you're there. It rolls on past you, leaving you lost and disorientated and unable to reconnect with the present. He said he had tried to wean himself off going too deep. For him it was the academic approach that kept him sane. He said there was nothing like statistics and political treatises to keep one on the straight and narrow. If one wanted to smell anything of the past it had to be dust, not shit or pomanders.' He gave her an apologetic smile. 'All I'm saying is, be careful.'

And so it was done. The marriage had been completed, the children were made legitimate under the law of Scotland, Sarah was his wife. When Davy arrived in a chaise and four, sweating and furiously angry after his futile chase the length of the country, it was too late. Thomas persuaded him to take a glass of wine with him and the new Lady Erskine and Davy's small half-brother and smaller half-sister and then waved his eldest son goodbye. He watched his son's chaise disappear into the distance with a heavy heart. He knew things would never again be the same between him and his older children again. Davy had told Thomas privately that Margaret was planning to move down to Sussex to live permanently with Frances and Samuel. They would not see her under Thomas's roof again.

The trip south took place more slowly and in considerably more comfort than the journey north. Sarah did her best to be charming and she was happy. She had achieved her every ambition, her children were secure and they were heading back towards Evergreen Hill where henceforth she would be the undisputed lady of the house.

It was as they pulled up under the porch and disembarked from the coach and Thomas followed Sarah into his beloved home, that he realised his troubles were only just beginning. The staff were lined up to greet them, the male servants bowing to their new mistress and the maids bobbing curtsies, none trying to hide their reserve, when Thomas raised his eyes briefly towards the great staircase that led to the upper floor of the house from the wide entrance hall and there, halfway up the first flight, crouching below the stained-glass window resplendent with Thomas's coat of arms, he saw the figure of a man. He knew his mouth had fallen open in horror. He saw some of the servants turn to see what it was he was looking at. Sarah, who had been stooping to remove little Agnes's mittens, sensed the silence and the concern and looked up.

'Oh, sweet Jesus,' she gasped.

There on the stairs was Andrew Farquhar, his twisted body hunched as he sat on a step, his eyes gleaming, his face a study in triumphant hatred. For a second no one moved or spoke, then one of the housemaids let out a long piercing scream. The sound was followed by pandemonium as half the servants made for the door that led down to the kitchens, Roberts shouting in vain for them to stand still and remember their manners. Thomas had frozen, unable to drag his gaze away from the staircase as Sarah hugged Agnes to her and wrapped her in her cloak, unable to move, overwhelmed with horror and fear.

As Thomas watched, the figure faded, then it was gone. Erskine crept towards him and clung silently to his coat. 'Has the bad man come to live here with us, Papa?' he whispered.

Thomas cleared his throat. 'Take the staff away, Roberts,' he commanded the butler. 'And see to it that the fires are lit. That was a shadow on the staircase, caused by the light coming through the window, as I think you will agree. Please see that the maid is all right, then chide her for the noise she made. She has frightened the children, to say nothing of the rest of the servants. And,' he paused for a fraction of a second, 'please have one of the footmen go to Church Row immediately and ask the parson to come here as soon as is convenient and tell Mrs Ford to send her ladyship's maids to her. She will need to change for dinner and the children must go to the nursery.'

He turned abruptly and went into the small morning room where a fire had already been lit. He always thought of this room as his own, his favourite retreat, where over the years neither Fanny nor his children had come without invitation.

Sarah followed him without hesitation and closed the door behind her. 'You are not to blame me for this. I never invited that man in.'

'Nevertheless you allowed him to follow you here.'

'I did not do it deliberately, you must realise that.' She moved closer to the fire, shivering. 'He came with your wife.'

'My wife!' Thomas turned on her furiously. 'You are my wife!'

'I meant your first wife,' she repeated sullenly. 'As you well know! He clings to her. If he has frequented me, it is because he cannot leave her alone.'

The look he gave her made her quail. 'Are you saying he has followed my beloved wife to the next world? My wife who hadn't an evil bone in her body! How is that possible? Why is he not in hell?'

'Well, he clearly isn't!' she retorted. 'He's an earthbound spirit. And if your wife,' she emphasised the word bitterly, 'is earthbound as well, that's your fault as you persist in summoning her back. Let the poor woman go and perhaps Farquhar will leave you alone.'

She turned to the door. 'I take it I'm to share the best bedroom with you? Did you give the housekeeper orders accordingly before we left for Scotland?'

She stalked out of the room. Thomas stared after her. He had not thought where she would be sleeping. The thought of her in his room, in the bed he had shared for so many years with Fanny, filled him with something like revulsion.

Within two hours he had bidden Benjamin to pack a fresh valise and while he was away to move all his things into his dressing room and he had left a note for Sarah as he called for his formal carriage, the one with his coat of arms on the doors. 'I am commanded to Carlton House. I will return as soon as I can. Your humble and obedient servant, TE.' He did not bother to say farewell.

When the parson arrived there was no one to greet him. He stood in the hall, his hat in his hand, staring round as the footman waited patiently by the open front door. He could feel it, the restless, angry spirit wandering the house and he murmured a prayer, wondering if the occupants of this beautiful place were aware of it, and whether this was the reason for his sudden summons. All he could do was pray for these parishioners as he prayed for them all and take his leave. As he walked back under the lofty porte cochère he thought he heard the sound of demonic laughter behind him and he fervently wished the Anglican church provided him with a sacrament of exorcism.

Max's warning had no effect. As soon as she had wished him and Fin goodnight and slipped back into her bedroom Ruth reached for the letters again. She read on for a while, half listening to the muted conversation coming from the drawing room next door. She wasn't aware she had fallen asleep. The story continued in her dreams.

Writing, always writing, as though by clutching the pen in his hand he could keep the ghosts at bay. Thomas had taken his notes and files with him to Buchan Hill. Ruth had noted the different addresses at the top of the letters. It seemed he could write there in peace, assiduously keeping his journal and walking with his dogs the wild acres of the Sussex Weald that he called his own. His purchase of this land might have proved a disaster commercially, the soil too arid and barren ever to make money, or so his advisors told him now it was too late, leaving him as the somewhat perplexed owner of a broom-making business, but the acres were peaceful and lovely and his nemeses did not follow him there; Sarah did not care for the country and Farquhar had never shown himself in Sussex.

He found himself wondering whether the presence of his precious fetish doll only a few miles away at Poynings with Frances extended its protection this far. He had no way of knowing if she had even kept the thing and he could not ask her, but he liked to picture a golden net of peace and safety thrown across the county from end to end. Certainly the very air itself, so fresh and pure compared to the stinking smoky miasmas of London, was a blessing and a comfort, better even than the wind-swept heights of Hampstead, and he loved to think about the dragons that his steward had told him had once lived here, in St Leonard's Forest. If any still lurked in a little glen or down a winding path amongst the gorse and heather and birch trees, they would be, perhaps, an added protection.

As summer leached into autumn he had begun working on what he considered would be one of his most important speeches in the Lords for a long time, a defence of Queen Caroline against accusations of adultery by her husband the king. Since his friend and patron the prince regent had become king the man had been very ill, but he was well enough to make it clear to Thomas if he defended his wife they could no longer be friends.

Yet again, Thomas's conscience could not allow him to give up on the case. The woman was undoubtedly as guilty as sin, but she deserved the best defence and that was him. London was as always a ferment of excitement and disorder, concentrating its restless and often violent displeasure against its rulers by avidly supporting Caroline against the king's demand for an annulment of their marriage.

It was as he sat by the fire, the pile of notes about the queen on his knee, a glass of port in his hand, that the idea came to Thomas. He was here alone in the country because he and Sarah did not get on. Never had. Never would. He pushed the king's papers onto the floor and leaned back in his chair taking another sip from his glass. Divorce. He could not seek annulment, not with two children, but surely he of all people, with his experience of the law, could find a way of obtaining a divorce.

79

Mal caught the early train home. Ensconced in his window seat, a cup of coffee on the table in front of him, his briefcase on the seat beside him, he was engrossed in one of his favourite history books, reminding himself about the intricacies, complexities and sheer bloody excitements of Georgian London as the train thundered north. By the time they pulled into Waverley station he had slipped seamlessly back into Thomas's world.

The mutual infidelities and scandals surrounding the marriage of the prince regent and Princess Caroline had culminated in her leaving the country for a riotous life abroad, but on his ascent to the throne at last as King George IV, she returned to claim her place at his side as queen. The move was wildly popular with Londoners but appalled George. It was at that point that he decided that the only course of action open to him was divorce. Battle lines were drawn. The king was as dissolute and extravagant as she was and widely disliked in the country. The whole nation was engaged. The divorce proceedings went as far as a bill in the House of Commons, but in the Lords it was a different matter. There, opposition to the king's wishes became more and more entrenched.

In the end there would be no divorce, not for Caroline, but not for Thomas either. Thomas was sitting in his morning room back in Hampstead while a footman poured coffee from the elegant silver pot on the tray. He was enjoying the warmth of the sun streaming through the window. London was delirious with excitement, and Thomas, one of the architects of Caroline's triumph after the eleven-week hearing in the House of Lords, found himself one of the most popular men in town. Much to the king's disgust, he had as usual taken the role his conscience dictated and he found himself grievously offending his one-time friend, the king, but a hero of the hour. They were selling little copies of a marble bust of him all over London and he was told it was as though every house in the land had one on its mantel-piece. Only yesterday, much to his alarm, the cheering mob had brought his coach to a halt, unharnessed his horses and insisted on dragging the coach themselves all the way to the House of Lords.

'Congratulations, my lord.' Even the footman was smiling. 'A glorious victory for Her Majesty, if I may say so.'

Thomas's pleasure in the moment was short-lived as Sarah appeared in the doorway, her face like thunder as she commanded the footman to leave and close the door behind him.

Thomas looked up, his heart sinking. Sarah had a sheet of paper in her hand and was waving it at him. 'So, you thought you could cast me off! So pleased with yourself now, you thought you would take the chance to get rid of me!'

'What is that, dear?' He knew very well what it was. It was one of the notes he had so carefully penned to draw up his own plea. He sighed. There was no point in pretending. 'Where did you get that? Those papers are private. The matter of the king's affairs is of the utmost confidentiality.'

'The king?' she shouted. 'This is nothing to do with the king! This is about you. Look! You, you, you! You plan to divorce me!'

He sighed. 'And can you blame me, shrew that you are. I want no more of this, Sarah. Listen to yourself.'

There was a long silence. He stood up warily as he watched her face, seeing it darken, working with fury. For an instant he wondered with a pang of disgust if Farquhar was going to speak through her, but when she opened her mouth the voice was gentle, kind. 'Darling Tom,' it was Fanny's voice. 'Don't be so silly. You know you love Sarah. What would we do without her?'

'No!' he shouted. 'This is nonsense. You are not Fanny! This is all make-believe! Get out!' He pointed at the door. 'Leave me alone. I cannot stand this another moment! Roberts!' He shouted for his butler. 'Roberts!'

There was a roaring in his ears. He was dimly aware of Sarah running from the room sobbing loudly, of the butler appearing at the door, his face a picture of anxiety, then everything went black.

When he woke at last, Frances and Samuel were there, and his son, Davy. He was dimly aware of them in his darkened bedroom. Samuel had prescribed more laudanum and a warm fire and rest. There was no sign of Sarah.

It was several days before he was well enough to get up. Restored by nourishing soups and peace and quiet Thomas was sitting by the fire in his bedroom, wrapped in a dressing gown, his feet on a stool. 'Sam?' He indicated that his son-in-law should sit down opposite him. 'Tell me what happened. Am I dying?'

Sam laughed. 'No, you're not dying. You are well on the mend.'

'I had a seizure like this before when I was speaking in the Lords.' It had terrified him at the time, and those around him. They had suspended the sitting.

'You were suffering from exhaustion, then and now,' Sam said slowly. He scanned his father-in-law's face. 'You have been under terrible strain.'

'Where is Sarah?'

'She has returned to her house with the children for now. We deemed it better. They were too noisy to be here with someone who was so ill.'

He smiled sadly. 'Noisy? Agnes and Erskine? Poor little mites, they are too frightened ever to be noisy.' He saw Sam's lips tighten with disapproval.

'They will be well looked after,' Sam persisted. 'Their

nursemaids and the cook we found are answerable to, and paid by Davy. The children will want for nothing.' He stood up. 'Frances wants to speak to you. Do you feel strong enough to see her?'

Thomas grinned. 'Will I need strength? Is she very angry with me?'

Sam laughed. 'All she wants is your welfare and happiness,' he said.

Frances bent to kiss him on the forehead. 'You gave us such a fright, Papa. When Davy sent for us to come we thought you would have breathed your last by the time we got here.'

She was still neat and slim and pretty, this eldest daughter of his, for all her children, so like her mother it hurt to look at her. He reached out for her hand. 'My darling, I have caused you all so much worry.'

'Indeed you have.' Her voice was brisk. 'Papa,' for the first time she hesitated. 'Davy and Henry and Thomas and Sam and I have been talking about what to do for the best.' She paused, waiting for him to say something. When he remained silent, she went on. 'We feel it right that you and Sarah live apart for a while. She clearly upsets you.' Again she hesitated, waiting for him to object. 'There is something in this house when she is here,' she shivered. 'We can all feel it.' Again a pause, then she took a deep breath. 'You mentioned to Davy that you could no longer afford to live here, Papa. It is a large house and expensive to run. It is time to give it up. We have all been so happy here. With Mama here, our childhood was idyllic. You made us so happy . . . ' She slipped off her chair and knelt before him, taking his hands in her own as tears began to roll down his cheeks. 'It's not a happy place any more. Would you not wish to remember it as it was?'

He sighed. They were right. About Sarah, and the children, and about the house. Sarah had spoiled it for him. And the money. They were right about the money too. 'I have investments,' he said at last.

'No, Papa. Your investments have gone. You remember? At Davy's suggestion, you invested in securities in America, but they were not sold in time, and with the war they disappeared.

And Buchan Hill, beautiful as it is, is worth nothing as an agri-cultural estate. Birch brooms will not make your fortune.' She smiled, teasing. 'You have to live on your income now.'

'Which is far from inconsiderable.'

'For most people, yes.' She smiled fondly. 'But your way of life is extravagant, Papa. You entertain princes and politicians and poets and playwrights, you hold court here; and that is as it should be, you are a great man, but you can no longer afford this place, nor the house in Lincoln's Inn.' Her voice was firm and he was reminded so strongly of her mother he almost wept out loud.

'You will not take Buchan Hill from me,' he said, determined to win that point at least.

'No, Papa, no one will take Buchan Hill, with its legends and its dragons.' He had told her children the stories. 'We know how much you love it. Besides, no one in their right mind would buy it!' Again the spark she had inherited from her mother. 'You will still have your beautiful little house in Arabella Row which is so close to the heart of things, to the House of Lords, to Carlton House and to Buckingham House, and from there you can visit Sarah and the children whenever you want to. You know this is for the best.'

'The king will longer speak to me, since I defended Caroline.' He was wistful.

'He will. He is too fond of you to give up your friendship.' She scrambled back to her feet. 'Papa, I have something for you.' She had had a reticule hanging from her wrist when she came in, and she turned to pick it up off the chair. 'You gave me this when I married, to keep me safe.' She handed him the bag. 'I want you to have it back. I know it is powerful and I know what it does.' She hesitated with a half glance over her shoulder towards the door. 'I have never told Samuel. He would not have approved. I have him to keep me safe now, and I want you to have it back. There is something evil here in this house, something that came with Sarah, and it's wearing you down. You need this more than I do.' She bent and kissed him again.

He sat without moving for a long time after she had left the room, the bag lying on his knee. He knew what was in it without having to look. He could feel its magic, its power and its strength spreading slowly out around him. He rested his hand over it and smiled. Andrew Farquhar would not come back to this house. Future generations who lived there, whoever they were, would not be bothered by his malicious presence. He felt it as a certainty.

As Mal turned up the drive he was stopped by a police car parked diagonally in front of him. For a moment he was paralysed with fear. Had something happened to Ruth? But the young policeman on duty reassured him. 'It was thought best she go and stay with friends, sir. Bradford was here yesterday, ringing the doorbell.'

Mal and Ruth spoke on the phone for twenty minutes. 'You must be exhausted,' she said. 'You don't want to drive all the way back to Edinburgh to fetch me tonight. It's my fault. I didn't tell you I was here because I didn't want to worry you. Come tomorrow.'

The house was empty without her. He had collected the dogs on his way home and he could tell they were missing her too. Pol came and sat at his feet, his huge spaniel eyes full of reproach. He took the hint. Locking the door behind him he set off to walk to the chapel. In his head he was still in the nineteenth century and Thomas too had headed north to Edinburgh once more.

Thomas found it strange to be back in Edinburgh without his mother or Harry there. The invitation had come, not from a member of the family but from the city corporation. They planned to give a dinner on 21 February in his honour. Everyone who was anyone was coming; even his brother, the earl, had accepted an invitation.

He allowed himself time to see his nephews and nieces, Harry's children and, much as he enjoyed being feted as a hero of Scotland, managing to escape his hosts and their overwhelming attentions he allowed himself one afternoon to wander incognito through the old town of his childhood.

It was snowing and a bitter wind blew down the High Street, but undaunted he walked alone down towards the old palace of Holyrood, to the now-ruined abbey where his parents were buried, then up past the entry to Gray's Close where he had been born, and on towards St Giles' kirk where as a wee boy he had seen the ghost of a murdered man rise from his body. He remembered the incident as though it were yesterday. Standing there in the street, the snow drifting down, clinging to his greatcoat, he shivered violently.

'My lord?' A man had stopped beside him, elderly, swathed in a rough coat and scarves. 'Do you remember me?'

A swirl of snow surrounded Thomas and he pulled his collar up around his ears. He had assumed no one would recognise him without his entourage.

Studying the old man's face he felt a stirring of memory. 'Forgive me . . . ?'

'I worked for your father when he lived here. When he left, his steward failed to pay me what was owed. I asked your brother, the earl, but he said he would not pay his father's debts.' Again a flurry of snow blew down the street. There was no one about, no sound but the howl of the wind in the high tenement roofs, the eerie squeak of an inn sign swinging back and forth over the deserted thoroughfare. 'I was his butler. I knew you to be an honourable man. I knew you would pay.'

Thomas took a step forward, but the man had gone, hidden in the whirling snow. He shivered, feeling the familiar prickle at the back of his neck. If the man had worked for his father that would have been long ago, when he himself was a boy. The name was coming to him. John Barnett. He had been kind to the little boy then. He and his wife had lived near the book-shop close to the university and had welcomed Thomas in to browse amongst the shelves.

Almost without meaning to he turned and began to walk back down over the slippery cobbles, skirting piles of rubbish and broken slates that had come off the roofs in the wind, following his memory, unable to leave without finding out if anyone remembered John Barnett and his family.

The bookshop was still there. He did not expect to find the man's wife still alive, the old lady huddled over a brazier of coals in a small ground-floor flat at the end of a dark close, cared for by her son's family. She remembered the incident, remembered to the last bawbee the sum owed and Thomas dug in his pockets to find the money, appalled that such a small amount had meant so much to them. As he pressed his purse into the old lady's hand and received her strangely dignified thanks he felt humble. 'How did you know?' She looked up at him, her eyes milky with age, glistening with tears in the light of the tallow candle that stood at her elbow. He smiled gently. He could never tell her he had seen her husband's ghost. As he turned away and walked back into the street he felt sharply the ironies of parting with a purse full of coins to that family, to whom the debt had meant so much, while he was on his way to a banquet which would cost thousands.

He attended plays and concerts while he was in Edinburgh, dinners and parties, he planned to travel more widely as the spring approached, to reclaim the childhood so abruptly cut off by the family's flit to St Andrews, but far too soon he was summoned back to London to attend a banquet being held to celebrate Queen Caroline's victory, his victory, if he was given his due, against the king. 'I will come back to Scotland,' he whispered to his younger self. 'I will come back and we will visit Mama's cave at St Andrews, and we will row again across the loch to Inchmahome, and we will ride in the Pentland Hills and sail on the Forth to the Bass Rock to see the whirling birds as they fight over the ledges on the cliffs.'

In truth, he dreaded returning south. In London he had to face two insuperable sources of torment. Sarah and Andrew Farquhar.

80

It was good to be outside again. Even two days in London was too long! The dogs ran ahead of Malcolm up the path through the trees, barking with excitement, and he found his heart was lifting as his optimism came back. When the dogs reappeared from the trees and returned to his side, quiet and watchful, their exuberance gone, he felt a lurch of anxiety. They were near the chapel now, on the narrow track that wound up through the larches.

At first he didn't see anything wrong; it looked much as usual. But he could feel it. The energies of the glade were jagged, the birds were silent, not even the harsh call of a pheasant ringing across the hillside. He moved closer. The dogs hung back. He could see now that the door was open a few inches and with a feeling of deep foreboding he looked inside. The place had been trashed, the little table and chairs overturned and broken, the candles and crystals gone, the little statue of the Mother and Child broken into a dozen pieces. Whoever had done this had tried to set fire to the place, piling bits of broken chair and handfuls of dried leaves in the centre of the floor. They had flared and charred and then the flames had died. As a final insult the whole place stank of urine.

Stooping to pick up a small quartz crystal that had rolled

near the door Malcolm slipped it into his pocket, turned and walked outside again. He took a deep breath and almost blindly made his way over to the ancient oak tree that overlooked the glade. Ever since he was a boy he had regarded this old tree as his friend and advisor and he leaned against the trunk now, trying to draw strength from it. 'Who did this?' he asked the tree but he already knew. It was Timothy.

'You will not, cannot divorce me!' Sarah was backed against the wall in her small sitting room, her fists clenched. 'To divorce requires an act of parliament and you will not get it!'

He gave a grim smile. 'You do not have to teach me the law, madam!'

'You want to make my children illegitimate!'

'I do not want to make *my* children illegitimate!' he repeated, emphasising the word, 'and I would not do so. Besides, divorce does not result in illegitimacy.' He sighed. 'There are other ways to solve our problems. I will seek a legal separation. You will be looked after as you are now, with your own house and sufficient money for your needs and for the children's. You will want for nothing, Sarah. You will keep your title.'

'What use is a title when your friends do not recognise me? When I am shunned and belittled and mocked.'

'We are both mocked, as is everyone regarded as newsworthy,' he said, more gently now. He recognised her loneliness. Her own family kept their distance from her as far as he knew, and his acted as though she didn't exist. He sighed. 'Sarah, you must realise that you can make this so much easier for yourself. People do not like a shrew.'

He wished he could take back the word as soon as it left his mouth as he saw the shock and genuine hurt in her eyes. Surely she realised how unpleasant she was to people; she must understand why her servants never stayed, why she had no friends of her own. He moved towards her and held out his hand. 'My dear, between us we can sort this out.'

With a sob she threw herself into his arms; he stepped back, but she was clinging to him and he didn't have the heart to push her away. 'It will be all right, Sarah.'

'Why?' she looked up at him, and her eyes had changed. They were Fanny's eyes. 'Why don't you love me any more? Why have you forgotten me?' Her voice had softened, it was pleading, it was Fanny's voice. He fell his heart lurch. He reached up without being aware of doing it, to pull off her pretty lace cap, and as her hair tumbled free he could smell the hair dressing that Fanny used, the aroma of sandalwood and orange and musk. The soft lips that reached up to his were Fanny's lips and the hand that took his, and led him towards the staircase, was Fanny's hand.

When he woke he was lying alone on Sarah's bed. He closed his eyes again with a groan. What had he done? 'Fanny, my darling, forgive me,' he murmured out loud; all he could hear were the rattle of wheels and the sound of horses' hooves on the cobbles outside the window. The room was growing dark. In the distance the night watch called the hour and closer, downstairs, he heard Erskine's voice as he shouted at his sister who was crying.

Wearily adjusting his clothing he went downstairs. Candles and a fire had been lit in the sitting room but there was no sign of Sarah. He didn't bother to call the servant. Letting himself out of the front door he beckoned his coach forward and climbed in. When he reached his house in Arabella Row he called for hot water for a bath and the brandy decanter and drank himself almost insensible as he sat there, barely noticing when Benjamin called a footman to help him heave his master up out of the water, swathed him in towels and guided him to bed. He fell asleep wondering how long it would be before he heard Andrew Farquhar's spiteful laughter.

It was already growing dark when Mal turned and made his way back towards home, leaving the door of the chapel wedged wide to let in the cleansing moonlight and the wind and the rain. He already knew he would pull the place down; the gods and creatures of the woods and mountains would take it back for themselves.

Locking himself into the house he picked up his mobile and pressed Ruth's number. He discovered his hands were shaking.

'Ruth? I have to talk to you. Are Max and Fin with you? Listen. You need to be careful. The police still haven't found Timothy. Apparently they were here all day yesterday. They had a helicopter up looking for him in the hills. I've just been out with the dogs, up to the chapel and he'd been in there. He's wrecked the place. Desecrated it.'

'Oh no! Mal. I'm so sorry.'

They talked for half an hour, then Malcolm went up to his study, staring down bleakly at his desk. Two more of Thomas's notebooks lay there; they had obviously been supplied to him by a bookseller in the Strand. Mal noted the printed insignia on the back of the flimsy leather covers. Sitting down he opened one. There was no date, it merely said Thursday at the top of the entry, and Thomas launched into his narrative, his writing cramped and hasty, his anguish almost tangibly pouring off the page.

'I am with child!'

Sarah, swathed in silks and with a new hat, aswirl with egret feathers, stood in the middle of his drawing room in Arabella Row, smiling triumphantly.

'If you are, someone else is the father!' His shock and disgust were palpable.

'You know that's not true.' She was so confident now, this woman. 'My servants will swear that you have visited me and they will swear they saw you in my bed.' Her smile was heavy with sickly charm. 'I have the date exactly when you came to me. The child will be born at Christmas.' She waited to see what else he was going to say and when he said nothing she turned and sailed out of the room. He heard her shout abuse at the footman when he was slow to open the front door and he heard her call someone else, presumably a maid, as the sharp click of her heels died away. Then the door closed. The house fell silent. He tensed. There was something there, something that had entered the room with Sarah and that had remained when she had gone.

He walked over to his desk and, stooping, pulled open the bottom drawer. There, in a box, still in its woven bag was the doll that had the power to keep him and his family safe. He picked it up wearily and carried it with him to his chair. Whatever else its powers, it had no magic that would save him from Sarah, but surely it could hold Farquhar at bay. Opening the drawstring that held the bag closed he looked inside. The small figure looked dusty and forlorn and it smelled faintly of nutmeg and cinnamon. The stones that made its eyes were dull.

Malcolm looked up from the journal. A doll. Thomas referred to the fetish as a doll. Well, perhaps it was. It had legs and arms, well one arm, of sorts, and a head and eyes and perhaps two hundred years ago it looked more like a natural figure.

He felt vaguely guilty about doing it, invading her privacy even more than he had already, but he couldn't resist. Taking the stone steps two at a time, round and round up the spiral, he went into Ruth's room, both dogs following. There was no sign anywhere of the doll. He sighed with relief. She was not likely to have forgotten to take it with her. Even if he wasn't there to keep her safe, the fetish would watch over her.

Timothy had slept deeply and it was late afternoon when he finally went downstairs. The house felt very empty. There was still no sign of April. Suddenly suspicious, he turned and ran back up the stairs two at a time and pushed open her bedroom door. Her stuff had gone. He went over and opened the cupboard. It was empty.

He didn't see the upturned corner of carpet until he had tripped over it and almost fallen. With a yell of fright, he recovered his balance and stood looking down at the floorboards under it. One of them was slightly raised and, dropping on his knees, he ran his fingers over it. He scrabbled round the edge of it, tearing his nails as he did so. However hard he tried, he couldn't quite get enough purchase to lift it and with an exclamation of impatience he went downstairs to the kitchen and rummaged through the drawers until he found a sturdy carving knife. It took several seconds of violent waggling to loosen the board and lever it up an inch or so, then wrench it up so violently it snapped it with a loud splintering sound to reveal a dusty space between the joists. He sat back staring down. This was where she had been keeping her stash of money. If it hadn't been for the carpet he would never have spotted it. He backed away to sit down on the edge of the bed and stared at the empty space for several minutes. The mix of frustration, fury and the sense of abandonment that possessed him as he realised what had happened left him incapable of thought.

When at last he went back downstairs he crept automatically into the front room to peer through the curtains. He couldn't see a police car anywhere. Turning back into the kitchen he slumped down at the table, his head in his hands, as the room grew darker around him.

Time to go out soon, Timo!

It was a whisper, a faint hiss in his ears.

Come on. We need some excitement. Who needs April anyway?

Samuel leaned forward to ask the coachman to stop. 'I am going to drop you off at your father's, then I will go on to see his wife,' he said to Frances. 'I don't think it right that you accompany me there.'

She looked back at him, her face pained. 'I'm coming with you, Sam,' she said firmly. 'The law has decreed that she's his legal wife, and that they must stay married, even if separated, so it is right that I as his daughter recognise her as such. You will give her the consolation of the church; I will offer her friendship. We both know neither Davy nor Henry or Thomas will do anything for her, and Margaret has made it clear she will not stay under the same roof. You and I live far away. It is the least I can do to call in just this once.'

'Your father will be furious with you.' He knew better than to argue.

She smiled sweetly. 'My father will not know, at least not from me. If she chooses to tell him, that is her prerogative.' Her hand strayed to her throat where the golden cross Sam had given her on their wedding anniversary nestled against her skin.

Sarah kept them waiting ten minutes after they were shown into her sitting room. When she swept in to greet them she was dressed in an extravagant gown of cerise silk. It was obvious at once from the flow of the lightweight fabric that she was pregnant. Horrified, Frances glanced at her husband; Sam refused to meet her eye.

'How kind of you to find the time in your busy schedule to call on your stepmother,' Sarah said. She seated herself by the fire before asking Frances to sit down. She ignored Samuel and he was forced to collect a chair for himself from where it stood by the table.

'We wanted to see how you were,' Frances said politely. The woman was younger than herself by a good ten years. 'And see how the children are. May we see them?'

'Why?' Sarah's voice was sharp. 'None of the family have shown any interest in their welfare so far.'

'And for that I'm sorry,' Frances went on. 'Can we make up for that now? I have brought some little gifts for them.'

'We don't need your gifts,' Sarah snapped. 'Your father gives us everything we need, as is his legal duty.'

She seated herself more comfortably, one hand on her stomach, then she raised her head to gaze at Frances. 'In some ways you are very like your mother,' she said at last. 'You have her eyes.' Noting with satisfaction the look of shock and distaste that fleetingly crossed Frances's face, Sarah leaned forward to the side table and reached for a small hand bell. 'Will you take tea? Now that you're here, I don't want to fail in my attempts to behave like a lady.' The sarcasm of the remark left Frances speechless. This time her helpless glance towards her husband was answered. He sat forward.

'My mother-in-law was a lovely, gentle soul, you must agree.'

'Indeed,' Sarah retorted. The door opened and she ordered the tea. 'Thomas has told you how I came to meet him, I presume?'

'We never discuss it,' Frances managed to reply.

'Fanny introduced us. It was her need to go on speaking to him that led to our first encounter. It was your eldest brother's wife who arranged the meeting; the American woman. She came to a séance where I was communicating with those who have departed and your mother spoke to her begging to speak to Thomas. He came the moment he heard about me.' She smiled complacently. 'So you see, it was your mother who introduced your father to me. I thought you knew.' There was a long pause as the housemaid and a manservant came in with the tea trays. They set up a table, laid out the cups and saucers and produced a cake which the maid cut into the neat slices, after which with a curtsy and a quick, curious glance at the visitors, she left the room with her companion. Sarah smiled and now her eyes were Fanny's eyes and her voice was Fanny's voice. 'Perhaps you would pour out, my dear,' she spoke gently to Frances, 'as you see it is difficult for me to do so in my condition.'

Frances let out a whimper of misery. 'Mama?' she whispered.

'Enough!' Samuel stood up. 'You call yourself a medium, I presume, madam?' His voice was frosty.

'I presume I do.'

He took a deep breath. 'I fear the church does not approve of attempts to contact the dead.'

'How sad. I fear I don't care what the church thinks.' She gave him an insincere smile. Her voice was her own again. 'I don't *attempt* to contact her, I succeed with ease. I speak for Fanny whenever Thomas asks me.'

'Dear God!' Frances stood up so abruptly she almost knocked the table over and slopped the tea over the lace cloth. 'You pretend to be my mother! That's how you lured Papa into your clutches?'

'I pretend nothing.' Sarah was still complacent, then she gave a gasp and clutched her stomach.

'What is it?' Frances was gazing at her in horror. 'Is it the baby?'

'No.' Sarah's voice was deeper now, coarser, her face twisted, her eyes narrow slits. 'No, it's not the baby. I met you when you were a child, Frances. Have you forgotten?' The voice grew louder and more alien.

'Sam!' Frances clutched at her husband's arm. He was standing, looking down at Sarah in horror. 'What's happening? What's wrong with her?'

'She's possessed,' he cried desperately. 'In the name of our Blessed Lord, Jesus Christ, leave this woman!' he shouted. 'This cannot be happening! Sarah, Sarah, fight him!'

'She can't fight me, no one can.' The voice coming from Sarah's mouth was a man's, and obviously amused. 'Look at her, she's helpless. Foolish woman.' Sarah did indeed seem almost unconscious. Her eyes had rolled up in her head and she was lying back in the chair, her arms hanging limply at her sides.

Samuel glanced at Frances. 'Get out. Get out of here. Now. Please, my darling, leave this to me.'

Frances didn't argue. She ran for the door, pulled it open and fled into the hall. A manservant was lighting a lamp on the table by the front door. 'Let me out!' Frances cried. 'I have to find our carriage!'

He reached for her coat and somewhat unceremoniously draped it over her shoulders before opening the door, preceding her out onto the pavement and waving forward the coach that had been waiting in a side mews. 'Don't be afraid,' he murmured as he handed Frances in. 'This happens quite often. She'll be herself again soon.'

'You heard?' She turned and stared at him. 'You know she does that and you still work in that house?'

He nodded. 'Most of the servants leave at once, but someone has to stay there for her little ones. Cook and I stay. Lord Erskine pays us well.' He pushed the door closed. 'You wait there, ma'am, and I'll fetch your husband.'

She sat back on the seat, huddled in her coat, amazed to find she was actually shaking. It was several minutes before she noticed the denser patch of shadow on the seat in the opposite corner and heard the quiet sound of mocking laughter.

Caddy found her vinaigrette and waved it under Frances's nose then called for brandy and sal volatile, then as Davy took Sam out into the garden of their house for a serious talk, she drew her sister-in-law to the sofa.

'Tell me what happened.'

Frances took a deep breath. She was not proud of herself. She was not a woman to resort to the vapours. Standing up, she went over to the door to make sure it was shut. 'Sam and I went to see Papa's wife.' She steadied her voice with an effort then she related what had happened.

'Oh my!' Caddy was appalled. 'I felt so guilty about the way that woman attached herself to your father. When he took up with her we were as shocked as you were. We never ever expected him to marry her. I promised myself I would never tell anyone how he met her. It seemed so shocking.'

'She forced him.'

'Honey, your papa is a strong man, a clever man—'

'Not when it comes to Mama. He loved her to distraction. If he thought he could contact her, speak to her again he would do anything to have her back. I heard her. I heard Mama's voice coming out of that woman's mouth. And someone else's.' She drew in another quavering breath, clutching at her cross. 'A man's voice. She seemed really frightened. Sam tried to bless her, to chase away the demon but it, he, followed me out to the carriage.'

There was a long silence as Caddy stared at her, speechless.

'I didn't imagine him. The carriage was so cold. I could smell him, the stink of him clung to upholstery. He was only there for a few seconds. He disappeared when Sam arrived. Our coachman saw nothing. He said it was a shadow from the carriage lamp.'

Caddy reached for the brandy glass and pressed it into Frances's hands again. 'Have another sip, honey. At least you have Sam to deal with this now. He's a man of the church. He will know what to do. He and Davy between them will come up with a plan.'

81

Ruth sat looking down at the letter before her. The letters were blurred, swimming before her eyes. The cross. The gold cross. Was that the same cross she was wearing now? Her fingers strayed towards it. She had left it on, taking comfort from it, illogically, knowing it had been her mother's. She could make sure, she could date it from the hallmark, but somehow that didn't seem important now; she knew in some inner part of herself that it had been Frances's cross and as such it had been there in the sitting room with Sarah, in the carriage with the ghost of Andrew Farquhar, in the presence of her father, in all the places Frances had been and it had kept her safe.

Timothy found a bowl in the cupboard then a whisk, then as he reached for the eggs he heard the doorbell ring. He froze. He turned off the light, holding his breath.

'Ruth? Are you there?' A woman's voice echoed through the house. She must have put her mouth close to the letter box. 'Ruth?'

He waited by the kitchen door without moving.

She didn't call again and after a full five minutes he tiptoed out into the hallway and crept into the front room, peering through the gap in the curtains. The street light outside threw a cold light over the doorstep. There was no one there. He guessed it had been the nosy neighbour from next door.

Walking back into the kitchen he shut the door firmly and went over to the small TV which sat on the worktop. He turned it on quietly and began to break the eggs one by one into the bowl.

Thomas sat for a long time by the dying embers of the fire after his son and son-in-law had left. He had sent the servants to bed knowing he would not sleep that night. It was in the early hours he got up wearily to reach for the tongs and feed lumps of coal onto the fire, poking it back into life. He knew what he had to do. He turned to his desk and pulled open the bottom drawer.

Sitting down again, the bag on his knee, he waited a few more minutes then slowly he pulled the drawstrings open and took out the doll. It had changed. Somehow it looked less shabby, less dusty and its eyes had grown bright. 'So, you know we need you, little one,' he murmured. 'Tomorrow, I'm going to take you back to Frances. I want you to keep her safe. Frances and her children and her children's children.' He laid his hand gently on the doll, with a glance at the two dogs lying by the fire. Neither had stirred.

Caddy led Thomas into her morning room. He had missed Frances by three hours. 'They didn't feel there was anything else they could do here. Papa,' she hesitated, suddenly embarrassed, 'I'm so sorry. I've caused so much trouble in the family.'

'You've done no such thing.' He looked at her sternly. 'I presume you mean by indirectly introducing me to Sarah? None of this is your fault. Sarah is genuine. She's not to blame, nor are you, nor is Margaret for passing on your message. If anyone has proved ill-advised in this whole sorry business it's me, and it's for me to sort it out. And as for the evil spirit that is or was Andrew Farquhar, Sarah isn't strong enough to fight it on her own. That's for me to do. All I can do now is try and deflect it from Frances.'

'Can Sam and Henry not have him exorcised?'

He smiled at her use of the word, reminding himself that

Caddy had believed enough in all this to go to that fateful séance in the first place. 'Sam and Henry, as men of the cloth, have learned their religious sensitivities from the Bible, and they can pray, but neither of them "see" other worlds. Frances alone has inherited that ability of all my sons and daughters. It gives her special insights as it does me, but it also makes her especially vulnerable. It brings pain and terrifying experiences.'

'And prayer is not enough to keep you both safe?' Caddy was shocked.

He shook his head slowly. 'No. And that is the fault of the man and not the prayers. I have always been a bit of a rebel as far as the kirk was concerned, and my conversion to the Church of England was required by my position in society. That does not suit me either.'

He did not mention that he put his faith in a small doll made of straw and beads, given him by a woman whose skin was black and whose heart was gold, or that the only person apart from her to understand his gifts and curse had been his family's sennachie, a man with the second sight himself and the knowledge of generations of men and women with the same gift from the secret places of his native land, a man who had been dead now for years.

He arrived at Poynings by dusk in a phaeton driven by the son of a friend who was not afraid to let his horses gallop. By a stroke of luck Samuel was out amongst his parishioners and he was able to speak to Frances alone.

'You have to keep it,' he said. 'For the rest of your life. Promise me.' He pressed the bag into her hands.

They were in the low-ceilinged parlour of the old parsonage, warmed by a log fire. Frances had asked her cook to make hot chocolate for them both.

'You think I've brought Farquhar with me?' she asked. She looked unutterably weary.

'I am afraid that's possible. He seems to cling to people with tentacles that are hard to dislodge.'

She shuddered. Opening the bag, she brought out the doll. 'The woman who gave you this conferred an enormous blessing. She meant it for you.'

'And my children.'

'What about the others?' She held his gaze.

'You are the only one who has inherited the sight. That is a gift, but . . . ' He did not finish the sentence.

She nodded. 'My little Mary Ann has it too. She's the only one of mine.'

'Then she too will need this one day.' He nodded at the doll.

'She shall have it.' She smiled.

He stayed the night with them and the next day Samuel offered to drive him back to Buchan Hill.

It was as they were bidding one another farewell under the ancient oak tree outside Thomas's newly built house that Sam held out a small package. 'Frances asked me to give you this.'

Thomas waited until Samuel was out of sight then he walked over to the bench he had had set against the south-facing wall of the house and sitting down in the last rays of the warm autumn sunlight he opened the packet. He read the letter first.

Papa. I was looking at the doll last night and her right arm came off in my hand. I did nothing to pull it off, I promise. The doll meant it to be given to you, her blessing and gift of safety. Keep it close; never part with it and I will keep the rest. Your loving daughter, F.

He unfolded the scrap of silk that wrapped the detached limb. There was no way of telling what it was supposed to be. A few twigs, a few strands of thread, some dried berries, so old now, they looked like little black beads. He smiled and dropped a kiss on the scrap then carefully rewrapped it. The silk came, he noticed, from an old torn handkerchief. He saw the ornate initial F embroidered in the corner and for a moment he wondered if it had belonged to Fanny. He kissed the bundle again and tucked it into his pocket.

'This must be some story Ruth and Mal are reading.' Max was in the kitchen as Fin walked in. 'I hope Ruth lets me represent her if she ever wants to publish.' Judging from the bag in Fin's hand he had been shopping at the deli in Leith Walk again.

Ruth had barely emerged from her room all day.

'Good old Max, ever the agent.' Fin began laying packets of cheese and smoked hams and salami on the counter.

'I hadn't realised how truly obsessed she is. I'll be pleased when Malcolm comes to collect her tomorrow. Hopefully he'll find ways of distracting her.'

Max sighed. 'I hope they catch that bastard Bradford soon. And in the meantime all we have to do is keep Ruth safe. That last girl Bradford attacked is in a critical condition apparently. She might die.'

Fin groaned. 'Ruth's probably safest in the past, Max. Leave her there for now.'

Thomas had the baby removed from Sarah's house the day it was born and had it baptised Hampden after his hero, John Hampden, who had stood for the people against King Charles I's ship tax. The other two children were taken a day later, with their nursemaids. He installed them all on the top floor of the house in Arabella Row and promised himself next spring he would send them down to Buchan Hill to be brought up in the countryside. There, they could run through the gardens and play in the woods and hunt dragons to their hearts' content.

Sarah had been drunk when he visited her, sprawling on the sofa in a room where the fire remained unlit, a bottle of gin lying spilled on the floor at her feet. It was the housekeeper who had begged him to take the children away, but he had planned to do it anyway. He wanted so badly to see little Erskine lose his anxious angry scowl and run laughing round a house, any house, where he could find happiness.

Farquhar had been there, Thomas was sure of it. He could feel evil in the room. He stood looking down at Sarah, surprised to find so much compassion in himself, but there was nothing to be done. He went down to the kitchen and found the housekeeper still there, alone. 'Will you look after her for me?' He sat down wearily at the kitchen table.

'He's still here,' she said. She poured a glass of sherry for him and then one for herself. 'This bottle is all I have left, my lord. She has drunk her way through the rest.'

'When you say he's still here . . . ?' he asked cautiously.

'The bastard evil spirit in her head. She opens her mouth but it isn't her speaking. He shouts, he yells at her, he tells her to go after you.' She looked up at him anxiously.

'Go after me?' He felt in his pocket for the little silk-wrapped packet.

'He wants you dead, my lord, begging your pardon. You shouldn't come here any more. I'll look after her. Once she's sober, we'll sort something out for her.'

'Farquhar won't go just because she's sober,' Thomas said gravely.

'I know that, sir,' she sighed, 'but I'll think of something. And please, my lord, no offence, but will you give my love to those precious tots of yours. They deserve so much better than this and I'm pleased they're going to get it now they're with you.'

Four days later the woman was dead.

Davy was there when Sarah came to his door in Arabella Row in tears, her hair awry and her dress smeared with food. 'She fell down the stairs. I don't know how. She must have tripped. Please, I want to see my children.'

When Thomas refused, she began to scream and her voice changed. It deepened and grew more powerful.

'Let the woman see her children. She's your wife, you miserable man.' Even Davy could see it, the change in her face, the squaring of her shoulders as she moved towards them.

'Dear God, what's the matter with her?' Davy exclaimed.

'Nothing is the matter with her. She's mine!' The voice was coming from Sarah's mouth and she launched herself at Thomas, punching him in the face. He staggered and fell backwards. As Davy dragged her away from his father he felt the strength in her arms, a man's strength, then she collapsed in tears. She was Sarah again.

Davy helped Thomas to his feet, appalled at what had just happened. Settling his father into a chair he propelled Sarah towards the front door. 'Never let me see you here again,' he hissed.

As soon as she had gone, wailing, down the street followed at a discreet distance by one of the footmen to make sure she got home safely, Thomas knew she had left something behind. Only his pride had been hurt, but he had felt the evil like a poisoned veil trailing after her, winding round the furniture. It didn't come near him now she had gone, but it was prowling, looking for an opening. It would only be a matter of time before it found a way of coming closer.

Thomas made Davy swear not to tell anyone what had happened then he paid for the housekeeper's funeral and sent money to her family. What else could he do?

'Oh my God, Ruthie! Have you seen it? It's all over the news! That girl died.' Harriet had called just after Fin had tiptoed into Ruth's bedroom with a gin and tonic which, with exaggerated silence and his finger to his lips, he put down on the table beside her with a rattle of ice cubes. She could hear the tonic fizzing gently.

Ruth sat back in her chair and looked down from the window towards Queen Street Gardens, dark behind the old-fashioned street lights. 'Oh God, that's awful. Tragic.' She dragged her thoughts back to the present. 'I still can't believe Tim would do such a thing.' But it wasn't Tim, it was Farquhar.

'Where are you? Are you still in the Tower House?'

Ruth felt a pang of misery and loneliness. 'No, the police brought me to Max's.'

There was a short silence as Harriet digested this news. 'Didn't it work out with Malcolm?'

'It's not that. Mal had to go to London and they felt I'd be safer here.' Ruth reached for the gin and took a sip. From the other end of the flat she could hear the faint murmur of voices. Fin and Max were assembling their supper. She was safe here, but still she was afraid and, she realised, she was more afraid for Mal than herself. He was alone out there.

'Take care of yourself, Ruthie.' Harriet was signing off. 'If there's anything I can do to help, call me, and if you come to a conclusion about our ascended master—'

'I'll let you know, I promise.'

'I have to go away, for the children's sake. If I'm not there, then he – and Sarah – won't pester them.' Thomas was outlining his plans to his eldest son. 'I'm going to Scotland. I've been exchanging letters with your Uncle Harry's widow and she's asked me to stay with her at Almondell for Christmas and to remain there until the spring.' He looked more cheerful than he had for months.

'That's wonderful, Papa.' Davy embraced his father with relief. It would be a weight off all their minds if his father removed himself from London. It wasn't just Sarah's presence that was hanging over them all, it was the constant publicity, the cartoons and gossip columns in the newspapers, and the nagging fear that she would think of some even worse way of harassing him.

'Will you come with me?' Thomas gripped his son's arm.

'Me? To Scotland?'

'Just for a few weeks. I've decided to go by sea. I can't face any more racing around in carriages, not for such a long journey. Not any more. And I fancy another voyage before I die.'

'You're not going to die, Papa. You'll outlive the rest of us.' Davy laughed uncomfortably.

'Please come, Davy.' He slapped his son on the back. 'I have the tickets. We're booked on a smack bound for Leith. It leaves from Wapping in two weeks' time.'

Before he left he wrote a letter to Frances. 'I have a superstitious certainty that evil cannot travel over water, like the witches of old, and so I trust my evil twin will not be able to follow me north, hence my eccentric desire to travel by sea. However, should anything untoward happen to me, I trust you to come to Arabella Row and remove my personal papers. I am vain enough to believe that my public doings should be a matter of record, but my journals and letters are no one's business but my own. Burn them. Likewise, please, my darling, make yourself the overseer of my youngest children. Ensure they are brought up safely and well.'

He locked his papers in his desk, all but his current journal. That would go with him. He kissed the children and he made sure his little amulet of twigs was tucked in his breast pocket as he left the house to join Davy in the carriage that would take them to Wapping. He had no sense that he was followed. Andrew Farquhar and all his evil intentions were left safely behind.

April was watching the news on the hotel room TV. She was sitting on the end of her bed, numb with horror, as picture after picture of Tim appeared. There was only a quick shot of her but she wasn't mentioned. They seemed to have lost interest in her.

When the news moved on to another story she lay back on the bed, her arm across her eyes as tears trickled down her face. How could this have happened? What had gone wrong? She wished fervently they had never come to Edinburgh, never met Donald Dunbar, never set eyes on Number 26. The laughing face of the pretty girl he had murdered was branded into her brain. A girl, a child almost, who had her whole life ahead of her and Timothy, her brother, had killed her in the vilest way possible.

Where was he now? Apparently he had gone out to the Tower House again, still hunting Ruth. Was it Ruth he thought he was raping when he had attacked that poor girl? The police were supposed to be keeping an eye on Number 26 but she had seen how ineffective that had been; he was there when she had left the house and he would want her there with him now, to comfort him, to tell him that it didn't matter. That what he had done was OK.

Except of course it wasn't OK. It would never be OK again.

She sat up. Her keys to Number 26 were lying there on the dressing table with her purse and her mobile. Should she ring the police now? Tell them to go and look. Tell them how easy it had been to live in the back of the house where no lights could be seen from the street. Tell them to get there before he killed again. She picked up the keys and weighed them in her hand for a few seconds, then she reached for her coat.

'Papa! For God's sake come into the cabin!'

The weather had grown worse as the smack turned out of the Thames estuary and beat north-eastwards into the teeth of the wind.

Thomas glanced at Davy and grinned. 'Go in if you want to. I love this weather! I hadn't realised how much I missed the sea.' He was shouting against the roar of the wind in the ochre red sails. A large wave hit the boat broadside and showered them with icy spray. In his head Thomas was a midshipman again. The skipper had told them both to get below several times, but Thomas refused. He was soaked to the skin and shivering, but he was enjoying every minute of the experience. A flash of lightning lit the horizon and there was a rumble of thunder as huge black clouds rolled in from the north-east. It was growing darker all the time.

They were off Harwich when the full force of the storm struck. The sails had been reduced and the boat was bucking through gigantic waves. Thomas had gone below for a brief respite from the noise and the power of the wind, but he could not resist going on deck again as the lightning sliced into the water round them, clinging to the rail as he watched the full force of the storm. The skipper was at the helm with two of the sailors, fighting to point the smack's bow away from the coast; they were heading almost into wind when a sizzling flash and a bang shook the boat from stem to stern. In the brief second of intense white light he thought he caught sight of a figure in the bow, a wild shadowy figure, standing upright, not touched by the wind. The figure turned and raised a hand in triumphal greeting but the flash was spent, the sea was black once more. Thomas had imagined it. Farquhar could not be on the boat. It wasn't possible.

The next wave almost swamped them, crashing across the deck in a solid wall of water that swirled into the scuppers in a fury of wild foam, dragging Thomas's fingers from the shrouds to which he was clinging and hurling him down into the body of the boat as another bolt of lightning hit the mast beside him.

The news was just starting. 'The Edinburgh rape case has now turned into a full-scale murder enquiry.' The newscaster was looking solemn, her voice even and low pitched. 'The rapist's third victim died today in Edinburgh Royal Infirmary from injuries sustained two nights ago in a vicious attack. Timothy Bradford, believed to be in his early forties, is being sought in connection with the incident. He was last seen in the Scottish Borders Region. The public is warned not to approach him but to contact the police immediately if they see him.'

Timothy went on beating the eggs. On and on. So, the stupid girl had died. That was her fault. She shouldn't have fought him. He felt nothing. He didn't remember much about the incident at all. It had all been the other one, the strange invader who took charge of his body with such confidence, the man who, if he were honest with himself, he would like to have been.

Putting the frying pan on the gas he cut a wedge of butter and threw it in, waited until it melted and poured in the eggs. He had forgotten to grate the cheese. It didn't matter. He picked up a knife and sliced a few pieces off the lump then tossed them in the pan with the eggs. The smell was marvellous and he felt his mouth watering. On the TV the woman had moved over to a discussion of European economic policy. It was intensely boring. As the eggs cooked he switched over to another station and started to watch an American cartoon.

The man in his head could smell the food too. He was hungry and now he had a way of satiating that hunger, through the taste buds of another. He licked his lips and so, unconsciously, did Timothy.

The Tower House was lonely without Ruth there. Malcolm missed her; the dogs missed her. He had seen Pol plodding upstairs on his own, clearly on a mission, and without checking he knew the animal had gone up to Ruth's bedroom in the hope she might be there somewhere, hiding. When he came down again he looked at Malcolm with something like reproach. 'I know!' he replied.

He looked at his desk and the journal. He was reluctant to read on without Ruth there, but he ached to open it and continue the story. He needed to know what happened.

Sitting down he stared at it for several seconds, seconds that felt like an eternity, then slowly he reached across and opened it.

82

When Thomas came to he was in his berth below, wrapped in several thick blankets that smelt of tar and fish. The motion of the waves had eased slightly but all he could hear was the rush and scream of the wind. There was no more thunder.

'Are you awake, Papa?' Davy was there. The anxiety on his face clearly etched. He put his arm round his father's shoulders and helped him sit up so he could have a sip of brandy. 'We thought we'd lost you.'

Thomas managed a smile, the heat of the brandy spreading through him. 'I'm an old sailor! It would take more than a storm at sea to finish me.' His teeth were chattering. His soaking clothes were gone, he realised, and he was naked under the rugs; his body was racked with shivers and he began to cough.

Davy held the cup to his lips again and he took another gulp of the brandy. 'The lightning damaged the mast. It knocked you unconscious and you were drenched and chilled to the bone,' Davy said sternly. 'I have some dry clothes for you here from your trunk.' His irritation alternated with anxiety as he saw his father's pallor deepen. 'This whole trip was madness! I knew it. I should never have let you come.'

Thomas lay back on the bunk, too exhausted to argue. He felt his eyes close then suddenly they flew open. 'My jacket!' he said. 'Where's my jacket?'

'There. Your clothes are all there. I've hung them up to dry them. They were all but torn off you.'

'Bring it to me. My jacket.' Thomas was fighting to free his arms from the blankets.

With a sigh, Davy reached for it. The small cabin was lit by a single swinging lantern hanging from the bulkhead and grabbing the coat in the wildly leaping shadows, Thomas began to search the pockets. The sea water had made the wet woollen cloth sticky and cold and he fumbled desperately with numb icy fingers, trying to find the inner breast pocket. When at last he found it he turned it inside out, then did the same to all his other pockets. The amulet may have saved him from the figure on the bow and from the lightning, but now it was gone.

Malcolm was sitting by the stove, the journal on his knee. He looked up as a gust of wind blew down the chimney and the embers brightened. He had been picturing so intensely the storm at sea, feeling the wind and the rain, the heave of the great North Sea swell that it was a shock to find himself inside by the fire.

He wondered where Timothy was now. He should be letting the dogs outside to have a final pee before bed but he was reluctant to unlock the front door. As though reading his thoughts Cas and Pol sat up expectantly. They always acted as if this was the high point of their day; but then, bless them, they always acted as though everything was the high point of their day. He put the journal down. It was strange to think he now knew where the missing arm of the doll had gone. And frightening.

Walking over to the window he looked down at the area in front of the house where his car was parked.

He had always resisted the idea of putting in outside security lights but there was a bulb above the front door and its light was enough to show that the weather had deteriorated and it was raining hard. He could see it drumming down on the car roof. If Timothy was still outside on the hill he would be very cold and very wet. Another gust of wind drove the rain sideways, sending ripples across the puddles on the drive. The dogs had got the message and lain down again in front of the stove. He went over and threw on another couple of logs and glanced down at the journal lying on the table, wondering in spite of himself what had happened to Thomas next. He picked it up. There weren't many more pages that were still legible. The last few had been scorched as though the little book had been burnt.

The mast had been repaired, but by the time the boat was opposite Flamborough Head, Thomas's fever had set in in earnest. After a hurried consultation with the skipper, it was decided they would put in at Scarborough and Davy would seek medical help for his father from a local doctor. Thomas was furious, but he was too weak to argue and in the end he had to admit it was the right decision.

Two weeks taking the famous waters improved his health enormously and he was certain he knew what he wanted to do next. They argued for hours. 'You know it would be foolish to go on!' Davy repeated for the fourth time. 'For God's sake, Papa, be reasonable. We can travel back home in comfort, in stages, staying at the best hostelries. I don't understand your obsession with Scotland. Leave it for now. You can always try again in the spring when the weather's more clement.'

'My plans are made,' Thomas said firmly. He was not accustomed to losing arguments, least of all with his own son. 'I will travel in stages and in comfort, but I will go north. I will not return to London. I fully appreciate that you need to go back. I'll be fine to travel on alone. I can hire people to look after me and have every care I need.'

'You know I can't let you do that!' Davy was beside himself with frustration.

'Then you will need to come too.' Thomas still had a cough but the fever had subsided and a spell of fine weather had allowed him to take a few short bracing walks along the cliffs. 'I intend to hire the best conveyance I can find to take me north to Scotland. I plan to stay with your uncle at Dryburgh for a few days, then slowly make my way onwards to stay at Almondell as arranged.'

There was no point in arguing.

They stayed a week with the earl in the great house next to Dryburgh Abbey, visiting Elizabeth's grave in St Monan's chapel in the beautiful ruins, walking by the River Tweed, the two brothers reminiscing about their childhood and introducing the younger Davy to family legends and stories of childhood adventures. Thomas was still frail and anxious to continue their journey; he had chest pains that he hid not altogether successfully from the others, and he wanted very much to reach his final destination before the weather deteriorated any further. On the last day of October he set off with Davy along the post roads north.

Ruth was sitting on the edge of her bed. She was, she realised, missing Malcolm more than she could bear. She picked up her phone again.

He answered on the second ring. 'Ruth? Are you all right?'

She smiled at the sound of his voice. 'I'm fine. I'm safe here. I was worried about you. Timothy's loose out there somewhere and it's dark and you're alone.'

'I have the dogs.'

'They're a couple of softies.'

'My doors are locked.'

'But we both know that won't keep him out. Not Farquhar. The police don't know what they're dealing with.' She realised he could probably hear the fear in her voice.

'They are dealing with a man in the bodily form of Timothy Bradford, Ruth, and it is Timothy they need to catch. It won't be long now,' he added reassuringly. 'He's taking insane risks. The police will find him. I'm coming to fetch you first thing in the morning. Stay there now, where you're safe.'

'I will. And you. Don't go wandering off into the woods again.' There was a catch in her voice as she ended the call.

Snuggling up against her pillows she reached over for the next letter from her pile. At least that would distract her from thinking about Malcolm and the darkness outside his windows.

Almondell was a week's drive away, and the turnpikes north led across wild hilly country. The days were growing shorter when they finally arrived at Harry's dream house in the valley of the River Almond and Thomas was exhausted. Harry's widow, Kate, greeted them on the doorstep and ushered them in herself, shocked at Thomas's obvious weakness. 'Why didn't you stay on with David at Dryburgh?' she scolded. 'Men are so foolish!'

She led Thomas indoors, taking him by the hand, leading him straight into the drawing room where a huge fire was burning. She ordered tea and scones and cakes and sat him down close to the hearth before turning round and giving Davy a piece of her mind. 'How could you let your father wear himself out like this? Why did you let him set out on this visit at all? I'd no idea he was ill!'

It was later, when Thomas was feeling more restored, that she brought over a salver on which were piled some letters. 'Frances has been writing to you. She must have thought you would have been here long before this. Shall I leave you to read them while I show Davy round the house? Harry would have so loved to show you both himself . . . '

Thomas heard her voice retreating into the distance as he pushed aside his teacup and sipped from the glass of whisky she had put on a small table beside him.

There were three letters on the pile. He looked at the dates and broke the seal on the earliest which had been written only four days after they left London.

All is well here, Papa

Sam and I have been talking and we have decided to bring your little children down to Poynings. I am taking the liberty of thinking that you would agree that it would be nicer for them to stay with us here and our brood has agreed with alacrity. The girls particularly

are looking forward to taking care of baby Hampden.
When you return you can take them with you to Buchan
Hill if that suits you, or back to London to keep them at
Arabella Row.

The autumn colours here in Sussex are wonderful and
the weather is still clement. Sam and I will drive up to
London tomorrow or the next day to collect them.

With all my love from your dutiful daughter, Frances

Thomas put the letter down with a smile. 'Dutiful, eh,' he
murmured. He had guessed this might happen, indeed had
hoped it would, but the suggestion had to come from them.

He took another sip of whisky, savouring its strength, wishing
he didn't still feel so weak, then he reached for the next letter.
It was dated three days after the first.

Papa, something terrible has happened. When we
reached Arabella Row we found the house in complete
disarray. Sarah's brother Charles had come and taken
the children away. The servants didn't dare argue with
him; he did not allow the nursery maids to go too and
carried the little ones off in much distress at leaving
their toys. He had a note from a magistrate entitling
Sarah to take them, apparently. Obviously the man
didn't know who you were. Samuel went round at once
to the house you rented for Sarah but she had gone.
The house is closed and there is no one there. A
neighbour said the new housekeeper was sent away
without notice or character. He went on to the
magistrate who had dealt with Sarah and the man was
appalled at what he had inadvertently been a party
to, and he has suggested we notify the Watch to look for
them, and take all legal steps to get the children back,
which Sam did at once. I am so sorry to have to tell you
this. Please let us know by return if we have done the right
thing and if there is anyone else we should contact . . .

The glass slipped from his hand to the rug. He lay back in his chair too stunned to move for several minutes, his heart thudding uncomfortably, then he took a deep breath and reached for the third letter. It was dated a full week after the last and headed Arabella Row.

I hear from Uncle David that you stayed with him at Dryburgh and are only now on the way to stay with Aunt Kate. Oh, Papa, I am so sorry to have been the transmitter of such terrible news. We are no nearer finding the children. The whole of London is in ferment and looking for them. The Watch went to Stonecutters Court where Sarah's family live and searched the place for them but the children weren't there and the Bucks say they know nothing of the matter. Sam and I went back to Sarah's house to see if we could find any clues. There is nothing there to say where they are or what their plans were but oh, Papa, I felt such discomfort when I went there. It was as if that dreadful man who speaks through her mouth had infiltrated every room. I saw nothing, I am pleased to say, but it was as though he had left an echo of evil there. I had brought the doll with me to Arabella Row and left it there in my writing box. I went back and held it in my arms, praying that it would watch over the little ones, and keep me free of such a tainted spirit. I trust you still have your special piece of her magic safe, Papa, and that you are now feeling much better. I wish I could give you better news. I am sure that Sarah would never knowingly hurt them, and if her brother is with her perhaps he is able to guide her to a more sensible way of life.

I will write to you at once when I have further news,

Your loving daughter, F

When Kate and Davy came in some half an hour later they found Thomas lying unconscious in his chair. Davy picked up

567

his sister's letters and read them later when Thomas had been put to bed and the best doctors in Edinburgh had been called. Davy and Kate concocted a letter to be sent at once to Frances, but in his heart Davy knew it would reach her too late. Whatever happened to those children, they would never see their father again.

Timothy could hear the rain lashing against the kitchen window. He had finished his meal and put the plates and the pan in the sink. April could wash them up when she returned. He wondered again, briefly, where she was as he made himself a mug of instant coffee.

Time to go out.

The voice was back.

Let's find another girl.

'No.' Timothy spoke out loud. He surprised himself at how forceful he sounded.

He banged the coffee mug down on the table. It slopped everywhere and he stood looking down at the brown puddle, transfixed. 'That girl died.' It was as if he had only just realised the significance of what had happened.

Shall we go and find Ruth then?

'No! I said, no!' Timothy was growing agitated. 'Leave me alone!'

Let's take the knife you used on the floorboards. That would be perfect. In case the police come.

Timothy's head was splitting. 'Leave me alone!' There was a roaring in his ears. He clamped his hands against them and shook his head violently, trying to dislodge the intruder.

Now. Let's go now!

The knife was lying on the table. As Timothy watched, it slowly began to spin round in circles. He stared at it, mesmerised for several seconds and then he pounced on it. He waved it in the air. 'Where are you? I can't see you.'

Here!

The voice was behind him.

Here!

Now it was near the door. Then it was all round him,

reverberating in his head. He began to turn round and round and suddenly he was shouting in a frenzy of despair and fear and lust.

Outside, April inserted her key in the lock. She hesitated as she heard him yell. All her instincts told her to run. It wasn't too late. All she had to do was reach for her phone and dial 999. His shouts died away and for several seconds there was silence, then she heard him give a heart-rending sob. That was it. He needed her. Turning the key, she pushed open the door and, slamming it behind her, ran across the hall towards the kitchen as his screams of fury began again. 'Tim? What's wrong? What's happened?' She stood in the doorway and stared at him in horror.

He didn't recognise her. He didn't even think. The man who had hold of him, mind and body, launched himself towards her, and slamming her against the fridge, began to tear at her clothes.

'Tim! Tim, it's me, Tim! It's April!' She clawed at his eyes. 'Let me go, you bastard!' She grabbed his wrist, twisting it as hard as she could. 'Let me go!'

He didn't hear her. The roar in his ears was deafening, the blinding pain in his head overwhelming.

He was far too strong for her. She never stood a chance. She didn't even feel the knife go in under her ribs. For several seconds she stayed standing but she was no longer fighting.

The knife fell to the floor with a clatter and Timothy stood back as April slid down into a sitting position, leaning against the fridge door.

'April?' He was looking down at her in horror. 'April? What's wrong? Stand up!'

Blood was pooling in her lap. Her eyes were open but they were strangely vacant.

Timothy stared round the kitchen in a daze. The house of his dreams, the future. It was gone. In an instant. All gone. Without April, he was nothing but an echoing void; a blank man in an empty shell. The voice had deserted him.

'Damn your eyes, you vicious cowardly monster,' he screamed. 'I hope you burn in hellfire for this. I shall make sure you do. I shall take you there myself!'

Staggering across the floor he scrabbled for a box of matches from the drawer and, grabbing the newspaper, he tore it to

569

shreds. He struck a match with a shaking hand, lit the paper and as it flared held a handful of blazing strips to the curtains. Then he turned on the gas. April had had the guts to burn a house; he could do no less for her. Turning back to her he knelt beside her body and kissed her on the top of her head.

Thomas's illness worsened daily and his brother was summoned from Dryburgh. The doctors diagnosed severe inflammation of the lungs. They listened to his labouring chest and bled him and gave him various potions. It did no good. It was no surprise to Thomas to find himself from time to time watching their efforts to prolong his life from somewhere outside that poor old body. He had known from the moment he lost the amulet that he was doomed, that his battles were over. His dogs would miss him, but he knew Frances would take them. For the rest, he was tired. His children, all of them, must fend for themselves now, but from wherever he was bound, he would watch over them.

'Davy!' Thomas drifted in and out of consciousness now, but as Davy sat at his bedside alone he reached out to his son, who took his hand. 'I have a journal. There, in my portmanteau. I want you to burn it.'

'But, Papa, that would be sacrilege!' Davy tried to force himself to smile, to make a joke of it. 'Do you remember Lord Byron said all your writings would one day be valuable!'

'Do it now. Please.' Thomas was visibly irritated. 'What is in there is private and of no concern to anyone but me and my maker.'

Reluctantly Davy stood up and went to lift the lid of the valise. He found the leather-covered notebook, filled with his father's cramped handwriting in a writing case lying on the top of his folded shirts.

'Do it now, while I watch.' Thomas leaned forward on his pillows, gesturing towards the brightly burning fire.

Reluctantly Davy took the notebook and walked towards the hearth. He hesitated for only a moment then he tossed the small volume into the flames.

* * *

Sally Laidlaw was in her kitchen when she smelt smoke. By the time the police and the firemen arrived the downstairs of Number 26 was well alight. They found the bodies in the kitchen; Timothy was holding his sister in his arms.

Thomas

How strange that I can talk dispassionately about my own demise. It was a relief when it happened, though I was sad to see Kate's tears and my brother and my son, the two Davids in my life, sobbing on one another's shoulders. It was decided to inter me there, in the old Kirk of St Nicholas near Kirkhill where my brother Harry already lay in a tomb with others of my family. The Davids suggested that I should be embalmed and my body taken south to lie in Westminster Abbey. What tosh. My living ego might have loved such an honour but I was content now with Kate's firm decision that I should be taken in a simple procession, led by a soberly black-clad minister of the kirk, with no fripperies or even music, to lie in a quiet corner, where my old corpse could, if it were able to rise from its vault, view the glories of the distant Pentland Hills. I was to lie in Scotland and I was content.

My son Davy disappointed me. When the fire died after he had disposed of my journal he found it lying there only half burned. He took it out of the ashes and carried it to his bedroom where he wrapped it in a cravat and buried it in his own trunk. Later he would give it to Frances, with a plaited clipping of my hair in a gold locket, as consolation in her distress.

My youngest children did not fare well. They were traced at last to Stonecutters Court where Sarah had returned to live with her brother's family. As their mother she regained custody of them from that same fool magistrate now that their father was gone, and she complained bitterly to all who would listen that I had left her without maintenance. Davy tried to persuade her to send Hampden to a good school, offering to pay all the expenses himself, but in her bitterness she would not allow it, demanding help and money from any who would give it and at the same time claiming she was without friends or help from my family. My heart broke for those little ones but for the family, for the time being at least, they were gone.

She tried to earn a living as a dressmaker, then a bonnet-maker as she was when I first met her. Her gift of speaking with the dead had deserted her. Once she even tried to summon me to use me as her mouthpiece. It did not work.

And what of Andrew Farquhar?

He too was silenced, swept away in the storm, perhaps, though not, I now know, forever. Frances had the gift of the sight, but also that inestimable quality of serenity; through her, the slave woman's doll kept our family safe. Did Farquhar hunt me through the echoing spaces of the universe? Perhaps, in his endless bitterness, he did. I did not encounter him, not until my life was dragged from the old and dusty papers Frances had left hidden and unread until they were laid bare on the desk of my great-great-great-great-great-grandchild, a woman called Ruth.

Epilogue

'Neither neighbouring property was damaged and structurally your house is sound. The damage is superficial except in the kitchen where the fire started.' James Reid looked at Ruth over his glasses. 'Once the paperwork is complete you can do what you like with it. I assume you will want to sell?'

She nodded. 'I want nothing to do with it.'

'I can't say I blame you.' For a moment he almost lost his professional dispassion. 'Though, I can't help feeling,' he hesitated, 'that fire cleanses as well as destroys.' He cleared his throat. 'As far as the money is concerned you have the likely final figures there and the jewellery and cash found in April Bradford's hotel room have been recognised as yours by the court – the money being the cash paid for two diamond rings and a selection of Victorian and other jewellery from your mother's collection. Would you believe, the woman kept the receipts? No next of kin for the Bradfords have responded to challenge the ruling and as far as the courts can establish there are none.' He stood up and held out his hand. 'Goodbye for now, Ruth. I hope you can put all the trauma and unhappiness you have experienced in the last few months behind you for good. I understand you will be living in the Borders for the foreseeable future?'

She noted the quizzical lift of his eyebrow and laughed. 'I

will indeed. You have my address, James. As you well know, I am lodging with a fellow author.'

Hers was not the only property that was going on the market. Fin had decided to sell the Old Mill House and planned to go back to the Isle of Skye in the spring. 'But it's not forever. Some more filming and some downtime then I'll be back,' he told her with a hug. 'I have an eye on a flat near Max. I don't have the strength or time to live in a big house any more. A flat is all I need and this one has a magnificent kitchen.'

Lachy came down to the Tower House to help Malcolm demolish what was left of the chapel after the winter winds had cleansed it, helped, in an advisory capacity, by Cas and Pol who ran round in wild excitement and Ruth who watched from a safe distance.

After Lachy had gone, Ruth and Malcolm walked back up the track to stand on the site. For a while they just stood there, arm in arm, then Mal nodded. 'There is nothing here. No ghosts. The spirit of the woods will move back soon.'

'Will you build a new chapel?'

'No. There are hundreds of acres of woods here. That's all I need. And my special tree.' He slapped the old oak tree on the trunk affectionately.

'Your family tree.'

'When we go over to Dryburgh I'll show you an ancient yew in the abbey grounds that would have been a thousand years old when Thomas and his brother were there. That could be yours.'

She shook her head. 'It turned out my family tree was full of ghosts,' she said. 'A ghost tree.'

He laughed. 'Everyone's is,' he said. 'It's just that not everyone sees them.'

Later, she went up to the room that had been her bedroom and was now her study.

Pol and Cas were up there with her as usual, lying patiently on the rug, but now, suddenly, they both stood up. One after the other they slipped out of the door and down the spiral stairs.

Ruth had been about to turn on the lamp but now she waited.

It was almost no surprise when she saw Thomas's familiar figure in the shadows by the window.

His story, with its heroes and its villains, had been told, the ghosts laid to rest, at least for now. He had come to say goodbye.

Author's Note

This story is fiction, woven around and through the very real life of my great-great-great-great-great-grandfather and his family. Like Ruth and her mother, both fictional characters, I became fascinated by Thomas from an early age because of the stories I heard about him and the fact that his name was treated with such reverence by the family that many of them, myself included, found themselves given his name. He intrigued me, not least because I wondered why we, as such distant relations, should possess so much memorabilia about him. Alas, no letters or journals (or silver!) in the quantity that Ruth inherits – they too are fictional, but nevertheless enough to make him seem very real and very close.

As soon as I realised I was a writer, beguiled and enchanted by all the branches of our family history, I dreamed of one day writing a novel based on Thomas's life and *The Ghost Tree* is the result at last of an attempt to make sense of all the material assembled by my great-aunt and after her by my father, research that revealed a man far more complex, more interesting and more human than I ever expected.

Thomas was the youngest child in an ambitious, highly motivated, brilliant family. That much is clear. The basic facts of his life mostly come from a book called *Volume VI of the Lives of the Lord Chancellors* by Lord Campbell, that was published in 1847, only twenty-four years after Thomas's death. He wrote in close collaboration with his son, Thomas, who obviously gave him access to much detail, but also a certain amount of disingenuous obfuscation.

Subsequent biographies have mostly followed Campbell's version. I have worked with two, *Erskine* by J.A. Lovat-Fraser (1932) and *Thomas Erskine and Trial by Jury*, by John Hostettler (1996). But we now have the benefit of much original material which is online and it is relatively easy to follow up each strand of his career, his education, his time in the navy, of which I knew nothing except for the lightning strike. (The first of three, according to family legend. I remember my mother showing me the reference in an old edition of the Guinness Book of Records. His record is long broken.) His army career, his legal and political careers, his marriages and his children are all on record to explore. Though, as always on the internet, the facts are not always consistent.

His time as Lord Chancellor turned out to be fairly brief, but his passion for civil rights and his reputation as the most brilliant barrister of his age, his involvement with the anti-slavery bill of 1806 and his devotion to animal welfare lasted a lifetime. His animal rights bill came in 1809, fifteen years before the founding of the RSPCA. I also had that most invaluable source, family stories and, for me, in a way far more interesting than all these was his publicly admitted ability to see ghosts.

His marriages were a source of much interest. Here was a man who ran away to Gretna Green not once but twice (although even that is not certain; his marriage to Frances, according to some records, happened in Guernsey) and whose second marriage was a well-recorded public and private scandal. That Sarah Buck was a spirit medium was part of the family legend, and I have found nothing to substantiate it. Some of her bizarre behaviour has been attributed more prosaically to post-puerperal fever rather than possession. The fact that she attacked Thomas was witnessed and recounted in a letter by his son David. My theory that Sarah channelled Thomas's beloved Fanny is fiction (or guesswork!). As is the character Andrew Farquhar. When I started writing the book

I realised I needed a fictional link to carry such a powerful story and to explain so many of the puzzling facts that have survived as profound enigmas. Farquhar is one of those people who, if he didn't exist, had to be invented to explain the unexplained.

Sarah survived Thomas by thirty-three years. As far as history seems to relate he had three surviving children from his second marriage; I haven't attempted to follow up their history as it lies beyond the scope of the novel. It appears in some records that Erskine went to live in Sussex, so I hope Frances and Samuel made contact with them in the end, and at some point after their mother died he and Agnes seem to have left England for a life in New Zealand.

Following up the family stories and visiting scenes I have written about in the book have brought the connections and motivations, friendships and animosities into a wonderful focus for me.

Thomas seems to have had at least twenty-six grandchildren from his first marriage, and possibly twelve more from his second, which goes some way to explaining the number of descendants he has all over the world. I have met some of them and it has been a delight to find I have so many distant cousins!

And me, where do I fit in? My grandmother was the granddaughter of Mary Ann Catherine, who was Frances and Sam Holland's third daughter. My grandmother and her siblings inherited the Sussex connection, the passion for Scotland, the obsession with ancient ancestry (going back long before the eighteenth century) and from somewhere, and perhaps most interesting of all, the second sight and the ability to see ghosts.

And so to Dion Fortune. While researching my novel *Time's Legacy* I came across her story and it was when I found out that she believed herself to be communicating with the very same Lord Erskine that this novel was born – a weird and most unexpected connection!

My sincere thanks for help with this story go as always to so many people who have thrown themselves with so much enthusiasm into helping me. First to Carole Blake, who was my agent when we first discussed this novel and who, as always, whole-heartedly supported the project, but sadly died before it was completed. And to Isobel Dixon who has taken over as Carole's successor. Next there are all the cousins, immediate, distant and even more distant! Passing strangers, curators, guides, the lovely lady skipper who allowed us to embark on the ferry to Inchmahome as Storm Ophelia roared towards us across the hills. It was the last ferry of the season. Following my habit of visiting the scenes of my fiction at the end of the summer when the world has sent the year's tourists away I revelled in the wildness of the weather, especially as my son Jon, research assistant, chauffeur and dispenser of soothing wisdom and co-conspirator in all our adventures, was with me.

The team at HarperCollins have been wonderful, coaxing me on to finish the book after the sadness of my father's last illness and death. He would have loved to read this. I hope that maybe he is even now sharing a dram or two with Thomas and scanning some ethereal version of the manuscript. Especial thanks to my editors, Kim, Susan, Anne and Eloisa, for their dedicated patience. Also to Richard Woodman for correcting the naval references and to Peter Buneman for abandoning his professorial desk to hunt the alleyways and closes of Edinburgh for clues and Rachel and Hugh who did the same; to Annie McBrearty for walking with me in Ruth's footsteps (or did she walk in ours?) To Robert Lindsey (one of those other descendants) for sending me his essay on Thomas, and to so many others. The liberties I have taken with history were for the purposes of the plot. The errors are mine, or are the result of the mists of time.

Reading Group Questions

- What are the key themes of the novel?

- The book is written from multiple perspectives. What does this narrative structure add to the novel? And how do the various threads entwine?

- Who is your favourite character and why?

- What connections can you draw between Thomas and Ruth?

- 'History is a good story, in my humble opinion.' What is Malcolm trying to tell Ruth here? And how might this statement reflect the author's broader preoccupations in the novel?

- It has been the author's dream, ever since hearing about her famous ancestor Thomas Erskine at an early age, to write a book based on his life. How much do you know about your own family tree? Do you have any famous ancestors?

- What role does the weather play in the book's representation of the supernatural?

- In the first few chapters, we learn that Ruth had a difficult relationship with her father. Can you think of any other examples of complex familial relationships in the book?

- The character of Thomas Erskine is, of course, drawn from real life. Did you feel you wanted to find out more about him?

LET TIME STAND STILL
DISCOVER EVEN MORE OF THE MAGIC

BARBARA
ERSKINE
3 MILLION COPIES SOLD
Lady of Hay
The International Bestseller

BARBARA
ERSKINE
Bestselling author of Lady of Hay
Kingdom of
Shadows

BARBARA
ERSKINE
Sunday Times bestselling author of Lady of Hay
Child of the
Phoenix

BARBARA
ERSKINE
Sunday Times bestselling author of Lady of Hay
Midnight is a
Lonely Place

BARBARA
ERSKINE
Sunday Times bestselling author of Lady of Hay
House of
Echoes

BARBARA
ERSKINE
Sunday Times bestselling author of Lady of Hay
On the Edge
of Darkness

BARBARA
ERSKINE
Sunday Times bestselling author of Lady of Hay

Whispers *in*
the Sand

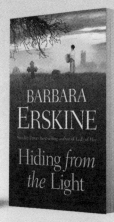

BARBARA
ERSKINE
Sunday Times bestselling author of Lady of Hay

Hiding *from*
the Light

BARBARA
ERSKINE
Sunday Times bestselling author of Lady of Hay

Daughters
of Fire

BARBARA
ERSKINE
Sunday Times bestselling author of Lady of Hay

The Warrior's
Princess

BARBARA
ERSKINE
Sunday Times bestselling author of Lady of Hay

Time's Legacy

BARBARA
ERSKINE
Sunday Times bestselling author of Lady of Hay

River *of*
Destiny

BARBARA
ERSKINE
Sunday Times bestselling author of Lady of Hay

The Darkest
Hour

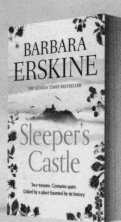

BARBARA
ERSKINE
THE SUNDAY TIMES BESTSELLER

Sleeper's
Castle

Two women. Centuries apart.
Linked by a place haunted by its history.